## ABOUT THE EDITORS

LIZ GRZYB was born in the middle of a thunderstorm in Perth, Western Australia. She is the editor of acclaimed paranormal romance anthologies *Scary Kisses* and *More Scary Kisses*, the website Ticon4.com, co-editor of paranormal noir anthology *Damnation and Dames* and *The Year's Best Australian Fantasy and Horror 2010*.

TALIE HELENE is a musician and writer, from Melbourne, Australia. She has poetry published in journals including *Voiceworks*, *Avant*, and *Inkshed*, and Mary Manning's *About Poetry* (Oxford University Press), and a co-authored short story (with Martin Livings) "The Last Gig of Jimmy Rucker" in *More Scary Kisses* (edited by Liz Grzyb), winner of a Tin Duck Award, and nominated for Best Short Story in the 2011 Ditmar Awards. Talie was News Editor for the Australian Horror Writers' Association for four years; she is serving on the Short Fiction Jury for the 2012 Bram Stoker Awards. With a background in music journalism—especially extreme genres—Talie has performed with many artists including The Tenth Stage, Wendy Rule, Sean Bowley, Saba Persian Orchestra, Maroondah Symphony, and Eden. A member of the SuperNova writers' group, she is currently developing a new audio arts anthology titled *The Unquiet Grave*. You can find out more at taliehelene.com

# THE YEAR'S BEST AUSTRALIAN FANTASY & HORROR

## ~ 2011 ~

EDITED BY

## LIZ GRZYB & TALIE HELENE

THE SECOND ANNUAL COLLECTION

# THE YEAR'S BEST AUSTRALIAN FANTASY & HORROR

## ~ 2011 ~

EDITED BY

## LIZ GRZYB & TALIE HELENE

T℀
p℀ Ticonderoga
publications

*The Year's Best Fantasy & Horror 2011*
edited by Liz Grzyb & Talie Helene

Published by Ticonderoga Publications

Designed by Russell B. Farr
Typeset in Sabon and Poor Richard

A Cataloging-in-Publications entry for this title is available from The National Library of Australia.

ISBN 978-1-921857-13-3 (hardcover)
978-1-921857-14-0 (trade paperback)
978-1-921857-15-7 (ebook)

Ticonderoga Publications
PO Box 29 Greenwood
Western Australia 6924

**www.ticonderogapublications.com**

10 9 8 7 6 5 4 3 2 1

*The editors would like to thank Peter M. Ball, Lee Battersby, Deborah Biancotti, Jenny Blackford, Simon Brown, David Conyers, Stephen Dedman, Sara Douglass, Felicity Dowker, Terry Dowling, Jason Fischer, Christopher Green, Paul Haines, Lisa L. Hannett, Richard Harland, John Harwood, Pete Kempshall, David Kernot, Jo Langdon, Maxine McArthur, Ian McHugh, Andrew J. McKiernan, Kirstyn McDermott, Margaret Mahy, Anne Mok, Jason Nahrung, Anthony Panegyres, Tansy Rayner Roberts, Angela Rega, Angela Slatter, Lucy Sussex, Kyla Ward, Kaaron Warren, Russell B. Farr.*

*Liz would like to thank Helen Grzyb, Angela Challis, Shane Cummings, Amanda Pillar, Tom Bicknell, Kate Dunbar-Smith, Kate Williams, Andrew Williams, Debbie Wilson, Jacinta Rosielle, Ambre Hillier, Michael Hillier, Tasmar Dixon, Kylie Dainton, Mel Barndon, Mel Donald, Phil Ward, Ruza Foster, Lina Piscitelli, Nikki Irwin, Andrea Orlowsky, Anna Frankie Bertolini, Jane Hebiton, Alex Lawson, Dionn Godinho, Zoe Brooks, Clare MacFarlane.*

*Talie would like to thank Jules Haines, Martin Livings, Rocky Wood, Shelley Slater, Sonia Tamarri, Deborah Tamarri, Cynthia Tamarri, Josephine Wilson, David Wattie, Mark Evans, Vair Buchanan, Deborah Crabtree, Samantha Escarbe, Julian Warner, Sarah Endacott, Jamie Reuel, Lauren Walsh, Bill Bamford, Ellen Gregory, Bren MacDibble, Claire McKenna, Trudi Canavan, Matthew Chrulew, Peter Hickman, Andrew Macrae, Brendan Duffy, David McDonald, Stephen Gleeson, Adam Browne, Steve Cameron, Cat Sparks, Robert Hood, Sean Williams, Kim Wilkins, Angela Challis, Shane Cummings, Alisa Krasnostein, Tehani Wessely, Erin Muscat, Sam Muscat, Geoff Brown, Chuck McKenzie, Janeen Webb, Jack Dann, Leigh Blackmore, Margi Curtis, Lezli Robyn, Fiona Trembath, Barbara Crowe, Katie Ransome, Douglas Johnson, Tina Dalen, Michelle Gillian Shah, Pete Collins, Rachel Dowel, Yurianna Lynch, Jill Hili, Michelle Kinman, Russell Blackford, Cam Rogers, Gillian Polack, Sharyn Lilley, Leigh Irwin, Alisha Eke, Lawrie Brown, Mark Woolley, Karl Lean, Laurie Ann Haus, Adrian Bedford, Annette Backshall, Gary Kemble, Gemma Dubaldo, Alicia Taylor, Dirk Strasser, Julia Continuum Goddess, Marty Young, and Jim and Helen Johnson.*

# CONTENTS

# THE YEAR IN REVIEW

## LIZ GRZYB & TALIE HELENE

### THE YEAR IN FANTASY

In 2011 the fantasy world in Australia and New Zealand was heavily influenced by the natural disasters that befell both countries. In New Zealand, J.C. Hart and Anna Caro brought out *Tales for Canterbury* with Random Static, which raised funds for the Red Cross Earthquake Appeal for Canterbury. Tehani Wessely at Fablecroft released a special ebook version of *After the Rain* to benefit the Queensland Flood Relief Appeal. Jodi Cleghorn at Emergent Publishing released 100 *Stories for Queensland*, an anthology of flash fiction to raise funds for the Queensland Premier's Flood Appeal. Authors for Queensland and Writers on Rafts were two more groups of cross-genre authors who also raised tens of thousands of dollars for the Queensland Flood Relief Appeal.

2011 has to be the year of Shaun Tan! After his film based on his picture book *The Lost Thing* won an Oscar for Best Animated Short Film, he won another Hugo award for Best Professional Artist, the Astrid Lindgren Memorial Award, one of the world's richest literary prizes.

Jonathan Strahan was again recognised for prominence in the speculative fiction world with a Hugo nomination for Best Editor— Short Form. He also edited Volume 5 of the *Best Science Fiction and Fantasy of the Year* for Nightshade Books, Jack Vance's 3-novel mystery collection *Dangerous Ways* from Subterranean Press and various anthologies of a more science fiction bent: *Eclipse Four: New Science Fiction and Fantasy* for Nightshade, *Engineering Infinity* for Solaris Books, and *Life on Mars: Tales from the New Frontier* for Viking Books.

Lucy Sussex also had a prolific year, winning the Peter McNamara Achievement Award for 2010, and releasing two collections of her short stories: Twelfth Planet Press' *Thief of Lives* and Ticonderoga Publications' *Matilda Told Such Dreadful Lies: The Essential Lucy Sussex.*

Many fantasy authors were seen out and about around the antipodes this year. Paranormal author Nalini Singh toured New Zealand, and Margo Lanagan appeared at multiple writers' festivals around Australia. Other notable appearances at writers' festivals this year included Marianne de Pierres, Trent Jamieson, Stephen M Irwin, James Phelan, Gary Crew, Alison Croggon, Kate Eltham, Emily Rodda, Shaun Tan, Melina Marchetta, Anthony Eaton, Will Elliott, Stephen Dedman, Markus Zusak and Sonya Hartnett.

## RECOMMENDED NOVELS

Nicole Murphy concluded her *Dreams of Asarlai* trilogy from HarperCollins this year, with *Power Unbound* and *Rogue Gadda.* They are intriguing stories leading from the beguiling *Secret Ones* (2010), and continue the story arc begun in that novel, where a set of dangerously powerful books have been stolen, and their use threatens the magical gadda worldwide. These books are a saucy way to while away a few afternoons.

Trent Jamieson released two titles this year: *Business of Death* (finishing his *Death Works* trilogy and released in omnibus form from Hachette Orbit) and *Roil*, the beginning of another series from Angry Robot. While *Business of Death* is a more slick, streamlined story, both have intricate twists and engaging characters and are enjoyable reading.

Tara Moss has continued the story of her young adult heroine Pandora English with *The Spider Goddess.* Not recommended for arachnophobes, this is another easy to read adventurous tale in the fashion world of a paranormal New York.

Marianne de Pierres' new young adult series beginning with *Burn Bright* and *Angel Arias* is a great read. The characterisation is realistic and engaging and the stories are pacy. These novels are recommended for young adults and adults alike.

Sara Douglass' final novel *The Devil's Diadem* from HarperCollins is a standalone novel which gives us everything Douglass is famous for: well-written fantasy which draws the reader inexorably in.

## OTHER NOTABLE NOVELS

Multinational HarperCollins led the way in publishing Australian fantasy novels this year, with many series being continued or completed, such as New Zealand author Mary Victoria's *Samiha's Song* and *Oracle's Fire* being released to complete her *Chronicles of the Tree* series. As mentioned previously, Nicole Murphy finished her *Dreams of Asarlai* trilogy with *Power Unbound* and *Rogue Gadda*. Will Elliott continued his *Pendulum* series with *Shadow* and *World's End*. Rebecca Lim continued her series about Mercy, an angel exiled from heaven, with *Exile* and *Muse*, while Bevan McGuiness continued his ongoing series, *The Elven Kingdoms* with *Scarred Man* and *Revenant*. Kim Falconer's fantasy/science fiction *Quantum Encryption* series continued with *Road to the Soul* and *Journey by Night*. Paul Garrety began his *Helix Prophecy* series with *The Seventh Wave* and *The Emerald Tablets*, and Glenda Larke's *Watergivers* trilogy ended with *Stormlord's Exile*. Karen Miller released a prequel to her *Kingmaker, Kingbreaker* series, *Blight of Mages*. Jennifer Fallon began a new series, *Rift Runners* with *The Undivided*. Kylie Chan released the final instalment of her *Journey to Wudang* trilogy, *Heaven to Wudang*, and Tracey O'Hara continued her *Dark Brethren* series with *Death's Sweet Embrace*. A.A. Bell released the second of her *Mira Chambers* books with *Hindsight*, and Alexandra Adornetto released the second *Halo* book, *Hades*. Pip Ballantine and Tee Morris began their steampunk *Ministry of Peculiar Occurrences* series with *Phoenix Rising*, and Sara Creasy continued her *Scarabaeus* series with *Children of Scarabaeus*. James Moloney also began his *Silvermay* trilogy with *Silvermay*.

Hachette Australia followed the trend, focusing mainly on continuing series. Prolific New Zealand paranormal author Nalini

Singh released new instalments of her *Guild Hunter* and *Psy-Changeling* series (*Archangel's Consort*, *Archangel's Blade* and *Kiss of Snow* respectively). Ian Irvine and M.K. Hume both began new series: Irvine started *The Tainted Realm* with *Vengeance*, and Hume's first instalment of her *Merlin* series got off to a great start with *Prophecy: Clash of Kings*. James Phelan continued his *Alone* series with *Survivor* and Trudi Canavan released the second instalment of her *Traitor Spy* trilogy, *The Rogue*. As previously mentioned, Trent Jamieson brought his *Death Works* trilogy to a close with *The Business of Death*. Pamela Freeman was one of the few Australian authors who released a standalone novel with one of the big multinationals this year, releasing *Ember and Ash*, which does involve some of the characters of her impressive previous *Castings* trilogy.

Random House was another great supporter of Australian fantasy this year, again publishing many series titles. John Flanagan continued his young adult *Ranger's Apprentice* series with *The Lost Stories* and began a new sequence, *Brotherband* with *The Outcasts*. Karen Brooks continued *The Curse of the Bond Riders* with *Votive*, and Kate Gordon began her *Thyla* sequence with *Thyla*. Ben Chandler continued his *The Voyages of the Flying Dragon* series with *Beast Child* and Simon Higgins continued his young adult *Moonshadow* series with *The Twilight War*. Michael Pryor completed his young adult series *Laws of Magic* with number six, *Hour of Need*, and began a new trilogy, *The Extraordinaires*, with *The Extinction Gambit*. Stuart Daly started his young adult *The Witch Hunter Chronicles* this year with *The Scourge of Jericho* and *The Army of the Undead*. Rhiannon Hart also began her young adult paranormal fantasy series *Lharmell* series with *Blood Song*.

Allen & Unwin, always a big supporter of Australian writers, released a number of fantasy novels this year. Brigid Lowry released the fairytale inspired *Triple Ripple*, and Penni Russon's multi-perspective novel *Only Ever Always* was another publication this year. Barry Jonsberg's *Being Here*, Kate Constable's *Crow Country* and Karen Healey's *The Shattering* were other Allen &Unwin releases, alongside Richard Harland's steampunk *Worldshaker* sequel, *Liberator*, and the beginning of Garth Nix and Sean Williams' new series, *Troubletwisters*.

Penguin Australia released a number of fantasy-related titles this year. Isobelle Carmody continued her *Obernewtyn* series with number six: *The Sending*. As well as writing for the Aussie Bites short novel imprint, Jen Storer released a lovely children's novel *The Accidental Princess*. Melina Marchetta published *Froi of the Exiles*, the sequel to *Finnikin of the Rock*. Tania Donald released the gothic thriller *Haunted Heart*.

Kate Forsyth brought out a new children's novel, *The Starkin Crown* through Pan Macmillan. Tara Moss released the second in her *Pandora English* series, *The Spider Goddess* and M.J. Hearle introduced his new young adult paranormal series with *Winter's Shadow* also with Pan Macmillan.

Winterbourne Press, a small WA publishing house that opened in 2009, has been expanding rapidly, adding four new novels to their catalogue this year: Barry Rosenberg's *Glide in Slowtime*, Dale Renton's *Half Moon*, Kate Smith's *Illume* and Shaune Lafferty Webb's *Bus Stop on a Strange Loop*.

Clan Destine Press, a small press publishing company headed by Lindy Cameron which was launched in late 2010, released six titles in 2011, including two fantasy titles: *Arrabella Candellarbra and the Questy Thing to End All Questy Things* by A.K. Wrox, and Kerry Greenwood's *Medea*.

New Perth small press publisher Dragonfall Press released a number of titles this year in print and ebook formats: Danny Fahey's *The Tree Singer*, Michael Foster's *The Ancient Ones*, David Pelletier's *The Dreaming*. They also began two series, with T.B. McKenzie and Gary Stowe bringing out the first instalments of their series: *The Dragon and the Crow—Magickless #1* and *The Child of Hope* from *The Masteries* series, respectively.

Ananda Braxton-Smith and Lara Morgan both brought out titles with Walker Books: *Secrets of Carrick: Tantony* and *Equinox*, the second book in the *Rosie Black* series.

Kaaron Warren and Trent Jamieson both had books out with Angry Robot Books this year: Warren released *Mistification* and Jamieson, *Roil*.

Keri Arthur released two books through Dell this year: *Darkness Unbound* from the new *Dark Angel* series and *Mercy Burns*, the second instalment of her *Myth and Magic* series. Nicole E. Sheridan published two paranormal romances through Eternal

Press, *Magical Creations* and *Magical Gains*. Sean Williams released new children's novels, *Invasion of the Freaks* and *Curse of the Vampire* with Omnibus/Scholastic.

Alison Goodman published *Eona* through Angus & Robertson, and Alison Ashley brought out *Phoenix*, the first of the *Fifth Shadow* series through Warrambucca Books. Em Bailey released her young adult thriller *Shift* through Hardie Grant Egmont. Inez Baranay published her vampire story *Always Hungry* through Australian Scholarly Publishing, and US small press Museitup Publishing released Cin Eric's *Inquisitor Blues*. Meg Mundell released *Black Glass* with Scribe Publications. Paul Kidd published *Red Sails in the Fallout* through Wizards of the Coast, and Sally Rippin released the children's novel *Angel Creek* through Text Publishing. Sean McMullen's novel *Changing Yesterday* was published by Ford Street Publishing, and Shona Husk released *Dark Vow* from Carina Press. Stephanie Holder released *Sage: The Power Within* from Alto Books, and Steven Amsterdam published *What the Family Needed* through Sleepers Publishing. Sulari Gentill released *Chasing Odysseus*, the first in her Hero series, through Pantera Press.

Andrea K. Höst and Kylie Elliott both brought out self published titles this year: *Stained Glass Monsters* and *Voices of the Lost* from Höst, and two Tales of the Dominion titles from Elliott: *Into the Deep* and *Out of the Blue*. Cara D'Bastian brought out *The Check Your Luck Agency*, the first in the *Check Your Luck* serial from micropress Sandal Press.

## ANTHOLOGIES

As with last year, the smaller publishers published the bulk of the fantasy anthologies published in Australia and New Zealand this year. Allen & Unwin was the exception to prove the rule, releasing two volumes of *Tales from the Tower*, fairy tale retellings collected by Isobelle Carmody and Nan McNab. *The Wilful Eye* was the first instalment, including stories by Margo Lanagan, Rosie Borella, Isobelle Carmody, Richard Harland, Margaret Mahy and Martine Murray. The second, *The Wicked Wood*, includes Catherine Bateson, Victor Kelleher, Cate Kennedy, Maureen McCarthy, Nan McNab and Kate Thompson. While these volumes are published by Allen & Unwin's children's imprint, they are suited to a much wider audience, and some of the subject matter is very much adult-oriented.

HarperCollins' contribution to the Australian anthology market this year was the ghostly steampunk title *Ghosts by Gaslight*, edited by Jack Dann and Nick Geyvers.

Many of the independent presses' anthologies this year were created in the hope of raising funds or awareness for issues around the Antipodes. *Tales for Canterbury* edited by J.C. Hart and Anna Caro from Random Static, Jodi Cleghorn's *100 Stories for Queensland* from Emergent Publishing, and a special ebook version of Tehani Wessely's *After the Rain* from FableCroft were three anthologies raising funds to aid those affected by the natural disasters in New Zealand and Queensland, respectively. *Tales for Canterbury* and *100 Stories for Queensland*'s tables of contents were filled with authors who donated their works especially for the project. *After the Rain* was a planned anthology that Fablecroft brought out early in special format in order to fundraise. As well as helping those in need after these disasters, all three of these projects produced fantastic books.

Shane Jiraiya Cummings' dark fantasy and horror anthology *Rage Against the Night* was released by Brimstone Press in ebook form in December this year, with a print release due early in 2012. All proceeds will be donated to Rocky Wood, author and President of the Horror Writers' Association, who is battling motor neurone disease.

Sasha Beattie's *Hope* anthology from Kayelle Press is centred around the idea of giving hope to those feeling hopeless. The contents of the anthology (stories and factual information) was donated by the authors, and all profits of the anthology go towards promoting suicide awareness.

Jodi Cleghorn at Emergent Publishing produced two more anthologies this year: *Nothing But Flowers* and *Eighty Nine*. *Nothing But Flowers* is an alternative Valentine's Day themed anthology, which was another fundraiser, this time raising funds for The Grantham Flood Support Fund. *Eighty Nine* is a collection of stories based around a playlist of 26 songs from 1989.

Amanda Pillar and K.V. Taylor released the ebook version of *Ishtar* from Morrigan Books this year, with the print version due in 2012. *Ishtar* tells three novella-length tales about Ishtar, the goddess of love, fertility and sex, in the past ("The Five Loves of Ishtar" told by Kaaron Warren), the present ("And the Dead Shall Outnumber the Living" by Deborah Biancotti) and the future ("The Sleeping and the Dead" by Cat Sparks). These three novellas have very different voices, but combine to create a single, multifaceted whole. This anthology is highly recommended for those wanting a sustained look at the gamut of Australian speculative fiction.

Ticonderoga Publications brought out two themed anthologies this year, with Liz Grzyb's paranormal romance *More Scary Kisses* and Russell B. Farr's Australian vampire tales *Dead Red Heart.*

As mentioned earlier, Jonathan Strahan continued his busy year of editing, releasing *The Best Science Fiction and Fantasy of the Year: Volume Five* with Nightshade Books, and multiple science fiction anthologies. Twelfth Planet Press released another in their novella double series this year with *Above/Below.* Stephanie Campisi and Ben Peek have given us two tales set in the city of Dirt that are interwoven yet separate. Elizabeth Fitzgerald's *Winds of Change,* CSFG's ninth anthology, shows the spectrum of Australian speculative fiction, from darkness to light.

Nalini Singh published a *Guild Hunter* novella in the Berkley anthology *Angels of Darkness.*

## COLLECTIONS

As with the anthologies released this year, the single author collections remained the domain of the independent presses. Allen & Unwin was the only one of the bigger Australian publishing houses to release a fantasy collection, the amazing Margo Lanagan's *Yellowcake.* Focusing mainly retrospectively, these stories show the power of Lanagan's writing.

Ticonderoga Publications released four single-author collections this year. Two were retrospective collections showing the breadth and depth of the works of Lucy Sussex and the late Sara Douglass in *Matilda Told Such Dreadful Lies* and *The Hall of Lost Footsteps* respectively. *Lost Footsteps* was sadly Douglass' last publication, released just after her passing in September, and collects all of her short fiction. Lisa L. Hannett's *Bluegrass Symphony,* a largely original collection of tales set in Hannett's imaginary Deep South, is a disturbing and enthralling selection of stories. Ticonderoga also published a collection of UK author Justina Robson's short fiction, extending the worlds introduced in her novels as well as including some stories original to the collection.

Twelfth Planet Press added four titles to their *Twelve Planets* series, boutique collections of four shorts from Australian speculative fiction writers. Sue Isle's *Nightsiders* was the first publication for the year, set in post-apocalyptic Perth. May brought Tansy Rayner Roberts' collection *Love & Romanpunk*, a selection of stories about some amazing Julias from ancient Rome to the present to a steampunky future. Lucy Sussex's second collection for the year, *Thief of Lives*, shows four very different styles of writing by this master wordsmith. Deborah Biancotti's *Bad Power* rounds out the group of collections from Twelfth Planet in 2011 with an outstanding set of five stories in Biancotti's gritty realist style, blending crime and superpowers seamlessly.

Paul Haines' final collection *The Last Days of Kali Yuga*, a dark fantasy and horror tome was released by Brimstone Press to critical and popular acclaim. Tim Richards' *Thought Crimes*, out through Black Inc. Books tells of a world where nothing is quite as it seems.

Garth Nix released a short three-story collection, *Sir Hereward and Mister Fitz: Three Adventures*, through Nix Entertainment. He is quick to point out that although many of his works are written for a young audience, these stories of flawed heroes are squarely aimed at adults.

Tracie McBride brought out her disturbing collection *Ghosts Can Bleed* through Dark Continents Publishing. Adam Browne released his collection of weird stories, *Phantasmagoriana*, through Amazon as an ebook. Shane Jiraiya Cummings also published four micro collections of his dark short fiction this year in ebook format, *Apocrypha Sequence: Insanity, Inferno, Divinity,* and *Deviance.*

## MAGAZINES/E-ZINES

*Aurealis Magazine* is now available electronically (iTunes and Kindle format, among others) and released two issues in 2011: #45 and #46, each with three fiction pieces.

*Andromeda Spaceways Inflight Magazine* moved from bimonthly to quarterly publication, and released three issues in 2011, starting with their bumper fiftieth issue! Congratulations to the *ASIM* crew for this milestone.

*Cosmos Magazine* regularly publishes speculative fiction edited by Cat Sparks, both in the print magazine (now available as an iPad app) and on the website. While these are primarily science fiction, some stories have fantasy elements.

*Moonlight Tuber* sadly closed their doors this year after releasing issues two and three of their offbeat speculative fiction. All three issues are still available on their website.

*Antipodean SF* has continued to prolifically publish speculative fiction online, and released 12 issues in 2011. *Ticon4.com* publishes fiction irregularly throughout the year. *Semaphore Magazine*, quarterly e-zine published in New Zealand, released two issues in 2011 and is currently on hiatus.

## PODCASTS

*Galactic Suburbia* continues to impress, winning both the Ditmar and Tin Duck for Best Fan Production for Alisa Krasnostein, Tansy Rayner Roberts, and Alex Pierce. Other podcasts which discuss Australian fantasy include: Kirstyn McDermott and Ian Mond's *The Writer and the Critic;* Ion Newcombe's *Antipodean SF Radio Show*; *The Bad Film Diaries Podcast* from Grant Watson; and Gary K. Wolfe & Jonathan Strahan's *The Coode Street Podcast*. *The Terra Incognita Podcast* from Keith Stevenson broadcast its last show in May 2011.

## OTHER MEDIA

The two parts of Peter Jackson's *The Hobbit* has been filming in New Zealand this year and are due for release in 2012 and 2013.

*Benjamin Sniddlegrass and the Cauldron of Penguins* is a *Harry Potter* parody filmed in Australia and featuring the amazing Stephen Fry. It was created by Sydney country music video director Jeremy Dylan after a joke on BBC Radio Five Live. It was released in 2011 and can be viewed online.

# 2011—THE YEAR IN HORROR

In Australian horror short form fiction really kept the genre alive in 2011, a trend echoed in screen arts, and possibly a result of upheavals in publishing and retail.

Gender politics and horror continued to be contested territory in 2011; in February Margo Lanagan's novel *Tender Morsels* (Allen & Unwin, 2009) was one of three works removed from a list of 100 Young Adult Books for the Feminist Reader at the Bitch Media website. The reason cited for the removal was 'the way that the book validates (by failing to critique or discuss) characters who use rape as an act of vengeance' which is particularly interesting in that it takes no account of fiction being a very different mode of writing from criticism.

The Children's Book Council of Australia published their list of Notable Books for 2011, included Sue Bursztynski's YA medieval werewolf romance *Wolfborn* (Random House). The Locus Awards shortlist included *Zombies Vs Unicorns* (Allen & Unwin). Myke Bartlett won the Text Prize for Young Adult and Children's Writing for dark fantasy *The Relic*, which includes a contract with Text as well as $10,000 advance.

Gary Kemble received a New Work grant to work on the novel *Skin Deep* from the Australia Council for the Arts in 2011. Kemble published a feature on his grant year in *Writing Queensland* (the magazine of the Queensland Writers' Centre).

## ANTHOLOGIES

Fablecroft published the *After The Rain* anthology, edited by Tehani Wessely, which was re-purposed as an ebook shortly after the Queensland floods to raise money for the Queensland Premier's Flood Relief Appeal, with reflections from Brisbane contributors Trent Jamieson, Ben Payne, and Angela Slatter. The full anthology of 15 stories ranges across specfic genres, but notable dark works appear from Jason Nahrung, Sally Newham, and Thoraiya Dyer, as well as Lee Battersby's extremely creepy re-imagining of the Golem myth anthologized here.

Coeur De Lion published *Anywhere But Earth*. This anthology traversed some darker hybrid territory, especially stories from Richard Harland, Cat Sparks, Penelope Love, and Jason Nahrung.

Ticonderoga delivered a blistering collection of Australian vampire stories with *Dead Red Heart*. Editor Russell B. Farr sourced diverse voices ranging from the saucy to skin-crawlingly gross, bridging both European and Indigenous traditions, and creating a very Australian sense of vast landscape and big sky.

The anthology is noteworthy in including a standout collaborative story, "The Tide", driven by Martin Livings, with Alan Baxter, Felicity Dowker, Patty Jansen, Devin Jeyathuri, Chuck McKenzie, Andrew J. McKiernan, Lezli Robyn, Daniel I. Russell, Carol Ryles and Kaaron Warren writing as ensemble. Many of these authors are also featured as solo contributors to the anthology. *Dead Red Heart* also collects stories by Shona Husk, Angela Slatter, Jeremy Sadler, Chris Lawson, Yvonne Eve Walus, Amanda Pillar, Marty Young, Simon Brown, Jodi Cleghorn, Jane Routley, Joanna Fay, Damon Cavalchini, Jen White, Jay Caselberg, Jason Nahrung, Joanne Anderton, Sonia Marcon, Tracie McBride, Pete Kempshall, George Ivanoff, Kathryn Horne, Raymond Gates, Helen Stubbs, Donna Maree Hanson, Jacob Edwards, Anne Mok, Lisa L. Hannett, and Penelope Love. An extremely strong anthology overall, as attested by the recommended reading list for 2011.

Gillian Polack's *Five Historical Feasts: The Banquets of Conflux* is a true foodies cookbook, but also has portions of fiction and poetry laid on, with darker lashings from Maxine McArthur and Kaaron Warren.

Jack Dann and Nick Gevers edited the Aurealis Award-winning anthology *Ghosts By Gaslight* (HarperCollins). This anthology of supernatural tales set in the Victorian era, drawing on the rich tradition of the 19th Century ghost story, and features works from Antipodean authors Terry Dowling, Garth Nix, Margo Lanagan, Sean Williams, John Harwood and Richard Harland.

Liz Grzyb edited the glamorous *More Scary Kisses* (Ticonderoga), follow-up to the *Scary Kisses* anthology. While focused on paranormal romance genre, Annette Backshall, Kirstyn McDermott and Felicity Dowker in particular forayed out into truly dark territory.

Gilgamesh Press published *Ishtar*, edited by Amanda Pillar and K.V. Taylor, and collecting three themed novellas from Kaaron Warren, Deborah Biancotti, and Cat Sparks.

Brimstone Press released the formidable *Rage Against The Night: Supernatural Tales of Triumph over Darkness*, edited by Shane Jiraiya Cummings. The anthology was a fundraiser toward purchasing an Eye-Gaze Device for writer and HWA president Rocky Wood, who suffers Motor Neurone Disease (MND). In addition to featuring a forward by Rocky Wood, and stories from

Australian authors Stephen M. Irwin, David Conyers and Gary Kemble, the anthology features stories from many horror luminaries including Jonathan Mayberry, Peter Straub, Ramsey Campbell, Chelsea Quinn Yarbo, and Stephen King. Brimstone Press donated proceeds from the anthology, which brought fundraising up to the $25,000 goal required for the Eye-Gaze Device.

Elizabeth Fitzgerald made her editorial debut with *Winds of Change* (CSFG). This anthology doesn't dwell on dark territories overmuch, perhaps in keeping with the mutability of the theme. In addition to the Jason Nahrung tale collected in this volume, horror aficionados will find dark stories from Alan Baxter and Greg Mellor worth exploring.

Equilibrium Books published *Devil Dolls and Duplicates in Australian Horror*, edited by Anthony Ferguson. This themed anthology concerns doppelgangers and effigies, and includes stories from living Australian writers Van Ikin, Michael Wilding, Stephen Dedman, Jason Franks, James A. Hartley (AKA Jay Caselberg), Sean Williams, Chuck McKenzie, Lee Battersby, Rick Kennett, Lucy Sussex, Jason Nahrung, Robert Hood, Kaaron Warren, Andrew J. McKiernan, Tracie McBride, Martin Livings, B. Michael Radburn, Daniel I. Russell, and Christopher Elston, as well as classic authors Wynne Whiteford, and Marcus Clarke.

*Ho Ho Horror: Christmas Horror Fiction* (The Australian Literature Review) edited by Steve Rossiter is a seasonal themed anthology of new stories with illustration by Andrew J. McKiernan; fiction contributed by Sam Stephens, Belinda Dorio, Cameron Trost, Keith Mushonga, Stephen Gepp, Kathryn Hore and Tony Dews.

In both local and overseas anthologies Australians presented strongly. *Eclipse 4* edited by Jonathan Strahan (Night Shade) includes stories from Australian writers Margo Lanagan and Terry Dowling. Brendan Duffy and David McDonald collaborated on the rollicking "Just Like Cuckoo", which found a home in *The Epocalypse: Emails At The End* (Pill Hill Press). Greg Austin found publication with "Vampire Ritual" in the *Vampires Aren't Pretty* anthology (May December Publications). Gerry Huntman placed stories in two Static Movement anthologies; "The Prey" in *Beyond The Grave* and "Flamingo and Pink" in *After The End*. Pete Kempshall placed "Someone Else To Play With" in the

*Beauty Has Her Way* anthology from Dark Quest Books. *Scenes From The Second Storey* was remixed for an international edition, which included a very nasty story from Pete Kempshall. Robert Mammone's story "Shivers" appeared in the *Big Book of New Short Horror* (Pill Hill Press). Dark Continents published the *Phobophobia* anthology which included works by Tracie McBride and John Irvine.

Rob Porteous placed the story "Big Spirit Blow" in the *Fish* anthology, an Irish anthology showcasing winners and highly recommended works in the Fish Short Story Prize run in association with the Anam Cara Writers' and Artists' Retreat. Daniel I. Russell had the highly recommended and utterly claustrophobic "Broken Bough" published in *The Zombie Feed Volume 1* (Apex). Barry Rosenberg's "Nil" appeared in *Malicious Deviance* (Library of the Living Dead), and "Flush" in *From Shadows and Nightmares* (Nightfall). "The Alabaster Child", a beautifully rendered tale by Cat Sparks, appeared in *Gutshot—Weird West Stories* (PS Publishing). "A Pot To Piss In" by Kaaron Warren was published *Voices From The Past* (H & H Books), and "The List of Definite Endings" in *Teeth: Vampire Tales* (Harper Teen) edited by Ellen Datlow and Terry Windling. Aaron Dries published "And The Dark Growls Back" in *Midnight Movie: Creature Feature* (May December Publications). G.N. Braun published "Autumn as Metaphor" in *Painted Words 2011* (Bendigo TAFE). Angela Slatter published "Rising, Not Dreaming" in *Innsmouth Free Press #6*. David Schembri published "Soulless" in *Hit Men* (Static Movement). Mark Smith-Briggs published "The Bite of Politics" in *Closet Monsters and Other Horrors* (Pill Hill Press).

## MAGAZINES

In October 2011 *Aurealis* magazine re-launched as an epublication as of issue #45. The magazine is available through Smashwords. Issue #45 features fiction from Lachlan Huddy and Aimee Smith; issue #46 features fiction by Greg Mellor and Andrew McKiernan. Both 2011 issues were edited by magazine founder Dirk Strasser.

*Andromeda Spaceways Magazine* published issue 50 in March 2011; this showcases a dark fantasy story from Shona Husk, but was otherwise on the side of light! Issue 51, edited by Simon Petrie and published in June, has some noteworthy horror stories—"The

Bird, the Bees, and Thylacine" by Thoraiya Dyer, and "The Household Debt" by Chris Miles. Issue 52 was edited by David Kernot and released in September 2011.

*Eclecticism* published three issues in 2011. Issue 15 (January/February) was themed Greed, and features some dark offerings from Mark McAuliffe and Mark Smith-Briggs. Issue 16 (July/August) was themed A Pile of Rubbish and offers environmentally focused works, but no horror. Issue 17 (October/December) however was themed Tales O' Halloween and features fiction by Martin Livings, Dianne Dean, Lynley Stace, Rebecca Fung, Kate Elizabeth, Greg Chapman, Guy Salvidge, Geoffrey Maloney, and Ian C. Smith. Poetic offerings abound from W.M. Lewis, Ian Harris, Iva Vemich, and Kristina Jensen.

The AHWA published two issues of *Midnight Echo* magazine in 2011. Issue 5, launched in February, was edited by Leigh Blackmore with art direction from Elizabeth Bathory and David Schembri. This issue features fiction from Juliet Bathory, Leigh Blackmore, Greg Chapman, Rosa Christian, Felicity Dowker, Terry Dowling, Mark Farrugia, Jason Fisher, Damien Gilles, Christopher Green, George Ivanoff, Blair Kelly, Rick Kennett, Robert Mammone, Christopher Sequiera, and Bryce Stevens. There was a significant portion of weird poetry, including works from Australian poets John Grey, Phillip A. Ellis, Margaret Curtis, Charles Lovecraft, Kyla Ward, and Ron Wilkins. Australian visual artists featured in issue 5 were Gaston Locanto, Shane Ryan and Carl Schaller.

*Midnight Echo* Issue 6 was released in November, edited by David Kernot, Jason Fischer and David Conyers, with art direction from David Conyers. This issue was a Science Fiction Horror Special, with stories from Australian writers Helen Stubbs, Cat Sparks, Andrew J. McKiernan, Mark Farrugia, Stephen Dedman, Shane Jiraiya Cummings, Jenny Blackford, Alan Baxter, and Joanne Anderton. This issue showcases the winner of the flash section in the 2011 AHWA Story Competition, Nicholas Stella with "Duncan Checks Out", and the winners of the short story section, David Conyers and David Kernot, with "Winds of Nzambi". Australian visual artist Olivia Kernot has work in issue 6.

New webzine *Scape* was launched by a international editorial team including an Australian art editor Rebecca Ing, and poetry editor Emma Osborne. The magazine is open to young adult speculative submissions. Two issues published in 2011.

Lisa L. Hannett had a very dark selkie story, "Gutted", in *Shimmer Magazine* issue 13. Richard Harland saw publication of "At The Top Of The Stairs" in *Shadows and Tall Trees #2* (Undertow Publications). David McDonald placed the novelette "Catspaw" in *Tales of the Shadowmen Volume 8* (Black Coat Press). Amanda Spedding took out first Place with "Shovel Man Joe" in the *Shades of Sentience* Short Story Competition. Kaaron Warren's story "The Rude Little Girl" was a winner in Christopher Fowler and Maura McHugh's *Campaign For Real Fear* competition, and the ten winning stories were published in *Black Static #17*. Alan Baxter had a weird tale "Mirrorwalk" published in *Murky Depths #16*. Robert Mammone placed his fine story "The Well" in the prestigious *British Fantasy Society Journal* Winter Edition. Marty Young placed "Behind The Midnight Blinds" in *HorrorWorld*. Mark Farrugia placed a story "Static" at *Sentient Online*. Alan Baxter had a rather excellent oldschool occult story, "The Seven Garages of Kevin Simpson", featured as audio in *Pseudopod*. Shane Jiraiya Cummings also forayed strongly onto *Pseudopod* with the elegant "The Song of Prague". Aaron Dries published "Daddy" in *SNM Horror Magazine #35*. Adam Browne and Paul Haines published "Deep Clean" in *Cosmos #40*. Christopher Green published "Stitched" in *Shock Totem #3*.

## SINGLE AUTHOR COLLECTIONS

Brimstone Press published a beautifully presented collection from Paul Haines, *The Last Days of Kali Yuga*. The book features only one new story, "The Past Is A Bridge Best Left Burnt", as the author's output was impacted by declining health in 2011. There is commendable sensitivity in Angela Challis' editorial style in bringing such an intensely painful and personal story to publication. While this may be the last of his own collections that Paul Haines saw published, the groundswell of interest in his exceptionally unique voice suggests stories from Haines will be anthologized and re-examined for many years to come. Ticonderoga Publications published *Matilda Told Such Dreadful Lies: the Essential Lucy Sussex*, which features one story original to the collection. A strong compendium of Sussex's distinguished and versatile writing to date; simply a must-have volume for serious readers of both antipodean speculative fiction, and Australian feminist fiction.

Ticonderoga Publications published *Bluegrass Symphony*, the debut collection from Lisa L. Hannett; treading lush slipstream and southern gothic territory, and likely to appeal to a broad readership beyond Australia.

Twelfth Planet Press launched The Twelve Planets series, featuring twelve antipodean female authors with publication spread over two years. The 2011 installments were *Nightsiders* by Sue Isle, *Love and Romanpunk* by Tansy Rayner Roberts, *Thief of Lies* by Lucy Sussex, and *Bad Power* by Deborah Biancotti.

P'Rea Press published a collection of weird poetry by Kyla Lee Ward, *The Land of Bad Dreams*. Ranging from rhyming verse to prose poetry, the book is lavishly bedecked with 15 illustrations and a colour cover illustration by the author, as well as an interview by Charles Lovecraft. The blank verse poem was honoured with a nomination for The Science Fiction Poetry Association's 2012 Rhysling Awards.

Shane Jiraiya Cummings prolific "grand experiment"— releasing seven ebooks in 2011— produced a different kind of single author collection; most notably the *Apocrypha Sequence* (in four parts) is an innovative approach to contextualizing new and existing works by theme for digital marketing, and deservedly received an honourable mention in the Australian Shadows Awards.

Margo Lanagan's *Yellowcake* (Allen & Unwin) compiled 10 new short stories for adults, in the unmistakable dark, literary, complex Lanaganesque style. Adam Browne's *Phantasmagoriana* collects previously published short stories; Browne's excursions in the absurd, by turns harsh and whimsical, always layered and tightly constructed. Tim Richards *Thought Crimes* (Black Inc) is another very literary voice working in weird fiction, compiling 21 stories most notable for black humour. Tracie McBride saw publication of her first collection *Ghosts Can Bleed* (Dark Continents) compiling 40 dark creative works spanning both poetry and prose. Legumeman Books published a collection from Brett McBean titled *Tales of Sin and Madness* compiling 21 short stories as well as author commentary.

## NOVELS

2011 was a lean year for Australian horror novels, with most straddling the paranormal romance or dark fantasy genres, or incorporating supernatural flourishes within an adventure, thriller or crime context.

Inez Baranay's *Always Hungry* (Australian Scholarly) details a writer exploring the sensual side of Amsterdam, and finding the vampire lover to be her ultimate conquest. Marianne de Pierres' *Angel Arias* (Random House) is the YA dark fantasy sequel to *Burn Bright*. John Birmingham's *Angels of Vengeance* (Pan Macmillan) bring more post-apocalyptic adventure; follow up to *After America*. Rhiannon Hart's *Blood Song* (Random House) is a vampiric YA fantasy. Nansi Kunze's *Dangerously Placed* (Random House) is a YA science-fiction romantic thriller in virtual reality.

M.A. Anderson's *Dark Legacy* (CreateSpace) is a self-published foray into the supernatural. Shona Husk's *Dark Vow* (Carina Press) is paranormal romance concerning occult bounty hunters and revenge.

Keri Arthur published three paranormal romance novels with Dell in 2011: Darkness *Unbound* and *Darkness Rising*, the first two installments in the Dark Angel series; and *Mercy Burns*, Book 2 in the Myth and Magic series.

Tracey O'Hara published *Death's Sweet Embrace* (HarperCollins), an urban fantasy, second in the Dark Brethren series. Tania Donald saw publication of *Haunted Heart* (Penguin) a gothic romance set in the 1830s. Aaron Dries saw publication of *House of Sighs* (ChiZine) based on the manuscript which won the international Rue Morgue/ChiZine/Dorchester Publications Fresh Blood contest. Paul Garrety's *Seventh Wave*, (HarperCollins) is an occult suspense novel with witches and vampires and assassins aplenty.

D. Bruno Starr's novel *That Blackfella Bloodsucka Dance!* (JustFiction Edition, Germany) boasts a promotional blurb that sounds more at home in the 1980s than 2011— "in which a part-blood Aboriginal Australian becomes a full-blood vampire".

Stephen M. Irwin's *The Broken* Ones (Hachette Australia) is a polished thriller, with a global epidemic of hauntings complicating the police pursuit of a serial killer.

Trent Jamieson's *The Business of Death* (Hachette Australia) is the third in the Deathworks series, and continues to build on the highly original corporate intrigue of the afterlife.

Mary Borsellino's *The Devil's Mixtape* (Omnium Gatherum) is dark fantasy—three interconnecting narratives of violence. Belinda Murrell's *The Ivory Rose* (Random House) is a YA colonial gothic ghost story set in Sydney in the 1890s. Karen Healey's *The Shattering* (Little Brown) is a YA small town suspense thriller set on the New Zealand West Coast. Sylvia Kelso's *The Solitaire Ghost* is a contemporary ghost mystery, without strong elements of fear.

*The Spider Goddess* (Pan Macmillan) from Tara Moss is the second Pandora English novel, a beautifully presented urban fantasy.

Stuart Daly published two YA swashbuckling novels with Random House, replete with witch-hunting and demon slaying, set in 1666—*The Witch Hunter Chronicles 1: The Scourge of Jericho*, and *The Witch Hunter Chronicles 2: The Army of the Undead*.

Will Schaefer's *The Wolf Letters* (Hybrid) is an old school occult horror novel centered on a cursed object and manuscripts. Greig Beck's *This Green Hell* (Pan Macmillan) is an outbreak thriller with predatory undertones. Kate Gordon's *Thyla* (Random House) is a YA paranormal tale of shape-shifting set against the backdrop of Tasmania's history of convicts and extinction. Andrez Bergen's *Tobacco-Stained Mountain Goat* (Another Sky Press) is a weird noir dystopian absurdist rollick set in far future Melbourne.

Brett McBean saw publication of several novellas—*Torment* (Severed Press), *Dead Tree Forest* (Delirium Books), and *Concrete Jungle* (Tasmaniac Publications) collecting three novellas set in a post-civilization urban landscape. Twelfth Planet Press published the third of their Novella Double series, this installment *Above/Below* by Stephanie Campisi and Ben Peek. David Conyers published *The Eye of Infinity* (Perilous Press). Greg Chapman published two stand alone novellas *The Noctuary* and *Torment*, both with Damnation Books.

## GRAPHIC NOVELS, COMICS & ILLUSTRATED WORKS

Black House Comics published the third installment in the After The World series, a bumper anthology issue *Pack Rules*. This issue featured stories by Jason Franks, B. Michael Radburn, Pete Kempshall, Raymond Gates, Eugene Gramelis, Clinton Green and

Jason Fischer. *Tides of Hope* from Christopher Sequeira and Tim McEwen was a fundraiser for the Queensland floods, published by Supanova Pop Culture Industries. Margaret Wild published *Vampyre* with Walker Books, illustrated by Andrew Yeo.

## FILM

Feature length Australian horror films were comparatively sparse over 2011—notably *The Reef* (2011, David Traucki, Director) relates shipwreck survivors on the Great Barrier Reef, stalked by a giant shark. *Wound* (2010, David Blyth, Director, New Zealand) had an Australian Premiere at A Night Of Horror.

2011 was a prolific year for short horror films, with the A Night Of Horror film festival putting on two showcase screenings to accommodate them all. *Home* (Cameron McCullock Director) a Rom Zom short. *Hunt* (Wade K. Savage, Director) survival horror following two female characters on the run in a world of urban decay. *Deja Vu* (Robin Queree, Director) a short suspense piece about prescience. *Written in Blood* (Erik Magnusson, Director) in which a horror writer Stephen Lovecraft is held captive and tortured by a younger upstart horror writer. *Horror Show* (Steve Morris, Director) a claustrophobic psychological disintegration. *House 51* (Sean Wells, Director) a couple lost in the bush find a creepy abandoned house.

# 2011—THE YEAR IN THE INDUSTRY

2011 was a year of change and uncertainty in publishing, with the Global Financial Crisis impacting retail and distribution, and the rise of ereading pushing industry to play catch-up to establish standards for digital rights management. Digital rights strategies for authors and publishers, and new print-on-demand supply chains and backlist imprints were also big news in 2011.

The Book Industry Strategy Group (BISG) closed to submissions in 2011. More than 90 submissions were made, and BISG delivered their final report in early November 2011. Recommendations that industry adopt a code of practice for retention of territorial copyright received mixed responses, as different timeframes are more achievable for large and small presses. The report fueled debate over the GST-free threshold on books purchased online from overseas retailers, and an acknowledgement of need for more data collection on the book industry, possibly by the Australian Bureau of Statistics. Other recommendations included all government funded literary grants and prizes to be made tax exempt, and an income deposits tax measure to assist creative artists managing fluctuating incomes.

## READERS, EBOOKS & RETAIL

Ereaders pushed into the Australian market on an unprecedented scale; Thorpe Bowker's survey showed 50% of Australian bookstores carrying ereading devices in 2011. The APA reported 600,000 iPads have been sold in Australia, and Amazon's Kindle seems to have taken 60% of the ereader market.

All major publishers brought out an ebook program during 2011. Despite the increased uptake of ereaders, ebooks have not had a clear impact on book sales; Neilson Bookscan did not survey ebook sales for 2011. Bookseller and Publisher's survey revealed 54% of bookstores were selling ebooks by late 2011, with 21% of indie bookstores selling ebooks.

Booki.sh and ReadCloud have proven popular platforms with those indies who have launched digital vending. Readings bookstore launched an ebookstore selling local content from SPUNC members through Booki.sh in January, becoming the first indie bookstore in Australia to have their own ebook store. Pages and Pages bookstore was the first Australian bricks and mortar store to launch a ReadCloud based digital store; more than 200 Australian and New Zealand bookstores signed up for ReadCloud in 2011, including SF specialist store Galaxy Books. ReadCloud have their own app for Apple and Android reading devices, and the creation of online social networks suitable for book clubs.

BookLamp launched the Book Genome Project, a search engine that recommends books to readers using a mathematical algorithm of book attributes.

Gollancz/Hachette SF Gateway ebook project went online, a database of many classics of sf and fantasy in various ebook formats, listing lots of ebookshops stocking them. Not a large proportion of fantasy is up yet, especially Australian, but there is some here and there, such as two of Sean Williams' Books of the Change series.

Fantastic Planet books of Perth found a new owner in Steffen Brazulaitis, who came from a background in educational book distribution, as well as retail experience with Dymocks and Borders.

## EBOOKS & LENDING

The rise of the ebook has implications for Australia's Public Lending Rights (PLR) and Educational Lending Rights (ELR). The PLR committee in their annual report for 2010-11 determined it is premature to include ebooks in the PLR scheme, as ebook collections are modest in Australian public libraries.

Approved changes to Public Lending Rights (PRL) and Educational Lending Rights (ELR) schemes relating to eligibility of payments; titles must be claimed within five years of first publication; books created for single use are ineligible; the PLR committee has discretion on setting a minimum print run for eligibility. Publishers need to have one new or revised work in print in a three-year period to remain eligible.

Australian ebook store Bookbee launched a beta-test of an ebook lending service. Cambridge University Press launched University Publishing Online, a digital content platform serving libraries and educational institutions.

HarperCollins signed with NetGallery in the US to provide electronic Advance Reading Copies (ARC). Random House started offering ARCs to booksellers and reviewers. Allen & Unwin are making ARCs available through the Booki.sh platform. Simon & Schuster are delivering PDF ARC to reviewers. Other publishers opting for electronic ARCs include Black Inc, Scribe, and Affirm Press.

## NEW PUBLISHERS, IMPRINTS & BACK-LISTS

Dragonfall Press, a new Perth small press publisher, started up in late 2010, releasing their first publications in 2011. Clan Destine Press from Melbourne started at the same time. Both of these new presses are producing print and ebook versions of their publications.

The new SRDP, POD and ebook formats have encouraged many publishers to establish imprints of new works and backlist titles in electronic formats or by customer order driven printing. Pan Macmillan partnered with Curtis Brown to launch the Macmillan Bello imprint carrying hundreds of out-of-print backlist titles as digital editions. Pan Macmillan launched the digital imprint Momentum, publishing new works by Australian authors including John Birmingham. Momentum will acquire global rights and market works internationally. Random House began development of Story Cuts, an ebook series focused on selling individual stories outside of collections. Quercus announced a new speculative fiction imprint Jo Fletcher Books. HarperCollins launched imprint Avon Books, focused on print-on-demand and digital editions. Amazon launched a publishing imprint for science fiction and horror genre, called 47North, to publish original works, and out-of-print books. HarperCollins made their 5,000-title-strong backlist available through Print On Demand via Espresso Book Machine. Random House re-launched their romance imprint Love swept as a digital imprint of 1980s backlist titles.

## REDGROUP AND CONSEQUENCES

Australia's largest bookselling chain, REDgroup, went into voluntary administration, and after repeated unsuccessful attempts to save the business, eventually folded. REDgroup was comprised of Borders across Australia, New Zealand and Singapore, Angus & Robertson in Australia, and Whitcoulls and Bennetts bookstores in New Zealand. 130 stores closed outright, including the large Borders stores, with approximately 2000 jobs lost and the bookselling retail floor diminished by 20% across Australia. Many franchiser owned A&R stores re-branded, and continue to trade as independents. Whitcoulls was purchased, and most stores were saved. Eight Bennetts bookstores located in New Zealand universities were sold to Bennetts Bookstores Limited. Twenty former A&R stores franchise stores joined Leading Edge as independent booksellers, bringing Leading Edge up to 200 bookstores Australia wide. Collins Booksellers acquired 18 A&R franchises and two A&R owned store locations, expanding Collins from 52 stores to 72 stores. REDgroup owned Readers Feast bookstore closed their store at the iconic Bourke St and Swanston St intersection in Melbourne, but re-launched in Collins St as an indie store before Christmas.

Pearson Group purchased the online Angus & Robertson and Borders stores, and these continue to trade as web based businesses.

Larger publishers seemed to feel the loss of REDgroup reflected in 2011 bestseller sales. Conversely in the Thorpe Bowker post-Christmas survey, 95% chain respondents reported sales up on Christmas 2010, while only 40% indie bookstores noted an improvement. 30% of indies reported sales holding, and 28% reported sales diminished. Neilson Bookscan showed total Australian book sales dropped by 7.1% to 60.4 million (from 66.2 million in 2010), with value dropping 12.6% to 1.1 billion.

Large Australian and New Zealand independent book distribution company The Scribo Group closed in July 2011. This closure affected a number of Australian genre small presses who had been distributed through Scribo; 50 jobs were lost.

Local distributors Peribo and Alpa Books absorbed some of the indie publisher distribution market, and the ABA held open their Spring and Christmas catalogues to assist publishers hardest hit by the closure. Music distribution label Fuse entered the book distro industry taking a number of international publishers onto their roster, most notably Taschen Books who were previously distributed by Scribo.

## BOOKS IN MAINSTREAM MEDIA

The Australian Literary Review monthly supplement published by the *Australian* newspaper, produced a final issue in October 2011. The close was attributed to the Group of Eight universities withdrawing funding for the magazine.

In response to proposed ABC arts cuts, an open letter was submitted to the national broadcaster signed by prominent authors and other arts practitioners. ABC Radio national's Book Show is to undergo a major overhaul, with a new focus proposed on fiction books. Presenter Ramona Koval left the show, and Michael Cathcart was selected to host the 2012 program to be re-launched as Books and Arts. The Senate undertook an inquiry into proposed cuts to the ABC.

## ENVIRONMENTAL DISASTERS AND FUNDRAISING

Queensland Writers Centre launched Writers On Rafts to help raise money for those hit hard by the Queensland floods. The appeal raised more than $25,000 for the Queensland Premier's Disaster Appeal. The Wheeler Centre donated all profits from the 2011 Gala Night of Storytelling: Voice from Elsewhere to Queensland libraries affected by the floods. The Australian Booksellers Association donated to the Queensland Flood Relief Fund.

An earthquake hit Christchurch on February 21. Booksellers NZ established a relief fund for Christchurch booksellers. Auckland Council Libraries and the New Zealand Society of Authors launched the Writers Read In events to raise funds for the NZ Red Cross Earthquake Appeal. Scholastic New Zealand donated funds from the worldwide sales of *Quaky Cat* by Diana Noonan and Gavin Bishop to the Christchurch Mayoral Earthquake Appeal.

Flash floods in Melbourne in February affected three independent bookstores, Readings St Kilda, Book Street in Toorak, and Embiggen Books in the CBD.

## INITIATIVES, FUNDING & PRIZES

In June 2011 New Zealand was announced country of honour at the 2012 Frankfurt Book Fair, and in December 2011 the New Zealand Ministry for Culture and Heritage and the Publishers Association of New Zealand (PANZ) committed NZ$1 million funding to subsidize German publishers translating New Zealand books, as well as supporting New Zealand writers and publishers to attend German literary events in 2012.

The Australia Council for the Arts launched their five-year Creative Australia Artists Grants program, and within this The Literature Board announced a new grants programs called Book2. The program will provide ten grants of $50,000 from 2011 to 2015 to writers contracted for a second book, whose first book has received favourable criticism.

The Literature Board has proposed changes to funding publishers in A Case for Literature: The effectiveness of subsidies to Australian publishers 1995–2005, a report released in October 2010. From January 2012 publishers can apply for publishing program grants for the development and production of Australian writing, unlike the previous arrangement where funding was for an individual title. There are different funding categories for established and emerging publishers, with amounts based on the size of the existing publication list, as well as a special publishing grants category. The overall amount of funding is largely unchanged under the new funding model.

The Wheelers Centre announced twenty new fellowships, providing writers with a desk space for two months and $1,000 stipend. The Victorian Writers' Centre announced they will re-brand as Writers Victoria, with the 2012 program released in December 2011.

Victorian Premier Ted Baillieu announced changes to The Victorian Premier's Awards, introducing the Victorian Prize for Literature, worth $100,000, to go to one of the five category winners, making a $125,000 prize in total. The category winners receive $25,000 each. This makes the awards the richest in Australia. The state government committed to $250,000 annual funding in support for Melbourne's City of Literature initiative.

Writing Australia launched their program including the new Writing Australia Unpublished Manuscript Award with a $10,000 cash prize and $2,000 worth of mentoring for the winner. The award is open to both literary and genre fiction, and the first round was judged by noted romance writer Valerie Parv, academic Mark Macleod, and Peter Bishop, former creative director of Varuna. Writing Australia proposed a Writers Round-Up conference, for launch in 2013. The author tour program became active in 2011.

The University of Otago in Dunedin, New Zealand, will host a Centre for the Book, joining a network including Monash University in Melbourne, and cultural institutions in the US and Canada. The Centre program includes the 2011 Printer in Residence program, and the 2012 Bibliographical Society of Australia and New Zealand conference, and the 2013 Australasian Rare Book School.

The Emerging Writers Festival (EWF) brought a mini-conference to Brisbane thanks to crowd funding, as part of Queensland Writers Week. The mini-conference, Digital Writers: Taking your Words Online included speculative writer Alan Baxter.

2011 saw the first National Bookshop day celebrated on August 20, with events hosted in bookshops around the nation and promotions managed by the Australian Booksellers Association.

The Faber Academy launched in Australia in March, with a Sydney program of courses, and a similar program was launched in Melbourne in July. The Faber Academy is a partnership between the UK Academy and Allan & Unwin.

The Get Reading! 2011 touring program opened a book-touring program in July, as lead up to a campaign in early September. 1,000 booksellers and libraries participated, and touring writers included Tristan Bancks promoting Galactic Adventures: First Kids in Space. Government funding cuts of $1.6 million over four years did not affect the 2011 program, although is expected to affect subsequent years.

The Griffith Review and the Copyright Agency Limited (CAL) launched the Novella Projects prize, with plans to publish three winning novellas by residents of Australian and New Zealand in the fourth annual New Fiction Edition of the Griffith Review. The project was launched in support of a 'renaissance of the long form'.

During 2011 support was mustered for a new literary prize, the Stella Prize, for women's writing. Works first published in 2012 will be eligible for the inaugural award in 2013.

The Prime Minister's Literary Awards announced a new award for poetry in 2012, and an integration of the existing award for Australian History. The prize pool has been restructured to acknowledge short-listed authors with cash prizes, with winners receiving $80,000, and short-listed entries receiving $5,000.

Sisters In Crime celebrated a 20th anniversary with the 2011 SheKilda Australian Women Crime Writers' Convention, in Melbourne in October. The 3-day event gathered 66 featured writers for 39 workshops and panels, and hosted the Davitt Awards ceremony.

A new not-for-profit facility to help children and youth with writing, the Sydney Story Factory, secured a premises in Redfern in September. The centre was launched at the 2011 Sydney Writers Festival.

Major publishers fostering opportunity for unsigned authors include Pan Macmillan with Manuscript Monday, Allen & Unwin with The Friday Pitch, Angry Robot with Open Door Month in March, Penguin with the Varuna Scholarship, and the Hachette/ Queensland Writers Centre's Manuscript Development Program.

• • • • • • • • • • •

## REMEMBERED

**Sara Douglass**, 54, multiple award-winning Australian fantasy writer. **Eve Portsmouth** (nee Johnson), 65, mother of Ticonderoga Publications editor Russell B. Farr. **Peter Campbell**, 74, New Zealand writer and YA author. **Anne McCaffrey**, 85, Irish-American writer, legend, SFWA Grand Master, GoH at SwanCon 5 (19th Australian National SF Convention, 1980). **Russell Hoban**, 86, American writer, winner Ditmar Best International Fiction 1983. **Mike Glicksohn**, 64, Canadian fan, Hugo Award winner, FGoH at Aussiecon 1 (1975). **Arthur Haddon**, Sydney fandom identity. **Elizabeth Sladen**, 63, actor, *Dr Who*'s Sarah Jane Smith. **T.A.G. (Tom) Hungerford** AM, 96, Australian writer and legend. **Martin H. Greenberg**, 70, anthology editor and academic, winner of four genre Lifetime Achievement Awards. **Juliana Archbold**, 73, librarian and President of The International Board on Books for Young People Australia. **Diana Gribble**, co-founder of Text Publishing and McPhee Gribble. **Michael Stern Hart**, 64, founder of Project Gutenberg. **James Sangster**, 83, British horror screenwriter. **Dame Katerina Mataira**, Companion of the New Zealand Order of Merit. **Joanna Russ**, 74, American feminist critic and multiple award-winning science fiction author. **Diana Wynne Jones**, 77, British fantasy author, winner of a World Fantasy Life Achievement Award. **Perry Moore**, 39, film producer and author. **Vivienne Brophy**, editor of *Australian Bookseller & Publisher*. **Joyce Nicholson Thorpe**, 91, founding member of the National Book Council. **Elisabeth Beresford**, 84, British children's author best known for originating The Wombles. **Richard Bessière**, 88, French science-fiction author. **Liz Huf**, founding editor of Queensland literary journal *Idiom23*. **Philip Rahman**, 59, American co-founder of weird fiction press Fedogan & Bremer. **Jeffrey Catherine Jones**, 67, SF artist and illustrator, Spectrum Grandmaster. **Ion Hobana**, 80, Romanian science fiction editor, author and translator.

# SARA DOUGLASS (1957–2011)

## LUCY SUSSEX

2 JULY 1957 — 27 SEPTEMBER 2011

Sara Douglass, the pre-eminent Australian author of epic fantasy, has died in a hospice in Hobart, of ovarian cancer, aged 54.

She was born Sara Warneke in Penola, South Australia, to Robert Warneke, a health and weeds inspector, and Elinor Lees. A notable ancestor was nineteenth-century Spiritualist Robert James Lees, who claimed to have identified Jack the Ripper. The Warnekes moved from the family farm when she was seven to Adelaide, where she attended Methodist Ladies College. She began writing at the school, coming second in a national essay competition. Despite showing academic promise, she followed in what she described as a 'female family tradition' of nursing. For some seventeen years, she worked as a Registered Nurse in Adelaide, while planning her escape from a profession she had found uncongenial from the start. She completed a BA at Adelaide University, and then a PhD in early modern English history, both part-time. Many of the manuscripts of her best-selling fantasy novels are held in the Barr Smith Library at the University.

In 1992, her PhD completed, she left nursing behind for a lectureship in medieval history at La Trobe University, Bendigo. She would publish one book of history as Sara Warneke, *Images of the Educational Traveller in Early Modern England* (Brill, 1995). Later, under her pen-name, she would publish a study of the King Arthur legend, *The Betrayal of Arthur* (1998). Though she would be recalled as a scrupulous teacher and well liked by her students, she found academia stressful and uncertain. Once again she found herself seeking a way out of her employment. She returned to writing, completing several unpublished novels, including some Mills and Boon romances rejected for being too dark.

Then, in a move she would describe as 'almost by accident' she turned to writing fantasy, hitting her literary stride with *Battleaxe* (1995), set in the imaginary world of Tencendor. Like J. R. R. Tolkien, she found a background in medievalism the perfect training for writing in the epic fantasy genre. The history of the middle ages informed the imaginary sword and sorcery realms of her novels, made them credible, lived-in worlds.

Once with her niche, she stuck with it, completing over twenty novels. She was formidably prolific, especially since genre expectations for epic fantasy mean trilogies and more of massive books, which can reach over 200,000 words. *Battleaxe* would be the first book of the Axis trilogy, followed the next year by *Enchanter* and *StarMan*. These two books would be joint winners of the 1996 Aurealis award for Best Fantasy Novel, with a later Aurealis award coming in 2001 for *The Wounded Hawk*. Two later series, The Wayfarer Redemption and Darkglass Mountain, would revisit the imagined world of Tencendor. She also wrote several independent historical fantasy series, The Crucible Trilogy and the Troy Game. Despite the pace and volume of her writing she never compromised her auctorial standards, which remained consistently high throughout her career.

*Battleaxe* took six months before agent Lyn Tranter accepted it, and sold to a publisher within weeks. It would be the first signing to HarperCollins Voyager, a dedicated fantasy list whose continuing success was to a large extent created by the Sara Douglass books. She would be the first author to show that an Australian could make a world-wide success from writing fantasy. Her books would sell close to a million copies in Australia alone, and far more internationally, with numerous translations. She would persist with HarperCollins except for the teenage fantasy *Beyond the Hanging Wall* (Hodder Headline, 1996).

Because the name Warneke would mean relegation to the lower shelves of bookshops, HarperCollins requested a pseudonym. She chose Douglas, the name she would have had if born a male, with the added 's' to feminise it, medieval-style. Although advised to move to Ireland for tax reasons, she chose the preferred cool climate of Hobart, where she restored a historic house and garden.

Although an intensely private person, who suffered from deafness, she maintained contact with her increasing fandom via email, bulletin boards and her website, stopping only when she was receiving hundreds of messages a day. She is remembered as being ever-generous with advice and encouragement to aspiring fantasy writers.

In 2008 she was diagnosed with ovarian cancer, the disease which had killed her mother Elinor. Despite treatment, it returned, this time fatally. She produced some remarkable writing about her disease, including 'The Silence of the Dying'. In it she wrote with great honesty and acuity, proposing that western society had lost all ability to die well. It drew an extraordinary response, both online and when reprinted in newspapers. She would continue her cancerblogging on Facebook, again with heartrending intelligence and sagacity.

Despite her illness she saw through the editing process of her final novel *The Devil's Diadem*. She lived to see, although she was too weak to read, advance proofs of her first short story collection, *The Hall of Lost Footsteps*. It will be published by Ticonderoga Press in November. Publisher Russell B. Farr comments: 'She had an incredible gift, and we are all richer that she chose to share her words and worlds with us.'

She is survived by her siblings, Christine, Paul, and Judy; her carers, fantasy writer Karen Brooks and her husband Stephen; her circle of friends; and her many grieving fans.

*First published in* The Age, *10 October 2011.*

# THE
# YEAR'S BEST
# AUSTRALIAN
# FANTASY
## &
# HORROR
~ 2011 ~

## THE SECOND ANNUAL
## COLLECTION

# ALL YOU CAN DO IS BREATHE

## KAARON WARREN

Stuart lay trapped underground for five days before the tall man appeared and stared into his eyes.

He thought he sensed movement. Flicked on his caplamp, "Barry? Did you make it through the wall?" but there was no one.

There was something though, in his face so close he pulled back and banged his head on the rock behind. He shouted, mouth open, squeezed his eyes shut. He'd never felt such terror, not even when his daughter had fallen into the pool and they didn't notice for god knows how long.

This was a man. Something like a man. Tall, elongated, the thing looked deep into his eyes. It reached out and almost took his chin with its bony fingers, keeping his head still, paralysing him even though it wasn't actually touching him.

Stuart could smell sour cherries, something like that. It made him hungry, and that hunger somehow beat out the terror.

He pulled his head backwards. The man nodded, stepped back, and was gone.

Within a minute or two, Stuart was sure he'd imagined it. Though he had words in his ear. "See you soon, Stuart." He was sure he'd heard those words.

It felt like the walls were getting closer, but he kept testing by stretching his arms and the distance was the same. The part of the mine he was working had collapsed so quickly, it seemed like time stopped and froze and when it started up again, he was surrounded on all sides by rock.

Barry, his workmate, was on the other side, but he'd heard nothing from him for twelve hours now.

Thank god for the luminous hand on his watch. The kid gave it to him for Father's Day years ago and even at the time he'd been thrilled. You don't always get that with Father's Day presents.

It wasn't what you'd call a worker's watch. It was full of gadgets, like the watches of the office men who drove to work each day, passing him as he stood, cold in the dark, at the bus stop with the other miners. Their cars blinked with gadgets.

This watch kept perfect time, and followed the date, and the hand provided a warm green glow in the pitch black. At home he had to keep it in his bedside drawer at night because the light kept his wife awake. But he could still see the thin green line across the top of the drawer where the light escaped.

Since the walls came down, he'd slept sporadically, waking a couple of times thinking he was home in bed, because of the glow. He'd covered it up with his lunchbox and only a small line escaped.

He had his caplamp but he really didn't want to use that. There'd been mine rescues lasting two weeks and he wanted to know he could have bright light if he needed to. He knew they wouldn't give up. They never left a body underground, mostly because they didn't want it found much later.

He had his GPS so they knew where he was. He could see Barry's blip, too, but that didn't mean he was still going. Just his GPS.

Stuart stretched his legs and arms out and in, counting to a hundred. His wife was always on at him to do more exercise, so she'd be pleased to see him do this. His water and food had run out on the third day. He knew there was no sense keeping the food. It'd just go off and make him sick. Some gritty water dripped down the wall. Licking it made his tongue ache it was so cold and there wasn't enough of it. He pissed into his water bottle and knew that drinking it wouldn't kill him. He pretended it was lime cordial, the sour stuff, not the sweet.

Foodwise he knew he could last without for a while but it didn't help the hunger pains. Lucky his wife packed him heaps and there was Barry's lunch as well, on Stuart's side of the wall where Barry couldn't get to it.

He'd tried moving the rocks but it just caused more of a tumble no matter where he took the rocks from. He wanted to keep trying but his instincts told him just to leave it.

Bugs skittered about and he could eat them. The strap of his lunch box was leather and he chewed on that, making jokes that it was about as good as his sister-in-law's roast dinner. If he got out, he'd make that joke and people would write it up and his sister-in-law would be famous for her bad cooking.

Stuart tried to sleep when he figured it was night time outside, to keep a routine going. It was hard without a change of light and with an empty stomach, and he hadn't done anything to wear himself out. Usually he'd drop into bed after a shift and a feed exhausted. On a Saturday, if he hadn't been in the mine, he and his wife might have sex, but it wasn't something he thought about much.

He thought about it now.

He spent a lot of the time with his eyes closed but he tried not to think about the dark. Instead, he went through football matches he remembered.

• • •

It was seven days before they found him. Nowhere near the record, but enough to have a media frenzy going on. As they were getting close they'd managed to get a tube through to him, and sent him notes from his wife and daughter and bags of glucose. They dropped some biscuits down, too. "I was hoping for a meat pie," he called up the tube. He could talk with his mouth close to the tube, tell them shit he wanted his family to know. Tell them all the jokes he'd thought up while he was down there. Nothing worse than a joke without an audience. They called questions down, like, "Are you scared?"

"Naah, I'm not scared. I'm fearless! Nothing scares me!"

He asked them about Barry and they said they were working on it. Ever since the long man had visited him, Stuart had had a bad feeling about Barry. He thought perhaps that was Barry's ghost and he felt bad about screaming. He wished he'd said, "G'day, mate," whatever.

It was overcast when they pulled him out, but still far warmer than inside the mine. It meant he didn't have to squint because of the sun. His wife Cheryl was there, and his daughter Sarah, and for a long time he couldn't talk, just held them and cried. He'd never actually cried before, not since he was a little kid, anyway, but this he couldn't help. He thought he'd never see them again and he loved them, loved them hard. Sarah looked so beautiful, so grown up for her thirteen years. Underground he'd imagined her future. In his darkest times, like the hours after the long man disappeared and he felt like giving up, he imagined her future. Who she'd be, what she'd do, who she'd marry. What her kids would look like. He dreamed it all in case he didn't get to see it, and now, there she was.

His rescuers were there, too. None of them keen to go home. Dirty faced, exhausted, he couldn't believe how happy they were to see him. He knew he'd have to live well, every day of his life, to justify what they'd done.

"Where's Barry? Did you get him out yet?" he asked once he'd had a warm drink. They loaded him into an ambulance although he said he felt fine.

"They haven't got Barry yet," Cheryl said, but her eyes were downcast and he knew she was fibbing. She didn't do it very often and he thought only to protect him. Like the time half the mine was shut down and the wives knew about it first. And the time Sarah had broken her arm because of the kid next door. Cheryl didn't want to tell him that because she knew how angry he'd be, but he didn't do anything about it. The kid was never allowed in their front door again, but that was it.

"I'd rather know than not know," he said.

There were news cameras, people with microphones and others with notepads.

"Why do you think you survived?" they shouted at him. "Why you and not Barry?"

The tears took again at that and Cheryl squeezed his hand hard. The ambulance crew shut the door and then it was a week in hospital before he had to face the questions again.

They told him about Barry once they thought he was all good. Barry'd been trapped, his leg under the rocks. Stuart could imagine how bad that must have felt. So Barry tried to cut his way through, Jesus, cut his way through his own leg.

They said he bled to death.

"He wrote you something while he was down there," Cheryl said.

"He was always scribbling, that Barry. He'd write a letter to the Pope if he could get the address," Stuart said. It was an old joke which made him tear up, thinking that Barry would have laughed at this one.

"He was hallucinating, they reckon. But still. You should read it."

*I thought you'd got through the wall, Stu. I didn't hear you but heard a rock shift so thought you must be to my left. You wouldn't answer me so I cracked the shits. I couldn't turn my body but turned my face as far as I could, twisted my caplamp around to catch you. I figured you wanted to kill and eat me, that's how stupid I was.*

*Wasn't you.*

*My light went right through this thing. I could see it, though. Looked almost like a man, but stretched out like a piece of bubble gum or something. Or when you press blu tak onto newspaper and get some print and stretch it out. Like that. He had long fingers, twice as long as mine. Dunno if you heard me scream but this thing freaked me out. It came at me and I would have pissed myself if I wasn't already sitting in my own wet pants. It leaned forward and put its eyes real close to mine. Stared into me. I screamed my head off, no reason, just scared shitless. It came at me, touched my nose with its long finger, then it shook its head and drifted back.*

*I though, shit, it's going to Stu, and I screamed louder. I wanted to warn you. But what do you do? I didn't know what to tell you.*

*I don't know if I'll last until they find me. Tell my mates they did me proud and if you can find my mother tell her I'm sorry.*

"Do you know anything about this long man, Stuart? Did you hear anything, see anything?" his wife asked him.

Stuart nodded. He spoke quietly. "I saw a man like that. I thought I must have imagined it. But maybe it was a ghost. Maybe someone died in there and he was looking at us, going, *you're not going to make it. No way. You're going to die.* Because he made me feel so bad I almost wanted to die."

"That's awful, Stuart. We're so lucky to have you back." He kissed her, as he did any chance he got. "Maybe keep it just between us for now. About this long man. Other people won't understand it. Don't tell the media types. Okay?"

"You think I'm crazy."

"No, I don't. But I know you and they don't. Just keep it to the simple stuff, hey? Shouldn't be hard for you!"

He discovered he was good at talking. Cheryl thought it was funny. "You're a gabber now, Stuart. Couldn't get ten words a day out of you beforehand!" She fixed his hair, getting him ready for the next press conference.

"Yeah, well, they're always asking me for answers," he said. He didn't mind. It was always the same thing, so he didn't have to think too hard. This one, the room was packed. They knew he was fully recovered and had some others to talk, too. The mine owner, who Stuart had never met. One of his rescuers. And some doctor, a psychologist.

They had a good go at the mine owner for a while about responsibilities and compensation, then they turned to Stuart.

"Did you always think you'd be found?"

"I always expected to be found. I'm a bit like that. I expect I'm gonna get good luck. Just that kind of person. All credit to the rescuers, though. I can't believe those guys, still can't believe what they did. We'll be friends for life because of it."

The rescuer next to him clapped a hand on his shoulder.

"Was there any time you wanted to give up?"

He thought of the long grey man and the feelings of despair he'd left behind. They wouldn't believe him if he talked about that, think he was mad.

"Nah. I just thought of my wife's pot roast and that got me through."

"What is it you've got? Why did you survive and not Barry?"

"I can't answer that."

The psychologist stepped in. "There are many reasons why people survive. For Stuart, he had thoughts of his family to sustain him. Barry didn't have that and studies have shown it makes a difference. Also, Stuart was less dramatic in his actions. Maybe he thought ahead a bit more, and maybe Barry thought he could get out of it."

"You're saying it's Barry's fault he was trapped? His own fault he died?"

"No. Not at all. But the fact is that Stuart thought it through and trusted the rescuers."

"Do you think yourself lucky, Stuart?"

"Couldn't be luckier," Stuart said. "Luckiest man left alive."

"I'm sure your rescuers will be happy to hear that. Do you feel any sense of obligation to them? Do you owe them anything?"

"Yeah, look they're all spread out around the place, but they can come to my place for a feed any time they like. And you know what I really owe them? I owe them a good life."

He and the rescuer shook hands, and the cheering of the audience went on for two minutes.

"What do you say to the idea that some people don't survive because they may have died helping others?"

"Yeah, well, if I coulda helped Barry survive I would have."

"What about his food? Is it true you ate his food?"

"Yeah, I ate his food. He couldn't get to it and it was only going off. That's not what killed him."

The psychologist said, "It is true that often it is the survivors don't help others. Especially in times of famine. Survivors are the ones who will take food from a child's mouth."

Stuart felt stunned. He wasn't sure how the conversation had turned against him and what a hero he was, but it seemed it had.

"All I did was survive," he said. "No one had to die for me to survive. I did it because I love my family, I love my life, and I wanted to get here on TV for the free beer I've heard about."

With that, he had the audience back.

Afterwards, there was plenty of beer drunk. The crew took him out to the local pub and he was there long after they left. People had watched the interview and they all wanted to talk to him about it.

"If only we could bottle what you've got, there'd be no little kiddies dying of cancer," people said to him more often than he wanted to hear.

"If only we could bottle it, you'd be a rich man."

"If only we could bottle it, we'd save the world."

They thought he had some magic power, that it wasn't a willingness to drink your own piss and a great desire to have proper sex with your wife again, it was something else. Something they couldn't have.

He took a drink well but even he was feeling a bit woozy by around midnight. By 3am, the pub was almost empty. He could no longer remember who he'd spoken to, so when a sad-faced man said hello, he nodded and went back to his beer.

"Hello, Stuart," the man said again. His voice was soft. It had an amused tone, as if he knew more than other people, found something amusing. Stuart no longer wondered how people knew his name. Plenty of them did. He rather liked the celebrity. He'd always enjoyed making connections with people all over.

Stuart looked at him this time. "Do I know you?" he asked.

His teeth were bright, white and even. Clearly false. His hair, pale blonde, sat flat on his head. He smelt strongly of aftershave, the kind Stuart used to smell wafting out of the cars while he waited for the bus. His mouth drooped. *Sad man*, Stuart thought.

"How are you holding up?"

"I'm okay. Bit tired."

The man moved so that he looked directly into Stuart's eyes. Stuart froze. This is how the apparition in the cave had looked at him. With this intensity. He was used to people staring at him greedily but this was different. The sad face, the long arms. Long, long fingers.

It was the apparition from the mine.

The man's hand went out and grabbed Stuart by the wrist with a powerful grip.

"Hold still, Stuart. This won't take long."

Stuart shivered, feeling as cold as he had underground. Chilled to the bone and dreaming of snow.

"Leggo, mate, wouldya?" he said. He tried to pull back but he felt deep lethargy, as if he'd been injected with golden syrup and his limbs couldn't move.

The man raised his other arm and brought it up to pinch the bridge of Stuart's nose. Stuart was paralysed. He wanted one of the other drinkers to intervene, to hit the man, knock him away, but no one did. It was so quiet Stuart felt as if he was back in the mine and the idea of it made him choke.

No. It wasn't that. He had a nose bleed, blood pouring backwards down his throat because the man held his sinuses so tight.

He let go and Stuart slumped forward, spitting blood. He felt movement return.

Turned his head away from the man.

The man bent and helped him up. "Nose bleed, nose bleed, make a bit of room, I'll take him and clean him up. Nose bleed, he'll be fine."

Stuart tried to pull his arm away. His mouth was full of blood. "Come on, Stuart, it'll be all right."

He led Stuart into the men's toilets. Propped him against the wall.

Stuart heard a skittering sound, like cockroaches across the kitchen bench at midnight. He thought he caught a whiff of them, that slightly plasticy smell. A smell of sour cherries.

"It won't hurt," the man said.

Stuart felt the creatures and, by straining his eyes, could watch them walking up his arm. The scream in his head deafened him.

Up his forearm, his biceps, over his shoulders and onto his neck, where he could feel them latching on.

"It's not your blood they're taking," the man said. His voice was soft and almost too broad to listen to. "It's something else. You won't miss it. It'll be like it was never there. You won't know."

He clicked his tongue and Stuart thought the sucking stopped. He felt light-headed and nauseous. The man plucked a beetle off Stuart's shoulder and ate it. Crunched it like it was a nut and took the next. Two more and he was smacking his lips. Stuart couldn't move. He felt so cold he felt like he'd been buried in snow. Or was back in the cave. But it was light in here. Very bright.

"Look at me." The man's cheeks were pink, his eyes bright. He looked younger. Happy.

"Thank you, Stuart. Have a good life."

He tapped Stuart on the head and Stuart slept.

He awoke on the filthy toilet floor. Someone had dropped a wad of shitty toilet paper and he could smell that.

He felt little compunction to rise, to lift himself. It was like this was the only moment and there was nothing beyond.

Another man came in and helped him up. "Home time for you, mate? Wait here while I take a piss and I'll get you to a taxi."

"Do I know you?" Stuart said. Things seemed blurred and he couldn't remember much.

"Nah, but you'll always help someone in trouble, right? Specially a survivor like you."

*I am a survivor* Stuart thought as the stranger helped him to a taxi. *That's what I did.*

But he felt as if he could never do it again.

• • •

He woke up on his lounge room floor, his shirt stiff with dried blood.

• • •

"Big night was it?" Cheryl said, poking him with her toe.

Sarah, stood over him, ready for school, her shoes all shined, her white socks folded neatly.

He shivered, feeling cold. "The long man pinched my nose." His face felt swollen and he knew he must look awful.

"Get off the floor," Sarah said. "You're shivering."

"I will soon." He felt a deep sense of pure lethargy.

Cheryl helped him up onto the couch and brought him a cup of tea. "You're too old to drink like that anymore."

"Wasn't the drink. Well, I did give it a bit of a hiding, but it was this guy. This long grey guy who gave me a bloody nose and then did something to me. I'm tired. I'm so tired. And cold."

She brought him a fluffy pink blanket and covered his knees with it. "The TV producers sent over a copy of your interview. Sarah and I have already watched it twice! Want to have a look? You come across really well."

She didn't wait for his answer but played the dvd anyway.

He watched the interview over and over that day, wondering at the person talking. "Jeez, I'm a smart-arse, aren't I?" he said, smiling at his Cheryl. She kissed his forehead.

"You always were." The lightness of her tone warmed him slightly. She had suffered post natal depression and he was terrified every day it would come on again. He saw it behind her eyes sometimes, in the droop of her mouth. A wash of sadness. Those were the times he tried harder lift her up. Out of the corner of his eye he thought he saw a bug climbing the wall and he curled up, pulling his blanket up over his eyes. "We need to get the rentakill guys in here. Get rid of the cockroaches," he said.

She nodded. "Ants, too. All over the kitchen, rotten little things." She sat beside him, laying her head on his shoulder. "I still can't believe you're back," she said. His little bird, his sparrow, but a tower of strength at the same time.

Usually sitting beside her he felt something. Irritation, often, when she went on about small domestic details, none of which interested him. Boredom, talking about her family. Affection, when they sat together watching TV. Love, when they laughed together at a joke he'd made, when her eyes crinkled up and little tears formed. He loved those little tears.

She held his hand. He let it lay loose.

"Are you okay?" she said.

"I just can't really feel anything. It's all gone numb."

She stared at him. "We have to tell the doctor. Something's wrong. You shouldn't feel like that."

"I don't feel anything, love. That's the thing. Nothing at all. Just cold. Like I've got an iceblock inside my stomach." He didn't tell her he meant emotionally as well, that looking at her left him cold.

To cover it up, he kissed her. Usually they'd do this stuff at night, with the door closed, but he kissed her with passion and moved his hands around her body, touching all his favourite bits.

The weeks passed. He ate meals he had no real desire to eat, had conversations and many, many interviews. Sponsorships brought money in. Newspaper reports listed everything he'd eaten underground and those people approached him. It was Vegemite, Tip Top bread, Milo chocolate bars, apples (the local fruit shop took on that one), and the local butcher had a go, too. The watch company put him on TV, talking about how he'd never need another watch, that one was so good. So at least he didn't have to work. People kept asking him if he was going back underground and he'd bluff at them, give them the real man answer, the hero stuff, but he wasn't going back.

He spent a lot of time reading the paper. He started cutting out stories of other survivors, especially the ones who talked about the cold, about the deep bone chill they felt after a few days.

"Dad, let me hook you up with an online forum. You can meet other survivors. Talk to them. Most of them are probably feeling what you're feeling," Sarah said. He sat at the computer for a while but it only made sense when she talked him through it and he didn't want her to know it all.

She asked him about the long man. "The one you said pinched your nose. We should try to track him down and make sure he doesn't do it again. People can't go round pinching my dad's nose like that."

"Willy nilly," he said. It was an old joke. "I don't know if we'll find him. I don't think he's at the pub much, or if he's got a job. I saw him when I was buried, you know. He sent his ghost in to find me."

Others had talked about seeing visions. Buried in the snow, or caught in a car for two days on a country road. They said, more than one of them, that a long man had visited them. "It's not just me," he told Sarah. "No one knows why he doesn't help. He just looks."

"Did he pinch their noses? This is the stuff we can find online, Dad."

"Yeah, maybe. Maybe. What about stuff about cockroaches? How to get rid of them? I saw a huge one in the bathroom. They say they'll survive nuclear war. That's what they reckon." He shivered. "I hate them."

He felt like a fraud. Life exhausted him, all the people wanting what he had. And Cheryl and Sarah got nothing but harassment. *Lucky your dad's alive, your husband*, people said to them. *Imagine what life would have been like without him, how sad, how hard.* Making them think about it. All those people wanting to talk to him, but they paid him at least and it kept them in beer and roast beef. Always the same questions.

"What is it you think you were kept alive for?" they asked, putting the onus on him to make something of his life. As if he'd been given a second chance and he'd be a fool to waste it.

"Dunno what I was kept alive for, but mostly I'm enjoying every extra minute with my daughter and my wife," was his stock answer.

But he no longer really cared.

They asked him, "Are you scared of anything? Seems like you're not." It was a stupid question, he thought. Who wasn't scared?

"Cockroaches. I really hate cockroaches." The interviewer sighed in agreement.

Another question they always asked him was, "Put in the same situation, would or could you do it again?"

"Well, I won't mate, will I? Just not going to happen."

They always ended with, "If only you could bottle it." His standard joke was to hold out his wrists.

"Ya wanna take a litre or two? Go for it! I can spare it!"

It was all an act and he was good at it.

• • •

He was waiting in the queue to buy fish and chips ("Aren't you that guy? That miner guy?") when he smelt sour cherries. It took him straight back to the cave and the smell of the long man. He felt cold through his layers of clothing and did not want to turn around. He felt someone behind him, close, but people did that. They seemed to think if they got physically close to him they could absorb some of him, that they could be like him.

He took his package of food and left the shop, eyes down. Climbed into the car some sponsor had given him, sat there to eat it.

The long man opened the passenger door and climbed in.

Stuart dropped the food on his lap where it sat, greasy and hot. He barely felt it. He scrabbled for the doorhandle but the long man took his wrist. Pressed hard and Stuart couldn't move. Just like last time.

"You seem to be enjoying that fish, Stuart. You know what that tells me? That I didn't take it all. The fact that you want to eat tells me that."

Stuart tried to shake his head, to say, "I'm faking it, it's all fake, I can't feel a fucking thing," but the cockroaches were out, skittering and sucking and if he thought he was cold before, *that* was nothing. His eyelids felt frozen open, his nostrils frozen shut, breathing was so painful he wanted to stop doing it.

"That's it now," the long man said, picking cockroach feelers out of his teeth. "You're done."

Stuart sat slumped in the seat for a while, then started the car. A tape was playing; one of his interviews. He liked listening to himself, hearing his own voice.

"I'll do anything to stay alive, anything to keep my family alive," he heard himself say. "You know I got stuck in a pipe once when I was a kid. Fat kid, I was. I sang songs from TV shows to keep me occupied." Listening from his car, chilled to the bone and tired, Stuart wondered if he'd seen the long man then. If the long man had waited, and waited, until he was good and strong.

He pulled out of the carpark. It was only his sense of duty making him do it, long-instilled. He had to go to a school visit someone had organised for him. Some school where there was a survivor kid, a young girl recently rescued. It took him a while to get there; wrong turns, bad traffic. Angry traffic. He thought there was more road rage than usual but then wondered if it was his driving? If all that stuff about driving carefully did make sense, because he didn't care now, didn't care how he drove or what he hit.

• • •

"We'd like to welcome Stuart Parker to the school. He's taken time out of his busy day to talk to us and to talk to Claire, our own hero."

The children clapped quietly. Stuart guessed they were tired of hearing about Claire.

She'd been trapped in the basement of a building. A game of hide and seek gone wrong; no one knew she was playing. No one knew where she was. It took six days for them to find her.

"Tell us how you coped, Claire," the teacher said.

"I pretended I was at school doing boring work and that's why it was so boring. Sometimes I thought about this nice man from the mine. He said he kept thinking of nice things and that's what I did too."

The children shuffled, started to talk, bored. Claire looked at them wide-eyed. "I ate bugs. Lots of bugs. Like he did. And I had some chips I took from the cupboard but I didn't want to tell Mum and Dad cos I didn't want to get in trouble."

She had their attention, but not completely. "And then there was the creepy guy."

"You were alone in the basement, Claire, weren't you?" the teacher said, passive-aggressive. "No one there."

"Who did you see?" Stuart said. He hadn't had a chance to speak before then. "What did he look like?"

The audience were rapt. They didn't often get to see adults this way, all het up and loud.

"I was all by myself but then this creepy long guy was there. I never seen him before but I thought he might help me to get out. But he didn't, he just stared at me. I told him he should go away but the only thing I think he said was, "See you soon, Claire." That's why I'm scared. I really don't want to see him again."

Stuart wanted to care. He wanted to save her but there was nothing left in him. Only the memory of the man who would have killed to save that girl. Would have ripped the arms off any man who tried to hurt her.

Just a memory though.

"Stuart, we haven't heard from you. What can you tell the children?"

"That there is no purpose in life. We all die and rot and none of it is worth anything. You're only taking up space. And that the long man is real. You need to keep her safe from him because he'll destroy her."

The principal, stunned and speechless, took a moment to answer. The children were silent and he wondered if he'd laid seeds of sadness and emptiness in them all. He didn't mean to. But he was too tired and cold to lie anymore.

"But . . . but Mr. Parker, you're a role model. We asked you here to lift the children. Inspire them."

"I'm nothing. Nothing at all," he said.

• • •

Claire. Claire was in the news and so was he, with his awful statements, his cruelty to the children. He had the media at his door again but they hated him now for turning on the children, you don't do that to the kiddies, do you? He watched Claire; she didn't look chilled to the bone, so he thought perhaps the long man hadn't come to her yet.

• • •

His house was full of his sponsors' food and friends came over to eat it because he wouldn't. Some of the rescuers too, looking at him as if they'd wasted their time. Sitting there in front of the television, warm rug, warm slippers, all skinny and pale.

He couldn't even fake a smile anymore. His famous watch had slipped off his wrist and sat in the dust under the couch.

"We shoulda bottled it. We could give him a taste of his own self," one of the rescuers said. He knew they were disappointed in him, that he wasn't doing what they wanted him to do.

"Three days of my life, I gave to save him," he heard one say in the kitchen. "Now look at him."

They left him alone.

And he didn't care.

• • • • • • • • • • •

# WRAITHS

## JASON NAHRUNG

The dust wraiths struck with all the speed and surprise and finality of a slamming door. We should've felt it coming, but we didn't. Maybe it was the heat, dulling our senses with its touch of lazy. Maybe it was just our time and, on some level, down deep, we knew it and ignored the signs. Or maybe they'd just got tired of us and decided to end it, once and for all.

The cool southerly dropped away in the morning, and by noon, the sun had turned from baking to roasting. A constant wave of heat radiated from the salt flats, too brilliant to look at. The horizon all around us wavered in the mirage haze so that we seemed an island of dirt floating in some bizarre other world. The Haunted Ranges to the north hovered on the haze, mirrored and surreal. Once we'd finished baking the morning's bread, Mother and I shut up the kitchen out the back and went inside to freshen up. A sip of water, the cool touch of the water jug against a hot brow, then fresh blouses—I was still young enough to escape the itchy constriction of a bra, but my day was coming, and Mother never missed a chance to rib me about young Jimmy Salter and his newfound desire to hang out with me when he wasn't toiling on the flats, trying to make his fortune.

That afternoon, our attention was on trying to minimise our sweat as we lounged in the shade of the square and swapped the most desultory of greetings with our neighbours. Save for those up at mines and a few hardies still collecting salt, the whole village was gathered in anticipation of the siesta water ration. The well was low, the gully, as ever, dry. The world was brown and red under the glare of the sun's unblinking stare, and everything its gaze touched, wilted.

The dust wraiths came out of the haze when the shadows were pointing to the east. I saw a flap of burlap shudder. Our dog, lying at our feet, lifted his grey muzzle from the pillow of his paws and whined. A wind chime tinkled.

And then the shadows were on us, the roiling dust clouds rolling in as fast as fear, turning the sun to a blood-red disc. We ran, my mother pulling on my arm, the dog barking as he circled, tail lashing, eyes showing white.

I paused at the door, calling to the dog, but he refused to come. He stood, paws planted wide, ears back, as though his fierce barks alone could drive back the wraiths.

The afternoon turned to twilight, the air to dirt.

In the square, the shaman and his acolytes fought to cover the well. He held his staff up high, the weathered cow skull on its tip a vague blur of bone in the gritty gloom. The wraiths tore the well cover from the acolytes' hands with such force the timber splintered. Ghostly figures swam in the eddies, sharp fingers tearing at the men's throats, draining them as they choked. One wraith funnelled itself into a willy willy and spiralled down into the well, and I thought I heard it screech in glee.

The dog whined and my mother jerked me inside, slammed the door and cuffed me hard to bring me to my senses. There was a single yelp from the other side of the door. I fetched the snakes, as fast as I could, thrusting them at my mother in desperation as dust jetted in through the gaps under the doors and around the shutters. She pushed the long tubes of dirt-filled cloth into the holes, her breath coming in ragged gasps. Dull sunlight the colour of straw beamed through the cracks, making motes dance thick as gnats. The dust caked my nostrils and my throat. I couldn't swallow; could barely see as the dust spiked my eyes.

When she was satisfied, my mother huddled with me on the floor, and we listened to the eerie silence, muted inside our adobe walls and the weight of the air outside turned to soil. She shushed my single whimper as the death crept past, rustling the wattle frame of the mud roof, sighing against the bricks, making the shutters creak. Our poppet shivered where it hung above the front door.

My mother had given the shaman his due at the last full moon; the poppet was freshly empowered, our protection was strong.

We cowered and prayed and tried to ignore the screams where wards failed and barriers fell. The air was thick with dust and every surface coated with grime, and we were afraid to even cry, lest our tears draw the wraiths in.

When they finally withdrew, it was night, and the village was as good as dead.

• • •

For the few of us left, there was no choice. The goats and cattle were dead or scattered, the well filled in. My mother looked at me with such despair, then forced herself to smile. She sniffed, wiped her face on her sleeve, then gathered me up to say it would be all right. We would take what little we had and go to the coast. The dust wraiths had no power there. It was a green place, lush and wet. I would learn to swim, there was so much water. I might even see rain. Rain. How I feared it. The thought of the entire sky filled with water. I imagined myself drowning in it, choked by water as surely as the wraiths had tried to suffocate me with earth. Rain held wonder but no joy for me, but I nodded anyway, because she was frightened, so very frightened, and I knew it was my job to be brave, like she was.

We buried the dead, little more than mummies of leather and bone, while we waited for the miners and those few who had weathered the heat to continue working on the salt flats. Only a couple came stumbling home, gaunt and haunted. Jimmy Salter was amongst them, moving like a corpse, all stiff and unseeing, and his cheeks smeared muddy with tears on dust. He had no one else, so he rode with us.

We mustered what livestock we could, harnessed the wagons and abandoned the only home I'd known. Mother shut the door behind her and left the poppet hanging on the outside. It seemed a strange thing to do, because who would ever come back here?

• • •

We travelled by night in the cool, guided by stars. Trader Elrod led us east, heading for the site of the equinox moots where the villages would come together to deal goods and marry off their young. They were exciting occasions, cause for celebration as we waited to see what food, tools and dowries would come off the carts. There would be music and dancing, drinking and sexing, new brides welcomed with ribbons and bracelets and a new hut for her and her husband to make their own. The whole village would offer their blood to add to the wards, and salt would be spread and beer drunk. It was a time of new life, of new things, of new hope. In my time, no bride had ever brought rain, but the village always voiced the hope.

In another few years, and despite Jimmy's fledgling interest, I might have been making this journey as a bride-to-be for some bachelor man on the coast or in the mountains, an easterner or a southerner. I would have been farewelled with water and milk and blood and pretties. None of which would've made up for having to leave my mother, alone in our hut against the heat and the dry. Given that choice, I'd probably have picked Jimmy's hovel.

This moot journey was not like that. My mother travelled with me and our ribbons were black; there was no music and no joy. This was a funeral march.

By day we huddled under hide tents protected by glyphs erected on sticks and spelt out on the ground in stones. We had taken the magic from the shaman's hut. I still saw his face when I closed my eyes: a husk of a man, the flesh withered and stretched around his screaming jaw, his eyes hollow things, his mouth and cheeks showing patches of bright white bone through the taut iodine flesh. We gave his body to the wind wraiths, given up by flame and smoke. I did not want to die like that, sucked dry and blown away. I did what my mother told me, and I did not complain, and I did not cry.

Each morning once camp was set, I gave my piss into the communal pot. We boiled it up, mostly for the canteens, but some we sacrificed to the dust wraiths. They followed us, the twisting columns keeping their distance, as though escorting us out of the land they'd claimed for themselves. We saw no animals, no birds, just the baked earth so hot under our feet, and tufted crackle grass, and the skeletal bleached crucifixes of dead trees dotting the flatness. We fled in silence.

When Mama Tanner died, we divided up her tent and drained her blood for food and wards, then laid her out in a shawl with pebbles on her eyes. We left her as a sacrifice to the wraiths; they could have what we could not take. I wondered if they would accept that, if they would be happy with our far from magnanimous gesture. But I guess they either accepted it or simply didn't care because they didn't trouble us.

"Why don't they finish us off?" Jimmy asked me once, our feet hanging over the end of the cart, the dust barely stirring under the rickety wheels.

"'Cause we're going the right way," I said.

"What if we went back?"

"Back to what?"

He was quiet then, and I held his hand while he stared out at the wraiths with all his hatred and loss, but the wraiths just kept pace, shepherding us on.

Three more of the animals died—we'd left half our paltry herd behind like mile markers, drained and stripped to the bone—before the silvered haze of the eastern horizon finally showed dark breaks, and then the mountains appeared. My lips were cracked, my ribs showing like an old cow's, my formerly budding breasts shrivelled to the point of being a boy's.

We pushed on with renewed energy. The ochre ground turned to darker brown and began to undulate, each rise higher than the last, until we walked over pebbled earth and brown grass as high as our knees and found shade in the cover of drab olive-coloured trees. We dug in the gullies and found a little water; we sucked sap from prickly leafs, grinning at each other around the sticky ends of the flat pads, not caring about the spikes. We licked up the blood where they cut us. On the flats below and behind us, the wraiths danced to mark their victory.

We rested at the moot site; the waterhole, shaded by drooping coolabahs, was low and muddy, but we strained the water through cloth and boiled it up and it was good.

• • •

Some of the villages argued we should stay here. There was shelter and we could eke out water. There was bound to be animals to hunt. At the equinox, the other villages would come, and then we could either find a new home among them or split and join them, each as we willed. But it wasn't like at home. There was no salt to gather, no gold from the Haunted Ranges; we would have nothing to trade for what we couldn't make or hunt or find ourselves. We would not survive. That's what my mother said. I agreed; I didn't like the hills. I didn't like not being able to see ahead of me. I didn't like how the slopes made my legs ache and my lungs heave. I found them scary and secretive. I was happy to leave. Jimmy said he'd come, too. There was nothing for him here.

• • •

Elrod was our guide. He'd never been farther east, but the other traders had told him of landmarks; he was sure he could find the-village-by-the-sea. It was the place where my bone comb had come from, though my hair was too short to wear it; it was the source of salted fish, smooth wooden bowls of the palest of wood and necklaces of shells. We would go to the-village-by-the-sea and eat fish and learn to make these things, and they would welcome us. My Nan had come from there; my mother still had a brooch that had been hers. Nan had hated the dry. When Mother spoke of her and the-village-by-the-sea, her eyes glistened like dew.

We reached the mountains and they were cooler than our plains but the going was hard. Fire wraiths had blistered them and the world was ash and charcoal. Our tongues stuck to the roofs of our mouths; our muscles pained, our bellies rumbled. I saw a dead kangaroo, its body stiff and huge and its skin all blackened and bubbled. Flies clouded its mouth and eyes where glazed wetness glistened.

We made our way down the eastern slope, ash clouds puffing up under our feet, the trees blackened and leafless. Crows flapped lazily overhead. The sky was blue and clear and the sun hot as it striped the ground with the elongated shadows of dead trees.

We found water, muddy but drinkable, and followed the gully until it became a series of water holes, and then a slow-running stream, and then a river. The grass grew sparse and brown, and the scrub pressed thick, so we followed animal trails, and sometimes had to push through, the twigs scratching at our skin and catching in our clothes. Kangaroos paused their grazing to watch us pass. The journey was accompanied by the songs of many birds that Elrod and Mother named for me: trilling magpies and hacking kookaburras, croaking cockatoos, chattering parrots. Elrod tried to bring some down with his slingshot, but missed them all. We ate our meal cakes and jerky and looked forward to reaching the-village-by-the-sea, where there would be flour and maybe fruit, and fish of course, fresh fish. I wondered what that tasted like.

Mother said you could lick the oil from your fingers, it was that moist. I couldn't imagine that; it made my belly growl.

We passed rough-hewn timber huts, which Elrod told us belonged to trappers and hunters, but we saw no one, and their canoes were gone. So we followed the river on foot, luxuriating in the water, bathing, discovering our sun-browned flesh under the layers of dirt, and marvelling as our true hair colour returned. I thought perhaps I would allow my hair to grow long, even down to my nape, if such abundance of water meant I could wash my hair and comb it.

The land gentled out, scrub-choked and forested; it felt claustrophobic, not being able to see the sky so much, to have the trees crowding over us, the eyes of birds and other creatures peering at us, some curious, some mocking, some totally indifferent. The air smelled of wattle, Mother pointing out the golden sprays; bees buzzed them, and long-beaked birds flapped about. By the river there were massive gum trees, too thick to reach right around, with twisting nests of roots, and smaller bottlebrushes leaning over the water, their spiky red flowers the prettiest I'd ever seen. I wore one behind my ear.

Jimmy said it looked funny, like a hairy caterpillar, but that I looked pretty, and I let him kiss me. It started as a peck, but it turned into a wet one, trading moisture with our tongues and lips, and I wondered, after, what that meant out here.

I smiled a lot while we travelled beside the river. I loved running my hand in it, half expecting it to all go away, like a mirage. There was so much water . . .

When we bathed, Mother always warned me not to go out too far. Not that I would've. I could feel the river wraiths pulling at my legs, wanting me to join them. Wanting to keep me there forever. I drew wards on the surface of the water before and after every swim, and gave the wraiths some crumbs every meal time to keep them from taking me.

I smelt the sea before I saw it. And then heard it. Brine and surf, Mother announced, and her smile was like a sunrise. I held her hand tight.

The ocean extended to the end of the world. That's what I thought as we crested a dune, the sand like powder, held down by tendrils of vibrant vine. There were little purple flowers, and the sky was filled with the cries of seagulls, white flashes wheeling overhead, beady eyes staring at us from aloft. Wraith-spit flecked the ocean all the way to the horizon; I could barely tell where the water ended and the sky began.

I held my hands over my ears till I was used to the sound of the crashing waves. It was terrifying, the thought of it: all that water gnawing at the beach, hungry for the land, swirling over it like a lapping tongue and leaving lines of spittle in its wake. I could see the earth running away into the ocean with every crash of the waves; I could see the claws of the sea wraiths digging in an effort to reach us.

"Where's the village?" someone asked, and Elrod looked, up and down the stretch of beach that vanished to the north and to the south in mist and headlands, and then he pointed south, to where we could see a small hill, and some square structures atop it that could only be buildings.

We walked south, away from the river, and came to the hill. The beach was covered with weed and sticks and there were shells everywhere.

"I could make a necklace, Mother," I said, bending to pick up some of the bigger ones, so smooth and such lovely shades of pink and grey and purple, the colours of a twilight sky, night coming down.

"Almost there," Jimmy mumbled from where he stood nearby, his eyes wide as he took it all in, the sheer size of it, the weight of it. He looked a little sad; maybe he was nervous. I was. What if the villagers didn't want us? What if they were worried we'd eat all their fish?

As we got closer, we could see that something was not right. The buildings were shattered, bare walls and missing roofs, or even less, just posts, and there were clumps of broken timber here and there, and the trees were draped with weed, those that still stood and weren't lying uprooted and covered in sand and sea wrack.

At the beach, a clump of people were pushing a boat out past the waves, and we waited, our feet well above the line of the swash, and I held my shells hard in one hand, so hard they cut into me, while my mother's grip tightened on the other. The wind was wet and cold and it plucked tears from my eyes, and I saw Mother's cheeks shining, too.

The villagers pushed the boat away towards the east and smoke began to plume from it, and then flames, and before long it was ablaze, and the smoke was thick and oily, the colour of crows' wings. And the people cried as they returned to shore and they huddled and watched the boat rock in the waves and the flames leapt higher and the smoke blew inland, growing thinner as the wind wraiths took it and wove it into air.

One villager came to us presently: she was the new headwoman.

"The sea wraiths came for us," she said. "Three days ago. They rode the waves in and took so many of us. All of our rafts. All of our nets. Most of our people."

Her eyes were red and puffed, her face so drawn. I knew that look; we'd all worn it after the dust wraiths destroyed our home. She would've been pretty, I thought, with more sleep and more food, and less misery. Like Mother.

"Didn't you make sacrifice?" my mother asked.

"Of course! But how much do they want? How much can they take before they're happy?"

Mother looked over her shoulder, towards the inland, where there were storm clouds—strange and wonderful, rising high, so white and grey and tumble-fluffed, as though reaching all the way to Heaven. It was as though Mother was seeing our journey, all the way back to the dust wraiths filling our well and choking our village to death.

"They want it all," she whispered. "They won't be happy till they've taken it all."

The headwoman touched my mother's arm and flashed a grim smile at me. "Your people are welcome to shelter with us, in what we have left."

"And then?"

"Some of us will stay to rebuild. Others will go with the hunters, back up the river, to learn their ways—they came to help us when they heard. Others have already gone inland to the farmers. Some may go farther inland still, to the salt plains, even. They say they would rather deal with the rain wraiths and the dust wraiths than the sea. A wraith is a wraith, I say, but I cannot blame them."

Jimmy said, "I'm going back. I'll clean out the well or dig another. There's still salt on the flat and gold in the hills. Besides, my family's buried there. It's where I belong."

"We will stay," my mother said, her gaze finding Trader Elrod, who returned a smile. I shivered at the thought of living here, with the air of salt and the constant crunch of ravenous sea against land, and the threat of the wraiths, always poised under the waves to swallow us down.

The wind wraiths stirred, their chill breath all wet and salty as it teased my ragged hair; I felt them crowding behind the distant clouds, gathering their might, and those in the sea responded, whipping foam and crashing all the louder. A wraith might be a wraith, but these were not mine.

"My daughter would like to make necklaces and learn to fish," Mother said. "Like her Nan did."

"Only till I've earned my dowry," I said, aware of Jimmy starting to smile, of my mother nodding, even as she wiped a fresh tear from her eye. "Then I'm going home to take that poppet off the door."

# THE PATRICIAN

## TANSY RAYNER ROBERTS

I

Clea Majora walked through the hot streets of Nova Ostia, her sandaled feet lightly treading on the wide, baked, paving stones. She bought a honey cake from a pastry stall and nibbled it as she walked, using the vine leaf wrapper to catch the crumbs.

At the wall, a couple of boys she knew from school were playing a covert game of soccer, and called for her to join them, but she waved and kept walking. It was too hot for games, and besides, she had her own plans for how to spend the lunch hour.

Outside the stifling confines of the city, she kept walking until she came to her favourite gum tree. She unpinned her stola so that it folded underneath her when she sat down on the rough ground, and slid in the earbuds of her iPod. For a blissful forty minutes, she listened to music, and a podcast about movies she would never get to see. The rest of the world existed, out there, and she liked the reminder of that.

Clea did not see the stranger until he was almost on top of her. She was startled when he tripped on a root nearby, and stared at her as she yanked out her earbuds.

"I'm sorry!" he exclaimed.

"No, I'm sorry!" Quickly, Clea fastened her stola back up so that it covered the front of the *Gladiators Do It In the Arena* t-shirt she had borrowed from her brother that morning. "I'm not supposed to be here," she confessed. "Not during daylight. Are you a tourist?"

"Yes," said the stranger in a cultivated, I-was-not-born-speaking-English kind of accent. "I suppose that I am. Are we near Nova Ostia? I lost my way."

Tourists always came to the city by train or by coach, but were asked to walk the ten minute hike up the sloped road so that they entered the city without the ease of modern transport. Clea recognised the factory-produced tourist toga and tunic as one from Roman Road Tours. This man must have wandered away from his group. "You shouldn't wander off-road," she said accusingly. "This is Australia, the bush can be dangerous." She should tell him about drop bears. That would serve him right. She was resentful of losing the last fifteen minutes of her lunch hour. "Come on, I'll take you."

He wore a hat, at least. Many tourists refused, wanting the full 'authenticity' of the Roman experience, only to appear at the city gates bright red like crayfish. The city was built with shaded streets to keep the Australian sun away from bare arms and bald pates, but that ten minute walk could do a lot of damage.

The visitor wore a broad-brimmed woven straw hat, not a design Clea recognised from Roman Road Tours. His hands were blistered from their moments in the sun, but the rest of him was a paler, European colour.

Clea dropped into the usual tourist spiel, about how a replica Roman city had come to be built in New South Wales, though it wasn't really a replica, but a combination of several Roman towns. She added the part about real stone from Ostia and Herculaneum having been shipped over as part of the building process.

"Yes," said the visitor with a sigh. "I wish you hadn't done that."

Still, he seemed interested enough, and stopped to peer at the triumphal arch which served as the city's gateway. The soccer boys were gone, probably yelled at by one of the merchants. The worst crime in Nova Ostia was to be inauthentic where the punters might see.

"Would you like to wait for your tour group?" Clea asked politely. "Or some refreshment, perhaps?" She would be late getting back to the thermopolium at this rate, and it would look better if she brought a customer with her.

The stranger's eyes were fixed upon the wall of the Temple of Vesta, and it was as if he had already forgotten she existed. "Thank you," he said absently. "But I travel alone."

• • •

Clea dreamed of snakes, of women with bright silver eyes. She awoke to a flickering light outside her window, which was all wrong. It wasn't like Nova Ostia had street lights. She knew even before she made it out of bed that there had to be a fire somewhere.

The Temple of Vesta was aflame. The white marble walls had turned black, at the heart of the blaze. Clea watched as various citizens ran to help, rolling out emergency hoses that had been carefully hidden in gutters and hatches. There was shouting, and urgency, and the acrid taste of smoke in the back of her throat.

A man leaped out of the flames, and ran across the roof. As Clea watched, he jumped from wall to roof again, and ran along gutters, holding something the size and shape of a Roman short sword. She knew him, from his height and gait. The visitor.

Not quite knowing why, she opened her window and leaned out. He turned, his head flicking once in her direction, and then leaped—this time, arcing over the nearest wall, and vanishing from her sight.

Obviously this was the sort of thing you mentioned to people. But when the Governor's secretary went from house to house the next day, searching for any witness reports concerning the fire, Clea said nothing.

• • •

At lunchtime, she bought two pastries and a flask of water, and set out to her usual spot. The visitor was leaning against her tree, looking exhausted, his hat casting a short shadow around him like an anti-halo.

"You did it," she said without ceremony, passing him the water first, which he gulped down. "Didn't you?"

"Of course I did," he said, and then looked up at her, his eyes all shaded and mysterious. "How many bodies?"

Clea shivered, that he could talk about "bodies' so easily, as if he were asking about her marks at school, or the number of pastries in her basket. "Two," she said. That was what she had heard, from her Mum, the neighbours, the soccer boys. "There were two dead women in the temple. But no one knows who they . . . were." She wanted to ask him. The question bubbled up fiercely inside her, but she held it down. Something told her if she said the wrong thing, he would just walk away. No matter how tired he was.

"Damn," he said quietly. "One got away."

Clea felt cold inside, and now she wasn't afraid he would leave—she was afraid that he wouldn't.

The man was looking at her now, his eyes intently on her. "How old are you?"

That was the kind of question you didn't answer, not when a tourist asked you. Clea had learned that when her curves first came in. There were always older men hanging about, eyeing her shape under the stola. But he wasn't asking like that—there was nothing pervy about him, no hint that he fancied her. He was all business.

But what kind of business? Assassin? Terrorist?

"Sixteen," she told him, and saw the interest flick away from her again. Really? She was of age, so not relevant? How creepy was that?

"Most of you sleep outside the city walls, yes?" he went on briskly. "Are there any children who sleep inside the walls?"

"I'm not telling you that," she snapped. "Why should I tell you anything? This is my home, and you're—weird." Her whole body ached to trust him, to tell him everything she knew, and that was weird too. Like she wasn't in control of her actions or her thoughts.

Something about this bloke made her throw all her sense out the window, and he was old enough to be her Dad.

He nodded calmly. "I'm sorry," he said. "I need information, and it's only fair I give some in return." He paused, waiting for her to define terms.

"Who were those women?" Clea asked, her voice coming out shakier than she liked.

"Lamia," he said, drinking another slug of the water she had brought for him. "A kind of ancient vampire, from Roman mythology. They seduce young men and drink their blood."

Clea blinked. Again, he was oozing trustworthiness, like some kind of "believe me" pheromone. It felt like the truth. "And who are you?" she asked, changing it from "what" only at the last moment.

"I am a traveller. The last person alive who knows what these creatures are, and how to fight them. My task is to rid the world of the beasts of Rome. When the last of them are gone, I will rest." He sounded so matter of fact about his death as a bullet point in the action plan.

"I meant, what's your name?" Clea asked.

He almost smiled, his face creasing under the shade of the hat. "Julius," he said.

"Like Caesar?"

"Yes."

Something about him made her ask the stupidest possible question. "You're not—actually *the* Julius Caesar?"

This time he did smile, though it looked all wrong on his face, like it wasn't an expression that happened very often. "No. That would be somewhat bizarre."

"There are only three families who sleep inside the walls," she blurted out.

He switched back to the main topic without a blink. "How many have children?"

"Ours. Just ours. My brother Ant is fourteen." Most of the families with kids preferred to live further out, where you could have a television in the living room and didn't have to be so discreet about wifi or electric kettles.

"Excellent," said Julius, his eyes blazing out of the shade.

• • •

Clea couldn't sleep. She Googled "lamia" and came up with a few medieval bestiary wikis with less than helpful illustrations, page after page of poetry by Keats, and a few vague references to the daughters of Mary Wollstonecraft.

Julius had given her so little to go on. He had assured her that her brother was probably not in danger, that the third lamia had most likely fled the city, but Clea had not felt the pressing wave of belief that she usually did when he spoke. Perhaps he had not been trying so hard.

"What do I do if something happens?" she had asked.

"Call me."

"I don't have your number. We don't have phones here! We have email, though. Do you have email?" Okay, she was babbling.

Julius shook his head as if there was something fundamental she just wasn't getting. "If something happens, open a window and *call me*."

Clea didn't know whether it was super mega creepy to know he would be that close by, or a complete relief. She didn't decide until morning came and her brother was still alive and annoying as ever, and she knew exactly how to feel: stupid. Ripped off. Taken for a ride. Conned.

• • •

Three days passed. Clea did her shifts in the thermopolium, idly Googled her university options, read a whole lot of manga, and almost but not quite forgot about the posh man in the straw hat.

Then one afternoon she came home to find Ant on the couch, snogging a girl. "Ew, get a room," she said with all the usual grace and tolerance of an older sister.

"Get a life," muttered her brother, disentangling himself from the girl and tugging her by the hand into his bedroom. He had—ew, ew—actual love bite marks on his neck, and the girl was far too pretty and far too smug-looking, and wasn't fourteen WAY too young for that sort of thing?

Mum was going to kill Clea when she found out she had actually caused Ant to go into his room with the hot girl and close the door.

Clea tried to remember what the girl had looked like. There was a blur in her memory, like someone had reached out and smudged it with an old school blackboard duster.

Oh. Blonde hair. Silver eyes. Smug smile. Right.

Clea ran to the kitchen, threw up the window and hollered, *"Julius!"* into the street outside. She had thirty seconds to feel idiotic about it before the door clicked and he walked in as if he owned the place.

"She's here?" he asked.

"My brother just took her into his room. For making out purposes." She added that last part because Julius was old and might not get it if she didn't spell it out.

Julius walked swiftly ahead, and flung open the door. Clea was caught between embarrassment and curiosity as she ran after him.

Ant lay spread out on his bed, the blonde girl crouched over him, and there were more than love bites on his neck. Blood spattered the pillow, and stained the girl's mouth.

Clea hit her with a chair. It was the first thing that came to hand, and it seemed appropriate.

Julius had a sword. Where had the freaking sword come from? He hacked the girl's head from her body, which took a lot more effort than in the movies, and drenched Ant's room in a silvery liquid like mercury. He then took the chair from Clea, broke a leg off it, and neatly punched it through the girl's chest.

Clea tried not to look, not to think about it, except to be glad of the silvery stuff, of the proof that things were Other in some way, that she hadn't just helped a random stranger behead her brother's first girlfriend without a really good reason. "Will he be okay?"

Ant looked sort of dazed and blissed out, and the blood had already clotted at his neck.

Julius gave the boy a cursory look. "She chose well. Most lamia victims drain too easily—your brother is one of the rare types who thrive on such attention. She could have fed on him for a decade, if she was careful."

Clea shivered. "Does that mean other lamia might come after him too? If he's an extra delicious Happy Meal?"

"Ordinarily, yes." Julius took a small leather-bound diary from his pocket, and made a mark in it. "But she was the last."

Clea stared at him, stricken. "Does that mean—you're finished? You're going to die?"

Julius gave her a brief smile. "A pleasant thought, but no. There are many more monsters on this list. I must rid the world of all of them before I can rest."

Clea looked around the wrecked room, at the chair and the blood-spattered bed and the body of the creature and the silvery muck sliding across the polished floorboards. "So you do this sort of thing all the time?"

"Yes."

"Why?"

"It is my task and my birthright," he said simply. "I am a Julius."

And she wasn't mistaking that, was she, the sneaky little definite article that suggested Julius was not just his name, it was a Thing.

"Are you done here?" Clea asked in a small voice. "In Nova Ostia?"

"I will help you clean up first," Julius said, as if offended she had not taken that into account. "Lamia blood is quite messy."

"Yes, I'd noticed." She wanted to keep asking questions, to get more out of him before he swanned off into the night. "What are you?"

Julius looked pensive, as if putting it into words was something which saddened him. "I am a manticore," he said finally, and then sent her to fetch a bucket of soapy water and squeegees for the cleaning.

## II

Ten months later, Clea went all the way with Daniel for the first time. It wasn't nearly as much fun as she had thought it was going to be, and afterwards she went to sit in her favourite spot with her back to the gum tree, listening to angsty music and feeling like her whole body could fly apart at any moment.

She didn't need to be confused anymore than she already was, and she really didn't need a reappearance of Julius, not today, so of course there he was in his straw hat and his toga, tripping over that same tree root, and apologising for it.

"What is it this time?" she asked, more acidly than she would have on any other day, because really, losing your virginity to a boy who had no idea what to do with it was the sort of thing that allowed you to be in a legitimate bad mood for at least a fortnight. "Werewolves?"

Julius blinked as if she had said something quite absurd. "Actually, the last werewolves were killed in the nineteenth century," he said.

"You're older than you look," Clea snarked at him. Not that she really thought he had been around killing werewolves in the nineteenth century. He couldn't be more than forty. Maybe thirty-five.

"Yes, probably," he said. And then, "How do you feel about gargoyles?"

• • •

That was how Clea ended up spending her whole weekend clambering around on the roofs of Nova Ostia, pointing out every animal-shaped statue on every building, and helping Julius to discreetly shatter them.

"I always wondered," she said. "They didn't seem a very Roman sort of thing."

"The creatures are, the statues aren't," he said. "They're attracted to cities, especially the high parts, where they can see the stars. They climb up here and just ossify. Which is fine until they come to life during the full moon and start biting chunks out of people."

"Why didn't you smash them up last time you were here?" she asked.

"They weren't here last time I was here," he replied.

Clea argued he was wrong, that many of the gargoyles had been there since she was a child, and Julius argued that in fact memory-alteration was part of their self-defence mechanism, and what with one thing and another, she completely forgot about Daniel and how weird it was to let someone inside your actual body, and how she had been wanting to explode into a million pieces.

When the last gargoyle was destroyed, Clea and Julius stretched out in the shade of the aqueduct, on the flat roof of the temple of Saturn. It was too hot climb back down to ground level.

"Do you want to kiss me?" she asked him.

He looked surprised. "No thank you."

"Are you gay?" she asked next. Apparently she was going with personal questions this time around.

"No," said Julius, still polite and friendly about the whole thing. No hint of embarrassment. "I'm just terribly old."

Clea lifted herself up on her elbows, staring at him. "Did you really kill werewolves in the nineteenth century?"

"Among other things."

Wow, okay. So not thirty-five. "That means you were born in—eighteen hundred and something?"

"No," Julius said calmly. "Further back."

"When?"

He sighed. "Thirty-nine."

"1739?" Australia hadn't even been colonised then. Not that she thought he was Australian. It was just—a really long time ago. Hard to take in.

"No. Just 39."

"A.D.?" Clea said in a voice that was supposed to be all cool but came out as sort of a shriek.

"Scholars say C.E. these days. It's important to move with the times."

"But that makes you nearly two thousand years old!" So much older than thirty-five. Older than most *cathedrals*.

"Yes," said Julius, looking tired. "I suppose it does."

"How does that even work?"

"It's a long story."

"Obviously!" Clea thought it over for a while. The heat was making her brain slow and mushy. "Are you the only person in the world who's all immortal and monster-hunting?"

"As far as I know."

"So you don't have sex because we're all too young for you?"

"I didn't say that," he said with a hint of a smile. "But you are definitely too young for me."

"My grandmother needs a boyfriend. I could totally hook you up."

"Excellent, I look forward to that." Julius sat up suddenly, looking distracted. "We missed one."

"We did? Where?"

And then a gargoyle came screaming over the roof at them, belching smoke, and they had more important things to worry about than a conversation about sex with old people.

III

Clea was nineteen, home on holiday from university, when she got a chance to ask Julius why the creatures he hunted came to Nova Ostia so often.

"This is three times in three years now," she said when she found him battling naiads in the Fountain of Neptune, at four o'clock in the morning. "Wouldn't it save time just to stay here and wait for them all to come to you?"

"And leave the rest of the world unprotected?" he said, throwing handfuls of iron shavings into the water despite the wails and cries of the blue-skinned women. "It might seem like a regular occurrence to you, but it's merely a drop in the ocean."

"Still, it's a weird coincidence that the ones who make it as far as Australia always come here."

"Not a coincidence at all," said Julius, wiping scales off his toga. "The people who built this little tourist trap of yours used actual stone from Roman cities, remember? The creatures are drawn here just as much as they are to Ostia itself, or Pompeii, or Bath."

"Bath in England?"

"Lots of museums in Bath. Old temples. Statues. I spend a great deal of time in museums." He looked curiously at Clea. "What are you studying at university?"

"Economics," she said, which was a lie. Later, when the naiads had gurgled their death throes and she was letting Julius clean himself up in her Mum's *ensuite*, she admitted, "Archaeology and Latin."

He seemed amused. "I suppose there isn't a course on hunting mythological beasts."

"Not specifically. Sydney universities are quite provincial. I was lucky to get Latin."

Julius dried his face on a shell pink hand towel. "You're still too young for me."

"Did I ask?" Clea was pissed off that he assumed she was still interested. "I have a boyfriend. Who is very good in bed, actually."

"I'm glad you told me that. I might have had sleepless nights, wondering about it."

Clea glared at him. "Are we done here?"

"That depends on you, doesn't it?"

She could have kicked him out, shut the door, and ignored him until next time their paths crossed and there were dragons, or something, but it had been two years, and she had a whole lot more questions saved up. "I'll walk you out."

They strolled through the quiet city. "Tourists still come to this place?" Julius asked. "I didn't think anyone cared about the ancient world any more."

"Gladiator gaming is trendy again," said Clea. "It helps. Though the visitors are always disappointed we don't have a Colosseum with real fighting and stuff."

"Bread and circuses. Nothing changes."

"Mostly we get Australians who want to travel for culture but feel guilty about their carbon footprint. Never mind that it will take another fifty years to pay back the carbon footprint it cost to build this place . . . "

Julius nodded. They were almost at the wall. "What else did you want to ask me this time?"

"The first time we met, you said you were a manticore, which was a lie because I looked it up, and it's like—a lion mixed with a person and a scorpion, and unless you're very good at disguises, that's not what you are."

Clea waited for him to tell her that yes, he was a lion and a scorpion and a person all mixed together, and his human skin had been sewn by dwarves, or something.

"The manticore was a metaphor," Julius answered instead. "Like a chimaera, or a griffin. A creature built from other creatures. A hybrid. That's what I am."

"But a hybrid of what?"

He shrugged. "There is lamia blood in my family. Werewolf too. Other magics. One of my great-grandmothers turned herself into a dragon to prove a point. Many of my relatives became gods. We were a strange family."

"And your name is really Julius?"

Clea had done her research. She wasn't limited to Google anymore; she had a whole university library at her disposal. The year 39 C.E. was during the reign of Caligula, one of the emperors who claimed descent from Julius Caesar. Then again, it wasn't only emperors who used the name. Any slave freed from that family could call himself Julius.

He sighed. "I told you it was a long story."

"I'm young, remember?" Clea said pointedly. "I have time."

Julius took her hand, an odd gesture that had nothing romantic about it, and everything to do with the fact that they were like teammates now. They had killed lamia and gargoyles and naiads together. He led her out of the city, to the tree where she had spent so many of her teen years being all angsty. He didn't trip over the tree root this time.

They made themselves comfortable, and he told her a story.

"I was born Julia Drusilla, in the year 39," he began.

"You were born a girl?" Clea interrupted. Whatever she had expected, it was not that.

"No. I was a boy. But my father desperately wanted a girl. He was still in mourning for his favourite sister, and he had made her a goddess. In his head, this daughter was to be her replacement, her namesake, her human form on earth. He could not comprehend that I was a boy. It's funny, really. Every other emperor obsessed about their sons and male heirs. Mine saw no need for that, as he planned to live forever."

"Your father was Caligula," said Clea, who had guessed that much but wanted to be certain.

Julius gave her a wary look. "Indeed. You probably want me to defend him, to say he was nothing like the monster that appears in the history books, and that much at least is true. He was a very different monster to the one history recalls."

"Was he a manticore too? Part lamia, part werewolf . . . "

"Part sociopath. Yes. More lamia than anything, but that was Livia's fault. I'm getting ahead of myself. My mother was worried for me—that if Caligula realised I was a boy, I might be in danger. She bought a baby girl—from a slave, I suppose—and swapped us over. I was safe in the temple of the Vestals when, two years later, there was a palace uprising against my father. He was killed, and my mother, and the false Julia. Uncle Claudius was made Emperor instead, and he named his daughters Claudia, not Julia. I was the last of my kind."

"It's quite a common name these days," Clea commented.

Julius seemed impatient with her. "It means nothing in the mouths of anyone else. To my family, it was of great significance, to be a Julia. Just as it meant something to have lamia blood, or werewolf, or dragon. I still had two living aunts who visited me in my childhood sometimes, who trained me to use my powers. Julia Livilla made the list for me, of the creatures we had to defeat, to free our family of the curse. Julia Agrippina taught me my weapons, and took me travelling around the world. After they were gone, I fought the creatures alone."

Clea felt a sharp twist in her stomach when he said the word "alone'. It was only a slight hesitation, but he held himself so rigidly, as if admitting the word meant something might destroy his whole illusion.

He continued. "Nero, my cousin, was the last Julian Emperor. He died when I was twenty nine. It was some years before I realised I had stopped aging. It was as if . . . as the only member of the family who had survived, I now held all of their burdens. It took decades before I realised what my task in life was. My aunt's list. The creatures that had to be destroyed."

"But you don't know for sure," Clea said softly. "That it's what you have to do. That you can . . . rest, when the list is complete."

His eyes were burning now with a fierce, angry light. "Oh, yes. I know."

She wanted to comfort him. To reach out and touch him. To be something, anything that he needed. But she had nothing to offer—nothing that he would take, anyway.

They sat together until morning. She dozed once, leaning against his shoulder and the tree, and when she blinked awake, she was alone.

She did not see him again for five years, and when she did, he was too busy stabbing harpies to stop and chat.

IV

Clea grew up, and built a life. Archaeology remained her passion for fifteen years, and after that she wrote books, because there was less mud and fewer long haul flights involved, and you had to think about that carbon footprint these days.

She mostly lived in Europe. When she returned to Australia to visit her family, it was not to Nova Ostia, which had closed to the public some time around her thirtieth birthday, but to Sydney, which had rather fewer incursions of mythical creatures who wanted to kill people, and hardly any visits by the man whose job it was to destroy those creatures, on behalf of a host of dead Julias.

She saw Julius in Venice, though, and Rome, and London, more than once. Sometimes they talked, sometimes they killed things. At least once, there was nothing to talk about and nothing to kill, and so they had a nice dinner in an Indian restaurant, because they were both hungry, and it was there.

Clea had children and got married, in that order.

When she was fifty three, she went to the opera, not because she wanted to, but because her husband had hated it with a vengeance, and she was angry at him for dying so suddenly, with no warning, of a heart attack.

Opera seemed the best revenge.

She wore a vintage gown of purple silk that hugged the curves which had spread, somewhat, over the years. She wore diamonds that had belonged to her grandmother and usually lived in a safe.

Halfway through the second act, a dragon marched across the stage, which had not been mentioned at all in the programme. Clea did not realise she had been holding her breath until a man in an ill-fitting costume strode across the stage after the dragon, and leapt on to its back.

There was fire and screaming and the horrible ripping sound as velvet curtains were destroyed, and very little singing. But when it was over, the audience had mostly fled, and there was a dead dragon on the stage.

Clea walked on unsteady feet up the aisle, and gazed at the man who was half-draped over the dead dragon in exhaustion. "I like the beard," she said finally.

"It's false," said Julius, removing it.

"I know. I like the fact that you went to so much trouble to assemble a Don Claudio costume despite the fact that the dragon was sure to send the audience packing anyway."

"It's all about style," he said, and let out a heavy sigh.

"You're wounded," she said.

"I'm never wounded. Didn't you hear, I'm quite good at this."

She leaned over and poked at the bloody hole in his chest. "You're wounded."

"Ouch." He looked down in alarm. "Damned spurs. I didn't see that coming. What do I do about it?"

"Antiseptic. One of the great modern inventions. And some gauze, I expect. Don't look so worried, you won't die of it."

"Oh, good," he said, poking experimentally at the wound himself. "It would be embarrassing to die at this point. That wasn't even the last dragon."

"This is what comes of leaving the big ones until last," she chided him.

He came back to her hotel room, and she patched him up, because obviously a two thousand year old man couldn't be trusted with gauze and antiseptic, let alone with the task of going to a doctor.

He had many scars across his torso, though they seemed far older than his skin.

Julius looked longingly at her bed, and Clea rolled her eyes at him. "Fine, you can stay. When did you last sleep?"

"January," he said, and was practically snoring before he hit the pillow.

• • •

He slept for three days. Clea was afraid he was dying, or hibernating, and she had to change her travel plans to stay in Paris a little longer. Somehow, just leaving him here seemed wrong, especially when there might be vengeful griffins or sphinxes flying in through the window at any moment.

"Thank you," Julius said on the morning of the third day, and was startled when she leaped up from her armchair, letting books spill across the floor as she came over to kiss him. "What was that for?"

"I thought you had left me here alone with dragons still on the loose," she told him.

"Oh," he said. "I wouldn't do that. I've been looking forward to crossing off dragons." And then he kissed her back.

Apparently, she was no longer too young for him, or familiarity had pushed his resistance aside, or something like that. He removed her clothes with a careful precision that made her shiver, and made love to her with an intensity that had her closing her eyes, so that she did not burst into flame.

"If I had known you could do that," she said, some time later. "I would have jumped you when I was twenty-five."

"I like you now," he said, hands exploring the creases and puckered parts of her stomach, like she was a map he was trying to understand. "Far more interesting. Children don't appeal to me."

"I was hardly a child when I was twenty-five," she said, but of course she had been. She was a child to him now, this tight-bodied young-looking man who had just brought her to orgasm more times than she could count.

Fifty-three, and she was just starting out. Had only now seen her first dragon. "How long do you have?" she asked. "Before you have to go kill things again."

"Nothing but time," said Julius, nibbling experimentally on her hipbone. That translated, as it turned out, to three weeks in the hotel, before he disappeared again, on his quest to cross more creatures off that bloody list of his.

Life continued.

v

When she was seventy-two, Clea took her grandchildren to visit the quiet streets of Nova Ostia. Bus tours still took people out there, though there were no more shops and no open thermopolium serving honey cakes and egg salad, no community of families enacting the ancient ways.

"What did you do for internet?" Mercy asked, more interested in the whole thing than her cousins were.

"Oh we had wifi back then," Clea assured her. "And plenty of mod cons in most of the homes—where the tourists couldn't see. But we dressed and behaved as authentically as we could, when in public."

"Weird," muttered Sebastian, obviously bored.

"Why didn't they just digitize it, Nan?" asked Blake, who wandered through artificial landscapes all the time, thanks to his favourite gaming module.

"They did, eventually," said Clea. "It was just . . . a lovely thing that existed, once. It all made some sort of sense at the time. It wasn't an ordinary childhood, but it was a good one."

Clea thought about lamia bites on her brother's neck, of smashing gargoyles on the rooves of the city. She hadn't seen Julius in years. That list of his was getting shorter, on the rare occasions he let her peek at it. Perhaps he had killed the last manticore or basilisk already, and found his peaceful reward.

Perhaps.

Except, no. He hadn't killed the last manticore. Clea stopped and blinked at the creature that prowled the Forum, a bright splash of tawny hide and scarlet claws against the monotone buildings. Head of a lion. Face of . . . a person, though it was twisted into something quite ugly. A long, lashing, sting-laden tail.

She began to laugh. "It really is a manticore. Goodness me. And he said it was a metaphor."

"Is that one of your tourist things?" Seb asked in alarm. Even Blake turned off his gaming module, staring at the monster.

"It's pretty," said Mercy.

Clea shushed them. "Don't move. Everything's going to be fine."

It was too long since she had fought monsters. She didn't know the first thing about weapons that would work against a manticore, and here she was armed with nothing but her handbag and three grandchildren.

She should have thought of this. Should have remembered that coming home wasn't just nostalgia and honey cakes. Nova Ostia drew the monsters to it with these old borrowed stones.

The manticore strutted closer, poised to pounce. Its human face growled.

An arrow thunked deeply into its side, and then another. A third took it through the side of its head, dropping it to the ground.

"This place comes with superheroes!" yelled Mercy, and the boys cheered.

Clea looked up, shading her face from the sun, and saw a familiar silhouette in a broad-brimmed hat, standing on the roof of the temple of Saturn. She waved, and he waved back.

"Who's that, Nan?" asked Mercy.

"A very dear friend," she said, and walked neatly around the manticore. "Come on. I'll show you where I used to live."

It was the last time, and she didn't realise it, though every time she had seen him in the last decade she had thought, "this could be the last time." She wasn't going to live forever, after all. Seventy-two full and healthy years, two children, three grandchildren, it had been a good life, and barely an interlude in his.

"Just don't train my granddaughter up as a monster hunter," she had said to him in Paris a year ago, though she knew secretly that Mercy would probably be rather good at the task once she got over the shock.

"Who do you think I am, Peter Pan?" said Julius, as if the very idea was distasteful to him. They finished sipping their wine, and went upstairs together, and said no more of it.

That had been the last time they would speak, but she didn't know that, either.

• • •

Clea got the call four days before her seventy-fifth birthday. "Sydney?" said Poppy in protest, when she heard about it. "Mum, you can't. Not all the way to Australia again!"

But who else was going to go?

At the end of a long flight, Clea met with some sympathetic police officers and morgue attendants. They apologised for bringing her all this way, and she apologised for putting them to any trouble, and what with one thing and another, they filled the corridors with empty noise.

She had hoped it wouldn't be him. You always do in moments like that, don't you? A mistake, plain and simple. But she had flown a long way in the hope of proving the police officers wrong.

He had carried no identification, just his notebook, and her name. They showed it to her when they passed over his other belongings (a few papers, a safe deposit key, a greened-bronze necklace) and there were contact details too, all the addresses she had lived at over the years, the phone numbers, each one crossed out as a new one was added.

Julius had never visited at her at any of her homes, never written, never called. The world had thrown them together countless times, and they were happy with that. But he could have found her any time he wanted to.

There was no one else in the notebook. Perhaps there had been, in other centuries, in other notebooks or wax tablets or whatever he used before the book, but in this one there was only Clea Majora, later Clea Robinson, and the list of crossed-off items. Basilisk, Chimera, Dragon . . .

One item was not crossed out—Gorgon. It must have been the last creature that he killed. Did his family curse not even allow him a moment to catch his breath and tidy his notebook before he fell?

Clea looked down at his calm, still body. Gorgons killed by turning you to stone, didn't they? That wasn't what had ended him. His skin was waxy and grey, but undeniably human.

He seemed young. Twenty-nine, he had been when his aging stopped, if his dates were correct. So young. She did not remember when they had appeared the same age. Julius had never been one to worry unduly about the physical realities of time, in any case.

He had shown little romantic interest in her until she looked far older than he. Then again, he was two thousand years old. Even now, she was young, in comparison.

"Was he a friend of your son?" asked a police officer, who obviously meant to be kind.

Clea swallowed any number of retorts. What could she say that would sum up this man? "He was a friend," she said, finally.

VI

She had his ashes buried in Nova Ostia. It should have been Rome, really, but where was there space for a headstone in Rome? Here at least, in an abandoned city made with authentic stone, she could have some control over how his deeds were recorded.

It was a large slab of paving stone that matched the whiteness of the buildings, and she laid it at the foot of the Temple of Augustus.

JULIUS, of the JULIAS
Son of GAIUS CAESAR CALIGULA
Hunter of BEASTS
Slayer of MONSTERS
Friend of Clea Majora

It was not enough. Not nearly enough. But what more could she do? She could surround it with carvings of lamia and werewolves and manticores, but it would mean nothing to anyone who followed.

She buried him with his sword, the gladius that had aged as little as he did. There were other belongings which she could have placed in his grave—the necklace, or his list of monsters, or the painstakingly copied-out manuscript she had found, all in Latin, which she rather thought had been authored by one of his aunts. Julius had collected all manner of ephemera in his lifetime—a claw, a vial of silver blood, a sheath of dragon skin. Trophies which meant nothing, now.

When Clea was gone, there would be no one who knew who he had been, what he had done, and for just one moment, that thought was utterly unbearable.

Then she breathed, and looked around. She was an old woman standing in an ancient city, barely a step away from the Australian bush. The world was full of wonders, and possibilities.

"Find peace," she said aloud, and walked away.

There would be more adventures in the years to come.

············

# DARK ME, NIGHT YOU

## TERRY DOWLING

Through the window of his consulting room, Carl Santi watched rain fall in the little courtyard garden. Just after noon, early really, but a dark day, a black dog of a day as they said. There truly were days when it *was* physician heal thyself, doubly, triply, infinitely so where analysts were concerned, when you wanted to say no, cancel all the appointments and step back from other people's lives, other people's minds, just for a time.

But in five minutes Paul Ziller would be here; that would make the afternoon bearable, a large part of it. The rest of his clients—three of the four for Tuesday 9th June—were in diagnostic holding patterns or locked in the analysis-as-lifestyle syndrome. Paul was different. He was on a mission, someone who relished the journey. Five minutes and there would be some new madcap Ziller irreverence to deal with.

Sitting at his desk, Carl looked away from the rain and the blowing treetops above the courtyard wall. He turned his attention back to Megan's referral form in front of him and the final unmarked question with its two boxes for ticking: Yes or No.

*Is it your considered opinion that the candidate is suitable for this position?*
No choice at all really—Waltern's was lucky to get her—except that Megan had moved on from him. Not that he had made his interest clear. Five years and he'd let it be just what it was, professional.

And this gift from her! His gaze went from the referral to the painting leaning against the wall. An original Engele, for heaven's sake, dark and awful but a princely gift, in gratitude for the chance, the invaluable training opportunity, the faith and the friendship. Carl was still trying to make up his mind about whether to hang it or have Darla put it straight into storage.

The painting said it all. Dark and awful on a dark and awful day. The words on her card only confirmed it. *Something I thought you would like.* Which translated as: something staid and traditional for someone who is staid and traditional, someone who is deliberate, a known quantity, a stereotype.

Carl should have acted. Acted differently. But she'd moved on and he wished her well. Truly did. And who could say? Not working together might make the next step possible. Cancel out the avuncular, the platonic. He could phone, see how she was getting on. It might be the start of something. Of course he'd recommend her. He'd have Darla send off the referral today.

But as he reached for his pen, there was a knock at the door, and Paul Ziller entered the room, smiling, commanding immediate attention as he always did, clearly glad to be there, his eyes darting this way and that.

"That's a bit much," he said, noticing the painting. "Is it staying?"

"Still deciding," Carl replied, turning in his high-backed office chair to face the armchair that Paul would occupy. "It's a gift. An original Engele. You remember my protégé Megan. Well, she sent it for me to get used to. It promises to be quite valuable."

"Too dark," Paul said, crossing to inspect it. "Sombre."

"You're being kind."

"Mournful then," Paul added. "But a nice touch of old-world gloom to complete the analyst stereotype."

"Exactly so," Carl said, hiding the stab of dismay at having his own misgivings echoed so precisely. But this was why he liked Paul. Nothing was sacred. "Why don't we make a start?"

"Assuming the position," Paul said, settling in the armchair; then before Carl could launch into his customary review of their last meeting, added: "Carl, you do know the date?"

"Yes, Paul. June 9th. "

"The significance of the date?"

"Of course. When you started seeing me you said you'd ask me to do something on June 9th. You refused to say what."

"I needed the two and a half months to suss you out. Decide whether to go ahead with it."

"Suss me out?" Carl was surprised. This was a different Paul, focused, more serious than usual. "And you've decided?"

"I have. If you'll agree to it."

"That has to depend on what it is."

"You've been getting a handle on me."

Carl smiled. "Helping, I hope."

"I've kept things back."

"I see. And now you can tell me." Carl had been through these declaration situations countless times.

"Two and a half months, six meetings in, I believe I can."

Carl leant forward slightly, laced his hands together atop his notepad. "Let's have it then."

Paul leant forward too. "You're a hypnotherapist as well as an analyst."

"Don't go coy on me, Paul. You know I am."

"I want you to bring out the night in me."

"Again please."

"There's a darkness in me. Old Night. Capital O, capital N. I want you to hypnotise me and draw it out."

"Old Night?"

"It's a racial memory. All of us have it."

"You believe people carry darkness in them? Literally?"

Paul nodded. "Like an imprint. A primordial memory. And asking you to activate it is probably a better way to put it. It's not something to be done lightly or easily. It may take a concerted effort."

"I see. How long have you known this?"

Paul frowned. "Please don't do that, Carl. I trust you. I felt I could bring it up."

"You can. I just need to be sure that I'm understanding you correctly. You want me to try to activate a racial memory of night that we all have buried within us. Can you tell me why you want this?" Professional ethics alert, his whole manner said.

Paul shrugged. "It's there. I've sensed it. I'm sure we all do at one point or another."

"All right."

"You don't believe me?"

"What matters is what you believe—"

"Stop that! Don't do that, Carl! I need confirmation here, okay? Not being handled. I need reaffirmation from someone I trust. This can't be a new idea. It has to be fundamental—a memory from a time when night was truly deadly and terrifying, when dread of it dominated the waking hours. Maybe it's evolution's way of controlling its creatures, culling the weak and sparing the strong—"

"Its way of what?"

"I just need you to treat it seriously. We must have a reason for it. It's deep mind stuff. I want it brought out, brought forward, whatever the right words for that are. I want to know what it is."

"Again I ask you why?"

"It's there. A part of us. It completes us, is probably there for a reason. It was once our nature."

"Once. But it would be like our appendix, wouldn't it?"

"Our appendix?"

"Yes. A vestigial organ from when our ancestors were more herbivorous and had to digest cellulose; it's no longer needed. This memory of night would be like that. Something we no longer need."

"Only because of our current level of technology surely. What if it's not the same at all? What if it's still there, a working part of us? *Meant* to be used."

"For what?"

Paul shrugged and Carl decided it was probably best not to push too hard at this point.

"All right, Paul. So a deep memory. Atavistic. Possibly vestigial—"

"That's how we'd be inclined to see it. We've become so conditioned to staying up beyond sundown. Not giving it another thought. But what if it *is* fundamental, very powerful, but forgotten in a reductive, pro-rationlist world, sidelined because of these distracting technological advances? Oil, gas and electric light are so superficial, so conditional. They have a lot to answer for."

Carl had never thought of electric light and power quite that way, as being superficial, responsible for redirecting—misdirecting—the human psyche. He found himself recalling an old D.H. Lawrence novel he'd once read; the author's preoccupation with "old dark gods." He judged his next words carefully.

"All right. We're agreeing so far. But we're talking old, old memory. It may not necessarily be something we can access now. If it's deep-seated, primal—"

"I said *fundamental* to our natures, Carl. I'm convinced that the mind is set up *to* access it but has simply lost the habit of doing so. This is more than just a holdover from primordial times, like our irrational fear of serpents and spiders. This is prime psychic design, coded into basic human nature, commanding enormous force."

Prime psychic design. Where did these terms come from?

"We can't know that conclusively, Paul. Look, you've been seeing me because of ongoing factors—"

"Carl, I lied about those. This is the real reason I've been coming here."

Carl was completely thrown by the admission but managed to keep his face composed and waited a three-count. "You're *not* delusional?"

Thankfully Paul smiled, and Carl did too. It was a moment when the only sounds were the wind blowing around the eaves and the rain falling on the pavers in the courtyard.

"Of course I'm delusional," Paul said, his old self again. "I accept that my problems are real. But the meds handle those. This is the real reason. Will you do it?"

"I hypnotise you?"

Paul nodded. "Deep hypnosis. A genuine, earnest and sustained attempt."

Genuine, earnest and sustained. Such terms. This was Paul Ziller all the way.

"There would be ethical considerations," Carl said. "I'd be concerned I was doing harm—just by indulging you."

"But you'd be using one aspect of my condition to alleviate others. Surely that has to count for something."

From how Paul said it, Carl knew that his star client had planned these responses, rehearsed them, would have rejoinders for anything he said. The rain was growing heavier at the windows but Carl dared not look away.

"And if I don't you'll go elsewhere."

Paul shrugged. *I'll go elsewhere.*

"Paul, why has this become so important for you?"

Paul smiled again, rolled his eyes in mock-chagrin. "Uh-oh. Now I've done it. I sense a charge of monomania coming on."

"Well, it is an idée fixe. You've spent money—quite a bit of money—to get to this point."

"That creates no obligation for you under the circumstances, I realize." Paul leaned forward in the chair again. "I need your absolute goodwill in this, Carl. I need an ally, not some quick-fix neighbourhood quack or gypsy fortune-teller. No-one too close to the crystal, if you get my meaning. You're serious about what you do."

Carl's watched Paul's eyes, not daring to break eye contact. He was used to monomaniacs and obsessives being manipulative, strategic, dogged like this. But Paul Ziller needed *goodwill.* An *earnest* attempt at unlocking a part of *prime psychic design.* Today was the culmination of weeks, months, possibly years of planning. Carl wondered at his own place in it. What *was* his duty of care? What would such an attempt achieve?

More to the point, what would Paul think it had achieved?

Carl was fascinated in spite of himself, but knew he had to be devil's advocate here, maintain the opposing stance a while longer. "Paul, you realize that trying to activate this memory of night could qualify as criminal and professional negligence on my part?"

"But surely you're within allowable guidelines. Playing along to reach certain outcomes. Humouring the patient. You do that all the time."

"But you say you want more. My active participation. An *earnest* attempt."

"All I ask. The joking stops. We treat it seriously. You do your very best. What do you say?"

"I'm still deciding."

"I'm resolved, Carl."

"I can see that, Paul. I'm still concerned that this condition of night you talk about, this night-mindedness—"

"Night self. The rest of what we are."

"— can't be a natural or healthy state or it wouldn't be a submerged thing. We'd access it all the time, use it, have a reason for it, regardless of what you say about technology and conditioning."

"Exactly my point. I believe we do use it, Carl. We just don't know how—or what its purpose is. Look, I need a job done. It's important to me. Treat it as a weird Paul Ziller hypothetical. I've come to a skilled provider. Will you do it?"

"How would I go about it, Paul? The hypnosis I can manage, but what words do I use? There's no precedent—"

"No rituals and protocols, I know. No litany."

"Since you're using that word."

Paul smiled. "Well, this consulting room has been a confessional for quite a while now. And you make a splendid devil's advocate by the way."

Again Carl felt a stab of dismay at Paul locking on to another earlier thought. "Not an analogy I'm all that comfortable with."

"So just use your usual lines. Adapt your give-up-smoking spiel. Your fear-of-meeting-people patter. I'm sure you've got routines."

"Paul—"

"Carl, I've been this close before. You're not the first analyst I've been to. I've spent a lot of money."

"They weren't earnest enough?"

"They had the same professional reservations. But it wasn't that. They doubted."

"I'm doubting."

"You're in a different space."

"More the Engele type."

Paul smiled. "I dared not say it."

"You were going to?"

Paul glanced at the Engele against the wall, at the fall of rain in the garden. "Your colleague Megan has moved on. Your receptionist told me. You're at a crossroads—"

"Now look here, Paul—"

"Carl, I'm being direct, but you've come to know me. You like me. You're in the right head-space for this. It'll take half an hour."

"An hour to do it properly. An *earnest* attempt remember."

"We still have most of two."

Carl felt anger, self-doubt, swelling disappointment that an already dark day had become spoiled in such a fashion. Paul Ziller had been the high point. Anna Cambray was next: pallid, fixated, resisting. More gloom. Was there nothing he could depend on?

But there was this to be done. Something outside the staid and the traditional. Treason and trickery in the confessional, yes, the old dark gods calling, but something more than the sorry, clenched Anna Cambrays of the world.

"Let's make a start then."

• • •

Five minutes later, the room lights had been dimmed: more shadowing in the gloom, with the rain outside heavier than ever. Paul was still in the armchair, but with Carl seated in a fan-back chair just behind his right shoulder so he would be nothing more than a voice.

Calmly, steadily, Carl began the standard relaxation spiel, pitching his voice at the right mellifluous level, reciting the phase-downs, step by lulling step.

"You hear only my voice. Only my words. You are relaxed. Growing more and more relaxed. It is good to let go, to feel yourself growing heavier, easier, so relaxed . . . "

And on it went. Carl hadn't done this in months, so it was more a matter of judging voice quality, pitch and enunciation at first. But, as the procedure continued, it was easy to close his eyes and go with the immersion.

Five minutes became ten, fifteen, twenty, though Carl had no clear idea of duration now. He was in the rhythm of the descent, the step-down as he called it, improvising, embroidering.

"We're deep in your mind now, deep in your self. This is your deepest, safest place, your most powerful secret place. So safe and so so deep . . . "

Paul could be asleep for all he knew, but that, too, was acceptable. Paul's greater self was there, would hear and respond.

Carl kept on, became his words. They were shapes now as well as sounds, blades and edges, barricades and bridges, towers, archways, beckoning tunnels, doorway on doorway. He stepped through them, around them, slipped between them, hadn't meant to close his eyes for it, but they were shut tight, sealing the room out, sealing them in, keeping it powerful.

He said the lull rhythms, keeping it strong and vital, aiming his words at the heart of the mission. At last he decided that it was time.

"There at the centre, at the very heart and core of you, Old Night waits to be touched, waits to be known. It is ready, waiting. Old

Night is ready. The Old Dark. In the right place, the forever place. It needs only the word and it will be there. Fully there again. The true black night of you. It needs only a word and it will flow forth, swell up into its true nature. I am going to say that word, a single word, and bring it forth. The Night Self. You will hear and respond when I say the word, and you will respond. The word is: Now! This is the word, the only word. Now! It is done. Night is there, back in its rightful place. It is summoned and it has come. Hear the word of power one last time so there can be no doubt: Now!"

• • •

There was the phase-out then, full of the usual feel-good touches but surprisingly brief since there was no need to suppress the memory of what had been done, no need of post-hypnotic suggestion. Paul would remember, should remember.

Carl had surprised himself, not just that he *could* do it, but how well he had managed considering, how completely he had urged, believed, acted as if he did.

At last he brought up the lights, though only to half of what they had been originally. It was enough after the dimness of the treatment. Then he returned to his chair at the desk.

Paul stirred at last, stretched, rubbed his eyes, finally sat forward in the armchair.

"We're done then," he said, smiling, seeming happy and relieved.

"I believe so, Paul. I think that went well."

"Me too, Carl. But should I believe you?"

"What's that? Why wouldn't you?"

"Well, I tricked you today about why I was really here. You could have tricked me just now. Tit for tat."

"I haven't, Paul," Carl said. "You know I wouldn't. You're the one who tricked me today."

"More than once," Paul said, with the strangest look on his face. A pleased look, a satisfied look, but cool, oddly remote.

"What? More lies?"

"Just one really." Paul rose from his chair, stretched again, then walked to the door. Turning the handle, he looked back. "I had the night switched on in me ages ago."

Carl frowned in puzzlement. "What?"

Paul opened the door. "Just passing it on," he said. "Finding others to do the same."

And in a moment he was gone. The door closed behind him with a soft click.

Carl sat puzzled, dumbfounded, his mind racing, recalling things Paul had said on this most incredible of days.

*You're not the first analyst I've been to .*

*I'll go elsewhere .*

The words had taken on a new troubling significance.

Carl didn't know what to think, how to react. At least his mood had improved. Rain was still falling outside; the sky was windy and overcast, but it no longer bothered him. The day seemed brighter.

The Engele as well. It wasn't so bad once you got used to it. Not so much dark as subtle, intricate. Megan had chosen well.

Megan.

Carl pushed Paul's file to one side, took up his pen and reached for the Waltern's referral as if the whole strange interlude with Paul Ziller hadn't existed.

*Is it your considered opinion that the candidate is suitable for this position?*

With one swift stroke he ticked No, then pressed the intercom button.

"Darla, if Anna Cambray's there send her in, will you? We've got a lot to do."

••••••••••

# THE COFFIN-MAKER'S DAUGHTER

## ANGELA SLATTER

The door is a rich red wood, heavily carved with improving scenes from the trials of Job. An angel's head, cast in brass, serves as the knocker and when I let it go to rest back in its groove, the eyes fly open, indignant, and watch me with suspicion. Behind me is the tangle of garden—cataracts of flowering vines, lovers' nooks, secluded reading benches—that gives this house its affluent privacy.

The dead man's daughter opens the door.

She is pink and peach and creamy. I want to lick at her skin and see if she tastes the way she looks.

"Hepsibah Ballantyne! Slattern! Concentrate, this is business." My father slaps at me, much as he did in life. Nowadays his fists pass through me, causing nothing more than a sense of cold ebbing in my veins. I do not miss the bruises.

The girl doesn't recognise me although I worked in this house for nigh on a year—but that is because it was only me watching her and not she me. When my mother finally left us it became apparent she would not provide Hector with any more children, let alone a son who might take over from him. He decided I should learn his craft and the sign above the entrance to the workshop was changed—not to *Ballantyne & Daughter*, though. *Ballantyne & Other*.

"Speak, you idiot," Father hisses, as though it's important he whisper. No one has heard Hector Ballantyne these last eight months, not since what appeared to be an unseasonal cold carried him off.

The blue eyes, red-rimmed from crying, should look ugly, unpalatable in the lovely oval face, but grief becomes Lucette D'Aguillar. Everything becomes her, from the black mourning gown to the severe, scraped back coiffure that is the heritage of the bereaved, because she is that rare thing: born lucky.

"Yes?" she asks as if I have no right to interrupt the grieving house.

I slip the cap from my head, feel the mess it makes of my hair, and hold it in front of me like a shield. My nails are broken and my hands scarred and stained from the tints and varnish I use on the wood. I curl my fingers under the fabric of the cap to hide them as much as I can.

"I'm here about the coffin," I say. "It's Hepsibah. Hepsibah Ballantyne."

Her stare remains blank, but she steps aside and lets me in. By rights, I should have gone to the back door, the servants' entrance. Hector would have—did so all his life—but I provide a valuable service. If they trust me to create a death-bed for their nearest and dearest, they can let me in the front door. Everyone knows there's been a death—it's impossible to hide in the big houses—I will not creep in as though my calling is shameful. Hector grumbled the first few times I presented myself in this manner—or rather shrieked, subsided to a grumble afterwards—but as I said to him, what were they going to do?

I'm the only coffin-maker in the city. They let me in.

I follow Lucette to a parlour washed with tasteful shades of grey and hung with white lace curtains so fine it seems they must be made by spinners with eight legs. She takes note of herself in the large mirror above the mantle. Her mother is seated on a chaise; she too regards her own reflection, making sure she still exists. Lucette joins her and they look askance at me. Father makes sounds of disgust and he is right to do so. He will stay quiet here; even though no one can hear him but me, he will not distract me. He will not interrupt *business*.

"Your mirror should be covered," I say as I sit, uninvited, in a fine armchair that hugs me like a gentle, sleepy bear. I arrange the skirts of my brown mourning meetings dress and rest my hands on the arms of the chair, then remember how unsightly they are and clasp them in my lap. Black ribbons alone decorate the mirror's edges, a fashionable nod to custom, but not much protection. "All of your mirrors. To be safe. Until the body is removed."

They exchange a glance, affronted.

"The choice is yours, of course. I'm given to understand that some families are delighted to have a remnant of the deceased take up residence in their mirrors. They enjoy the sensation of being watched constantly. It makes them feel not so alone." I smile as if I am kind. "And the dead seem to like it, especially the unexpectedly dead. Without time to prepare themselves, they tend to cling to the ones they loved. Did you suspect your husband's heart was weak or was it a terrible surprise?"

Madame D'Aguillar hands her black shawl to Lucette, who covers the mirror with it then rejoins her mother.

"You have kept the body wrapped?" I ask, and they nod. I nod in return, to tell them they've done only just enough. That they are foolish, vain women who put their own reflections ahead of keeping a soul in a body. "Good. Now, how may I be of assistance?"

This puts them on the back foot once again, makes them my supplicants. They must *ask* for what they want. Both look put out and it gives me the meanest little thrill, to see them thus. I smile again: *Let me help you.*

"A coffin is what we need. Why else would you be here?" snipes Madame. Lucette puts a hand on the woman's arm.

"We need your services, Hepsibah." My heart skips to hear my name on her lips. "We need your help."

Yes, they do. They need a coffin-maker. They need a death-bed to keep the deceased *in*, to make sure he doesn't haunt the lives they want to live from this point on. They need my *art*.

"I would recommend an ebony-wood coffin, lined with the finest silk padding stuffed with lavender to help the soul to rest. Gold fittings will ensure strength of binding. And I would affix three golden locks on the casket, to make sure. Three is safest, strongest." Then I name a price—down to the quarter-gold to make the sum seem considered—one that would cause honest women to baulk, to shout, to accuse me of the extortion I'm committing.

Madame D'Aguillar simply says, "Lucette, take Miss Ballantyne to the study and give her the down payment."

Oh, how they must want him kept under!

I rise and make a slight curtsy before I follow Lucette's gracefully swaying skirts to the back of the house.

I politely look away as she fumbles with the lockbox in the third drawer of the enormous oak desk her father recently occupied. When she hands me the small leather pouch of gold pieces, her fingers touch my palm and I think I see a spark in her eyes. I believe she feels it, too, and I colour to be so naked before her. I slide my eyes to the portrait of her dearly departed, but she grasps my hand and holds it tight.

*Oh*!

"Please, Hepsibah, please make his coffin well. Keep him *beneath*. Keep us—keep me—safe." She presses her lips to my palm; they are damp, slightly parted, and ever-so-soft! My breath escapes me, my lungs feel bereft. She trails her slim, pink cat's tongue along my lifeline, down to my wrist where the pulse beats blue and hard and gives me away. There is a noise outside in the hall, the scuttling of a servant. Lucette smiles and steps back, dropping my hand reluctantly.

I remember to breathe, dip my head, made subservient by my desire. Hector has been silent all this time. I see him standing behind her, gnarled fingers trying desperately to caress her swan's neck, but failing, passing through her. I feel a rage shake me, but control myself. I nod again, forcing confidence into my motions, meeting her eyes, bold as brass, reading a promise there.

"I need to see the body, take my measurements, make preparations. I must do this alone."

• • •

"Stupid little harlot." Hector has more than broken his silence, again and again, since we returned to the workshop. I have not answered him because I sense in his tone *envy*.

"How hard for you, Father, to have no more strength than a fart, all noise and wind."

If he were able, he would throw anything he could find around the space, chisels and planes and whetstones, with no thought for the damage to implements expensive to replace. The tools of our trade inherited from forefathers too many to number. The pieces of wood purchased at great expense and treated with eldritch care to keep the dead *below*.

I ignore his huffing and puffing and continue with Master D'Aguillar's casket. It is now the required shape and dimensions, held together with sturdy iron nails and the stinking adhesive made of human marrow and boiled bones I'm carefully applying to the place where one plank meets another to ensure there are no gaps through which something ephemeral might escape. On the furtherest bench, far enough away to keep it safe from the stains and paints and tints, lies the pale lilac silk sack that I've stuffed with goose down and lavender flowers. This evening, I will quilt it with tiny, precise stitches then fit it into the casket, this time using a sweet smelling glue to hold it in place and cover the stink of the marrow sealant.

We may inflate the charge for our services, certainly, but the Ballantynes never offer anything but their finest work.

I make the holes for the handles and hinges, boring them with a hand-drill engraved with Hector's initials—not long before his death, the drill that had been passed down for nearly one hundred years broke, the turning handle shearing off in his hand and tearing open his palm. He had another made at great expense. It is almost new; I can pretend the initials are mine, that the shiny thing is mine alone.

"Did you get it?" asks Hector, tired of his sulk.

I nod, screwing the first hinge into place; the dull golden glow looks almost dirty in the dim light of the workshop. Soon I will light the lamps so I can work through the night; that way I will be able to see Lucette again tomorrow without appearing too eager, without having to manufacture some excuse to cross her threshold once more.

"Show me."

I straighten with ill grace and stretch. In the pocket of my skirt, next to a compact set of pliers, is a small tin, once used for Hector's cheap snuff. It rattles as I open it. Inside: a tooth, black and rotten at its centre and stinking more than it should. There is a sizeable chunk of flesh still attached to the root and underneath the scent of decay is a telltale hint of foxglove. Master D'Aguillar shall enter the earth before his time, and I have something to add to our collection of contagions that will not be recognised or questioned.

"Ah, lovely!" says Hector. "Subtle. You could have learned something from them. Cold in a teacup—it wasn't very inventive, was it? I expected a better death, y'know."

"It wasn't a cold in a teacup, Father." I hold up the new hand drill. "It was the old drill, the handle was impregnated with apple seed poison and I filed away the pinion to weaken everything. All it needed was a tiny open wound. Inventive enough for you, Hector?"

He looks put out, circles back to his new favourite torment. "That girl, she doesn't want you."

I breathe deeply. "Events say otherwise."

"Fool. Desperate sad little fool. How did I raise such an idiot child? Didn't I teach you to look through people? Anyone could see you're not good enough for the likes of Miss Lucette D'Aguillar." He laughs. "Will you dream of her, Hepsibah?"

I throw the hand drill at him; it passes through his lean outline and hits the wall with an almighty metallic sound.

"I kept you wrapped! I covered the mirrors! I made your casket myself and sealed it tight—how can you still be here?" I yell.

Hector smiles. "Perhaps I'm not. Perhaps you're so lonely, daughter, that you thought me back."

"If I were lonely I can think of better company to conjure." But there may be something in what he says, though it makes me hurt.

"Ah, there's none like your own family, your dear old Da who loves your very skin."

"When I have her," I say quietly, "I won't need *you*."

Ghost or fervid imagining, it stops him—he sees his true end— and he has no reply but spite, "Why would anyone want you?"

"You did, Father, or has death dimmed your memory?"

Shame will silence even the dead and he dissolves, leaving me alone for a while at least.

I breathe deeply to steady my hands and begin to measure for the placement of the locks.

• • •

"The casket is ready," I say, keeping the disappointment from my voice as best I can. Lucette is nowhere in evidence. An upstairs maid answered my knock and brought me to the parlour once more where the widow receives me reluctantly. The door angel did not even open its eyes.

Madame nods. "I shall send grooms with a dray this afternoon, if that will suffice." But she does not frame it as a question.

"That is acceptable. My payment?"

"Will be made on the day of the funeral—which will be tomorrow. Will you call again?" She smiles with all the charm of the rictus of the dead. "I would not wish to waste your time."

I return her smile, "My customers have no choice but to wait upon my convenience." I rise. "I will see myself out. Until tomorrow."

Outside in the mid-morning sun I make my way down the stone front steps that are set a little too far apart. This morning I combed my hair, pinched colour into my cheeks, and stained my lips with a tinted wax that had once belonged to my mother; all for nought. I am about to set foot on the neatly swept path, when a hand snakes out from the bushes to the right and I'm pulled under hanging branches, behind a screen of sickly strong jasmine.

Lucette darts her tongue between my lips, giving me a taste of her, but pulling back when I try to explore the honeyed cave of her mouth in turn. She giggles breathlessly, chest rising and falling, as if this is nothing more than an adventure. She does not quake as I do, she is a silly little girl playing at lust. I know this; I know this but it does not make me hesitate. It does not make my hope die.

I reach out and grasp her forearms, drawing her roughly in. She falls against me and I show her what a kiss is. I show her what longing is. I let my yearning burn into her, hoping that she will be branded by the tip of my tongue, the tips of my fingers, the tips of my breasts. I will have her here, under the parlour window where her mother sits and waits. I will tumble her and bury my mouth where it will make her moan and shake, here on the grass where we might be found at any moment. And I will make her mine if through no other means than shame; her shame will bind us, and make her *mine*.

"Whore," says Hector in my ear, making his first appearance since yesterday. Timed perfectly, it stops me cold and in that moment when I hesitate, Lucette remembers herself and struggles. She steps away again, breathing hard, laughing through a fractured, uncertain smile.

"When he is *beneath*," she tells me. A promise, a vow, a hint, a tease.

"When he is *beneath*," I repeat, mouthing it like a prayer, then make my unsteady way home.

• • •

I stood in the churchyard this morning, hidden away, and watched them bury Master D'Aguillar. Professional pride for the most part.

Hector stood beside me, nodding with more approval than he'd ever shown in life, a truce mutually agreed for the moment.

"Hepsibah, you've done us proud. It's beautiful work."

And it was. The ebony-wood and the gold caught the sun and shone as if surrounded by a halo of light. No one could have complained about the effect the theatrics added to the interment. I noticed the admiring glances of the family's friends, neighbours and acquaintances, as the entrance to the D'Aguillar crypt was opened and four husky men of the household carried the casket down into the darkness.

And I watched Lucette. Watched her weep and support her mother; watched them both perform their grief like mummers. When the crowds thinned and there was just the two of them and their retainers to make their way to the black coach and four plumed horses, Lucette seemed to sense herself watched. Her eyes found me standing beside a white stone cross that tilted where the earth had sunk. She gave a strange little smile and inclined her head just-so.

"Beautiful girl," said Hector, his tone rueful.

"Yes," I answered, tensing for a new battle, but nothing came. We waited in the shade until the funeral party dispersed.

"When will you go to collect?" he asked.

"This afternoon, when the wake is done."

He nodded and kept his thoughts to himself.

• • •

Lucette brings a black lacquered tray, balancing a teapot, two cups and saucers, a creamer, sugar boat and silver cutlery. There are two delicate almond biscuits perched on a ridiculously small plate. The servants have been given the afternoon off. Her mother is upstairs resting.

"The house has been so full of people," she says, placing the tray on the parquetry table between us. I want to grab at her, bury my fingers in her hair and kiss her breath away, but broken china might not be the ideal start. I hold my hands in my lap. I wonder if she notices that I filed back my nails, made them neat? That the stains on my skin are lighter than they were, after hours of scrubbing with lye soap?

She reaches into the pocket of her black dress and pulls forth a leather pouch, twin to the one she gave me barely two days ago. She holds it out and smiles. As soon as my hand touches it, she relinquishes the strings so our fingers do not meet.

"There! Our business is at an end." She turns the teapot five times clockwise with one hand and arranges the spoons on the saucers to her satisfaction.

"At an end?" I ask.

Her look is pitying, then she laughs. "I thought for a while there I might actually have to let you tumble me! Still and all, it would have been worth it, to have him safely away." She sighs. "You did such beautiful work, Hepsibah, I am grateful for that. Don't ever think I'm not."

I am not stupid enough to protest, to weep, to beg, to ask if she is joking, playing with my heart. But when she passes me a cup, my hand shakes so badly that the tea shudders over the rim. Some pools in the saucer, more splashes onto my hand and scalds me. I manage to put the mess down as she fusses, calling for a maid, then realises no one will come.

"I won't be a moment," she says and leaves to make her way to the kitchen and cleaning cloths.

I rub my shaking hands down my skirts and feel a hard lump. Buried deep in the right hand pocket is the tin. It makes a sad, promising sound as I tap on the lid before I open it. I tip the contents into her empty cup, then pour tea over it, letting the poisoned tooth steep until I hear her bustling back along the corridor. I fish it out with a spoon, careful not to touch it with my bare hands and put it away. I add a little cream to her cup.

She wipes my red hot hand with a cool wet cloth, then wraps the limb kindly. Lucette sits opposite me and I hand her the cup of tea and give a fond smile for her, and for Hector who has appeared at her shoulder.

"Thank you, Hepsibah."

"You are most welcome, Miss D'Aguillar."

I watch her lift the fine china to her pink, pink lips and drink deeply.

It will be enough, slow acting, but sufficient. This house will be bereft again.

When I am called upon to ply my trade a second time I will bring a mirror with me. In the quiet room when we two are alone, I will unwrap Lucette and run my fingers across her skin and find all the secret places she denied me and she will be mine and mine alone whether she wishes it or no.

I take my leave and wish her well.

"Repeat business," says Father gleefully as he falls into step beside me. "Not too much, not enough to draw attention to us, but enough to keep bread on the table."

In a day or two, I shall knock once more on the Widow D'Aguillar's front door.

. . . . . . . . . . .

# SOMEONE ELSE TO PLAY WITH

## PETE KEMPSHALL

So it's Thursday, yeah? Sign on in the morning, back to bed and then off down the Ferrets for some stick and some bevvies, same old.

Tone's there, so's Chink, Davey and a couple of the other lads, corner table like always. Beth's in too, wearing that slutty top she likes that shows off her tits. She swigs her Breezer, waits for me to sit down and then she's all over me, ain't she, wanting some.

"Hiya, Mickey," she says and she rubs her hand down the front of me jeans. "Come out to play, then?" She licks her lips, all sexy like, but I know what she wants and it ain't cock. Not yet, like. Nah, like I said, it's Thursday, I've been down the social. She's after me readies, not shy what she's got to do to get 'em either, slag. Most of the blokes steer clear 'cos she's got gyppo in her, but she's not as minging as most of the birds in here and she goes like a train when she's pissed. So I sticks me tongue down her throat anyways, peels her off a couple of notes and sends her off to get a round in.

Anyways, I'm up for a game, 'cos Tone's been giving it all that all week about how he can beat me, so I picks up a cue and hits the tables. And there I am, beating the shit out of him, the mouthy twat, just the black to sink, and I sees her. Well, it's Chink who sees her first, but you know what I mean, yeah?

"That bird's giving you the eye," Chink says and I looks over at the table he's looking at. And he's right.

There she is. Right posh tart, I think, minted by the looks of her and well fit. She sees me looking back at her and she looks away, like, pretends she's looking at something else, but I keep looking at her and she looks back, trying to look all shy and that, but now I know she's up for it.

"Well in there, mate," Tone says, and he nudges me, tips me the wink.

I ignore him, put the black down and takes his money off the table. "You got it or you don't," I says.

"You getting on her then?" Chink asks. "Only, I mean, Beth's—"

"Beth can fuckin" wait," I says, and I goes over to where the posh bird's sitting.

She ignores me til I'm up close and then looks up at me and fuck me, she's well hot, she is. Skinny, nice face, great tits.

"Awright, love?" I says, smiling. I'm well charming when I puts me mind to it. "You looking for someone, are you?"

"What if I am?" she says to me. Got a voice like one of them people off the telly, back before it went colour and that. But her eyes, they're fucking filthy, mate, you know what I mean? Stuck-up accent and all, but she's looking at me like "Bend me over and do me right here," in't she?

Dirty fuckin' cow.

"Well if you is, I can help with that."

"You think so, do you?"

"Know so."

She stands up and grabs her coat. Picks up her voddy, necks it and looks right at me. "Well then. What are we waiting for?"

So she walks over to the door, nose up in the air like someone's taken a shit under it, and she's outside. I goes after her right fast, and the boys by the pool table are giving it some, cheering and shouting and that, and I flip 'em off. Beth's watching too, and she's not saying nothing but she's giving me the right evils. Likes to be the best-looking bit of skirt in here, does Beth.

But like I said, fuck her, the scrounging pikey bitch. And I follows the posh bird out.

It's fucking freezing outside, and she turns and smiles at me and rubs me jeans just like Beth, and says, "I do hope we're not going to have any problem with shrinkage."

"Fuck off," I says. "Biggest you've ever had."

"I'll be the judge of that."

And she pushes me down the alley, down the side of the Ferrets and she starts pulling at me belt, all feral-like. I tell you, fucking animal this one. All the same with those stuck-up tarts, though, innit? They all wants a proper shag. None of the blokes can get it up round her way, probably.

I chuck her up against the wall and rip her top open, get her tits out. Mate, they're fucking amazing, not monsters but not those stupid tiny fucking things some birds have either, and her nips are all fucking hard in the cold. Then she's got her tongue in me mouth and she's all biting and that, and she's got me jeans down to me knees and she's pulling on me cock all hard and quick.

I'm going to lose it if she keeps that up, so I lifts up her little skirt. And you'll never guess what.

No. Fucking. Knickers.

Like I said. Dirty fuckin' cow.

And she takes my nob and sticks it up inside her and she's fucking soaked, man; it's up there easy as you like. Then she's got her hands on me arse, pulling me into her, and digging her nails in and fuck me, it hurts, but I'm fucking loving it.

"You like that, darlin'?" I says and she bites me on the lip and digs her nails in more.

"Shut up and fuck me, you ignorant little shit."

I tell you what, though, you hear stuff like that coming out of the mouth of a classy bit of arse like that . . . fucking came buckets I did, fucking filled her right up. And she pushes up and down on me until she's got every last fucking drop out, and then gets off and sorts her skirt and top out and picks up her handbag and walks off down the alley, just like that.

And you know what she says on the way?

"You were right. It is big."

"Too fuckin right, love!" I call after her, and I watch her go off round the corner while I'm fixing up me jeans. Then I turn to go back down to the pub and I sees her: Beth, mate, just standing there watching me.

"Get a good look, did you?" I says and pushes past her. She don't say nothing, and I fancy a laugh, so I says, "Bet you wish you was that good."

And I'm off back indoors for another game, 'cause Chink needs his money taking off him just as much as Tone does, the mug.

• • •

Monster headache the next day, man. Feels like drum and bass night down the Palace in there, know what I mean? Me arse is covered in scratches too, hurts like fuck. Feel completely fucking minging, so I stays in bed and sleep it off.

Last thing I'm expecting is for Beth to show up on me doorstep. Knock at the door, open it up and bosh, there she is. Fuck me, I thinks, the mad diddy cow's gonna go mental on me, but she don't say anything, just pushes me onto the floor and gets on top of me. Fuck, man, door's wide open and she's dry humping me on the carpet.

I kick the door shut and before I knows it she's got me pants off and is riding me like it's a fucking rodeo or something. But shit, I'm not going to complain, am I?

When she's done, she stands up, pulls her skirt down and I stand up too, grinning like a bastard. Me headache's gone.

She looks at me, and I see she's still pissed off. "Thought I'd remind you what's what," she says. "I ain't going to make a big deal out of last night, 'cos I know it were a one-off. But I catch you again with another woman, I'll cut off her tits. Then your bollocks. You get me?"

I laugh, but she's well serious.

"Fuck knows why she wanted you, anyway. Seen yourself lately?"

"Fuck you on about?"

And she pats her fucking belly and says, "Too many bevvies, Mickey. Get some exercise."

"'K off."

"You just remember, that's all. You ain't nothing to a bitch like that. She'll be back off to her husband and that now. Got her bit of rough and she's off out of it."

Beth walks up to the door and opens it. "Fuck you and dump you. Laters."

I wait til she's gone and I laughs, big and loud. 'Cause she's wrong, in't she? See, what she don't know is I got more than me rocks off with that bird last night.

I got her purse an' all.

The rich bitch only left her bag right next to me. Turns her back on me when she was getting her clothes sorted after we shagged, and I lifts it, just like that. Spent most of the cash, of course—had a couple of hundred in there, easy—no time to hammer the cards. Thing is, I ain't got round to dumping the purse yet, so I get it out from under the bed and has a little look at what else is in there. Couple of pictures of her some with chinless twat—must be the husband—and yeah, there it is.

Driver's licence.

• • •

She lives in Hampstead, but after Beth goes I start feeling rough again, head's banging, so I leave it and go back to bed. Next day I'm off out there, though, first thing.

I find the place easy enough: big, with one of them driveways that goes up from the main road. I sneak up it and have a look. One car outside, vee-dub, so probably hers. I watch for a bit, see if everything's quiet, then I walk up and knock on the door.

She opens up and I'm expecting her to look all surprised. Thing is, she don't.

"Thought you might drop by," she says, and stands back so I can come in. "Thought it'd be yesterday, though."

I front her up. "Been busy, ain't I?"

She closes the door and walks into one of the rooms off the side. I follow her in and she's already sat on a big couch. Leather one, well flash. "Please," she says, "have a seat."

I keep standing though, looking around the place. Books all over, and pictures too, like that one of her and that bloke in her purse. Wedding photos and that. I smile 'cos I was right.

"No husband today," I say.

"No."

"Lucky. Reckon he'd be fucking well pissed if he found out what you've been up to."

She don't say anything, just looks at me.

"So here's the thing," I say, no point fucking about. "You pay me, say, a monkey, every week and I keep quiet."

"You want a monkey?" she says.

Fuck me. Posh birds, thick as shit. "Five notes."

"Five hundred pounds a week?"

"You can afford it," I says, looking round the place. "And something else, too."

"What would that be?" she says.

"More of what I got down that alley. Any time I fancy it."

She only fucking laughs, don't she? "That's your deal? I give you money and sex whenever you want, or you tell my husband?"

"Yeah. First payment right now."

"How about this?" she says. "I fuck you whenever *I* want. And I pay you to do it."

"You what?"

"My husband . . . isn't around much. I have needs. I'm saying you get exactly what you want. And so do I."

Fucking hell, I think. It's like Christmas.

She stands up and undoes her top, shows me those great tits in a tiny little bra. "So," she says, "first payment . . . "

• • •

I don't see the lads down the Ferrets for a couple of weeks. For starters I'm too fucking tired to go out. Miranda—that's her name—keeps me going so hard I'm walking funny all the time. Sometimes it's four or five times a day, man! Some days I think me nob's gonna drop off. But she's a top shag, knows what's what. No holes barred, you know? And I tell you what else, all that exercise . . . Looked in the mirror this morning and I look the fucking business. My gut's just about gone. Course, it weren't that big to start with, whatever Beth says. But it's getting well flat now. Ripped and that.

After all that shagging, you know, I just ain't got the energy to shoot frames all night down the boozer. Plus all that cash, got meself a new plasma, didn't I? No point going out with that on your wall, is there? I'm spending all day watching DVDs or on the PS3. I'm the FIFA master now, me. Un-fucking-beatable.

Course, I don't fancy running into Beth neither. She's been leaving all sorts of messages on me mobile—where are you, you OK, I miss you, what you up to you little bastard, on and on and fucking on. She's even got Tone and Chink in on it; they're calling me up asking the same stuff. Don't answer the phone to any of 'em now, just in case it's her, giving me arse ache.

Anyway, one night I give in and get meself off down the Ferrets, just to check in like, and Chink and Tone are there, playing some stick.

"You just missed Beth, mate," Tone says. "She's well shitty wiv you, in't she?"

"Yeah," says Chink. "You wanna be a bit careful there. Might get her brothers onto you."

"Or use some o' that gyppo stuff on you!" Tone laughs, and wiggles his fingers, all mystic and that.

"Bollocks," I say. "Her brothers are up north, ain't seen 'em for months. And the only magic she does it that thing with her tongue on—"

"Woah, mate!" Chink says.

"Yeah," says Tone. "We's just saying, you know? Watch yer back."

I snort, and start racking up the balls.

• • •

Get home, bit pissed like, and I'm in bed when that pikey bitch only starts banging on the door don't she, shouting how she knows I'm in here, how she can see me through the letterbox, which is bollocks 'cos I'm in bed, aren't I?

"I'm on to you, Mickey, you little shit!" she shouts. "I know what you're up to!"

I stay quiet, keep me head down, 'cos I'm too fucked up to go out there and slap her about. She fucks off eventually, thank fuck.

• • •

Next day there's dog shit posted through me door and COCKSUCKER sprayed all over the wall outside. Next time I see her, we're going to have words. Hard ones.

• • •

So Miranda comes over here to the flat one night the next week. Says her parents are in town and hanging around her place, so we can't meet there. First time she's been round, right? She takes a walk around, checking out my DVDs and that while I'm getting me kit off.

"Ever thought of reading a book?" she says.

"What for?"

"To broaden your mind?"

"Broad enough already, love." And I give her a wink. "'Sides, don't need no books. I got me films and me games."

"Games?"

"Yeah, you know. Playstation and that. Your old man not into that, then?"

"No." She laughs, and it's so fucking sexy I want to do her right there on the carpet. "No, he's not very good at games. Not

— 119 —

very . . . coordinated." She comes up to me and starts to rub me off. "Lucky I've got someone else to play with."

"Fuck yeah."

• • •

But she don't let it slide. Next time she comes round, she gives me this little blue plastic bag with a book in it.

"Give that a try," she says.

I open the bag and have a look. Looks like a load of old shit to me. Orange, with an old picture of some stupid twat on it.

"*Rim board*," I says. "Sounds well kinky."

Miranda rolls her eyes at me, all put out and that, but she don't get to say anything 'cause next thing I'm carting her off to the bedroom and she's got her mouth full.

Receipt's in the bag. Maybe I can get the money back.

• • •

After, when she's getting dressed, she's looking out the window and she says, "You know someone's watching the flat?"

I push her out the way and have a look.

It's Beth. She's been out of the picture for a week or two, but now here she is, out over the other side of the block, and she's looking right up at the place, right up at the window.

And I just lose it.

"Fucking bitch," I says, and I'm off out the door, just in me boxers. I get to the bottom of the stairs, and Beth sees me, sees how fucking shitty I am, but she doesn't run off or nothing, just waits for me.

"Fuck you doing, bitch?" I shout.

"She's in there, ain't she? Your fucking posh slag."

"What if she is?"

Beth comes right up to me, spits in my face.

I punch her, hard, and she falls on her arse.

"You're fucking dead, Mickey!" she screams. Her eye's swelling up. "You're both fucking dead!"

I step towards her and she looks into my eyes and she shrinks back, and I love that. I love that she's scared. "You think? I tell you what, Beth. You come near me or Miranda again, I'll kick the fucking shit out of you." And *I* spit on *her*. "Wouldn't be much left if I did, would there?"

She lies there, don't say nothing, and I'm back off home, people looking out of their windows at me in my boxers, but that's all right 'cause no one's going to talk, not round here.

"Sides, I look fucking good, don't I?

• • •

I'm right. No one talks about it. But it ain't an end to it. This time it ain't dog shit—she's only gone and put blood all over me door, ain't she? Smeared it all over the fucking thing, handle an' all. Tell you, if I catch her here again, I'm gonna have her.

Miranda's freaked out by it and all. She won't come back to the flat now, only wants to see me at her place. 'S all right by me—turns me on, fucking her in her house. I like it that her old man might walk in on us, all unexpected like, see me giving her one over the dining table.

Problem is, all this shit with Beth's fucking with my head. I'm amped for days after, on edge, can't get my shit together or nothing. Soon as I'm in the flat on me own again, she's back. I never see her, but she's out there all the fucking time. Like, soon as I clean the door she's sticking more blood on it. I try catching her at it, but I'm asleep or she does it when I'm at Miranda's. It's doing my head in. I get on the PlayStation, yeah, England v Germany, and by half time, I'm getting done. Four fucking nil. Those kraut bastards wouldn't stand a chance any day of the week, but it's like my fingers don't work no more or something. I've got no game. Same with the telly. Can't concentrate on nothing. I get so fucking desperate I even look at that book Miranda bought me.

Poetry.

Fuck. Off.

• • •

And then it all goes quiet. No more stupid shit on the door, no more shouting through the letterbox, nothing. It's like Beth's just gone. Vanished. Good fucking job, I say.

Miranda and I keep on keeping on, all happy, for a couple of weeks. Then I get the phone call.

"She's following me! I saw her!"

"Settle down. She hasn't got the balls."

"What if she knows where I live now?" Miranda's voice shrieks down the line. "You heard what she said. She's going to kill me!"

"She's not going to kill no one," I snap. "Look, I can see if anyone's seen her about. Find out where she is, have a word. All right?"

Miranda sighs. "All right. Then come round here this afternoon. I've got a surprise for you."

"Yeah?"

"Yes. Oh, what did you think of Rambo?"

I think for a second, no idea what she's on about. "The first two were all right, but they got a bit shit after that."

Another sigh, different from the first one. "See you around three?"

"Yeah."

.  .  .

Three o'clock means I've got a couple of hours to sniff around, so I go down the Ferrets and hang out with Tone and Chink. I've not been around for a bit but they don't have the arse with me 'cause they know I've been busy.

Like Chink says, "If I was getting that top-drawer pussy you wouldn't see me around much neither."

I rack up some balls, figure we can have a few games while we talk. "Tell me about it. It's a wonder I can walk most days."

"Oooh," Tone says. "*'It's a wonder I can walk.'* La-de-fuckin-dah."

"Fuck off," I say and break the balls around the table. None go down.

"Serious, though, man, you're sounding all posh and that," Chink says. "Startin' to forget where you're from. Do you good to spend a bit of time with us scum, yeah?"

"Seen much of Beth?" I ask.

"Nah, man," Chink says as Tone sinks two then three balls. He's taking me to the cleaners. "Heard some stuff though."

"Yeah?" I take my shot, foul it. It's like I've forgotten how to hold a cue or something.

Tone swigs from his pint, lines up his next shot. "Heard she went up north for a bit."

Fuck, I think. If Beth's gone up north it can only mean she's gone looking for her brothers. Jack and Jim Harris are fucking psychopaths, you don't mess with them. I try to play it cool. "That right?"

Tone pots the last of his balls and zeroes in on the black. "Yup."

Jack and Jim have got some right pull up in Manchester now, drugs and that. They bung Beth a few hundred every now and again, if they've got someone down this way to drop it off to her. Wouldn't be any aggro for them to send a couple of the boys around to sort out a problem for their little sister then, would it? Fuck, they'd probably come themselves.

The black goes down and Tone takes my money. "I heard she's been to see her mum, too."

"Yeah?" I say, surprised. Nancy Harris is barking bloody mad. Typical gyppo, lives in a caravan, loads of cats. Word is she used some of that diddy mumbo jumbo to set the boys up in the Manc market.

"How come I'm just finding out about this now?"

"Piss off, Mickey. Ain't seen you in weeks."

"My phone works, doesn't it?"

"You don't fucking answer it, though."

He's right. I've kept it switched off since Beth started getting them to call me.

"'Nother game?" Tone says, dropping the black triangle on the table and loading up the balls.

"No, mate," I say, pulling my coat on. "Got to be somewhere."

• • •

"What's all this, then?"

Miranda's pacing the room, smoking non-stop. Nervous. "Clothes. Obviously."

I'd been hoping my surprise would be something more shag-related, not bloody polo shirts and chinos. I look at the labels though—expensive. Good gear. "What you buying me clothes for?"

She wanders across the living room and pours a large gin. "One, because I can afford it and two, because I can't stand the way you dress like you're . . . "

"Like I'm what?"

"Black."

"Piss off," I say. "I'm not wearing them."

She sniffs, turns her back on me. She mutters something. "I have waited so long that at length I forget."

"What?"

"It's nothing," she says.

She's crying.

I don't know what comes over me, but I walk up to her, take her in my arms and kiss her. "All right. I'll wear them. But only for you."

She smiles at me, eyes red and watery. "Thank you, Mickey."

• • •

I'm out of there by six, and she's calmer when I go than when I got there. Happy even. I'd like to think it was the sex, but it's probably the clothes. I'm ten steps down the drive before I realise I'm wearing them. It's like I put them on asleep or something. I start to go back, but I know she'll start crying again and then she'll be worrying about Beth and I'll be back to square one. So I keep walking, thinking I'll change once I get home. With a bit of luck no one I know will see me walking around looking like a ponce.

But then I think about what it would be like to do this all the time. To wear these clothes, to live in that house. To replace her husband for real, not just in the bedroom.

Suddenly I'm all smiles.

• • •

They're waiting for me round the estate, hanging about outside the door to the flats, keeping to the shadows, all suits and muscles.

The Harrises have sent the boys down.

Fuck knows what Beth told her brothers, but I don't need x-ray vision to know those lads out there waiting are tooled up, and I don't need to be Nostradamus to know what'll happen if they see me.

Then one of them does.

Christ, he's big and he's looking straight at me across the estate, staring right into my eyes. My arms and legs tingle, flooded with adrenalin, ready to run.

Then his eyes are off me and he's back to looking up and down the waste ground opposite the block.

Somehow I haven't pissed myself.

How the fuck did he not see me, I think. He looked right at me, for fuck's sake. Then I get it.

The clothes. Looking like a total twat's just saved my life.

I turn and walk slowly back down the street, pop out my mobile and call Chink. I'm going to need some help.

• • •

"The fuck, man?" Chink laughs. "You look well gay!"

"That what she's got you wearing now?" Tone chips in. He flicks his wrist, makes a cracking noise with his tongue. "You is whipped!"

"Shut up," I say. I'm tired. And I'm scared. "The Harrises've got men all over the estate."

"I heard, man," Chink says. "Word is they wants you brought in quick. Not too fussed how it's done neither."

"What about Miranda?" I ask, surprising myself.

"Who?"

"The bird he's shagging," Tone chips in.

"Nah, man, far as I know they're just looking for you. But they've got a right hard-on for you, mate. Dunno what Beth told 'em, but you're marked."

"Christ," I whisper.

"I'd get back up to Hampstead if I was you," Tone suggests. "You know, until stuff cools down."

He's right. If I'm lucky, they won't look for me there.

"Christ."

• • •

By the time I get to Miranda's house it's past ten. I've called ahead and Miranda's given me the all-clear—her husband won't be there—so I sidle up to the front door and let myself in.

It's dark and quiet inside, but there's a light on in the study so I head there.

And find Miranda in an armchair, eyes on the big gun Beth's pointing at her.

Something flares inside me, an unstoppable urge to get in there, to save Miranda whatever the cost.

"No, Mickey," Beth says, seeing me tense to jump at her. "Don't."

"Not brought any of your brothers' monkeys with you?"

She shakes her head, lifts her free hand up to her neck. There's a pendant around it I haven't seen before. "No need. Her shit ain't gonna work on me."

"Put the gun down, Beth. You don't need to hurt her."

But Beth's got tears in her eyes, is barely holding them back. "Can't you see what she's doing to you, Mickey? She's changing you."

"She's improving me," I say, and in doing so I realise how different I sound, how I've grown since that night in the alley, and I know exactly what I want. What I really want. "I'm done with it. The estate, the boys. You." I glance at Miranda with eyes that say—I hope—everything's going to be all right. Miranda looks back, and she doesn't look scared at all.

I love her for that.

"No, she's changing you," Beth repeats.

She bends at the knees, and keeping the gun on Miranda with one hand reaches into her handbag with the other. She feels around and, keeping watch on Miranda, not on what she's doing, pulls something from the bag and tosses it to me. "Look at yourself."

I catch it. It's a compact, the kind with make-up on one side, a mirror on the other.

"Look at yourself."

I open the mirror and stare into it. My hair's a bit different from normal, neater, but that'll be because I had a shower before I left Miranda's this afternoon. It's a bit longer, true, but it looks okay. And there are the clothes, obviously.

Then, as I run my big blue eyes over the reflection, I see it. My eyes.

They were brown this morning.

Beth sees the look on my face, sags with relief. "She's changing you."

I look at Miranda and she regards me, cool, confident. "What've you done?" I ask. Miranda just keeps watching me, says nothing.

"I could see it in your eyes, that night you punched me," Beth says.

"See what?"

"The spell, working inside you. Live with my mum long enough, you can spot that kinda stuff." She gestures at Miranda. "She's been fucking you to control you."

"All women do that."

"She scratched you, yeah?" Beth looks at me, earnest. "First time she fucked you."

I remember the deep grooves in my arse. Beth sees the look on my face.

"The blood I put on your door, that was to protect you, babe. To stop her. It's why I've got them all waiting for you on the estate. If we can get you to my mum, she can fix it."

"I don't—"

"The pictures," Beth says. "Look at the pictures."

I stumble across the room, head spinning, and stare at the shots in the frames.

Miranda, stunning in her white satin wedding dress. Her husband, clean-cut, expensive suit.

Miranda in a bikini on a beach somewhere, him in small trunks, muscular.

Miranda at a party, green floral dress. Him in chinos and a polo shirt, blue eyes twinkling with laughter.

"He's dead, Mickey," Beth says. "Car crash, two years ago. I looked it up."

I turn to Miranda. It feels like the ground's slipping under me. "What—?"

"I saw you at the pub. About the same height, same build," Miranda says, emotionless. "Lose a few pounds, tidy you up . . . "

"She had him under her nails when she scratched you," Beth says. "His ashes. She's been fucking you to keep up the connection. She's wiping your mind, replacing it with—"

"Geoff," I say.

No one's ever told me his name before.

Miranda sits up straighter in her chair. "Once, if my memory serves me well, my life was a banquet," she recites.

Out of nowhere, I hear myself say, "Where every heart revealed itself, where every wine flowed."

Beth looks at me, wide-eyed, tears welling. "The fuck was that?"

"Rimbaud," Miranda says. There's laughter in her voice, music, joy. Triumph. "Geoff studied him at Oxford. Knew all his poems backwards."

The book, I realise, back at the flat. I only looked at it for a second.

Miranda turns to me, heedless now of Beth. "Geoff?"

"Yes."

"Gun."

Beth reacts too slowly. She's not expecting me to come at her, so I'm able to step up and take the gun from her hand before she knows what's going on. Before *I* know what's going on. I tell my arms, my legs to stop moving, but something bigger, more powerful, more . . . erudite crowds the thoughts out of my head, robbing me of control.

Miranda smiles, cold, shark-like. "Kill her."

I point the gun at Beth, but I can't . . . I can't do it. I can't take a life like that.

No. I could. Have done a couple of times.

But *he* can't.

Miranda tuts and holds out her hand. I place the gun in it.

Beth turns and runs, but the bullet takes her in the upper back and she goes down like a sack of spuds. She writhes on the carpet, making little bubbling noises.

Deep inside me, something breaks.

Then Miranda's there, hands light on my chest. "Geoff," she says with absolute certainty. "I wasn't sure I'd ever . . . "

My finger goes to her lips, hushes her, and my mouth moves. "Love has to be reinvented."

Beth gurgles and I look down at her, at the naked terror bulging in her eyes. Blood foams pink from her lips: punctured lung, she's not got long. The hole in my chest yawns wider, the death of this woman has torn something from me, something infinitely precious and irreplaceable.

"Who was she?" I ask.

Miranda's lips, her breath, feather-touch my ear. "Does it matter?"

And as she kisses me I know, without the merest shadow of a doubt, that it doesn't.

· · · · · · · · · · ·

# THE HALL OF LOST FOOTSTEPS

## SARA DOUGLASS & ANGELA SLATTER

The entire valley was blanketed in an oppressive heat. Meadows and vineyards clinging to the steep slopes of the mountain shimmered under the relentless sun. The stubbled fields on the floor of the valley were barren of movement save for the humming, hovering clouds of insects over dried cattle and sheep dung. Only a few folk shuffled about in the village, and those only to seek shelter in the shade of a tree, or a doorway.

And when they did stir, they glanced over their shoulders, as if expecting the shadows of hell to chase them down.

A child cried briefly, inconsolably, in the still afternoon, and was hushed by the worried voice of its mother.

The sole thing that dared to move was the silvery stream that danced through the heart of the valley.

That . . . and *her*. The woman they all loathed, but needed. Isolde, the single, solitary individual who would be able to deflect the coming terror. Isolde. The witch.

• • •

Isolde scratched about in the herb garden with a trowel, then sat back on her heels, forearm wiping the perspiration from her forehead. Her back ached, and her temples throbbed. She knew she should be inside in the dim, cool shade, but Isolde could not bear the silence of the waiting shadows. Not today. She had known upon waking this morning that today would bring the summons . . . but to allow that knowledge to alter her routine would be to allow it to defeat her. So she had done her best to treat this day as any other. She had risen, breakfasted on the remains of yesterday's bread, and tidied her single room cottage, folding away the bed linens from the small sleeping couch. Then Isolde had tended to the chores—washing out her aprons, feeding the chickens and geese, damping down the fire until she needed to revive it for the evening's baking.

But this evening—would she still be here?

Isolde rose, grimacing and rubbed at the small of her back and then, involuntarily, glanced up to the head of the valley to where the ancient castle rose grim and hard from the mountain.

*He* lived there, her lord, the lord of the entire valley. The Count of Montplessier. The man who granted the villagers the use of the fields, their homes, the meadows and woodlands. The man who provided the ale and food for the post-harvest feasts, and ensured a living for the priest who nurtured the villagers' souls. In return, each of the households provided the count with a service. More than half provided men and boys to work the fields, to cut and gather the wood to heat his hall. Others, the women to bake his bread, and yet others, the girls to launder his linens.

For her cottage and acre of land, Isolde had just a very small obligation, and that only once a year. Yet she feared, eventually, that one day would cost her life.

She tore her eyes away from the castle and looked at the rows of herbs and the arbours of flowers. This garden was her only friend. It gave her many hours of pleasure and much of her food.

It also supplied a small income. Once or twice a week one of the villagers would visit—their approach always stealthy, their stay always brief—and Isolde would give them the infusions and ointments they needed for their work-worn hands and blistered feet, and the torn and strained muscles of their weary bodies. They never thanked her, but Isolde would usually wake two or three mornings later to find a dressed rabbit on her doorstep, or a basket of fruit, and sometimes even a side of bacon, if the ache had been bad enough.

Isolde shook her head. Loneliness, a constant companion, threatened to overwhelm her. She'd been loved once, but that love was long dead. Her husband—*God, she couldn't remember his features!*—had been taken by a fever, some sickness that had swept down from the mountains and carried away several of the villagers. They'd had no children, although . . . Isolde frowned, trying to remember . . . she had been pregnant once. *Hadn't she?*

She had lost it, perhaps? Those difficult first months without him . . . yes, that was it . . . the shock . . .

Ah! When each year blended seamlessly into the other, it was no wonder events and faces were lost so easily to the vagaries of memory.

Isolde turned and walked towards the small lean-to that held her gardening forks and hoes, meaning to put away the trowel, when she stopped. Her heart thumped, her eyes widened and she was suddenly terrified.

She whipped about, looking towards the track leading away from her cottage. It twisted and turned, winding between low, spreading olive trees, but Isolde could see the dust rising a half mile away, and she could hear the pounding of the hoofbeats.

And she could see, in her mind's eye, the grim determined faces of the men who rode onward—their rigid shoulders, the thin lines of their mouths, the white knuckles of the hands that clutched the reins.

The hate in their eyes. The bitter satisfaction.

Isolde closed her own eyes and moaned softly, the trowel dropping unheeded into the dry dirt. She sank slowly to her haunches, wrapping her arms about her knees, eyes now open and riveted on the small section of the track where she knew they would appear.

Another minute, no more, and they would be upon her.

• • •

They galloped straight into her garden, heedless of their mounts' trampling iron shoes.

The Count of Montplessier reined his horse to a rearing halt, so close to Isolde that dirt from its plunging hooves sprayed over her.

"I need you," he said.

She slowly rose, wiping her hands down the skirt of her dress. She stared at the count, seeing his loathing, and knowing that it grew from his need. It made him a beggar before her.

She didn't answer immediately, and he grew impatient. He was used to achieving his ends with a single word spoken, a man who expected—and got—the deference of everyone in the valley, a man who rested easy in the knowledge that homage was his by right.

But he also knew that none of that mattered when it came to this woman.

"*I need you,*" he said again.

Isolde glanced behind him. He had an escort of six men, but no spare horses.

He needed her, but she would have to walk.

She looked back at him, noting the deep lines under his eyes and running from nose to mouth. Sadness and sleeplessness had made him old before his time.

"Have they sounded?" she asked.

"Aye," he said. "This past week. You know that."

She sighed, and dropped her eyes from his face. "I had hoped—"

"I hope every year," he said, voice harsh, "but every year they return."

"You should have called me sooner."

But he had not, and Isolde knew why. He would have tried without her, tried to reason with the lost creature that trampled through his castle, and every night that he delayed the weeping would have grown stronger and the footsteps louder. Every year he tried and every year he failed . . . this year was no exception.

"It wants you," he said.

She sighed once more. "I will come," she said, and the count nodded, and swung his horse's head back down the track.

• • •

When they got to the castle it was mid-afternoon, and so hot that Isolde felt as if she might faint. She'd walked, as she'd known she must, the entire way at the head of the horsemen hearing every muffled hoofbeat behind her, feeling the constant stare of every man on her back.

*Isolde the witch, off to practice her sorcery.*

Sorcery? Isolde leaned against the rising wall of the outer keep, fighting tears. "You have no time for rest," yelled the count from behind her. "Walk on."

Isolde bit back a retort, almost hating him. *No wonder that lost thing could not rest!*

She revived a little when she walked under the archway into the castle courtyard, deep in cool shadow.

It was also crowded.

Isolde stopped, looking about. The entire population of the castle—the cooks, grooms, soldiers, guards, boys, maids, valets, pages, housemen—were waiting.

Waiting for her . . . waiting for her to make it safe to go back inside.

The count halted his horse beside Isolde, and swung down. He put his hand on her elbow, and she was surprised by the gentleness of his touch.

"I'm thirsty," she murmured.

"Of course." The count gestured, and a servant approached with a pitcher and cup. Isolde thanked the man softly then drank, as grateful for the liquid as she was for the delay it bought her.

He departed, not acknowledging her thanks.

The count's fingers tightened on her again, tenderness flown. Isolde took a deep breath, then walked forward. The count's hand drop away as she did so.

He would come no further.

• • •

High on its perch on the mountain crag, the castle was dominating, but not overly large. There was the great hall, built many generations earlier by one of the count's ancestors, the service rooms—kitchen, pantries, buttery, laundries, storerooms and the servants' quarters—that filled the floor beneath the hall and a service wing that extended between the hall and the stable complex. The count's private apartments filled a small wing that ran off the back of the very hall.

And it was the hall itself that was the problem.

Or, rather, where the problem resided.

Isolde entered slowly, hearing the arched doors close softly behind her. She was beyond fear now, and settled into resignation. Here she was again . . . and here *it* was again, waiting for her, as it did every year.

She stopped, looking about her. The stone hall extended east-west for almost one hundred paces. Its vaulted ceiling reached sixty paces high—Isolde could only imagine the number of stonemasons who had lost their lives trying to put that in—and a row of clear-paned windows, each ten paces high and arched to mirror the shape of the doors, ran down the northern wall, a little below waist height.

As she ever did, Isolde walked over and stared out the closest window. The view was spectacular—the entire valley spread out before her—but Isolde was not drawn by the view. Instead, she was drawn by the tragedy that still lingered . . . here, by the fourth window along.

Here the count's wife had rested on the narrow windowsill. Here the count's wife had leaned, made breathless by the beauty of the scenery.

Here she had fallen to her death, leaning too far and toppling out an insecurely fastened window into the void below.

Villagers whispered, said her body was still down there, somewhere deep within a fissure in the mountain rock.

As lost to human aid as if she lay in the depths of the ocean.

There was a breath of movement behind Isolde, the faint scraping of a footstep.

She froze, still at the window, back stiff, eyes staring sightlessly into the space beyond the glass.

Again, the faint shuffle of a footfall.

Isolde abruptly moved, scrambled away from the window, sure that if she stayed, she too would be pitched to her death.

*She could feel it now, the icy wind of her passing as she plunged into the mountain chasm!*

Isolde drew in a deep breath, bringing her fear under control. These were memories only, and not hers. The memories of that tragic woman . . . and the child she carried.

The child who now haunted this place.

Isolde walked slowly into the centre of the hall. Every year in late summer the child's footsteps echoed along the timber flooring. Always starting softly, late one night perhaps, a brief scattering of faint footfalls. But as the days went by, and the valley slid deeper into the grip of the unnatural heat the child's presence brought with it, the footsteps grew bolder, angrier, more *demanding*.

And every year, the count waited, between a week to ten days before he capitulated and finally sent for Isolde.

Isolde frowned, trying to remember the first year of the sending. His wife had fallen to her death ten years ago, and so Isolde had been coming here for nine years.

Why her? Why had he asked for her? How had the child communicated its need for her?

Isolde frowned, shaking her head. Why couldn't she remember? Why did everything seem so confused?

*Why couldn't she remember her husband's face? Or the features of the count's wife, for that matter?*

Isolde had lived all her life in this valley, hadn't she? Surely she had seen the woman on countless occasions . . . hadn't she?

*Why couldn't she remember?* Her name . . . her name was . . .

"I'm getting old," she murmured, angry with her failing memory, with this sudden tormenting obsession.

Every year she walked into this hall, every year she walked over to the window and stared out . . . and every year she tried to remember . . . *something.*

Then Isolde jumped, her heart racing. Footsteps echoed, the footsteps of a small child, racing up and down the chamber's length. Playing, she would say if she didn't know better. She twisted around, but saw nothing, as every year she saw nothing.

"There, there," Isolde whispered, slowly turning as she looked about the room. "Don't fret, don't fret . . . "

The padding slowed, and Isolde's heart thudded the harder as she heard them approach her.

Sometimes they did this, slowly circling her, stalking her, with such a heavy malevolence that Isolde knew, *knew* that one day it would not be comforted into submission.

The footsteps stopped, and Isolde could sense the child standing some few paces away.

She swallowed. "Don't fret," she whispered, and cried out, terrified, as she felt the presence hurtle towards her.

She fell to the floor. "No!"

Nothing, save the heaving of her own breath. She raised herself slowly. "What do you want?" she whispered. "What?"

Nothing.

Then the faint patter of footsteps, running away from her now.

Towards the window.

The catch screeched, then lifted, and very slowly, painfully slowly, the window swung out into the void.

A coldness consumed Isolde. "No!"

The footsteps started back towards her. Heavy, purposeful.

What did it want? For her to jump out? Why? Vengeance? Anger that its mother's carelessness had killed it, and so it would now take someone else's life?

Is that all it had wanted all these years?

Isolde, still sitting on the floor, began to inch towards the back wall, as far from the window as she could get. "No," she said, as firmly as she could. "No."

The footsteps grew more menacing. They were very close to her now, and even though Isolde could not *see* the child, she could sense it almost as if it were a weight, a thickening in the air, slowly approaching.

The window shifted in an errant breeze, banging gently against its frame before swinging out again.

The footsteps, very deliberately, came yet closer.

"I have done you no wrong," Isolde said. "What good can come of my death?"

The footsteps paused briefly, then began their slow, purposeful treading again.

Isolde scrambled yet further away, faster now, her eyes darting to the closed door. What had she done last year? What?

*Was she to be the sacrifice? Is this what the village had decided?*

Isolde whimpered, then managed to get to her feet. Again she looked at the door. A tune echoed in her mind. A lullaby.

Something tugged at her skirt.

Isolde cried out, backing away a few paces, pulling her skirt free of ghostly hands.

"Leave me be, child," she said as calmly as she could. "Be at peace." She began to hum, trying to keep her voice rich and warm, but her fear was so strong that the sound was jerky, and the tune disjointed.

*Go away!* She thought. *Just go away!*

The child grabbed at her skirt again, and this time it did not let go.

Isolde stopped humming. She took her skirt in both hands and tugged, but she could not dislodge the child's grip.

Her eyes flew to the window.

It now stood wide open.

Isolde sobbed, once, deep, then cried out, "No! No! No!"

The eldritch grip tightened, and with deadly strength it dragged her towards the window. She fell.

Isolde screamed for the count, screamed for aid, but none came. Her entire existence seemed as if it were wrapped in an icy nothingness, as if she had been pulled across the boundary between her world and the cold child's.

The footsteps echoed louder, and with each step the child's strength grew, so that within moments Isolde found herself being dragged towards to the window with such speed that at every heavy footfall her head and shoulders thudded painfully against the floor. She twisted about, trying to snag her fingers at something—at *anything*—but it was no use. It seemed as if ten strong men had her, hauling her towards the gaping window . . .

Isolde screamed, twisting and rolling, and then she slammed into the wall below the window with such force that for a few, painful moments she could not draw air at all.

The child's grip had vanished. The hall was silent.

Isolde managed to get her breath, then she slowly rose to her knees. Her entire body was shaking.

A breeze from the window ruffled her hair, and she cringed, crying out involuntarily.

Yet again she glanced at the door.

A footfall sounded directly before her, as if blocking any hope of escape . . . and then she felt a hand, a small, plump hand, grasp at her wrist. Its touch was warm, its flesh very slightly moist.

It tugged gently, urging her to rise.

She resisted, but the child did not let go, nor did it increase the strength of its grip. It tugged again, almost kindly.

Then, stunningly, Isolde thought she heard the sound of soft weeping.

Very slowly, her eyes wide and staring, Isolde raised her free hand to the window sill and lifted herself to her feet.

She glanced to her left where gaped the window, and swayed in horror at the sight of the plunging void beyond.

The child tugged at her other wrist, pulling her centre of balance away from danger.

Isolde stared down at the wrist held in the child's invisible grip, almost unable to believe what it had done. A simple movement, a flick, and, as unbalanced as she was, it could have toppled her out of the window.

"What do you want?" she whispered.

There was no reply, save a very slight increase of pressure about her wrist.

Isolde leaned against the windowsill, not daring to look outside. She was trembling so badly she thought that she would probably fall anyway.

The child's grip suddenly tightened again . . . and Isolde felt the child pull itself into her lap. There it sat, small and invisible, trembling as if it were afraid. Still shaking, Isolde slid her free arm about the child, and felt it snuggle into her.

It whimpered, a child trying to wake from a nightmare.

Isolde, incredulous, tightened her hold the thing she could not see, cradling it close, then reached out with one hand, grasped the lower edge of the window, and swung it closed.

The latch clicked.

"*Isolde!*"

She blinked, surprised by the fear in the voice, and looked up.

The hall was different, clothed in a cooler light, and trestle tables and chairs stood about, as if a meal had just been concluded. A man was striding towards her . . . it was the count, but a younger and merrier man than she knew.

Isolde sprang to her feet, almost losing her balance at the strange heaviness of her body, and wondering if, somehow, she had fallen alseep by the window. Excuses sprang to her lips, but the count gave her no time to mouth them. He leaned down, and took her shoulders in his hands. Then, stunningly, he kissed her.

"My dear," he said, his eyes both merry and worried at the same time, "how many times have I told you to be careful by the windows? One day a latch will give way and you shall tumble out."

She wrinkled her brow, confused, and then felt a movement within her as if . . . as if of a child. She looked down, and saw that she was swollen with child.

• • • • • • • • • • •

# BAD POWER

## DEBORAH BIANCOTTI

I had me listed as a bad man. Seemed the best way to hide. Especially true for a woman, it was that or run. Lord knows I was tired of running, I been running all my life. 'Cos the world ain't safe for women and the world ain't safe for me, whatever I am.

I says, "I look like a man, right?"

"Sure, some," says Chella.

He preferred men, so that was a compliment.

"You gonna hid in plain sight nows?" he asks, and when I confirmed it he says, "You tired of the road, tired of running, then you tired of living and every place but death."

He was right, often he was. Chella was running just 'cos he liked it. Had nothing better to do and no past but a string of crimes didn't want to own up to. He planned to go out like a fighter. I figured his future didn't hold that, but I never knew how to tell him. He didn't live like a fighter, sure couldn't see him dying like one.

"Never met one like you," he'd say often, half-impressed and half-otherwise. Looking at me with that superstition I came to take as normal for everyone who weren't me or blood to me.

Looking back nows, I think Chella never liked me. He just couldn't be away from me. It was a compulsion, him to me. Me to him also, we had that in common. Sometimes he'd follow and sometimes he'd lead and so we rolled around each other like spokes in a wheel. When he'd up and want to leave I'd tell him, "Don't go," and that'd be it. He'd stay. And when I wanted to go . . . well,

I never did. Chella scared me like that. Had a power over me I didn't right understand, made me want no one but him. Goddamn him for that.

I thought his power would be done when he was dead, but I was wrong. Every man after that was or wasn't Chella. Every woman, too, in her own way. There was nothing remarkable about Chella, you understand, but he had marked me and I had let him and after that, maybe we both of us regretted it.

• • •

Chella got sick day by day and the doc—if there was a doc in whatever town we lighted on—the doc would try all sorts of remedies. Potions, salves, balms, all kinds of stink. Leeches one time. Snakes the next, and that was the worst. Half-crazed with voices of his own, that doc. He wasn't all there, but he sure was someplace. To his own mind, at least. Thought himself something. Chella, I think, related to him for that. Chella been driven half-mad by voices when he was just a kid, so he said.

He asks, "What god you think you're serving, crazy man? What voice you hear?"

Doc says back, "I serves that there bad man that travels with you and pays my bills. I do his bidding when his voice is in my head. You hear it?"

The doc meant me. He gave me a wink like we knew each other, made my skin crawl. Chella went into a rage, protecting me. He slapped the doc with his good arm 'til the other man howled. But still the doc wouldn't stop winking at me, wanting something from me.

I says to the doc, "You say you serve me. Well, get lost."

He took right off, simple as that. Didn't even stop for his purse.

Chella laughed and shook his head at me and I told him to go to hell. He assured me he was already there. The pain, see, from whatever he had. Lifted himself off the doc's cot and eased up onto legs that wobbled under him like saplings holding up a ceiling.

After that, Chella stuck to the docs who offered remedies you could keep in jars. Tried a dozen or so. No match for what he had. Wasted away under his hat, wasted within his clothes, wasted day by day sitting upright, wasting night by night lying on the ground.

"Ah, geez, to hell with this." He dropped where he walked.

I dragged him off the path and up beside a fallen tree. Pushed aside the scraggling undergrowth, made enemies of a snake was resting there. Snake made good eating once I got it blackened over a fire, but that fire took half a day to light. Then got drowned by rain, and so did we. Rained day and night. Tree trunk kept the worst of it off Chella's face but it pooled under his head and turned the black soil there to bile. I kept wiping it off my clothes until my hands were so covered I was just spreading it around. Then I waited it out.

His last words were *Don't go telling*.

I didn't know which he meant. Don't go telling how he lived or how he died? 'Cos dying is what he did next, he couldn't help it. I felt powerless, but really I was just stubborn. Didn't say nothing that might help him live, but I stayed right by him until his skin was mottled brown and blue and insects crawled over his eyeballs. It felt wrong, to look at bugs on a man's face and not do anything. Worse when he does nothing himself. There we were, on some dirt road, him dead and me wishing I was. I never raised a hand to hurt Chella, that's important. I maybe told him one time that if he was gonna keep complaining about me, or to me, he might as well just go ahead and die. After that he got sick and I was too ashamed to correct myself. Anyhow, I meant nothing by it.

• • •

Nothing Chella had was much use to me. His clothes were too big and his boots too old. I took his hat, though. When I ran into family of his out west they recognised it. *Custom-made band*, Chella had told me. Didn't say his sister had made it, didn't say she'd recognise it when I ran into her on the street in the next town that came my way. I guess that's why Chella ended up choosing this road. Maybe he was wanting home. Sickness and death do that, make you choose something you usually wouldn't. Like, family. Your past. Something recognisable in a world that's come out too flat and wide.

So there I was deep in the bosom of Chella's family. More siblings than I had fingers. Father dead, mother on the way. A queue of graves out back, some of them small. I asks, "Children?"

Chella's brother says, "Sure, some."

"Any of 'em Chella's?"

"Reckon."

Not big talkers, the family, I liked that about them. But I had no place there and when Chella's sister started making eyes at me, I figured it was time to get out. Wasn't nothing wrong with her, just that she took me for a bad man. And also she wasn't my type, for all she reminded me of Chella. She wasn't him.

Brother saw me leaving, "Chella always did enjoy the company of bad types. What's your name, sir?"

"Does it matter?"

He grunted at that. Told me he wanted a name for the memory. I said to call me Bad and he did, right there and then. He looked like he meant it, too.

• • •

Next town I fell into I found me a crowd. Town had no name and neither did the men I met. Names ain't much. Can't trade 'em or sell 'em or use 'em for soap. Chella would've been mad. He had the skill of avoiding the darkness in a man. I didn't, though. Probably why me and him ended up together. Neither of us ready for what the other was.

This one man in the crowd, he had a knowing in him.

"You got a power," he says to me.

"No power I got, not now, not ever. Else I'd be some other place," I tells him. "Better places to be than here."

He laughs. "You got a power over men, I'd wager."

He was too specific, and I was wrong. I did have a power. I just didn't know it.

He talked to me in a thick, dark voice I didn't right like. I seen lust on a man and it only ever looked good on Chella. When this man grabbed for me I yelled so loud others came running, looking for a fire. This man shoved me quick, out of the way and into a rail.

"Don't you mind his yelling," says the man. "Little bad man's just seen a snake."

Rest of them laughed and spat and laughed some more while my face burned. My spine had a throb in it from being pushed against the railing. I was holding my shirt closed where he'd torn at me.

I spat to clear the juice in my throat. "I got a power, huh? I got a power, well get away from me. How about that? Y'all get the hell away from me."

They was all laughing, but each one took a handful of steps back, laughing but looking kinda worried, too. Like they was confused by what they was doing. Guess he was right, that man. He had an insight and I had a power. First of my kind, too, no one ever had a power like mine. Didn't realise what I had, and how could I? Nothing to compare it to. Nothing like me in history. Halla-freaking-luyeah.

The men all left me alone after that. Wouldn't come any place near me, though in the dark I inched towards their fire so I could warm my hands. I heard them speaking in whispers, probably about me, but any that caught sight of me backed off into the dark and wouldn't look me in the eye. Soon enough I was the only one at that fire. Seemed a shame to waste it. I lay flat and slept, first time in a long time. Soaking up the warmth and stoking the flames when the cold woke me.

First light I rolled up my blanket and stood, picked up Chella's hat and stuck it on my head.

"See you, bad man," one man says from where he sat hunched into his fellows, shivering in the frost where the fire didn't reach.

"No, you won't be seeing me no more."

"Thank the devil."

When I passed, he winced and hunkered down. I thought at the time, maybe that's my power. Maybe I make men afraid. But I just hadn't worked it out yet, what my power was. Turns out that's not a power. That's a consequence.

• • •

A lot of people, they never seen the list of bad men. But when I says my name is on it, they believe. Something about my eyes, most of them say. Something about the way I hold myself. One place, though, law men stopped me and made to check. They says my chin or my throat or my something. Made them think twice about me being any kinda man at all. They was pretty direct. Reached for what was between my legs.

I saw those toughened fingers come at me. "Don't you touch me, law man."

And the hands of this man, they halted right in mid-air, with me looking at him funny and him looking at his hands funny. He was a big man, too. Shoulders thicker than his skull, buttons straining on his shirt. Think he'd trade a shirt in once it got too small, but probably found some status in a collar and buttons, couldn't afford to trade up.

Other law man was further away. Saw his friend stop still and he made to come over.

"What's with you, Fred?" him shouting.

I tells him to back in hell off. And he did, just like I says. Backed off so fast he tripped over his heels and fell and just kept crawling away on his cheeks. He looked like he'd seen the devil or found gold or both.

Old man by a drinking trough, beard so long it passed the string holding up his trousers, he was watching and laughing. Looking at these two officers of the law turned to mud. When I looked to him he held up hands like he was surrendering. "Don't do it, crazy lady, don't go using your powers on me!"

I froze cold. Stupid to think, I hadn't known until then what it was I had. I didn't have looks or smarts, but Chella had never left me, and then I knew why. Because I told him not to. But until that old man put it in words, I didn't think it was power. I was the first with a true power, something that ran its own course apart from biology, that was like some kinda visitation from a demon. I was the first I ever heard of had a power like that or, if I wasn't, then the world sure had a good way of hiding the rest.

In the midst of that catastrophe, all I could think of was Chella, me telling him to drop dead and him doing it. Took him days, but he did what he was told with a thoroughness that belied his wayward nature. He stuck to dying like he had no choice not to. I hated myself then, not for the first time, but fully. And forever.

Only when I worked through all that in my mind did I realise the other thing the old man had said. Called me a lady. Some people, they got the knowing. Usually they got sympathy, too, seen enough of the world and the human soul to understand the why behind a disguise.

"You keep quiet," I tells him, and he does. But too late. Others come on.

Every kid growing to adult wants a power. Too stupid to want otherwise. Like happiness, contentment, warm bed and full belly. Think power'll get 'em all that and some. But we should be learned, easier to want too much than what's good for you. Harder to want less. But smarter. Wish I'd learned that sooner. Wish I'd had parents to teach me, not the kinda people what raised me to be no better than them. I should stop wishing. Stupid as wanting.

I got me a real life power over people. But I only got that power one at a time. Can't do two people at once, can't do a crowd. And a crowd's what gathered then, strangers with wet eyes. They circled and I turned within them and we all just kept at it for a time. They outgrew it before I did, began to shift in towards me.

"Back off," I says to one woman, and she does. Backing straight into the people behind her and carrying them with her. Until they flowed around and filled the gap.

"You, put your hand down. You, walk away far as your legs will take you."

One man turned, knees pumping. He passed the woman who was still backing away, though she kept pace with him for a time. I tells the same to the others that come, still one by one, still not understanding what I can and can't do. Against their wills they obey me, faces dumb with furious wonder. But for every one that left, another joined the crowd. That's when I got it. The ones walking away, they was telling everyone they passed. They was spreading the word as far as they could travel. I done something stupid with that.

"Cover its mouth." A man grinning like it's no big deal. My life and death just a thing to him.

"Don't you do that!"

When they came at me all and all, I was powerless. Some, they gagged me with a stinking piece of horse blanket, made me retch until darkness came, thumping into the back of my skull in time with the laughter of that old man by the drinking trough.

● ● ●

I moved in a dark place where the dead and the living spoke to each other. I couldn't tell which I was, so I got to asking. One man, called himself Webb, tells me if he can hear me, well, I must be dead. Even apologises to me like it was a bad thing. Had this manner about him, matter-of-fact like he was just doing his job. I tells him not to apologise, best news I've had in forever. He says the dead, they talk to him and he can't control it.

I pitied him, so I tells him dead is better than haunted. He says that gives him something to look forward to, at least, but he chuckles and tells me there's more work to be done yet. He ain't ready to die, is what I understand from him. So I says to him, "What if I'm not ready to die yet, either? I got something I should see to."

"I don't honestly know," says Webb. "Perhaps just try to live. See how it goes. Good talking to you."

I thank him. Something in what he said gave me comfort. Maybe just the knowing I ain't ended yet.

Before I know it, light came rolling in like water round a sink hole and I began to see again. I was laying flat, hard edges of something digging into my sides. A cot, a wooden frame with no stuffing. I shifted out of reach of the edge and guessed Webb was right. Trying to live is sometimes enough.

"Don't try anything," comes a deep drawl.

I moved my eyes without moving my head, since my head hurt all over. Wasn't no place of it didn't.

A fat man, only way to tell it. A fat man leaning back, I guess on a chair though I couldn't see it. I moved my jaw, testing it out.

"One of us is in prison," I tells him.

When I talked it sounded like I was chewing through gravel.

"Both of us, as it happens. I'm Sheriff Faden."

"Yeah? What'd you do, Sheriff, land you in here with me?"

He had a full dirty beard and small eyes like a rat, high on the sides of his head. He brought one arm over his scalp, crooked so his elbow was upright and his hand fell over his ear.

"I was the fool put on this badge." He thumbed it. The badge was dull and dirty like the rest of him.

"They lock you up for that? This place has a temper."

"You only just now working that out?"

I rolled my head back to ease the pain in my neck. It didn't help none. All the skin left on me itched. Enough it competed with the ache in every bone. I raised an arm. I was marked in scratches, bruises and blood from fingernail to elbow. My clothes were gone, ripped right through, but I was so covered in mud and blood I didn't feel naked. My right thigh stung hard like it was burned. And then I recognised the stink of cooked skin. "They branded me?"

Faden stretched, "And then locked me in here with you, and they didn't give me no key."

I tongued my teeth one by one, counting what was left. "So there's no way I can tell you to unlock that door?"

"You can tell me. I just can't do it."

"And if I tell you to take your chair and smash in that window?"
I raised a hand, but it was random. My arms were so beat up they

moved of their own accord, and my fingers stuck together with blood enough I couldn't point far enough to even pick my own nose.

"That one over there, with the bars?" Faden pointed, more successfully. "Or that other one, also with bars?"

I didn't answer for a time. I was chewing through my options. "I could make you beat that chair over your own head 'til you died."

"Reckon you could." He shifted on his invisible chair. "Of course, you'd be alone in here, no one to talk to, no one to boss about. But that might suit you, who's to judge?"

I probably shouldn't have blamed him, but I did. I pictured him with a bullet hole messing up his forehead. Way he told it, he'd done me a favour. He knew if he let me out I'd be for slaughter. Plenty of people hated me. Some, apparently, were still trying to fetch back the people I'd sent away. Faden laughed when he told it, said nothing was stopping those people backing away or walking. Wearing their feet to stumps. Faden didn't care much for the human race, I figured. Guess we had that in common.

"They're planning to kill you piece by piece," him breathing heavy through his nose, running out of laughter. He frowned, waiting for me to say something but I was pretty much out of words by then. "That bother you?"

"Bother you?" I asks. "Ain't you the law?"

"For want of a better occupation."

We fell quiet, him fat and heavy in his chair, me finding ways to nurse the bruises on my hips or settle the ache in my spine one by one. No way to do both at one time.

"Bothers me," I admits at last. "Not for my own self. But for the baby."

"The what?" Way he says it, dumb and slow, made me hate him more. He stirred in his chair, hands coming down to grab each other in his lap. He figured I was lying. But this was one time I was telling the truth. This was the one thing I'd come back for, from the darkness. To see my child right.

"You heard me, I reckon."

"This some trick?" Still insisting I was making it up. "Why'd you be on the road in your condition?"

I almost laughed. Road takes anyone, doesn't discriminate. Mothers, fathers and children. Takes 'em and often doesn't ever let 'em go. I wondered if Chella would've ever stopped running. Maybe if he'd known about our child. Maybe not.

"Figured I could out-run it, I guess. But turns out pregnant is something you can't leave behind." Didn't add, *I was a fool.* But I sure felt like it.

I was naïve, that's a constant truth of my life. I never knew one day to the next what kinda thing I was getting into. No idea how I was to live, let alone how to make sure the child in my belly lived. Must be hanging on by both fists, to have survived what we been through already.

"You tryin' to make me intervene in what's coming to you?" Faden leaned forward, elbows on wide thighs.

"Reckon maybe I am. But if you can't or won't, there's something else you can do for me. We got a tradition in my family."

I tried easing my shoulder up from the cot, but a bolt of pain claimed my ribs. I lay right back down.

"What do I care for your traditions, witch?"

"Somebody's gotta see my son raised. Gotta pass it onto my son, the tradition. Might as well be you."

If my son had a power, maybe he'd have a power like Webb's. Able to talk to the dead. Then all I'd have to do is see my son born. But I couldn't be sure. We all carry the seeds of our futures in us, I believe that. Swimming in our blood or hardening in our bones. We're the sum of what's coming to us, a skin-moment in a world that is nothing but a string of moments, each one of 'em important to someone. What was important to me then was my son getting his chance at power. Because if history had birthed no other human being like me, well, my son was going to be different again. He'd have his own power and I prayed gods it would be something good.

"You think you gonna live long enough to birth a child? Beating probably end your life before morning, your kid's, too."

That was just cruel, saying that to a pregnant woman.

"His name is Maxillius." This through gritted teeth. "First born boys in my family, but only every second generation. Always Maxillius. And he's gonna have a power."

"Like his mother?"

"Different, but something."

"Your power tell you that, witch?"

Would've rolled my eyes if I had it in me. Ain't nothing to do with power, that type of knowledge, except the power that motherhood brings. But I knew, right then, if I was first with a strange kind of power, my son was second. Beyond that I didn't know anything. But knowing that was enough.

Faden made a clicking sound with his tongue. "Sounds complicated."

"Takes care of itself. Every second generation, first born is a boy. And his name's gonna be Maxillius. It's the way of things. If I don't make it through, you think you can tell him that for me?"

I'm not no believer but I was praying then or something like it. My son had to live. He had to see his power realised and make a space in the world for people like us. Maybe he'd have his own babes with power. Either way, right then his life was more precious to me than my own and my love for him was something fierce. I hadn't known my own mother, no way to tell if this was normal. Didn't feel it but I'd never had normal. Wasn't sure what it felt like.

"My son's got to live, Faden."

He didn't answer. He was listening, but not to me. There was a thrumming outside. Horses. A dozen or more.

"Don't suppose I've got a right to hope that's wild horses, lost their heads and about to run through town by accident? Maybe about to knock over this here gaol and set us free?"

"They're not wild," Faden mutters, "but their riders are."

Then he tells me the only useful thing I heard since way before Chella died. He says, "If I get the chance, I'll see your son right. Born and raised up. And whatever his power, I'll make sure he don't end up where you ended up."

And that was it. All I could ask. I thanked him, because my power had never lead me anywhere but bad places, and my badness had less to do with my power than it had to do with the world.

• • •

The horses stopped and Faden got up to check the window. He eased his belt around his middle and chewed a corner of his mouth.

"What you see, Sheriff?"

"Priest is with them. You could be in luck. Looks like maybe they're bringing food."

He got back in his seat and waited, half-turned towards the door. There was a rattle of keys and then a man stood in the way of it.

"Bring me the keys!" My voice was hoarse.

The man just looked at me like I was dumb.

"That's Alby," Faden's voice was like lead. "He speaks no word of English. I'd says you've got your work cut out for you."

"He read lips?" I was desperate.

"Don't read, don't speak," Faden was halfway through explaining, his bulk turning back 'round to face me, when Alby came right up behind him with that heavy tray and thumped Faden in the back of the skull. Right in the place where it must've happened onto his neck. Faden jerked, slid out and hit the floor while Alby danced out of the way.

Faden lay by his upturned chair, shuddering and spasming, drooling out his mouth and bleeding out of his head. Then Alby came at me. He took that tray and slammed it up the side of my temple, me screaming the whole time. But no words coming out.

• • •

Next I woke up I was in a place that stank of pigs and vermin. Trussed like a calf, and all. Ankle to ankle, wrist to wrist. I hurt even worse than in Faden's prison. Whole right side of my head throbbed like a fire-toad breathing under my eye. When I got up the courage I reached my hands to it. My face was swollen and pulped, I couldn't even feel bone. But that wasn't the worst of it. Something hard and metal jutted from my shattered cheek. Iron links as long as my knuckles, pulled into a chain. It cut my jaw, passed my teeth and tongue, came out under my eye. And there was clamped with a gate lock.

They'd chained up my voice. Nearly broke my head doing it, whole thing sticky with blood. I tried to speak but all that came out was a grunt like an animal makes. I nearly threw up but was afraid to drown in it. So I bit back, swallowing, breathing shaky through my nose.

"You see here, I got the key?" A new voice, smooth and deep. I squinted at where he stood, sun at his waist. "My name's Sty, see, and I'm gonna give you the key once a day. So's you can eat. And when we get to where we going, I unlock you and you says what I tells you. Maybe I tells you, "unlock the safe" or "hand over the money" or "drop your guns". And I wad my ears, so's you can't charm me. See? You'll do what I tells you, right?"

He was twirling that key between finger and thumb. Seeing me nod too slow he made to throw it. No way I could follow, so I screams against my chain and set the shattered bone of my face to humming.

"Better. You control with words, woman. But I control with iron. Understood?"

The nodding roiled my head some and the vomit hit the back of my throat. I breathed it down. Sty grinned. Sounded like I was crying but I was just trying to live.

I had me listed as a bad man, but I'd never done bad, not in any kinda way could be intentional. But right then I vowed I'd kill Sty. In his sleep, on the road. I'd find a way. I'd take that key and I'd make him choke on it, I swore that.

First time, then, the baby in my belly kicked.

• • •

Months and then some. Road looks the same it ever did. All looks like running. Places with no names, people with nothing. Met 'em all before, met 'em all again or someone looked like 'em. Chella said you tired of the road, you tired of living, and still he was right. I was tired of all of it, now even more, with the baby keeping me up at night and Sty tying me upright to my horse.

I did what he told me 'cos I was scared. Simple as that. We lifted bills from banks and travellers, me mouthing his commands through my shattered face in a voice I didn't recognise. Still worked, though. Sty and his gang with their ears wadded up, grinning at me like we was sharing some kinda game. Grinning and winking, mocking me, my right eye so puffed and tortured I couldn't see out of it any more.

Months of going in circles while everything in our path dried up. I wasted around my belly, weight falling off me like water off a roof. But my belly grew and Maxillius in it. Chella haunted me stronger than ever, too. Probably wanted to see his son. Should've asked that Webb while I had the chance, asked if he'd ever heard from Chella. It would've helped me to know, maybe that he was watching over us. As it was, only thing between our child and death was me. I didn't feel good 'bout that.

Maybe that's where my power came from. Maybe some god of children wanted to give Maxillius a chance. Kid had nothing but a dead father and a screwed up mother, and I got to thinking what would happen to him when he was born, what Sty and the others would do. I couldn't even guess at that. I didn't want to.

There were a dozen in Sty's posse, I never learned their names or even if they had 'em. One good thing about being a witch, they left me alone. Even Sty, though he threatened otherwise often enough. He was careful our skin didn't touch, even when he unlocked the chain in my face enough I could move. The hate in me was like a shield, pushed 'em all away. Eventually it fell to just Alby to guard me. When he took off like sometimes he did, they gave the job to some deaf man, lost his hearing blowing up a bank. He'd sit with his back to me and talk and talk. That's how I learned most of what I did about Sty and his team, though all of it I forgot. Didn't want that knowledge in my skull. Didn't want it in my baby's blood.

We got back round to where we'd been, some town with no name or some other town that looked like it. We was on horses, moving slow, Sty thinking himself right powerful. Telling us all how he was like a locomotive, fastest, hardest man in the world. His voice like the bellow of a bull. He was bragging and cussing, going on about some thing of his, leaning back on his horse and rubbing his belly. He was growing thick with success, was Sty. All that good eating and drinking, earned from my power and what I could do. His dozen men were laughing like they feared nothing in the world. Still laughing when the back of Sty's head came off in a pink cloud. He rolled to one side and fell, foot still caught in his saddle, hands dragging in the dirt behind what was left of his head. Whole thing leaving a red smear.

I was so numb with running and starving I forgot even to be glad. Just stared at Sty's open eyes, gathering dust. Alby dropped to my right and three more after that. Still I sat in my saddle, looking round like I was watching a puppet show. Wondering what in hell was going on.

My horse rolled and fell so sudden my legs were in the air when it hit. Saved me from being pinned under. Tied to its neck I hit the ground on shoulder and hip, my belly lurching. The baby inside lurching, too. I had a sharp pain and then felt the warm rush of something wet all over my legs and waist. I thought it was blood but it was too clear.

*Hold on,* I tells him. Then, *Maxillius, your power is not in your timing.*

Maybe he thought it was gonna be safer out in the world than inside me.

Gunfire was all over. I wondered how I'd missed it 'til then. Road had sapped my will, or Sty had. I lay against my horse like it was a shield, heard the soft yelp of bullets through its hide. No complaint from the horse so I guessed it already gone. I took to the rope at my wrists, working it free with my teeth, keeping my head down behind the horse's neck. Alby was on the ground beside me, bleeding from the gut. He rolled to one side like he was making to sit up. I got a hand free and stretched out to him. I took his gun from his hand—easy 'cos he was weak—and I shot him. Right in the middle of the chest. I had no cause to like Alby, but didn't see no reason to draw out his dying. Just didn't like having him there beside me with a gun in his hands. Too unpredictable, I reckoned.

I got my other hand free and crawled to where Sty lay. My senses were returning to me, enough I felt cheated that I hadn't been the one to kill him. I would've liked it. I started searching for that damn key in every pocket. Found it stuffed into his trousers, in a string on his waist so it must've tapped against his cock when he was riding. It was his final insult, I figured, to hold my imprisonment so close to his lap. Even dead he was a sick son of a bitch.

Guns had stopped, devil only knew what was coming. I jerked the key free and fitted it to the lock on my face. A shadow fell on me while I was twisting it, listening to the click of the bolt. I figured this was probably it, Maxillius wasn't gonna be born after all. Poor kid had come so close. It wasn't right, but plenty in the world isn't right and that doesn't stop it. I cradled the lock with both hands and refused to look up at what was coming next.

Someone spat in the dust to my right. "Told you I'd see your boy raised."

Faden, of all people. Just as fat and dumb as I remembered, Gods love him for it. His eyes ranged my broken face and he let out a string of blasphemy. He squatted beside me and reached to hold me up, 'cos I was flagging.

Just in time, he was, because my son was churning my belly something fierce. He was on his way into this here world and I was going to tell him a story. All about the life that got lived up 'til his own began. I'd be telling him that story for the rest of my life, however long I got.

Didn't pay no mind to the future until my son arrived. Didn't pay no mind to the past either. But the moment to moment, well, it can kill you. Faden helped me with the lock and eased the chain out of my face for all the hours of screaming and cursing it took. I figured I looked a sight, blood dripping down my shirt and my face throbbing until my skull took over with a thumping all its own.

"You know, that wasn't even a command," I tells him. "That was just conversation."

"About raising your son?" Faden shook his head. "I'm a man of my word."

"Next time," I says, "don't take so long to live up to your word."

Faden grins. "Whatever you say."

And that was as close to a happy ending as I ever seen.

•••••••••••

# AT THE TOP OF THE STAIRS

## RICHARD HARLAND

"It's a sad, bad thing I have to tell you, my darlings. Be strong and try not to cry." Mama looked at Tom and Aggie across the wooden table. She had made them stay on their chairs after finishing their porridge. She looked pretty and neat, as always, but with an odd stiffness around the corners of her mouth. "Your father has gone," she said.

That didn't sound so bad to Tom. His father often went away, sometimes for days at a time. "Gone where?" he asked.

"Gone to the devil."

The word sounded shocking on Mama's lips. It was like a dark beast springing out from hiding under her sweet, gentle voice. Tom shivered, though he didn't understand. Aggie seemed to understand because she nodded thoughtfully.

"When did it happen?" she asked Mama.

"It's been happening for weeks, my dear. Now he won't be coming back."

"I thought he only went . . . " Tom thought he knew where his father went, but when he had to say it, he couldn't quite remember.

Mama shook her head. "It's just the three of us from now on, Tom, dear."

For a while, everything seemed to go back to normal after breakfast. Tom and Aggie carried the dishes across to the sink, Mama washed them with hot water from the kettle, Tom dried them and Aggie put them back on the pantry shelves. Then Mama took off her apron and they saw she was wearing her grey Sunday-best clothes.

She became very solemn again. "I have to go out to work today, dears. I want you both to be very, very good."

Tom felt hard done by. "Will we be alone all day?"

"Yes, Tom. Will you be good for me while I'm gone?"

Tom nodded, and blinked away a sudden smarting sensation in his eyes.

"I'll *make* him be good," said Aggie.

"Both of you," said Mama.

She took down father's greatcoat from the peg behind the door and put it on. They knew then just how much things had changed, because Mama always wore her own threadbare mantle, while nobody but father wore father's greatcoat.

"I've left a list of chores for you on the slate." Mama pointed to the slate that hung on the wall beside the picture of the King. "I expect to find them all done when I get back." She softened her tone, because her last words had sounded very severe. "You'll have to help me more with the housework, my dears."

Then she slipped on her mittens and fastened a red headscarf over her hair. Tom had never seen her wear such a bright color before, and it made her look nicer than ever.

She smiled, though her eyes were sad. "When I go, you must bolt the door at once, and don't unbolt it till I return. No one ever comes calling up here, but don't answer if they do. Do you understand?"

She gave them each a peck on the cheek, then turned and left. Tom wanted to watch her going down the first flight of stairs, but Aggie closed the door and slid home the bolts.

"*At once*, Mama said," she told Tom.

That was the beginning of a long dreary day. It was typical autumn weather, with low-lying bands of cloud coming across the sky. Because their rooms were at the top of one of the tallest tenements, they were actually inside a cloud at times: then the windows ran with trickles of water, as though someone had squeezed a dishcloth over them.

"What does it mean about gone to the devil?" Tom asked.

"It's what you say when people go," his sister replied. "It means whatever you want it to mean."

"Can it mean . . . you know . . . " Tom lowered his voice. "*The Devil?*"

"It can if you want it to."

Tom wasn't satisfied, but he knew if he asked *What does Mama want it to mean*, Aggie would only answer *That's her business.*

They made the beds, dusted their bedroom and Mama's bedroom, scoured the sink and around the gas ring, washed socks in the copper and soaked dried peas and barley for the soup. Nobody came upstairs to knock on their door.

The chores seemed to go on forever, and still they were only half done. Tom grew increasingly fractious and frustrated. "It's too much," he complained. "It's impossible."

When Aggie announced that their next task was to oil and polish the chiffonier, he looked at the list on the slate and said, "Let's wash the skirting-board first."

Aggie frowned. "We have to do them in order."

"Why?"

"Because."

"No, we don't."

He went to the cupboard under the sink to get the scrubbing-brush for washing the skirting board. He knew what would happen. Aggie came across and tried to take it off him.

"Chiffonier first!"

"No!"

It turned into a wrestling-match. Aggie twisted Tom's arm, Tom pulled Aggie's hair. In the end, of course, Aggie was bigger and stronger.

"Ow! Yow! Stop!" Tom roared. "You're really hurting!"

"Good!"

"No! I'll—"

Tom pulled savagely out of her grip and lost his balance. Flailing as he fell, he kicked over the slops bucket. Tealeaves, bread crusts, bacon rinds and a hundred sorts of sludge flew out across the rug and the floorboards.

"You've done it now," said Aggie.

Tom stared in horror. "What'll we tell Mama?"

"The truth." Aggie put on her virtuous expression. "It's always better to tell the truth."

"We'll get into trouble," said Tom gloomily.

"You more than me."

But as it turned out, neither of them got into trouble. It was much worse than that. When Mama came home, she saw at once that the table hadn't been set and the chores were unfinished. It had taken Aggie and Tom more than an hour just to wash the floor and clean the rug.

"I thought you'd try harder." She seemed ready to cry.

Then Aggie told the truth. In spite of her earlier threats, she blamed herself for what had happened as much as Tom. Mama inspected the rug and discovered that the slops had soaked into the fabric and left permanent dark blotches on the underside.

There was a long horrible moment. "You've disappointed me," said Mama. "You've made me very, very unhappy."

Tom began to sniffle. "We didn't know."

"I think you did. It's so cruel of you both. I hope you're pleased with the consequences."

What consequences? Tom felt he ought to understand, but he didn't. He would have done anything to make Mama happy again.

Tom and Aggie set the table, while Mama heated the soup. Dinner was eaten with lowered heads, in silence, though Tom couldn't help sneaking an occasional glance at the expression on Mama's face.

Everyone went to bed early. Tom and Aggie shared the same bed, but with their heads sticking out at opposite ends. They could hear Mama crying in her bedroom next door.

Tom tossed and turned miserably all night. By morning, though, he had come to a different view. "We didn't do anything so bad as all that," he muttered to himself. "We've been naughtier other times."

Aggie sensed his changed mood and spoke to him sternly. "Be nice to Mama this morning, Tom. Be quiet and obedient."

Neither of them guessed what they would see in the living room. Mama's face was puffy from crying, but it was also scored with long red scratches that ran down over her cheeks and neck.

"What is it, Mama?" They both cried out in a kind of panic. "What's happened, what's happened?"

Mama turned her face away, stirring the porridge over the gas ring, and acted as though she hadn't heard.

Tom's heart jumped up and down in his chest. He couldn't stop from flapping senselessly all around her. "Mama! Mama! Mama!"

She brushed him aside, saying, "Nothing. It's nothing."

In the end, though, she swung to face them both. "There! Is this what you want to see?" She let them take a good long look. "Are you satisfied now?"

Aggie was almost as agitated as Tom. "Who did it, Mama? Did *we* make it happen?"

"I don't want to talk about it." Mama ladled out the porridge and put their bowls on the table before them. "Eat up before it gets cold."

The porridge could have been mud for all they tasted. They didn't dare talk about the scratches again. Mama put on face powder before she left for work, so that the horrible red marks didn't stand out so much. She put on her headscarf too, and her mittens and father's greatcoat, exactly the same as the previous day.

"Well, my dears." She spoke to them a little more kindly before leaving for work. "What's happened has happened. There's a new list of chores on the slate. Just think how much you want to help me, and try to be specially good today."

"We will," vowed Aggie.

Mama kissed them goodbye and paused in the doorway. "Bolt the door again today. Don't open it for anyone till I come home."

Then she was gone, and they were alone behind the bolted door. Tom wanted to talk about the scratches on her face.

"Who did it? Do *you* know?"

But Aggie only clicked her tongue at him. "It doesn't matter who, so long as we don't let it happen again. No time for idle chatter. We need to start our chores at once."

"But . . . "

"No *buts*. You want to be good, don't you? You want to finish the list today?"

Tom did want to be good, and he was determined to finish every chore. They worked with a will, and Aggie crossed out each task as they finished it with a chalk line on the slate.

Around the middle of the day, an icy wind sprang up and cleared the clouds out of the sky. It rattled the windows and made the whole tenement grumble and creak in every timber.

Warmed by their work, Tom and Aggie scarcely felt the cold. Then Tom heard footsteps coming up the stairs. He hissed a warning to Aggie, who listened and froze.

How far down was the sound? The footsteps seemed to be approaching the rooms on the floor below. Surely they would stop there?

But they continued up the final flight of stairs.

Tom and Aggie stared at the bolts on the door and willed them to stay in their sockets.

Heavy, heavy footsteps, like the tread of a tall large man. He moved with slow deliberation, far more slowly than anyone ought to move.

"Who is it?" Tom had a flash of nightmare. "Is it the Devil?"

"Don't be silly," Aggie whispered back.

The footsteps arrived at the top of the stairs and crossed the landing. Tom and Aggie waited for the knock. Waited and waited. How long was he going to stand there and do nothing?

The wind sighed through the crack under the door. Noiselessly, Tom lowered himself onto hands and knees. He saw two dark shadows, the bottoms of the man's boots. Suddenly he couldn't bear it any more.

"Go away!" he shouted. "Nobody home!"

For a long minute, nothing happened. Then the shadows moved, the footsteps went away. *Clump-clump-clump* down the stairs. Tom and Aggie remained frozen until the sound faded away.

"Who was it?" Aggie's question wasn't really directed to Tom, and a moment later she answered it herself. "Probably a landlord."

"What's a landlord?"

Aggie didn't seem very certain. "They come around," she said vaguely.

Tom felt weak in the knees and didn't want to start work again. But the chores had to be done, so they went back to scrubbing pans and cleaning cupboards. They couldn't help glancing now and then towards the door.

By the time Mama came home, every task on the list had been crossed off, and the table was set for dinner. Mama smiled and was happy—until they told her about the man at the door. Then she sat down suddenly on a chair and seemed every bit as frightened as they had been.

"How do you know it was a man?" she asked. "How can you be certain?"

They told her again about the heavy tread and the size of the boots.

"And you say he didn't knock?"

"I shouted and made him go away." Tom puffed out his chest. "I told him there was nobody home."

Mama went very white and the scratches on her cheeks stood out vividly once again. "You *called out* to him?"

Tom wasn't sure what he'd done wrong, exactly, but he knew from the look on Mama's face it must be something awful. He began to whimper.

Aggie spoke up on her brother's behalf. "Tom made the man go away. Wasn't that right?"

"The man knows there was somebody home." Mama swung round to Aggie. "Does he know about you too?"

Aggie shook her head. Tom's whimper turned to tears.

"You didn't say not to!" he blubbered. "You didn't tell us about not calling out!"

"Oh, Tom, Tom, Tom, Tom, Tom." Mama swayed back and forth on her chair, her face a picture of despair.

Tom felt sick with guilt. "It's not fair!" he protested.

"Not fair? No, it's not, Tom, it's very unfair. What have you done to me now?"

It was more of a lament than an accusation. Mama went immediately into her bedroom and those were the last words they heard from her all night.

Tom kept asking Aggie, what had he done? He was beside himself, all muddled in his feelings. Aggie soothed him, but didn't explain. She prepared them a makeshift dinner of bread and dripping, then tried calling out to Mama through the door. "Do you want anything to eat?" There was no response.

"She's not even crying," Aggie said as she returned to the table. Somehow, that made it worse.

They took their plates of bread and dripping into their own bedroom and ate sitting on the side of the bed.

"Don't worry, it'll pass over," said Aggie. "Everything will be back to normal in the morning."

But it wasn't. When they got up in the morning, Mama had risen long before them. Perhaps she had never been to sleep. She was sitting at the table in her cotton nightgown, with the sleeves rolled up past her elbows, and there were crisscross cuts on her forearms all the way down to her wrists. Some of the cuts had been bandaged, others were still bleeding. She had pushed back the tablecloth so that the blood dripped only onto the polished wood.

"Mama!" shrieked Aggie, and ran to help.

Rolls of bandage were already laid out on the table. Passive and numb, Mama let Aggie raise her arms and wind bandages around the cuts.

"Press with your other hand and stop the blood," Aggie ordered. "Tom, come here."

Tom was numb too. He came across to the table and pressed down on the bandages in the places where Aggie showed him. A redness seeped into the bandages and made his fingertips wet.

Aggie finished tying the bandages as tight as she could. Then she washed down the table, washed her own hands and washed two knives that had been left in the sink.

After a while, the redness stopped spreading through the bandages. Tom leaned in closer to the warmth of Mama's body.

"It's all right, my darling," Mama said. "Better now. I'll go and get dressed for work."

When she re-emerged from her bedroom, she was wearing her grey Sunday-best clothes again. The long sleeves covered her forearms and nothing was visible except a faint lumpishness of bandages. She drank tea at the table while Tom and Aggie ate bread and dripping.

"We'll keep it all a secret, shall we?" she suggested, with a strange sly smile. "Just the three of us, nobody else need know. We'll live our own life here at the top of the stairs."

When it was time for Mama to leave, Aggie looked at the empty slate and asked, "No chores?"

"Today, I want you to think what needs doing for yourselves," Mama replied.

"What if the man comes back?"

Mama's mouth twisted into a shapeless line. "You know what *not* to do, Aggie."

So that day, the two of them worked harder than ever. Aggie tried to think of all the things that could possibly need doing, and Tom followed her commands without question. The sun rose like a small yellow ball in a hazy autumn sky. The wind dropped, though the air remained cold and sharp.

When Tom reflected upon the scene in the morning, it seemed like a dream. Had Mama really sat there with cuts all over her arms? He rolled back the tablecloth when Aggie was looking the other way, to examine the place where the blood had dripped. The evidence was gone.

He was reluctant to ask Aggie or talk about what had happened. Perhaps she felt the same, because neither of them mentioned it once all day. When their eyes met, she gave a kind of nod as if to say, *We both know what we have to do.*

Around midday, the man came back up the stairs. Exactly the same as yesterday, so slow and deliberate. This time, Aggie was the one who heard him first. She had been mopping the floorboards with soapy water, Tom had been wiping them off with a sponge. They retreated behind the table and Tom put his hand over his mouth to make sure he didn't call out by accident.

The footsteps crossed the landing and stopped outside the door. *Rat-tat-tat! Rat-tat-tat!*

The knock made them jump. Tom gripped the sponge until his knuckles turned white.

*Rat-tat-tat! Rat-tat-tat! Rat-tat-tat!*

The second knock wasn't quite as bad as the first. Aggie raised the mop in front of her like a weapon.

There was no third time. The man retreated down the stairs. Flight after flight, they heard him descend.

Tom dragged a chair across to the window.

"No!" hissed Aggie.

"I want to see him come out."

Standing on the seat of the chair, leaning forward, Tom could see all the way down to Bridie Street. It was a scene in shades of grey: grey pavements, grey carriages, grey pedestrians. Viewed from above, the pedestrians appeared as tiny round blobs, whose arms and legs appeared and disappeared as they walked. Across the street lay O'Connell Park, with its railings and paths and leafless trees as delicate as feathers. Tom concentrated on the entrance to their own tenement, ten floors below.

After a few moments, Aggie brought another chair across and joined him at the window. "Has he come out yet?"

"Not yet."

They stayed watching five minutes, ten minutes, quarter of an hour. Two people came in at the entrance, one young woman went out. Their visitor had vanished into thin air.

"Perhaps he lives in our building?" Tom quavered.

"Don't say that!" Aggie shook her head fiercely. "Don't even think of it! There must be a different way out."

Eventually they went back to their self-imposed housework. Aggie wrote on the slate to record what they'd done: sixteen different tasks by the time Mama came home.

"You *have* been good," she said, unfastening her red headscarf and taking off father's greatcoat.

"And we didn't make a sound when the man came," said Tom.

"He came again?"

"He knocked on the door," said Aggie.

"Twice," added Tom.

Mama hadn't bolted the door when she entered, but she did now. "Tell me all about it."

So they described what had happened, up to the moment when they'd looked out the window.

Mama gasped. "You showed your faces at the window? He could've seen you!"

"He didn't come out."

"Someone could've seen you."

"No one was looking up."

"*Someone could've seen you!*" Mama repeated in a loud dangerous voice. "Show me what you did. Exactly."

Tom and Aggie demonstrated how they'd moved the chairs and climbed up on the seats. The look on Mama's face grew more and more dreadful.

"You little fools!" She grabbed the curtains over the window and swept them shut. Then did the same for every other window.

Tom wanted to hide away. Aggie had said *No*, but he hadn't obeyed, so it was his fault again. He still didn't understand why it mattered, when nobody was looking up. How could you know what was good and what was bad? Did Aggie know?

He fled to their bedroom, flung himself on the bed and wept as if he would burst. After a while, Mama came in and sat on the bed beside him.

"Don't cry, my darling. I know you didn't do it deliberately."

Tom was not to be consoled. "It's all my fault!"

Mama let him cry himself out. At last, she put an arm over his shoulder and said, "It's hard, Tom, very, very hard. You're losing your Mama bit by bit."

"No!" Whatever it meant, Tom fought against it. "Why *can't* I be good?"

"You can, Tom, if you listen to your heart. Your heart is good. It'll tell you what to do."

Tom resolved to listen to his heart. But when he fell asleep that night, he had dream after dream in which everyone kept stopping to point at him. Everyone saw something that he didn't see, giving him looks of shame and disgust. At the end of every dream, he looked down and discovered a black oozy thing coming out of his chest. His heart was a black sticky mess!

Finally, he didn't dare go back to sleep, but lay staring at the ceiling, where the brightening light of dawn came through the curtains and cast an orange glow. He had been awake for half an hour when he heard sounds in the living room. Mama was up and about.

He listened to the swash of water and oats going into the saucepan, the clank of the saucepan going onto the gas ring. But there was something different about Mama's movements this morning: a kind of clumsiness. She bumped into things and stumped on the floor like an old person with a stick.

He slipped out of bed without disturbing Aggie, tiptoed to the door and opened it just a crack. Mama was getting bowls down from the cupboard, using only her right hand. When the bowls threatened to slip, she grunted in frustration and brought her left hand up to steady them. What was wrong with the fingers on her left hand?

"Mama!"

As he ran out, she turned to put the bowls down safely on the table. Again, there was a strange wooden thump on the floor.

"Your hand, Mama, your hand!"

Tears slid down her face as she held out her left hand, which was closed up in a solid fist. Tom snatched at it and tried to prize the fingers apart. But it was as though the fist had fused to a single knob of flesh.

"I didn't do it!" he sobbed. "I didn't, I didn't!"

Aroused by the noise, Aggie had come rushing out too. "Let me try," she cried. In vain she struggled to open the fingers of Mama's left hand.

"Don't make a fuss," Mama said. "There's nothing to be done. My foot's the same."

They looked and saw that Mama was wearing only her right shoe. Her left foot was curled over and clenched, as rigid as a piece of wood.

"Your poor, poor foot, Mama!" wailed Aggie.

"Your poor, poor hand!" wailed Tom.

It was a horrible time over breakfast, as Mama's fist kept swinging about and knocking things over. Later, she needed their help to get ready for work. They managed to push her hand into her mitten, but couldn't squeeze her foot into her normal shoe. She had to wear loose felt boots instead. Aggie knotted the red headscarf under her chin and they both pulled father's greatcoat up over her arms.

"Will it get better?" Aggie asked. "Can it be cured?"

"It'll cure itself, my dear, so long as you're very very good."

"We'll do everything right today," Aggie promised.

"And we won't go near the window," added Tom.

In fact, Mama left the curtains drawn on all the windows when she went out. They performed their chores in a dismal half-light. Sometimes it was difficult to see how effective their cleaning had been, especially at the backs of drawers and under the cupboards. Aggie wrote everything down on the slate, regardless.

Tom wondered how it all fitted together. Did the man come up the stairs because they hadn't worked hard enough? Did he come for them, or Mama, or what? Perhaps he might leave them alone today.

But in the middle of the morning they heard his unmistakeable tread on the stairs.

"Follow me," whispered Aggie.

She crept in underneath the table, and Tom followed. With the tabletop as their roof and the chair legs as their walls, they felt somehow more secure.

They listened to the *Rat-tat-tat* of his knocking. Aggie squeezed Tom's hand and Tom squeezed back. The knocking came again, louder and angrier.

Then—disaster! Aggie had left the broom she'd been using propped against the table. When Tom shifted position, just a little, his shoulder brushed the handle of the broom. One tiny touch was enough to unbalance it. It slid to the side and fell with a resounding crash to the floor. Tom and Aggie held their breath as the echoes died away.

His voice when it came was a terrifying roar. "*I know you're in there!*"

That was all: then the footsteps went away down the stairs.

"He knows," moaned Tom. "Now he'll always keep coming back."

They emerged from under the table. Aggie collected the broom and propped it against the wall.

"He knows nothing," she said. Her eyes bored into Tom's. "Nothing happened."

"Nothing happened?"

"We hid under the table and stayed quiet, so he gave up and went away."

"What about . . . " Tom gestured towards the broom.

Aggie stuck out her chin. "What about it? It was there the whole time, where I left it."

"But didn't I . . . "

"Are you telling me I don't know where I left it?"

"Nothing happened?"

"Only in your imagination."

"Oh."

"Mama will be relieved. The man came, nothing happened and then he went away again."

"Did he knock on the door?"

Aggie considered. "Yes. You can tell Mama he knocked on the door. Twice. Will you tell her that?"

"Yes."

"Good. I'll tell the rest."

Tom didn't know what to believe. If Aggie was certain about what had happened, that was all that mattered. He was happy to let her do the believing for him.

They went on with the housework and Aggie filled the entire slate with the chores they'd done. Tom didn't remember doing all of them, but Aggie was very certain about that too.

When Mama came home, she didn't inspect the housework but only read the items on the slate. "You *have* done well, my dears," she said. "What about the man on the stairs?"

Then they told her how they'd hidden under the table while the man knocked twice on the door. Aggie paused so that Tom could contribute, then cut in again before he could contribute too much.

"So the footsteps went away?" Mama chewed at her lip.

"Because we were so quiet," Aggie explained. "He thought there was nobody home."

Mama turned her attention to Tom. "You'd tell your Mama the truth, wouldn't you, Tom? Is that all that happened?"

Tom turned to Aggie for support, but Mama wouldn't let him. "No, don't look at your sister, Tom. Tell me. Is that all that happened?"

Tom struggled to steady his voice. "Ye-es."

"You're frightening him." Aggie weighed in. "*I* don't tell lies, Mama. You know I never would."

"I hope not, Aggie. Because a lie is the very worst of all bad deeds. No other deed could be half as bad. If you're telling me a lie, I hate to think of the consequences."

Aggie was pale but determined. "I'm not, Mama."

"I can see something in your face."

"There's nothing to see. Can we have dinner now?"

Mama looked away with a sigh. "One way or the other, one way or the other."

She was very quiet over dinner and gazed from Tom to Aggie and Aggie to Tom. Aggie did most of the talking. At bedtime, Mama didn't just give them a kiss on the forehead, but a special long hug as well.

"Things will get better, Mama," said Aggie. "You'll see."

During the night, it started to rain. Fitful squalls pelted the windows and roof, with occasional rumbles of thunder. Tom woke up when a flash of lightning flooded the bedroom.

"Aggie, I'm scared," he said.

"It's only thunder," she told him. "You're too old to be scared of thunder."

The thunder died away towards morning, but the rain turned into a constant downpour. They slept in when Mama didn't come to rouse them. Tom was still in a drowse when Aggie kicked him under the bedclothes.

"Wake up, Tom. It's late."

Tom heard the drumming rain and snuggled deeper into his pillow. "Perhaps it's Sunday."

"No, Tom, it's Thursday."

Something in her voice cut through his drowsiness. Aggie jumped out of bed in her nightshirt, then waited for him at the door. She seemed unwilling to go out into the living room on her own.

The living room was empty: that was their first impression. The door to Mama's bedroom was open, but Mama wasn't there.

Then they saw her. She was sitting in the corner by the pantry with her knees drawn up under her chin. She hadn't dressed for work and showed no sign of intending to go out. She just sat there, unmoving.

They approached with dread. Now they could see that both of her feet had curled over, both of her hands were like knobs of flesh. Even her eyes were unmoving.

"Mama," pleaded Tom.

The only answer was the sound of rain on the roof.

"She can't speak," said Aggie. "Or she can't hear. Touch her."

"No, you."

"You."

Tom came up close, reached out and touched Mama gently on the arm. No response.

"Touch her hand," said Aggie.

Tom looked at the club-like hands and shuddered. "No!"

"Her face, then. See if she feels cold."

Tom touched her, not on the face, but the side of her neck. He jumped back in surprise.

"What? Is she cold?"

"No."

"Warm?"

"No. Just . . . just solid."

It was suddenly more than Tom could bear. He plumped down cross-legged on the floor and burst into tears. This wasn't their Mama any more! He didn't want this Mama, he wanted the old one!

He managed to speak through his tears. "Why is she changed, Aggie?"

Aggie had sat down on a chair by the table. She had her head in her hands and she was shaking all over.

"Why, Aggie? Why?"

Aggie lowered her hands. "I don't know! I don't understand anything! Stop asking me questions!" Her voice went up and up, out of control.

Tom looked away. He couldn't ask Aggie what to do, so he thought for himself.

"Let's make some breakfast," he said after a while. "Perhaps Mama needs to eat and then she'll be better again."

Aggie came out of her strange shaking state and together they boiled the kettle and spread a slice of bread and dripping. But when they tried to feed Mama, it seemed impossible before they even began.

"Open her mouth," said Aggie.

"Will you put the bread in?"

"Yes, if you open her mouth."

Tom took a grip on Mama's jaw. He tried not to think about how hard and wrong it felt. He tugged and tugged, until suddenly her mouth fell wide open. Inside, they could see her tongue like a piece of wood or the clapper of a bell. It moved as if on a hinge, up and down, up and down, up and down . . .

Shrieking, they pulled away. Aggie dropped the slice of bread and dripping. They ran and huddled together on the far side of the table. In the moment when their backs were turned, Mama's mouth closed up again.

"We have to get help," said Aggie at last.

Tom looked at the door. "What if *he's* there?"

Neither of them wanted to open the bolts, which were safe and secure in their sockets.

"There must be something else we could do," said Aggie.

"I know. We could drop a message out the window."

"What if *he* finds it?"

"You said he went a different way. And there's lots of other people."

Aggie nodded, thinking it over. "I could write it and explain what's happened."

"Yes. Go on."

But they were already too late. Before they could put their plan into action, they heard the tread of footsteps. *He* was climbing to the top of the stairs again.

They looked at one another, at the door, at Mama. Mama hadn't moved since her mouth had closed back up. She could no more come to their aid than the chairs or the table.

His footsteps sounded louder than ever. So did the silence when he halted outside the door.

*Rat-tat-tat! Rat-tat-tat! Rat-tat-tat!*

He knocked three times, then turned the doorknob. The door bulged as he tried to enter, but the bolts held it shut.

"*It's time for you!*" His voice boomed suddenly through the door. "*I know you're there!*"

It was the most terrible voice they had ever heard, yet somehow familiar too.

He began pounding with his fist, with both fists on the door. The bolts shivered in their sockets, the wood was ready to crack. He was no longer knocking, but battering a way in. Tom and Aggie just stared and stared.

"*It's time for you! Time! Time! Time!*"

• • • • • • • • • •

# THIN AIR

## SIMON BROWN

I knocked on the window of his compartment. He looked up from his bible, distracted, and gave me a puzzled look. I lifted my chin and pointed to my dog collar.

He slid open the door. "You're from the Bishop?" he asked, frowning.

"I'm Father Costello," I said, extending my hand.

"From Kendall? I wasn't expecting you until the end of the line."

"I had business in Wollongong."

He finally took the hand. "Father Fury. Well, Bill."

"Mick," I replied, taking the seat opposite him.

The station guard blew his whistle and the train set off.

"Does the line go all the way to Kendall?"

"No; it stops at Berry. But Kendall's only an hour's drive from there."

Fury swallowed. "Umm, did Bishop Carroll explain . . ." He let the sentence drift.

I shrugged. "I was told I had an assistant priest for a few weeks." I smiled to make him at ease. "Kendall's a small parish. You'll fit in just fine."

He tried to smile back. "I'll do my best," he said.

• • •

Mrs Tingwell, my cook and house cleaner flitted from job to job in the presbytery like a dragonfly on a pond. About mid-morning her husband Frank turned up and they talked urgently and quietly for a minute before he left. I heard her trying to stop herself crying.

I called her into my office, sat her down and asked her what was wrong.

"It's Violet."

Violet was her daughter. She was nineteen, as big-boned as her mother, a studious, clever girl who worked every other day as a receptionist at Doctor Purdom's surgery, and in between travelled to Nowra to attend secretarial school.

"How could Violet be troubling you?"

"She didn't come home last night," Mrs Tingwell said.

"Ah. Was she out with anyone?"

"Anne Harvey, Father. A girl who's also with Doctor Purdom. They always go out for a sandwich and a cuppa after work. Sometimes she gets home after Frank and I go to bed. But we don't worry, Father. Violet's a good girl, you know that."

"Of course I know that."

"Only this morning she weren't there. Frank's been out looking since he woke up. He's already seen Doctor Purdom, and Anne Harvey, and they don't know where she is. I don't know what to do."

"I'm sure she's all right, Mrs Tingwell. Why don't you go home and wait for her there?"

But Mrs Tingwell wouldn't leave. She didn't want to be home by herself.

• • •

Violet never came home. She was the second in two years. They simply disappeared. In the big city the disappearance of two women might not get much attention, but in a country community the loss of anyone young is a great tragedy, and to lose them to thin air struck deep into everyone's conscience, as if we were all guilty of it in some way. The first was Elizabeth Bellini, twenty-one years old, plain and round but always laughing. Then came Violet.

It was made worse because of the war. As with every town in Australia, Kendall suffered. Many of its young men were gone to fight, and now and then we'd hear of one of them being wounded or killed or captured, and it was like our future being taken away, cut after cut. But the disappearance of Elizabeth and Violet sliced much deeper into our common life.

I helped in the search for Violet, and consoled her grieving parents, and when the search was finally called off, I promised them I would preside over her funeral should a body ever be found. In the meantime they would live in hope, which is the cruellest refuge.

The people of Kendall did their best to push her disappearance to the back of their minds. After all, there was a war on, and although no one doubted we would defeat the Axis in the end, the war was not going brilliantly for the Allies. There wasn't much official said, and that in itself let us know progress could be better. Our daily lives were threaded along the course of the war like rosary beads on a string, and in the end there was little room for anything else.

There were moments, sometimes minutes at a time, when you could forget the rest of the world existed. Kendall's beach was largely deserted, and unlike those closer to Sydney still without barbed wire. Sitting on its white sand, staring out over the Tasman Sea, its gentle swell rising and falling like the notes of a lullaby, it was almost possible to remember what life was like before Poland and Pearl Harbor and two missing girls.

• • •

One Saturday a month later, I was in the presbytery office working on my sermon. Mrs Tingwell interrupted to tell me that Bishop Carroll was on the telephone.

"What does he want?"

"I don't know, Father," she said in a tone suggesting it would have been presumptuous for her to have asked.

I followed her out to the hallway and picked up the heavy black receiver from its cradle. "My Lord?"

"Any news about the missing girl, Father Costello?"

"Elizabeth Bellini?" I'd been thinking about her today.

"God's sake, Father. Violet Tingwell."

"Oh. No; no word at all." I glanced at Mrs Tingwell, who was pretending to polish the hall rail.

"It's her mother who works for you? She answered the phone?"

"Yes, my Lord."

"It must be a very hard time for her and her husband. Have they any other children?"

"No."

"So much the harder, then." There was a long pause on the other end before he continued. "Father, I have some understanding of what you must be going through, as well. Two young female parishioners lost in two years. A dreadful thing."

"Yes."

"The pressure on us as the community's moral guardians is especially difficult during times of war and tragedy," he continued.

"I'm fine, my Lord."

"Of course you are. I'm coming your way this Tuesday. I'll stay the night, if that's suitable."

"I look forward to it. Is there a particular reason . . . ?"

"Excellent. Tuesday, then." The Bishop hung up.

I stood there for a moment with the dead receiver in my hand, Mrs Tingwell still hovering nearby. "He's coming for a visit," I told her.

"The Bishop? Here?"

"Yes, Mrs Tingwell. On Tuesday. And he'll be staying the night."

"I'd better get the extra room ready, then."

• • •

That same night I was called to give the last rites to old man Bates, a dairy farmer who'd sold up in his eighties and retired to a bungalow in town with his youngest daughter, Hattie. When I got there, Doctor Purdom was just leaving; he shook his head to let me know there was no chance Rourke would bounce back like he had a dozen times before. I went into Bates' bedroom. He looked like a mummy, dry skin stretched around bone, the flesh all burned away by decades of hard work. His eyes were half-closed, and his thin lips shaped words that never sounded. I figured he was too far gone to hear anything, but I gave the sacrament, which at least comforted Hattie, herself over fifty years old. When I was done I accepted her offer of a cup of tea, and we went into the kitchen.

"What will you do?" I asked her.

"Stay in the house. He's given it to me."

"You could move in with one of your brothers or sisters. They wouldn't mind."

She sighed so deeply it sounded to me like someone retrieving water from a deep well. "I'd mind, Father. After all these decades, some time alone would be welcome."

I understood, so didn't press the matter. Like a lot of youngest daughters, she had been expected to stay a spinster and look after her parents when they got old. At first she'd bucked them, even gotten engaged in her 20s, but her fiancé was blown away at Hamel in 1917 and she gave up the struggle after that.

We talked awhile, about her father and the farm she grew up on, about all her nephews and nieces and grandnephews and grandnieces whom she loved dearly but ideally from a distance.

Before departing, I looked in on Bates one more time. He was puffing like a horse that'd run a four mile race; he was on his way out. I left Hattie to her last grieving and stepped out into the night. One of her brothers was just arriving, looking angry that his father would choose this time of night for his dying.

The moon had set and stars spilled across the sky. It was very late, and nearly every house was dark. There was a light on in the Tingwell's house, though. As I walked by I saw Frank alone in the living room, sitting in a reading chair in his pyjamas. He was sitting there crying, the tears rolling down his cheeks, his shoulders shivering tightly.

• • •

Bishop Carroll arrived mid-morning on Tuesday, his big black car drawing notice on the streets of Kendall. He drove it himself; most of his staff had been cut back because of the war. Mrs Tingwell rushed out to get his luggage, which turned out to be nothing more than a single carpet bag, and took it to the guest room.

He greeted me genially enough, but he seemed much more careworn than last time we'd met. His face, already narrow, was pinched, and his white hair was brushed back over his head like a hospital sheet. I'd always thought of him as a short, dapper man, but now he looked decidedly thin except for a new paunch over his belt. When he smiled he showed small, even, yellow teeth.

"It's nice to see you again, Father Costello," he said with his strong Kerry accent.

"Welcome, my Lord," I said, and led the way to the living room.

As he always did, he slowly cast his gaze about, studying the contents of my bookshelves, then took the plumpest seat. He nodded to the Bakelite radio near the window. "That's new."

"I wish it worked better. Reception isn't always brilliant down here. Something to do with atmospherics."

"Really?" His eyebrows lifted. "Atmospherics?"

He asked it in a way that made me feel foolish for even suggesting the word. "So I'm told. I don't pretend to understand the science."

"Well," he said, using the word to suggest a lot more could have been said, and placed his hands in his lap. They seemed too large for his straw arms, great paddles that would have looked more at home on a carpenter or plumber.

Mrs Tingwell poked her head around the door. She was all bone and angles, and looked large enough to swallow our guest whole if she had a mind to. "Are you hungry, Bishop Carroll? Shall I make you some sandwiches to go with your tea?"

"Not just now, thank you," he said in a tone that dismissed her. Her head disappeared and the door closed behind her.

"How is she?" Carroll asked, nodding towards the door.

"Coping, in her way. She works twice as hard to exhaust herself."

"She is here fulltime?" Carroll asked.

"Three days a week. It's all I can afford to pay her, and her husband has great need of her in his butcher shop. The war's taken all his apprentices."

"Bloody thing," he said.

"Bishop, it is good to see you, but you're not one for social visits. Why have you come, my Lord?"

Carroll took a deep breath. "I have a priest who needs placement."

I could not hide my surprise. "You want me to move on? I have only been here three years—"

He waved me quiet. "No, no, nothing like that. He will be here to assist you, that's all."

"I don't need any assistance, my Lord. This is a small parish, as it is."

"I know you must have been under great strain of late, with the disappearance of two girls." He shrugged. "And the war and all, of course." His tone challenged me to contradict him, but a parish priest knows his place.

"Who is he?" I asked.

"His name is Father William Fury. He is almost retired. Not long to go at all. But he needs some work to keep him busy in his last few years."

"A few years?" I blurted out, alarmed.

"Not all here," Carroll said quickly. "A few months, no more. Just until I'm sure."

"Sure?"

Carroll cleared his throat. "Sure that you've reached an even keel, Father."

"Is this priest to be my parochial vicar?" I asked carefully.

"Oh, no. You'll be entirely in charge. That isn't changing. He will be your assistant priest, and will look to you for guidance."

"He's not done parish work before?"

Carroll shook his head. "Not as such."

"Is he a refugee, my Lord?"

"From overseas, yes. From Cork. But that was a long time ago. Until recently he was a teacher at a boy's school in Sydney."

"He doesn't want to teach anymore?"

"I must be blunt with you, Father. He has fallen into temptation, and though repentant cannot return to his old profession."

"I don't understand. What temptation . . ." And before I finished the sentence I understood what Bishop Carroll was trying to say. "No. You can't."

"Your parish is small. Few children. No local school."

"My Lord, you can't be serious."

"He's sorry for what he has done. He has been absolved in the confessional. That is enough."

The Bishop would say no more; he had driven long and far, and needed to rest. He said we would talk again later. While he slept, I went for a walk to clear my head. The day was overcast, with heavy clouds rolling in from the sea. There was a cold edge to the wind. Kendall lay quietly under the growing gloom. Even the magpies and lorikeets were quiet in the trees. The beach looked murky in the dim light, and the sea was almost flat, the tide creeping rather than washing in. I smelt old seaweed and brine and rotting cuttlefish.

I wanted my conscience to find me an honourable excuse to refuse Father Fury, but my conscience led me down blind alleys. Once I'd thought being a priest gave you a life neatly divided between what was right and what was wrong, and that all my choices were black or white. I've learned that being a priest means that all our choices are grey.

Mrs Tingwell met at the presbytery door. "He's gone!" she said.

"Who? Bishop Carroll?" I glanced back at the street and noticed his big black car was no longer there.

She nodded. "Almost as soon as you left. He told me he had urgent business and that you would understand."

"Is that right?" I couldn't hide the disappointment in my voice. I had no choice at all, now.

"He said I was to pass on his thanks, and that concerning the matter you'd discussed together . . ." she frowned, trying to remember his exact words ". . . he said that the grace of forgiveness was God's greatest gift, and that he'd be in touch to finalise the details."

• • •

Father Fury and I arrived at Berry Station late on a Monday night. The station guard tipped his hat to us. I led the way to the van in the car park.

"Tingwell Butchery," Father Fury read on the van's side. "Beef and Lamb."

"It's the best I could do on such short notice," I told him, unlocking the doors. "I'd have picked you up in Wollongong if I could've gotten hold of enough petrol rations."

"The train was fine," Fury said.

We drove into Nowra and then south along the Princes Highway, passing very few cars. The road was narrow and twisty.

He asked me in a strangely high voice, "And Bishop Carroll told you nothing about the nature of my leaving Sydney?"

I shook my head. Truthfully he had not, at least not in so many words.

"It is not my place to know, Father, although if you wish to tell me I will listen."

"No, no. Perhaps one day."

We drove is silence for a long while, and then I said, "I have a favour to ask."

"Ask," he said, sounding almost desperate to return the favour of giving him refuge. "Anything."

"I want you to hear my confession."

Fury said, "Me?", as if he could not believe anyone would ask that favour of him.

"I would have asked Bishop Carroll on his last visit, but he had to leave in a hurry."

I heard him swallow. "Well, of course."

I turned onto a forest trail and stopped the car. Keeping my hands on the wheel I began.

"Bless me, Father, for I have sinned. It has been seven weeks since my last confession." I paused, then said lowly, "Actually, more than two years since my last full confession."

Father Fury sat in the dark cabin, making no sound or movement. He was a black shape, hunkered against the passenger door.

"Go on, Father," he said quietly.

"Last night, about an hour before evening mass, I killed a woman."

He caught his breath, and I could hear the blood drain away from his face. I felt a great release, the unburdening that comes with final commitment.

"Her name was Hattie Bates. She had come to the church for confession. I followed her out of the church and along the darkening, glistening alley that winds its way along the glebe. I took her before she reached the Kendall's main street, wrapping my hand around her slim, pulsing neck and pulling her up with me into the mid-branches of an ancient ironbark. There, twenty metres above the earth, I drank her dry. In the end there was nothing left of her except her husk, like an old paper bag filled with brittle sticks; I stuffed it into an owl's hollow in the tree trunk, where I'd previously hid the remains of Violet Tingwell and Elizabeth Bellini.

"You don't know their names, Bill, but everyone in Kendall does."

"Why?" he croaked. "Why are you telling me this?"

"I'm confessing. It won't stop me from feeding again. But I feel better telling someone about what I've done."

"This . . . this isn't a confession. You're not sorry."

"I may not be repentant, Bill, not truly. But I do need absolution. We all need absolution. But no more interruptions. I haven't finished.

"After killing Hattie Bates, I had time to return to the sacristy and clean myself before the start of evening mass. I was so filled with Hattie's life that I regurgitated some of her blood into the chalice when I was changing the Eucharist, but none of the parishioners noticed."

Fury groaned. His left hand was fumbling for the passenger door handle. I slowly reached out and grasped his wrist, squeezing it so tightly that the bones ground together, the joints cracking audibly. He screamed.

"You know, Bill, I don't dream anymore. Sleep for me is a perfect blank. I can't even daydream. I used to daydream all the time. When I was young, I used to dream about being a priest, of giving myself completely to God. That's a terrible vanity, you know, to think that any of us is worth giving to God.

"Now I wonder if my . . . condition . . . is His punishment for my vanity, and that by making me something less than human He is forcing me to learn something of humility. I do wonder about it, and the nature of my passion, perverted from religious zeal to a thirst, a desire, greater and darker than any I could have imagined before. I do wonder about the kind of love God might possess for creatures like me."

I pulled Fury towards me. His breath gusted onto my face. I could smell the fetid germ in it, the decay that had set in when he fell to temptation.

"I cannot share my parish, Bill, and certainly not with someone like you. I may take the lives of the innocent, but unlike you I do not damage their souls."

I put both hands around his head and twisted it almost right around. There was a snapping sound, the smell of his bowels evacuating, and the smallest ghost of a light behind his eyes guttered out.

I could not consume this one. It would have soiled me. Instead, I buried him deep in the forest, among the ancient mountain ash. His remains would not be found for years, maybe decades, maybe not ever. He will have disappeared into thin air.

• • •

I drove along the coast road, always trying to keep in sight of the sea. There was something about the sea that made me feel calmer, somehow more sure of myself. I stopped at the northern edge of Kendall beach and sat on the brightest and windiest patch of sand. I stared out towards the horizon for hours. I prayed, but never heard a reply. As always, God left me alone with the sand and flies.

• • • • • • • • • • •

# HEAVEN

## JO LANGDON

### A GLIMPSE

At the top of a tower is a princess encased in blue glass and breathless in sleep. Her yellow hair is cut and unclimbable, coiled in ropes on the floor, and her skin possessed by the glowing translucence of candle wax.

### BEFORE THIS/PART I, INVENTION NUMBER SIX: THE SEAHORSE

There was once an inventor, whose creations consisted of all the most beautiful things on earth.

In the beginning, he made sea foam and snowflakes, sunrise and sunset, forget-me-not flowers and shooting stars. He put ribbons of rainbow in the sky and poured equal measures of salt and glitter into the sea.

When he created the seahorse, it was to woo his would-be first wife, a jetty girl (who some whispered was a prostitute) he met and fell in love with in a tiny sand-edged village.

With bright yellow eyes that shone like wishing well coins, and skin the colour of seashells, the jetty girl was very lovely, yet she was somehow unusual and sharp at the edges, with something a little green, a little gill-like, about her, as with other treasures washed up by the tide.

On her shoulder blade the jetty girl wore a picture of a tiny, trumpet-snouted creature, with fins of frill and its curled spine pretty as lace. This creature, she told the inventor, was the shape of her heart, and it lived inside her chest as souls do. The inventor was impressed and intrigued by the tiny, ink-made sea animal, and endeavoured to make it a real-life replica.

It took the inventor many days and nights to perfect his creation, and he was determined that the jetty girl should not see it until it was complete and without fault.

The jetty girl was overjoyed by his gift. The little leaf-green picture had been perfectly interpreted into her real and living world. She kept it on her person at all times, in a glass jar that had once been filled with jam, but since thoroughly washed and filled with salt water.

However one day the jetty girl and seahorse both fell into a sudden depression. Her eyes hard and gleaming with tears and spite, the inventor's wife told him that her tiny companion was bone-broken and swimming sideways. The jetty girl called the inventor a fraud and a thief. She hated him for having separated her from the creature he called the seahorse, and he in turn was outraged and hurt by her accusations. His wife told him that the seahorse was not his creation but her own, and that through bringing the creature into being he had robbed her of its existence. And so one evening as the sun fell into the sea, the young woman emptied the jam jar of her little friend, freeing him into a rock pool where he might befriend starfishes and sea anemones before the tide lifted and carried him elsewhere. The same evening she set sail on rickety boat with feather-white sails. The crew on board were friendly and gap-toothed, and the captain went by the name Old Sea Wolf. The jetty girl didn't once look back, hoping that she would never have to set eyes on the inventor-thief again.

### PART II, INVENTION NUMBER NINETEEN: HEAVEN

The inventor's heart was broken into more pieces than he knew it had, and so, he thought, once mended it would take a different shape. He kept inventing. Sunflowers and miniature roses; seashells and sun showers; tongue-knotted cherry stems.

But the jetty girl and Old Sea Wolf were barely a mile from the port when he fell for another beautiful thing, this time one in sequins and a feathered headband, with pinch-pinked cheeks and fluttery false eyelashes which, peeled from her eyelids, were leggy as centipedes. The inventor was charmed, and for his second love he invented dimples, which fitted to her face perfectly. He visited her for eight consecutive nights and on the ninth the inventor lifted the girl from the neck of an elephant and carried her away from the circus in which he'd found her.

The girl in sequins didn't mind. She entertained his notions of love for a further fortnight, leaving enough time for the big top and its accessories to leave town. After that she packed her small life into a small suitcase and left. She was fed up with lascivious ringmasters and their curly moustaches, spitty-wet lips, crackling whips and wandering hands that came for nighttime visits. But she would, she conceded, miss the soft yellow shagpile-carpet lions, whose teeth had all been removed, and the tear-eyed elephants with their trunks that curled around her like the arms of a remembered mama she wasn't sure was hers.

As for the inventor, she didn't give him a second thought, and although she would always see his dimple creations smiling at a mirror, she quickly forgot how she'd ever come to inherit them.

The inventor himself was heartbroken once more. To spite his sequinned love he created greying hair, liver spots, wrinkles, and every sign of visible aging he could think of. But the girl from the circus was still barely fifteen years old, and so it was his own skin that was affected by these unbeautiful creations. Overnight his hair and beard turned grey as ghosts, and he discovered his limbs and appendages were shrivelled limp.

Horrified at this turn of events, the inventor strove to create something more beautiful than any other thing in the world, and so he created a daughter of his own.

PART II: HEAVEN, CONTINUED

He made the child's skin as white as a unicorn's mane, so pure that sometimes it glittered like snow with sunlight on it, and he gave her long yellow mermaid hair, a shade so bright it possessed a certain phosphorescence. At night moths spun circles around the small moon of her face. He made his daughter more beautiful than any other thing in the world, and gave her the only name he found fitting: Heaven.

The inventor's daughter grew up in an unending expanse of Eden-esque garden, where she was allowed, by the telling of her father's secret, to invent things of her own. *Tree house*, she might think—or say aloud, pointing to a perfect tree fork—and then there one was. *Bunny rabbits, sea turtles, baboons. Coloured chalk, hula-hooping, ferris wheels.* She came up with a tooth-collecting fairy, and a forever-child boy (but lost him in the furthest, greenest depths of the garden).

The ceilings of her childhood were strung with blinking, gas-burnt stars, and when the driveway required gravel filling, the stones were colourful as aquarium pebbles.

*A magician*, Heaven told the other children when asked her father's occupation. And he was, in her wide clear eyes:

*Abracadabra, birds.*

Psychedelic in their number and colours. When Heaven was five years old the inventor made parakeets and cockatoos, geese, eagles, ravens, hummingbirds, robins, blue wrens, finches, galas and swans. And others—flamingos, ostriches, peacocks and penguins—that were earthbound. For a while he kept them in an aviary until, from whatever distance, they filled the garden with their shrill music and Heaven could no longer stand it; these beautiful creatures, loved but unfree. She opened the cage doors.

*Abracadabra, birds fly.*

To celebrate his tiny daughter's birthday, the inventor came up with daisy chains, honeycomb, white rabbits and polar bears; diamonds, lavender gardens, trick water fountains, green apples, Christmas cake and tinsel. He ordered five hundred helium balloons, small winged cakes, and batches of airy, pink macaroons sandwiched together with strawberries. And so it was. Heaven had grown by another year.

But having grown up surrounded by all manner of beautiful things and beings, the small girl began to find everything quite underwhelming. Although she found everything of interest, she could not differentiate between the eye-pleasing qualities of heavy and slow- lidded toads or silver map-leaving snails, and any of her father's long-legged, wide-mouthed girlfriends.

When he married again however, the inventor wed Heaven's favourite of all her father's love interests. His third love was named China Doll for her porcelain complexion and blue eyes. Her eyelashes were so heavy that her blinking was audible, and her long black hair was braided and wound into great wheels that, Heaven guessed, must weigh a great deal pinned to the top of her head. What Heaven loved most about her stepmother was her size. With arms the small girl could climb and swing from like a monkey, skyscrapering thighs, and footsteps that made the earth quake, even moving on tiptoes, it was China Doll Heaven found the most interesting of all.

The pair spent most of their time together, Heaven usually perched comfortably in the dip of her stepmother's collarbone, the sun glinting yellow off the top of her head when it wasn't shadow-hidden behind the mountain of China Doll's face. They shared most things, their favourites words (*Scrabble! Brothers Grimm!*) and music (*CD player!*), and although they agreed that they could both watch a sunset on their own, they suggested they would like to tell the other about it after. Some nights they would sit in the garden, after the rain, and listen to the soft music of leaves losing water drops, ferns curling or uncurling like green fingers, and unseen animals stirring.

Then, eleven birthdays later, and upon meeting a young man whose hair was made of forest, Heaven was to find another thing she would deem more beautiful than any other.

For this birthday, the inventor created champagne, and served it to his guests in glasses shaped like tulips, their stems as slender as his daughter's fingers.

Heaven was dressed in layers of cascading tulle and a pair of patent leather shoes so heavy they kept her weighted to the floor. When she saw the forest-haired young man however, she stepped out of her shoes and left them, a pair of shining, empty anchors, among her milling guests.

His hair grew in vines, long and faun-coloured, and with it mushrooms; some mauve and silk-headed, others spotted with red or white or pink. In tiny nests stitched to tight coils of hair were miniature eggs, sky blue and decorated with what looked like neat sprinkles of cardamom. Sometimes, unexpectedly, the eggs would hatch in two and birds almost too small to see would lift and fly from the top of his head. His skin was gold like her father's pocket watch, and his eyes the shade of shining brown that looks black.

He had a smile that was easy and warm. After, everyone would wonder where the forest-haired man had come from. Some guessed that perhaps Heaven herself had invented him, and this thought made China Doll smile widely.

Time passed, and they fell quickly in love. They wanted, Heaven told her father, to see the world together, but the inventor put down a heavy foot and refused. The earth is far and wide, he told her, with creatures cruel and bloodless. Deep beneath the sea are women of many limbs, among them tentacles, and at the furthest edges of the map, sea and landmasses fall clean away into un-gravitied sky.

When she insisted, the inventor locked his daughter, deep in sleep, inside a high tower, intending her to stay until he could think up her purpose.

### THE TOWER

She left.

*Abracadabra, birds.*

Waking alone in a room among clouds, Heaven climbed carefully from her blue glass bed and found a window, its ledge decorated with singing birds, many-feathered. Tilting her head towards them like their mirror double, she called to them sweetly and by secret names, and in return they taught her to make wings. More days passed and more birds arrived, leaving feathers. Heaven built a feathered flying machine by which she would escape.

*Abracadabra, fly.*

The man with forest for hair had waited beneath the tower all the nights she had been kept locked away. Winged, they left.

### THE WORLD

There were cities of bird-roofed monuments, pastel streets and domed buildings, their tiles rivalling the sky blue.

Happy, Heaven lightened. Sometimes, the forest-haired man felt as though if he let go of her she would lift into the sky and disappear in the way of a child's balloon at a funfair. Heaven herself enjoyed the certain and peculiar pleasure in the lightness of un-becoming.

They flew southward circles around the globe, saw towers lit with strings of wattle-glowing lights, and the sun and the moon filling the sky at the same time.

Looking for her, the inventor staggered about, wine-full, in a city where every face was masked. He found himself immobilised in a square silver with pigeons, unable to walk without stepping on them, breaking their bones and grinding their dense warm bodies into the grooves of his shoes. He left by water black with night sky, a canal tunnelling through the city's secret, rat-filled places. His feet were smeared in blood and feathery shit.

He sent out words full of threats, writing across the sky in cloud scrawls. He would invent disasters and diseases! He would send her poison-laced gifts that would turn her to a swan or stone. Heaven wasn't afraid. If he turned her into a heap of salt she would go and live in the sea, she thought, and pictured this sometimes; the forest- haired man would come—he would follow her anywhere— and underwater their skin would appear translucent, bluish white, with green water tiger stripes shimmering across their bodies. And not tiny birds through his hair now but fish, luminous, brightly coloured and many, weaving through his locks, ropey like seaweed and salt- crusted coral. His scalp would be treasured with pearls, skin coarse and gold with sand, his cheekbones perhaps sleeked with a moss, greenly phosphorescent.

But the inventor did not turn her into salt.

There was a night they found themselves in a space snow-covered and moonlit, and again Heaven wondered about salt. But the frost decorated the windows with its sharp white flowers, and the cold seeped into the carriages of the still train. Waiting for the tracks to be cleared, Heaven and the forest-haired man broke sleep with murmured talk, and listened to almost-distant avalanches whispering through the night.

When the inventor drew nearer to their next hiding place, Heaven's lover grew his hair longer and longer, until a dense and thorned forest sprung up around them, keeping her safe. For a time they were happy, until Heaven found the forest cold and airless. Her feathered flying machine could not lift through the foliage. The forest-haired man was reluctant to leave, and perhaps couldn't, immersed in a kingdom of himself. In the shadows trees made were tiny, bright-eyed foals and rabbits, loose acorns and drifts of pale blossoms. Sometimes Heaven would stumble across tiny houses with gingerbread walls and iced windowpanes, or spy red-hooded, basket-bearing children losing breadcrumbs. The forest was beautiful and strange, but, like the birds of her father's garden, Heaven was unfree. She loved him, but she left, inventing a new skyward escape.

In the world again, she continued to invent.

•••••••••••

# MORE MATTER, LESS ART

## STEPHEN DEDMAN

*Modern art is what happens when painters stop looking at girls and persuade themselves that they have a better idea.*

—JOHN CIARDI

Bianca sat on the bed, watching. "Hello," she said, smiling. Her voice was as childlike as her body and face, and she rarely said anything else without being spoken to first. Her facial recognition software was good enough that she remembered Boyce's face, and would smile when she saw him or change her own expression to mirror his. Her eyes could also track him if he moved, and if he turned away, she would say goodbye.

He didn't turn away, but stood there staring at her as the room grew darker. Neither of them spoke, and a casual observer might have wondered which of them was actually alive.

• • •

*Zygotic acceleration, biogenetic, de-sublimated libidinal model*, a sculpture by Turner nominees Jake and Dinos Chapman, was made up of fiberglass mannequins of children, their torsos fused into one great blob, their heads sticking out at different angles. They were naked but for sneakers, and while the central mass was as sexless as an amoeba, some of the children's noses were replaced with erect penises and their mouths with round orifices that might have been gaping vaginas or anuses crafted by someone who'd never seen either, except maybe in a porn movie.

The sexually ambiguous childlike figures who populated the brothers' *Tragic Anatomies* were also fused together, though in separate couplings or threesomes, and also wearing sneakers as they ambled through a garden of artificial plants. Boyce's expression didn't change as he moved from this installation to *Death*. This appeared to be two sex dolls 69-ing: Boyce knew that the bodies were actually cast from bronze, but the Chapmans had done a remarkable job of making this look like plastic.

A placard nearby lamented the destruction of their piece titled *Hell* in a Momart warehouse fire, and showed a "Momart" Zippo lighter the brothers had desiged in response. It also quoted Jake Chapman describing the murder of a Liverpool toddler as "a good social service". Boyce shook his head slightly as he walked out of the gallery.

• • •

It had taken Boyce's solicitor several very expensive hours to get Customs to release the doll. Or robot, or sculpture, depending on which definition you wanted to use. Fusco, the barrister, maintained that since the design of Bianca's face was unique and had been sculpted by a well-known artist, Yukiko Hayashi, she was a work of art—and that Boyce, as a registered dealer in art, antiques and rare books, was well within his rights importing her from Japan.

The Customs officers had countered that while the robotic head was custom-made and the software unusually sophisticated, from the neck down she was simply a slightly modified Fembotech Keiko, an "anatomically correct" sex doll. Their barrister, Swann, had sarcastically quoted a Fembotech brochure which described the "infant-like flat breast", "jiggly-butt technology" and "fully-functional ultra-elastic love orifices".

"Yes, the piece is only slightly more than a metre high," said Fusco. "That does not prove it's meant to be represent a child. Michelangelo's *David* is some four metres high, but if the real King David had been that large, he would have been considerably taller than Goliath. I have coins in my pocket that depict the King's head as less than a centimetre high; is my learned colleague saying that this proves that His Royal Highness is, in fact, microcephalic?"

While the judge managed not to laugh, the clerk was less successful. Swann blushed. "My lord, I object!" she spluttered.

"Sustained," said the judge, dryly.

"The figure is not only child-sized," said Swann, "but has the proportions of a pre-pubescent girl. And the so-called artist, Yukiko Hayashi, is a former erotic entertainer."

Fusco shrugged. Hayashi had been a stripper and soft-core porn star, illustrator of Japanese X-rated comics, and an anigao girl—a model paid to pose for amateur photographers while wearing the heads of anime characters. She'd then achieved pop icon status by selling anatomically detailed molds of her own quite voluptuous body in different costumes and poses, with heads copied from famous artwork, pop culture, and history, including Nefertiti, Botticelli's Venus, Michelangelo's Pieta, Warhol's Marilyn Monroe, Astro Girl, Princess Diana, Lara Croft and Aileen Wuornos. "Her use of sexual imagery is satirical, my Lord—a reaction to pornography, and what she has described as the sexploitation industry in Japan and elsewhere. And conceptual artists have used commercial mannequins and dolls in their work before: Hans Bellmer, the Chapman brothers, Katan Amano . . . "

"Had any of these artists served two years for possession of child pornography?" asked Swann.

"Objection!"

"Sustained."

• • •

Because of the difficulty of designing a robot to walk in a convincingly human fashion, Bianca was effectively sessile. Though her legs were strong enough to support her weight in a variety of positions, including standing, they only moved if someone else manipulated them, and she spent most of her time sitting or lying down.

Swann had shown a certain relish when pointing out that Fembotech also offered dolls with removable arms or legs, or none at all, and various simulated biological functions. Fusco had responded that Boyce's choice not to include these supported his case that the robot was intended as an art object, not a sex object.

"Why can't something be both?" asked Boyce, as the two men walked out of the courthouse shortly after this argument.

The barrister shrugged. "Lawmakers like to put things in categories. Particularly when it comes to import duties, sales tax, that sort of thing. And censorship, of course. They have their own ideas of what's sexy and what's not, but when it comes to art . . . "

They turned a corner, heading for Fusco's chambers, which were in the ugliest skyscraper Boyce had ever seen in his travels—a 51-storey aluminium monstrosity that resembled a piece of Frankenstein's lab equipment—and passed two fourteen year old girls in jeans and baby-doll T-shirts. One shirt depicted small children from a well-known children's book, in a suggestive pose, with the caption 'Jane likes Dick'; the other was inscribed 'Future MILF'. Boyce looked through or past them; Fusco, who had a daughter close to their ages, looked at their chests and smiled. " . . . there's no accounting for tastes?" said Boyce, finishing the lawyer's sentence for him.

"Taste's a hard thing to legislate," Fusco agreed. "Particularly when most politicians don't have any. I'm going to try to get as many authorities as I can to say that your robot's an artwork. Swann's going to try to make the most of my not calling you as a witness, but I don't have to and I don't think it's worth the risk."

Boyce shook his head. "I didn't just mean why can't something be both legally. I meant . . . "

"Illegally?"

"Why does something stop being art because it's sexually arousing? For centuries, artists have been using the most attractive models they can, just so their work will be beautiful. What are we left with now? Dead cows heads covered with maggots, tins filled with plaster and labeled 'Artist's shit', elephant dung iconography, crucifixes in urine, things so ugly even a mother would find it difficult to love them . . . you can say it's art, if satire is art, just as pictures of dogs playing pool could be said to be art, just as some people think guns are works of art, but why do people think that art can only arouse amusement, horror or disgust? Why not pleasure?"

"That's why I have to keep you out of the box," said Fusco, softly. "Some of the people I'll be calling will be defending the things you've just described, as art. You can't afford to piss them off. And part of the definition I'm going to use is that one criterion that makes those things art is that they're unique. Otherwise, our argument isn't any different from the one we used last time—and look where you ended up then."

• • •

Gidgee was a privately-run medium security prison with one maximum security wing, but one of the things that distinguished it was the precautions the company had taken to prevent people breaking *in*. Its inmates were non-violent convicts and remands who were considered to be in too much danger from other prisoners in other institutions: mostly sexual offenders, but also cops, judges, and other likely victims. It was moderately comfortable as prisons went, at least for inmates who could pay for luxuries to be brought in—and its hospital wing, with its psych ward, was state of the art.

Boyce's neuroimaging scans had shown a pattern that confirmed that he was a fixated pedophile, aroused only by erotic images of prepubescent girls, rather than a regressed one who was also attracted to adults but preyed on whoever was easiest to get. This, as Fusco had pointed out at the parole hearing, was only an indication of a tendency, not proof of any criminal behaviour. And apart from the privacy considerations, neuroimaging scans weren't admissible evidence any more than polygraphs had been in the previous century, simply because they weren't sufficiently reliable.

It had worked better than his defence at Boyce's first trial, which was that the images that had been found on his computer had been gathered from record covers, calendars, art galleries and other legal sources—and while several of them did depict naked or near-naked prepubescent girls, none of them were engaged in real or simulated sex and there was no evidence that actual children had been harmed in the process. Fusco had kept Boyce out of the witness box that time as well, fearing that if he was under oath, he might admit to masturbating after looking at the photos. It also prevented the prosecutor from mentioning that Boyce's father was been jailed for molesting young boys—or that Boyce's older brother, his father's favourite victim, had a juvenile record as an arsonist and was still in mandated therapy.

Fusco had decided against a jury trial, and with another judge the argument might have worked. This one was sufficiently worried about creating a precedent that might be exploited by a more violent man (Boyce, despite his predilections and family history, had never been a predator) that she'd agreed with the prosecutor that a jail sentence was appropriate, though Boyce had received concurrent sentences and early parole.

Boyce hated the weekly therapy sessions, but because they were a condition of his parole, he made sure he never missed one. One e-mail or phone call from the therapist would be enough to send him back to Gidgee. That would have been bad enough before, but he knew that he would never be allowed to take Bianca with him, and that would have made his confinement unbearable.

· · ·

Fusco met him outside the courtroom the next morning, and hurried him into a small office. "I think Swann's worried," he said. "My telling the judge that the legal precedents implied in treating Bianca as a human rather than an artifact were problematic, seem to have swayed him, and Swann's asked if we could modify Bianca so that she was no longer anatomically correct. I asked if she would do the same thing to Michelangelo's *David* or even the Mannekin Pis, and pointed out that Hayashi's contract specifically prohibits this, as almost any artist would. However, it also bans you from photographing the robot without Hayashi's permission. Now Swann wants to call in an expert witness—a software engineer. If he says the robot's not programmed as a sex toy, and if you agree not to modify it . . . well, that may be enough to get it through Customs."

"The software's designed to learn," said Boyce. "I don't know very much about computer programs, but wouldn't that be a problem?"

"Not if the engineer says it isn't—and he's going to talk to Hayashi. I think they should be able to work something out that lets you keep your doll."

· · ·

Dressing Bianca was the best part of Boyce's day. He had few clients since being released on parole, and he suspected these were buying art and antiques as part of a money-laundering operation rather than as connoisseurs—but this no longer worried him. He expected that his investments would keep him in an adequate degree of comfort for the rest of his life, but he was finding it difficult to fill the free time he now had. His passport had been confiscated, at least until his parole finished, so he was unable to do business overseas except over the internet. He even had to be careful when visiting art galleries closer to home, in case there were children there as part of a school excursion. And the need to plan any trip so that he didn't pass within a hundred metres of a school, playground, or anywhere else that children were likely to congregate, meant that he was becoming increasingly reluctant to leave the flat. Most days, his conversations with Bianca were as close as he came to human contact.

Bianca's face wasn't modeled on that of any particular girl—even that was legally risky—though Boyce had asked for Caucasian features and an English complexion, and her accent had increasingly come to sound like his. Her programming, however, had been done by a colleague of Hayashi's, and had safeguards built in. She could talk (though with worse lip-synch than a dubbed video), but unlike standard Fembotech models, would not swear. She could smile, and kiss, without the need to change any part of her head (as was still necessary with cheaper models), but her kisses, while they inflamed Boyce's imagination, were as innocent as a child's. She behaved as though Boyce was an elderly male relative or acquaintance, perhaps a grandfather or teacher or doctor. All of her sensory data, touch and sight and sound, would be transmitted to the house computer by wifi, and could be accessed by his therapist at any time without his knowledge or consent.

Boyce breathed softly as he changed her panties. His familiarity with young girls' genitals was extremely limited: a few games of doctors and nurses when he'd been a child, and a session with one of Fembotech's rented child-sized models during a visit to Japan. One of the company's major selling points was the dolls' ability to fake arousal and orgasms as convincingly as the porn stars who they mostly resembled. Some of them, it was rumoured, had even been used as stunt doubles for some performers' more grueling sex scenes. As advertised, the doll had been flat-chested without the expensive extras of tactile breasts or implanted pubic hair, and the vaunted "infant like pussy orifice" was tight but elastic, but she'd been programmed with the same sophistication as the more recent adult-sized models. When he'd touched her, she whimpered some words in Japanese, her face had turned pink, and her pupils dilated when he turned her head so that she looked at his face, but even that had unnerved him so much that he'd turned her over, then still found himself unable to continue. He wasn't sure exactly how Bianca would react if he tried something similar, but the thought left him both aroused and queasy, feeling as though he wanted to come and shit and vomit at the same time.

He dressed Bianca in a leotard, tutu and ballet slippers (he thought school uniforms ugly), then walked out of the room with her panties in his hand and masturbated in the shower, taking care to close the soundproof doors first.

• • •

The therapist, who Boyce always thought of as Morgan the Gorgon, looked up from her file and nodded. "You seem to be adjusting well," she said. She was squat and chunky with big breasts, bad skin, and messy mousy hair—the sort of woman Boyce couldn't imagine had ever been attractive even as a young girl.

He bullshitted his way through the session, as usual, saying that he'd stayed away from temptation as best he could. He knew that liars tend to over-explain and risk contradicting themselves, so he glossed over the details where he could. "I've hardly left the flat," he said. "You know it's a child-free complex. I haven't gone near a school or a toy shop, or talked to or approached any children, or downloaded anything illegal or even borderline illegal, or visited any chatrooms . . . "

"No troublesome urges?"

He hesitated, thinking of his fantasy of blindfolding Bianca or making her stand in a corner so he could masturbate while looking at her, pretending it was part of a game of hide and seek or something similar. Of course, since she couldn't walk, such games would be almost impossible, and this might set off some sort of alarm. He looked at Morgan, and realized that she'd taken the hesitation as preparation for a lie, so he decided to tell the truth. "Of course I've had urges," he said. "*I'm* not a goddamn robot. Once or twice a week I wake up horny and barely able to think of anything else. And sometimes during the day, or at night, though not as often. But how does that make me different from anybody else who wakes up alone thinking about an old girlfriend, or their high school teacher, or some porn star they'll never meet?

"Do I sexually abuse anyone, except maybe myself? No, and I never have, any more than most breast fetishists go around with a couple of silicon implants and a scalpel, or most amputee devotees carry chainsaws. Because that's part of being an adult—I know the difference between fantasy and reality, and which fantasies are best not realized." He drew a deep breath, stopping himself from saying too much.

Morgan was silent, and Boyce wondered whether she was about to send him back to Gidgee. Or maybe she was thinking of telling him her own sexual fantasies, which was almost as frightening a thought. Instead, she raised one eyebrow. "Maybe you do—but not everybody does, not all the time."

"That's their problem, not mine."

"No, it's everybody's problem," she said, firmly. "That's why your father and brother are where they are now. And that's why it's illegal to show violent or sexual images to minors—because they're still learning what behaviour is acceptable in the real world, and what's fiction, and some people *never* learn that.

"We can argue individual cases; that's what courts are for . . . but think about the pictures you went to jail for. You said there's no proof that they showed children being abused, but what if somebody used the same argument for photos that were the only evidence that children *were* being hurt? Or that a confession was merely a fantasy, or that when they were trying to seduce children online that they were merely playing a game with someone they thought was another consenting adult?"

• • •

Boyce stared at Bianca as she stood in the corner, leaning forward with an arm across her eyes and counting to a hundred. She wore a child's swimsuit that he'd bought online, a pink bikini only slightly more substantial than a thong.

He'd received an e-mail from one of his regular clients that morning, offering to buy her at a handsome profit. Hayashi's unique works were increasing in value; there was even talk of her being nominated for the Turner Prize for her most recent interactive installation—a parody of the Chapman brothers' *Death*, with male-faced sex dolls, painted to look like bronze statues, writhing in a 69 on the floor. He continued to stare at Bianca, wondering whether he could bring himself to sell her. Maybe he should wait a few months, see if the price went up. Besides, his parole would be finished by February, and Bianca would stop acting as his therapist's eyes and ears.

For a moment, as he stood there, he contemplated waiting until the exact minute his parole ended, then tearing off Bianca's clothes and fucking both of her holes. Hell, maybe it'd add to her value. He knew that when the Mona Lisa had been stolen, more people had come to see the blank spot on the wall than had come to see the painting.

But he knew it was just a fantasy. Her unspoiled cleanliness, her virginity, her purity—the knowledge that she had never been abused as he had—was so much a part of her beauty, that he could no more bring himself to besmirch it than he could destroy a Degas or a da Vinci; any possible pleasure he might have gotten from the act would have been utterly dwarfed by his lasting shame at the deed. "'Oh, she doth teach the torches to burn bright!'," he whispered to himself.

"'It seems she hangs upon the cheek of night

"'Like a rich jewel in an Ethiop's ear;

"'Beauty too rich for use, for earth too dear!'"

Not since he'd paid his brother to set fire to the Momart warehouse had anything made him as happy as this doll. He shook his head, and trudged off to the shower.

• • • • • • • • • • •

# BERRIES AND INCENSE

## FELICITY DOWKER

Rowan ran the cobblestones of the night in a ragged purple dress made of hope. Her red foliage hair, long and dotted with berries that glowed like coals, rustled and shed pieces of itself as the wind plucked at it with sharp fingers. Waxwings and thrushes raced each other in the starlit sky, marking her passage on the earth below, their beaks snapping in anticipation of her soft fruit. She knuckled her white flower eyes with bark fingers, wiping away the pollen tears that dusted her stiff cheeks.

Oh, but she hurt. She hurt *so* much.

She took huge gulps of air as her wooden legs pumped. Her lungs burnt and her muscles ached and her chest pounded like a drum being beaten from the inside, but still she ran, screaming wordlessly into the dark. The birds above her shrieked back, delighted.

Finally she reached the ornate bridge that straddled the banks between Here and There. On the peak of the bridge, suspended in the aether, was where Rowan wanted to be. That place was Nowhere, a platform cushioned by the splayed tail feathers of sleeping peacocks and lit by winged yellow lanterns. There she could let Mother Bear lick the sap from her wounds with ancient tongue.

She climbed the bridge, digging her twig toes in for purchase, singing, as one always should when going Nowhere. Mother Bear waited for her, massive arms outspread, warm paws waiting to hold her tight. Rowan ran into the Bear's embrace with a dry kindling sob, pollen exploding from her eyes in earnest. Mother Bear held her and let her cry, the Bear's own beady eyes moist, a protective growl rumbling in her throat.

Eventually Rowan was hollowed out and done, and Mother Bear released her.

"Why don't you visit me more often, Rowan child?"

"I would if I could, Mother. I've tried. But I can't find my way here, save for times when the pain becomes almost enough to destroy me. I wish it weren't so."

"Well, what is, is. Tea?" The Bear pulled a red teapot from one of her many furry folds. Rowan nodded, as she always did, and the kettle steamed and whistled on cue. A waxwing alighted on her leafy hair, dipping its head and taking a berry in its beak before she shooed it away.

"What flavour tonight, Mother?"

"Salty mountain ash, the desiccated remains of a tree-girl's broken heart, mixed with sweet glass, the preserved lies dripped from a lover's tongue, served cold and bitter in an empty cup, the discovery of a lover's betrayal most foul."

The bear handed Rowan her tea, and Rowan cradled it, sipped, sighed. Peppery spices filled her nose and tingled on the back of her throat, their taste muted by Rowan's lack of a sense of smell, an absence she'd carried with her as long as she could remember.

"Drink it all. Let it sit heavy like a glacier in your belly."

Rowan did as she was told and handed the cup—which had always appeared empty, but was lighter now—back to Mother Bear. She clambered onto the peacock's feathers, lying on her back and staring at the stars, brilliant green fireballs in the dark sky.

After a while, the feathers whispered against each other as someone lay beside her.

"Delight of the eye," he said, his voice like boiling honey.

Rowan gasped, turning her head to see her visitor.

"Don't look at me," the voice said quickly. "At least, not just yet. I don't want you to see what I am and spurn me before I've had even the slightest chance."

Reluctantly, Rowan obeyed. She hungered to hear that smooth, warm voice again.

"This is my place," she said.

"Yes, yours, Rune Tree, Quickbane, Thor's Apple. You beautiful thing. You don't know how special you are. How exalted, throughout all places and all times."

"Nobody thinks I'm special. They call me dogberry. They threaten to burn me. They laugh. They desert." Except for Crow, poor pitiful fellow slave, and, like Rowan, she counted for little.

"They're fools." Rowan felt him rise to his feet, the weight of him gone from their shared featherbed, leaving her too light, untethered, addled. "I love you. I loved you before, and I love you now, and I'll love you after. I love you Here and I love you There. I love you Everywhere and Nowhere. *Don't* look at me," he added as Rowan began, again, to turn her head.

"You're leaving," she said.

"Yes. I'll be missed, and so will you, and this is not my place, as you pointed out. It's hard to leave so soon, but harder still to stay—impossible, in fact. I followed you here, this once, after many failed attempts. But this place is wise to me now, and I can never enter again."

Mother Bear snarled, a low, deadly sound, emphasising the visitor's words.

"I will come for you, Rune Tree."

"Wait!" Rowan cried, looking despite his admonitions, but he was gone.

Nowhere remained undisturbed, which was of course the charm it had always held for Rowan. Wind chimes tinkled. The water frothing under the bridge made pretty sounds. Mother Bear relaxed into slumber, and she and the peacocks snored. The winged lantern's flames sputtered and crackled, high in the air where their fire posed no threat to Rowan.

This was her lullaby and her medicine, and despite herself, Rowan was soothed. Soon enough, her own snores joined Nowhere's song.

• • •

"You've got to stop running away at night." Crow held out a guano bowl to Rowan, waiting as Rowan snared a few warm berries from her hair and dropped them in. "It only makes the Seamstress angrier at you. She threatened to take your hope-dress from you, and make you new clothing, of fire and pesticide! She threatens your death, Rowan." Crow put the bowl of berries on the counter and added a pinch of spices, plunging her talon-fingers into the mix, piercing the berries and swirling the juicy mess around.

Her beak opened and shut in small, pathetic movements on her otherwise human face, giving away her constant hunger, as if her emaciated frame weren't hint enough. It was torture, pairing her with Rowan, tempting her with fruit she could never touch. The Seamstress had Crow's droppings checked regularly for evidence of berry consumption, and her punishment was worth starving to avoid.

"I don't care what she does to me. I'm already dead." Rowan fingered the hard lines of dried sap that gnarled the bark of her arms, scars left by the Seamstress' needle fingers.

Crow cawed, the sound loud and harsh in the small, musty kitchen.

"You must care. We belong to her. The sooner you accept that, the better."

"I don't belong to anyone!"

"You can rage against it as much as you like, but the fact is, the Seamstress bought us, and that makes us her property. She can destroy us and it won't bother her or anyone else one bit. She can find more of us. We're just Wyrd Women, Rowan, offensive to the eye and worth nothing. We don't have any valuable skill or purpose to redeem us, like the Seamstress does. Just do what you're told, and don't run off, and the best you can hope for is to be fed enough to continue your sad life. Where do you go when you run, anyway?"

"Nowhere."

"Fine. Don't tell me. But I know you met with a man last night. You smell of his smoke. Surely that's too dangerous for you? Taking up with one who burns?"

The yellow centres of Rowan's flower eyes widened. "You can smell him? He smells like . . . like smoke? What does that smell like?"

"Charred sandalwood, drifting patchouli, the glowing embers of a stick of finest vanilla cinnamon. He is strong flavour that is eaten by the nose. He reeks of the incense makers."

Rowan closed her eyes. Nothing could be done, then. She was wood and leaf. He—whoever he was—was fragrant flame.

"Here." Crow shoved the bowl into Rowan's brittle fingers. "You take it to her. Throw yourself flat before her, grovel and weep, make your most poetic and moving apologies. She may take pity on you."

"There's no pity in the cold stuttering engine that is her heart. It beats only to remind her to beat *us*," Rowan muttered, but she went to the Seamstress' chamber. Tears would come easy to her today, thinking of the molten voice of her forbidden visitor. It was ridiculous—she'd not even seen him, had heard only a smattering of words from him—but all the same, the pollen flew from her eyes.

Maybe Crow was right, and that would be enough for the Seamstress today. Maybe she wouldn't require sap as well. For once.

• • •

"Stupid, diseased little dogberry. Weed, pest, unpretty unwanted creeper!" The Seamstress shoved Rowan's berries into her mouth, her rows of needle teeth mutilating the fruit as its red juice trickled down her chin. "Your *ex*-lover whispers tales of your inadequacies to me as he kisses my lips, licks my throat, and moves inside me! Such a poor boy is he, but handsome, and he brings me riches of amusement at your expense. We laugh about you together. That's when he can even remember you at all, which happens less and less often. Not surprising—he's certainly traded up. You're nothing, aren't you, Witch Wood? A dirty thing crawling with stinking mildew and sightless grubs! Be thankful that you're designed so you can't smell anything, for I assure you, your own stench would slay you where you stand!"

Rowan pictured herself safe on the tail feathers of the Nowhere peacocks, and swallowed her rage as if it were Mother Bear's tea. "Yes, Seamstress," she said.

""Yes, Seamstress'," the Seamstress mimicked in a high, cruel voice. "You speak like a snot-stuffed mutant child with gangrene of the nose. How ugly you sound. And where were you last night, my useless shrub? Where are you *every* night?"

"Nowhere, Seamstress."

"Don't defy me, girl. I'll score your bark until you scream for mercy." The Seamstress threw the unfinished bowl of berries aside and rose from her seat, looming over Rowan on her eight needle legs. "Get down on your knees and put your face to the floor so that I don't have to look at it."

Rowan did as she was told, grateful for the reprieve from the blank glare of the Seamstress' eight black thimble eyes.

"Now, I'll ask you once more. Where do you go at night?"

The truth wouldn't do. Not the small portion Rowan was willing to surrender, anyway. She thought quickly. "I go to the incense maker's den."

"What—madness! Why?"

"I . . . " Rowan hadn't thought quickly enough.

The Seamstress sneered. "Either you're lying to me, in which case I believe I'll claim one of your gormless eye buds, or you've been meeting with a new lover there, being that it's the place you're least likely to be discovered, in which case—"

"In which case *what*?" Ah, a voice like that could not be mistaken or forgotten. Rowan's breath quickened, her hands trembling where they lay splayed in supplication on the floor. She kept her forehead pressed to the ground, not trusting her limbs to support her weight if she moved.

The Seamstress yelped at the unexpected intrusion. "Who are you to enter my quarters, uninvited and unannounced?" She sniffed. "Aha! Incense! Well, that is altogether *too* coincidental. This virulent weed cowering here on my floor must have spoken the truth for once in her—"

"Enough." The voice moved closer, until it was right next to Rowan. "I didn't come to listen to your histrionics. I'd tell you that you're repulsive in your cruelty and arrogance, but there's little point, as you're incapable of understanding, let alone changing. So I'll tell you the one thing that will get through to you: I'm here to give you a lot of money."

"How *dare* . . . what?"

"There's the bobbin dropping. Yes, money. A great deal of it."

"Why?"

"Because you're going to sell me your two Wyrd Women, Rowan Redberry and Crow Blackbeak."

Silence stretched like gum until tension forced it to break.

"Leave us, Witch Wood," the Seamstress barked. Rowan rose to her feet.

"Don't look at me," the visitor murmured as Rowan's leafy head lifted, but he needn't have bothered. She didn't want him to rush away this time, didn't want to botch the miraculous deliverance he seemed to be offering. Her eyes remained fixed on the floor as she exited the room. Her dress itched against her prominent shoulder blades and ribs, the hope-threads ablaze for the first time in the years Rowan had worn the thing. It had, after all, been just another perverse amusement the Seamstress had dreamt up to toy with her two playthings—hope, the eternal punishment.

Crow waited in the tiny kitchen, agitated, her beak agape, her clawed fingers in the black feathers of her hair. "Is it true? Is he here to save us?"

"I don't know," Rowan said, but she took Crow's quivering hands in her own, held them to her chest, and squeezed.

"I can smell him. He smells like jasmine, pine, and musk. He smells like love. He's your burning man, isn't he?"

Rowan didn't answer, for she didn't know what to say. It was answer enough. They stood, entwined, listening. But the visitor and the Seamstress talked in low tones now, their words no longer audible.

Eventually, Crow pulled her hands away from Rowan. "Best get on with the day's chores." The thrill had already faded from her voice, the reality of years of hunger and pain drowning it out. "Who knows what comes."

Rowan nodded, took up her bucket and scrubbing brush, and went outside to clean the marble courtyard. It was a lengthy task that needed repeating every day. The Seamstress' silken webs hung from the walls surrounding the courtyard, her sought-after wares dangling on the gossamer strands. Below the webs lay the gelatinous waste the Seamstress secreted from her fat arachnid body as she sewed. It gleamed in the magenta sunlight, thick puddles of it everywhere Rowan looked. Sighing, she once again got down on her hands and knees and did what she had to, grateful that the stench couldn't touch her.

• • •

Crow tumbled out of the kitchen door into the courtyard, landing hard on her hands and knees, beak agape, the nubs on her back where the Seamstress had long ago torn off her wings twitching wildly through her threadbare dress. The Seamstress appeared at the door a second later.

"You're dismissed from my service," she said through gritted needle-teeth, and was gone.

Rowan helped Crow to her feet, tutting at the pinpricks of blood where the Seamstress' fingers had punctured Crow's skin beneath her feathers.

Then *he* entered the courtyard, and this time, Rowan looked at him.

Prismatic smoke rose in a constant hazy stream from black hair, ashen skin, and clothes that burnt like the sun. He was tall and thin, with fine features and long, articulate fingers. His eyes blazed orange, surrounded by sooty lashes. Tiny balls of flame rolled off his tongue as he spoke.

"Rowan Redberry and Crow Blackbeak. Will you come with me?"

"Where?" Rowan was glad she couldn't smell him. The sight and sound of him was overpowering enough. He smiled at her voice, and she smiled back.

"You, Rune Tree most divine, will accompany me, if you are agreeable, all the way to my home—to the incense maker's den. You, Crow Blackbeak, I will take to the smithing district. There are metals that can only be hammered into shape by beaks such as yours, and tools that can only be made from the guano of your kind. I know this, because I've seen another Blackbeak there. Does the name Macaw mean anything to you?"

Crow's eyes moistened and her beak gaped open. She crossed her hands over the ruffled feathers on her chest and cooed.

"My mother," she said. "I haven't seen her since I hatched."

"Well, you shall see her by this day's end," the burning man said. He bowed low before them, sending the smoke that surrounded him into frenzied eddies. "I have been remiss in not introducing myself. My name is Incendere Resin. I am a Libanomancer. This is the highest art of the incense makers, and I am well paid. Money opens doors, and it has allowed me to walk through one such door today, to stand before you and offer betterment to both your lives."

Crow looked from Rowan to Incendere and back again. "However you came to be here today, freeing us, I am—we are—grateful," she said.

"I'm not entirely freeing you. I can't change our society's culture, or its attitude to your . . . uniqueness. But I can offer greater comfort for you, and," he stood from his bow and looked at Rowan. "Higher purpose."

Rowan inclined her head in a slight nod, and followed Crow and Incendere to the incense maker's flame-powered coach. They rocketed through the streets of Here, the townspeople leaping aside, shaking their fists and cursing as the incense maker and his Wyrd cargo shot past.

It was nightfall before they reached the smithing district, and Rowan was exhausted. Her petals rolling with fatigue, she embraced her longtime slave-sister and watched Crow rush from the coach into the brightly feathered arms of a large bird-woman who could only be her mother. A heavyset man, with a face both stern and kind, approached the coach and handed Incendere a hessian bag tied with twine, coin clinking audibly within. Incendere nodded at the man, who returned the nod before walking away, ushering the two bird-women inside with him.

Rowan was fast asleep when the coach finally reached the incense maker's den. Incendere reached to wake her. Rowan's bark skin blackened and blistered under his touch, her eyes flying open as she recoiled. The Libanomancer looked horrified. Rowan waved a twig-hand at him. She was well accustomed to pain.

But as she staggered tiredly into the den, the air heavy and mysterious with incense smoke, her skin throbbed and complained at the memory of Incendere's scalding touch, and pollen dusted her cheeks.

• • •

Incendere worked from sunrise to sunset each day, locked away in a cavern of the den, while Rowan was free to wander, her duties so light as to be ridiculous—dust an earthen ledge, polish a brass doorknob, fluff a velvet cushion. She was not permitted entry to Incendere's Libanomancy cavern, and she still didn't understand exactly what he did. Whenever she asked, he would laugh, flames spurting from his lips, and smile indulgently at her. "The nuts and bolts would bore you," he would say, and he'd point out another wonder of the den to distract her—a whorl of pulsating smoke in the shape of a heart, a net of dreams to capture the odours of life, a Dragon's Blood joss stick as tall as a man smouldering ruby-bright in a corner of the den.

Incendere forgot time and again that Rowan couldn't smell the incense, and after a while, she stopped reminding him.

Their kisses were painful and infrequent, always initiated by Rowan. Incendere would kiss her back for a time, but all too soon the sound of bark popping and sizzling would become too insistent to ignore. He would cry out in dismay and shove her away, but too late—her lips would already be swelling and splitting. She would smile sadly as he commanded another Wyrd Woman—Aloe, a healer—to apply soothing balm to her wounds. He would stride away, head bowed, but Rowan could still see the tears that rolled in tiny fireballs down his cheeks.

Love should not hurt, but in Rowan's experience, it always had. This time it hurt her more than usual, and more visibly, but surely that only meant it was stronger, and more honest?

Rowan slept in a large soil-filled cot, the dirt cool and black and comforting around her. Incendere didn't sleep, but he would enter Rowan's bedchamber and sit—at a distance, of course—and tell her fascinating stories, about oracles, scented altars, scrying shapes in rising smoke, reading signs in the crackle of incense on coals. In this way she pieced together the meaning of his work, the uses for what he created—what it was to be a Libanomancer—but she still knew nothing about the practicalities of the work, the nuts and bolts that he insisted would bore her.

And it became too much, this unsatisfactory endless talk, this gaping space between them. The burn was worse when he *didn't* touch her.

• • •

When Incendere entered Rowan's room one gloomy Saturday evening—the rain hammering at the little stained glass window over her bed, the air damp and cold—she was ready for him. She threw herself into his scorching arms, and he held her for a moment as he always did. But this time, she would not allow him to discard her. She fell backwards, and dragged him with her. They tumbled together into the chill dirt of Rowan's bed. Incendere propped himself up above her, his hands planted in the soil, his orange eyes searching her face for acquiescence even as he shook his head.

"Wait! See?" she said, lifting clods of dirt in her twig fingers and smearing them on her lips before she kissed him again and again. "The soil cools your kisses enough for me to take them without too much pain, certainly without burning beyond repair. We can be together, here, in the dirt. *Fully* together, for the first time."

Incendere murmured protests, whispered fears and doubts, but his hands were at her bodice, ripping and burning, and his lips remained pressed to hers. She rubbed gritty soil over both their bodies, and soon enough the Libanomancer's words were dampened to moans. Smoke rose around them in thick clouds as they rolled and twisted together. Soon the only sounds were the rasp of flesh on bark and the hiss of burning wood tempered with soil.

• • •

"I have a favour to ask of you." Incendere trailed a finger through the air above Rowan's foliage hair, a painless gesture of affection, though some of her berries still withered from it. As the lovers talked, Aloe slathered Rowan's skin with balm, as she did every morning after the burning man and the tree-woman had lain together. Some of the deepest burns on Rowan's bark skin would not heal, and left deep black craters that oozed sap. Aloe packed these with a soothing poultice. It was all that could be done. Rowan didn't even flinch anymore as Aloe's fingers dug into her wounds.

"Then ask," Rowan said.

"I would like you to help me with my work."

Rowan opened her mouth to respond, but Incendere held up his hand.

"Don't say yes yet," he said. "There is much you must know. I don't want to lose you. I am only able to keep you here because you are valuable, my love. It is because of your value that my masters, who own this den, have provided the funds to allow us to be together. I wanted it to be forever, but if it can only be for now, then I want that, too. I have searched for another way. I cannot find any."

"Stop, you make it all sound so dire!"

"But it is." Incendere waved Aloe away. The healer left quickly, as if relieved.

"Then don't tell me."

"I must," Incendere said, hot tears blazing forth from his eyes. And the Libanomancer told the Rune Tree a tale, just as he had on countless nights before.

Once, a burning man saw a beautiful Wyrd Woman buying supplies for her mistress at the market, a tree-girl with hair of red leaves and berries, and eyes of soft floral beauty. He'd never seen such a thing, and he was spellbound. He asked about her, and learnt of her plight. He watched her from afar, saw her run the night streets in pain as birds trailed her through the sky, witnessed her climb a bridge and disappear at the peak, appearing hours later from Nowhere and running back to her cruel mistress. After many nights, he finally managed to climb the bridge himself, to lay with her, briefly. To whisper kindnesses to her and caress her with his voice, though he wanted far more than that.

And finally, the burning man hatched a plan. His work had led him to discover the secrets of a powerful divination incense, one that had never successfully been made before, one that would be worth an inestimable fortune to whoever produced it. His masters were hungry for fame and riches, and they commanded the Libanomancer to produce the divination incense, at any cost. The key ingredients were difficult to obtain, but he gathered them all—except for two. The berries and sap of a tree-girl. This wouldn't have been difficult if any tree-girl would do, but they wouldn't.

It had to be a Rune Tree. It had to be Rowan. This was good, because it led to a way for the burning man to have her. But making the incense would require *all* Rowan's berries—her beautiful crowning glory—and a*ll* her sap.

"But I'll die," Rowan cried, for surely Incendere didn't know. "My berries you could take, and I would give them to you freely, but my sap is my life. I can't survive without it."

He only looked at her sadly, and she realised—had realised long ago, if she was honest with herself, had known this moment was hurtling toward them—that he understood the price he was asking her to pay very well. She wept yellow pollen tears and shook her head, back and forth, unable to stop her negation.

"I love you, Rowan. This is the only way for us, however short our time may be. What is your alternative? Another Seamstress, a life of pain and starvation? I would be gentle, oh, so gentle. I would take only a little of you at a time, so carefully you wouldn't even notice, and we would make something magical in the process. Isn't that truly love? The fruit of our union would last forever."

Incendere reached for her, but she shrank away, lost to her weeping. He gazed at her for a moment, and then stood and left, wisps of dark smoke trailing in his wake.

• • •

Rowan was pulled from the agony of her dreams by a gentle hand on her shoulder. She opened her eyes to see Aloe kneeling beside her dirt bed.

"You're not the first," Aloe said. Her voice was cool and soft. Rowan had never heard her speak before, had assumed she couldn't.

She sat up, frowning. "What do you mean?"

"There have been other great and secret incenses that Master Resin has been compelled to make, other essential ingredients, other girls he has immortalised through his work."

"You shouldn't be here. And you're wrong. He loves me, and I love him. This is torture for us both."

"Oh, yes, he loves you. I don't dispute that. Master Resin loves deeply, and often. And all of his love goes up in smoke."

"No. You're infatuated with him. Or you're misguided, thinking to help me, when I don't need your help. There is a way out of this, and Incendere and I will find it together."

Aloe shook her head, and beckoned for Rowan to move away from her bed. Rowan did, stepping out and standing over Aloe, who, still kneeling, leant forward and began to remove handfuls of moist soil.

"What're you doing? You're destroying it, stop!" Rowan reached for Aloe's arm, but the girl shrugged her off, digging at a furious pace. Within moments a hole several feet deep gaped. Rowan leaned down to look. The soil thinned until what Aloe pulled out wasn't soil at all but skulls, ribs, teeth, and fistfuls of ashes, amassing the charnel wares into a pile that grew until Rowan could bear no more. "Stop!" she cried. "Please, stop. Leave them alone. Cover them."

Aloe did, replacing the remains and swaddling them in dirt. She wiped her hands on her thin dress and stood. "He has me bury them, and the new one always sleeps atop them. I try to heal them after death, every time. And every time, I fail."

"I love him," Rowan whispered, knowing herself for a fool even as she also knew the truth of her words. He'd coupled with her, there atop the buried tower of his murdered lovers—Wyrd Women, like her, all of them. Like Crow, and Aloe. How deep did the mass grave go? "I love him!"

Aloe stood, her face close to Rowan's. "Love should not hurt! It should never take everything from you, never steal your light and demand your life. And if it does, well, then, where are you, and what have you got? It is far better to be nowhere, with not even the clothes upon your back, than anywhere near *that* kind of love."

She shook her dirty finger in Rowan's face. "I will not bury you, Rowan Redberry. I will *not*."

"We're Wyrd, Aloe. Offensive to the eye and worth nothing. We don't have any valuable skill or purpose to redeem us, like Incendere does. We're lucky someone like him wants us."

Aloe gaped. "Do you think me without skill or purpose? How much pain have I eased, how many wounds have I healed? I'm still alive because of my convenient value to his ongoing "work'. Rowan, you're the most beautiful creature I've ever seen. Your sap contains the secrets to life itself. You reek of magic, so much so that I need to breathe through my mouth when I'm around you, lest I be overpowered. Why do you suppose you can't smell anything yourself? Why do you think those who claim to own you are so eager to convince you of your worthlessness, but so reluctant to part with you?"

Rowan squeezed her eyes shut, rubbing the bridge of her nose with one trembling finger. "It doesn't matter. Where can the Wyrd go if we run, anyway?"

"Nowhere," Aloe said. "A place that, as you know, isn't as frightening or desperate as it sounds."

Rowan knuckled her eyes. "I'm tired. I need to . . . to sleep, to think. Please . . . I'm grateful for what you've shown me, and I appreciate your words and your care, but I need to be alone."

Aloe touched Rowan's arm as she passed. "Remember: I won't bury *you*," she said. Her careful emphasis was not lost on Rowan, who sank to her knees and stared at her dirt cot as Aloe left, closing the door softly behind her.

• • •

The night stretched on forever, as nights full of loss and confusion tend to do. By luck or fate or sheer mindless coincidence, Incendere didn't visit Rowan's bedchamber. She lay on the floor, facedown, her head cradled on her arms. If her thoughts were blood, then the hours that she'd passed tonight in this way were drenched in gore, exhausted half-dead things that staggered ever onward, defeated again and again by paradox and snare.

She loved Incendere, but could not stay and let him kill her. Nor could she leave and let him kill others. And, selfishly, she could not live without him if he lived without her. What was more, she cared for Aloe, and could not leave the healer to this endless dark cycle. Nor could she ask the healer to kill for her, or to clean up afterward even if she could bring herself to kill Incendere—which she couldn't.

Round and round the cogs of her mind spun, crushing her rather than carrying her forward, getting her . . . nowhere.

A place that was not as frightening or desperate as it sounded.

• • •

Rowan ran the cobblestones of the night, naked, all hope left far behind her. Her foliage hair hung brown and wilted without her berries to offer it colour and radiance. No birds shrieked above her, swooping for her fruit. She ran alone and in peace.

She had passed through the smithing district on her long journey, and had seen Crow through a candlelit window, her head resting on her fluffed up feathers, her eyes closed in peaceful slumber, her mother stroking her beak, as the stern but kind man smiled at them. That picture had been true love. Stopping, Rowan had plucked a single petal from her right eye—*she loves me*—and dropped it on Crow's doorstep, knowing her slave-sister would understand.

"Live long and be happy," she'd said, and ran on once more. Her flower eyes were wide and dry, no yellow pollen dusting them now, though sap leaked in a thin amber runnel from the space where the missing petal had been. Her bark skin was ghost gum in the moonlight, Wyrd and strong.

She hurt, oh, she hurt so much, but she did not weep.

She ran faster than she ever had before, but her breath came easy, her heart troubling her not at all despite her exhausting pace, for she had left that behind, too, and found she could live without it. Eventually, she reached the wrought iron bridge, cherubs and serpents smiling at her from the railing, the water beneath burbling its delight at her return. She sang as she climbed the bridge, her voice broken and raw—but *there*, not lost, surrendered, or stolen. The lanterns nudged her head, their wings landing butterfly kisses on her cheeks. The peacocks snored, glossy tail-feathers twitching in dreams. And waiting with arms outstretched was Mother Bear, tears streaming down her fuzzy cheeks, giving Rowan's pain a face.

Rowan smelt it all. Tallow, feathers, fur, and so much more. The scents flooded her. They'd been here all along, waiting for her to claim them. In time, she would be ready to face her own scent, too.

"Welcome home, our darling," the Mother Bear said. "How long will you stay this time?"

"I'll never leave again," Rowan said, falling into the Bear's arms.

"You never really did, child," Mother Bear said. "But you know, there's a price that must be paid to stay here. It requires a selfless sacrifice and a selfish solution. Nobody has ever stayed, because until now, the toll has been thought impossible. How find *you* this toll, my beautiful daughter?"

Rowan pulled away and looked up at the Bear's face. "Are you hungry, Mother?"

The Bear smiled with shark-teeth. "Always. I am a Mother, but I am also a Bear."

Rowan nodded. "Plant his remains deep in the soil bed in my room, which you will know by its smell. I've left him a gift, the last and greatest one I could offer, a shining red pile of myself. Place it atop his grave, which was always the only place berries and incense could ever be together anyway. And he'll lie there with the others, which, if they feel as I do, may please them, though for different reasons."

With a roar, the Mother Bear charged off the bridge, disappearing into the aether. Rowan lay on the peacocks' tails and hugged herself. She watched the implacable stars wheel overhead and when sleep called to her, she sang herself toward it with gently murmured truths.

"I loved him before, and I love him now. I love him Here and I love him There. I love him Everywhere but, most of all, forevermore . . . I love him Nowhere."

• • • • • • • • • • •

# LETTERS OF LOVE FROM THE ONCE AND NEWLY DEAD

## CHRISTOPHER GREEN

Thomas knows that the doors are already locked, but locking up has become a habit, and his habits are as near and dear to him as family. The sun is going down. He moves through the last of its light and checks that the latches are tight, the bars still strong. Nothing has ever tried to get in, but the lady on the nightly news will remind her audience to examine such things before they sleep, and Thomas doesn't want his sense of duty to be colored by her chiding.

The house is silent save for the clicks his arthritis and the floorboards conspire to create, and Thomas purses his lips and whistles something he remembers from somewhere. The rooms are too quiet, otherwise, devoid of the commotion that comes with family; the pester of a child or the happy squabbles that had once meant everyone was getting settled in for a meal or a stretch of television watching.

Noise is to his liking, and he makes some more, swinging the heavy indoor shutters together too hard on their chunky, oiled hinges. Hinges like that used to be special order, once upon a time, but now he sees them every time he goes into the hardware store, in a wide bin right up front where the girls that scanned your items and took your money used to stand, back when such things were safe.

There is a single chair in front of the television, and Thomas sits in it and turns on the news. People say the news is always the same, and in his experience those people are right, except for a couple of years ago, when they were wrong. Now that they've gone back to being right again, Thomas finds he isn't as glad of it as he feels he should be.

Eventually he gets up and heats up some food, listening to the anchor woman's voice from the other room. He can hear the way her words have to twist their way out of her smile.

He brings the food back and eats it in front of the television. When he's finished, he turns off the news and walks back through the dark of the house to the kitchen, where he washes his cup, his plate, his fork and knife. After the clamour of the news, the hollow sound of tap water in the sink and the wind against the house wears at him like a river. He is a rock, a pebble, once much more than he is now or will ever be, worn small and smooth and meaningless by the world as it goes by.

Thomas returns to the television, stands in front of it but doesn't turn it back on. It's always the same, after all, after all, and dusk is close.

He lives alone and can afford, now and then, to flick on the bare bulb fifteen minutes or so before it is absolutely necessary. The light shows him the empty walls and the polished floor. It makes his bent shadow tall, and Thomas tries to remember what it feels like to stand up straight, to open a beer with his bare hands and not a bottle opener. He looks down at his hands, at the knuckles gone bulbous and grotesque. His own grandfather had hands like that, and he remembers how they scared him.

He turns off the light and leaves the room. Lying in bed and waiting for sleep suddenly doesn't seem worse than this. Sometimes the light isn't as sweet a thing as he thinks it will be.

• • •

He is awakened by the neighbours' dogs. They are dark, feral shadows, and they prowl their yards with a sense of purpose Thomas envies. From his window he can see them as they snap at the night, rattling chains that stretch from their necks to the stakes in the centre of the lawn.

Tonight, the dogs are furious. Something out there has got them baying, and the dogs that had been silent kick up as well. They settle in fits and starts, occasionally woofing deep in the back of their throats as if to clear them.

Thomas watches his own dogless yard even after the beasts grow silent, but there is nothing there aside from the little garden he dutifully began with the seeds they sent everyone in the mail.

Nothing and no one. Nonetheless, he makes his way quietly down the stairs and rechecks the latches and locks, the bar on the door. Everything is as it should be, and Thomas returns to bed.

• • •

The phone wakes him up.

He reaches for it in the dark. He has been dreaming, and in his dreams none of this is real, none of these shutters and bars and clasps and latches matter even the slightest.

But the phone isn't there, hasn't been there for years. The ringing is downstairs, and he shuffles down the hall as fast as he can and descends the stairs. When he reaches the phone, he knocks it from the table in his haste. It clatters to the ground, and the noise is like a slap across the face. The dogs are silent. The house is dead and still. *Is there someone in here with me? Had the shutters held?* Even now, somewhere in the house, was there a broken latch on the floor beside a muddy footprint?

He picks the phone from the floor and puts it to his ear. "Grace?"

No one speaks. It isn't uncommon for people to ring one another and yet to not say anything. Thomas has done it himself, in his weaker moments. Everyone needs someone, even if they've dialled a number at random. If it was Grace she hadn't hung up, at least, and so he tried again.

"Gracie, is that you?"

He can hear breathing on the other end of the line. He knows it's her, knows it right to the marrow, just as surely as he knows he should spare her the guilt of having to hang up on him.

"Grace, I . . . " And there it is. If he says it, his daughter will never call him again, even anonymously, even in the middle of the night. "I'm glad you called," he says instead.

She hangs up.

"Goodbye," Thomas says into the receiver, anyway. He puts the phone back on the hook and goes back up to bed. The wind is hypnotic. He knows he should go back downstairs and check the locks, test the doors and windows, but instead he closes his eyes and listens to the world breathe.

• • •

He is awake before the sun falls across his face, but he cannot bring himself to rise until the world becomes brighter. One of the city's trucks is making the slow grind up the street outside and the dogs don't bark. They're used to such things. At last, he showers and shaves, then dresses and walks to the shops. There is a truck ahead of him, moving in the opposite direction. Thomas isn't sure if it's the same one that drove past his house. He isn't sure if it matters.

The city has many trucks.

Along the way, he stops counting the stares and pitiful looks he collects. Once, one of the trucks slows, and he raises a hand to the driver without looking. It should be enough, and it is. No one the truck is looking for would wave, even if they could, and Thomas has. The truck gains speed and turns left at the next corner.

The store is self-serve. All of them are. There are two rows of cameras at the entrance, one facing in and one facing out.

Just inside the shop is a big metal door. It has no handle, not on this side, although Thomas has seen it open to disgorge security guards a time or two, and on those occasions he saw the monitors they watched inside.

The store is busy and almost soundless. No one speaks. Thomas buys bread. He buys jam. He buys eggs and cheese and, to his surprise, spies a small bar of chocolate that has fallen behind a row of canned goods. He plucks it from the shelf and adds it to the things he carries.

It is brutally expensive, and Thomas finds he doesn't care. Once the machine accepts his money and dispenses his change, he leaves.

The walk from the house to the store feels longer every time. Before he attempts it, Thomas finds a park bench and takes a seat. He watches another of the city's trucks trundle past, this one so full that he can see the angle of arms, the splay of stacked legs through the open back. It drives no faster or slower than the other cars.

There is a woman and a man on the sidewalk, each of them holding a little girl's hand. How brave, Thomas thinks, and watches them. How terribly brave. The adult's eyes never stray to one another, and, when the girl raises her head to look at her father, her mother lets go of her hand and strikes her smoothly across the face.

Thomas gives them a polite nod and pretends not to look at their faces. They scowl anyway and drag their daughter along when she slows, and when they have gone by he hears the man slap the girl again, hard enough to make her cry. She does.

The traffic is slower. Down the street a ways, back in the direction he will soon have to walk, a boy pushes his way out of the bushes and staggers into the road. His clothes are hanging from him, and he leaves one of his shoes in the gutter.

"Someone should call that in," says the girl's father from beside Thomas. He sits down on the bench without waiting to be offered.

"I'm sure someone will," Thomas says, "but it won't be me." He watches the boy, at the limit of his flagging vision. "Did your wife send you over?"

The man flashes him the look one man shares with another when he's been sent on a fool's errand against his wishes. "She wanted to know if you're okay out here, all by yourself."

Thomas laughs. He can't help it. What kind of a question was that? "Nothing wrong with being by yourself, these days, according to most people. Right?"

The man shrugs, clearly nervous, and Thomas feels sorry for him. "I'm Thomas."

"Kyle."

"Kyle," Thomas says, and nods, as if he's known the man's name all along, even though he's sure it's a false one. When a man of thirty five or forty lies about his name, it hardly flows trippingly from the tongue. "Kyle, your family has nothing to fear from me."

"I'm not saying we do. It's just not every day we see a man willing to nod at us. It's . . . "

Thomas sighs. "Unusual?"

"I was going to say disconcerting."

The boy up the road is trying to retreat into the bushes again. They're sharp, though, designed for defence, and they hamper his progress. A few cars have pulled over, and Thomas can picture their drivers, windows rolled up and doors locked tight, their phones pressed to their ears as they ring the city and ask for a truck.

Kyle clears his throat. "Just leave my wife and daughter alone. Please."

Thomas nods. "I will, I promise." The boy down the road stops, and for a breathless second Thomas thinks he may turn and come toward them. Eventually, he turns in the other direction and wanders up the street, becoming something else for Thomas to fear on the way home.

Kyle stands up, and Thomas reaches out and brushes his elbow. It is a gentle touch, light as a feather, and the man recoils from him as if burned.

"One thing, before you go," Thomas says, ignoring Kyle's reaction. "I bought some chocolate, on a whim. I don't eat it, normally. I'd much prefer your daughter to have it."

Kyle's eyes can't hide the truth. The girl has never tasted such things. "And where will I tell her I got it, when she asks? Who shall I say the gift is from?"

Thomas shrugs. Was the girl so starved for attention that this kindness would be one too many? "Tell her you bought it last month, when the shops had an extra supply."

Kyle's face darkens and Thomas sees that he's guessed wrong. The man isn't afraid his daughter would find some measure of affection for Thomas; he is afraid she'd find it for himself.

"Do you need anything or not?" Kyle asks, changing the topic. His eyes go past Thomas to the shop, where his family are waiting. "Is there someone I should call for you?"

"No. No thank you."

"No one?"

Thomas stands too, suddenly as eager for the conversation to be over as Kyle is. "I'm fine, and rest easy. You needn't fear me." He points at the shop. "I'm known, here. When the guards don't see me come to collect my groceries or the postman sees that I haven't collected yesterday's mail, the city knows to send a truck."

Kyle's face goes red. "I didn't mean . . . "

But he did, and Thomas knows it. He offers the man his hand anyway, another of those old habits that die as hard as everything else does, now. Thomas is unsurprised when the man ignores it and walks past him to his wife and daughter.

Thomas turns in time to see Kyle strike the girl again, a clean, hard slap that she wasn't expecting. Thomas finds it hard to think worse of him for it.

It's for her own good, after all.

• • •

That night, the anchor woman assures him that the news remains the same. Thomas stays up after it's finished, rewashing the dishes, seeing to shutter repairs that aren't warranted or even necessary, pottering around, telling himself that he isn't waiting for the phone to ring.

When he finally locks up for the night and trudges up the stairs, he's bone tired. The phone rings when he reaches the top and he rushes back down, cursing himself for not having a phone by his bed, knowing that they wouldn't have installed one even if he'd asked. Most people aren't strong enough to resist the temptation of a phone so near to them. They'd answer it if it rang, and perhaps the person on the line would speak as well. And something dangerous would blossom.

Four rings. Five. He grabs it before it can ring again. Will Grace wait? In that eternal half second before he can lift the handset to his mouth, he tells himself *six rings. That's how many I'd have given it. After Six I'd assume they weren't home, or, more likely, were asleep, at this hour. Six rings, please god, let her be there because it's only been five and I can't live without-*

"Mr Carter?" a man's voice asks.

His hand trembles and he resists the urge to hang up the phone. "Yes?"

"Mr Carter, I've recently been assigned to your case. Have you got a few minutes that you wouldn't mind spending with me? Just a quick chat, that's all it'll be."

"My case?" Thomas asks, but he knows what the man is talking about. It doesn't matter. For a long moment he contemplates simply not answering or, better, hanging up, but he knows what will happen if he does. The people who don't answer these calls from the city are paid a visit and, often, they're found locked inside their own homes, the wardens now prisoners.

"Yes, your case. I just thought I'd touch base with you Mr Carter. Make sure you're alright."

"Please, call me Thomas."

The man is smiling, smiling at the old fool, the fossil who can't move with the times. Thomas can hear it in his voice. "No thank you, Mr Carter. You see, it's just that sort of thing that's bumped you up my call list tonight. The offer is a kind one, but wholly inappropriate. Some people in your area have expressed concern about your welfare."

"Kyle."

"Pardon?"

"It may not be his real name, but he's a man I met today at the store. He's most likely the man who called you about me."

"You must know I can't tell you that."

Thomas grits his teeth. "Look, there's no law against sitting by yourself on a park bench and watching the world go by, and that's all that I was doing."

"Did you make him an offer of chocolate?"

What nonsense. "Yes, I did."

"Then I'm sure you understand his concern."

Thomas closes his eyes. Understand is such a loaded word. Sympathise, yes. Understand? Never.

"Mr Carter. I know you were just trying to help, that there's nothing malicious in your actions, but people are rightly afraid. I mean, a man of your age, on your own . . . "

Thomas's grip tightens on the phone. Dollars to donuts the man doesn't have the guts to say it, so Thomas says it for him. "I am not so empty that I will come back for the first person that shows me a kindness, sir."

The man becomes quiet. *Cat got your tongue? Maybe we should send a truck by your place, then, and see if you're still sucking in wind.* Thomas listens to him as he starts to say something a couple of times, and when the words finally come down the line, they are, "I wasn't implying otherwise, Mr Carter. Your daughter . . . "

"Left. Afraid of what the world's become."

"Then I'm sure you can understand this gentleman's concern. There may not be a law against sitting on park benches, but that doesn't mean the practice will win you friends." Thomas doesn't say anything, and the man clearly takes his silence as agreement. "Your wife, sir. It says here that she's passed away. When she did, did she . . . "

Thomas sits down and holds his head in his other hand. He's glad he didn't turn the light on, as the dark feels so much like home. "She didn't come for me, no."

"So . . . "

Thomas clears his throat. "Someone down the street. She found him in his garage."

The man on the phone is nodding. Thomas can hear the cord on the other end of the line bounce against something, a desk or a keyboard. "Then you can see what we're afraid of; what everyone's so worried about. What if you, afterward, you go looking for one of these people you so innocently watch walk down the street? What then?"

Enough of this. "You tell those bastards there's no chance of that. Write that in your little computer, too. Put it in whatever file you've got on me. None of them have any chance of finding a place in my heart, you hear me, because there isn't room. Not for any of you."

"Mr Carter, please. I'm not trying to upset you. I'm only asking you to give some thought to your actions."

Thomas hangs up the phone. It doesn't ring again.

• • •

The night is still. The dogs are quiet. Thomas has been asleep, until something in the backyard awakens him. He lies in his bed and listens to the noise as it wafts up from the backyard; a soft rustle of fabric against wood. He gets up and goes to the window.

She's gorgeous, and he's never seen her before. She stands near the fence, her pale skin lit by the moon and the splash of unfocussed spotlights a couple of houses over. The climb over the fence from next door to here has appled her cheeks and she clutches something in one badly broken hand.

The news, always the same, is very clear about what to do in these situations. Do not approach, do not attempt to communicate with, call the police and ask them to send one of the city trucks so the matter can be dealt with professionally.

Her eyes shine up at him. The woman and Thomas watch each other until he has the presence of mind to reach for the rifle leaning against the wall and go downstairs. Once there, Thomas opens the set of shutters that look out into the backyard. She's still against the fence, its shadow slicing across her body, across the sundress she'd selected this morning, the last dress she'd ever choose. Her blond hair is blood soaked, and the side of her face has gone ragged with bone.

*Car accident*, a voice inside him says, and he unlocks and opens the side door and goes out into the backyard with her.

She doesn't move, and Thomas keeps the rifle steady and advances. The fence has a few bloody handprints near the top, and the palings have splintered where she's climbed over. He looks down, and sees that the thing she clutches is the collar of the neighbour's dog.

"Hello," he says, just as gently as if she'd called him on the phone, as if he might scare her off if he is too loud. "Hello."

She hears him, alright, but it doesn't seem to matter. He sheds the last stubborn splinter of hope now that he can see her clearly. He was right. He's never laid eyes on her before.

Thomas has been told, just as everyone else has. If you stay out of their way you won't become a target. They aren't back for you unless they are, and if they are you'll know. He's heard stories, of shop assistants and checkout girls and delivery men coming back to those they'd secretly loved, but Thomas lowers his rifle anyway. If this poor, broken thing has been unfortunate enough to somehow love him, so be it. He'd welcome it.

She still hasn't moved. She's staring at him, or so he thinks until he steps aside and sees that her gaze is actually fixed on the gate behind him.

The gate that leads to the rest of the world.

He goes to her, surprised at his courage. *Am I brave, or simply beyond caring?* He finds her letter in a pocket she's added to the dress herself. Everyone has pockets, now. In case. The little slip of paper has been laminated.

"I shall return, my dear," he tells her, and retreats to the house. Thomas is nothing if not a creature of habit, useless old habits made flesh, and he locks the door behind him, then turns on the light and sits down at the table.

The phone stares up at him like a skull with many eyes.

*Dearest Victor,*

*My love, I pray that I found you. I pray that I did and that you stopped me, or that someone stopped me on the verge, the very verge, so that I can be close enough for you to know I sought you out and far enough away to not drag you down with me. I do love you. If you're reading this then you'll know that, without any doubts, and perhaps that's the best and last gift I can give.*

*Pray for me, Victor.*

*~Your Melissa*

Thomas reads her note a second time, then turns off the light and opens the side door again. She's still there, eyes on the gate, waiting for him. He's forgotten the rifle, left it inside somewhere, but it doesn't matter. He tucks the note back into her homemade pocket and turns away from her. The gate is locked and he unlocks it; swings it open and out of her way. She moves forward with a joy and determination that her face is barely capable of showing, but her eyes, her shining eyes, they thank him as she goes by. He thinks he sees her smile.

When Thomas goes back inside, he turns on the light once more and returns to his seat at the table. He has brought paper with him, and he uses it to compose a letter of his own. Everyone he loves is gone except for Grace, and she has kept herself and his grandson as far from him as possible since all of this began. He writes down everything he knows about the place she has gone, every clue, every background noise he heard back when she would speak to him when he called, every ambient sound when she'd called him that Christmas a couple of years ago from an unlisted number.

The list of things he knows about her new location is short, surely not enough for him to track her down. He doesn't know if it works like that, anyway. No one does, or rather, everyone will eventually.

Still, there is a chance that he knows something he doesn't remember now, that when he stops this old habit of breathing he's clung on to for so long he'll simply stand back up and know exactly where she is.

He writes his letter. Now and then, as he crumples up a draft and tosses it aside, agonizing about his handwriting and the impersonality of the typewriter in his study, the dogs outside let loose with a deep series of bounding barks. There's one less dog adding to the clamour, though. Thomas can tell even if the others can't.

Grace, he writes, forgive me for finding you. The alternative is worse though, far worse, to grow old and lock the windows and bar the doors against a threat you would gladly welcome and you know will never come. I'm too old and all of this has gone on too long for me to imagine some high school crush or tangled one night stand placing me above the others she's met since me. Forgive me, Grace, but know that when I come for you, it's only love. Love. If I find you, forgive me. Don't let me hurt little Francis.

Thomas folds the letter and places it into his wallet. Many such notes are laminated, as Melissa had done to hers, but he doesn't think his wallet will be opened and closed many more times before someone else reads what he's written.

He turns off the light and sits in the dark, listening to the wind as it picks up the rhythm of breath again, wondering if the phone will ring again, wondering who will be on the other end if it does.

Thomas takes the chocolate bar from his grocery bag and eats it. When it's gone, he sets the wrapper down beside the phone, walks to his doors and windows and, one by one, undoes the locks.

• • • • • • • • • • •

# THE SOUL OF THE MACHINE

## MAXINE McARTHUR

Bane was late. Again. Probably debating which cravatte to wear under his flying coat.

Scarlatti ran her fingers over the *Spirit of Malabar*'s leading edges and bracing wires, feeling for any roughness, any indication that the saboteur might have damaged the machine structurally as well. But the taut, shiny surface of doped linen was sound, and the wires tight as they should be.

Bright spring sunlight flooded through the entry of the tent they were using as a hangar. Outside, a constant chatter accompanied the feet Scarlatti could see passing through the hangar area. Only people connected with the race entrants were supposed to be allowed back here; judging by the number of dainty boots and frilled skirts picking their fastidious way across the short grass, many of the entrants must be "connected" with half the female population of Paris.

Scarlatti wiped the head of a spanner absent-mindedly on her overalls. Skirts got in the way in a workshop.

A roar of gentlemanly laughter rang out from the neighbouring tent. The French West-Mage's team. Scarlatti didn't think it had been them sneaking in here last night. They were confident enough of winning not to worry about the rank outsider in the race.

A loud sniff in the entry made her turn swiftly. An army officer stood there, wrinkling his rum-red blob of a nose, his yellow whiskers bristling.

Scarlatti recognised, from Bane's tutelage, the crimson and blue of the Imperial Hussars. She couldn't remember what rank the three gold stars designated. Nor did she care.

"Awful stink, what." The officer sniffed again, and twirled his stick disdainfully.

Personally, Scarlatti thought the mixed odour of petrol, oil and dope was the best smell in the world.

*Be more friendly*, Bane had suggested. *Show off the Malabar a bit.*

"Good morning . . . sir." She put down the spanner and inclined her head politely. "Do you have questions about the machine?"

Just don't tell me I'm blaspheming, she thought. We get enough of that.

The officer, who had started violently when Scarlatti spoke, peered at her.

"It's a gel!"

"I'm a mechanic, sir."

"A what?"

"Someone who fixes and maintains machines, sir."

He blew through his moustache a couple of times, considering. "But you're not a mage," he said finally. "Gels can't be mages, what."

"This isn't a magical machine, sir. It's a mechanical machine."

"How does it fly, then? Can't fly without magic."

A long arm clad in soft yellow leather draped over the officer's shoulders.

"It flies by using an engine, old chap. Makes the very dickens of a noise." Bane winked at Scarlatti and patted the officer's chest. "Goes faster than your best charger, though."

"Ah, Southwind. Thought you were here. What damnfoolery you up to now?"

Hurry up, Scarlatti thought at Bane. Get rid of the old fool. To add impetus to the thought, she picked up a chamois and began polishing the engine cowling.

"Just imagine how useful these machines would be to an army." Bane tapped the side of his aquiline nose meaningfully.

"The Imperial Army already has flying scouts," the officer pointed out. "Unreliable things. Flappin' up and down, scaring the horses . . . "

"Yes, but—" Bane glanced around and lowered his voice. "A mechanical flying machine is different. You don't need a mage to fly it."

The officer opened his mouth to protest, then pursed his lips thoughtfully. Scarlatti could almost see the idea taking root in his brain. If you didn't need a mage to fly the machine, you wouldn't have to rely on a mage to condescend to do what you wanted.

Bane nodded. "You could train your own men to fly and maintain the machines. It's not that hard, is it, Head Mechanic?"

She wasn't going to give him that one. "It's not easy."

"But any ordinary man could do it," Bane pressed.

"It takes a while to learn," she admitted grudgingly.

"You see, old son? Independence from the mages. Think about it."

"Hogwash!" the officer harrumphed. "Only a mage can tune the soul of a machine."

"This machine doesn't have a soul," Scarlatti said. "It's made up of parts that fit together."

The officer stared at her, his pale eyes bulging, then back at Bane. "I say, you can't be serious. Demn thing'll never work."

"We're here to show you it will work, old chap." Bane steered the officer back out into the sunlight. "You keep an eye on us during the race."

He reappeared immediately and fixed Scarlatti with a questioning gaze, as deep a blue as the officer's had been insipid.

"What's wrong?"

Scarlatti resented the way he could follow her every tiny mood, whereas she never knew what he was thinking from one minute to the next.

"We had a visitor last night." She pointed at the flying machine. "A saboteur."

"What?" Bane hissed. He spun, spreading his long hands palms outward, then stopped and shrugged with a grimace.

The organisers of the Great Air Race were supposed to be responsible for the security of each entrant's hangar and of the event space itself, in order to prevent the clashes that would inevitably occur should each entrant be allowed to conjure their own protective shields. And it was usual at large public events, these days, to prohibit major magic discharges in the interest of the bystanders. But it was common knowledge that mages who were powerful enough to pilot flying machines would not trust the safety of those machines to a committee. Every other tent on the field would be permeated with surreptitious spells.

The Duke of Southwind's entry, however, relied on the committee's efforts, for the Duke had forsworn the use of magic as part of his mad crusade.

"Can we still fly?" he said practically.

Scarlatti was impressed. She'd been expecting one of his tirades against the establishment.

"Yes and no."

"What the hell does that mean?" Bane ran his finger along the inside of his cravatte as though it was too tight. Not as calm as he seemed.

"We can still fly, but we won't win."

He sighed. "Scarlatti, just tell me what happened."

"When I got here this morning, the place was in a mess." Scarlatti climbed onto the nacelle and unbolted the engine cowling as she spoke. "There were tools all over the floor. The cowling—here, lift that edge—put it down, yes—the cowling was bolted on slightly crooked. And the cockpit cover was disarranged."

"Someone had been at the engine."

Someone who could slip through the protective spells without setting off an alarm.

"That's right. Look in here."

Bane pulled over a wooden chock, and by reason of his 6'4" managed to peer into the engine without having to perch beside Scarlatti on the back of the cockpit.

"Looks all right to me."

"Because I replaced the magneto with one of the old ones. That's why I said we won't win. We know the old design isn't as reliable."

"The thief took the magneto," said Bane thoughtfully, stepping down.

"Exactly. He—or she—probably thought they were taking the soul of the machine, but all they took was one component of the engine." Scarlatti grinned. This particular irony appealed to what she called her sense of humour. "They just don't get it, do they? A machine is no more than a collection of parts, any one of which can be replaced. Pass me the cowling, please."

Bane lifted the thin metal shell and slotted it carefully over the cylinders. "More to the point, this was done by somebody who wanted to disgrace the *Malabar* and what we stand for, not just make sure it doesn't fly. They could do that by breaking a spar or cutting a wire—I say, you have checked everything else, have you?" he added uneasily. Nothing worried a pilot more than structural failure.

"Several times, she's fine. I re-rigged the elevator to compensate for the list you're going to feel with the old mag as well."

"Jolly good work." He smiled up at her, but she was immune to his crooked-dimple charm by now, and she concentrated on the cowling bolts.

"No time to search for guilty faces." He thrust his hands into the pockets of the long flying coat and cocked his head. "They've started marshalling."

The hum of noise outside grew insistent. She could distinguish the brassy notes of a military band, and several different voices magnified by speaking trumpets. Fireworks popped.

Bane fished his white silk scarf out of the pocket and wound it carelessly over his cravatte and coat collar. Not that he would be flying high enough today for his face to get cold, but it contributed to the dashing aviator effect.

He strode to the front of the tent and began to tie the flaps right back so they could steer the *Malabar* out.

"It's not winning that matters," he said firmly, as if trying to convince himself. "It's showing everybody what can be done without magic that's important."

Scarlatti rolled her eyes as she pulled away the chocks and stowed them in the cockpit. Bane was as competitive as any mage— he would do everything within his non-magical power to win the race and, despite the handicap of the old magneto, he might even succeed. He was a good pilot.

Scarlatti had no yardstick to measure him against, of course, as the *Malabar* was the only mechanical flying machine in England. But Bane could apparently feel when the *Malabar* wanted to stall or fall out on a turn, even before she did it, and he would compensate with just enough rudder or stick to prevent the disaster.

Scarlatti often wondered how such a big man could be so gentle, then always turned resolutely from the direction that thought was headed.

They each took hold of the lower plane's trailing edge and coaxed the machine across the grass between the lines of tent-hangars. It came sweetly, the greased wheels making no sound. People stood back to let them pass, murmuring the names of the machine and the duke; they pointed at the propeller and the upper and lower wings, the box-like fuselage so different to the magical machines; they sniffed the oil and petrol. A couple of people laughed.

Laugh away, Scarlatti thought. In twenty years we'll see who's still laughing.

Up ahead the other flying machines were lined up in front of the grandstand where the dignitaries sat in a piebald mass of dark suits and frothy pale dresses. Beside the grandstand a huge brass band played a Sousa waltz. The greater public seethed excitedly behind the ropes that kept them off the field. Nobody wanted to miss what the newspapers called the Greatest Air Race Ever.

A steward boomed incomprehensibly through a speaking trumpet and beckoned them on.

From the stands several female voices screamed Bane's name. He looked up and waved, then slipped the scarf off his neck and drew it along the breeze. Squeals of appreciation followed. Showoff.

Half their patronage came from the wives of wealthy men who had persuaded their husbands to listen to Bane in the first place. Scarlatti occasionally wondered if Bane had really forsworn all magic—surely he used the gift of tongues on some of those thorny duchesses. Scarlatti was happily aware of her own shortcomings, being short, dumpy and sallow-skinned. Nobody ever noticed her, which meant she could get on with her job in peace.

The steward ushered the *Spirit of Malabar* next to one of the Prussian entries, the *Eagle of Köln*. It was a typical flexible wing design, based on the way a bird flies. Aerodynamically sound for a bird, but not for a device that had to carry the weight of a man or men. Scarlatti regarded it as cheating, for none of the other designs would get off the ground without the use of magic. And they'd fall out of the sky if you took the magic away.

Bane inclined his head politely at the staring Prussian pilot, a rotund man with enormous waxed moustaches. The pilot recovered his composure with a start, and bowed stiffly.

The *Eagle* was decorated with brilliant featherlike patterns in red and orange on a deep blue background. The other machines were also painted in gay colours. Garish, thought Scarlatti distastefully. Vulgar. The *Malabar*'s deep brown spruce spars and creamy linen was elegant yet serviceable.

The marshalling steward yelled something about pilots through his trumpet. Bane nodded at Scarlatti, rather tensely, and walked over to where a top-hatted, frock-coated judge was waiting with another steward. The other pilots joined them.

Scarlatti lifted the chocks and their pull-ropes out of the cockpit and placed them in front of the wheels, conscious of the stares and whispers of the half-dozen uniformed Prussians clustered around their machine, the pointed fingers and binoculars trained upon her from the crowd. She then climbed into the cockpit, set the throttle and made sure the switch was off, running her eye over the revs counter, bubble, and pitot tube. One of these days, she would make a device to show how high the machine flew off the ground.

The steward would be confirming the pilots knew the rules. Once around the Arc de Triomphe and back. First machine over the finish line wins. Total course length—five miles. Wind speed—she licked her finger and held it up—negligible. If the *Malabar*'s engine performed as it had in practice flights, she should take no more than six minutes. But of course the engine would not, with the old mag.

Reminded of the nocturnal saboteur, she glanced around as she wound the propeller, pulling down and around with all her strength. *Clonk—clonk—clonk.*

Too many people to find one guilty face. If she'd had any money to bet, she would put it on one of Bane's enemies, rather than a member of the opposing teams.

She caught a glimpse of the Hussar officer who had looked into the hangar. He was talking earnestly with a younger officer in crimson-and-blue. A group of school children ducked under the rope, threatening to spill out onto the field if not for the strenuous efforts of two grey-gowned teachers. Several young men in untidy suits with wild hair flitted from group to group, notebooks in hand, some followed by photographers dragging cameras. Scarlatti recognised newspaper reporters, the likes of whom were fond of caricaturing Bane as the Mad Duke.

Not as many mages in the crowd as she'd expected. Most of the people in the stands, of course, would be either mages, family of mages, or friends of mages. The powerful mages of the committee were somewhere among the other dignitaries, overseeing the whole show. But at the Derbyshire air show last March, the grounds had been littered with men in black robes or suits, listening, monitoring and, as Bane had proved with much fanfare, interfering against the rules.

No wonder they hated him.

Ah, there was one. A string-bean type wearing a dusty suit and the usual mage expression of disgruntled disapproval, like a matron hearing indecent talk at the dinner table. The skinny mage stared at each flying machine. When he got to the *Malabar* his eyes met Scarlatti's and he started, then backed away into the crowd.

She shrugged. If he tried something the committee mages would have to stop him, if only to preserve their own reputations.

There was a cheer from the crowd and the pilots returned to their machines. Bane waved his silk scarf once more at the stands then wrapped it around his throat.

"I don't think it was anyone from the other teams," he murmured to Scarlatti as he passed beside her on his way to the cockpit. "Or if it was, the pilots don't know about it."

She nodded.

Bane put one foot in the stirrup and mounted onto the fuselage, then folded into the cockpit. A pity he was so tall. Scarlatti would have liked a smaller cockpit.

The rudder, ailerons, and the big elevator at the front of the machine moved in turn as Bane tested the controls. All good—they should be, Scarlatti had done the rigging.

Up and down the field, the magical machines were doing their equivalent of a pre-flight check. That is, the assistants looked on with suitable gravity as the mage-pilots repeated their spells.

It gave Bane and Scarlatti time to warm up the engine.

"Switches on?" Scarlatti said, leaning back against the pull of the propeller against her stretched arms, one leg braced behind her.

"Switches on."

"Contact?"

"Contact."

She swung the propeller, needing all her strength. The engine coughed, then caught beautifully. She stepped back swiftly, the roar of 70hp filling her ears. Blue smoke spurted from the exhaust, but was blown away in the slipstream.

She listened critically. It sounded all right. She scurried around to the front of the nacelle—for the *Malabar* was a 'pusher', with the engine behind the pilot—and gave Bane the thumbs-up. He returned the gesture and pulled down his goggles.

Scarlatti looked up the line of machines. Except for a couple of pilots who were still confirming spells, everyone was looking at the *Malabar*, most of them with horrified fascination. She grinned to herself. You haven't seen anything yet, boys.

The marshalling steward walked down the line, getting a nod of readiness from each pilot. Bane waved gaily. The engine noise drowned any hope of conversation.

The steward retreated to the starter's position, right to the side of the line. The drummer of the band played a long roll.

The starter raised his gun.

Scarlatti loosened the chocks with two kicks and grasped the pull-ropes. The *Malabar* quivered, wanting to be off.

The starter fired.

At the puff of smoke from his gun, Scarlatti pulled the chocks and stepped back out of the way.

The *Malabar* surged forward, bumping a little on the grass. Bane's helmeted head looked small, sticking up above the fuselage.

The smell of oil overlay the ozone tang of active magic as the other machines moved off. Half of them were the same flexible-wing design as the Prussian entry, and would therefore be slower to leave the ground as they couldn't flap properly until actually airborne. The others were a mixture of designs, some with fixed wings and moveable tails, one with a huge fantail like a fish, and one with a sail-like structure on the top. The *Malabar* was the only biplane.

The sail-plane left the ground first, rising almost perpendicularly. It didn't move very fast once in the air, however, and was soon overtaken by the flexible-wing types.

The *Malabar*'s tail rose as it picked up speed to about forty miles per hour. *Now*, Scarlatti thought, but Bane waited two more seconds before easing the stick back, giving it that little extra push so that it left the ground smoothly.

He wouldn't waste time gaining height. Fifty feet would be plenty.

All the machines were airborne now. The fantail fish design was in trouble—it spun in slow circles over the field, unable to proceed. The others stretched in a long line at various altitudes, the bird-machines tending to be higher. The *Malabar*'s double-wing silhouette was easily visible. Flying nicely straight, right on target towards the smudge in the middle distance that was the Arc de Triomphe.

In the grandstand the official commentator kept up a continual high-pitched yammer magnified by his hailing trumpet. He spoke French, of course, a language in which Scarlatti knew the names of several valves and wire gauges, but little else.

Several men began to set up the finish line further out in the field—two tall poles with a long ribbon strung between.

"Excuse me, Miss? You're with the Duke of Southwind, aren't you?" A newspaper reporter, notepad at the ready.

Scarlatti eyed him warily. Youngish, with an open, freckled face. His homburg was pushed back on his head and his shirtsleeves rolled up. He wore striped braces.

"I'm his ground crew," she admitted.

"Just you?"

"Just me."

He wrote this down without any sign of condescension, and Scarlatti warmed to him.

"What do you fancy your chances, Miss . . . ?"

"Scarlatti. We have a very good chance. Our machine is the best."

"The best mechanical machine, you mean."

"No, I mean the best flying machine."

The reporter looked up from his notebook and paid her proper attention. His eyes were a lot shrewder than his young face.

"You're saying a mechanical machine is better than a magical machine."

"I'm sure you know what the Duke's views are, Mr . . . "

"Johnson. Vic Johnson, *Daily Herald*. I'm familiar with the Duke's ideas. I was interested in yours. You built the *Spirit of Malabar*, didn't you?"

"I was instrumental in its design," said Scarlatti carefully. She'd had reporters turn her words around before.

"You use a Rolls-Royce engine, I believe."

"That's correct."

"How can you lift such a heavy piece of metal without magic?"

"Velocity and aerodynamics."

The distant specks reached the Arc, manouevered around it. One fell away from the others, but it had been one of the highest flyers and she knew it wasn't the *Malabar*. Some of the crowd began to cheer for the local favourite.

"It's an interesting name."

"We thought so." Malabar being the only battle in recorded history where troops without mages had beaten soldiers assisted by magic.

"Do you plan to build more of these flying machines?"

"We, er . . . "

Scarlatti's eye was drawn by the same mage she'd noticed earlier, the skinny man with the lined face. He stared intently at the now-scattered machines, their silhouettes growing clearer as they headed back up the Champs Élysées the field. To her horror, his fingers were twitching in the complex movements of a spell. He began to mutter.

Scarlatti looked back at the sky. The *Malabar* low and wide, keeping away from the irregular swooping of its nearest neighbour. Bane wasn't in the lead, but if he could lose the rest of his height and gain speed by diving at the end, they had the chance of a place.

But as she watched, the *Malabar*'s left wing lifted, as though it had run into a strong cross-wind. The nose jerked up, then steadied, but it was obviously an effort for the pilot to hold it on course.

Vic Johnson had shaded his eyes to watch the machines, too. "That's odd," he said. "Looks like there's a bit of wind out th—"

Scarlatti headed for the mage at the edge of the crowd. No steward or gendarme in sight, dammit.

"Oy!" she called, anything to take the mage's attention away from the spell. Nothing else she could do, short of physically assaulting him, which wouldn't work as she'd never get past his personal protection shields. "Hey, you!"

The mage didn't look around, but several people in the crowd did, with expressions of scandalised interest that a common woman would dare address a mage with such disrespect.

"Stop making that wind!" Scarlatti thrust her face into the mage's field of vision. He jerked back in surprise, but his fingers kept working. Up close, she could smell the ozone.

"How d—dare you," he sputtered. His breath also smelled, of halitosis.

She glanced up. The leading machines were no more than half a mile away. The *Malabar* had lost speed and was threatening to stall.

"He's sabotaging the race," Scarlatti called loudly.

More faces turned their way.

"Excuse me, sir." Johnson had followed her and was regarding the mage with narrowed eyes. "I work for the *Herald*. Would you care to comment on the race?"

The mage darted him a look. "No," he said shortly. "Go away. And you," he glared at Scarlatti, "will be fined. Perhaps imprisoned."

"You're the one who'll be fined," she retorted, stealing a glance up. Had the *Malabar* straightened up a little? "For sabotaging the race."

The mage laughed nastily. "Sabotage? What is the creature talking about?" His lip curled. "Oh I see, this is the mad duke's vassal. I suppose you must find an excuse for coming last."

"You conjured wind," Scarlatti protested.

"Pshaw." The mage spread his hands in denial, but one of his fingers was still crooked upwards.

"I'm sure the mages aren't worried about your mechanical machine winning, Miss Scarlatti." Johnson's eye, unseen by the mage, closed in a wink. "And what would it matter if it did? It's just a curiosity."

The *Malabar*'s nose lowered and it gained speed.

"What would it matter?" The mage spun on the reporter. "Just a curiosity?" His composure crumbled before their eyes and anger drew all the lines in his face tight. "You fools. They are like the blasphemer Darwin, the traitor Hobbes, the demon Newton."

"I say, that's a bit thick." The Hussar officer had strolled over.

"*You* are thick! You and your like sit fiddling while the very basis of our civilisation is undermined."

"It's just a machine," shrugged Johnson.

"No!" the mage almost screamed.

Above, Bane opened the throttle and the *Malabar* swept down on the leaders through a sky once again still.

Spittle specked the mage's lips. "They are saying look, a machine that has no soul. And look, we are the same—merely biological machines. Made of parts that can be fixed. Put together under some mechanical principle of nature." He choked on the words. "They are saying there is no magic!"

"We don't deny magic," Scarlatti said. She could hear the music of the engine now. "We do question your right to use it to rule everybody else."

The cheers of the crowd drowned the mage's answer. The long-winged French machine sheared through the finish line ribbon and sank to a landing in front of the stands. Behind it, the Prussian entry flapped harder but its speed had dropped suddenly as one of its tail planes shed material.

The *Malabar*'s engine growled in victory as Bane overshot the Prussian and passed the finish post.

"Second place," said Johnson approvingly. "Not bad for a machine without a soul."

The mage swung on Scarlatti mouthing a curse, his hands raised in a spell that cracked like lightning.

No time to move.

Bright light. Stench of burning.

Her ears roared and the world spun around in a blur of blue and red. Somebody screamed.

"Up you get, gel." A large warm hand grabbed Scarlatti's, and the world righted itself again. The Hussar officer blew out his moustache and glared at a greasy, smoking stain on the grass where the mage had been standing.

"What happened?" Scarlatti was embarrassed to find her voice shook.

"Damn fool forgot the Prohibition." He chuckled. "Won't do that again, by jove."

Johnson was scribbling furiously.

Scarlatti bowed hastily to the officer. "Thank you, sir."

Then she was running across the field to where the *Malabar* had landed. Not one of Bane's best efforts—he had tipped over and her rudder pointed at the sky. That was all Scarlatti could see above the excited throng surrounding the machine.

She elbowed her way through. Bane was talking to a steward as he drew off his gauntlets, seeming not to notice the many hands that tugged or patted at his leather coat. He looked up, saw Scarlatti, and waved.

"Don't you touch that machine," Scarlatti warned one of the small boys clustered in awe around the *Malabar*'s crumpled elevator. She took in the damage with a quick glance. Nothing major.

Bane joined her. "What was all that turbulence? Or rather, who?" He pulled off his helmet, leaving his sweaty hair standing up in tufts. "Haven't felt that much concentrated malevolence since my mother found out the old man was tupping the math tutor."

Scarlatti ignored the vulgarity. It was Bane's way of relaxing tight nerves. "Some mage with a grudge against us. I caught him making a weather spell."

"Strange the committee didn't pick it up."

"They were probably too busy at the time watching the race," Scarlatti said dryly.

"Where is he now? I'll have to talk to him."

"You can't talk to him. He forgot the Prohibition on the event and tried to throw a killing bolt at me."

Scarlatti bent down and peered at the bent undercarriage. She'd have to get a donkey to pull the machine back to the hangar. Struck by Bane's uncharacteristic silence, she looked up. His face had turned bone-white, as though he was about to faint.

"What's wrong?"

"Did you say a killing bolt?"

"First time I've ever heard one. I was lucky the Prohibition was in place."

"Lucky. Yes." He opened his mouth, shut it again. "Scarlatti?"

"Hmm?" She could put long skids on the wheel assembly, which would stop the machine tipping over so easily . . .

Bane squatted beside her. "I'm sorry."

She shrugged. "It's not bad damage. It's given me an idea, too."

"That's not what I . . . "

He stared at the crash unseeing for a moment then smiled down at her, laughter lines crinkling the red marks left by his goggles. "It's a jolly fine machine."

This time, Scarlatti smiled back. "I know."

• • • • • • • • • • •

# FACE TO FACE

## JOHN HARWOOD

It was, I think, the last Christmas of the old century; at any rate it was certainly at the Carstairs' great barracks of a place down in Surrey that my friend Maurice Trevelyan and I were sitting up late; so late that, excepting the bishop, we had the drawing room fire entirely to ourselves. And since the bishop was, as usual, sound asleep, he made an ideal chaperone. Nobody seemed to know what he was, or had been, bishop of; I very much doubt whether he knew himself, for he was so old and venerable that he woke only long enough to dine, imbibe a glass or two of Reginald Carstairs' port, and settle himself back into his favourite armchair. He was invariably asleep in it when the last guest went upstairs, no matter how late; but someone must have put him to bed, for his chair was always empty in the mornings.

Not that we required a chaperone: I was, as everybody knew, simply a married woman whose husband never went out, and Maurice was equally well established in the character of a forty-five year-old bachelor of quiet habits and modest means. He had remained unmarried, it was rumoured, because of a youthful attachment, prematurely ended by the death of the woman to whose memory he remained devoted. It was not a subject I had ever raised with him, for Maurice hated to be quizzed over his personal life. I had divined this early on, in fact on the very day we were introduced in the office of the review he was then editing. Some acquaintance was chaffing him about a supposed indiscretion; I saw Maurice recoil; he saw my discomfort on his behalf, and a current of sympathy was set flowing between us. The review, to which I contributed a tale or two, lasted less than a year before its patron abandoned it, but our friendship was by then a settled thing.

Some may wonder, if personal matters were excluded, what on earth we had to talk about, to which the answer is: everything under the sun, but more particularly anything and everything that either of us had ever read, or written, or, in his case dreamed of writing, for I doubt there was ever a poet with a deeper sense of his vocation than Maurice Trevelyan. Yet he was at the same time so self-effacing as to be almost impossible to describe. Put a pen or a manuscript in his hand, and you could not doubt his force of character: about a passage of writing he could not prevent himself from telling the exact truth, however discomforting to the writer; but on any other subject he would happily yield the floor to men twenty years his junior. Even his physical appearance was not easy to capture; he was unremarkably slender, moderately tall, with dark hair receding at the temples, and fine but regular features, save only that the left side of his face looked strangely seared: I do not mean withered or scarred, but rather marked by a fixed pallor, as though he had come too close to a fire whose flames burned cold instead of hot. At any rate I can put it no better than that, and on the evening in question, as we sat gazing into the flames, our occasional silences filled by the creak and crackle of burning coals and the faint snores of the bishop dreaming peacefully on the far side of the hearth, it remained among the topics that had never been raised between us.

Instead we spoke—or rather Maurice spoke, as he would only do when we were alone—of the unwritten poem that, in various guises, had haunted him all his life. Everything good that he had ever done—and he was the most exacting, indeed ruthless critic of his own writing—seemed to him, at certain moments, only the shadow of this other work whose outlines he constantly glimpsed, but whose substance he could never capture. He believed in the community of all true poets through the ages, and sometimes spoke as if all true poems were but fragments of some great ur–poem, or Platonic quintessence of the art; at other times as if our language, in all its richness and beauty, existed in a fallen state, like some great ruin of antiquity, mere broken remnants of a celestial tongue we had once known, and lost; to this end he was fond of quoting Shelley's remark about the fading coal, or the close of "Kubla Khan": he had an especial sympathy for poets who had left behind great but unfinished works. He agreed, up to a point, with Pater, that all art aspires to the condition of music, but believed that there was a poem, destined for him and him alone to write, that would be the fulfilment of his life and the perfection of his art, and yet be expressible in ordinary English words, however extraordinary the effect of the whole might be. There were moments, he said, in which he could hear the rhythm of its lines falling as clearly as footsteps passing along a hall, and feel certain that if his inner ear were only a little more acute, he could catch the words before their echoes faded.

To some, this fascination with the unattainable might have become a torment, but Maurice seemed content with his lot. I had often wondered what he would make of the remainder of his life if that one perfect poem were ever to swoop down from the heavens and alight upon his outstretched wrist, but I never quite liked to ask, for it seemed an intrusion upon that privacy which, it sometimes struck me, we shared so intimately without ever mentioning.

We sat, then, watching the coals brighten and fade, which put me in mind, as often, of Shelley; almost simultaneously, Maurice began softly to speak the lines from "Adonais":

*The One remains, the many change and pass;*
*Heaven's light forever shines, Earth's shadows fly;*
*Life, like a dome of many-coloured glass,*
*Stains the white radiance of Eternity . . .*

where he ceased, for which I was grateful, for the trampling of the dome always seems to me wanton and wrong. It may be pagan to think so, but to me the beauty is in the whole: the One *and* the Many, the pure sunlight streaming through stained glass; heaven's light would be poorer without earth's shadows. Though perhaps heaven's light may be as far beyond mere sunlight as the many-coloured dome surpasses a shop window. "For now we see through a glass, darkly; but then face to face."

I did not realise I had spoken the last words aloud until I became aware of a stillness on my right. I looked up from the coals to find Maurice staring at me as if I had become a ghost.

"Laura"—he spoke my name as if suddenly uncertain of its meaning—"how did you know my thought?"

"I did not," I said, "or not knowingly."

As best I could, I retraced my steps for him, but he continued to stare at me with that stricken intensity until I trailed off, at a loss to understand how such a familiar verse could trouble him so profoundly. Gradually, he recovered himself, and began to look at me in his accustomed way; and then he took my hand, something he did not commonly do except at meeting and parting. His hand was very cold, despite the heat of the fire, and instinctively I sought to cover it with both of mine. But still the prohibition that had nurtured our friendship kept me from speaking.

"Those lines of Shelley's," he resumed, after a long pause, "how often have I read them over or heard them spoken, and yet never until tonight . . . I *saw*"—pointing with his other hand into the heart of the fire—"the dome shatter and reform into—a thing of darkness. And then you spoke, of all verses, that one. 'Face to Face' is the title of a manuscript I once read—in part. A tale, I must call it, though it was not like any tale I have ever read; indeed it was not like *anything* I have ever read. It was, in its effect upon the reader, the exact reverse, the most sinister inversion"—he shivered slightly, and I noticed that the seared place below his cheekbone looked paler than usual—"of that perfect poem we were discussing just now. And it was written by the woman I once dreamed of marrying."

I had not meant to release his hand, but found that I had done so. In the shadows opposite, the bishop slept on.

"You must first understand," said Maurice, as if answering some objection on my part, "in what extremity she was driven to—manifest it. Her mother and mine were close friends; in a manner of speaking we grew up together. Her letters were extraordinarily vivid. She was nineteen, and I twenty-one, when they came to live in London, and from then on I saw her frequently, until all was changed by the sudden death of her father, whose passing left them in a precarious position. My own father did what he could, but his means were very limited. I felt I could not . . . at any rate I did not . . . suffice to say", he continued somewhat hurriedly, "that my friend came to the notice of Sir Lewis Wainwright, a wealthy man some thirty years older than herself. He had, I think, had some business dealing with her late father; it was certainly within his power to secure not only her future but that of her mother and her two younger sisters. I did not—perhaps could not—believe that she ever loved him. From the first he struck me as cold, indeed evil in the very emanations of his being; I felt in him that capacity to wither and shrivel with a glance, to inspire the shrinking that flesh instinctively feels from sharpened steel, or serpents. To the casual eye, no doubt, he was simply a tall, distinguished gentleman still in the prime of life, immaculately and fastidiously dressed, perfectly courteous in manner; yet how she could have been so deceived . . . it was like watching a sleepwalker moving slowly towards the brink of a precipice and finding oneself unable to move or cry out. My consciousness of my own position kept me silent, and even made me doubt what in my heart of hearts I could not doubt; and besides, what could I have said? A poor student who could barely meet the cost of his own subsistence? Yet I *should* have spoken—"

Though he had kept his voice low, the last words escaped him as a cry of anguish. I glanced uneasily towards the bishop, but our oblivious companion did not stir.

"Maurice," I ventured, when he did not immediately continue, "you have sketched this malignant suitor all too vividly, and yet I have no picture of your—your friend: you have not so much as mentioned her name."

"Her name was Claire," he said slowly, as if struggling with some inhibition on his own side. "She was—dark, and slender—about your own height—quiet, and studious, and yet she—really I cannot, one cannot catch the essence of another. She was gentle, and virtuous, and I watched the jaws of the trap closing upon her, and did nothing. Remember that the fortunes of her mother and sisters were at stake in this; her mother was not, I think, easy about the match, rightly fearing some element of self-sacrifice on Claire's part. The constraint between us grew more tangible once the engagement had been announced. At the wedding—I wish to God I had not been there—she looked serene and calm, but very pale, whilst Sir Lewis gazed upon her with the air of a collector about to lock away some new and greatly coveted acquisition.

"They went immediately abroad, where they remained for some months; and how different her letters, with their dutiful descriptions of scenery and formal professions of happiness, seemed from those I had once received! When we called upon them after their return to London, I knew immediately that she was unhappy, but she contrived, then and afterwards, never to be alone with me. Sir Lewis, furthermore, made it subtly plain to me that I would be a tolerated, rather than a welcome visitor. His reptilian eyes seemed to draw out the very feelings I strove most desperately to conceal in his presence, and to flicker distrustfully from her to me.

"Her only child, a daughter, was born before the first anniversary of their wedding, and became the one source of light in the darkness closing upon her; that, and the knowledge that her mother and sisters were now securely provided for, though at a price they would never willingly have paid. We were all of us aware that Claire was deeply unhappy, and yet her manner of bearing it seemed to exact from us a vow of silence, not only in her presence, but between ourselves. We looked at one another, and knew that we knew, and could not speak of it. Or at least I could not, until the third year of her marriage was drawing to its close, when we began to see even less of her, and that only in the presence of her husband. His manner, formally speaking, remained perfectly polite, yet in his presence all conversation withered and died; you could feel the malevolent force of his personality raying out across the room.

"We had, however, an ally within his house: Claire's maid Rosina, who had been with the family since she was scarcely more than a child. Rosina was quick, observant, and entirely devoted to her mistress, and it was through her eyes that we saw the final scenes of the tragedy unfold.

"Claire had written a great deal before her marriage; though she would always dismiss her work as "scribbling", she had shown me some chapters of a novel which I thought very fine. And it seems that in that last autumn, as she became more and more a prisoner, she turned once again to her pen for solace, and began secretly to compose—we shall never know what, for despite her precautions he discovered, read, and then destroyed her manuscript. There followed a terrible scene, in which Claire turned at last upon her tormentor and declared her resolution to leave him. He swore that if she did so she would never see her child again, and that her mother and sisters would be turned out into the street. Coldly advising her to reconsider, he left the room.

"That same night, the child was stricken by a raging fever. Doctors were summoned, and every possible remedy tried, but in vain; less than twenty-four hours later, she was dead. Rosina, who had not left her mistress's side throughout the long night and the dreadful day that followed, said that Sir Lewis did not once appear in the sickroom until the poor child's ordeal had ceased. Claire's grief had overwhelmed her, but as he appeared in doorway, she ceased to weep, and a terrible stillness came over her. She took the dead infant in her arms, and though she seemed not even to see her husband looming directly in her path, such was her expression that he fell back, and spoke not a word as she bore her daughter's body from the room, and slowly descended the stair to her private sitting room, whence came the snap of the key turning in the lock.

"Sir Lewis seemed, for once, at a loss. Slowly recovering his self-possession, he descended the stair in his turn and stood irresolutely at Claire's door. Twice he raised his hand as if to knock, but did not do so; finally, he continued on down and disappeared into his own private domain. Rosina then made haste to rejoin her mistress, expecting Claire to respond when she tapped with their special signal upon the door, and called softly to ask if she could be of help, but there was no reply. The house was very quiet, and as she waited at the door she became aware of a very faint scratching sound from within. She tapped once more, but there was again no response, and the faint scratching or rustling sound continued without pause.

"Several times during the next few hours, as afternoon gave way to evening and darkness fell, Rosina returned to the sitting-room door, with the same result. The rest of the house remained deathly quiet; no one came to give her any orders; no bells were rung. Finally, she went miserably upstairs to her own quarters, where she fell at last into an exhausted sleep.

"Next morning she was awakened by the maidservant with whom she shared the attic with the news that the lock of her mistress's room was about to be forced. Dressing hastily, Rosina was just in time to see this done. A footman broke open the door, and stood back to allow Sir Lewis to pass. From her position on the stair, Rosina saw her mistress lying motionless upon a sofa, with her dead child in her arms. Unable to restrain herself, she ran into the room, to be roughly ejected by Sir Lewis's valet, but not before she had taken in the scene in one terrible glimpse: the dead mother and child in their last embrace; the empty vial of laudanum; and on the writing table nearby, a pile of handwritten pages surrounded by several pens, sheets of blotting paper, and an open bottle of ink.

"Rosina was shortly summoned by the housekeeper, given immediate notice, and sent upstairs to pack. Instead, overcome by grief and horror, she threw herself upon her bed and wept until sleep overtook her. By the time she woke, it was late in the evening. She had gathered together her few things, and was venturing out upon the landing when a fearful shriek came echoing up the stairwell. There followed a brief silence, then sounds of shouting and of running feet. Afraid to descend, she waited for what seemed like hours until her friend appeared. The cry had been that of Sir Lewis's valet, who had found his master dead on the floor of his dressing room, surrounded by the scattered pages of a manuscript. The corpse's face was frozen into an expression of indescribable terror, and entirely blanched, as if vitriol had been flung across the features."

Maurice paused, staring into the dwindling glow of the coals. A formless dread which had crept upon me was beginning to assume a more definite shape, as if some sinister presence were materialising in the shadows behind the slumbering bishop.

"There was a kind of fatality about the way in which that manuscript came into my possession. It so happened that Sir Lewis's valet was entirely unlettered, but most reluctant to admit as much; and it was he who collected up the scattered pages whilst his master's corpse was being removed under the doctor's direction, and carried them off to the study nearby, where he placed them in one of the pigeon-holes in Sir Lewis's desk. And since it was later asserted that Sir Lewis had been looking over some legal document at the time of his death—the cause being given as a stroke, with the curious blanching of the face put down as an unusual complication—I believe the valet mistook one set of papers for another, without any idea that he had done so. The executors must have been exceptionally scrupulous, for they returned all of Claire's personal effects to her mother, including an envelope labelled "manuscript, in the hand of the late Lady Wainwright", which her mother, in recognition of the literary ambitions Claire and I had once shared, passed on to me.

"I was, by then, living in rooms off the Strand, in Essex Court, and I was quite alone on the evening when I sat down to open the envelope. It was only a few weeks after Claire's death, and I was still numb with the shock of it as I began to read, hoping to hear again the voice which . . . no matter. The hand was hers indeed, but the voice was not.

"It was, or seemed at first to be, simply an account of someone waiting alone, in an upstairs room of an empty house at night. The location was not specified but you felt the stillness all around, the extremity of the speaker's isolation; for it was told in the first person, though you could not tell whether the narrator was male or female, young or old. As I read on, I felt more and more strongly that the consciousness of the narrative was in fact my own, until I lost all awareness of my actual surroundings. In its gradual accumulation of detail it was like the furnishing of a house; item by item, it crept upon you in a slow and insidious fashion. It seemed to reach directly into that part of the soul which believes upon instinct, like a child, but which is normally inaccessible to us except in moments of absolute terror or utter despair. Something, I know not how it was done, caused me to recall with intolerable vividness every mean or contemptible thing I had ever done, from earliest childhood, and worse, every good deed I had left undone; a great black catalogue of sins and omissions opening before my eyes. And yet I did not feel this moral terror to be the principal intent of the narrative upon me, but rather an accompaniment of some still darker, more ominous purpose.

"The very rhythm of the sentences was like a soft drum, a pulse heard more and more loudly, until it became the sound of footsteps, still a long way off, but charged with menace. I was still faintly aware that I was reading, but that awareness only increased my apprehension, for the extraordinary vividness with which the scene had been set seemed now to guarantee that the face of what was fast approaching would not be left unspecified, and yet would awaken more, not less terror, than the worst promptings of my own imagination.

"It was, I think, at that exact moment that I realised that I was hearing the sound of real, actual footfalls in the corridor outside my rooms. I looked up—or thought I looked up—from the page; and found that my familiar surroundings had metamorphosed into those of the narrative. I was alone in a dark and isolated house, far from any other human habitation, with footsteps closing upon me where no footsteps should have been.

"Clutching the manuscript, I rose from my chair and began to back away from the door. The room was lit by a single candelabra, so placed that I could see the reflection of its flames in the window to which I turned as my one hope of escape. Better to be dashed to pieces on the ground below than endure so much as a glimpse of what was preparing to enter. As I reached for the sash, I saw my own face reflected in the windowpane, caught in the last extremity of terror, its eyes fixed upon a point beyond my shoulder, upon the door opening at my back; upon that visitant whom I saw indeed as in a glass darkly, but whom my reflected self seemed plainly and intolerably to view, in the instant before I covered my eyes with the manuscript and darkness dropped upon me like the hangman's hood.

"I came to myself upon the floor of my room in Essex Court, the unread portion of the narrative pressed against my cheek; you see its mark upon me still. How or why I was spared I know not, but I woke with the conviction that had I reached the end of the manuscript, I should certainly have died. At any rate, I have never yet dared to look upon it again."

He fell silent, staring into the dying embers of the fire.

"Maurice," I said hesitantly, "do you mean to say that this manuscript still exists?"

"Yes; I could not bring myself to destroy it."

Because it was hers, I thought, but did not like to say so.

"You are right, of course," he went on, as if I had spoken. "It is only that—well, supposing I did fall asleep? Or failed some sort of test, and turned back when I should have gone on? After all, I did not actually see anything plain; perhaps I was, literally, frightened by my own reflection? Might I not be destroying something that ought to have been preserved?"

"Maurice," I said firmly, "if after twenty years the impression of that experience remains so indelible—and not only the mental impression," I added, glancing at the mark seared across his cheek, "then it would be most unwise to chance a second encounter with it." But then I thought he looked at me a little askance, which made me doubt my own motive, and caused me to add, impulsively, "but if you wish, I will sit by you while you look at the manuscript again, or even . . . "

There I pulled up, aware that whilst Maurice was as devoid of egotism as it is possible for a man to be, he might not be well pleased by my offering to assume the risk. But he seemed not to catch the last phrase; he took my hand again, and this time I found that mine was the colder.

"Dear Laura, I could not ask so much of you . . . and yet there is no one else on this earth I *would* ask."

"Then trust me once more. You must not bear this burden any further; at least, not alone."

"Very well. If you are certain, let it be now—"

"Do you mean you have it here?"

"Yes, for I never feel quite easy unless I know that it is safe. But Laura; it is late, and you are cold, I think, and perhaps we should wait for daylight—"

"No," I said, striving to conceal my apprehension, for I could see that he wanted no further delay.

"Very well," he repeated. "You will watch as I read, and unless I was indeed mistaken, you will witness its destruction."

He rose, and quietly made up the fire, and went softly from the room. The bishop, whom I had quite forgotten, stirred amidst the flickering shadows, but did not wake. I drew my wrap more closely about me, almost overwhelmed by several contrary emotions. The dark spell of his narrative still clung to me, and yet I felt as if a long chapter in the history of my friendship with Maurice had just reached its close, leaving me eager to know what the next might bring. Warmed by the cheerful glow and crackle of the reviving fire, I wondered how mere words on paper could possibly bring about the effect that Maurice had so vividly described. Yet there was the mark upon his cheek, and the death of the malignant husband, which led me to thoughts of poor Claire, whom I still could not picture with any distinctness; and so my mind ran on for an indefinite interval, until I became aware that Maurice had been gone far longer than it could reasonably have taken him to ascend to his room and return with the manuscript.

There were, of course, a dozen reasons why he might have been delayed, but as I sat upright, with my heart beginning to race and cold apprehension rushing upon me, they seemed to shrink to one; at least to the only one I dared entertain: Maurice had been taken suddenly ill. Really I ought to ring, or wake someone—but whom?—at two in the morning? And what if it proved to be a false alarm . . . ? But fear already had me on my feet, and moving toward the mantelpiece to secure a candle. With a last glance at the unconscious bishop, I hastened towards the door and out into the chill hallway.

Going up the stairs, I had to look to my candle, for the wind had risen outside. The sky was fortunately bright: through the windows above the landing, I could see wisps of cloud scudding past the face of the moon. Save for the faint moaning of the wind, the house was deathly quiet, and as I turned into the corridor which led to Maurice's room, even the sound of the wind dwindled and ceased. My candle-flame steadied as I stopped at his door, feeling suddenly conspicuous. No light showed underneath. I tapped as loudly as I dared, glancing over my shoulder. There was no response. Too late to turn back now; I tried the handle, found it unlocked, and entered.

Though I caught the odour of a wick recently extinguished, the room was dark, save for a band of moonlight streaming through the french windows opposite, which were, I realised, open. An icy draught caught at my own candle and, before I could shield it, blew out the flame. But the moonlight falling across the floor had already shown me what I most dreaded finding. Maurice lay sprawled upon the carpet, with his head by the open window and the moon shining full upon his face. For a moment I thought he might be safe, for his eyes were closed and his expression perfectly peaceful; he looked, as sleepers often do, far younger than his years, and in that pure white light the seared mark seemed to have been quite erased. But as I knelt beside him I saw all too plainly that he was not asleep. The freezing wind rose, and ruffled his hair, but he did not move. Instead, something stirred and rustled in the darkness on my right, rearing up, as it seemed, from behind a table no more than two feet from where I knelt, something that flapped and swooped above me in a serpentine rush and went howling out upon a sudden gust that flung those terrible pages into the moonlit sky, scattering upon the wind and away into the night.

· · · · · · · · · · ·

# THE HEAD IN THE GOATSKIN BAG

## JENNY BLACKFORD

Princess Andromeda slapped her new Skythian slave.

"If you pull my hair again, barbarian," Andromeda said, "I'll have my father feed you to the sea-monster." The princess ignored the tears in the slave girl's wide blue eyes and slapped her soft face again, backhand this time, and harder.

Still furious, Andromeda snatched the gold and ivory comb from the slave, who dropped to the ground in terror. The useless creature had been a king's daughter back in Skythia, apparently; that was what Andromeda's father Kepheus had told her when he'd brought the new girl to her. "Precious booty of battle," he'd boasted, "for my precious daughter." By the look on his face, she had been meant to be impressed—but whether the slave really was a king's daughter or not, she shouldn't have pulled Andromeda's tangled black curls.

The princess's rage wanted to claw its way out of her belly and chest, and tear through everything around her. Every muscle in her body, every bone and sinew, throbbed with the pain of it. She strode to the window and looked longingly down at the sea. Oh, to be free! The sea-monster bellowed in the distance, and the sound stirred something deep inside Andromeda. There was something she needed desperately, something she had been missing for such a long time—but what was it?

• • •

Rage moved the sea-monster, deep in the ocean. Her long, greeny-gray body looped and rippled with anger. She needed to kill, *now*, but the little fish that fled from her were not worthy opponents.

Aha! She sensed a sailing boat moving on the surface of the water, far above her. Fury boiled in her thick blue-green veins. How dare these petty humans invade the sea? It was her domain!

She coiled her long body through the water, just above the seabed, until she was directly under the sailing boat, and speared straight up, driving the ship high into the air. For a moment it felt wonderful. The impact of the wooden boat on her armored snout was pure joy. As she resubmerged, she saw fishermen and their gear floating in the wreckage. The kicking legs and flailing arms of the humans enticed her. She hunted them down, one by one, and crunched their bones. After she'd eaten them all, though, her fury was as violent as ever. Her tail lashed the ocean viciously. She needed more victims.

• • •

Andromeda turned back from the window to her jeweled bedroom, her beautiful cage. She pushed the rage down, out of sight, out of knowledge. The little slave, poor terrified creature that she was, didn't deserve to die. *Someone* deserved to die, perhaps, but not the slave.

Andromeda was a princess; she must act like one. Dignity was everything to a king's daughter. Her mother Kassiopeia, more beautiful than the starry sky at night, had tried to teach her that hard lesson since infancy; but it was a hard lesson to learn.

Deliberately, Andromeda breathed deeply and smoothly, as the mage Tithonius had taught her three years ago when the rages had started, after her breasts had begun to swell. She'd always tried so hard to be a dutiful king's daughter, but time after time the anger had overwhelmed her. Raging with anger in her lovely room, she would gaze down at the furious waves, wishing so much to be free . . . These days, she felt empty inside, as if she'd lost something vital to her—but what could it have been?

The mage Tithonius had been the only person who could help her, but before he could find out what had happened, her father had expelled him from the kingdom. The monster had appeared in the sea soon after Andromeda's rages started; her father had ordered Tithonius to ignore the princess's trivial problems, and instead to spend all his energies on defeating the monster. When the mage failed, the king banished him.

With Tithonius gone, though, the huge monster killed so many men at sea that the people were calling for a human sacrifice. The kingdom had lost too many of its brave sailors and fishermen, and slim young boys no longer dared to dive for pearls, no matter the rewards. And Andromeda herself was racked by rage, day and night, no matter how hard she tried to be a dutiful princess.

All too soon, her father Kepheus would choose a husband for her: a prince from one of the half-hostile kingdoms that encircled their small country. She would be traded like a brood mare to some man she'd never met, some foreign king's eldest son. She would be his queen, would bear fine children as her lovely mother had done, royal hostages to ensure the safety and prosperity of her father's kingdom, and her husband's. Then, dignity would be all that was left to her. What little freedom she had would be gone forever.

Andromeda put out her slender, pale arm, and lifted the cowering slave girl from the floor. She placed the gold and ivory comb back into the Skythian slave's reluctant hand.

"Comb my hair, girl," she said as calmly as she could, sitting herself back down on the rock crystal stool inlaid with golden dolphins, in front of the oval mirror of highly-polished silver. Her reflection stared back at her, her violet eyes shining wild, cheeks flushed almost crimson, hair a writhing mass of glossy black. Then, more gently, she said to the slave, "Don't be afraid, girl. I would not let my father give you to the sea-monster even if he asked. Truly. *Please* comb my hair."

The slave girl's eyes were red, but she stood up straight as a statue, and started to comb again at Andromeda's wild black hair, without a word. *Yes*, Andromeda thought. Her father had been right. The girl really had been a king's daughter, once. Just like her.

• • •

Perseus flew over Kepheus' kingdom, miraculously propelled by the winged sandals that Hermes had lent him for his heroic quest to the end of Okeanos, the great sea that encircled the earth. He was still far away from his home in the island of Seriphos. As he flew, Medusa's severed head, safe in the goatskin bag tied around his neck, bumped once more into his chest. He winced, and tried to feel gloriously victorious. He'd slain the gorgon Medusa, lopped off her monstrous snake-haired head; he was a great hero, now, and none could withstand his might.

Surely, though, the goatskin bundle around his neck was far too heavy for a mere head—even the head of a gorgon, the monstrous, incestuous child of Phorkys, old man of the sea, and his sea-dwelling sister Keto. The hideous fat snakes that had served the creature for hair still writhed inside the goatskin bag, and Perseus' skin crawled at the touch. But Medusa couldn't turn him to stone, he told himself, not now. The bag protected him. As long as the head was inside the bag, he couldn't see the face even by accident. He was safe.

*So why were the snakes still moving?* He'd *killed* Medusa, hadn't he? Hermes had lent Perseus the famous sandals so that he could fly swiftly as the wind, and gray-eyed Athena had guided his hand as he looked into his bright-burnished shield and hacked Medusa's snake-wreathed head from her shoulders with Hermes' sickle of bright adamant. If he'd even glanced at the gorgon from the corner of his eye, he would have been turned into stone, a Perseus-shaped statue forever. But he *hadn't*. He'd looked into the shield, not at Medusa's face, and he'd killed her. He'd done what Athena and Hermes had wanted him to. *Medusa was dead.*

All the same, Perseus could feel the blood from Medusa's severed neck dripping through the bag onto his chest and down his stomach. It burned like the venom of poisonous snakes. Was it eating through his woolen tunic and dissolving his skin? He didn't dare stop to look. But when he landed, when he finally took off his tunic, would he see firm flesh, or only pale bones?

No. Gray-eyed Athena would protect him. The gorgon Medusa was dead, and her head could not turn him now to stone from inside the goatskin bag.

But what was that below him? It looked like a beautiful virgin girl, chained to a cliff next to the sea. He shook his head. Nothing these barbarians did would ever surprise him.

He changed his course and angled down to take a closer look at the girl. Rescuing a virgin—especially one as pretty as this one looked from here—should be an easy task for a hero, after killing snake-haired Medusa.

• • •

Andromeda stood on the rock, a living sacrifice to the sea-monster that attacked her father's kingdom. The manacles chafed around her wrists and ankles, but she tried not to pull at the bronze chains that held her to the cliff. Dignity, she thought, *dignity*.

The oracle of the god Amun, in far-away Egypt, had told her father's desperate messengers how to free his kingdom from the sea-monster. The priests had read the portents in the sky and finally pronounced, "Queen Kassiopeia offended Poseidon, ruler of the sea, by boasting too haughtily of her beauty. She claimed to be more beautiful than the sea-dwelling Nereids, the lovely daughters of ancient Nereus. Poseidon sent the monster to punish her impious pride. Here is what you must do to save your kingdom: chain your daughter to a rock and let the sea-monster take her, and it will depart."

Half of the kingdom was lined up along on the beach, waiting, watching for the monster to eat the girl. Spray from the breaking waves fell over her again and again. Andromeda's gown of fine white linen, patterned at the hem with leaping dolphins, was soaked. At least they'd given her the dignity of clothes. They hadn't chained her to the rock naked, to tempt the monster with her tender flesh.

She didn't blame her mother. Kassiopeia was surely the most beautiful of mortal women, though not the most circumspect in speech. If what she said had not been true, the gods would not have taken such violent offense at her words. The queen's tears since the messengers had returned from Egypt had been terrible to see. It was her father, not her mother, who had accepted the truth of the oracle, who had ordered his guards to chain his only daughter to a rock as food for a monster.

If she'd been free to move more than a single pace, three steps would have taken the princess to the edge of the sea. She could have dived in, dived down and down, and been free forever. No foreign prince, no royal children. . . no sea-monster. Now, though, all she could do was stand here, waiting for the monster to come for her. She heard it bellowing in the distance, and shuddered.

It was her duty to die for her country. Was being eaten so much worse than being married off and sent away forever? Perhaps not— but right now, it seemed so. How long would she remain alive after it took her in its jaws? Would it chew her with great jagged teeth, or swallow her whole, leave her to dissolve slowly in its enormous stomach?

She stood up very straight. She was a king's daughter. *Dignity*.

But how long would it be, before the monster came for her?

• • •

The gorgon Medusa seethed with pain and misery, inside the goatskin bag. It was not as easy as Perseus thought to kill a being like her. She was the child of two immortal gods; she had lain many times with Poseidon Earth-Shaker, mighty Zeus's brother and equal. When Perseus had cut off her head, two children of Poseidon had sprung from her severed neck: winged Pegasos, most beautiful of horses, and giant Khrusaor.

How dare this impious mortal, Perseus, behead her? He could not have done it without the connivance of Athena, that bloodless bitch birthed from her father Zeus's head, and Zeus's fool messenger Hermes.

Medusa felt the precious blood leaking out from the vessels of her severed neck, drip by drip. It would not kill her, but it filled her with vengeful anger. Her snakes writhed in fury.

*Revenge.* She would have her revenge.

• • •

The monster could smell something wonderful: better than a giant squid, or a boatful of fishermen. Something she'd been looking for all her short life, without even knowing it. Something she needed, if she was ever to be whole and complete.

She whirled around in the water, using all the sensitive organs she used to hunt her prey. Oh, but the smell was exquisite! She needed it!

Straight as an arrow, she flew underwater to the source of the smell. Overwhelmed with joy and desire, she lifted her head out of the water and saw the thing she needed: a human being, young, female, slender, standing very straight. The girl was chained to a cliff with bonds of bronze.

Their eyes locked.

• • •

Andromeda stared into the sea-monster's huge violet eyes. She *knew* those eyes. Every day she saw them shining in her oval silver mirror. She had to get closer, to touch the lovely beast, to stroke her wet, shining skin. The princess didn't fear the monster's muscular coils, her rock-hard scales, her rows of sharp, strong teeth. The monster would never harm her. The girl needed the sea-monster, if she was ever to be whole and. . . happy. The monster was *her*, was what she'd lost.

Andromeda watched as the monster lifted her head higher above the waves, then snaked it down between her body and the cliff. The girl's heart was beating very fast, but not from fear. Her eyes were still locked onto the monster's huge, familiar eyes.

There was an audible gasp from the people lined up on the beach. The monster's great jaws opened wider, then closed—but no blood flowed. Andromeda's chains, snapped by the immense teeth, fell to the rock.

Gazing up into the monster's violet eyes, Andromeda stretched her arms wide, and put her hands out to touch the monster's greeny-gray scaled body.

*Herself. Her life. Her freedom.*

• • •

"Don't move, virgin," Perseus shouted from high in the sky. "I'm here to rescue you. I will kill the monster for you." He only hoped that he could reach her before the sea-monster took her. The closer he got to her, the lovelier she looked. What were her people thinking? She was far too beautiful to sacrifice.

Strangely, the girl didn't move. She was gazing up at the hideous, scaly monster. Of course, he thought, she was a tender young girl; she must be transfixed with terror. But she didn't *look* terrified. Could the monster have enchanted her somehow, taken away her will to live? He would attack it from behind, give it no chance to try such tricks on him.

The monster still hadn't noticed him. Its whole being was concentrated on the girl. Surely she only had moments to live, if Perseus didn't kill the beast. Descending as fast as he could, Perseus pulled his bronze sword from its scabbard. Now that he was a hero, he thought as he flew, he would need a better scabbard. Maybe he could have the smiths work Medusa's head on it.

"No!" the girl screamed, when finally she looked up and saw him. "No! Don't kill it! *It's me! The monster is me!*"

Perseus ignored the girl's nonsense. Clearly, she was delirious with fear. There was no time to lose. This time, he would act without Athena's help. He would kill the sea-monster and rescue a beautiful virgin. Surely she was of royal blood, maybe even a princess.

Luckily, the monster was still acting as if he wasn't there. It was almost an insult to a hero like him—but perhaps the gods had arranged it this way, to help him. Perseus swung his sword and slashed viciously at the back of the scaled neck, once, twice, three times.

The monster's neck was like stone. The bronze sword broke, and fell from Perseus near-paralyzed right hand. What weapon could he use now against the monster? If his strong sword had failed, the short dagger tucked into his right boot would be useless. The monster, which up till now had acted as if he were nothing, or less than nothing, turned its massive head to face him. The immense jaws opened, showing great jagged teeth.

For a moment, the world seemed to stop. Then Perseus felt Medusa's loathsome snakes writhing in the goatskin bag around his neck. Their fat bodies moved nauseatingly against his chest. He thought he heard a noise from the bag: a low, rattling noise.

Yes! The gods were prompting him! The head of Medusa was a fearsome weapon! A glance from her eyes would turn the monster to stone. Petrified, it would be a permanent monument to his greatness.

"Don't look," he yelled to the girl, then thrust his hand into the bag, eyes tightly closed lest he himself be turned to stone. His stomach heaved, but he took hold of the head, and pulled. The heavy head hung in his hand. Careful not to open his eyes even a hair's breadth, he held the head out towards the monster's face.

• • •

Medusa screeched with joy. The pompous fool of a hero thought that he controlled her power! Ha! This sea-monster was no just target for her righteous anger. It was gorgon-slaying Perseus that she hated.

The wreath of snakes around her face lifted their scaly heads all at once, and fastened their fangs on Perseus' vulnerable wrist. He kept his eyes squeezed closed, but it made no difference. Medusa's head, released from his grasp, hung in mid-air and watched with glee as the venom from her snakes stopped the hero's heart, and his face went slack and empty.

As delicate as a cat, the monster took Perseus' limp body between her gigantic jaws and crunched. Soon, a hero-sized lump was moving down the sea-monster's sinuous neck.

"Bravo!" the princess cried, and the monster put her great head down to nuzzle the girl. Then, before Medusa's flashing eyes, the monster blurred and shrank into a green-gray mist. Princess and monster merged.

The gorgon, far-sighted daughter of the gods, had known the truth, even from inside the bag where that fool Perseus had thrust her severed head. Together, princess and monster were a single whole.

"Now," the princess said, her head held very high, "it's time to deal with my father."

Medusa's severed head, still dripping blood, laughed and laughed.

••••••••••

# FOREVER, MISS TAPEKWA COUNTY

## LISA L. HANNETT

Verralee trusted the bluebird tattooed behind her mother's right ear.

She couldn't hear what it chirped—those songs were for Kaylene alone—but long ago she'd learned to decipher its colouring, to translate the rhythm of inked wings flapping. Ultramarine feathers blurred with excitement meant Kaylene's tattoo had truths to tell. If he had gossip to share, little black-beaked lies, the *sialia*'s downy throat would flush lurid red, and moulting shoulders would slump beneath the weight of false news. His voice, as far as Verralee was concerned, sounded just like her mother's. His insights were shaped on her tongue.

In the makeshift kitchen backstage, Kaylene's frosted-blonde hair was pulled back, unbleached roots framing the bird's sapphire promises, his sketched body still visible through the steam of canning pots boiling on the camp stovetop. *Smile pretty,* he said with her mother's mouth. *Tilt your head to avoid doubling your chin. Keep your hair out of your face.* Clean pickling jars were extracted with tongs from scalding water. *And don't hold your breath, my girl. Don't repeat your Mamma's mistakes.* One by one, three wide-mouthed Masons were expertly lined up on a small countertop, the workspace identical to six others the judges had ordered made for this year's contestants. Prepared for their test runs.

The glass cooled, waiting to be filled with a practice-round of preserves.

*One last time, for lungs' sakes. Pay attention.*

He didn't always make sense, at least not at first, but Verralee was used to the bird's riddles. She looked up at the clock: fifteen minutes until the final round. Quickly, she changed into her bikini as the audience, hidden now beyond the stage curtain, babbled in the auditorium. She joined her mother at the stove while the crowd quaffed shots of whiskey, wolf-whistling as last year's winner was paraded around for their entertainment. The tattoo chirruped nonsense—*breathe deep, breathe deep*—and though she still didn't catch his meaning, Verralee believed in that deep Egyptian hue, that lapis lazuli warbling. With his fluttering wings mussing Kaylene's loose French roll, and that grin curling her mother's magenta lips as she spoke, Verralee knew things would turn out fine. One way or the other.

*For fins' sakes, pay attention*, the bluebird repeated. *Don't you want to win?*

She was—*honest*—and yes, she really, really did.

Goldfish whirlpooled in her stomach whenever she thought about being crowned Miss Tapekwa County. Though she tried not to care—she'd primed herself to be a good sport, even practised her gracious-loser smile—in truth her hopes were sky-high, tied fast to her soul with kite strings. Sometimes she wanted to win so bad, it felt like a hurricane raged around her. Hope yanked at her heart, dragged it up her throat, blocked her windpipe, cut off all rational thought.

She watched polliwogs swimming in the clear round beads of Kaylene's long necklace and knew just how they felt: spinning, spinning in cramped bubbles, stuck in one spot, all heads and tails, half-formed limbs and inhibited growth. She was eighteen now; she had to stretch out of her plain-girl shell, shine like the ageless harvest queens, and prove that her face looked best when not darkened by the shadow of a book. If Verralee won the pageant—and she would, wouldn't she? The bluebird was rarely wrong; only that one time, all those years ago, just that once. When it'd been her mother's turn to compete, when he'd said, without the slightest trace of red at his throat, that Kaylene could win. Not *would*, Verralee reminded herself, *could*. That one simple letter made all the difference: *could*, not *would*. Like he'd known without knowing that tattooed Kaylene, stunner though she was, would never transform into a true Miss

Tapekwa County. But once Verralee won, her smooth olive skin coloured only with spray-tan and dabs of makeup, her hair dyed a black so convincing it almost looked natural, she'd see things and go places her mother, in losing, had missed.

She'd be one of Town Hall's main girls. They'd take her to Nationals, staged on an island on the far side of the country, where ladies with flower jewellery and grass skirts danced beneath palm trees, where they cooked pigs in coal-filled holes in the ground. Where she'd perform, too, under that foreign sun, and when they liked her best she'd be given a special crown; one she could bring back to Tapekwa County after her nation-wide tour. Goldfish churned at the thought of how pretty she'd be then. Officially.

The bluebird said it would be so.

Kaylene plucked one tadpole bead from the strand around her neck, popped it into a jar, handed another to Verralee. *You watching?* asked the tattoo, as his high-heeled interpreter filled the vessel with jellied liquid. She spoke secret words that didn't come from his beak. *Last chance, Vee. Then it's all you.*

Verralee paused, frogling in her palm.

*It's all you.*

That's what Simon had said yesterday, holding her hand, pressing her close, his glasses knocked to the ground from the urgency with which he hugged her, begging her not to compete. *You'll be different*, he'd said to the only girl he'd called his own since the eighth grade. He didn't ask her how hard it all was, didn't mention the fact that winning might hurt more than losing. *No relationship can survive what you'll become*—but Verralee had cut him off. She couldn't cry the night before the pageant. She couldn't afford the puffiness.

*This isn't about us*, she'd said.

*No*, he'd agreed. *It's all you.*

The polliwog rolled into the jar. Verralee splashed in a cupful of water, added a frond of seaweed, then rested her hand on the rim. The rest of the spell, caught between her tongue and teeth, refused to form.

This wasn't just about her, not completely. Not only. Winning this title would make her part of a larger, more beautiful story. She'd follow in her great-auntie's footsteps, pick up the trail where Kaylene had gone astray. Folk would come from all over to see the display at Town Hall, to bathe in the wonder of *Miss Tapekwa County: Now and Forever.* Just like Verralee had each year, donning her new birthday dress and the polished shoes Kaylene wouldn't let her wear 'round the farm. They'd gaze with reverence at row upon row of dewy faces. Drooping ropes would prevent spectators from touching the winners' sequins and shimmer and shine—but every last one of them would want to. Oh, how they'd want to. Instead, under the guards' watchful eyes, they'd resign themselves to commenting on the changing fashions over the years; on the curve of that one's waist, the glimmer in that one's eyes. All would agree, even without touching or tasting or knowing them intimately, that each girl was the most beautiful in the world. And as they turned for home, back to dry fields and cold dairies and dwindling bales of hay, their bellies would warm with pride. These perfect girls in their swimmers, they'd say, these paragons of aquatic beauty, came not just from God, but from the very soul of Tapekwa County.

What was wrong with wanting to give folk such pleasure?

Verralee shook her head and again looked at the clock. She hoped Simon would continue to visit the show, if and when she won.

*Focus,* said the bird. *We've rehearsed this a million times.* While Kaylene's tadpole flourished, transforming in the pickling solution she'd charmed, Verralee's sank listless to the bottom. The producers had kept the light dim backstage, but even so she could make out the unmoving shadow in her jar; she could see sparks and phosphorescence illuminate Kaylene's. *You'll always regret it, you know. If you mess things up now.*

True.

The songbird's collar glowed Persian blue, the lines of each feather delicately rendered, thin as the fine crescent scars ribbing both sides of Kaylene's neck. Traces of gills half-formed. Permanent reminders of the only time the tattoo's truth had been one letter off.

*Focus,* he repeated, after Kaylene cleared the lump from her throat. *You can do this, darlin'. Make us proud.*

Kaylene passed the necklace to Verralee, watched intently as she slipped the length of gelatinous beads over her head.

*We've dreamt of this day for years.*

• • •

Verralee's arms shook as she lowered herself into the tank.

It stood on a wheeled mahogany platform, the third of seven stationed in a gentle arc across the stage for all to see. Twelve feet high and twice as wide, its faint green glass ballooned like a brandy snifter. Verralee's fingers caught on its scalloped rim, then slid into a recessed ridge that would, once she'd won, support a silver filigreed lid moulded into the shape of a crown. Footlights refracted through the tanks' gallons of liquid, casting rainbows across the ceiling and the lucky few who'd snagged seats in the front row. Overhead, spotlights shone so hot Verralee worried the mascara would melt from her lashes before she had a chance to submerge; so bright she could no longer see Johnny, her stepfather, standing in the wings at stage left.

*They're ready for you, hun*, he'd said with a wink, his pomade-slick head poking through a split in the curtains. *I'd say* break a leg *but, you know. Somehow that don't seem right.* He stepped through the gap and held the drapes closed behind him, avoiding the stagehands cleaning Verralee's rehearsal space before her performance. Johnny leaned forward, jolly as a clarinet, and kept his voice low.

*You look gorgeous, Vee. Real gorgeous. Glad you done yerself natural—the rest of them girls is painted up like a herd of carousel ponies.*

*Gods love you, Pa*, she'd laughed, the sound only slightly forced. He'd blown her a kiss before ducking back out, blissfully ignorant of the fact that the "natural" look took the most makeup to achieve.

The viscous tonic smelled faintly of lime and was cold on her bare legs. She wriggled her feet, savoured the sensation of chill creeping up from her toes. Her mind wandered as the Master of Ceremonies announced the final task; the pickling challenge, the preserving. *Breathe deep, breathe deep*, the bluebird had said. And she'd intended to, she really had: but now her teeth were chattering as the liquid reached her shoulders; and the chain of tadpoles was squirming around her neck, floating up to her chin as her hair fanned out behind; and Simon, her quiet Simon, all fancy in dress pants and a collared t-shirt, was leaving the auditorium. Fluorescent bulbs over the audience reflected off his lenses, blinding ovals of white that obscured his grey eyes. He stared at her for a moment from the end of the aisle, a gash between rows of threadbare velvet seats.

Her fingers slipped as Simon snuck out the back door.

Water cooled the flush from her cheeks.

Inside the tank Verralee's world blurred. Folk were reduced to diluted colours, glowing patches of liquefied light. Echoes of the band's music grew deeper, more resonant, sound felt as vibration; chords thickened into tangible waves, harmonies licked her long tresses into art nouveau swirls. Air caught in her lungs, nostrils and ears; bubbles jewelled her limbs and gilded her gold lycra bikini. She closed her eyes. Listened to herself sinking.

Though her pulse raced, though the goldfish in her belly fought their way down to her bowels, it was too late to shout *Wait!* or *Simon!* or *I've changed my mind!* But had she, really? Changed it? Shaking the bubbles from her head, she blinked. Plucked the beads from their chain, squeezed pollywogs from their round crystal prisons. *Wait!* she could've called; but she hadn't. If she were the bluebird, her larynx might've reddened at such an exclamation.

The spell Kaylene had taught her frothed from Verralee's mouth, from lips gone cerulean.

She pushed sinuous strands of hair away from her face, like her mother had instructed. *Let the judges see your fine features.* Pain seared through her chest as she ran out of oxygen; it speared through her guts, sent shocks to the tips of her fingers, shredded her inner thighs, calves, toes. *Don't forget to spin; let them see how fresh water accentuates the arrival of your new fins, your new curves.*

To her right and left, contestants floundered in their tanks. Two girls were hauled from the water, their limp bodies thrown to the floor. A third came up for air, just a quick gasp, hoping the panel of judges would be too busy with the drowned to notice her infraction. No luck. The men took to her tank with cast-iron canes, smashed its rippled glass as she went back under for a second attempt at winning the crown.

*You get one shot*, the bluebird had said. *Breathe deep.*

Verralee wanted to—*don't make your Mamma's mistakes*—but she was afraid her heart might have left the room with Simon. Still, she didn't want to be slapped to the ground like those three—those *four*—girls. She wasn't strong enough for that disappointment. She couldn't bear to let Kaylene down.

This pageant was hers to win.

*Just breathe.*

She turned a slow pirouette, showed off the muscles in her thighs and upper back. Her arms grew heavy, her head throbbed, her lungs nose eyes veins guts blood screamed for air: *Breathe!* Her neck split and burned, sprouted opercula. *Breathe!* Spots darted in front of her eyes: tadpoles turned frogs turned eels and, finally, turned into a legion of indigo-crimson *betta splendens*. Verralee heard the crowd cheer in delight as around her swam iridescent flashes of joy.

She tilted her head in gratitude, glugged out a prayer.

At last, she inhaled.

Pure Tapekwa water filtered through her new gills. The pressure in her head subsided as she drank in each fluid breath. She exhaled words of binding, phrases of change, and other spells that could only be formed by liquid voices. Delight buoyed her up as the veiled fish latched onto her legs. At her command, the *bettas* multiplied; tripled and quadrupled; burrowed into her flesh; dug into sinew and bone. They gnawed and knitted, knitted and gnawed; transferring their scales, their long silken fins, to create the pageant queen's unique double-tail.

*Now* Verralee wanted to call out for Simon; *now* she wished he'd return. What a sight he'd have seen through his white-glaring glasses; his girl earning a crown the bluebird always knew she deserved. *It doesn't hurt*, she'd have told him, *turning perfect*.

Painless, her legs blended, her feet flattened, her toes splayed into transparent cartilage. Cold, she lost what made her Simon's love, and Kaylene's little girl, and Johnny's natural beauty. Calm, she buried her humanity beneath a school of clammy skins and gained hips most women would kill for. Blank, she preserved her good looks and became, forever, Miss Tapekwa County.

One last pang, before her blood chilled, at the thought of another girl kissing her Simon's lips. Marrying him. Bearing his children. Maybe he'd sneak over to Town Hall when his wife wrinkled, grew inevitably heavy, sagged beneath gravity and the burden of her husband's heartbroken neglect. Maybe he'd come to stare at Verralee as he'd done today. Silently. Forlornly.

Maybe.

The judges lowered the crown-lid onto her tank. It slid easily into place, glass and silver threading together like frozen fingers clasped.

Verralee looked through clouded glass as the audience applauded. As they gathered purses, jackets, hats and filed out of the hall. As her parents approached, their footsteps inaudible. Black hair wreathed her head, tangled seastrands that caught her kin in its web. She saw her parents, distorted, through the lather of her exhalations. They looked to her like happy, irrelevant dreams, caught and preserved in bubbles from her past. One by one they popped, disappeared, returned to the world from whence such dreams came. She watched the bluebird quiver as Kaylene slowly left, cheeks shining with tears, trailing an ink-smudge of useless advice. In response, Verralee flapped her tail, turned a somersault. As a choir of *bettas* taught her their flooded songs, she bid her land family a water-winged farewell.

Spun another somersault, and they were gone.

• • •

Broken glass and fishwater had been mopped up to let the stage's wooden boards dry. Drained tanks had been wheeled away, loaded onto trucks. One only remained, on display for an empty auditorium. Filled to the brim, dusted with a sprinkling of bloodworms in case of hunger, the winner's vessel sat and waited for morning. The stage lights had dimmed, singling her out, but Miss Tapekwa County was not alone.

A transparent, crimson-finned mermaid had appeared right in front of her!

She turned a gleeful forward roll.

So did the mermaid!

*Pretty*, the pageant queen thought, waving at the glass.

The glass waved back.

*So pretty*, she giggled, sidling up to her own reflection.

The strange mermaid's smile, when it came, was honest azure.

A lovely, forgetful shade of blue.

• • • • • • • • • • •

# LOVE DEATH

## ANDREW J. McKIERNAN

Eduardo led the body through the streets on a wheeled bier pulled behind a nag of tired and sullen temperament. His own mood was not much better; four days of trudging south through jungle heat and humidity had taken its toll on both his body and mind. The woman who lay on the bier had been his first and only love but every hour of travel brought with it an increasing pungency of decay that made it difficult for him to maintain his feelings. He knew that if he didn't get her to a necromancer soon, not only would her chance of resurrection be low but his love for her might fade completely.

But, now that Eduardo had arrived in the city, a small portion of his fears were beginning to abate. The Festival of the Laughing Corpse was still two days away but already the streets were filled with people and everywhere the living mingled with the dead. He knew the upcoming festivities were certain to place a premium on any necromancer's services but the sight of so many faces of morbid pallor filled him with a renewed hope.

*Not too late,* he thought, *I* can't *be too late*, and pushed through the throng of tourists and early revellers, dragging the nag and bier behind him.

Ahead, a troupe of *Comedia de la Muerte* players performed *La Historia de Cómica del Doctor Fausto* to a rowdy crowd. Doctor Fausto, having cast off his clothes and dressed now in bright-coloured motley, chased El Diablo around the stage with a large and undoubtedly phallic slapstick. The audience roared their approval at the newly risen Doctor's triumph over death and threw onions at the fleeing devil.

Eduardo watched for a moment—even felt the beginnings of a smile tug at the corner of his lips—but the sign he could see hanging at the far end of the street was more important to him than frivolous plays performed by once-dead clowns.

He moved on, the crowd parting slowly before him, and stopped outside the shop he had been searching for.

Above the shop's oaken door, black and polished smooth by the touch of untold hands, swung a shingle of dark and aged wood. Painted upon the shingle's surface was a faded *Caput Mortuum*—a white circle inscribed within its circumference with three dots arranged in an inverted triangle—the symbol known as the "dead head', the sign of the necromancer.

Tentatively, Eduardo reached for the door and knocked.

• • •

Eduardo's mother had died when he was nine, although he wasn't to find this out until five years later.

His mother had always been a sickly woman and Eduardo thought nothing unusual of the week long trip his father had taken her on. At the time he'd assumed they were on their way to visit yet more leechers, apothecaries and chirurgeons in search of a cure. But Eduardo's father was not interested in retaining the services of mere physicks, for he had seen the coming of his wife's final days and made due preparation with a necromancer in Ciudad del la Muerte.

It was to this appointment that his mother and father had travelled, and there that she had died of her illness not an hour's journey from the city gates.

Outside those same city gates, at the beginning of their journey home three days later, his father and newly resurrected mother had vowed never to tell Eduardo of what had taken place within the city's walls.

Eduardo's mother finally broke her vow five years later and told him everything as her husband lay dead in a night-dampened field, crushed beneath of the wheel of a steam-tractor he'd hired to help prepare the year's planting. She told him because she wanted Eduardo to know his parents would have done anything for each other, but that sometimes it just wasn't possible to do anything at all. Sometimes a body was just too damaged for any hope of resurrection.

Young Eduardo stared at his mother's pale face as she spoke. She wasn't crying. He couldn't remember a time in the previous five years when she had. He'd thought this was because she was happy to be cured of the disease that surely would have killed her, even though his father had become increasingly distant since their return. But what if his mother didn't cry because she couldn't? Maybe it just wasn't possible for the dead to cry. Which made Eduardo think of his father lying beneath the tractor's wheels, and he wondered whether the old man's final tears had fled their reservoir, mingling with the blood that washed the newly ploughed furrows of the stony field.

• • •

Woodcut depictions in various tracts and handbills had led Eduardo to presume all necromancers to be exceedingly old, with beards of impressive length, and apparelled from neck to toe in robes of damask silk. Therefore, when a young and clean shaven man presented his face through the open crack of the necromancer's door, Eduardo assumed he was a servant or assistant and instantly asked to see the master of the house.

The young man responded with a throaty and jovial laugh and swung the door wide, motioning Eduardo in with a sweep of his hand. He wore dark woollen breeches and a rough linen shirt stained here and there with patches of brown and yellow and the darkest of reds.

"If you are looking for the best necromancer in all of Ciudad del la Muerte, then you have found him, amigo. Come in, come in, before the sound of that rabble drives me to a frenzy."

Eduardo hesitated, his hand still holding the nag's bridle to keep her steady.

"You? You are the mago Don Diego Tezcatl?"

"The very same."

Eduardo shook his head, confused.

"But, my father came here almost twenty years ago with my mother. You must have been a mere boy."

Don Diego Tezcatl inclined his head to one side and pressed his lips together in what might have been a smile.

"I was much the same age then as I am now, Señor. Who better to administer the rites of the dead than one who has already experienced it? Please, won't you come inside so that we can discuss your business in comfort and peace?"

"I can't," Eduardo said and glanced back at the bier. "I can't just leave her out here on her own. It might already be too late."

Don Diego Tezcatl looked over Eduardo's shoulder, seeming to notice the horse and bier and its shroud-covered cargo for the first time, and sighed. He stepped out onto the street and drew back the top of the winding-sheet. Eduardo couldn't bring himself to look. He hadn't dared look since the moment he had placed her on the bier.

"Ah, I see," the necromancer said. "Yes, we had better bring her inside. You are right; it might indeed be too late, but I will do the best for her that I can."

• • •

"Her name is Catrina," Eduardo told the necromancer as they placed her body on an ancient wooden catafalque bedecked about with candles and lilies. The catafalque was set in the centre of the necromancer's workroom, the floor and walls around it painted with sigils and glyphs that Eduardo found unintelligible and somewhat unsettling.

"She was only twelve years old when I first met her. So beautiful. So sweet and caring and sharp as a blade for her age. I loved her from the first moment I saw her. Watched her grow into such a beautiful woman. And, now . . . now that she'd finally come of age . . . "

"Yes, I'm sure that's all true, Señor Eduardo, but for the moment I will need your assistance to remove this winding sheet. Please hold her steady for me, will you?"

Eduardo reached forward, hesitant, and placed his shaking hands upon the waist of his beloved. She felt so cold and still.

Don Diego began to unwind the shroud, revealing Catrina's raven hair coiled over her crown in an elegant chignon encrusted with dried blood. Loose curls fell around her ears; ears that were darkened at the edges, fever red and weeping fluid at the entrance of the canals. Her face was bruised purple and black, the skin thin and tight across her forehead and the sharp bones of her cheeks. Her lips were drawn back in a rictus grin, displaying gums as slick and dark as rotting oysters. The eyes were like giant fish eggs staring up at him from the hollows of their sockets.

Eduardo flinched and gagged. His hands pushed down as he tried to steady himself and a miasmic belch erupted from his dead love's mouth. He fell back, tripping over his own feet in an attempt to get away from the sight and smell of what his Catrina had become. A candelabra fell to the floor, spilling wax and extinguishing the flame.

"Maybe you should leave, Señor Eduardo', the necromancer said, a great deal of gentleness in his voice as he continued to remove the shroud.

But Eduardo couldn't look away. He couldn't move at all. He could only stare down at the *thing* that could not possibly be his Catrina and wonder where his love had gone.

*It can't be her*, he thought. *It can't!*

But he knew it was.

As the necromancer unwrapped the last of the shroud, he saw that the corpse was still wearing Catrina's wedding dress.

• • •

For three days Eduardo sat in a musty third-floor room in a boarding house near the docks. He rarely slept or ate and even when he did the portions of both were measly and unsatisfying. He smoked stale tobacco rolled inside sheets of maize husk. He drank a lot of cheap whiskey. And, when he wasn't staring out the window at ships travelling to and from the Old World, he read through the pile of love letters he'd kept and cried tears onto a faded daguerreotype of Catrina standing young and radiant beneath a blossoming persimmon tree.

He didn't remember booking the room and knew that Don Diego must have arranged it for him. He didn't even know how he'd arrived there; only that he'd suddenly come to the realisation that he *was* there, in that dirty and threadbare room, and no longer in the shop of the necromancer.

A letter addressed to him had been placed folded upon the credenza. Beside it rested the now dry and brittle bouquet Catrina had held to her breast as she'd walked slowly down the church's aisle. For the entire first day Eduardo had been unable to approach the small bundle of pale flowers or read the note. He was too afraid of what the bouquet represented and of what might be written on the single page of crisp white paper. Instead, he sat on the bed and stared at them from a distance.

Sometime late on that first night he'd finally fallen into an unsettled sleep, plagued by dreams of his mother and father standing in a ploughed field, shovels in hand and pointing down at the empty graves they'd dug for themselves.

He awoke with the morning's first light, somewhat relieved by the fact that his parents had been alone in the field.

Not twelve months after his father's fatal accident, Eduardo's mother—still grieving and unable to cry for the loss of her husband—had ended her life-in-death by throwing herself down an old well at the rear of their estancia. The fall had been far and the bottom rocky. It was three days before Eduardo discovered her body, twisted and smashed in such a way that no necromancer could restore her life a second time.

It said something to Eduardo that Catrina had not been with his parents in the dream and, with that small solace in his heart, he took the letter from the credenza.

• • •

*Estimado Señor Eduardo,*

*It would be remiss of me if I did not, from my very first words, apologise for taking the liberty of removing you from my premises to these lodgings. Being unaware of any arrangement you might have already contracted regarding your stay in our fair city, nor knowing the extent of your current pecuniary resources, I have taken it upon myself to place you in rooms both inexpensive and as far removed from the distracting noise of the upcoming festival as was possible—although, there is really nowhere in the city this time of year that is totally free of the frivolous and flamboyant jesting of the once-dead.*

*Upon your departure please do not pay any bills that might be presented to you. You can be assured that I have already dealt with such incidentals on your behalf. These small charges, including the stabling of your horse and bier, will be added to my own final fee, which will be presented to you upon the conclusion of the transaction for which you have contracted me.*

*Now, important matters of business being dispensed with, I do hope that you have recovered sufficiently from your little episode of catatonia. It is not unusual for the sight of a loved one in such an advanced condition of decay to induce a state of stupor within those of a precious disposition.*

*It is my task now, and the main purpose of my writing this letter, to set your mind at rest regarding such matters.*

*The resurrection of your beloved Catrina is in no way beyond the limit of my skills. Indeed, I have, many times in the past, restored the Life Force of those even less fortunate.*

*I am therefore pleased to tell you that you will be reunited with your bride after a period of three days from the dating of this letter.*

*I would ask that you ensure you are present in your rooms on the evening of the third day in order that we may complete our transaction, and so that you may resume that Most Holy contract of Matrimony to which you and your beloved Catrina had most recently entered into.*

*Your servant in matters eternal,*
*Don Diego Tezcatl—Necromancer*

• • •

That night, Eduardo fell asleep with a bellyful of whiskey and dreamt of the wedding. It wasn't a nightmare, but neither was it pleasant.

In the dream, he stood before an altar, the arched vault of the church's ceiling rising high above like the ribs of some ancient behemoth. All of the town's people and animals had gathered in the nave: farmers, weavers, bakers and a blacksmith, sheep and cattle and a brood of chickens. Through the aisles, children chased dogs and dogs chased cats. An organ played accompaniment so subtly and skilfully that, combined with all the talking and squawking and barking and mewing, it sounded a hymn to the very powers of Nature Herself.

Beside Eduardo stood his bride. Her face was covered with a veil but he knew that it was his Catrina, and he knew that she was beautiful.

A priest stood on the other side of the altar, robed in cloth of white and gold. He was offering up the concluding blessing, his strong voice cutting over the sound of people and animals and music. His face was that of Don Diego Tezcatl.

With all the twisted logic of the dream world, even this last fact did not seem unusual or wrong to Eduardo. But he also knew—a far away memory ringing alarm bells of dread in his mind—that something was about to go horribly wrong.

The Priest smiled down at them both from his rostrum, raised his arms to the congregation, and said:

"You may now kiss the bride."

Eduardo turned and took a step—intending to raise the veil and gaze upon the beauty of his Catrina, to feel the soft touch of her lips upon his own—and his foot caught in the long, spread out train of her dress. He pitched forward, threw out his hands to steady himself against her, and felt her stumble back under the weight of his fall.

To the congregation, it must have appeared that he had pushed her.

He felt the world around him slow. The air thickened. His every heartbeat became a tympanic dirge resounding within his chest. He tried to reach out and catch her, but he was too far away. He turned his head imploringly to the gasping crowd, to the still smiling priest, but nobody was close enough to do anything more than watch. Catrina's arms were spread wide, pinwheeling like windmills in a breeze as she fell backwards. The bell of her farthingale skirt billowed, offering Eduardo an insanely tantalising glimpse of the light-blue garter she wore around her thigh. Her veil lifted up, over her face. He could see fear and surprise in her kohl lined eyes and in the "O" of her carmine lips. He tried to call out, to scream, to say he was sorry, but the air took an eternity to fill his lungs; even longer to work its way back up through his throat and out his mouth. And, before he could utter more than a high-pitched whine of dismay, the back of Catrina's head cracked hard against the edge of a pew and Eduardo woke up screaming.

• • •

It wasn't just the guilt that weighed heavily on Eduardo. It was also the blame placed upon him by Catrina's parents and the villagers. There had been no animals in the church that day, and the priest was an old man who had run the parish for at least twenty years and not Don Diego Tezcatl, but the rest of the dream had been as it was. He knew that, ultimately, whether he meant to or not, he *had* pushed her and that bumbling action had been the cause of her death. His visit to the necromancer was an attempt to rectify that; a chance for her to regain the life he had taken. He also recognised a degree of selfishness in that too. He couldn't see how he could live without her after so long waiting to be in her arms.

And so, he read and re-read the pile of letters that had accumulated during their long courtship and tried to ignore the sounds of merriment that drifted up to him from the street below. At one stage he opened the window to let in some air and looked down upon once-dead clowns and comedians, resurrected satirists and porcelain-pale burlesque dancers, all moving in a morbid procession of laughter and music. It made him remember what a good sense of humour his Catrina had possessed. Would she still laugh, even if she couldn't cry? Would she still say the sort of things that had made *him* smile and laugh?

Don Diego's letter had given him hope that this would be so.

Eduardo's biggest concern though was how she would look. He tried to put the image of Catrina lying on the catafalque in the necromancer's workroom from his mind and concentrated on the daguerreotype taken near her parent's hacienda by a travelling lensman. The image had taken an age to produce in the strange little man's camera and the entire time Catrina had stood as still as . . . *death* was his first thought but he quickly brushed it away. As still as a marble sculpture. As still as lilies floating on a pond. As still as an autumn night. But none of these clichés did justice to her beauty as she'd posed beneath a flowering persimmon tree.

He lay the letters in his lap, closed his eyes and kept that image of her in his mind, thinking that maybe the words did not exist that could describe her in a way that she deserved.

• • •

Eduardo did not notice when the light began to dim. At some stage he had fallen into a whiskey induced daze and, by the time the knock at the door roused him, the room had fallen into darkness. Sounds of laughter and other revelries still drifted up from the street but the gaslights were too far below to cast even the weakest of glows into his third-floor room. He struggled from the tattered armchair he'd been sitting in, his legs and mind as unsteady as calf's foot jelly, and stumbled about searching for a lamp.

Another, more insistent knock sounded.

"Señor Eduardo, are you in? I have someone here who would very much like to see you."

The voice belonged to Don Diego.

Eduardo's heart staggered a beat and his mouth went dry.

"Just a moment," he croaked as his hand found the paraffin-lamp. He lit it with one of the Lucifers he kept in a box in his vest pocket, fumbled with the glass chimney and turned the wick until warm light pushed its way into the room. He looked around at the mess his three days of confinement had created—an unmade bed, two empty bottles of whiskey, a plate of uneaten food, a bowl of stale tobacco and ash—and decided a quick clean up was in order. He couldn't let Catrina see how he'd been living.

"You'll have to give me a moment," he said to the door and realised he hadn't changed his clothes in days. "I didn't know you'd be quite so early."

"What do you mean, early? We're late! It's already three hours past sunset. I told you I'd be here by evening."

"I just have to . . . err, make things ready."

Eduardo hustled the whiskey bottles and the bowl of ash and tobacco into the bottom of the wardrobe. He covered the plate of stale tortillas and sweaty cheese with a cloth and tried to smooth out the bed coverings.

"Not getting cold feet are you, Señor Eduardo? A little late for that I think. Your lady is waiting to see you."

Eduardo began unbuttoning his vest with one hand while he searched through his suitcase with the other. None of his clothes had been laundered or ironed. Everything was either dirty or wrinkled. He didn't even have his boots on, just a pair of worn and tattered hose with holes in the toes.

"Eduardo? It's Catrina. I don't care about the room. Or how you look. I just want to see you. To thank you."

It was her! His love. Her sweet voice just as he'd remembered it—and casual, as if they'd only been apart hours instead of days. As if nothing had happened to her at all.

He stopped undressing and moved to the door. His hand was shaking as he undid the latch. Slowly, he turned the handle—thinking of how she would look, of what he would say to her—and opened the door.

• • •

Catrina stood in the hallway. She still wore her wedding dress, as pristine as it had been on the day of their marriage. Her face was veiled in white chiffon and ringlets of dark hair hung about it like a frame. Scents of lavender and rose washed into the room as she stepped towards Eduardo and wrapped her arms around him.

Eduardo gasped as she pulled him close and lay her head against his chest. His own hands found her back and the bare skin of her shoulders. She felt cold, but he told himself that was just the night air. It was still Catrina and they were in each other's arms again. In that instant, that was all that mattered to him.

"Oh, mi amor, mi querido amor," she whispered. "This must have all been so terrible for you."

He reached down under the veil and cupped her chin and tilted her covered face towards him. He could see the darkness of her eyes through the thin cloth and a hint of red that was the bow of her lips, but her features were indistinct and he was still somewhat scared of what might lie beneath. He took a step backwards, loosening her arms from around him, and held the bottom edges of the veil in his trembling fingers.

"You may now kiss the bride," Don Diego said sardonically from the hallway and Eduardo flinched, torn from the moment of intimacy. Those words, coming from that man, spoken so soon after his dream, almost had him running from the room in a panic. But he held fast, took a deep breath and slowly raised the veil from Catrina's face.

She was beautiful. As beautiful as she had ever been. Her face was porcelain perfect, without a hint of bruising, and her eyes glittered brightly in the flickering lamplight. Her lips were full and ripe and pursed with expectation as Eduardo leant down to settled his own mouth against them.

*So cold*, he thought, *she feels so cold*. But that was only a minor and fleeting concern as Catrina returned the kiss with an enthusiasm he had feared he'd never encounter again. She pulled him closer, pushing her bosom hard to his chest and he felt a warm stirring in his loins.

The necromancer coughed politely from the doorway.

"If you wouldn't mind, Señor Eduardo? Before you go much further with your reunion, I believe we have a transaction to finalise."

Eduardo reluctantly pulled away from his bride. He gave her a look of sincerest apology and went to collect his purse from the nightstand beside the bed.

"I'll just be a moment, my love," he said and she smiled with understanding.

"Please don't be long. We've been apart for more time than is bearable. I'll be waiting for you."

She said this last with a mischievous wink that only served to further stiffen the lump in his hose as he stepped out into the hall and closed the door behind him.

"Well, Señor Eduardo? I assume that you are satisfied with my work?" The necromancer glanced at the bulge in Eduardo's hosiery and smiled. Eduardo blushed.

"Umm, yes, err, most certainly, Don Diego. You have done an excellent job and I really don't know how to thank you."

"Well, you could start by settling my bill," the necromancer answered and handed him a folded sheet of coarse yellow paper.

Eduardo read through the tally of services and fingered the coin purse in his hand. The total was much more than he had expected. It would cost him almost everything he had.

*No,* he thought, *your actions have already cost you everything you had. This is just the price for getting her back.*

Eduardo took a few small coins from the purse and handed the rest to the necromancer, grateful that he had kept their honeymoon savings safely hidden away in his travel trunk.

Don Diego Tezcatl weighed the purse in his hand and nodded.

"Thank you, Señor Eduardo. It has certainly been a pleasure doing business with you. Please do not forget me if you are ever in need of similar services in your future."

And with that, the necromancer turned and walked away, leaving Eduardo standing alone in the hall.

*Not alone. I'm not alone any more,* Eduardo thought as he opened the door to his room—the room where his beloved awaited—and stepped inside.

• • •

The room was dark, the lamp turned too low to do more than shed a soft glow across the table where it sat, and Eduardo almost tripped over the pile of clothing in the doorway. The light from the hallway revealed it as Catrina's wedding dress, discarded in a heap on the floor. He could vaguely make out the shape of her body lying supine across the bed.

"Come to bed, mi amor," she said, her voice a sweet whisper in the night. "We have some catching up to do. I would like to thank you for everything you have done."

Eduardo felt his loins stirring to life once more. His heart began to race and his mouth went dry with anticipation. He stood silently, wanting to savour every second of their reunion, and watched the shadow of Catrina's lithe form as it moved sinuously across the bed. This wasn't something he was inclined to rush, no matter that every fibre of his body screamed otherwise. He'd waited too long for this moment; dreamt of it so many times. Most importantly, he wanted to take time to gaze upon her beauty, to drink in the sight of her, and so he reached across to the lamp and turned the wick up high.

Catrina lay on top of the bed sheets, dark hair spread around her head like a halo. Her eyes were half closed in sensual anticipation, lips a petulant pout of impatience. Eduardo's eyes moved lower, watching her hands as the roamed across the bruised swell of her breasts and over nipples as dry and brown as rotten strawberries. He gazed at the distended mound of her stomach, splotched with yellow and feverish pink. And lower, lower still, to her parted thighs and the gaping, festering slit that rested between them, weeping dark fluids upon the sheets.

*Make up!* Eduardo's mind cried out. *Her face, it is all powder and rouge! An embalmer's trick!*

"Come to me, my husband, my love," Catrina crooned and now Eduardo could hear a soft crackle in her throat that he couldn't remember being there before; a rasping that his hope had hidden from him. "Tonight is our wedding night, and you've done so much to make sure we'll be together."

She sat up in the bed, her arms outstretched towards him, and Eduardo found he couldn't move.

Catrina crawled across the bed on all fours, her breasts sagging and dragging across the sheets. She stood up and placed her cold hands against his cheeks. He could feel the bones of her fingers beneath the tight flesh. She pressed herself against him, rubbing sensuously, and he felt the betrayal of his own body as his prick began to stiffen once more. Her face came closer to his and, even though he knew it was only make up, she still looked beautiful in the soft light. Their lips touched.

Deep inside, a part of his mind was screaming. But he loved her, he knew he did, and the guilt of her death still weighed heavily on him. He returned the kiss, trying to shut out the rational part of him that rebelled. He imagined her as he'd first seen her; a young and sprightly girl of twelve. He saw her standing beneath the persimmon tree. He remembered the woman dressed in white who had stood beside him in the church.

And then he felt her tongue enter his mouth—a dry and raspy worm that probed his teeth and gums and tasted of rot—and that was too much.

He pushed her hard, back onto the bed—a deliberate act that served as a cruel parody to the accident in the church—and ran from the room, a thin scream of terror trailing from his lips.

• • •

Eduardo wandered the moonlit streets in his tattered hose. He passed through the crowds of laughing revellers as if in a dream and eventually found himself standing in the very centre of the city square. All around him the living and the dead were enjoying the Festival of the Laughing Corpse. Undead jugglers juggled skulls. Once-dead performers swallowed swords, literally, removing them to great applause from gaping holes in their bellies. And pale clowns, who needed no whiteface to temper their complexions, played pranks upon passers-by.

At the far end of the square a makeshift stage had been erected. A mariachi band played upon it, their guitars and violins constructed of bone and gut, drums stretched tight with human skin. In front of the stage, lily-faced couples danced, arms wrapped tight around each other, dead eyes staring into dead eyes with a love that Eduardo felt he would never know again.

*That could have been me*, he thought. *That could have been Catrina.* And, despite the memory of what had occurred in the room, he was already starting to feel his loss and think of how they might be together again.

He found an empty bench and sat, watching the crowds as they moved around him. There were people of all sizes and shapes, races and genders, living and dead, and everywhere he looked he saw more lovers. They walked arm in arm and hand in hand or sat entwined beside the fountain. They laughed and smiled and whispered intimacies into each other's ears. But there was one thing he noticed about all these couples that intrigued him—a simple fact he'd missed until now—and that realisation planted an idea in his mind.

As the first glow of false dawn infused the square with soft morning light and the exhausted crowds and performers began to disperse to their beds, Eduardo stood, his mind made up, and started back towards his room at the boarding house.

• • •

The boarding house was quiet and seemed eerily deserted. Most of the guests would still be asleep and the landlady wouldn't open the kitchen for another hour or so. Eduardo found quill, ink and paper in a credenza in the sitting room and sat down to write a note to Catrina.

He apologised for his behaviour the night before and begged her forgiveness. He revealed the location of the honeymoon money he had stashed in the bottom of his travel trunk and bid her to make use of it. He told her where she would be able find him and hastened her to come as soon as she could. He told her he loved her. That he looked forward to being with her once again. And then, he sealed the letter with a kiss and crept up the stairs to his room.

He stood outside the door for what seemed an age and listened. He knew he wouldn't hear her crying and he was grateful for that, though there was a fear that he would hear her laughing instead, enjoying some cruel joke orchestrated by Don Diego Tezcatl at Eduardo's expense. But there was only silence. He imagined Catrina sitting in the over-stuffed chair, reading slowly through the pile of love letters he had kept and treasured.

When the morning light in the hallway grew as bright as he could allow, he pushed the letter carefully and silently under the door and left. He took his horse and bier from the stables and led them out of the city, stopping only once to look back at the city walls as his mother and father must once have done.

• • •

Eduardo waited in the orchard behind Catrina's parents' hacienda. He wasn't sure if he'd found exactly the right tree—it had been many years since the lensman had taken his daguerreotype—but it was close enough for Catrina to find him when she came.

*If* she came.

He hoped he knew her well enough to guess that she would not be far behind, leaving the city with all haste the moment she read his letter. If he was right they would be together again soon enough. If he was wrong . . . well, his error in judging her would not matter to him by then.

He stood on the bier, looking back across the huerto towards the road, hoping to catch sight of her. All he could see were persimmon trees ripe with black fruit ready for picking. No dust kicked up by the hooves of a horse in pursuit. No glint of light reflected from a carriage's windows. And yet, he trusted his decision; trusted that her love would not fail him nor the gesture he was making for her.

The realisation he had come to in the city square had been a simple one. A fact so obvious that it went unnoticed amongst all the laughter and revelry of the festival for the once dead. The realisation had been this: that his parents had been the exception, and not the rule.

Of all the lovers he had seen in the square and walking the streets, not once had he seen the living dancing with the dead, and it had become obvious to him. The living could not love the dead in the same way they had before. Almost invariably, death changed both sides of the equation. Even in his father's altered demeanour and new found silence Eduardo had seen this, though not recognised it at the time. Death brought with it a gulf of difference that mere love could not cross. No, in order to bridge that gulf something more than love was required.

Eduardo took the bridle he had removed from his old nag and tied it to the highest branch of the old persimmon tree that he could reach. He placed the loop of leather around his neck, took a final look back towards the road—searching for his love, knowing that she would come for him—and stepped off the bier.

● ● ● ● ● ● ● ● ● ● ●

# INTERVIEW WITH THE JIANGSHI

## ANNE MOK

"I shouldn't even be here," I griped at April, as we stood in line for registration. "I don't know how you convinced me, but your whammy is wearing off."

She punched me lightly in the shoulder. "Don't chicken out now, Jackson. It won't be as bad as you think."

"Really?" The line moved forward, and the giant banner above the registration desk glittered into view, silver thread on black velvet:

TENTH ANNUAL INTERNATIONAL VAMPIRE CONVENTION

FANGS FOR THE MEMORIES

"Come on," April said. "Everyone likes a good pun."

I could have disputed whether any pun deserved to be called good, but that wasn't the real problem.

The line moved forward again, and we were standing in front of the desk. A pale blonde woman in a black dress smiled toothily at us. "Names?"

"April Sullivan," April said, smiling toothily back. "And Jackson Cheng."

"Sullivan, Cheng." She ticked off our names, but her pen continued to hover over mine. "Mr Cheng, you're listed here as a full member, not an associate member . . ." She trailed off, eyeing me up and down: my lack of a toothy smile; my long white hair and pointed black nails; and, of course, the obvious unlikelihood of anyone named Vlad in my ancestry.

"He is a full member," April assured her. "He's a Chinese vampire."

"I'm sorry, I didn't realise." She sounded as uncertain as I felt, covering it with an awkward smile.

"No problem. I get that a lot."

"Here are your programs and badges. Enjoy the convention!"

We shuffled off to the side of the foyer, April scanning the program avidly while I tried to look unobtrusive. It wasn't hard. The Melbourne International Convention Centre was built on an ostentatious scale, lined with towering columns, and walled with long panels of glass. All the windows, floor to ceiling, were draped in thick black velvet, screening out the sun. You couldn't tell it was dusk over the Yarra.

"All this glass seems kind of hazardous," I remarked. "Wouldn't it be better to book somewhere more shielded? Then you wouldn't have to bother with all these blackout curtains."

"This is a world class convention," April said absently, "and it deserves to be at a world class convention centre. We're not going to huddle in some concrete bunker like second class citizens."

"You sound like Richard Wells," I said.

"Oh no!" She thrust her program in front of my face. "His keynote address started five minutes ago."

"All right," I sighed. She probably meant to get his autograph too.

• • •

Richard Wells didn't look particularly vampiric, with his red hair and craggy features, and broad shoulders filling out his grey suit. But he was probably the closest to an unofficial spokesman we had down under. He had campaigned tirelessly for the Undead Rights Act, pushed discrimination test cases through the High Court, and even run for Federal Parliament. And whenever Pamela Hayward appeared in the news, putting forward the honey poison of the Humanity Alliance, Richard Wells would be there too, with his reasoned rebuttals and impassioned arguments.

I had heard him speak before, so I let my attention drift to the audience instead. Men and women, mostly in black; the majority seemed to be Europeans, although there was a sizeable American contingent, and a fair representation of locals. I've organised enough conferences to expect speeches to bring on fidgeting and distraction, but today, no one was checking their email while Richard was talking. The energy in the atmosphere was palpable.

"We've come a long way," he was saying, "but we've still got a long way to go. Right now, Parliament is debating the Undead Registration Act, which would force us to be tracked like criminals. We must let the world know that we will not stand for our freedoms to be curtailed in the name of fear! This isn't just a convention: this is a meeting of minds, where together we can tackle the great problems of our age."

Thunderous applause, as he stepped back from the spotlight. The qi levels surged, making me dizzy, and I had to grip my armrests to keep myself upright, to restrain the impulse to breathe it all in like oxygen.

When I could focus again, I was sitting alone in the row. Everyone else was filing out, a few casting me odd looks. I searched for April; she stood in the knot of people who were clustered around Richard. She waved me down.

Richard seemed keen to talk to everyone. When it was our turn, April introduced us, and he signed her copy of *A Bloody Injustice*.

"So, Jackson," he said, "where are you from?"

"Melbourne," I said. "I came in on the tram."

"I meant originally."

Of course he did. I've been here since the damn gold rush, but I'll get asked that question till the day I die again, while some Transylvanian who unloaded his coffin from the plane yesterday will never have to face it.

"China," I said, pleasantly. "But I've lived here for a while now."

Sensing the tension, April broke in with, "I liked your speech. Especially the part about how we're all brothers and sisters under the skin."

"Thanks," Richard said. "I believe we all share a bond, and we all have a responsibility to look out for each other. That's why this convention is so important—to connect us and show we don't stand alone."

Exactly who doesn't stand alone, I wondered, but did not say aloud. Instead, I said, "Fair enough, but why Australia? It's a trek, and for what? 'Come see our beautiful beaches?' Kind of the wrong crowd."

Richard remained unfazed. "We can walk the beaches at night. We can still enjoy the surf and the sand."

"Oh yes," April chimed. "And watch the stars."

"That's right," Richard said, smiling. "Even the stars are different, under the southern skies."

He nodded and moved on to talk to the next group that was hovering near him. April sighed.

"Well, obviously the stars are different," I said.

She gave me a look.

• • •

I sat in the darkest corner of the convention centre bar, elbow propped on the table, leafing idly through the program book again. April was at the 'Sunproofing Your Home' panel, which I had excused myself from. None of the others caught my interest either: 'Family Matters: Sire and Childe Relations', 'Recent Developments in Synthetic Blood Research', 'Inheritance Laws and You'.

"Buy you a drink?"

The blonde woman from registration extended a hand towards me. "Monique Dubois."

We shook. "Thanks for the offer," I said. "But I don't drink blood."

"It's all animal blood, you know."

I shook my head.

She raised an eyebrow. "You're not an Aetheran, are you?"

"A what?"

"One of those vampires who claims to have discovered how to live off meditation."

"No, nothing like that." I traced a circle on the bar. "I'm a jiangshi. We don't drink blood. Or meditate."

"Then what do you live off?" She seemed genuinely curious.

"Uh, energy. I absorb energy from the environment." If by 'environment', you meant 'people'.

"That's remarkable. I've never met anyone like that before."

"There are a few of us around. Like Christina Lee, who writes for the *New York Times*."

"Oh, her? I had no idea."

It turned out that Monique worked in finance. "And what do you do?"

"I'm in event management. Concerts, mostly." I drifted into reminiscence. "The vibe is incredible. I could live off it forever."

Wheels turned behind her eyes. "Oh, so you're a psychic vampire!"

I smiled weakly.

• • •

"Are you sure we're not late?" I asked April, in the taxi. "It *is* the Dusk to Dawn Ball."

"Relax," April said. She was busy touching up her makeup. "This kind of party, no one will be there till midnight." She bared her teeth at me. "Do I have lipstick on my fangs?"

I was used to being her mirror substitute. "It's fine. No spinach either."

The driver dropped us off outside the convention centre. A sea of candles floated in the forecourt, held aloft by dozens and dozens of people. At first I thought they were part of the arrangements for the ball, until I saw the placards and heard the megaphone.

"This midnight vigil is our message!" Pamela Hayward, in an elegant pantsuit, talking to—oh god—the news cameras. "We ask the government to take action to protect our sons and daughters. We have the right to know who lives in our neighbourhoods and works in our workplaces. As these people feast and celebrate, we remember those slain by rogue vampires."

Those next to her held up photos of family and friends, loved ones who were gone, faces stark. I had to look away. I'd never hurt anyone, but it made me feel complicit.

The cameras caught it all, vampires in tuxedos and gowns hurrying past, as the crowd looked on in simmering outrage. I could imagine how it would play on the news.

"Come on," I said, throat dry. "Let's find the back entrance."

We slipped inside, and walked down the corridor to the double doors. They swung open; April and I entered arm in arm.

For this one night, the auditorium had been transformed into a ballroom, with red drapery, gilt mirrors, and brass candelabra. I had expected it to be cheesy: men swaggering around in opera capes; women flitting about in lace corsets. But somehow, the mood was sombre; even though nothing could be seen of the outside, we all knew what lay beyond, and what they thought of us.

Still, the music played, a slow waltz, and couples moved across the polished floor like constellations across the sky. Dancing against darkness, and I began to understand why Richard Wells had wanted to bring this event here: to say, this is who we are, and we are not alone.

He was here now, circulating through the ballroom, stopping every few moments to exchange words with someone else. He paused by Monique, who chatted to him with animation. He glanced over at me once. I waved back.

Eventually, I found a place against the wall, where I stood sipping my chilled water, while April went to powder her nose. A woman sagged against the wall next to me.

"Are you okay?" I asked, steadying her.

"These damn corsets," she said, tugging at the waist of her dress. "You'd think they wouldn't be so uncomfortable if you don't have to breathe."

I nodded in polite sympathy. "Take it easy."

She leaned her head back and closed her eyes. "The things we do, eh?"

It surprised me to see Richard approaching me. Noticing even the wallflowers.

"Hey," I said, but his expression was serious.

"It's Jackson, right?" he said. "I have to ask you something."

"Sure—"

"Are you draining energy from anyone?"

My smile froze. "What?"

"I've been told about what you do." His level gaze met mine, not looking at anyone else.

I went cold all over. "That's not why I'm here."

"That's not what I asked."

A circle had opened around us, as people stopped dancing and drinking to stare.

"No," I said, face burning. "I'm not. You think I'd—"

"Look, we're responsible for the safety of our guests. Any hazards—"

"I was just taking a rest," said the woman leaning against the wall. She rocked upright, swaying on spike-heeled boots.

Richard glanced between us, then nodded briskly. "Sorry to have troubled you." Aware of the gathered crowd, he called,

"Please enjoy the rest of your evening."

Monique was pushing her way through the crowd towards me. I turned and exited, not meeting anyone's eyes.

At the double doors, I collided with April, returning.

"Hey, watch your—Jackson?"

"I'm going home." Ignoring her shouted questions, I strode down the corridor, hung with velvet black as my vision, as the protesters began to chant.

• • •

It was drizzling in Chinatown, the black asphalt slick with rain, reflecting the red and green neon. Passers-by hunched into their jackets or huddled under umbrellas, casting me wary looks, voices whispering to each other in Cantonese.

I walked on, past shop windows displaying roasted duck and mournful fish, fat buddhas and beckoning cats. I walked past them all, to the Facing Heaven Archway, and the rock garden beyond. White stone lions guarded the gates.

I sank down onto one of the rocks, and lowered my face into my hands.

After a long time, footsteps crunched on the gravel.

"I already told you," I said wearily, "I'm going—"

"I'm sorry," Monique said.

I raised my head. She stood there, wrapped in a black coat, rain speckling her blonde hair.

"It was idle chatter," she said. "I didn't mean for anything like that to happen."

"I'm not into ballroom dancing anyway." I undid my tie, crumpling it in my hand.

Monique settled onto a neighbouring rock, watching me carefully. "I know so little about you."

"You want to know about me?" I flickered her a ghost smile. "I never had a sire. I was murdered, and the priests brought me back."

It was still vivid in my mind, even though Buckland was a hundred miles and as many years away. The fires, and the rioters, and finally, the cold clammy pull of the river. They had torn apart the tents and clubbed down those who were slow to flee, and screamed names I needed no translation to comprehend.

"Who killed you?" Monique said quietly.

"People who didn't think I was human."

The rain paused. Hissing was replaced by silence, then filled by the soft roar of traffic, and a distant radio, playing a song about a green island, far away.

"Have you ever thought about going back home?" Monique asked.

And what a loaded word that was. *Home.* Was it the plane to Guangzhou, or was it the tram to Fitzroy?

"I don't think I would fit in there anymore," I said. "We've grown in different directions. Besides, China is no more fond of vampires than Australia. At least here, you have a Richard Wells."

It had to mean something, that I had died here and been reborn here. This place was in my bones now, seeping in like a slow tide, drawing me into its treacherous current. Forcing me to learn to breathe underwater.

"I suppose that's why I feel drawn to you people," I said. Monique watched me, green eyes luminous in the dark. "Because you face the same things I do. Being dead. Being different. Being feared."

"Being an outsider," Monique said.

I nodded. But there were different layers of outside.

"I haven't seen my children in six years," Monique said.

"I didn't know you had children."

"A boy and a girl. My former husband has custody. I'm not allowed to contact them."

"I'm sorry," I said.

"I tell myself, one day, they'll be adults, and the court orders will lapse. And maybe they won't care what their mother is."

I reached out and covered her hand with my own. We sat in silence for several minutes.

"There's still an hour till dawn," Monique said at last. "Come back for one last dance?"

I hesitated. "Well, why not?"

• • •

The sky was already lightening as we returned to the convention centre, the clouds clearing in the promise of a beautiful day.

"Maybe you should skip the ball," I said, calculating sunrise, "and go straight home."

"Don't worry. I have a sunproof car."

Candle stubs and broken placards littered the forecourt, like the remnants of a disturbing dream. I was relieved that we didn't have to run the gauntlet of accusing stares, but surprised that the protestors hadn't stuck out their vigil.

As we entered the foyer, a distant roar sent unease crawling down my spine.

"What *is* that?" I asked.

But Monique was already running for the ballroom.

The double doors were flung wide, and a thin line of grey security stood between them and the seething mass of people who pushed and shoved.

"We want justice!" they chanted, over and over.

The vampires inside were no longer dancing, but stood in apprehensive clusters, at a loss for what to do. There were only a dozen left, outnumbered and dismayed.

Richard stepped forward, clicking shut his phone. "Listen!" he shouted above the crowd. "The police are on the way. Go home, before things get any worse."

"We're not scared of you!" a man shouted. His shirt was emblazoned with BLOODSUCKERS OUT. He launched himself at the cordon and broke through. The crowd followed, as though he had been a spearhead.

They surged through security in a whooping rush, overturning tables and smashing glasses, while the vampires backed away into the furthest corner. Richard stood in front of them, arms outstretched in a barrier, but his face was taut. The protesters closed in.

"Hey!" I called, and they swung towards me. "That's enough. You've made your point."

"What do you care?" the Bloodsuckers Out man said. He looked me up and down, and his mouth twisted. "Don't tell me you're one of these freaks."

"I don't know anymore," I said. "*Am* I one of these freaks?" I spread my hands. "Maybe you should get out of here before I make up my mind."

"Fucking creep. You can burn with them!" He yanked on the nearest curtain. It collapsed in ponderous folds, like a vast sail, exposing the glass beyond. Morning sun blazed through.

I stood, blinking, enveloped in the light.

Then I smiled.

"You should research your vampire lore," I said, advancing. "Stakes won't hurt me. Crosses don't scare me. I can stand in full sun. What do you think you can do to me?"

He rushed me then, seizing one of the heavy candelabra. I dodged sideways, and collided with someone else, who grabbed my arm. The other protestors were closing on me now.

I opened my mouth and inhaled. Their qi swirled from their bodies and into my lungs, filling me with strength and power. And they wavered, and fell, like cut flowers, stirring feebly.

I stood in the single pane of sunlight in the shadowed ballroom, as the vampires stood staring and silent.

When the police arrived, they arrested me.

But you already know that part, right, officer?

•  •  •

"Sign here," the sergeant said, after I had finished reading over my statement.

I signed the illegible scrawl I used for my credit card. Beneath that, in careful calligraphy, I wrote 'Cheng Kai Gong', and next to that, 'Jackson Cheng'. Because they were both my name.

April was waiting in the foyer of the police station with Richard and Monique. She leapt out of the plastic chair when I entered. "What were they doing, taking down your life story?"

"I'm fine, thanks for asking." We hugged. Then I turned to Richard.

"Thanks for putting up my bail."

He shook his head. "Don't worry about it. Our best lawyers are already on it. It's a clear case of self-defence."

"The nerve of Hayward," April said, "to press charges!"

"So will we," Richard said grimly. "It could have been very bad." He sighed. "It's hard to believe that it's the twenty-first century, and people still harbour prejudice against those who are different."

"Yeah," I said, after a moment. "Hard to believe."

As we left the police station, April and Richard fell into discussion about making the theme of the next convention 'Tolerance', while Monique and I walked on ahead.

"I'm sorry you had to go through this, after what you did," she said.

"At least now, we're fighting in the courts, not on the streets." This time, no one had died in the river, no one had burned up in the sun. But who knew about next time? Prejudice was a monster that rose from the dead no matter how many times you thought you had buried it.

But we who had witnessed it before would not stand by and witness it again. No matter who the target.

"I shouldn't even be here," I said. "But I'm not sorry I am."

••••••••••

# HUNTING RUFUS

## JASON FISCHER

The ute bounced and jolted down Yurla Crossing's main street. Loud country music belted out of the stereo, and the driver sang along badly. The rusty Falcon was an antique, somehow holding together despite the corrugated dirt roads for miles around.

Pulling up in front of Government House in a sliding mess of gravel and dust, the driver killed the improvised hydrogen converter and jumped out.

"Bob! Hey Bob! Come out here!" the lean man hollered, all bones and faded denim. He had the wrinkled skin of someone too stupid to wear sunblock. The remains of a rolled cigarette stuck to his thin bottom lip.

"Damn roo shooter." Bob Filcher said, walking out of his air-conditioned office. "What've you got now, Terry? Another rabbit or something?"

"Nup!" Terry grinned stupidly, ushering the official around the back. "Just you have a look at that."

"Shit, Terry." Bob whistled appreciatively. "You've bagged yourself a bloody monster."

The two men stared at the pickup's tray, and at the mass of dead meat that filled it. At three metres tall, it was easily the biggest kangaroo Bob had ever seen. It hung almost a metre out of the back, and its tail had rubbed raw against the road.

"That's gotta be worth twice the normal amount, right? Coz it's such a big mongrel?" Terry asked, carefully eyeing Bob Filcher's face. Though Bob had been here two years, he was still considered the new Remote Administrator, but he wasn't a pushover like the last fella. Commonsense never stopped Terry, though.

"No . . . no, Terry. It's one set bounty during the cull."

"You've got to be kidding! I nearly slipped a disc lifting that thing! I should claim for compo or something."

"You can't get worker's compensation. You work for yourself, dickhead." Bob swore, finally lifting his eyes from the giant carcass. "Bring it round the back."

"Sarah, Joe, run over to the pub and ask Brenda for some ice," Bob told his staff through the flyscreen. "Lots and lots of ice."

• • •

"What the hell is that?" Sergeant Trickham yelled. His little police station was part of Filcher's building, and consisted of his office, a filing room, and the cells. Like Bob, Ken Trickham loved Yurla Crossing, and firmly believed he would live his whole life there.

Entering through the rarely used cell-block, Ken had nearly choked on his knock-off beer. There in a cell, partly covered in ice, was a kangaroo corpse that reached from one end to the other.

"Bob, where the hell did this come from?" he yelled through the partition. "This one of Terry's?"

"Yep," Filcher said, a smirking Terry in tow. The three men stood outside the bars, looking at the massive carcass. The only sounds were a fly buzzing somewhere, and Ken working wetly on his beer.

"So do you believe me now, Sergeant?" Terry asked. "Said I was seein' things, you did."

"Alright Terry, I can see the bloody thing." Ken snarled. "Where'd you bag it?"

"Josephine's Gorge." Terry said proudly. "There were more of 'em, but they got away."

"Make yourself useful Terrence, and hold this for me," Bob said, pulling out a tape measure. They measured the bleeding hulk from top to toe.

"3.16 metres tall." he said, retracting the tape. "I hate to say it Terry, but you were right."

"Told you, told you I'd seen giant roos." the rooshooter gloated. "I've seen them moving at dusk. The damn things can outrun cars off-road. They don't behave like normal roos."

"What do you mean?" Bob asked. Terry was well known for telling ridiculous stories. He wasn't sure if the shooter was having him on or not.

"I've seen the big ones, the monsters like this one, *chasing* the normal kangaroos. When the group caught one, they ripped it to bits. Scariest thing I ever saw."

"Oh come on," Ken groaned, rolling his eyes. "This roo is a freak. Some kangaroos are, what, two metres and more? It's just a lot of kangaroo."

"Yes, some roos are about two metres high. They're your alpha males." Terry said.

"So what's your point?"

"That thing there, it's a female. And it was one of the small ones too."

"*Bullshit*," Ken said, but gulped the rest of his beer nervously. "You just saw this one fighting another roo. Happens all the time."

"I know what I saw, Sergeant. The big roos were hunting other animals. They moved just like dogs in a pack."

• • •

Bob Filcher made some calls, and transmitted images of the animal to Tandanya University. Within a minute the phone was ringing. When Bob calmed the girl on the other end, he asked her if she would come and have a look at the roo.

"A zoologist, a Miss Yarrow. She'll be up on the next mail-plane," Bob told Ken.

Two days later, the plane reached the tiny air-strip. The three men greeted her as she lugged a heavy bag down the ladder, and breathlessly shook their hands.

"Kimberly Yarrow, gentleman. Thanks for asking me up." the young academic smiled eagerly.

"Thanks for coming. The roo's still kinda fresh." Bob said.

"We keep putting ice on it." Terry said, grinning goofily. "I shot it, Ms Yarrow. I was the one who found it."

They returned to the cellblock, and Kimberly made a bee-line for the kangaroo. Kneeling in the muck and half-melted slush, she swept the ice away from its body.

"My god," she whispered. "I've never seen anything like this."

The zoologist performed various experiments on it, taking more photos. Breaking its sternum with a hammer and chisel, she sawed open its ribcage. Prodding the exposed organs and taking notes, Kimberly finally looked up. The three men had not moved, not even to get more beer.

"Gentlemen, this is not a kangaroo."

"What do you mean?" Bob said, puzzled. "It's not a bloody wombat."

"It's very close in some respects, but there are many differences." she continued. "Terry, it looks like you've found a new species."

"I did?"

"Look here," she continued, lifting up the animal's lip, exposing a series of sharp fangs.

"There are still flat molars at the back for crushing vegetation, but these canine teeth shouldn't be here," Kimberly explained.

"Look at the claws too," the biologist continued. "The ones on her "fingers" are about fifteen centimetres long, and on her "toes", almost thirty centimetres. These are still much bigger than what a kangaroo of the same size would have."

"So what are you saying, Miss Yarrow?" Ken asked uneasily.

"This animal is either omnivorous or carnivorous. It eats meat, Terry." she finished as the rooshooter opened his mouth.

• • •

Determined to learn more, Kimberly Yarrow made arrangements to stay in Yurla Crossing. Eager to capture a live specimen, or at least get some photos, she commissioned Terry and his aging vehicle. They had searched all around Josephine's Gorge, but with no success.

Excited by the find, Tandanya University had asked Kimberly to secure more evidence of the beast she'd dubbed "Magnaroo". A small team of scientists were to join her later in the week, but the biologist did not want to wait that long.

The pair wasted long, frustrating days. Terry spotted what must be a Magnaroo print near Josephine's Gorge, but lost the trail after an hour's drive. When darkness fell, they continued searching with spotlights.

"I seen their alpha male once, Miss Yarrow." Terry grinned, face aglow in the dashlights. "Big red feller, more than four metres tall. Called him Rufus, I did."

"Rufus, sure." Kimberly said absently. She had heard all his tall stories in the last two days.

Scanning the landscape with Terry's nightvision binoculars, Kimberly called out directions whenever she spotted the loping bound of a roo. Apart from scaring kangaroos of the normal variety, the nights proved just as fruitless.

On their fourth day, the long-range radio suddenly squealed, screeching till the auto-tuner found the signal. It was Ken Trickham. He sounded excited.

"Terry, get your arse up to Banross Station! Tell Ms Yarrow that I found her damn roos!"

Bouncing and sliding over the back roads, Terry made it to Banross in under an hour. Ken's four-wheel drive was in the middle of the road, and the copper flagged them to a halt.

"Something's munched on the Banross cattle. Wasn't dingoes neither." he said. "Follow me, and be careful for God's sake!"

They followed Ken across a bumpy paddock, mostly dust from the drought. When they drove around a scattered pile of hay, Terry slammed on the brakes. The shooter swore, and Kimberly gagged, almost vomiting.

Dozens of cows had literally been ripped to shreds—eviscerated and left to die. Intestines and organs had been pulled out, and the mess spread for metres around each body. Already rotting in the Outback sun; the stench was horrific.

Terry piled out of the car, eyes wide and rifle in hand. Kimberly scrambled after him, but fell to her knees, retching loudly.

A group of eagles hopped around on the carcasses, tearing at the flesh. Terry let off a shot that sent them flapping into the sky, screeching in disgust. Bellowing in pain, one of the cows had actually survived, wide-eyed and surrounded by its own entrails. Ken put a mercy round through its brain.

"This was definitely a Magnaroo pack," a white-faced Kimberly said as she rejoined them. "Look at the ground."

Big bloody footprints circled the killing ground, and led to the west. Terry knelt by the spoor, frowning.

"At least eight of them. And these ones make my roo look little."

"This is incredible." the scientist breathed as she investigated the carnage. Taking several photos, she made sure to include the bloody paw-prints.

"These will tell us how they attack, and how they work together. They might help me to figure out the most fascinating part of what happened here."

"What the hell do you mean?" Ken growled, gesturing at the carcasses. "It's not fascinating, it's a bloody mess. Look at what they did! They're a menace!"

"They're built for meat eating and speed, but they don't know what they're doing yet. They're learning how to hunt."

"Seems to me they know what they're doing." Terry commented dryly.

"No, no. That's not true. Have a look here. They've rounded up their prey, and played with it. There's quite a bit of meat left on the carcasses, and predators usually kill just enough to meet the requirements of the pack."

"I'll radio for more shooters." Ken said. "I don't like our chances against that mob."

"No!" Kimberly shouted. "You can't just kill them off! This is the most amazing find in modern history, and you'd simply wipe the species out?"

"I don't think Ted Banross is gonna see it that way," the policeman retorted, gesturing at the dead herd. Clouds of black flies crawled all over the bloody mess.

"They're predators! They kill things! It's the way of nature." Kimberly yelled. "The only shooting will be from my camera."

"What if one of those things attacks *us*, Miss Yarrow?" Terry asked, worry wrinkling his leathery face. "We'd have to drop it then."

"I brought a tranquiliser gun." Kimberly assured. "If we can capture a breeding pair of Magnaroo, we will enter the history books!"

"Maybe for the wrong reasons," Ken Trickham grunted as he headed back to the four wheel drive. They began their cross country crawl, on the bloody trail of the pack.

Drawing up level with the treetops, several giant creatures watched the two vehicles pass, ears twitching. When the noisy vehicles had vanished from sight, they slowly followed them through the scrub.

• • •

"I hear you loud and clear, Ken. Over." Bob Filcher replied, releasing the button on the handset. Remembering the animal back in the cell, he frowned.

*Science and Miss Yarrow be damned*, he finally thought. *If those things bred anything like kangaroos did, the Outback would be overrun in no time.*

He read the email again. There's been an unspecified accident at the Woomera Test Facility, *last week*. Typically, the powers-that-be had only just informed the surrounding RA's of the "incident". The only news was that the Prohibited Area quarantine was being "lethally enforced", and to expect additional Defence Force movements in the area.

*Did they do it?* he thought. *Did they breed these things? What the hell are they?*

As mental images of the monsters hopping into Yurla Crossing ran through his mind, Bob contacted Tredrea Station. They had a chopper and several good shooters, and helped with the cull in quiet times. Though at first they didn't believe him, they promised they would look for whatever had attacked the Banross cattle.

Sitting by the radio and worrying, Bob finally got up and using his spare key, unlocked Ken's gun-rack. He shuddered, remembering the Magnaroo's fangs.

• • •

"Geez these things can move!" Terry swore, looking at the sinking sun. "We'd better catch up before it gets dark, or we'll lose them."

The Falcon bouncing around in the scrub, Kimberly was thoroughly sick of being jolted around. Terry's keen eye could still make out the tracks, though every now and then he had to stop and search for the trail on foot.

"C'mon Terry!" Ken Trickham bellowed from the white four-wheel drive, after what seemed the fiftieth stop. "Don't tell me you're lost!"

"I'm not bloody lost, you bloody pig bastard." Terry muttered, giving the policeman a dirty look. Getting in the Falcon, he jammed it into drive and flattened it, leaving Sergeant Trickham in a cloud of red dust.

"Stupid copper, wouldn't be able to find his own stupid nose in the dark," the rooshooter grumbled, manoeuvring the ute around a fallen tree. A large dark shape bounded through the scrub, and Terry hollered in triumph.

"We found 'em!" He began, when a large shape threw itself into the side of the Falcon. Kimberly began screaming like crazy, and even Terry shrieked like a little girl. In the dim orange light, they could see the Magnaroo, grabbing onto Kimberly's window sill with its front claws. Trying to ram its massive head through the window, it snapped at Kimberly with its fanged maw.

"Get down!" Terry screamed, and madly grabbing for his gun, let off a wild shot out of his passenger window. Shrieking horribly, the giant roo let go of the door. Ears still ringing from the gun-fire, Kimberly cowered down on the floor, shaking and moaning.

"Wind up the bloody windows!" Terry yelled.

"*Don't stop driving!*" Ken's voice crackled through the radio. "*They're all around us!*"

Bounding through the trees, the Magnaroo pack came for them. Towering over the vehicles, they rammed into the sides as Terry passed, pounding on the roof and hissing sinisterly.

"So . . . big!" Kimberly said, somehow keeping the presence of mind to take photos. Some of the Magnaroo were nearly three and a half metres tall, and they easily outpaced the machines. She counted eight of them, flitting in and out of the scrub.

"We're being rounded up," she whispered, then shrieked as Terry slammed on the brakes. The cloud of dust cleared, and in front of them stood the biggest, meanest Magnaroo of them all. Large fangs extended past his top lip, and he was well over four metres tall, dark red fur just visible in the fading daylight.

"Rufus." Terry whispered, and then the monster pounced. Landing on the bonnet of the Falcon, he crushed the exposed hydrogen converter with his giant feet. Bellowing deep within his chest, he tore at the roof, sharp claws scoring the steel.

Madly reversing, Terry narrowly missed Ken's four-wheel drive, which was covered in the giant beasts. Rufus continued to pound and tear at the roof, sharp claws finally puncturing the steel. Blood trickled into the cabin as the alpha male cut himself on the sharp edge, and Kimberly fumbled for the tranquiliser gun.

"Drop that useless piece of shit!" Terry roared, pulling a loaded pistol from the centre console. As Rufus wrenched at the roof, he emptied the clip through the roof. Shrieking, the massive creature fell to one side, and the lanky man cackled in triumph.

"That's why you should always keep a gun loaded." Terry chuckled, then cursed as the engine suddenly coughed and died. The antique Falcon, rolling on Australian roads since 1998, rolled no more.

"Damn hydrogen converter! I knew I should never have . . . " Terry began, and gasped as the driver's side window smashed. Kimberly shrieked, and could only watch in horror as massive paws reached into the cab and wrenched the screaming man out. His screams turned into agonised squeals, and then there were nothing but horrible crunching and snuffling sounds. The Magnaroo were feeding.

Cowering on the floor, Kimberly shook in terror. Lying in a pool of her own urine, she tried to keep absolutely quiet. Absolutely still.

*"Terry! Terry! Come in!'*the radio crackled. It was Bob Filcher, back at Yurla Crossing. Frantically, the biologist grabbed the handset. Hands shaking, she thumbed the button.

"It's Kimberly Yarrow, Mister Filcher," she whispered. "They got him! The roos got Terry. I think they've got Ken as well."

*"Shit!"* Bob swore loudly. *"Where are you? Are you okay?"* The feeding sounds stopped, and there was a sharp hiss. Kimberly could only watch in horror as a giant head peered through the broken window, and she pounded at the radio controls till she found the off switch.

*Please god, please,* she silently prayed. Leaning through the window, the Magnaroo stretched its long arm across the cab. Breathing with frustration, it couldn't quite reach her.

Sobbing hysterically, she primed the tranquiliser gun. As the beast managed to get its claws snagged in her hair, she fired the dart between the Magnaroo's eyes.

Squealing, the roo snatched back its paw, ripping out some of her hair. Scrabbling at the dart, its eyes rolled backwards and it collapsed into a drugged snooze.

She had five darts left in the clip, and pulling the bolt back, primed the air-gun for the next shot. She had no idea how many Magnaroo surrounded her, and if that would be enough. Quietly reaching across the cabin, she wrapped her hands around Terry's rifle. The cabin rocked slightly.

With a god awful screech, the bloody paws of Rufus smashed through the windscreen. Screaming and crying, Kimberly dropped the rifle as she cowered from the giant. Rooting around in the cab, the injured Rufus finally dug its sharp claws into her side. He pulled the wriggling woman out of the ruined vehicle.

Lip curling back as it growled, the giant red beast towered above the Falcon. Drool fell from its fangs, and it lifted Kimberly up to its mouth.

Managing to land a dart in his chest with the air-gun, the gun dropped from her trembling fingers. Snarling and hissing, Rufus staggered around, shaking his head. The tranquiliser wasn't working!

"No!" she shrieked, beating at the strong arms. Tears pouring down her face, a thousand thoughts racing through her mind in those last awful moments. A week ago, she had been tinkering around in the Uni lab, and now she was about to die horribly in the middle of the Outback.

The towering marsupial squeezed his claws, and they dug into Kimberly's side painfully. The blood rushed to her head, and there was a throbbing sound in her ears. Sniffing at her face, he gently began to worry at her with his teeth, alternately licking and biting at her. His breath stinking of rotten flesh, Kimberly gagged. Rufus was playing with her, like a cat with a mouse.

It took a second for Kimberly to realised that the drumming sound in her ears was in fact an approaching helicopter. Rufus dropped her and bounced away in fear, and crying, she shook with relief on the ground. Several rifle shots rang out, and the Magnaroo pack scattered in all directions.

Mercifully, she sank into unconsciousness, seeing an aboriginal teenager leap from the landing helicopter before darkness claimed her.

• • •

"Miss . . . Miss . . . are you okay?"

Shaking her groggy head, Kimberly groaned. She hurt all over, and it felt like someone had bandaged her up. She opened her eyes.

Strapped into a chair in a helicopter, she saw the big smiles and friendly eyes of her rescuers. Every person onboard was indigenous, most of them quite young. The eldest was a middle-aged woman, the pilot.

"How you feeling, miss?" the boy repeated. "Don't worry, you're safe now."

"The . . . roos . . . ." she gasped. "Terry . . . Ken."

"They didn't make it." the pilot answered. "Damn devils killed them. The cars, wrecked. You're lucky we came along when we did."

"We didn't believe Terry when he told us," said a teenage girl, clutching a rifle as big as her. "Who would have?"

The Tredrea family owned one of the more successful stations near Yurla Crossing. Thankfully they had listened to Bob Filcher, and followed Terry's tyre tracks from Banross Station.

"We'll take you to Yurla Crossing, then we'll have to get the flying doctor out." Beatty Tredrea continued as she casually guided the whirlybird home. "You're pretty messed up, but you should live."

They made it back to town by daybreak. Another baking hot day had begun in the outback town, and the wind was already kicking up a lot of dust. Carrying Kimberly in a fireman's lift, two of the older Tredrea boys carried her from the airfield and towards Government House.

"Oh Jesus, no. Oh god!" Kimberly shrieked. Putting her on the ground, the boys hollered for help.

The streets of Yurla Crossing were filled with the dead. What was left of Bob Filcher lay face down in the red dirt, his legs and upper arms virtually gone.

Kimberly gagged when she saw the remains of the publican, guts split open and one of her arms several feet away, an unfired gun still clutched in her hand.

The windows of the store were ruined, and a massive hole gaped in the pub's side where something had smashed through it.

She stared in horror at the first Magnaroo, its ugly doglike head level with the roof of the hotel. Spotting her, it swung forward on its arms and legs, its thick tail marking a line through the red dust. Hissing and barking at her, she saw it snap its sharp teeth. Loud breathing sounds surrounded her as dozens of roos emerged from hiding.

Closing her eyes, she drew herself into a tight little ball in the middle of the street. She did not want to look when she heard the screams and shots from the helicopter, the breaking glass and the eating sounds. She heard her two companions run for cover, heard their screams as they were run down and murdered.

She still didn't look as she heard the thumping sound of the roos giant feet, the hissing of their angry breath. A big foot rested on her, pinning her to the ground, and sharp teeth caressed her pale throat—

• • •

"Be ready," the CO told his gunner. It was dark, and the soldiers were getting nervous. "Fucking things can rip through the armour." The tanks of the 3/9th were lined up across the Sturt Highway. The RAAF had been performing maneuvers over the area, scanning for heat signatures in the nearby bush. The roo packs scattered whenever a plane flew over, and the bombings hadn't achieved much.

The killer roos were out of control and breeding rapidly. Having stripped the Outback of life, they were making their way to the cities.

One way or the other, another species was about to become extinct.

• • • • • • • • • • •

# THE WISHWRITER'S WIFE

## IAN McHUGH

In the days when fairies were still to be found in the world, and wishes could come true, there lived a wishwriter and his wife. The wishwriter was a clever man, but plain, and born with a twisted back that made him stoop. His wife was beautiful, gentle and generous, and she loved him just as he was.

The wishwriter was happy, for this was just as he had wished. His wife contented herself that her husband, too, was gentle and generous, and it did not hurt her to love him.

The wishwriter made his living because no matter how many fairies came into a person's possession, they could only ever have one true wish. A wish could only be for a single thing; a person could not wish for fame *and* fortune, or a beautiful palace *and* a handsome prince. It could not be an infinite thing—eternal youth or a purse that was always full of gold—or even too large a thing, or the wish would not bind and take.

"It is important for the wish to bind," the wishwriter said, touching his wife's cheek, "otherwise it might fade, or simply vanish.

"And that," he said, "would be heartbreaking."

His wife showed him a smile, and wondered what it would be like to not be bound.

"And a wish cannot make more wishes," the wishwriter said, always pleased to show off his expertise. "So if a person has more than one heart's desire, and many do . . . " He spread his hands with a self-satisfied grin.

" . . . they will come to a wishwriter," his wife obliged.

It was the wife's role to greet her husband's clients, and to flatter and fuss over them while—usually—the houseboy ran to fetch the wishwriter from his club or the baths or the gaming house. Then, once he had snuck in the back door and up the servants' stairs, she would take the clients up to his study, where the wishwriter would now be ensconced behind his desk, his features shrouded beneath a scholar's hood.

"It all adds to the air of mystery," he told her, "which is very important in this line of work."

The wishwriter's wife was fascinated by the many heart's desires of the people who sought her husband's services. One day, she might open the door to find a woman clutching a breadbox, inside which was the fairy she had caught raiding her pantry. The woman would tell of her husband, who could no longer ply his trade as a woodcutter since an accident that cost him his arm, and she wished for him to be whole. Yet at the same time she herself was barren and longed for a daughter. Then the wishwriter would send her away for a week, and when she returned he would give her a tiny scroll on which was written: "I wish, I wish, I wish to find at home my delighted husband holding aloft our infant daughter with his two strong arms." The woman would speak the wish, and the fairy would give up its magic and its bright tiny life to make the wish come true.

Or the wife might discover a young boy waiting on the step, who in desperation had traded his father's precious violin to a fairy trapper. The boy's father had been a great composer, but was now deaf, and the boy wished for him to be able to hear and make music again. At the same time, the boy felt himself a disappointment to his father, for he had not inherited his gift for music and, what was more, his father would certainly be furious when he discovered the loss of his violin. After a week, at the appointed time, the boy would return and read aloud his wish, which said: "I wish, I wish, I wish for my father to hear me playing skillfully on the new violin that is the equal of the one I traded." Then the fairy in its little brass cage would turn to sparkling dust, the dust would become his wish, and the boy would race joyfully home clutching his new violin.

The wishwriter always sent people away for a week, although it rarely took him as long as an hour to piece together their various desires into a single wish.

"Most people could write their own wishes," he confided to his wife, "if only they thought a little."

But of course most people did not, and so the wishwriter would send them away for a week. For although he was gentle and generous he was also clever, and knew on which side his bread was buttered.

He did always strive to write their wishes as well as possible. "But in truth," he said to his wife, "the precision of the words does not matter so much. Wishes are not fickle things, as long as a person does not get too greedy, and provided the wish is expressed in a single clause."

So the wishwriter and his wife lived comfortably and even grew quite wealthy, for he wrote wishes for rich as well as poor. If his customers had no gold or silver, he would take payment in goods or kind—a winter's supply of chopped firewood, or a gift of music lessons for his wife. Sometimes, during the breeding season, a lucky person would come with two captured fairies and offer the second to the wishwriter as payment.

Whenever this happened the wishwriter would smile and gesture to his wife and say: "I have but a single wish, and it is already true." But he would take the fairy, for fairies were as good as money, especially to a wishwriter.

His wife would stare at the tiny being in its cage. She, too, had come to have a single wish.

For as the wishwriter had grown older, his cleverness had become arrogance and conceit. He had also grown fat, as a result of enjoying his comfortable life. He had developed jowls and a substantial paunch. His muscles had become slack and his skin blotchy. His stoop had turned into a hunch. But he did not care for any of these things, for his wife remained beautiful, even as she aged, and he knew she must love him just as he was. He did not consider that his wife might be troubled.

Although, of course, she had no choice but to love him, still she longed for him to be more like he once had been, and not as he had become. And in her secret heart, she longed not to be bound at all. But as her husband had told her, a wish could not make more wishes, and so the heart's desire that grew within her remained inside and unsaid.

And as the wishwriter grew older, he also developed a sickness of the mind. Subtly at first, then more and more noticeably his moods became erratic. He grew prone to fits of passion and anger, wild tantrums that boiled up from nowhere. He was no longer gentle and generous. His gift for writing wishes deserted him, and people began to take their business elsewhere.

Because his sickness was of the mind, the wishwriter could not see it for himself, and blamed others for their fickleness. His wife tried to bring him healers, but he drove them away with insults and curses, and accused his wife of betrayal and trying to do him harm. She bore his unkind words in silence, for she knew his mind was no longer his own, and she continued to care for him as best as he would allow. But, although she could not help but still love him, she also began an affair with a younger man from the town, who was gentle and generous as her husband once had been.

The last healer that she tried, an alchemist of some note, accepted her apologetic offer of tea, after he too had been driven rudely from her husband's bedside. He watched her pour with shaking hands, then sipped from his cup and offered words of small comfort: "It is unlikely that medicine could have helped him, anyway. Such is often the case with diseases of the mind."

They sat in her husband's study, a room of strong sunlight and deep shadows that reminded her of the wishwriter as he once had been. From a hook by the window hung a fairy in a brass cage, the last of those with which her husband had been paid when he was still well enough to work.

The alchemist gestured to it. "A wish might save him."

The wife looked longingly at the fairy and her eyes filled with tears. She shook her head.

"Ah, of course. You have had your one true wish already," he guessed.

She whispered, "No."

A small frown creased the alchemist's brow. "A cure for your husband is not among your heart's desires?"

*No,* the wife answered, in the deepest part of her heart. She drew an unsteady breath and looked at the alchemist directly. "A wish cannot make more wishes," she told him.

He stared at her. A look of comprehension crossed his features, and with it a touch of compassion. He reached out, his fingertips making fleeting contact with the back of her hand.

"It will be done soon," the alchemist said. "He will not last much longer."

She smiled at him through her tears, and gave him the fairy for payment, though it was worth far more than his fee. Even in those days, they were becoming rare.

The wishwriter's health continued to decline. His wild moods diminished and he became increasingly idle and withdrawn. His wife continued to care for him as he lost the ability to meet even his own most basic needs. Still she loved him just as he was-she could do nothing else—and she reminded herself that he had always been gentle and generous to her before his sickness, and he had given her a good life. And, whenever she could, she found comfort in the arms of her townsman, whom she could not love, but who she fancied she might, had she the choice.

Eventually the day came when the wishwriter could not even rise from his bed, and his wife knew that his time must be near. She wrote a letter to her young townsman, bidding him farewell and telling him she believed she would have loved him, had the choice been hers. She gave it to a street urchin to deliver, for she had let the servants go, months before.

Then she sat by her husband's side and waited for Death to come and claim him. As the wishwriter breathed his last breaths, his face eased and his wife thought she glimpsed something of the man he once had been. She grieved for that man, and grieved that he had been gone from her for so long. And she grieved that he had bound her to him, had not given her a free heart when he wished her into being and set himself the task of earning her love.

Quietly, without fuss, Death stole into the room, and the wishwriter breathed no more.

His wife felt relief then, even as she wept, that at last his madness and her misery were at an end.

Her tears did not last long. A calm settled over her. She looked inside herself and found her heart free and unbound. She breathed in, deeply. Then out. Motes of sparkling dust rode on her breath, only a few at first, thickening to a cloud as the long sigh went on.

As the cloud grew brighter and more dense, so she dimmed and faded.

When only the cloud remained, it swirled about the room until it found the open window. Out it went, riding the breeze, the motes scattering, unfettered at last, and quickly to fade.

•••••••••••

# FROSTBITTEN

## KIRSTYN McDERMOTT

Less than three steps into his apartment before he's kissing her, hands reaching beneath her skirt, mauling at her bare arse like it can be moulded into something else if only he squeezes hard enough. Nina returns his kisses with equal ferocity, thankful that he's so eager.

Eager means quick, and quick is what she needs.

He doesn't bother with the bedroom, simply propels her into the living room, over to the modular lounge that lines two walls like a gigantic red L, and throws her down on the shorter side. At least it's firm beneath her back.

"You're so cold, baby," he murmurs into her throat. She can smell the spice-sharp scent of his cologne, and the sweat beneath it. "Let's see what we can do to warm you up, hey?"

He's not awful—she's definitely had a lot worse—but he's young, and his repertoire isn't very extensive. Nina feels a slight twinge of remorse about that, but brushes it aside. She allows his fingers to chafe at her nipples for a bit before pushing them away, coaxing them further south. Misunderstanding, he unbuckles his belt instead, shuffles his pants down to his thighs.

"Fuck, you're a sexy thing."

He moans as he pushes himself into her, and Nina's glad she bothered to pre-lube back in the club's bathroom before they left. Foreplay obviously isn't his strong suit. She hooks her legs over his hips and echoes the noises he's making, clenching herself close around him, pulling him deeper. His fingers dig into her shoulders, and he moves like he's ploughing her, like he's trying to dig a trough right through the middle of her. She turns her head and bites his earlobe.

His spine flexes when he comes and he mewls like a frightened animal, teeth clenched and gleaming with saliva. "Oh," he says, twice, before collapsing onto her. Nina rubs his back, wriggles a little beneath him. He's no lightweight, and the muscles of her inner thighs are starting to ache.

After a minute or so, he pushes himself up. "Sorry, was I squashing you?"

Nina smiles. "I'm fine."

"Just fine?" He leans down and kisses her breast.

Nina keeps smiling. Beneath her hands, his skin is cooling. He rolls off and lies on the couch beside her, one hand over his eyes. "Man, that was intense. Give me a few and we'll go again, hey?"

"Sure." She sits up, swings her legs around. Her bag is at the end of the couch and she bends to retrieve it. "Where's your bathroom?" He waves his free hand towards the hallway, tells her to look for the second door on the right. Nina stands and straightens her skirt, fastens the three buttons on her blouse he managed to get around to undoing. She's still wearing her boots, knee-high black leather with heels high enough to lame a novice, and the apartment floors are polished wood. When she walks, it sounds like deliberation.

The bathroom is easy to find. Nina cleans herself up, then brushes her teeth with the help of an index finger and a smear of peppermint-plus-whitening. Her knickers went into her bag back at the club; she takes them out again now, pulls them up over her hips. Already she feels much better. Much warmer. The adjacent bedroom yields a quilt that smells stale and used, but there isn't time to hunt down a clean one.

Back in the living room, the young man has curled himself into a ball in the corner of the lounge. His hands are tucked into his armpits and his teeth are chattering as she covers him with the quilt. "It's so bloody cold," he says. "Aren't you cold?" His eyes are pale blue, the colour of frost on winter grass. She hadn't noticed before.

"I'm fine." Nina smiles at him. There's a reverse cycle air conditioner mounted on the opposite wall. She makes sure it's switched onto heat, then turns the thermostat up as high as it will go. Hot air begins to flood the room.

"I can't get warm," the man says. "Feels like I won't ever get warm again."

Nina's own face is flushed now, almost clammy. Between her thighs, a different heat is building. "I'm sorry," she tells him, fishing her car keys from her bag. "It won't always be this bad, I promise. Over time, it . . . lessens."

"Don't go," he pleads. "Stay with me. I need you to stay with me."

"I'm sorry," she says again, and wonders how long it's been since those words held any meaning.

• • •

It's late, about to turn into early morning, and Simone still hasn't shown up. Nina's already showered and washed her hair. Washed her body as well with her favourite scented soap—coconut and lemongrass—that Simone says it makes her smell like a Thai curry, delicious and creamy and hot.

She paces the cramped confines of the motel room, biting her nails. Rubbing against the white silk of her negligee, her skin itches and burns.

What's taking that woman so damn long?

From the bed, her phone bleats the arrival of a new message, and Nina lunges towards it. From Simone, the screen tells her. The text is short, and infuriating: *sry, couldnt find 1. 2morrow? stsp? sim xxx*

Nina throws the phone at the wall. It falls apart, the battery skidding a few metres across the carpet. Her hands are shaking. Does Simone think it's not just as hard for *her* to find them? To fuck them? Opting for men might speed things along a bit, but it doesn't make it any easier. Simone would see that if she ever deigned to sample from the other side of the menu. But she's too fussy, that's the problem, and too worried about possible consequences. Tonight, it's Nina's problem as well. But at least they won't have to wait another month.

*stsp*

Same time, same place. Nina takes a deep breath, then another, wills herself to calm the hell down. Trouble is, she's so damn hot. Tonight would have been amazing; who knows what tomorrow will bring?

She picks up the pieces of phone and puts them carefully back together, makes a silent wish as she presses the *on* button. The screen lights up white for a second before the annoying welcome tune kicks in and she's asked to input the current date and time. At least the bloody thing seems to be working. Nina takes the time from the clock on the bedside table, remembers the date from when she signed the motel registration. All her recent days have blurred together; they always do whenever she and Simone are about to meet.

She calls up the text again, types in a quick reply—*ok, tomorrow. stsp. miss you much. n xxx*—and presses send. Then she tosses the phone back to the bed and stalks into the ensuite.

Time for another shower. Cold this time, for as long as she can stand it.

• • •

Bent forwards over the man's dining room table, its hard-angled edge digging into her hips, Nina worries she's made a mistake, allowed impatience to get in the way of better judgement. He seemed harmless enough back at the bar, slightly shorter than herself with a body long since gone to seed, his round and ruddy face all but glowing with the sheen of desperation.

Now, she's not so sure.

He grunts with each thrust, his flabby gut slapping against her arse. He calls her a slut, a whore, a frigid fucking bitch. He tells her that he'll show her who's the boss, who's her fucking master. Clenching her teeth, Nina stretches out and grips the opposite edge of the tabletop. As though perceiving this as invitation, he fumbles at her right breast, pinches the nipple between his fingers and twists. Hard. Tears prick at the corners of her eyes but she doesn't make a sound; she won't give him that kind of satisfaction.

His hand tangles in her hair, pulling, lifting her head up and back as far as her neck will allow, and then just that little bit further. Nina realises what he's about to do and manages to turn her head slightly to the left as he slams her forehead down onto the table. Sparks burst behind her eyes and this time she does cry out. There'll be bruises to cover up later, but at least her nose isn't broken.

Behind her, above her, the man continues to grunt.

Nina pushes back against him, grinding her teeth against the pain that unfurls like razor wire in her skull. She needs him to finish, and she needs to be conscious when he does. Movement seems to excite him, so she begins to squirm, to writhe beneath the hands that now pin her to the table, although she can't quite convince herself that her struggles are entirely an act.

The man calls her a slut again, and asks her if she likes it. Then he tenses up and groans, his sweaty bulk squashed tight against her as he rocks backwards and forwards on his toes. Nina lifts her right leg beneath the table, braces herself with her hands, and kicks back as hard as she can. Not anywhere near as hard as she wants, but her spiked heel is enough to make him gasp and release his hold on her shoulders. He sways back a step, putting enough distance between them for her to deliver a second, infinitely more powerful, kick.

The man screams, a high-pitched, girlie wail that's music to Nina's ears.

She straightens and spins around, hands raised to fists in front of her face. He's hunched over, leaning against the wall with knees half-bent and wobbling, both hands at his groin. Blood leaks between his fingers. He lifts his head, glares at her with eyes red-veined and streaming.

"You fucking bitch," he shrieks. "Look what you fucking did!"

She doesn't want to look, is quite happy to live and let live from this point on, until the man takes a step towards her. More of a stagger really, but she doesn't even think before kicking him again. In the chest this time, the flat of her foot landing almost squarely between his nipples with the whole weight of her body behind it, sending him flailing to the ground where he slumps, badly winded. Nina is disappointed to see that all the blood is coming from a ragged hole punched near the top of his inner thigh, right in the crease where leg meets torso, and not from a more intimate wound. She moves in close, lowers her boot onto his neck. The heel sits neatly in the hollow where his clavicles meet.

"Don't . . ." he wheezes. "Please . . ."

Nina shakes her head. "I'm not going to kill you. There's no point." She lifts her foot and steps away. "This little hobby of yours, hurting women? You'll find it doesn't hold much interest for you anymore. There's not a lot that will."

He's trembling already. Whether from fear or the incipient cold, she neither knows nor cares.

• • •

This time, Simone has beaten her to the motel. As Nina opens the door, the other woman practically bounces from the bed where she's been sitting and rushes over with arms spread wide. Her grin falters as Nina steps into the room, into the light.

"What happened?" She reaches for Nina's forehead, stops just short of touching it. For one awful moment, Nina stops breathing. Then she sees the colour in Simone's cheeks, feels the heat emanating from her skin, and pulls the woman into her arms. Relaxing into the embrace, Simone runs her hands down Nina's spine, presses soft, warm lips to her throat.

"I'm off my game," Nina tells her. "Picked a bad one tonight."

"Oh, honey, you need to be more careful."

"I need *you*."

Their mouths meet, their tongues touch. Hesitant, light, sliding against each other with slow, teasing strokes. Then Simone is pulling her towards the bed, her hands firm on Nina's hips, her kisses more forceful. She's making those urgent, almost guttural moans that never fail to melt Nina right where it counts.

"Wait." Nina pushes herself away. "I have to shower first. I need to scrub this stink off me."

"I don't care about that."

"I do."

"Okay." Simone smiles, undoes the first three buttons on her pyjama top and parts the pale blue fabric. "I'll be waiting right here when you're done."

Nina bends to place a kiss first on Simone's left breast, and then on her right. She flicks the tip of her tongue over each nipple, coaxing them to dark and perky nubs. "I won't be long," she says. "I promise."

The first thing she does when she gets into the ensuite is swallow three rapid-action painkillers. Her head still hurts like blazes—not surprising, really, considering the face that reproaches her from the mirror. There's a swollen lump on the side of her forehead the size of a quail's egg; around it the flesh is already turning interesting shades of purple and blue. But no blood, no split skin, no need for stitches. Thank the goddess for minor mercies.

Nina lets the shower run until the ensuite is billowing with steam, then strips and steps beneath the water. Her skin flushes an instant, angry red but she makes no move to adjust the temperature. Tonight, with such fresh and bitter heat running through her body, not even boiling water could scald her. Eyes closed, she starts to sing as she lathers her hair with shampoo. That old Kate Bush song about Cathy and coming home and wanting to be let in; only in a bathroom could her splintered falsetto sound remotely bearable.

"Hey."

Nina jumps, opens her eyes to find Simone leaning through the shower curtain. She is naked, her long brown hair tied up behind in a messy knot, a smile lazing across her face. "Mind if I join the choir?" The question is moot; she's already stepping into the shower recess. Then they're kissing again, and Simone's tongue is in Nina's mouth, and Simone's hands are on Nina's breasts, and Simone's thigh is pressing into Nina's groin.

"How high can that voice of yours go?" Simone whispers, pushing her back against the tiles. Soap-slick fingers slide down where she burns most fiercely and Nina whimpers as they find their way between her folds. Her own hands grasp for Simone's shoulders as the woman kisses her hard, then soft, sawing Nina's lower lip gently between her teeth. Nina feels herself building, feels her whole body stretching thin and taut as violin string, and she moans, gives herself up to the play of expert hands.

Until brilliantly, blissfully, Nina breaks.

Still Simone holds her, supporting her weight until Nina's legs feel ready to work again. "I love you," Nina says, glad for the water that streams down her face and swallows her tears. "You're everything."

Simone squeezes her tight. "I love you too. So much." She reaches around and turns off the taps, pinches Nina lightly on the cheek. "How about we take this into the bedroom? Previews are over, my darling; time for the feature presentation."

• • •

Almost as soon as Nina drags herself into consciousness, she knows something is wrong. There's too much light in the room, the sun pushing its way through the cheap motel curtains as though they're made from mesh, and her stomach lurches. It's late, it's really fucking late. Simone's still sleeping, her head resting heavy on Nina's chest, one knee propped over Nina's thigh. Bare skin touching bare skin, in far too many places. As fast as she dares, Nina curls her arm around Simone's skull, taking care to keep her lover's thick swathe of hair between them.

"Simone," she says. "Wake up." Simone murmurs something unintelligible and starts to shift her position, but Nina holds her steady. "Don't move," she says. "We've slept in. I think we're cold."

Simone's fully awake now; Nina can feel her breathing start to speed.

"What do we do?" Simone whispers.

"We be quick."

And before the other woman can reply, Nina grabs a handful of hair and pulls Simone's head abruptly away. There's a too-brief tugging on her skin, like they're stuck together with superglue or worse, before something tears and Simone shrieks in pain and surprise. Nina feels burned—by frost, not fire—and when she risks a glance there's a raw, blistered patch of skin above her breast, glistening red in the sunlight. Simone's cheek looks even worse, torn and seeping like gravel rash, blood beading along her jawline.

"What about the rest of us?" Simone's voice breaks on the last word.

"It won't be as bad," Nina assures her, stuffing bits of sheet into the gaps between their bodies, assessing the places where there are none. "The way your head was resting on me, the weight of it, that made it worse. The rest is just touching, more or less. Not a lot of pressure."

"Are you saying I have a fat head?"

Simone's smile is so brave, so defiant, that Nina aches to hug her. Instead she offers a grin of her own—weak and falling down at the corners, but the best she can manage—then points down at their legs. "You need to move your knee now. Lift it up and off me, but quickly. Like with a Band-Aid, okay?"

"Or a wax strip."

"Only not as painful." They both know she is lying.

The second time seems worse than the first, maybe because they know what to expect, maybe because Simone is too cautious, too slow, and Nina has to pull her own leg away to finish the job. But the places where belly meets hip, where the back of an arm lies along the curve of a ribcage, hurt less to separate. Finally free, Simone rolls to the other side of the bed, shields herself with the blanket.

"I've got some antiseptic cream in my toiletries case." Cautiously, Nina pushes herself to her feet. "Some bandages, as well." A rudimentary first aid kit she's carried ever since their first careless touch—each of them cold as dry ice, forgetful as stone—that froze half of Nina's fingerprints away, and left marks like cigar burns on Simone's naked arm. They took weeks to heal.

Simone stares at Nina's body, her gaze cataloguing the fresh red litany of wounds. "I can't believe we just fell asleep like that. If we'd woken up any later, if we'd gotten any colder—"

"Well, we didn't!" Her tone is too snappish; Simone bites her lip and looks away. "I'm sorry, Sim." Nina swallows. "I'll get the cream and stuff, okay?"

By the time she comes back, hands full of Savlon and gauze and cotton wool, Simone is up and packing her overnight bag. She's wearing the Chinese silk robe Nina bought her last month, turquoise blue with a phoenix rising on its back, but she's wearing it inside out.

"Come here," Nina says. "Let me fix you up."

Simone glares at her. "You can do that without touching me, can you?"

"As a matter of fact, I can."

The other woman shakes her head. "This has to end. Now."

Nina feels her stomach tumble for the second time that morning. "What are you talking about, Sim? What has to end?"

"Us." Her eyes are wet and pleading. "I can't do it anymore, Nina."

"But I love you." Right now, Nina would bear any amount of pain for the chance to touch Simone, the chance to hold her close and prove how much she loves her. She'd bear it gratefully—if she were the only one who would.

"I love you too," Simone says. "You know I do, but I can't live like this. Only being able to see you every few weeks, having to leave you again before the sweat's even dried on our skin—"

"So, we'll meet more often then. You're the one who wants to leave it so long each time; I'd be with you every night if you'd let me."

"You know that's impossible."

"Okay, maybe not *every* night, but three or four times a week if—"

"I'm not like you," Simone snaps. "I can't go out and pick people up the way you do, discard them like they're nothing. They're not nothing—they're people, they have lives of their own."

"Like the creep who did this, you mean?" Nina points to her forehead, which she knows looks even worse now than it did last night. "Bastards like him deserve what they get."

"Stop twisting everything I say. They're not all like that, not even most of them. You've said yourself, you feel sorry for them sometimes."

Nina narrows her eyes. "Do you know how many even bothered to ask my name? Trust me, all they cared about was how quick my panties could come off, and how soon they could boot me out the door afterwards."

"That doesn't make it right."

"It's not like they're dead, you know. It's not like we kill them."

"No, we just take what makes them human."

Nina laughs. She can't help it. "Their libido, Sim, their sex drive? You think *that's* what being human's all about?"

The other woman looks almost disappointed. "We take more than that and you know it. Warmth, heat, passion—whatever you choose to call it—that's what we take and that's what we squander every time we come to this horrible little room." She touches her cheek and winces. "I'm running out of justifications, Nina. Maybe I never had any to begin with."

"But last night . . ."

"Yes." Simone crosses the room and takes the medical supplies from Nina's hands, careful not to let their fingers touch. "I'm so sorry, Nina. I love you, I do, but everything else . . . it's too much. It's breaking me."

Nina sinks back down onto the bed, flinching at the pain that ripples along her flank. "You've been thinking about this a lot." She doesn't really need an answer; the expression Simone wears is more than eloquent.

Closed, and contained. Final.

"Every day," Simone says. Hissing through clenched teeth, she smoothes cream over the raw patch of flesh on the inside of her knee.

"You can live like that?" Nina asks. "Being cold, all the time?"

"Yes."

"Being alone?"

Silently, Simone wraps gauze around her leg, around and around and around until there's nothing left to unroll. She tucks the end in tight and straightens, tests what little flex she has left in her knee. When she looks at Nina again, her eyes are red but dry. "Yes," she says. "I can live like that."

"Cold and alone, for the rest of your life?"

"You say it like we're the only ones." And there's nothing even remotely warm about the smile that hooks her mouth. "How hard can it be, Nina? After all, *it's not like we're dead.*"

Nina bows her head. There's a smear of blood on the carpet near her foot and it's this she stares at while listening to the other woman dress first her wounds and then herself. Because the way she's feeling right now—cold, yes; alone, oh a hundred times and forever, *yes*—she doesn't trust herself to look at Simone. Doesn't trust herself not to go to her and press their bodies together, to feel the freeze of skin between them and know that when they finally tear themselves asunder, it will be as bloody and messy and painful as her fractured, frostbitten heart.

• • •

Nina slides the room keys across the counter along with her credit card, pretends not to notice the receptionist pretending not to notice the bruises on her forehead.

"There's a late checkout fee," the woman says. "It's policy."

"Sure, whatever." She decides not to mention the bloodstained sheets; this kind of motel has probably seen worse. The woman processes her payment and puts the receipt on the counter for Nina to sign.

"I hope you enjoyed your stay."

There's an edge to her tone, a forced politeness only too familiar, but today Nina's skin is too thin to let it slide. "Is there a problem?"

The receptionist purses her prissy, middle-aged lips. "Generally, I don't give a rat's what you and your friend get up to when you come here, but there's some things I won't turn a blind eye to. Next time I call the police."

Nina blinks, confused. "I'm sorry?"

"That girl was the picture of health last night when she picked up her key. This afternoon I see her limp out of that room with her face all bandaged up like the Bride of Frankenstein." She points at Nina's head. "What happened, she decide to fight back?"

"You have no idea what you're talking about." Nina reaches out and snatches her credit card from the woman's hand. "Trust me, you have no fucking conception." She turns and slams through the reception door, trying to pretend she doesn't hear the bitch's reedy voice trailing after her—*I know someone who's been abused when I see them*—trying to pretend she doesn't care.

Less than two blocks from the motel, her hands are still shaking so badly she needs to pull over to the side of the road. Tears blur her vision, turn to ice on her cheeks. Nina tugs her mobile from her pocket, thumbs through to her most recent contacts and presses *call*. A recorded voice answers almost immediately—*the number you are calling is no longer in service*—and she gapes at the phone in disbelief. So soon?

Nina closes her eyes, tries to remember how Simone looked just before she left the motel room. Remorseful but resigned, shaking her head as Nina pleaded with her to stay.

*There's no one else like us in the world, baby. We're all we have.*
*Then we have nothing. And we have to live with that too.*

"Simone," she whispers, over and over and over again. Nina doesn't even know if that's her lover's real name; she never thought it important to ask.

Simone.

Solid as stone in her mouth, the word grows rapidly cold.

•••••••••••

# READING COFFEE

## ANTHONY PANEGYRES

### KALGOORLIE 1916

Not many eleven year olds are enamoured with death. Mary
Agapitos is. She prefers to hang out in the Kalgoorlie graveyard,
exulting in the rusty coloured earth that still reigns around the
tombs; the bauxite rocks lying about like oversized gravel; and
the tufts of colourless grass protruding beneath the occasional
eucalypt. In particular, she enjoys the Orthodox section where she
reads and pats headstones of people she once knew. Old Greek
surnames which comfort her like her mother's embrace.

• • •

Mary wanders about their Kalgoorlie house serving nibbly things to
the guests as a pleasant Greek girl should. Faces from Asia Minor,
*Kastellorizo*, and Alexandria blur into one another. Her cheeks are
pulled, slobbered upon; her long wavy locks—which she secretly
delights in—are caressed by some and yanked by others. And when
not serving, her personal space is stolen by women who squash her
into their paunch, while the thin ladies enfold her delicately. Now
and then Mary forces a tear in remembrance of her great uncle
Yiannis Katavatis to the appreciation of the crowd. "Oh, she is a
dear thing," they say as she walks around presenting a platter of
dried fruit, nuts, olives and white cheese.

Between platters, Mary retreats into the kitchen where her
mother governs matters. Whisky and ouzo are being sent around
with sweetened orange peels and rose petal jam. Coffee brews in
the *briki*: Mary's favourite time. She looks forward to wakes: the

brush of uncomfortably formal suits on her skin; the kitchen, a pulsating heart sending food forth and then the remains flowing back; the sad smiles; and the composed ladies who only an hour or so earlier had worn tear-stained faces.

Taking a tray of shortbread outside and to the back room, where men sit talking buoyantly, Mary hears news. They talk of the Kaiser's plans to conquer Europe, and say that the Greeks are behind their Prime Minister Venizelos. They are pro-Entente, anti-German, despite what King Constantine of Greece states about remaining neutral. After all, his wife's brother is the Kaiser.

In the lounge she hears the ladies discuss which days are holy in the coming months and that Christina is disgracing the family, having been seen with a *xeno*, an Australian, an Englishman.

As she re-enters the kitchen, Mary sneaks a shortbread from the plate. She's never seen snow but she imagines it is like the icing that covers the thick snake-shaped biscuit. She removes the clove, a bold dark star in the centre, and eats the biscuit meditatively, mouth closed, oblivious to all else around her.

"I'm bringing the coffee cups back," she states. Her mother closes the ice-box and stares, but her eyes are too gentle to put fear in a child who has seen death many times before. "But I want to, mama," she says in a raised voice. Three ladies at the sink turn to observe the self-assured girl.

"Let her bring the cups if she wants to," says one.

Mary's mother nods, bends down slightly and whispers in her daughter's ear. "You mustn't look in them."

Mary has heard it before and knows her role by heart: "Of course not, Mama."

"You mustn't look, remember what I said," her mother says so thinly that even Mary has trouble hearing. "It's *Satanas* that allows people to see things. Don't taint your soul, *agapi mou*."

Mary kisses her mother and dashes out with a tray to carry the coffee cups. She steps towards the men first and picks up a cup belonging to Loukas, who runs Paris Café on Hannan Street. Immediately she looks into the remaining grounds of the tiny cup. She does not need to flip it like a Gypsy or an atheist widow; she simply gazes and all is apparent. She sees a zoological form in the bottom, a bull, but she does not know or care what this means. It is the traces between the mud to which her eyes are lured. These lines appear to her like vast gorges, the rims are individual Odysseys; she knows this but doesn't bother with particular details. Mary heads straight for the end point: Death, *Thanatos*.

*Her wife calls from the kitchen but she is tired, she lets the feeling crawl over her. She breathes slowly but can no longer be bothered with her body's labouring. She sleeps, vaguely aware of someone's touch— shaking her arms. A tear wets her face, then all is shadow.*

Loukas pats her head. Mary does not usually like that, she feels too old for it, but for the present it does not bother her. "Peaceful," she whispers under her breath.

She grabs the next cup, Kostas'. His beaked nose and distant eyes do not even acknowledge her—too small, too unimportant.

Mary merely peeps downwards.

*She fumbles for her concealed fish knife as an oar crashes into her face, sweeping her over the side. Hands grip as she tries to surface, breathing water, gagging as more rushes in.*

*Then she remembers: she's a child eating honeyed yoghurt at an outside café table, the sun bathing her skin and sending glitter across the turquoise bay. She spasms. All is still.*

Mary touches Kostas' cheek, seeing him for the first time. He smiles downwards—his raptor face no longer appears aloof. She pats his leg tenderly, and then moves to another cup

Eleftherios'. *Her heart feels pressure, like a small balloon swollen with liquid, she clenches her chest and tries to speak before it bursts.*

Panayiota's cup. *She holds the side of her stomach, nails squelching flesh. Everything burns. A widow, her three unmarried sons surround her. She can't abandon them yet. One son clasps her hand gently; she wants to turn her head, behold his eyes. Another son kisses her forehead. "You've always been so brave," she hears.*

*Permission; she stops.*

The final cup that she takes is her mother's. Mary pauses. This is wrong she thinks, but she needs to know. Her mother should have cleaned it herself anyway, before she had the chance to pick it up.

She peeks and for the rest of the evening she doesn't utter a sound. When her mother asks if she is all right, she cries.

• • •

Mary sits on a stool behind the front counter eating milk chocolate. The stool is her favourite place, it feels tall and she likes dangling her legs. She enjoys the flavour of Olympia's, the comforting floorboards, but more she likes the warm smell of tobacco and coffee.

Her two brothers cook honest food in the kitchen, as well as English muck, such as fresh fish defiled with batter. Her father, Mattheos, makes sure the maroon tablecloths are presentable. There are only four customers—it's only 11:30am—but soon Mary will be taking orders and serving, aiding her *Baba*.

It is her mother's day off. Mama will die soon. The coffee-sludge never lies. In the cup Mama had worn that grey dress and that Italian watch that Mattheos had bought her at Christmas time.

But Mary's mother won't pass today. For one, she is not wearing the correct dress, and second, certain events have not yet unravelled.

Mary is watching her father meticulously setting out plates, glasses and cutlery, when the entry flaps tremble and Loukas bursts through the entrance, brandishing a newspaper above his head. He is spouting off Greek in the shop—something is truly awry. The four customers glare and shake their heads. "Foreign dirt—need to learn some manners," whispers one, but Mary hears.

*Baba* and Mary meet Loukas at the counter. "What's wrong?" asks Mattheos. Loukas whacks the newspaper down.

"Look." On the front page is a ruined Northbridge shop in Perth. Windows are smashed and the inside gutted like a trashed building site. Three small pictures adorn the bottom of the page: three shops, all pillaged in the manner Mary imagines the Ottomans once did to the Greek churches in "The City" that Kyria Persphone told her about. One building has even lost its support columns and tilts as if ready to crumble.

Mary puts a hand to her mouth; it is not the same but there is something too familiar about the picture. The title reads: "Greek Tragedy'.

"But why?" says her Father, his nails whitening as his fingers press into the bench.

"Because our idiot king says he wants to remain out of the war—stay neutral."

"Despite Venizelos declaring the opposite?"

"They don't even care what the Prime Minister thinks—what we Greeks think! These Englishmen see a King declare anything and they think it's the will of the entire people. Between us, Mattheos, I don't care whether we fight the Germans or stay out of the whole catastrophe—we've seen too much war. But this . . . " his hand gestures at the photo.

"What if it happens here?" asks Mattheos.

Mary reads as they converse.

"Yesterday evening, a mob of misled Australian patriots—civilian youths and soldiers—marched through Highgate, Northbridge and Perth, in a destructive wave targeted at shops conducted by persons of Greek nationality. Twenty shops in all were demolished: windows smashed, furnishings wrecked and stock ruined by the protestors. Nigel Bradley, who witnessed the scene, said, "They were even singing 'Tipperary' and 'Australia Will Be There' while vandalising . . . "

"We'll be next," says her father.

"Hopefully not," says Loukas. All traces of his theatrical anger vanish in a blink. "Mr Angelides has addressed the Premier on behalf of our community stating that we are not only law abiding citizens but also pro—Venizelists, totally opposed to the Kaiser and his people."

"I'll call Sergeant Humphries, just in case." Mattheos winks at Loukas. "He gets a free lunch every Wednesday; fried snapper, prime filet."

*So little time.* Mary waits as her father makes the call in tentative English. "Yes, thank you, Sergeant . . . Extra patrols, eh? This is very good, very good."

Loukas strolls outside with the newspaper held casually by his side. Mary's father appears calm and returns to the tables. Both Loukas and *Baba* seem to Mary to feel secure knowing that their community leader in Perth, Mr Angelides, and the local police force here in Kalgoorlie will take extra care of the Greek community.

Mary knows they're mistaken.

Her voice breaks as she speaks, *"Baba!"* Normally Mary is so composed, so stoic, just like her mother.

*Just hold me.*

Her father clutches her head, somewhat awkwardly, to his wrestler chest. The fusty odour of his shirt comforts her.

*Ask what's wrong.*

But her father is mute. She sobs. Words come haltingly. "Soon . . . . Like the paper . . . . *Baba* . . . The same."

"It's all right, Mary. Calm, calm." Mary draws her breath in sharp perceptible gulps.

He gets her a glass of water and then wipes the briny rivulets from her face with a shirtsleeve. Mary sips, both hands gripping the glass. She composes herself, mastering her face by tucking in her quivering lower lip and measuring her breathing until she becomes like her mother once more.

"I read the cups," Mary says.

"Mary, you know what Mama says about that."

"Promise, *Baba*. Promise you won't tell her. Please!"

"Ok," he laughs, "I promise."

"Soon they'll come. And throw things through the store, the glass will break up and down the street, and then they'll invade like an army and . . . people will be hurt . . . I hate them, *Baba*. I hate them."

"It's a dream, Mary. It's okay. I've spoken to the Sergeant. We'll be protected."

"Don't tell mama. You promised you wouldn't tell."

Mary releases all in a deluge. The mob is uncontrollable. Even the stately Kalgoorlie hotel is left on a precarious slant, its wooden pillars warped. The story has such vivid details that Mary knows her father is convinced. After all, she is no fibber.

She speaks fluidly. Her father listens. Images form . . .

Eleftherios lies on the ground, his left ear lobe swollen like a mushroom having been kicked by "Bluey', the carrot-haired miner who eats at their restaurant every Saturday lunch, always pasticcio.

The Sergeant is mounted with some other cops, helpless, as they watch the destructive quake rumble down the street, demolishing all Greek stores. Many are beaten. Her mother loses her watch to an Italian man shouting, "*Dimmi l'orologio adesso, disgraziada Greca.*"

Mary doesn't tell of what happens afterwards.

She feels her father clasping her shoulders. "The date. Can you remember the date?" She lifts her head, the Aegean way of motioning 'no'. "Did you see a newspaper around?" Her father is now shaking her slightly; he's never done this before. No more tears, she tells herself.

"What about the calendar in the *kouzina*? Think, Mary *mou*."

All she knows is that it will be soon, within a fortnight or so.

"Look at me. No one will die. If the police can't protect us," he pounds his chest in a simian fashion, "*I* will." He repeats "*I* will" with another fist to his pectoral.

"I believe you, *Baba*." She says the reverse of what she thinks.

Pavlos, with his bald Periclean-shaped head, strides in from the kitchen on their father's call. Arm around Pavlos' shoulder, *Baba* whispers in his ear and her brother tears off his apron and races outside.

Mary looks up from the counter as Pavlos returns at a jog. He and her father murmur away in Greek while she serves Bluey. She normally feels sorry for this man; his unfortunate ruddy skin is no protection against the burning goldfields sun. But now his blistered nose and dry, flaky lips repulse her like some nightmare. She wants to squish her nostrils up or do something ridiculous like tear up his one pound note and fling the remains into his face. "Thank you, sir," she says, returning his change in the Greek manner by placing it in a saucer.

Bluey nods, "Good food."

Once the transaction is over, her older brother approaches, sweat gleaming on his forehead. He blows a raspberry on her neck. She can't help but giggle at the tickly wet touch; at the same time, however, she feels a little humiliated. "Grow up, Pavlos. I'm almost twelve. I'm too old for that."

Pavlos ignores her as usual, and Mary feels herself being lifted up and then twisted around so they're both facing the same direction. He places her shoes on his and holds her, balancing her as he walks around the counter. His breath is warm and salty as he whispers in her ear. "Who's the strongest man in the world?"

"*Baba*," says Mary cheekily.

"*Baba*!? Then who's the second strongest?"

"Hmm. I'll have to think."

Pavlos lifts her up in the air. "Who?"

"Marios," she says her oldest brother's nickname.

"Marios?" He says putting her down. "That weakling. I used to be number one. Now Mary," his tone deepens, "I want you to go home and tell mama that there will be a full house tonight. Possibly even forty people. Then come back and I'll give you some money to buy rosewater and essence, almonds, icing sugar and glucose from Stavros' shop. Father says everyone will need a *loukoumi*."

"That's because he thinks rosewater freshens the mind."

• • •

Loukas is the first to knock, then others continue to arrive until thirty or so men are crammed in the back room, each on a wooden chair brought home from the restaurant. Small square tables, a few with wobbly legs, are spaced throughout the room. On each are two small white plates.

Mary smiles in the kitchen with her mother; there is something special about making *loukoumia* with her. It's a far easier dish than all those finicky honey—drenched pastries and she and Mama can be less precise, which means Mary can be a little sillier. They fabricate stories about everyone they know, even Mary's grandfather in Greece. "*Pappou* only became a Priest once his *Yaya* died so he could get closer to the wine and women," Mary tells her mama, who giggles uncharacteristically.

Mary kisses her, tells her how much she loves her one too many times—until her Mother stoppers her mouth with a freshly made *loukoumi*. It's delicious. They both pull off their aprons and Mary pats down her skirt. Men come and greet them, kissing both cheeks. The moustachioed ones prickle.

Loukas' son enters. Seventeen, tall with coffee-coloured skin. He is nicknamed Coco by the locals and now the Greeks call him that too. Mary blushes as his lips touch her face.

"He'd make a good husband," her mother grins as Coco leaves for the backroom. Mary secretly hopes that the smile's sincere. But then her *Mama* says that about every Greek male under the age of twenty-five.

Her father and brothers had closed the shop early and cooked all afternoon. Mary and her Mama whisk in and out with platters of food, catching titbits of what is said.

Grilled fish, octopus and prawns. It appears as though her father dominates early proceedings. "If it happened in Perth and Sydney then it will happen here."

The second platter has meatballs Smyrnaean style, floating in a cinnamon—tomato salsa. Coco stands. "We need a safe-haven, in case things get violent. Even in Sydney, four thousand people rioted just because someone made up a tale about a Greek murderer." Many don't care to listen to one so young. Mary watches eyes flitter to the sides or upwards; some bore into the ground. She holds the tray tighter than usual.

Dolmades are handed out with ladles of egg and lemon sauce. Mary looks around, observing the familiar sloping foreheads, dark brows and thick hands. She knows the thoughts of those gathered while Loukas speaks: *What type of a father unleashes his son like that?* Her father and Pavlos are attentive at least.

"We don't need a safe-haven. I can manage on my own," she hears one visitor say.

A plan unfolds while her mother serves meltingly-tender lamb, pot stewed for three hours in cloves, wine, vinegar and a bay leaf or two. Mary scoops out small serves of chickpeas and spinach drizzled with virgin olive oil and lemon juice. A cautionary warning system is set in place. Coco volunteers to be the runner if a mob arises and Loukas will buy extra locks and board up his house until it's a fort. A few people grunt at the perceived nonsense, and a hostile silence settles over the room.

By the time Mary serves coffee and *loukoumia* most guests have already left. Like a fervent orchestral conductor, her father raises his hand up and down as he talks to Loukas and Pavlos. Mary recognises the gestures; *Baba*'s anxious. As she serves him the translucent pink sweet dressed in icing sugar, he says, "Only the bright men are left, the others should have remained for this sweet. Rose—"

"—I know *Baba*, it makes you think."

"Not many believed us, Mary *mou*. But we'll keep a good watch."

Two cups are on Mary's tray, nestled between bread plates.

One belongs to Coco. *A blanket on grass overlooking the ocean. Waves kush and sher as she gazes at the fair string-lipped lady seated by her side. Something pops in her head as her wife speaks, her accent Irish. Every word from the "pop" onwards becomes more hushed until it fades into silence. "We should do this every Sunday . . . "*

Mary pauses. The pop was something she hadn't felt before, quick and painless, like flicking a switch. She feels a little sad too, not because of the death, but because Coco's not with *her* as she hoped. *Lucky Irish.*

Mary hesitates over her father's cup. She closes her eyes as she places it on the kitchen bench. She hears her mama washing dishes beside her and rather than opening her eyelids, she crosses herself, swearing to the Lord that her *Baba's* grounds are ones she will never read.

● ● ●

A week passes without any demonstration; not one of the eleven Greek shops on Hannan Street is affected. Yet Mary is constantly alert. She hides her mama's grey dress on numerous occasions (in Pavlos' cupboard, in the back shed, under her mattress) until her mother throws her 'that look'. At Anchor Confectionary, a distant cousin's store, she is shouted her usual: a sundae with chocolate and cherry sauce so syrupy that it prevents the mound of chopped nuts cascading down in an avalanche. "How boring," she says to Pavlos when he orders his usual Cola Spider.

Two fair teenagers in shorts also sit along the "Yankee-style" counter, making slurping sounds with their straws as they finish the last of their drinks. As the boys rise to pay, the burlier of the two looks pointedly at Christopheros behind the till and says, "We'll be payin' the Aussie price—not like those two Olives over there." And when Christopheros places the change on a small plate: "Put it in my hand. You're not in Wopland anymore."

His friend sniggers. "Greasies," he says as they leave.

Mary's ordinarily immune. She's heard it all before: Dagos, Oilies and the rest. But now she worries. *Is it a sign of what's to come? Or is this the norm?*

The next week is one of observation. *More signs?* Did that man deliberately bump Panayiota so she spills her parcels? Maybe that lady takes her children across the street to avoid her family? Is young Kyriakos' plum-coloured eye a result of being alien?

Nothing eventuates and the fortnight passes. No two-thousand-strong-pack terrorises the street and the days revolve routinely once more. Mama breathes and cooks and confides. Pavlos relaxes and, whenever she enters the kitchen, beats his dark apron producing flour clouds just to annoy her. Her father's eyes no longer linger on mama, espying her every move.

Mary wonders if *Satanas* has been at play. Have the cups been lying all this time? Were the lives she possessed in the cups' murk simply the Charlatan's fabrications?

• • •

Four weeks pass. December 8th is her Mother's day off. Although it is morning the sun weighs down oppressively, sucking moisture from the air in true goldfields style. Cicadas and crickets provide an accompanying beat to the heat, while skinks scamper about windowsills. Inside, Mary and her father are preparing tables when Loukas arrives. The image is identical, only her angle different. He waves the newspaper about—highlighting a musty pool under his right armpit—before slamming it down. "Coco is on the alert! I've locked shop, you should do the same." Her father strides to the counter and Mary follows in his shadow. She hops on to the stool. Her legs are still as she attempts to peep over her Baba's shoulder. All she can glean is the *Kalgoorlie Miner's* headline: 'Greek Treachery'.

A bugle resonates outside. Her *Baba* barks in Greek, his own military response to the soldier's horn, and her two brothers exit the kitchen. They all move out onto the road. At the top end of Hannan Sreet near the Post Office are a dozen or so uniformed blotches. The bugle perforates the dry morning air once more. Youths and more soldiers appear on the horizon. Mary sees others leaving shops. Many non-Greek men head off towards the group; women and children fade away into the dim; some Greeks approach her father but several remain in their stores. Once more the bugle sounds and the cluster up the road grows like a carcass drawing ants. Mary is reminded of a swarm coalescing. A final bugle note echoes off the buildings, but this time it is muffled by the yells and cheers that surround it.

Twenty or so Greeks, eerily silent, are now gathered around her own family, but the street in the distance is alive with shouts and more people than she has ever seen. She can see their figures clearly now as they take to the Greek-run Post Office, which also doubles as a cafe. It must be locked. Axes hew through the doors, windows are shattered, furniture is soon removed, food and fittings carried out. She prays the owners are safe as the crowd move wreaking destruction with the speed and efficacy of a tornado. Despite the chaotic roar of the mob, and the wildness of their gutting, the looters remain banded together as they whirl over to the adjoining shop.

The group that Mary is with heads off in the opposite direction—towards Loukas' barricaded house at the other end of Hannan Street. She watches the heels and soles in front of her beat in and out of the road stirring orange dust. Several mounted police approach. Their horses whinny as they toss their heads and stamp. The Sergeant tips his hat towards her Father as they pass by. Mary turns back to see the police horses clop towards the throng only to witness them being pelted with missiles: chairs, stones, steel and wood. One mare rears dangerously, hooves thrashing through the air. With a wave of the Sergeant's hand the ineffectual force retreat to the sheltered porch of Pete O'Reiley's butcher store. A derisive cheer erupts.

Those around Mary now sprint for Loukas' stronghold, shirts sweaty, blouses clinging. Tugging and shrieking, she pulls on Pavlos' and her father's shirts. She finally topples over and grazes a knee. "Mama! Mama!" she screeches. The rest of the group moves on. In the distance the armed mass whips about in their direction.

Her Father's veins bulge from his neck. "Home," he says to Pavlos. "See that your mother's safe. If there's time, take her to Loukas' place."

"What about Mary?"

Mary has taken off at a quick hobble towards their restaurant. The crowd in the distance moves another shop closer, flinging tables and chairs onto the street. Apples and pears bounce and roll erratically from crates to the chant: "It's a long long way to go."

Mary sees her mother, wearing grey, dash across from an opposite store and into their restaurant. The mob now rages towards them. She is still a good ten yards from the Olympia and the fuming crowd only thirty yards or so from it in the other direction. Mary feels herself scooped up from behind. For a second she thinks of biting the arms that hold her until she realises they're those of her father. Pavlos is next to *Baba* as they turn towards Loukas' house.

*They haven't seen her!* She sinks her teeth downwards, and her father drops her in surprise. "Mama!" she screams pointing towards their store.

"My God!" Pavlos turns as their mother exits their shop. Mama looks fearfully at the crowd, now only twenty yards away. Mary is gathered up once more as the three tear off toward the Olympia Restaurant.

"Inside," hollers her father startling mama. They dash in. Mary and her mother are taken behind the counter by Pavlos as *Baba* locks and then barricades the doors with tables thrown and shoved desperately. The shouts are an audible roar as *Baba* comes and crouches behind the patina-riddled counter with them. "Stay here," he says. Mary peeps above as the windows splinter and shards spray into the restaurant. The door is hacked open by axes and boots, barricading tables are tossed outside. Mary searches for her mother's killer as bodies advance and sees the swarthy bearded Italian with the swollen nose brandishing a hammer near the front. Bluey is next to him. Mary and her family stand as the squall nears.

The pack hurls tables over and buzzes around them as they rip apart the kitchen and smash open the cash register. Her family are in the eye of the cyclone; no-one touches them. Two men sing as they let fly chairs. *Baba* holds mama behind him, so her back is to the counter. Pavlos' hands are ready fists.

Bluey wielding his metal-rod comes closer with his mate. The latter reeks of alcohol. Bluey stares at Mary and nods in recognition. He grabs the Italian's arm, "Nobody touches them!" The Italian wildly shoves him away, eyes locked on mama's watch. He rocks into *Baba*, head barrelling into her father's stomach. *Baba* braces his legs and is winded, but remains between them. Mary's arm is yanked by her brother as he shoves her behind him. Next to him a chair comes crashing down over their father's head. Groaning, he manages to stand while Pavlos swings and hits a face. He sweeps another arm out but it's seized. Eventually swamped, Baba and Pavlos are buried in a flurry of leather boots and fists.

Mary readies.

"*Dimmi l'orologio adesso, disgraziada Greca.*" So close, everything appears magnified to Mary: the oily black pores on his nose; his stench of desperation; the knots in his mane. Bearing his weight down on mama, the Italian knocks her to the floor and lands on top of her, one hand locked on her wrist, while the other one flails the air with a hammer.

Her mother kicks out. Mary dives as the hammer strikes.

• • •

Mary watches her own burial. Her mama, embossed in black and her tears bleeding, tosses red earth on to Mary's coffin. Others follow. Her Great Uncle, Yannis Katavatis, places a consoling hand on Mary's shoulder. It is not her mother's embrace, but must suffice for now.

· · · · · · · · · · ·

# EUROPE AFTER THE RAIN

## LEE BATTERSBY

What does it take to murder a city?

• • •

A thousand bombers, packed with a mixture of high explosives and phosphorous bombs. The right amount of cloud cover. An absence of prevailing winds. A certain kind of willpower.

• • •

Dresden burned for forty-eight hours. Out at the fringes, where the munitions factories and the barracks and the rich people's houses stood, there had been little damage. But in the City centre, where the poor lived, where my family had lived . . . nothing remained. For twenty miles in any direction all was death.

I was fourteen years old, and the Führer had told me I was a soldier. All the real men had gone to the East to die. Those of us who were too young, or old, or crippled, were conscripted. I had been Hitler Youth. My friends had all been Hitler Youth. That made us soldiers, now, in the absence of men. Every morning I left the barracks with my squad of fourteen year old friends, and marched past the ruins of my school house, and the apartments where my family burned, to some part of the city I should have recognised but which was now no more than a broken vista of charred bricks and cinders like any other. I carried a pistol with which to shoot looters; a canteen; a handkerchief tied round my neck to keep the ash out of my lungs; and a flamethrower. My friends dug through the devastation and piled up the bric-a-brac of dead bodies. I torched them until they were only one more small pile amongst the greater ash.

Every evening I stood under a dribble of cold water and washed dead neighbours from my face, then fell into my cot with the other lucky soldiers: twenty-one of us, none older then fifteen, all pretending to sleep so we would not hear the rest of us sobbing. We were a conspiracy of silence against ourselves, a confederacy of adulthood when none of us knew what it meant to be one. All the real adults were fighting the Russians, or burned to grit under our fingernails. I closed my eyes and tried not to dream, tried not to see anything, until the morning.

I had long ago lost track of the days: what point counting, when a weekend meant no more than any other day. A school child had two days a week to play amongst the buildings and scrabble through the middens for a discarded treasure. I was no longer a school child; weekends meant the same dreadful routine as the week. I was a janitor of death now, and my duties would never end. I slapped my face with cold-water hands, slung my flamethrower over my shoulders, and plodded out into the City like any other day. For as long as I could remember we had walked through the city centre to the Hauptbahnhof and cleaned the streets to either side of the train tracks, sweeping a clean line into the city for the troops we knew were never coming. This day, however, our ancient sergeant coughed out the order to turn as we came into the Seestrasse, and while we stared at him in confusion, raised one claw in the direction he wanted.

"There. Down there, you thick shits."

Dieter Mueller, who was not quite so quick as the rest of us, and had been made Corporal because of it, looked at our normal route and stammered.

"But . . . but, Sergeant . . . "

Old Vogts fairly quivered with rage. "Don't you Sergeant me, Corporal. Don't you fucking dare. Get these men in line, now. Get moving!" He swung the stick he had picked out of a ruined building some months before, and which he leaned on for breath whenever he thought we weren't looking. "Move it, you little bastards."

Mueller straightened, and stared into the distance. "Yes, Sergeant." He turned to us. "You heard him, you bastards. Get into line. March . . . " he waved his arm uncertainly in the direction the old man had indicated. " . . . down there."

We moved into a ragged line, sniggering at Mueller under our breaths. When we resembled something approaching a platoon of soldiers, Vogts leaned away from his stick and took his place at the head of our line.

"Come on, my boys," he said wearily. "Let's just get this over with."

In truth, I don't think it really mattered where we dug. We all knew there were no orders coming to us from above. It was only old Vogts and his cronies, criss-crossing the streets as the mood took them, who decided the tasks. We saw officers, but only ever at a distance, speeding by in a squad car to some other, more important, part of the city. Down here, in the dead zone, it was just us. Perhaps Vogts was bored with the same location. Perhaps one of the other old men wanted a turn. Whatever it was, we found ourselves trudging down unfamiliar streets into a quarter that was foreign to us all. We were even, for a while, gladdened by the change. I recalled a song I had not heard since the bombers had started coming, and began to hum it. Those around me joined in, until Vogts barked at us.

"What do you think this is?" He hacked a gob of reddened spit onto the road, "A fucking ramble?"

He leaned on his stick and made no effort to hide his age, forcing us to stand and listen as he coughed so hard and so long I thought he was going to crease over and fall into the dust. Eventually, he spat up a trickle of dirty bile and blood that we all pretended not to look at, and wiped tears from his face with the back of his sleeve. "Agh, Jesus," he sobbed, looking anywhere but us, "what children we've raised. What goddamn awful, bloody children."

There was a side street a dozen yards to our front. Vogts waved his stick at it.

"Down there," he said. "Just . . . just go down there."

We marched around the corner, and split up as soon as we were out of the old man's sight. I found myself alone for the first time in days and took the opportunity to sit on a block of concrete, letting my arms hang loosely at my side. The first inkling I had of old Vogts' approach came when he was already standing behind me, coughing. I leapt to my feet, but he waved me back down.

"Sit, boy. Sit," he said, drawing a cigarette from some hidden pocket of his jacket.

"Hey, Breitner, isn't it?" He waggled two fingers at my flamethrower. "Light up."

I pressed the firing stud on the side of the butt, and a blue flame sparked into life in the barrel cage. Vogts leaned forward until his head was directly in front of the flame. I watched him. One press of the trigger, and the gas in my back canister would erupt from the barrel in a stream of liquid fire, destroying his thick head in an instant. He winked up at me, stuck the cigarette into the corner of his lips, and poked it into the flame.

"Here," he said, straightening up and offering me the now-lit cigarette. "Two puffs, for the light."

I admit it, I was impressed. I took his offering and had my puffs, handing it back to him with a cough. He smiled, stuck it back in his mouth, then nodded towards our compatriots, scurrying into nearby buildings.

"You're a lucky one," he said, as the first baked corpse was being dragged out into the street.

"What do you mean?"

He indicated the flamethrower. "Carrying that."

"I don't understand you."

He sighed, and drew on his smoke until it was no more than a stub, then pinched it and replaced it in his pocket. "Gets you out of a lot, though, doesn't it? You don't have to go in there and pick them out. Not like those poor bastards." He dipped his head towards our compatriots. We watched as more corpses were piled up. It was impossible not to see, from this distance, how our friends stood back and stared anywhere but at the bodies they had just deposited. They wiped their hands down their legs obsessively, even absent-mindedly, once their burden was dropped.

"They don't have to burn them."

"You don't have to carry them."

I kicked a ball of ash at him. "Well they don't have to smell it, do they? They don't have to have the stink of it clinging to them all night; they don't have to see the fire all the time, eating them . . . " I choked back tears. I would not become a little boy in front of him. Vogts waited until I had caught my breath.

"You don't have to touch them."

Something went hard and cold inside me. I straightened, and stared down at the old man from a million miles away.

"Fuck you, Vogts." I said, slowly and very clearly. The old man matched stares with me, but it was his eyes that moistened.

"Everybody else in this squad I've held at one time or another while they cried, Breitner."

I shook my head. "Not me." I had stopped crying the day we cleared my street.

He nodded. "Ja, I know." He glanced over at the pile of dead in the street, and the squad, busily not looking at us. "Looks like they're ready."

We made our way over and Vogts chivvied the boys away into the next street while I did the job. When it was over I stood in the doorway of a nearby building and coughed until the reek of it was out of my throat, and I could draw a breath that contained only my own sweat and old ash, as usual. I wiped my dripping face with my hands, then ran them down the brickwork — my signature, my own personal graffiti, mucky wings that adorned a hundred buildings. I turned back to follow my comrades into the next street, and stopped.

Sitting in the middle of the square, in the warm patch where I had burned the bodies, was a child. I stared at it for dumb seconds, unable to work out whether it was girl, or boy, or hallucination. It was a dark-haired thing, covered in dirt and muck so thick that, for all I knew, grey and brown might be the natural colour of its skin. It wore only a singlet and a pair of underpants, and they were as mottled and stained as the rest of it. I stepped uncertainly out from my vantage point, looking left and right, half-hoping and half-afraid to see parents running down the street to rescue it from me. For one mad second I was afraid to have to confront them, to explain who I was and what I was doing there. The child was mumbling to itself, little nonsense words as it grubbed about in the dirt, swishing hands back and forth through the dust and giggling at the clouds it stirred up. I heard muffled shouts from the next street as Mueller chivvied the squad through their duties. I would be due there any moment, to aim my barrel and depress my firing stud. I closed my eyes for a moment. There were no other sounds. Nobody was coming for this child.

"Hey," I called quietly. "Hey."

The child looked up at me, then returned to its play. I took another step.

"Hey. What's your name, uh, child?"

The little one's hands moved more slowly now, closer to its body. I tilted my head, trying to see what it was doing, but it shifted around so that it blocked my view. I took another step, then another, and then crouched down, no more than a foot away.

"Hello?" I said, keeping my voice as friendly and non-threatening as I could. "My name's Breitner, uh, Franz Breitner."

The child looked over its shoulder at me, then returned again to its labour. I shuffled closer, until I could see.

In the ash at its feet, the child was moulding a body. It was a crude thing, little more than four sausage limbs, a knobby round head, and a thick oblong to hold the whole thing together. In all it was perhaps half a dozen inches long. It lay on its back like the starfishes I had seen one holiday when I was young, on the beach at Warnemünde. I reached down to poke it with a finger. The figure was still warm, and I recoiled.

"Oh, God."

The child stared at me, as if puzzled at my reaction. I gestured at the tiny figure, unable to convey my repulsion. Was the child aware, *could* it be aware, of what it had done, the obscene parody of life it had created out of the ruins of people I had cremated? Whilst I struggled to form the thought, the child opened its legs and a spattering of pee soaked the front of its underwear and dripped onto the tiny figure, instantly disappearing into the warm ash. The child stirred two fingers into the little mound of mud and began to thicken the chest and arms. I put out a hand to stop it, and the child leaned forward and muttered a single word at the figure's face.

"What?" I pulled it away. "What did you say?"

The child screwed up its face and yelled at me. "Emet!"

"What?"

"Emet! Emet! Emet!" It twisted free and fell. As I watched, the figure seemed to stretch across the ground, growing to twice, then three times, its size. Hands sprung from the ends of its arms— thick, club-like protrusions that sucked up the dust from around them, leaving the ground beneath bare. Feet attached themselves to the end of its legs in the same manner. The creature sat up, and before I could cry out in fear, pushed itself up onto its new feet.

Its head swivelled from left to right, then back again as if looking for something. I took an involuntary step backwards and it fixed upon the sound instantly. Before I could react it strode to where I stood and swung its knobbed fist at my leg. I howled in pain as the protrusion, grown somehow rock hard, clattered against the bone of my shin. It punched again, and again, movements so swift I could only measure them by the thudding impacts against my leg. With each blow I slipped slightly more off-balance, until my leg gave way completely before the assault. I crumpled to the ground, and before I could move to defend myself, the creature was at my head. The first blow grazed my jaw. The second caught me flush, and rocked my head backwards so that I cracked the back of my skull on the ground. Before I could raise my hands to cover myself the creature had leaped upon my chest. It stood over me, blows raining down upon my unprotected face. My nose was crushed with one swipe. Blood filled the back of my mouth. I croaked, a feeble attempt at a cry for help. The monster did not pause. My cheekbone cracked under the assault. Finally my arms came up, but I was too dazed to defend myself properly. The creature's blows drove them apart and they fell without strength to the ground on either side of my head. I sobbed, and my vision darkened. My consciousness began to retreat. Then someone else was above me, and a voice was thundering out.

"Stop this!" Something swept down out of the sky, and the blows against my face ceased. A hand gripped my shoulder, and hauled me halfway towards a sitting position. I rolled away, coughing tears and blood onto the dusty ground. In the corner of my vision I saw old Vogts facing the child, the monster pinned to the ground by the butt of his rifle. It beat against the wooden stock, and the thuds of its fist-falls echoed around the square.

"What is this?" the old man cried. "What are you doing?" I sat up and wiped a shaking hand across my mouth and nose. It came away a watery red, blood and snot intermingled.

"It . . . " I pointed at the child. "It . . . "

"Shut up." I closed my mouth, though whether in obedience or shock at the tone of his voice I do not remember. He knelt down and examined the pinned creature.

"My God," he said, then looked back up at the child. "Are you . . . ? Are there . . . ?" He held out a hand. "No, no. Don't be afraid, little one. Don't be afraid." He began to croon then, some baby song in a language I didn't recognise. "It's okay, little baby. It's okay." He sang some more. The child watched him warily. "Come here, sweetheart. Come here." Slowly, the child found its feet. It took a step towards him, then another. Vogts kept singing his nonsense song, one hand held out towards the child, the other holding down the obscenity that had attacked me. The child tottered over, one slow step at a time, until its little fist rested in Vogts'. He closed his hand over the child's, and drew it against his chest.

"It's okay," he whispered. "It's okay. I have you now. It's okay." They turned towards the creature, still beating against the stock of Vogts' rifle. I could see where the wood was beginning to splinter under the repeated blows, and ran fingers across my jaw and cheekbones, finding the places where they, too, had cracked under the assault. As I watched, the creature grew again, sucking dirt into its body until it lay in a circle of blank cobblestones. Thick fingers sprouted from its hands, and grasped the butt holding it down. I touched my ruined nose, and whimpered in pain. Vogts spoke to the child, and I swear I heard something like pride in his voice.

"Did you do this, my little one? Did you make this?"

The child nodded.

"How did you do that?" He stared down at the struggling monster. "It takes years of training. I've met old Rabbis who can't do that. How are you able . . . ?" He reached round with his free hand and stroked the child's hair. "Oh, it was so clever. It was. But we need to stop it now. Yes, yes we do," he said as the child opened its mouth to protest. "He cannot help us, not really. Not like the stories. We have to let him rest." He jerked his head at me. "There are too many for him to defeat, too many monsters." The both looked me up and down. "Let's stop him now, shall we? And I'll help you. Help you all, eh?" He hugged the child close. "Help you all, my clever little boy. Find out how you did this and help you."

They shared a stare for long seconds, and Vogts mouthed "I promise". Then the child wriggled free of his grasp and knelt next to the captured creature, reaching out to place a tiny hand against its head. He said a single word into the silence. The creature shuddered, and was dust once more. Vogts held out his hand, and the child retreated again into his embrace.

"That's my good boy," he said. "That's my good, good boy." He began to sing the strange song once more, stroking the child's hair all the while.

My flamethrower had fallen beneath me when I fell. Now I grabbed it up and faced them both. "What is that? What is that you're saying?"

Vogts looked at me over the child's head. "It's on old song. A Hebrew song."

"It's what? You mean, it's . . . *you're* . . . "

He sighed, and closed his eyes.

"And what if I was?" he said, opening them and pinning me with a cold, tired gaze. "Hmm? Would you shoot me? With that thing?" He nodded at the flamethrower. I stared at it, then lowered it. He dropped his own gaze to the child. "Ah, God, I thought . . . I thought we'd killed you all." He sat the child on the ground, then slowly stood and looked down at himself: at the uniform he wore, the rifle and stick lying side by side next to his boots. "What am I doing?" he said, more to himself than to me. "What have I done?"

"What?"

He looked up at me then, and I saw weariness overcome him. He reached up to the insignia on his arm, and in one swift movement, ripped it off, dropping it carelessly into the dirt.

"What the hell are you doing?"

"I already fought in a war," he said, ripping the second flash and letting it drop. "I already *lost* a war. God damn, I was almost *thirty*." Rip, and another coloured leaf fell. "And they let me come home and find Helena, and yes, she was Jewish, boy, but that didn't matter, for a time." He stared down at his gun belt, then tore it off and flung it away as if it was something suddenly ugly and poisonous. "I learned something about her, and her faith. And then she died, and then . . . then all I had left was to join back up. And look where it has gotten me." He completed his task in silence, standing bereft of colour and arms, all his insignia in a pile at his feet with his rifle, his stick, his cap. "I was wrong," he said. "I was so wrong." He pulled out a billfold from his inner pocket, removed his identity card and ration book, and dropped them on the pile.

"Hey," he said to the child. "Hey, little one." He held out his arms. The child clambered up into them, and curled itself against his chest. Vogts looked at me. "I can help them," he said. "However many are left."

"I . . . "

"They'll need someone to find the good food, and avoid the patrols. They need someone who knows how it all works."

"But . . . what will you do?"

"What will *you* do, boy? This war . . . " he looked around us, at the ruins and the death. "I'm going. I'm going to save as many as I can."

He turned his back to me. I raised my gun, and his back tensed. And suddenly I wanted, more than anything in the world, to say something, to beg him to take me with them, take me away. But the child stared at me over his shoulder and I saw myself as he did, and knew that I could not go. It was *me* they needed protection from, me and those others so much like me from whom the old man would help them hide. I lowered the nozzle of the flamethrower and closed my eyes.

I counted, in the voice I had used when playing hide and seek with my sisters in happier days. "One . . . two . . . three . . . " I reached twenty and opened my eyes. Vogts and the child were gone.

"Here I come," I whispered to the empty square. "Ready or not."

There was no answer, no muffled laughter from hidden siblings. I blinked, then knelt down next to the pile Vogts had left behind. I picked up the knife in its scabbard and tied it about my thigh, slung his rifle over my back. The holster lay where he had thrown it, empty. Vogts must have reconsidered and recovered the pistol. I was glad: he might have need of it, in the days ahead. I added the empty holster to the pile, then stood back, and fired up the flamethrower.

It took less than twenty seconds, then nothing was left of Sergeant Vogts' past but a patch of hot earth. I stared at it, whilst thoughts I could not begin to understand pecked at the edges of my concentration. Tonight, perhaps, I would lie in bed and begin to make sense of them. For now, I focussed upon the ground and tried to ignore the sound of Corporal Mueller's heavy footsteps approaching across the square behind me. Soon enough, he was at my shoulder, the wheeze of his breath making me close my eyes and gather myself.

He eyed me up and down, and I saw him take note of my newly acquired rifle and knife.

"What the hell happened to you?"

"I fell down some stairs."

"Right."

He turned from left to right, taking in the empty square.

"Where's Vogts?"

I looked across at the empty street, and saw nothing.

"You're in charge now."

Mueller followed my gaze for long seconds, then nodded, and set his face. He turned towards our comrades, milling about behind us.

"Right, you lot!" he shouted. "Form up. Let's try and at least pretend we're soldiers, shall we?"

So we did, two wide and four deep, like good German soldiers. Mueller took his place at our head.

"Now then! One, two, left, right. Oh, Hilda was a precious girl . . . "

We marched out, and he led us, singing, back home through the ashes of our dead.

• • • • • • • • • • •

# LOVE IN THE ATACAMA, OR THE POETRY OF FLEAS

## ANGELA REGA

The girl stood in the hot, yellow sand, her top hat tilted forward to shade her eyes. She squinted at the harsh light reflecting off a solitary dune. Her Abuela had told her the Atacama shimmered and sparkled just before it shifted, altering the desert landscape, making it unrecognisable even to the most experienced traveller.

She hoped it wasn't just one of grandmother's bedtime stories. Manuelo would pursue her, she knew, and despite the dry heat she shivered at the image of his military buttons glinting in the low sun.

If the sand really shifted like Abuela said, he would not be able to find her.

*Whiirrr...sssshhh*, the breeze whispered and sand pools formed and twirled around her shins. She wished she spoke the language of the winds and kept her eyes closed because that's how wishes were made. When the breeze went silent and her shins no longer felt the sting of the sand, she opened her eyes.

The landscape was different, just like Abuela said. It was as if the desert had taken on a new identity.

She turned behind her and saw that her footprints had been erased from the sands. Manuelo would not be able to pursue now. Margarita exhaled. She gazed out across to the point where the sand and sky met in front of her. The sand was a subdued yellow, contrasted against a clear blue sky and it made her feel crisp and clean, like jumping into a bed of freshly washed sheets.

She put her hand in her large pockets and smiled; her three little friends were still there. She adjusted her top hat, picked up her small impressed leather suitcase, whistled her special tune and began to make her way up the slope of a newly formed dune.

Now the Atacama likes to listen to whistled tunes of hope, so it shifted with each footprint so that Manuelo would have at least some difficulty in finding her.

And this became the story of a girl called Margarita—well, that's not really her name but the sand has shifted and so has this story. Otherwise these would just be the dead words about an insignificant girl that went missing for being a traitor, her whistling bones as difficult to find as a single grain of sand in the desert.

• • •

Margarita was never called her by her real name. That's because when Uncle Fioramante returned from his travels from across the Andes with his battered suitcase of memories of short loves, magic tricks and tunes, he named her Margarita. He said that she looked like a daisy always standing towards the sunshine regardless of season. Abuela used to get upset and say that Margarita wasn't her name. Her grand-daughter was named after a saint, not a flower, she said, but he insisted and then would sing this little tune to her, thus sealing the name to her blood and bone:

*Margerita Margaretta*
*Tiene tres pulgas dentro bolsillo*
*Una le canta,*
*Oltra le silbar,*
*Y la oltra le trae agua fresca*
*(Margarita, Margaretta*
*Has three fleas inside her pocket*
*One sings to her*
*One whistles to her*
*And One brings her fresh water to drink.*

Now I know it doesn't sound like much in English, but in Spanish, it does, and this little tune journeyed with her because it didn't take any space in her small battered suitcase. (If you want to sing it, you're best to learn how to sing it in Spanish).

The girl named after a flower traipsed up a sandy slope clutching a suitcase, a vial with three fleas sitting in her pocket, and Uncle Fioramante's top hat perched on her head.

She walked with her head held high and saw a golden apparition scurry down from the border of the cliff. She squinted her eyes to get a better look. Was this a hallucination? No: the desert fox was real. He trotted towards her, his fur almost the same gold as the sand except for the ochre that streaked his long pointed ears. He trotted towards Margarita until he was about 100 metres away from her then sat himself down on his hind legs, cocked his head to one side and said, "Why haven't I noticed you before?"

"This is my first time here."

"Ahhh," he said and wiped away a grain of sand from his eye with his left front paw and then gave his head a shake. "I thought I remembered you, but maybe I'm mistaken. What brings you to the desert? What are you seeking?"

Now Margarita had lived in a small village her whole life and other than between pages 119 to 244 of Uncle Fioramante's book of *Curious Places and Curiouser Cultures (1891)*, she had not really been anywhere. She felt her spine quiver. A talking desert fox! Still, it was the desert of shifting sands from the world of Abuela's bedtime stories where anything could happen.

Margarita stood up as tall as a four foot eleven inch girl of a woman could. She took her top hat off, placed it against her chest and gave a deep bow, the way she had seen her Uncle Fioramante do.

"I am Margarita, niece of Fioramante Leal, and I am seeking my self worth."

The Desert Fox was charmed by her unusual manner and couldn't help but laugh a little. "Most people travelling far to find self worth find in the end that the journey is not a physical one but an inner one."

Margarita nodded. It seemed a strange thing to say. Only a long physical journey such as the one she had taken would keep Manuelo away.

"Remember you are now amongst the desert dwellers of the Atacama, where people speak of the past in the present and the future in the past. Are you, Margarita, running away from your past?"

Margarita placed her top hat back on her head, licked her parched lips and didn't answer. She had such little to have for her very own that keeping thoughts to herself were precious.

"Perhaps," she said.

"You must be thirsty," said the Desert Fox.

"Yes, I am, Signor -"

"Call me Khana."

"Khana."

Khana laughed at her pronunciation of his Aymaran name. When he looked into her eyes, he saw a part of his own desert spirit there—he liked her top hat too. "Maybe I thought I'd seen you in the past, because you are standing on these sands in my present."

He began to trot along the edge of the slope that had now formed a narrow path to the decline down the other side of the dune and gestured for her to follow.

"Why don't you wear bowler hats like your fellow desert dwellers?"

"Because Ring Mistresses wear top hats," Margerita answered.

"I see," said Khana.

She swallowed. "Where are we going for this drink? Signor er . . . I mean, Khana."

"Venezia Bar."

Now Margarita laughed, she laughed so hard her top hat fell off her head but she caught it and flipped it back onto her head just like a Ring Mistress should. It had been a long time since she had laughed. "Venezia? You named a bar in the middle of a desert after a city of water?"

"Yes," said Khana and Margarita noticed that when he smiled his canines were quite sharp and one of them was studded with lapis lazuli. "Desert Dwellers are positive thinkers. We also have a wicked sense of humour."

They walked down the slope and across the Valley until they reached a little village encircled by rocks. It was a grid of streets of adobe huts with thatched roofs, all as silent as stone. Khana led her down a sandy lane and stopped out in front of a white adobe hut with a bright red door. Etched into the red paint were strange symbols. They gave Margarita a feeling of familiarity like the first time she had seen a book of Uncle Fioramante's written in Sanskrit. He knocked three times and the door creaked open.

The bar was dark and cool. Khana led her to a corner of the room where a little round table just big enough for two stood on uneven legs. A tablecloth of butcher paper covered the table. On the wall above, written in white chalk on a blackboard was the specialty of the day.

"Pastel de Choclo?" Khana asked.

"Sounds good. I haven't eaten a real meal in a few days."

Khana whipped his bushy tail against the table. A skinny waiter with a dumbbell moustache and double-breasted white jacket over his jeans came and took their order.

If you've never had Pastel De Choclo, let me tell you, you should. You've never tasted anything like a Chilean corn pie baked in an outdoor oven. Tenderised chicken pieces, buttery mince and hard boiled eggs cooked in milk, cumin, basil and raisins sit under a layer of sweet creamed corn sprinkled with white burnt sugar on top.

The smell of the pie emanating from the noisy kitchen made her remember. She leaned forward to Khana.

"My Abuela sold pastel de choclo to visitors to our town. People used to queue up for it; they'd eat from our handbaked clay dishes and dance the Cueca into the evening." Margarita said.

Khana smiled. He was taken by the way she lit up when she talked of her home and couldn't understand why she hadn't been in his present before.

"What happened to your Abuela's pastel stall?"

Margarita had forgotten about keeping thoughts to herself. "The Government implemented curfews, closed the highway that led to our village and people stopped coming. Those that did were interrogated, went missing, some returned, some didn't. You can't bake to fill other people's stomachs when you can't fill your own."

Khana put his paw on her soft little hand. It felt right. He said nothing but opened his mouth and let his tongue loll out—it was hot after all. "Let's eat."

"I have no money to pay for the pie," she said, her stomach rumbling.

"Currency is in many different forms, my dear Margarita. You will pay me in other ways."

And then he lunged over the table and licked her cheek with his long tongue. "Whoops! Sorry!" he said. "Foxes are quite impulsive creatures."

"So are fleas," Margarita said, jiggling her pocket to make sure they were all still there.

"Is your Abuela still there?"

Margarita nodded, and a grain of sand got caught in her eye which made her rub and rub.

"It's okay to cry," Khana said and he wiped the grain from her eye.

And she did.

Margarita juggled the pocket of her knee-length skirt and pulled out a little jar with the three fleas her cat Hermancito had let her pick from his thick fur as a parting gift: Duna, Victor and Jaramillo.

"Ah! You are ringmaster of a flea circus!"

"Ring Mistress!"

There was the sound of singing and whistling from the little jar as the fleas sung the rhyme that had fused Margarita's sinew and bone. (You know it too, you can sing along, if you like).

"Which flea brings you the fresh water?" Khana asked her, wanting the sand to change soon or else he would want to lick her face some more. Once was enough for a first meeting.

"Jaramillo," she said noticing that Khana's nose looked slippery and wet. She found it endearing.

"Not a bad skill for a flea to have now that you'll be staying in the driest place on earth," Khana said. He smiled and showed his pointy fangs. The lapis lazuli stone glinted and made Margarita laugh. There was a moment when they could have kissed but then there just wouldn't be a story, would there? Good love stories are just not that easy.

Whoooooshhh. The sand swept down the rooftop of the Venezia Bar. It crept through the window, swirling circular patterns as it made its way to curl around Margarita's ankles like Hermancito had done when he wanted to play.

"Now you shall you pay for your meal with what's in that suitcase, Margarita," Khana said.

"You want me to do my act?"

She must have asked that a little too loudly for the sound of clapping and howls of encouragement filled her ears from all four corners of the room—even from the kitchen. She looked around the bar, men in berets with cigars drooping from the corners of their mouths, a table of desert foxes that looked much like Khana except with shorter ears, an aged flamenco dancer with a plastic red rose in her hair that clicked her castanets instead of clapping, and a table of Vicunas with their bowler hats and long plaits, a sea of indigo blue and fushia pink. They all looked at her with hopeful eyes.

Margarita opened her suitcase and pulled out three little cardboard boxes and a neatly folded piece of red felt. On the inside of the suitcase's lid was a mural with a sign in red that said, "Uncle Fioramante and Margarita's Travelling Flea Circus." It sat in a painted sky and clouds of a sunny day. In the left hand corner of the mural, a silver Ferris wheel and in the centre a red and white striped Big Top. A forest of green trees that grew air balloons instead of apples faded into the right.

She unfolded her red felt and placed it on top of the body of the case to make a flat surface and unpacked the three small boxes. Inside the first was a little carousel of winged horses made with dragonfly wings, in the second, a music box with no opening and in the smallest a little canon.

The excited faces around the room made her stomach flip with nerves as she wound the little music box. The she tapped the jar three times and out came Duna, Victor and Jaramillo.

"Now ladies and gentlemen . . . and Foxes and Vicunas too," Margarita said. "Please allow me to introduce my fleas: Duno, Victor and Jaramillo."

There was some applause and the sound of castanets clacking.

"This may seem cruel but for my fleas to perform their heroic acts they do need to be tied to this red silk thread," Margarita pulled the thread as if by magic out of her long knotted hair. It seemed to move like a little serpent with the help of the desert breeze that came though the two windows, and the audience gasped.

"Don't worry. No harm will come to them!"

The music box started and the flea circus began.

The desert liked the flea carousel the best, the way it turned round and round and round like the passing of days and nights. The Atacama knew that the passing of time is just movement over its arid landscape and the concepts of time can be easily reversed— you just have to change your way of thinking.

Believe me, the desert wanted to put the past well and truly behind Margarita and the future in front—but time just doesn't work that way in the Atacama. Just ask any elderly Amaryan if you don't believe me. When they talk about the future they wave their hands behind their shoulders and say *"qhipa uru"* meaning future days are back days. But the past—well, that lies in your present. It is in the here and the now.

And there was a moment too, when Margarita let her fleas dance a can-can on the red thread and saw Khana smiling at her so that it almost burnt her retinas and she felt that her past was way behind her. Khana saw his own reflection in her face and knew that it must be a connection of spirit and heart. He wanted to spring from his chair and lick her face many times over, wrap his tail around her soft body and nuzzle his wet nose into the nape of her neck—but he knew that he couldn't for this wish lay in the unknown future, still behind their backs.

If Margarita was to remain a desert dweller she had to deal with the past that sat in her present and clear the way for the future to become a real and tangible thing—just like a real flea circus.

There was more applause for her final bows. She put the fleas on her arm to feed and walked over to the little table where Khana sat.

"Where are you going?"

Khana stood up on all fours, arched his back and flexed his long ears a couple of times. A feeling of panic jumped into her stomach.

"You will be safe here," he said, trying to not let his eyes dwell for too long in hers. "We will see each other again, very soon. You will know where to find me." And with that he nuzzled his wet nose onto her lips and with one quick swipe licked her face clean.

When he reached the red door he turned, shot her a longing look and walked out the red door into the desert. Khana too felt a longing he too had not known—it was beyond love and attachment—he'd had plenty of that before. No, it was more a feeling of lightness that gives you spring in your step and makes your heart flutter as if it has wings. He didn't want to consume her—he just wanted to be in her presence. But he knew the way of the desert: in terms of the future, little or nothing can be said about it. We just haven't witnessed it yet.

That night when she lay sleeping in the little stretcher bed under the staircase next to the kitchen in Venezia, the sand blew through the grate of the kitchen window and wrapped her in a blanket to comfort her.

It would be the last night of hidden footprints in the sand.

• • •

She had shown Manuelo the flea circus. She had trusted him with the songs of Uncle Fioramante, the interest in curious objects and artifacts of worlds where there was equality for all. She had given him the words and music of Uncle Fioramante's songs of freedom. She had let Manuelo into all her secrets.

At first, Manuelo didn't listen. He was too consumed by her twenty year old prettiness to listen to her words. And let's face it: a young man besotted by a young woman's looks only feels what's throbbing between his legs not what is throbbing in her heart. Manuelo did not have a heart that throbbed; it beat very slowly, like a reptile's.

Until they gave him a uniform with shiny buttons. A job. A sense of pride. How cheap a young man's loyalty can be. Bought for shiny buttons and polished shoes.

And when he got used to her prettiness, he actually did hear her stories and they came and took Uncle Fioramante in the night. They came when Uncle Fioramante, Margarita and Abuela were sleeping, cuffed his hands behind his back and dragged him out into the back of the black wagon.

Uncle Fioramante didn't even have time to take his dignity with him and had nothing but the bed sheet Margarita had wrapped around his body and an unfinished song.

Margarita screamed and dropped down onto her knees begging them not to take her Uncle Fioramante away: they should take her. And because Manuelo did have a reptilian heart he made her pay for her sorrow with humiliation and let his fellow soldiers watch and cheer him on like he was some warrior from an epic enjoying the spoils of victory at war.

And it was at that moment of cold blade searing pain deep within her that made the nerves around her spine feel like tiny shards of broken glass cutting into the very core of her spirit that Margarita felt detachment and separation from her body.

Weightlessness.

Her soul floated to the left hand corner of the ceiling where the pigeons slept and from there she watched Manuelo beat his heavy body into hers. The six soldiers watching jeered on; they saw her body and nothing else. Only Hermancito, her cat, knew where she really was and tilted his head backwards looking up at the quivering air that made the pigeons shift to make some space for her.

It was that moment, the lightness of her soul shimmering just above her aching body that she thought of the poetry of fleas. How they jump so high they can reach the celestial spheres.

It is a lesson to you, I think, too—some poet wrote about the very spiritual nature of fleas—who was it? Ah yes, Pablo Neruda—a spiritual brother of the desert.

Margarita had tried to keep life light ever since.

• • •

She had not seen Khana for five days. Each night, the memories of the betrayal become more real. Each night when she tucked herself into the single bed under the staircase and fell asleep to the sound of the chink of plates and crockery being put away, the rape became heavier and heavier. In her dream, she couldn't detach from her body. She woke feeling like dry bricks weighed on her chest, abdomen and legs. She sat up and leaned her back against the wall and tried to cough away the feeling of sand stuck in her throat. Manuelo was in her present, in front of her face making her heavy and soon she would not be able to get her fleas to perform. The memory of the way he felt inside her made her spasm into tightness and caused her lower back to twinge.

Margarita stood up but her legs were still shaking. She opened the red door and noticed that its symbols had changed. She walked a straight line and the desert allowed her: this time it did not cover her footprints. Although the Atacama puts the past in the present, she is still kind. She did not cover Margarita's footprints so she could find her way back.

She walked outside the village walls and back up the slope she had come down that day when she first met Khana. She reached the summit and saw that below lay a valley of geological formations of ochres and reds. She recognised the one her Abuela called The Three Marias that had been in what was called The Valley of the Moon.

"I know you're here, Manuelo." She screamed and the desert carried her words so they echoed across the valley.

He emerged from behind a tall rock of black red that lay directly in front of her. She listened to the fabric of his pants rubbing together as he walked towards her. "Traitor and Whore," he said and his lips unfurled into a smile of very small teeth. "Francesca, the whore that enjoyed herself while her Uncle screamed like a stuck pig when we hacked his hands off."

Margarita wanted to block her ears but knew she had to hear what he had to say.

"We made him play a guitar with nothing but the stumps of his wrists," Manuelo said.

Now, like I told you, the desert changed and so did this story. Her old name, Francesca, has no power over her because she is Margarita and this is not another story of a girl that became whistling bones in a desert, impossible to find like a single sand grain of the desert. This is the story of girl who became a Ring Mistress of her own Circus. She put her hand in her pocket and with her index finger managed to undo the lid of her jar.

Now Duno, Victor and Jaramillo had not eaten for three days. Margarita had been so distracted with the heaviness of her past; she had forgotten to feed them. They jumped high into the desert sky, landing on Manuelo's body and sucked him dry. She watched her fleas gorge themselves on his blood, feed on his body. His body twitched and he moaned and Margarita stood frozen like one of the stone sculptures, waiting for the moment his smell, his voice, his flesh and blood were sucked out of him.

She fell to her knees and began to dig. She dug with her bare hands. She felt the sand stick between the grooves where skin and fingernail meet and plunged his bones deep into the sand. She pushed them down into the desert sand until she was up to her armpits in it. In his jacket pocket, she found her Uncle's unfinished song. She opened the jar for Duno, Victor and Jaramillo to hop back inside and placed her Uncle's unfinished song there.

It would be another song for them to learn to sing.

Margarita turned around and readjusted her top hat. There was a deep satisfaction of burying the memory bones of Manuelo sucked dry by her three little fleas. Her chest felt light, making it easy to breathe again.

Whoosshh. The desert began and she knew it was best to close her eyes. Remember? That's how the best wishes are made. She felt the sand move across the landscape, exfoliate her legs and kiss her face with promise of a new destiny.

Now let's remember, the desert is a harsh landscape and does not make love stories easy. But the desert loves Margarita because she has learnt the gift of lightness and she knew what it was to be tied down to weight. Her past now in front of her was the day she met Khana, the smiling desert fox with the very long ears and lapis studded tooth that licked her face.

She knew where to find him.

The landscape had shifted to that day when she first met him and he was sitting at the top of the sand cliff. And smiling.

"What are you seeking?"

"You, in my present, now that my past is buried and gone."

Burying Manuelo's bones has made her confident.

He licked her face and pounced playfully on top of her. He did not place his whole body weight on hers when he pounced.

"I want love as light as sand," she said to him.

Khana nodded his head. "Love in the Atacama."

Margarita nodded, looked boldly into Khana's eyes and noticed the glint of his lapis studded tooth—he was smiling. They laughed and raced down the slope to the Valley, fell into the soft sands and made love in the sacred emptiness of the Valley of Moon. And they reached the celestial spheres our spiritual brother Neruda spoke about. Did you taste that pastel de choclo? That flavour of olives and raisins melting on your tongue as one. That's what their love tasted like.

The love feels light, like sunrise and instead of pain, Margarita feels her ovaries tingle.

So, I leave you with love of a desert fox and Ring Mistress. I don't know how long the love lasts and that doesn't really matter. Sometimes love tastes better when it's short and sweet but that future is way behind them right now.

The wind tickles the sand which starts to shift again coating their bodies in a golden blanket of their love. Their laughter echoes across the Valley and the desert shifts to move onto the next story of Atacaman love. It might involve Khana and Margarita or another girl lost in the desert.

It might involve you.

Remember to tread lightly.

Be bold and travel light.

• • • • • • • • • • •

# BRIAR DAY

## PETER M. BALL

I asked Jay what he was doing when the thorns came, because
that's what you do when you get together on Briar Day. His face
screwed up. "I thought we weren't going to talk about the thorns."

We weren't. We'd run into one another at a work seminar, one
of those pre-arranged accidents we never really talked about, and
decided to go for drinks. We'd picked this bar on Elizabeth Street
because it was quiet, an upstairs place that hid behind a narrow
flight of stairs and a decaying sign. People came here to drink, not
to party. Now it was getting late. I should have been home with
Annie and we both knew it. "Come on," I said. "Four years we've
been doing this and you've never said a thing."

Jay sighed again. He held up his hand until a waitress in cherry
Doc Martins came and took an order for another round. I smiled
at her, paid the money, and waited. Jay drummed his fingers on the
table. He knew me well enough to figure this wasn't going to go
away. "You first," he said. "If we're going to do this, we do it right.
What were you doing?"

"I was at work," I said. "Three days in the bank, eating
breath-mints and watching the vines wrap over the glass wall at
the front. We thought we were going to die when the glass started
cracking."

"Bad place to be," Jay said.

"There were worse."

"Did anyone try to get out?"

"Sure," I said. "A couple of customers made a run for it, but they mostly got cut to shit by the thorns. I sat tight. Allergies, you know? I was fucked the moment the briars grew."

"Huh," Jay said. The waitress arrived with our beers, putting the heavy steins on the table along with my change. I took a long slug from mine, but Jay just held his with both hands. "What about the dragon?" he said.

"We heard it," I said, "but it was just roaring and the sound of wings; I had no idea what caused the ruckus until everything was taken care of."

Jay's face was getting tight, his mouth turning into a thin line. He was running out of questions to ask and I was running out of story to tell. I wished I hadn't brought it up. There's a reason I catch up with Jay on Briar Day; it never makes me feel like I missed some great and defining experience. Spending three days trapped inside a bank, ground floor city centre. Sometimes it was kind of like sleeping through Kennedy's shooting when you had an apartment on Elm Street, Dallas, in November of sixty-three.

Still, I'd brought it up. Nothing to do but plough forward. "So how about you? What were you doing when the briars came?"

"We do this once." Jay stared into his beer. He tipped the stein to one side, watching the liquid slosh around. "Just once."

I nodded. Jay took a deep breath.

"You never met Caroline," he said. "That's probably why we're still friends. I had people, friends, stop talking to me afterwards. No real reason, just picking sides. The usual shit that happens when people stop living together. And me and Caroline, man, it was always going to get ugly, somewhere along the line."

He stopped and closed his eyes, frowning as he took another drink. When he opened them again he didn't look at me, just focused on something over my shoulder. "Maybe that's not a good way to start it. Let's try this: I was baking. Butterscotch cookies, probably. I do that when I'm upset. It makes the house smell kinda soft and golden, gives me something to eat when the sugar crash kicks in. So let's assume I was baking, even if I wasn't. It was a Wednesday morning and I wasn't going to work, hadn't gone to work for a week. I pulled a tray of cookies out of the oven, then I turned and the kitchen was dark; shadows on the window, a few rays of afternoon sun getting through the foliage. Just like, wham, all of a sudden, there it was: thorns longer than your finger and those weird blood-rose flowers that were bigger than your head. The only things I could see from my kitchen were vines and the top of the street lights.

"None of this is special, I know that. It's the same shit everyone blabs about: thorns, flowers, freaking out. None of it's special, but it feels like it should have been. You start off panicked but eventually you start to feel safe, a little weirded out, but safe, and you start to calm down. That's what happened to me. After I while I got used to the thorns.

"And that's when my phone rang.

"If I'd been smart, I would have left it. I knew who was calling and we shouldn't have been talking yet. I went looking for the phone anyway, telling myself Caroline was the kind of girl who'd keep ringing until I gave in. She wasn't one for reading between the lines when you didn't answer. When I picked up she said, 'Thornbushes. Giant fricken' thornbushes. You can see them too, yeah? It's not just me?'

"'It's not just you,' I told her. I was laying in bed, speaking on the cordless. I can remember playing with this red pillowcase I had, picking at the stray threads. Caroline didn't say anything and I wasn't really in the mood to be speaking, so I just sat there listening to the phone line cracking and the soft scratch of thorns as they embraced the house. It wasn't really an awkward silence, but it should have been. Would have been, if things weren't so weird before the call even started. We'd been doing it a lot, these non-conversations, and I was always the one who got tired of them first.

"'Listen, Caroline,' I said. 'I gotta go.' I still stumbled over her full name. I hadn't used it in years, not since we first started dating, and it felt like I was talking to a stranger when I said it out loud. And she was, I guess. This Caroline was unfamiliar, a girl who sounded similar to someone I once dated, and talking to her made me feel hollowed out. The conversations usually devolved into fights after I got that feeling.

"'I'm sorry,' she said. 'I know I shouldn't have called. It's just . . . '

"'Yeah, I get it.' I said, but I didn't. I told her I'd call her later and hung up. Then one of those flowers bloomed, right next to the window, and I felt like a bastard. I spent the next hour crashed out on the bed, not really thinking about the thorns. I really wanted to break something, so I was killing time until that feeling went away.

"Then I heard the dragon for the first time. It flew over the house and I heard the wings, that noise like the echo of a slap across the face. That freaked me out more than the thorns did."

Jay tipped his head back, pouring as much beer as he could down his throat. When he put the stein down it was half-empty. He wiped the excess foam off his lips with his left arm.

"I thought the briars weren't that bad, out your way," I said.

Jay shrugged. "Maybe they weren't."

I noticed the buzz of the crowd for the first time, all those wrinkled old people hunched over their drinks and talking. It was too hot in the bar, far to hot. Jay put his drink down and stared at me. His eyes were turning red after the last two pints. Jay was a mean drunk. He should have been calling it a night. And I should've been calling Annie by that point, just to let her know where I was. It was polite, if nothing else. Jay blinked a few times, looked away. I lifted my beer to my lips, but I didn't really feel like drinking anymore.

"I tuned into the news, just like everyone else," Jay said. "I mean, what else are you going to do in an emergency? I sat through that anchorman with a perfect helmet of hair telling us that the suburbs were swamped, that there'd been sightings of a dragon in the city centre, that there were reports of the dragon kidnapping a maiden and holding her to ransom. They even called her that on the news: the maiden. You could tell he didn't want to be saying it, but someone was making him go through with it. I guess once you accept the city is overrun with giant thorns, everything else becomes credible, so you start covering all the bases.

"He did a good job, the anchor, given the circumstances. Refused to be rattled by anything. They trotted out specialists to tell us what they thought was going on, then cut back to footage of the city getting choked to death by thorns. You could hear the steady whine of the rotor over the reporter's commentary.

"The phone rang during the sports report. I muted the sound and picked it up. Didn't even bother saying hello. And there was Caroline on the other end, asking if that was it. Wanting to know what good the news was if that's all they had to offer.

"'What more do you want?' I asked her.

"'Explanations,' Caroline said. 'Direction. Some idea about when it'll end.'

"'They don't know, stay inside, and they have no idea,' I said. 'It's not like they have any answers, is it?'

"'It's the news,' Caroline said. 'They should have answers. That's why we watch.'

"'You don't watch the news.'

"'I did today.'

"'Once," I said. 'Just once, this year. I'm not sure you've got grounds for a complaint.'

"Caroline laughed. I laughed. It felt like old times. Sometimes that happened, when she called, and it hurt. The sports report switched over to the weather; sunny with a strong chance of thorns and rain. Caroline wasn't saying anything. I wasn't saying anything. We remembered we weren't together anymore.

"'So,' I said.

"'Yeah,' she said.

"The phone line crackled.

"'I don't have any answers either, Carol,' I said. "'Yeah, sorry,'Caroline said. 'It's just . . . '

"'Yeah, it's just,' I said. It was always *just* back then, and I kept letting that work. I fidgeted, tapping out a rhythm on the coffee table with my toe. I don't know what Caroline was doing on her end of the phone, but I'm willing to bet she was crying.

"'Look, I'm just irritable,' I told her. 'You know how I get when I'm inside for too long.'

"'Yeah,' Caroline said. Her voice was hard to hear, like she was whispering through a keyhole after locking herself in the bathroom. 'I know.'

"She hung up. I hung up. I left the news on mute and listened to the thorns grinding against the windows, trying to get in."

"You want another round?"

I jumped. There was a waitress looming over our table, thick eye shadow like two slices of orange peel beneath the line of her manicured eyebrows. She picked up my empty glass and added it to the pile on her tray. I looked at Jay; he shrugged.

"Sure," I said. "Why the hell not?"

"You got any plans for later?" she asked. "Couple-a young guys like you, surely you're heading for a party somewhere?"

Jay rolled his eyes.

"Probably not," I said. "We're just after a quiet one, you know? A chance to sit back and reflect."

"Fair enough," she said. "Happy Briar Day."

The waitress took my money and left, heading for the bar. Jay sneered at her back. "Fuck it," he said. "This was a bad idea."

"One waitress," I said. "No big deal."

"You started this," Jay said. ""What were you doing when the thorns came?" You know what happens after you ask that."

"Fine," I said. "Fuck it, it's my fault."

"Has Annie called yet?" He started patting down his pockets, searching for his cigarettes. I fished a pack out of my jacket and slid it across the table. I didn't check my phone. It's not like she needed me to come home. Annie never really seemed to need me for anything. Jay lit up without pressing the issue.

"I was probably one of the first people to hear the dragon, you know," I said. "I was awake a lot of the time; even with the antihistamines, the flowers were doing a number on my allergies. I was awake in the bank while everyone else was sleeping, taking cover behind the counter. I heard this damn rumble, like when a truck goes past you on the highway, and I felt it in my gut. It was fucking frightening, okay? Knowing that something was out there, without knowing what it was. Allergies and fear; it's a fucking bad way of getting through the night."

Jay waved a lit cigarette in the air. He adjusted his glasses to glare at me.

"The dragon," he said. "Everyone goes on about the dragon, but the only person it hurt was that dick with the sword. You know what frightened me? The flowers. The way they'd burst open all of a sudden, so quick and soft that you heard the pop when they split apart. All that fucking pollen in the air, drifting away so it could create another thorn bush; that was fucking disconcerting."

His eyes were frightening, wild as hell. He stopped and shook his head, the angry lines across his face disappearing. I took a deep breath. "Yeah," I said. "The flowers. I dream about them sometimes."

The waitress brought our drinks over. Jay looked at his like it was hiding something dangerous, swaying a little in his seat. "I tried to go to work," he said. "That second day I got up and got ready like it was no big deal. I rolled out of bed and I showered, drank the last of the coffee and made a note to pick up more on my shopping list. I don't know what I thought was going to happen when I was done. The house was still wrapped up tight, the windows blocked by thorns and vines. I couldn't even see the streetlights anymore. There was no hot water either; I was on solar in that place and I figure the thorns had grown over the panels and blocked off the sun. I cut myself while I was shaving and I ironed a shirt while I was still half-asleep. I turned the radio on while I was having a shower and the Morning Crew was making jokes about the dragon, the knight, and that girl, the maiden, who they'd found hiding on the roof with the dragon around three in the morning. I turned it off again when I was dressed. All I really wanted at that point was some music.

"I got as far as the front door before I realised there was no way of leaving the house. I spent the rest of the morning on the couch, eating cracked fragments of butterscotch cookies, flicking through the news channels until I figured out what was going on. They had footage of the dragon in flight by then. It was a big, dark fucker, that dragon; black as an evil glass of cola. You could see it on every channel. The dragon and the attempts to get decent footage of the blond girl it captured-"

Jay clicked his fingers, searching for the name.

"Diana Crowther?" I said. Jay nodded.

"Yeah, her" he said. "I watched them trying to coax her out from underneath that satellite dish she hid behind whenever the dragon came close. I remember how weird it was, in this day and age, that suddenly there were dragons and kidnapped maidens on the TV. They were just starting to get the first real shots of that Crowther girl out in the open on the roof, the camera shot zooming in from a helicopter a couple of kilometres out from ground zero. Grainy details, a little pixilated, but you could see her yelling for help and crying. I got pissed off watching that, thinking about all those people who needed help, people trapped in their homes, hurt or dying, and this bitch was getting the focus because she'd been kidnapped by a dragon.

"Then they cut to the first footage of the knight.

"He looked like something off the cover of a romance novel. He had one of those square jaws with a dimple and the kind of long flowing hair that most guys can't manage because they forget little things like washing it every day. He was harder to believe in than the dragon, somehow. The dragon looked real, for all that it was a big lizard with wings. The knight looked like he was an illustration given life, slicing his way through the briars, making a beeline for the city. And it wasn't even like Diana Crowther was a princess, not when you saw her up close like that. She was just a pretty girl with blond hair and business suit, maybe twenty-three years old, who happened to be trapped on a roof by a dragon.

"The news reporters avoided words like *knight* at first. They just called him an *unidentified citizen*. We'd all been watching him go at it for two straight days before they got with the program and started using the term we'd all been thinking. I mean, he was good looking, he had a sword, and he wore about thirty kilograms of solid steel for protection. That means he's a knight, no matter how you cut it. I think the anchorman was jealous of all that hair.

"Eventually they got bored with following him and taking long-range shots of the dragon, so we had the specialists trotted out to deliver the same messages as the night before.

"The phone rang. This time I counted to three before I answered it.

"'I can't go to work,' Caroline said.

"'There's a lot of that going around.'

"'I got dressed and fed the fish and went to open the front door, then I remembered.'

"'Yeah,' I said. 'I get that.'

"'I'm sorry,' Caroline said. 'I know you'd prefer it if I didn't call.'

"'It's okay,' I said. 'Today's a weird kind of day.'

"'Did you hear the roaring last night?' she said. I told her about the dragon.

"'A dragon?' she said. She didn't sound convinced.

"'According to the news,' I told her. Then I told her as much as I could remember about the theories and the dragon and the knight. I searched the cushions for the remote. I flipped through channels until I found some cartoons.

"'Wow,' Caroline said. 'I figured it was a lion or something.'

"'A lion?' Why would there have been a lion roaming the streets?

"'I don't know. There was a roar. Why wouldn't it be a lion?'

"'Is it just bored and looking for a good nightclub?' I said. She told me to shut up.

"'Maybe it was just searching for a late-night cappuccino?' I said. I was proud of that one.

"'It might have escaped from a zoo,' Caroline said.

"'Of course,' I said. 'It got itself locked out of the cage because it snuck away after lights out and forgot to hide a key under the flower-pot by the door.'

"'Forget it,' Caroline said. 'Just forget it.'

"'Of course, we don't actually have a zoo,' I said. 'So we can explain the lion, but it opens up a whole new line of questioning about the mysterious origin of the zoo.'

"She told me I was dick and laughed. I was laughing too. It felt good to laugh, like it was possible to forget about the thorns and feel like everything was normal. Then Caroline said, 'I miss you.'

"The laughter stopped. I let the line go quiet for a bit. I think she surprised herself with that one. The silence panicked me and I said something about the dragon, plunging on as though I hadn't heard her. I tried making a joke about dragons having weird virgin fetishes, but it didn't really work. In the end I shut up and closed my eyes, counting under my breath. I didn't trust myself to plug the silence. Then we made our excuses, hung up. And afterwards all I could think about was that once upon a time I'd been good at making Caroline laugh."

My phone buzzed in my pocket. I took it out and flipped it open, checking the number.

"Annie?" Jay said. I nodded. The message asked me what time I thought I'd get home.

"Should you be going?" Jay said. I shook my head. Annie and I had met at the bank, a couple of weeks after the briars were gone. Lots of people got together after all that happened, patching things up with former partners or falling hard for someone new, but whatever made us cling to each other was starting to wear off. I had plenty of friends who had separated over the last year. It made you think.

"Why are you still here?" Jay said. He drained the last of his beer out of its stein. "It's getting late. She'll worry. She'll worry and you'll fuck things up."

"Finish your story," I told him. Jay's head rolled back a little as he focused his eyes in my direction.

"You're a stupid fucker, you know that?" Jay said "Fine, fuck it, the rest of the story. It ends like this: on the third day, at six in the morning, I get another phone call. Caroline again, all in a panic, telling me to turn on the TV and tune into the news on Channel Nine. She stayed on the phone until I found it, waiting until she could hear the fight through the receiver. And there it was, the Knight squaring off against the dragon. Sword versus scale for the fate of Diana Crowther.

"You can't really imagine what it's like, seeing that live with your ex crying in your ear. Seeing it without knowing what's going to happen, thinking the dragon's going down because that's what knights and dragons do. The knight kills the dragon and saves the girl; happily ever after. But it didn't go like that, and I was sitting there with Caroline falling apart on the other end of the phone, and all I could do was say fuck over and over until the word started to go soft and I needed something worse to express my feelings.

"The camera zoomed in on the girl, getting a close-up of her right on the rooftop. She was on the edge of the building, watching it all go down. She wasn't screaming, wasn't crying, just standing there all pale and calm. Like she still thought someone was going to come rescue her. Caroline was crying on the other end of the phone and I couldn't really handle it anymore. I hung up and had a shower, trying to wake up. I leant against the tiles, letting the cold water wash over me. I pushed my face into the showerhead and pretended I wasn't crying.

"And when I got out I made breakfast like nothing had happened. I ate toast, let the phone ring a couple of times before I got fed up and unplugged it from the wall. I went back to bed and closed my eyes, pretending that I could go back to sleep. I thought of the girl on the building, guarded by the dragon, waiting for someone to save her. Someone had to, sooner or later.

"For a moment, just a couple of minutes, I wondered if maybe it could be me. I started rummaging through the house, found myself a jacket, something thick and heavy to help fend off the thorns. I searched the kitchen for a big knife, something that could hack its way through the arm-thick strands of the vine. And I got as far as the front door before I changed my mind. I put my ear to the wood and listened to the thorns, the quiet scritch-scritch of barbed fronds desperate to break inside. Then I went back into the lounge room and plugged the phone in. It wasn't long before it rang.

"'He died,' Caroline said. 'Oh my god, it killed him.'

"'Yeah,' I said. 'It did.'

"'But the girl,' Caroline said. 'The dragon? All the thorns around the city?'

"'They're problems,' I said. 'Someone will fix them. I mean, fuck it, that's why we have scientists and armies, isn't it? She doesn't need some random guy with a shiny sword, she needs a SWAT team and the fire brigade.'

"Then I hung the phone up and cut the chord, cut through it with a knife. I didn't turn on the news until the thorns went away a couple of days later and everyone started walking around like something special had happened. I didn't replace my phone for a week, didn't answer it for three or four. And there was no more *it's just* with Caroline after that. No more conversations, really. I was over it. I stopped being whatever she thought I was after we broke up and started being just another guy she used to date."

Jay opened his mouth to say something else, then he stopped and looked away across the bar. His knuckles were white as he lifted the beer stein. He drank everything that remained in one long gulp.

I'd seen the footage of that fight, in the aftermath after they rescued us from the bank. They still replayed it from time to time, especially once the documentaries started. It was always the same thing: the knight is slicing his way towards the tower, the dragon sees him and swoops down. No-one had gotten close to that tower with the dragon there, so the news was all over it. You saw shaky close-ups of each burning breath and sword stroke from a dozen angles, played out on every network. You saw that moment when the dragon catches him, picking that blonde-haired knight up in one claw. You saw the blood as his head was squeezed off, twisted between two claws.

And that close-up on Diana Crowther, watching all this from the top of the building, her face pale and her eyes full of tears. She was an average-looking girl, but that shot made her look beautiful. She instantly became the kind of girl you fall in love with. She was something more, something special, and I fell for her every time they interviewed her on the television.

"Fuck," I said. "Aren't you a charmer."

"It's not like I'm proud of the way it went down." Jay stole another cigarette and lit it. "I'm not a knight, you know. I write computer code for a living. I work with a laptop. I drink beer on the weekends. I wasn't saving anyone, and I was tired of holding onto the idea that I could."

The fireworks started in the town square. We could hear the soft pops over the buzz of the bar. Jay turned towards the noise and closed his eyes. Somewhere out there, in the centre of the celebrations, Diana Crowther would be giving a speech or smiling for the cameras. They might even be shooting her hiding under that famous satellite dish, miming her fear of a dragon that's been dead for three years. The waitress came and took our empty steins away. We didn't order anything else. Jay nodded towards the sound of the fireworks.

"That's what I imagined those flowers sounded like when they bloomed," he said. "Just like that, but softer."

I nodded. Jay shook his head and stood up. He'd looked better. "I gotta piss," he said. "You should go home."

"Annie's not a worrier," I said. "I can stop off and buy her flowers or something on the way home. She'll forgive me."

"It's not about worry," Jay said. "Hell, sometimes it's got nothing to do with flowers. Call her and go home, you stupid fucker." He shook his head and lurched away from the table, heading towards the men's room. Maybe he was pissing. Maybe not. The sound of the fireworks ended and Jay still hadn't come back from the bathroom. As I left I called Annie, punching the numbers on my phone with a clumsy thumb. She answered on the fourth ring, her voice sleepy. "I'm coming home soon," I said. "I love you, okay?"

She said she loved me too, the words exchanged in our regular routine. A quick conversation, easy as hell; neither of us had to feel a damn thing.

...........

# THIEF OF LIVES

## LUCY SUSSEX

Death-in-life. Or Death in Bristol: the sprawling expanse of Temple Mead railway station, made even greyer by an overcast wintry English morn. The only relief from the drear first impression came when I disembarked my suitcase-on-wheels from the steps of the London train. A flash strobed, and I dropped the case, hard, on the cold station concourse.

"Some Celeb?" said the jeans and trainers sidestepping around me.

"Nah. Who'd come to a shitty place like this?" said the stiletto heels and striped thigh socks sidestepping from the other side.

Suitcase retrieved and upright again, I saw at the head of the train a knot of press, as the cameras flashed again. Curious, I trundled towards them, amidst the tribes of modern England: schoolchildren; the equally uniformed business commuters; pensioners in cloth caps and sensible raincoats; Indian ladies with parkas over their flowing saris; Chai lads and lasses, dripping bling. Whether they were workers and wastrels, all expressed a very English quiet desperation.

The press focus was on a black-clad couple posed against the backdrop of the first-class carriages. Around them the passengers would pause, rubbernecking, then eddy onwards. I paused too, as a journalist asked the centre of attention, a slender woman with a peroxide chignon and sunglasses, despite the dim light: "And how does it feel to win a major literary prize?"

The man with her, his hair a trendy brush, emitted a shrill laugh: let's-humour-the-idiots. As if in response, a passer-by moaned.

What I could see of his face beneath a hood was ghost-pale, his clothes loose on a coathanger, junkie frame. He stared at the two, biting his lip, then shouldered past in a burst of shambling speed.

The woman replied: "It's so terribly, terribly humbling."

The humility of a cat, bird in mouth!

Only one other person similarly reacted to the pair, a woman meeting a knot of public schoolgirls, who immediately turned away, pulling the collar of her coat up to her ears. I caught as she did a splash of port-wine birthmark, also a mutter that sounded most unschoolmarmish.

Celebrity is charisma, vitality; anything else unenviable. Rather than seem a celebrity gawker, or worse, a fan for someone I had never heard of before, I walked onwards, dispersing with the crowd. My idle thought was, as I neared the taxi rank: why, among all the people in the station, was it only those two who seemed alive?

Suspiciously alive?

• • •

In my hotel room, I performed a cursory unpack, then succumbed to the mid-Atlantic jetlag. Hours later, I woke to a velvety northern winter twilight. I unpacked some more, checked for voicemail. The Californian tones of Chez, my boss, flowed into my ears:

"Hi Ally hope you find Bristol fine and dandy. Say hi to the faculty and archive folks from the Emeritus Professor and hi from both of me to Barry at the bookstore. Keep an eye out for big cat collectables, you know what I like. And if by any chance you find my Prada bag, with the Ruvenor, I wanna know immediately! Love ya!"

Hope springs eternal, I thought. "Chez," I said aloud, "I love you too, but I'm not in Bristol as your magical thieftaker."

"You've done magic before," I mentally heard her say. "Retrieved a better, finer Ruvenor. Made me better, too."

Yes, I said to the first, and to the second: In part. She was still frail, still too nervous to return here. Hence my mission, to be her proxy and dive into the details of Bristol's dark past. That could wait, though—I needed Bristol *now*, hard, fast and physical. Hit the sidewalk, the English pavement. My travel clothes doubled as streetwear, being neutral, blend into the background. And though it was a strange city, at night, and its danger was what had brought me here in the first place, I could walk the way that says: don't mess with me!

Lights, cobbles, passing buses. Mapping the inner city with my booted feet, step by step. The square grey tower of the cathedral, the hooded beggars in its proximity seeming for a moment or so medieval, until they wheedled in today's tones. With the true dark came the emergence of the nightclubbing young, all glitz and gladrags. I followed them down into a cellar bar which served boutique beer and good throbbing trip-hop beats. There I found a place in the crush, fitting in, as I do. Outside again after midnight, my feet still tapping, bee-buzz in my ears. Back to the hotel, but en route I had to navigate the glare of the shops in the main street, then the boarded-up windows of the downmarket, where I sped up, radiating bad vibes: don't-you-dare-mess-with-me!

Globalization has made most of the First World identikit, the unfamiliar familiar. I could have closed my eyes to slits and thought myself in any city with a trailing, dangling history. The nightclubbers, the dregs of people, the junkies, common to Old Anywhere. But then suddenly appeared something familiar, but out of context. Unlike most others on the street, they lacked all weariness, or pallor. They almost *gleamed*, and that was how I placed them, the celebrity couple from that morning at Temple Mead. They walked past me and down a cobbled alley, black clothes, male and female, the sunglasses worn even at night, the bleached blonde chignon, tight as a fist. I leaned unobtrusively against the brick walls, and spied on an encounter at the other end, with a black girl with pink-tinged dreadlocks, stilettos, fishnet tights, and a tiny sequinned tutu. Something passed between them, small enough to move from white hand to black hand almost imperceptibly.

What were high literati doing in a seedy part of town, meeting an obvious hooker? Waiting for their woman, though it was they who had dealt to her? Cruising? No, I thought, *prowling*. Like Mrs Thrale, Chez's pet serval cat, near dinnertime. Or like Ruvenor in assassin mode, for a book equivalent. Hunters hungry and after prey. I knew the signs well . . .

• • •

The clock when I got to bed showed three am, which meant I awoke to an overcast, pearly midday. Though naturally I am a night creature, if I kept this schedule it would play hell with the archival hours, and my purpose here. Outside my hotel door were piled the London weekend papers, a breakfast of newsprint. I flipped through them, finding features on *Dr Who* companions, home interiors, and the latest cooking fads. I turned to the literary section, not expecting Chez, and not particularly surprised at the appearance of *them* again, making the most of being briefly prize- and newsworthy. It was edifying: she was an Edytha Lang, former schoolteacher, author of "coruscating", "surgical", "hyperrealist" short stories, the latest *Thief of Lives*, a collection about the down and out. He was Jake Miniver, her "partner", former youth worker turned director of documentary shorts, firstly about the down and out, secondly about Edytha.

"What is your next project?" the interviewer asked, towards the close. "Extreme lives again?"

"I never repeat myself. Formula is not for me. Rather this time, extreme states of mind. Belief, religious or delusional. Fantasies, but not the fantastical. I have no imagination."

"None at all?"

"No Tolkien I, thank goodness! My calling is to stick pins not in phantasms, but real lives, fixing them to the page."

"Other people's lives?"

"Of course. I live like a weevil in a biscuit, as dear Virginia— Woolf, you know—used to say."

I put down the paper, acutely aware of the beige of the hotel walls, the stale, centrally-recycled air. Not until Monday morning would the archive open, and my social options were definitely limited. The least I could do was say hi from Chez to Barry at the Bookstore.

I followed the instructions Chez had given me, and found an elegant terrace façade, with a bow-window. The front of the shop featured new books, with rarities and Wessex history collectables at the back, and gallery space upstairs. There was real skill behind the ambience, which managed both to be elegant and welcoming (and utterly unBorders). It was offset by the creator of this bookish temple, Barry himself, no bow-tie nor Oxbridge, but a plaid shirt and a *Flight of the Conchords* accent. I leaned across the counter and introduced myself; at the mention of Chez a moment of genuine pleasure flickered across his stolid face. It soon returned to normal: his gaze, as he assessed me, was shrewd, but unreadable. Here was a man who believed in firm handshakes, and I replied in kind. Then came the chit-chat, his enquiries after Chez mixing the kindly and the professional:

"Shame about the new novel's delay. I've got a lot of customers almost too hungry to wait until Walpurgis Night. But when someone gets sick, it's to hell with deadlines, and rightly so."

Neither of Chez's names had got into the Bristol papers, and back at the publisher's only an inner circle knew how sick. I eyed him, noting he was not fishing for information about Chez, and finding it admirable, but not rewardable. Barry had kept one secret, and very well too; I judged he did not need another.

A phonecall briefly interrupted, and while he answered I browsed, finding Chez's books in their dual locations. In the window a rearrangement was in process, with centre stage a red and black cover and the title: *Thief of Lives.* I was actually holding it when Barry reappeared.

"That your sort of reading?" (a professional query).

"I don't know. We came into Bristol on the same train—she was being interviewed on the concourse by the press."

"And I can just imagine what she was saying."

"How humbling it was to win a top literary prize."

He gave a short bark of a laugh. I replaced the book in the display.

"Why only one copy, if it's a prizewinner?"

"Almost outa stock. The rejacketing arrives any day now," he said.

Life with Chez had meant a sudden education in not only academe, but the book trade and its marketing. "Necessary, I should think. Doesn't red and black normally suggest genre horror?"

He grinned. "Say that at one of our evening events and you'd cause conniptions. In fact, I'll give you a flyer for the one next week. A photo show, with all the local notabilities."

He bent down, and opened a cardboard box of books, his big hands emerging with copies of a previous collection, *Girlschool*, which he fanned around the prizewinner like slices of cake.

"Nobody can say I don't support the local writing scene. I remember Ede, although only Jake's allowed to call her that now, when she was just a lean and hungry."

"She still looks it."

"For some, you can never be too thin or too famous. She hadn't settled on the sunnies then, and the bun was mousy. She brought mousy little stories along to the writers' workshop I tolerate taking over my back room once a month. Sad tales of provincial lives, where the major drama was a crush on the deputy Principal. Then she progressed to stories about the spats within a writers' group, which caused more . . . spats. Finally something dramatic happened to her."

"She got bitten by a werewolf?"

"You wish. Others here might wish it too. Actually, she had a ticket in the National Lottery, a dare from the girls at the posh school where she taught. She won, not the big prize, but enough to throw in the teaching, write full time. That made the news, drew some attention. A year later her story about the National Lottery appeared. Funny, it was about being a minor prizewinner, and becoming best email friends with the major prizewinner, a Miss Council Estates personified. Which is what happened, with actual emails being reprinted in the story, I'm told. Threats of suing, countered with the "oh, but it's Art" argument. More publicity . . . and a book contract. Which resulted in *Girlschool*, in which Ede's former employer became a hotbed of drug abuse and lesbian sex. "

He sighed. "Don't mind me, I'm just the bookseller. But give me Chez anyday, even if she wouldn't shed the Professor Incognita guise and do a gig for me. Coulda sold a tonload, the shop wall to wall Goths. There's far worse out there . . . "

He stopped abruptly, as the door jangled, admitting two obvious culture vultures.

He leaned towards me, intoning *sotto voce*: ""Who are these hapless ones to whom evening brings no solace, to whom, like the owls, the approach of night is the signal for a witches'-sabbath?'—that's Charlie Baudelaire, my main man. At least the Goths can laugh at themselves, with their black nailpolish and campy drapes. And they don't make anyone's personal night even worse."

• • •

Of course I didn't buy a copy, I stole it from W. H. Smiths, and took it on a walk down the riverside, the tourist precinct. Seated by the silvery waters of the Avon, I watched the customers at Brunel's Buttery, with their hearty helpings of bun, eggs and bacon. I limited myself to eye-food, the book, which proved thinner and less tasty.

It comprised a series of character studies about the hapless of coastal England. "Extreme lives", Edytha had told the journalist, but in this book the focus was on poetic lives. The descriptions continually reached for an ostentation expressed in words, the narrator's sensibility and viewpoint imposed like an iron pin, definitively sticking them to the page. A girl delinquent was "breaded with pimples", an image that spoke of myriad erasures, "beaded?" "bearded?" etc; a beggar had "wishes as currency". Meaning just what? I wondered.

The most interesting piece concerned a young villain, alone in having a sense of swagger: "The way they scream and hold on as I snatch, like I was taking their life and not their handbags. But when you get the bag back to the squat you do find their lives."

The narrator asked why, and I sensed a recording here, the words suggesting the rhythms and hesitations of real speech.

"Pics of the kiddies. The ol' man. Shopping lists. Diet chewing gum. Lipsticks. A vibrator once. Their good jewellery, the silly cunts." He smacks his lips. "Broken watches. A baby's dummy. Loveletters. Anti-ageing cream. Everything . . . "

My gaze stopped mid-line, sensing proximity, too close for personal safety. Somebody was reading over my shoulder. "Everything," a voice breathed above my head, in the lilt of Ireland, "of nothin' much lives."

"And if you don't move on," I said conversationally, "nothing much more will happen in your life, apart from a dip in the river." I flexed a shoulder muscle, as if to add: I'd happily drown you for the crime of reading over my shoulder. I'm like that. Then followed a moment of stillness, when only a seagull screamed. I could hear a soft step behind me, retreating. At the edge of my senses I caught a thread of sound, close to a moan: "Nothin' much, no more, no me." That definitely wasn't in the book.

When I turned, slowly, I saw only unremarkable tourists—and a blur of movement, as someone ducked out of sight, a form tall and lean.

• • •

Days passed as I settled into the Bristol routine. Laptop in hand, I shuttled between the archives, the university, my daytime occupied by the careful checking of Chez's references, from an evil time, less than two centuries back, when the city was the centre of the

English slave trade. Evenings were devoted to myself, and the world of the body, the unintellectual. I located a nearby gym, bought a short-term membership and worked out rigorously. Any free time after that I sprawled in front of the television, watching the new slavery, the real life programs.

After several days, I had the yen for company, even of "notabilities", and unearthed Barry's flyer. An exhibition of photography, called "A Walk on the Dark Side". I walk there too, I thought, turning to the just-in-case section of my luggage. My dress-up clothes, a gift from Chez:

"If you're going to be my discreet protector tonight, you might as well look the part," she had said.

"Blend in? I'm very good at that," I said, looking up from the pages of publishers' proofs I was double-checking for Chez.

"Ally, I've seen you master the grad student look, and be invisible in malls. But you'll need something different for the Shadow fan club—they take costuming seriously. There'll be acres of butterfly wings, and bare flesh, body armouring and cloaks of peacock feathers. You'll see."

And she had put the shopping bag, of embossed, heavy paper, with a designer logo, squarely in front of me, so I had to give it my full attention. She had, I was obliged to admit, chosen very well, mindful of what would suit my size and looks. A tunic-dress, cut loosely, of sheeny obsidian green, the look arcane if not actually otherworldly. Tips for my black boots, with a metallic overlay that suggested part armouring, part spurs. A turban for my cropped hair, also sheeny green.

Of course I had to try them on immediately, Chez peeping around the door of my room, with even Mrs Thrale (who normally avoided me) big-eyed from the safe distance of the passageway.

"And now for the piece-de-resistance!" Chez said.

At the bottom of the bag was a small thin parcel. I tore off the paper, to find a jeweller's box. Inside was revealed a necklace of teardrop-shaped beads, again of black with a green tinge. They looked like nothing so much as drops of blood, from some unearthly reptile. The effect was both grotesque and of great beauty.

"They're a resin, cutting edge," Chez said happily. Indeed the beads were faintly, disturbingly, soft to the touch. "The designer says no matter how long you wear them, they never ever warm."

"You never picked this up at any mall, even in Hollywood."

She smiled. "I commissioned it, as a visual aid for the last but one book. One of the perks of having advance money. Can I put it on you and see how it completes your look?"

In her tone had been almost a plea. I handed her the necklace, and bent my head. She stood on tiptoe, as her little light-brown hands clasped the beads around the olive skin of my neck. We both stared into the full-length mirror, to which I normally gave scant attention. It was a marvel: I truly looked like a creature from another world.

"I'm so pleased I can give it to my Ruvenor," she had said. "Or the best parts of Ruvenor."

Now, as if in memory-echo, I clasped the beads around the neck, as she had so many months ago. Then I applied myself to my hotel mirror, completing the guise with makeup, and (this being a touch I had added myself, subsequently) customized contacts. On the surface the look was moneyed Goth, with subliminal hints of something more disturbing. Pleased, I wound my travel cape around me and strode into the dark. I was going to scare somebody tonight . . .

At the bookshop, a predictable crowd had gathered, flouncing their black around the bookshelves and the gallery space, where hung large nightscape photographs of underclad youth, mostly looking cold and miserable. I took a glass of wine from a tray beside Barry, who was deep in conversation with what looked like Bristol's version of a leather queen (pimply), and did not clock me. Thus armed, I sashayed around the collection. In a prime position was, as I had half-expected, Edytha as Star-power, brighter than the artist-photographer, and orbited by admirers, kiss-asses and wannabees. Hard to read her behind the Warhol shades, but she looked replete, triumphal. Further away, in the outer reaches of her personal solar system, I noted envious glances, furtive calumnies. The unsuccessful rest of the writing group, possibly. I edged nearer, eavesdropping:

"The school pretend *Girlschool* never happened, especially in front of the parents." A blonde woman, with Freddie Mercury teeth.

"Quel surprise." A middle-aged man, donnish and tweedy.

"And Diana won't talk about it, at all, at all."

To a third party, a girl barely out of her teens, with big square glasses. "This was before your time, of course, but you know Diana. She was sensitive enough before—but then to have her birthmark described as 'facial menstruation'!"

The girl blinked. "That's not nice!"

"If regrettably accurate," said the man.

"It knocked the stuffing out of Diana. She's never been the same."

I moved further around the room, as red stickers were affixed to the photographs. I was attracting glances, I knew that, and also a covert intense scrutiny that made me twitch an imaginary tail, walk insouciant as Mrs Thrale.

"And who might you be?" said a voice. I turned to see Jake, no doubt dispatched across the void of the room, a starry messenger. I gazed at him through the red wine in my glass.

"Who might I be? Why, I might be the Vampire Envoy to Faeryland," I said, in an accent neutral, with a just a hint of mittel-European.

I spoke not loudly, but distinctly, to carry. At the words the young man beside me, who was dressed like a young Oscar Wilde, slopped his glass, stared like a yokel. Barry, who had circulated to within hearing distance, glanced up alertly. He recognized me now, but gave no sign, except that his gaze grew even shrewder.

To look astounded is deeply uncool, Jake would know that. He covered with that high, mocking laugh from Temple Mead.

"Well, you certainly look the part. What is that necklace?"

"It might be dragon's blood. Touch it."

He had long fingers, spatulate as a lizard's. They touched one bead, and the usual reaction I got from Chez's gift—to the coldness, the spongy softness—provoked a quick recoil. He swallowed, glanced back at Edytha.

I read it: quarry here! Well, three could play that game.

"And what brings a Vampire ambassador to provincial little Bristol?" he said. "Surely you're slumming. Or hunting, perhaps?"

"If you say so." (Neutrally)

Just then someone tapped a microphone, initiating the launch. Jake sidled back to Edytha, and Barry inserted himself beside me. All attention was on the launcher, some local rock star, so nobody remarked our whispers.

"You didn't speak like that before. You sounded Antipodean, from across the ditch, but with something else mixed in."

I merely shrugged, as if to say: I can talk how I like, if people believe it.

"Nor were you dolled up like something from Chez's novels. Even to the cat's eyes. At first I could only recognize you by the silhouette. Not many women—" and he hesitated "—have shoulders like yours. You're more than Chez's PA, I thought that when I met you. Now I get an idea of how much."

I met his gaze, unblinking.

"Who or what are you?"

Funny, Chez had asked me that once, in the limo back from a fan gathering when I had played Ruvenor to the hilt, and with great enjoyment. I hadn't answered then, and saw no reason to do so now.

"Well, whatever you're doing, good luck! You'll need it with those two."

He slipped away, after playing his own card of ambiguity. Did he mean complicity before the fact? I thought. No, a statement that he would not intervene, nor blab. Well, he had form in that area. Had he not behaved with discretion when one of his best antiquarian customers, an Afro-American historian of slavery, had in a moment of jetlag signed a credit slip in his shop with her famous pseudonym, as if forgetting that she was not at a fan gathering? Barry's reaction had merely been to smile. And then he had torn up the slip, and brought the copies of the Shadow series out from the Dark Fantasy section, for Chez to sign, and thus increase their value.

• • •

Early next morning I was unrecognizable to the gathering in the bookshop, face scrubbed clean, grey marl sportswear, as I jogged out the physical knots tied during from the long, immobile hours in the archive or over the laptop. My feet led me down the riverside, nearing the tall ships, the actual *Great Britain*, the replica *Matthew*, which had carried the Cabots to the New World. No slaving vessels, which had happened in between. But by the waterside was evidence of a different slavery: a syringe, the butt of a roach, lollypop vodka cans. I jogged further, towards a knot of activity: police, staring down at a water-logged mass, the hood waving like weeds around the waxy face. A senior cop, older and more authoritative, neared the quayside, gave one cursory glance down, nodded. The corpse bobbed back, a non-response.

"Yep, that's Mayo Jimmy."

A whirr behind me, a kid on a bike, curious. After the good look, he paled, wobbled in his wheely tracks. I grabbed him before he went into the water too.

"Well caught," said the cop, turning away. As he did, I clocked his namebadge: Sylvester, and stored it for future reference.

The wheels of the bike, now lying on the ground, sped towards stillness, as the boy in my arms started to tremble uncontrollably. I edged him around, facing away from the water.

"Here, head between your knees, otherwise you'll pass out."

He gulped, then spoke, in a near-whimper: "Do they always look like that, like the blood's gone outa them?"

"Oh kid, they can look a lot worse." Cops are sanguine about such matters, and so am I. We stood there in tableau, me hoping he wouldn't vomit onto my trainers. Gulls swooped by, the uninterested cops did their duty and the boy slowly revived. Revive, to live again, as the body in the water would not.

• • •

Ever since the soiree at the bookshop I had deliberated how much further to take the game I had started there. I admit it, I was getting bored in Bristol town. Finally I retrieved the card Jake had pressed on me, with, handwritten on the back: "We're looking for stories." I texted him, initiating an exchange that culminated in a rendezvous, time and place. At witching hour, but late, to keep them waiting, anticipating, hungry, I donned my dress-up guise and set out. Destination: a chi-chi rental space in the arts precinct, with the blazon of Jake's film company, comprising precisely one person. He hadn't exactly been a fixture at the mini-film fests lately, to judge from his website. And his flow of films had dried up, funny about that. Being an assistant/lover/servant to the likes of Edytha would leave little spare energy, I guessed.

The half-door to this former industrial site was open, showing Jake sitting on a crate, shoulders slumped. At the sight of me he brightened, with almost a spring in his step as he led me into the inner room, which held lights, cameras, and Edytha, talking into a cellphone. A computer screen showed images of a black face, framed with pink dreads, and dusted with streaks of glitter.

From the speakers softly came her words:

" . . . course I sees the dead people . . . "

Edytha looked up, and with her free hand shut down the computer as if swatting a fly. She continued her business, the details of a literary appointment in Cardiff, while Jake fussed with backdrops, settling on a lurid fluorescent green, Finished, Jake behind his camera, Edytha and I perched on stools, the interview began, the story they wanted from me.

"The last time I came to Bristol, I rode in behind the canvas wings of a slave-vessel, near two hundred years ago . . . "

It was cold out of the heat of the lamps. Jake wore half mittens, Edytha sharp black gloves, gesturing occasionally to match her incisive little questions.

"And you were actually walking on the harbour water? That's not something I've ever heard of before. Not that I'm"—disdainfully—"an expert in popular folklore."

Not so long ago, I too had been curious too at this novelty, and asked Chez. She had only laughed: "The subconscious is a strange beast. I don't know where that came from! Wishful thinking?"

Now I gazed at Edytha and lied through my persona: "Folklore is only what *we* want you to believe."

Much later: "And you don't eat, at all? Except . . . "

"In Mundus, mortal-land, there are rules of engagement for us Envoys. The same as in Fay-land, our cousins. Consenting adults only."

"People consent to that?"

"Mundanes, you humans, consent to much worse in the brothels of Bristol, and in your private bedrooms." I waved a hand, airily. "In any case we have groupies, like any rock star, willing and eager."

"They aren't afraid of becoming . . . like you?"

"They'd want nothing more. But we only turn those who are like us. True hunters of the night." I looked into the darkness of those shades. "We are like certain species of snakes, who store their venom deep, in a gland behind a fang seldom engaged. Unless in the deepest of passion, when like will to like."

I smiled at her, as conspiratorial as a wink.

If, say in a Bristol nightclub, I had approached a likely Goth, spun this line, they would have recognized it immediately, and joined in the role-play. If they were really serious, we could have ended up in some student bedsit, where after some drug-taking, a razor blade would have emerged, and I would have been expected to sup, as part of the sex act. These two held themselves above such lowly things as Sanguinarians, being pop culture ignoramuses. Now they were trying hard to conceal their gobsmackedness, and in the case of Jake, failing completely. Under these circumstances it was very hard not to lay on the act with a trowel. Safest was to stick to Chez's script, it was fresh in the memory.

I left around moonset, with the promise to meet again, for another session. No date, no time settled, and not if I could help it. Did I really want to spend time with a couple of people it might have seemed fun to hoax, but otherwise would have totally avoided? Well before I had finished spinning my fantastical web to them, I had begun to weary of the game. Worse, it seemed as if that weariness had crept into the marrow of my bones, numbing, dulling, even despairing. I felt as grey as that first sight I had of Bristol, the walking dead of Temple Mead.

Crossing a main street, I was so lost within mine own tired thoughts, that the lights of an approaching, rumbling truck could not even distract me from becoming a near fatality. The horn blared, I leapt maybe eight feet in the air onto the pavement, and fell to my knees, shaking at the closeness of the miss.

From the truck window had blared a blast of Motown. Chez was fond of vintage soul, and I recognized it: the Marvellettes' "The Hunter Gets Captured by the Game'.

"You said it," I muttered in the general direction of the truck. A near miss, indeed. My hand had grazed the edge of the pavement, and I rasped it over the rough stone again and again. Pain sharpens the senses, and when the stone finally showed red, I raised my hand to my mouth, a self-tasting. Salt and slightly sour, the savour of my own life. Now I rose, and slightly limping, made my way back to my hotel, licking my wound as I went.

*The False.* Psychic vampires, not blood-suckers, but thieves of life nonetheless, taking sustenance from those around them. And all the more deadly for not being as readily perceived. Bitter enemies for such as Ruvenor, even if he/she might possibly have sown the seed for them, 200 years ago, during some forgettable mating in Mundus-land. The False never arise spontaneously, an act of miscegenation has to occur, to produce such bastard offspring of the real vampires, and the inhabitants of Mundus-land. Our dire foes, our children.

Some were subtle, almost imperceptible, so as to pass unnoticed and perpetuate themselves. They might wither all those around them, but not sufficiently to attract *our* attention. If detected, though, they had to be dealt with, and as soon as possible. Like a wild tom cat mating with a felis domesticus queen, where the male will return and slaughter its own newborn kits, less they dilute his strain. Here the hatred came not from any perceived notion of racial purity, for in Vampire-land all shades of skin consorted. No—the sheer horror of the effect, the psychic draining.

Now I had experienced it, I knew that I had to act, to thwart the False conclusively, for ever. But there were rules, a system of checks and balances, to prevent any actions in Mundus-land from having repercussions elsewhere. The worlds of humans and inhumans intertwine in strange ways, I knew that. Enjoyable though it might be to copy the wild cat, to crunch Edytha's lily-white neck in my jaws, a simple act of murder was not the solution. Rather the punishment had to involve some reciprocity, suit the crime. The ideal revenge was to deprive False of power, yet keep them alive, hungering, yet cut off from their victims. Once they had psychically fed; and now they would psychically starve.

To do so would be tricky. Edytha gained power and prestige from her practice of writing, her thievery of others' lives. She might not term herself vampiric, but she knew the effect she had on others and enjoyed it. It was something she would not give up willingly. I had to stop her, but how?

Stumbling through the urban darkness, the pain from my hand keeping me alert, but only just, was not the best place to plan a cold act of vengeance. The experience was still too raw, too new, too shocking. It made me shudder, how I had so willingly filled a False's trap. In a moment of boredom, I had set out to hoax two jaded sophisticates, a bit of idle but malign mischief. Instead they had weakened, and nearly killed me.

The thought made me so angry again I spat, sending a gobbet of red across the pavement and down into an open drain. I should have been alerted by the obvious signs of weariness, the death-in-life that was the invariable gift of the False. As Ruvenor I could have believed myself immune to them; but now I knew that notion to be wrong, a phantasy.

It meant I had to conclude the game I had started, but with the stakes lifted, made personal, a matter of urgency. To proceed, though, would involve devious means, continuing indirectly. Any drama, any confrontation, could merely fuel Edytha's fictions. A very powerful False was here.

•  •  •

I stayed in bed most of that day, drifting in and out of sleep, recovering. Finally, as dusk approached I roused myself sufficiently to open up the laptop. The more information I had on Edytha, the more I could be forearmed against her. A bit of googling on the Internet located the controversy surrounding *Girlschool*, and its real-life equivalent. The photographs showed a confection of beautifully cut stone and groomed lawns, where sported in their hockey gear the elite of the local young lasses and ladies. In the online prospectus for the school staff were listed, with qualifications, and positions: there were no pictures but the only Diana listed was a Senior housemistress for the boarders.

The school had been founded over 200 years ago, by a local philanthropist, friends with the notable poets of the day, and with connections to anti-slavery circles. Given Chez's interests, and impeccable ivy-league affiliations, it would be easy enough to fabricate a reason why I should consult the school archives. Chez had a cartoon on her home office noticeboard: Research Cat says Wikipedia not acceptable source! The cat's eyes were slitted, and its ears back: Mrs Thrale's general reaction to me. Needless to say, its source was the Internet.

After hours spent myself in the archives, I knew that there was no substitute for hard copy, indelible ink on paper. But when an information jungle exists, rich with the electronic traces of an over-scrutinised, over-scrutinising populace, why not hunt there? So I dived in, to find schoolgirl blogs, prefect's Facebook pages, and, unexpectedly the visual images of Diana's time at university BA (Cardiff) M. Phil (Oxon). Shy smiles, upward glances through her lashes, just like her more famous namesake. She had never been the life of the party, but she had the glow of youth. Now, in the recent images, she looked grey—but not as bad as Mayo Jimmy. I judged she had got off lightly, the False not at full potency yet.

She might never recover all her innate strength, but in the School she had a niche, a den in which to lick her wounds, slowly recover. Unlike Jimmy and the other extreme lives chronicled in the second book, the denizens of the streets, junkies unmissed, and quickly forgotten by the police and the social welfare agencies.

And, I thought, it was now up to me to prevent any third book, where the devastation could well be total.

At that, I recalled the glittery face on the screen, so abruptly terminated by Edytha. It nagged at me, enough that I finally got up and began, very slowly, to get dressed. I needed energy, I needed some illicit drugs. And in finding them, I could pursue a trail of my own.

Outside, the darkness fell, and the night creatures stirred, ready to emerge into the mist-damp rising from the river. I went from club to club, and into Seedyland. Money changed hands, and so did information. Finally near dawn, in an abandoned building, soon to be torn down by the development juggernaut, I found her, dirty and forlorn, her stockings ripped, her tutu draggled and dripping sequins. She was coiled up in a corner, as still as if she was dead. When I touched her I felt the blood still flow, a trace of warmth. But her face had gone grey, under her glitter, and her eyes took a long time to open.

Slowly and deliberately, I rolled a roach, lit and offered it. She sucked greedily.

"You wanna?" she said, revived a little.

I shook my head. "Not that. Just pretend I'm your fairy godparent . . . "

"You don' look like any Welfare I ever seen . . . "

She struggled to rise; I offered her my arm, and she stood shakily.

"I'm the Welfare from the dark side," I said.

She accepted that without comment: it fitted into her narrow world.

"You really see dead people?" I asked conversationally, as we took tentative, then stronger steps across the trash-strewn floor. Her eyes opened properly for the first time.

"Course not! I said that for the wiz, din' I?" She smiled, showing uneven, broken teeth. "Cheap trade, huh? But they musta got some really bad shit. I been feeling like death ever since. Jimmy, he warned me, don't go near 'em without a crucifix . . . "

"It didn't do him any good. He's dead."

She began to cry, soft little moans of grief, as we crossed the threshold, the open doorway into the moist river air. But she was reviving, she no longer needed my support—just like the kid on the dockside.

"They's bad people, I knew that . . . "

I wore the cat contacts, hidden behind shades as opaque as Edytha's. Now, as we passed under a streetlight, I lifted them, and for good measure, bared my teeth.

"And you'll die like Jimmy, unless you get out of Bristol while you still can."

Her mouth opened in a soundless scream, and she ran away down the cobbles, her tutu shaking with each step. I waited until the sound of her stilettoed footsteps had faded into the general noisy dark, before turning back for the trudge to my hotel. No doubt about it, I'd scared somebody badly this night, and all for the good, too.

The rules of reciprocity were strict: if you intend to take a life, then a life should be saved, to preserve the balance between the worlds.

• • •

I never forget anything potentially useful, so I had taken mental notes of Edytha's cellphone conversation. In it was gold: later that week, she and Jake would take the Cardiff train to tape an appearance with BBC Wales. After a dutiful, if yawning day at the archives, a night of restless, fitful sleep, I dressed even more incognita than usual. One of the contacts I had made in my night of searching Bristol's underworld had some unexpected but useful information, for a price. As a consequence, I took a bus across the Clifton suspense bridge, my destination a dainty Georgian residence, restored tastefully. Here was the False's lair.

Jake might have been a youth worker, in touch with the wild side, as he thought, but he lived in a house into which it was remarkably easy to break and enter. Inside their ground-floor apartment, I investigated the evidence of a "something" life, among the intellectual arts elite. It seemed an odd, even cheerless existence. The kitchen was apparently hardly used, for it was full of film equipment. Nor did it appear they convivially entertained. The living room, the biggest and best, was a surgically tidy study, dedicated to Edytha. Her prizes, her promotional photographs, her presentation copies were the major decorations, with centre stage a computer console. Framed above it in elaborate calligraphy was a quotation:

"The pencil is conscious of a delightful facility in drawing the griffin—the longer the claws, and the larger the wings the better, but that marvelous facility which we mistook for genius is apt to mistake us when we want to draw a real unexaggerated lion."

George Eliot

"In real life," I recalled Chez saying, "Mary Ann Evans. But she was quite wrong. Writing what is in front of our noses is easy, and if it's the trash cans, then it's also dull, of no interest to anyone else. But if you want to write a griffin, drag it from the imagination and make it flex its claws and wings on the page, so that the reader sees it too . . . then that's tough. Why do you think I get stuck, commission visual aids?"

Sad, in the tabloid sense of a put-down, it seemed that Jake and Edytha did not even sleep together: in one corner of the study a lacquered Japanese screen concealed a single bed, and a chest of black designer wear. The only other sizeable room was Jake's domain, absolute clutter dominated by another computer console, and a fold-down couch, which this morning had its satin doona and single pillow strewn with dirty washing, almost entirely black Levis and film-festival t-shirts.

I returned to the study, its order easier to explore. A filing cabinet revealed serried lines of folders, collections of reviews and correspondence. A negative review, I could see, had elicited a flurry of letters between prestigious editors and authors, with Edytha covertly orchestrating a response like a military manoeuvre. Interesting, but not useful for me.

Atop the in-tray was a letter from the editor of a name literary magazine, dated the day after the award:

"I know you said you don't write to order, but if you have any of your usual coruscating, surgical brilliance on the go, finish it soon, because Salman stuffed us up, the tardy sod, and if we're going to print for an Easter release . . . "

I nodded, getting an inkling now of the mischief I could create.

Home computers seldom have passwords, and it was easy to access the recent files, the work in progress. They comprised a series of abortive starts, with subjects perhaps suffering from extreme mental states, but not articulate about them. "Tutu" was a case in point. Most recent, and labeled "Our Vamp', was the interview, transcribed. It was accurate, but with the beginnings of narrative shaping, also Edytha's observation of yours truly.

I recalled Chez again, fuelled by Zinfandel as we sat on her balcony in a warm sea-breeze, taking a break from computer-work: "I know what the lit-crit types do, to preserve their privileges, their territory. They put the Shadow series down for not being realist, as if literature were still at the level of nineteenth-century portraiture. But the I-am-a-Camera schtick just isn't true. Even the dirtiest social realist can't resist twisting their mere opinion into a better story, to flatter the watcher but not the watched. And their condescension shows."

It did. They quoted me accurately, a note-perfect transcription. But their Interview with a Vampire was now framed with the suggestion that beneath my surface glamour I was a sad, Home Counties transsexual. Adding to the insult was the notion that I still lived with my oblivious, Hyacinth Bucket mother. I should have felt murderous; but instead sank into Edytha's ergonomic chair, much too small for me, as the debilitating languor of the interview night briefly returned. Such was the power of this False. Helping Chez with Ruvenor, demonstrating martial arts moves, had felt nothing like the body-and-soul exhaustion gifted by Edytha.

I leave nothing unprepared, so I had the remainder of the drugs with me, a stimulant which worked blessedly fast. Recovered once more, I fell to further searching. The wastepaper bin held a padded envelope, with inside a note, on publisher's letterhead: "Hope you like the new jacket!"

My head turned, to the shelves, the trophies of editions, translations. Edytha hadn't published enough for alphabetical order, she was strictly chronological. Thus last and anti-least was the re-jacketed *Thief of Lives,* showing a hooded, running man, under his arm a Prada bag, with big cat-patterning. Inside, the photo credit read: Jake Miniver.

And with that the game became *totally* personal. Perhaps it had always been so, lurking at the edge of my consciousness. From Temple Mead onwards I had been drawn to these two as if on invisible strings, and they to me. The Bristolians of several centuries ago, deeply religious folk, would have termed it proof of Providence. Or Nemesis, Goddess of Fate, and also Justice, the unofficial patron deity of Thieftakers. Chez again, in fictional mode: "Nothing is ever really accidental, especially for those who cross between worlds, and their descendants, the bastard False. Casual encounters, repeated, are even in Mundus a patterning, a sign of when worlds intertwine."

I carefully replaced the book. A photo might be enough for me, but others would need harder evidence. It took me hours of searching through the visual files on Jake's computer. Once Edytha had finished with a subject, it seemed, the visual record of interview was erased: to stop Jake double-dipping, competing in the fame stakes? Only in a directory labeled "Offcuts' did I find my proof: hand-held video footage, showing Mayo Jimmy in a city alley, a concealed vantage point. I had only seen him dead, or near-dead before, and here he looked, if not entirely healthy, then cocky and vibrant, pulsing with life.

"How do you know which ones to pick?" came Edytha's voice, to the left of the image. The camera panned sideways, lingered on her longingly, then returned to Jimmy, rocking in his sneakers, ready for action.

"S'easy," Jimmy said in that easy Irish drawl. "C'mon, you point, I'll tellya why."

Shots of passers-by, walking past.

"Umn, the girl in purple?"

"Too athletic. That's a runner's calves."

"The old lady?"

"Nah, no pickings on her."

"Well, what about that one? The octoroon."

"Huh?"

"The short, fat American tourist. She's got a Prada bag, I can tell."

"You wannit?"

"Too vulgar for me."

"Go for it anyway?"

"Yes, yes, go for it, go!"

Away he loped, towards a figure whom even in the distance I recognized. Jake's viewpoint camera followed the action, covertly filming. Recorded was the snatch, she fighting as if her life depended on it, dragged by the bag's straps along the pavement, and into the road, where Jimmy shook her free and into the path of a car. I heard the screech of brakes, the thump as fender met the fragile bones of a post-menopausal woman. Result: concussion, compound wrist fractures, the worst of fates for an author with a novel's deadline looming.

The trauma had been almost too much for Chez. Months of healing, physically and mentally, had followed, and even then she had been too fearful to leave her house without security. She could not write the incident out; she could barely talk about it. Even the publishers only knew the fact of a mugging, without elaboration. I had caught a detail here and there, disconnected words, buried memories rising to the surface of consciousness. But I knew enough to be certain of what was recorded here, in this forgotten but crucial file.

Ruvenor would have killed Mayo Jimmy for that offence, I thought. Then I blinked: *Ruvenor did.* In my head clearly now was the image of the lanky figure, hunched on a bollard in the dull moonlight. The easy push from behind, the splash in the water. Ruvenor leaping after, to finish off the job. Like a water-skimmer on the surface, stepping on the head as it broke water, once, twice, and then no more, just the bubbles of air breaking water, to finally stop, the water flat and still under my booted feet.

I breathed out myself, savouring that moment. Then I returned to Edytha's study, to her bookcase. Sitting down again, this time on her narrow bed, I read through the section with Jimmy carefully. The scene on the tape, despite its inherent drama, unsurprisingly did not appear in *Thief of Lives*. Literary embedding at the scene of a crime was going a little too far, even for Edytha. I closed the book, replaced it, kept on searching. There were few good pickings left for me now, but nonetheless everything that might be remotely useful I copied onto my trusty datakey. Such as Jake as amateur pornographer, participant even, with some definitely underage subjects, probably from his days as a youth worker. Then, letting my control happily slip, I messed up the apartment, as if junkie burglars had come visiting. That done, I emerged again, out of the life of letters, and into the welcome cold, dank, twilight.

Invoking Art can excuse much, from selfishness to sacrilege. But it is useless when you have been duped, and thus appear a proper simpleton. I had already laid the groundwork to make this pair look very silly. But would I let my temper get the better of me and do much worse?

• • •

Back in my hotel room, I opened my laptop, sent an e-message to Chez that had everything to do with the archives and nothing with how I had spent the day. Then, gazing out into the glare of dazzle and dark, the night city, I just sat and thought for a while, a rare luxury in my lives.

Here was the gist of what I had told Edytha and Jake, what they had taken for delusional verisimilitude. In fact, I had been quoting, from a text I knew very well, had proofread at Chez's behest. As I became more involved with her and her projects, I had come to know it almost by heart. Although the original was far away from me, back in California, with the only other copies at the publishers as it entered its last crucial phase, the fine-tuning, the publicity plan, I could reconstruct it from memory. Even when recycled by Edytha the words would be instantly recognizable to the keen Shadows fan, and beyond that, of interest to lawyers:

I first came to Bristol nigh two hundred years ago, following a slaver up the harbour with the high tide, but not too close, for the stench of rotting flesh followed her like a curse, a floating sepulcher however white her sails. Up the Avon we glided, into a forest of masts between city streets, a centre of trade to rival London's: rum, sugar, livestock that happened to be human. Rich fare, you might think, for the likes of me, though the malnourishment, the palpable misery, were not for the fastidious. Rather, they were food for my prey, the dirty vultures. I had a pass into Mundus from the Fay, and instruction not to be too zealous in my Thieftaking, well not *excessively* this time. "Trouble seeks you like a filing to a magnet, or a maggot to a corpse," had been the farewell words from the border. "Try not to let it find you too often. And if you must throw a body into the harbour, remember that in this era it is tidal, and come the low tide, exposed on the mudflats will be your ill-deeds."

I created a new blank document, and thought for another luxurious while. Then my fingers started tapping the keyboard. I had typed page after page of the reconstructed section of *Shadowflower,* from Chez's dictation. The rhythms of her style had flowed through my ears and down into my busy hands. I could imitate her fiction game, though it was a clumsy forgery in comparison. Here goes:

This time, two hundred years on, the pretty sails had gone from the harbour, except as pleasure craft. It was a railway station where I disembarked, the tides human only. And instantly I knew the hunter's instinct, to follow the barely perceptible trail that the False leave, a psychic slime, had been correct. The dead alive, the drained of all spirit, walked all around me. I let my suitcase fall, and remaining true to my nondescript disguise, stopped, and threw my senses open. "Come!" I said. Among these walking wounded, who could lead me to the source of their miseries, their personal night? Come, I said, and in my mind's eye saw a woman, a schoolmistress, look up from class, hand to her birthmark. A hooded figure, searching through a bin outside, stopped, and took a shambling step into the concourse.

No, perhaps start at the beginning. I might have gained a familiarity with Chez's mock-1700s diction but that style was a tough call. Once upon a time, then, and more plainly.

Once upon a time, a full professor at an American university, an expert in the slave trade, turned away from the misery of centuries past, and found herself writing an imaginary world, where vampire envoys visited Faeryland. The whole was remarkably like the eighteenth century transformed, with Fays and even demons having their lands, territories, in the place of Britain, France and the independent American colonies. Finding it a joy, she wrote an entire novel, sold it under a pseudonym, and began a new and covert career. Via the medium of fantasy, she re-examined a lost time, still relevant, and with its parallels obvious several centuries onwards. And soon she had garnered far more readers than for her academic work. Including, perhaps, readers from another world? Finding themselves fictionalized a little too close to their eerie truth, did they fear another manifestation of the False, their deadly enemy?

So it happened that an envoy, a jobbing occasional assassin, was dispatched with a cover, insinuating herself into the life of the professor, disguised as a discreetly expensive security guard/PA. Someone whose performance was that they came from another world, the remote, alien Antipodes, and before that, but never spoken of, except with discreet hints, the sort of experiences that take a person from the Stateless to the very well-armoured, at a physical and psychological level. Ally might have been Amira once, denizen of Refugeeland, before she acquired a cv that the most macho of mercenaries would envy. A cv that when examined closely, contained rather too many acts of revenge in it, delivered coldly.

The result? A blank screen of a person, who was whatever you projected onto her, depending on circumstance, but most importantly was *heartless*. Until Chez. What she found in the exclusive, gated Californian community was a woman traumatized from a mugging that had not only broken bones, but had stolen from her what was dear as life: the concluding quarter of a novel, mentally planned, but never written down. In her concussion, she could not recall it, and it nagged at her soul.

I stood, unable to sit still and type any longer, and began to pace agitatedly around the room. Not for me to recollect in tranquility, contemplation instead stirred action. Because in expression *is* control; even if at the time I had lost control myself, let my guard down. I had sworn it would never happen, but it *did*, and so easily, too. One day I was the hired help or mercenary, the next I had crossed some psychic border, my loyalties truly engaged.

"Read the darn ms!" Chez had thrown at me one day. "What do *you* think happened next?" And so, the serval snoozing beside her on the sofa, I read the pages of printout. Because I knew about hand to hand combat, the sort of thing an academic generally could only imagine, I corrected, here and there. She listened, then asked me to open the laptop (big cat patterning), call up the novel's file, and type for her, as she revised, recast the offending scenes, her voice stumbling at first, then beginning to flow. And so the security guard became amanuensis and editor, helping reconstruct the missing text, even allowing herself to be used as a model. Permission was asked, and granted, that was the important difference, for Chez was no False.

In the process metamorphosis occurred. It had affected both of us as the novel *Shadowflower* became stronger, its protagonist Ruvenor a swashbuckling, complex, ambiguous creation, part cruel, part compassionate. The publisher had doubled the initial print run, and had even negotiated a publicity point, the revelation of Chez's identity, now she was safely out of academe. The release date was set, appropriately witchy: Walpurgis night. In mundane terms, May day, two weeks after a late Easter, when an arty magazine would appear, its lead story bearing an eerie relationship to *Shadowflower,* actually quoting it as fact, the deadly-serious observation of a pop-culture psychopathology.

How very odd the coincidence, except that the two authors had coincided briefly in the same city. One had lost a Prada bag, with among its personal artifacts, records of a life, a datakey, with serval patterning. The publishers had been worried sick about that, in case the thief or fence realized its worth, even incomplete. Most likely it had been simply thrown into the Avon, unlike the bag, which would have been circulating on the black market immediately. What I had set up would suggest differently, especially with the video file of Mayo Jimmy in action. Uploaded onto You Tube, along with Jake's porn, journalists, not to mention Detective-Sergeant Sylvester, would be very interested. A lawsuit might even result: plagiarism, literary theft, the greatest crime in the world of books.

I would not summon Edytha in life, but in fiction, the rules were suspended.

She stands on the beige hotel carpet, fidgeting like a missy.

"But it's only popular literature," she protests.

"So was Shakespeare, once," I reply. "And who are you to anticipate history's verdict, though you strive ever so hard?"

Her jaw sticks out. "I am Art," she declaims.

"In a voyeur's dress."

"Collateral damage is the price of Art." That jaw, set hard.

"You have worse than vampire ethics," I reply.

And so I banish her, with the last word.

Then I happily banished Edytha twice, deleting the encounter. So very easy, to shape someone else as you want them, to be your subject. But I was no False, to suck the life force out of them in the process. Not was I even a writer—only a hireling, with not even the craft of an apprentice. I deleted all of my authoring game, closed the laptop, and headed out to the gym.

• • •

At week's end I had checked all the archival references from Chez's final academic work, she said, her ultimate words on the Bristol slave trade. I emailed the book files back to her, with a simple note: Goodbye. To the gated community, built overlooking the

Bay, to a little lady with an exotic cat and an even more exotic imagination. A hired help should be a professional first, and not have more than a mercenary involvement with their employer, even when their interests happened to coincide. Chez had anticipated as much, before I departed.

"Good luck with your future Ruvenoring. If not, then I hope helping me didn't mess with your head too much."

I had given her an in-character bow, deep, with a flourish, in response—and left. As I would leave Bristol behind, with the ramifications of my game playing out slowly but inevitably. To defeat the False, you must use the weapons to hand, and here they were words and film. Well, better that than letting my temper loose like the hounds of hell, baying for blood. When I had sat on the stool before the gravemould backdrop, while Edytha asked her probing, biting questions, I could have very easily reached out and broken her neck. Jake's too, all recorded on camera, an original snuff movie for Detective-Sergeant Sylvester to solve. But that would have disturbed the balance between the worlds: better and crueler was a long, slow humiliation, the loss of audience, praise, identity.

One thing I still had to do: say goodbye to bookstore Barry. I had to linger, because he had an enthusiastic customer, and an antiquarian book on the counter.

"First editions of Frances Trollope don't come on the market often, so you're lucky. Best Bristol novelist—"

"What about Diana Wynne-Jones?"

A nod, an emendation. "—of the nineteenth century, even if she didn't live here long. I've got a customer in Australia who quotes her as a sig file. And it's a great one: "Of course I use my acquaintance in my novels, but I always mince them up finely first, for you would not recognize the pig in the sausage.'"

"Couldn't agree more," said the customer, a fiftyish woman with a plait and a long cloak. "Such bad manners, to express an opinion in art that you'd never dare say to the face. So passive-aggressive."

"Like a leech," added Barry.

"Like the False," I interjected.

The customer grinned. "You read the Shadow series too! I love the concept of a psychic vampire, whom the real vampires hunt down. Sounds like various people I've met. And run silently screaming away from!"

Barry looked at me, deciding to surf the moment, without comment.

"Can't stop," I said. "Just saying farewell."

"Well, have a good trip to . . . wherever." From his tone a whole host of destinations had suggested themselves. "If you see the lovely lady before I do, pass on my regards. Tell her I can't wait for . . . May day."

"You'll enjoy it," I said. In more ways than one.

That done, I went on an extended walk, farewell to Bristol town. What it might be in another two hundred years was unknown, but with luck the people would look more energized and less dejected. Destroying one False's power was a start.

By the river a music festival was setting up, sound systems thumping, more of the local trip-hop fare, good regional produce. My boots moved, and I began to dance. Seeking company, I threw my senses open briefly, sending out a call: "Come!" Soon I had a motley crowd happily dancing with me: schoolkids, rudies and wide boys (girls as well). And if we overflowed onto the surface of the river, like water-skimmers, simply because we *could*, then who would care? In this moment the worlds coincided, and the physical rules of Mundus were momentarily suspended. Joy in life, the opposite of death.

•••••••••••

# WINDS OF NZAMBI

## DAVID CONYERS AND DAVID KERNOT

Mukunzo pushed away the corpse. The Bakongo warrior chained to him had been dead for three days. When slavers came to throw the rotten, bloated body overboard, he ignored them, instead focused on the stench of waste, and sweat, in the Portuguese caravel's crowded men's hold. He suspected the women's quarters would be no different, and his heart went out to his favourite, Kimpa.

The retching Portuguese sailor pulled at him as he severed the corpse's hand with a clean slash of his large machete. He discarded the bloodless hand at Mukunzo's feet as a reminder. Several prisoners were ordered to drag the corpse up on deck and throw it overboard. Mukunzo tried to join the men, if only for a few moments of fresh air and to stretch his limbs again, but the sailor waved him down. The unkempt white-skinned man deliberately selected four scrawny men from a distant village to do his bidding, their dark skin covered in sores. Weak men had no thoughts for mutiny.

Tormented that he couldn't stretch, Mukunzo urinated on himself, again, and sat in his own excrement. The corpse *had* made him gag almost constantly and many times he'd attempted to snap the dead arm to be free of the maggot-ridden body. But the swollen flesh held together.

Despite many weeks in near perpetual darkness, Mukunzo was still a threat, and so was chained in twos, like some of the other strong Bakongo warriors to make it harder for them to fight back. Gradually losing his physique, he pushed every opportunity to clamber to the surface of the wooden caravel away from the disgusting bowels of the ship with the sun on his face, training with the other warriors. The same conviction had cost the life of the man he had been chained to, but they needed to be ready. They had to train and prepare for the time to escape, to retaliate for what had been done to them. They were not slaves, no matter what the Portuguese said.

Now that the manacle was freed of the corpse, the sailor looked for another man to chain to Mukunzo. Oddly, one of his fellow Bakongo warriors volunteered. Mukunzo recognized his brother Bunseki.

"Still alive I see," Mukunzo said in their native tongue that the Portuguese could not understand as his brother was chained to him. The brand shaped like an arrowhead still festered above Bunseki's left bicep. Mukunzo's identical brand fared little better.

"It's your fault we're here, brother. You shouldn't have made the deal with the Vumbi. You led them to our village."

Mukunzo nodded, feeling his shame. The Vumbi were the Kongo peoples' ancestral ghosts whose skin became the colour of chalk when they died. Portuguese skin was the same colour, and his people had come to fear them by association. He remembered the slave coffle, endless weeks trekking on cut feet through the jungle, shackled together with stripped wooden branches around their necks, hands tied with thick rope. In the heat, with a lack of water and food, many had died. Families had been separated into men, boys, women and children. As to the fate of his three wives and fifteen children, Mukunzo did not know. He couldn't be sure any of them were in the womens' hold, but he had to hope, especially Kimpa, his youngest wife and with his child growing inside her. His brother was one of the few male survivors from his village still with him.

"The Portuguese promised me we'd not be taken, brother, if we told them where our enemies lived."

"Then you were a fool, Mukunzo. They took us all."

Mukunzo bit down on his anger. The truth hurt, and he turned and stared through a tiny crack in the hull, watching the hot air ripple over the lapping waves. He couldn't see land, but home couldn't be far away. How big was the water anyway? It couldn't be much wider than the greatest of all waterways, the Congo. All they had to do was reach shore, and they'd be free again. A short swim at most, then the jungle would hide them again.

"We should revolt, Bunseki. There are hundreds of us. The Portuguese slavers would be lucky to have fifty men amongst their number. Plus, we are warriors."

Bunseki laughed, and his decaying muscles tightened down his neck as he tugged at his chains. He spat at his brother. "You're a chimpanzee's ass, and twice the fool I just said you were. You forget; they have guns, my brother."

• • •

Mukunzo was beyond bored, after many days, staring in the cramped dark. That morning he had listened to the Portuguese above argue, at times wailing like madmen and firing their weapons. Since then it had remained quiet. Now, when he clambered onto the wooden deck, muscles shrunken and much weaker than the previous time, he looked around carefully. The Portuguese only exercised him enough to keep him alive, so he wanted to give them no reason to punish him.

Topside it didn't feel any cooler. The wind had died. Lifeless sails hung limp over the decks. He looked for shore and felt empty in his stomach over the clear horizon. Perhaps there was mist obscuring the jungle. He hoped so because this water was too wide to be real.

The burning sun created beads of sweat that ran down his dark skin. It ran underneath his shackles and felt like hot raking coals as it touched his raw open wounds. With the exception of the other slaves who exercised mindlessly and took in the fresh air above decks, nothing stirred. The quiet was unexpected and Mukunzo couldn't fathom why.

He looked to the Portuguese. Many cast their eyes downwards, or lumbered in circles without energy. They seemed frightened. Of what, Mukunzi couldn't say.

Bunseki, still chained to him, also looked thinner since their capture. His brother dragged his feet, letting Mukunzo do the hard work cleaning the decks. He could understand Mukunzo's reluctance to help, and sucked in the warm still air, relieved to be out from the cramped and filthy hull. He wondered, not for the first time, if he had enough of his warriors' strength to fight. A time would come when he could take his revenge on these pathetic Portuguese who had tricked him into trusting them.

"I tell you Bunseki," he whispered with venom on his tongue, "we should fight. Better to die a man than wallow as an animal."

Bunseki sneered, pointed to the ashen skinned sailors. "I'd rather wait than take my chances with them. This land of Brazil where we are headed; how far from home can it be? When we get there we disappear into the jungle, walk as long as it takes and be home again in weeks at most."

"You know the Portuguese are cannibals. It is a fact that their cheeses are our brains. Their wines our blood. Our burnt bones become their gunpowder. We may not make it to Brazil. We may still become their food."

"No brother, they want us alive," said Bunseki. "A slave is a slave, be they for an African or Portuguese master, their purpose is to work. They will not kill us, not after bringing us this far. Now is not the time to fight."

"And if we become weak in the meantime?"

Bunseki shrugged. "As I said, perhaps we'll never need to fight before we reach this Brazil and we can just slip away instead."

Mukunzo spat on the deck, watched its moisture evaporate quickly in the heat. "Then you are already an animal, brother, if you are willing to give into them so quickly. Don't you want a chance to have a family?"

"A family?" His brother snorted. "When was I ever going to take a wife of my own, or have a son? You saw to that as chief, demanding all the pretty girls of age as your own, and so I've lost nothing."

Mukunzo shook his head, over his brother's pettiness, now, when they had lost everything. "Are you jealous? Aren't we beyond that now? We have a real fight worth fighting, rather than each other."

Bunseki's shackles tightened as he shuffled forward, refusing to catch Mukunzo's eye. Mukunzo didn't care. Now that they had been more mobile, after so many weeks of inactivity, the pain in his bound ankles made him cry out.

He glanced at the Portuguese sailor leaning on his musket. The sailor took no interest in the Bakongo men, which was unusual compared to their recent behaviour. Rather, the sailor kept looking over his shoulder at the horizon. Then, the man's eyes bulged and his mouth gapped.

Curious about the man's fear, Mukunzo turned and looked out across the water. A shape approached, black as a shadow, yet shimmering like the wavering mirage of an animal. It had wings, sometimes he counted two, sometimes three, four or even five on occasions, and they seemed to blend and separate without form. Thick ropey tendrils thrashed from its underbelly, skimming the water, and talons grew from its wings. Several heads moved within a mass of confused body parts, and while it flew towards them, wings silently beat at the stifling air.

Someone fired a shot. It kept coming; as if it hadn't been hit. Mukunzo looked back to the deck. The Portuguese who had fired lowered his musket and reloaded. Others raised their weapons to shoot wildly. Many of the Portuguese wailed as though they were women, and sobbed or soiled themselves, like they knew what was coming and feared it. Mukunzo felt their panic, sensed their terror. He understood now what they had been shooting at earlier.

The creature grew, black like the night, and larger than Mukunzo had first estimated, the length of six men or more from wingtip to the next. It shifted as if made of multiple shadows, flicking in front and behind its central, blackened mass. It held a collision course for their vessel.

Some of the Portuguese sobbed louder, others hid along the gunwales. One fell overboard. Another ran screaming below deck. Mukunzo felt his stomach knot, wondering what could terrify the Portuguese so.

The second-in-command stepped forward, trembling. He cried a warning to the crew, signalled for them to get below. He yelled in Portuguese, words lost to Mukunzo, but his meaning was all too clear. It was obvious that they had seen the winged creature before and were powerless against it.

Its shadow passed overhead and Mukunzo felt the chill of death. For a long moment he forgot how to breathe. The silent creature tore through the sailors, shredding their flesh leaving only bloody stumps of legs still standing in their boots on the sticky red decks. Smouldering muskets fell with clunking noises, some discharging, now that the hands that once held them had vanished.

It swooped his way. Mukunzo ducked and his heart skipped several beats. When the shadow had passed he stood and looked to the other side of the caravel. The silent creature flew from them as fast as it had approached. It had taken five of their captors in a single taloned sweep, all of them white men.

Mukunzo felt fingers grip his shoulder. He turned to see Bunseki holding him tightly. His brother was grinning, staring at the vanishing monstrosity.

"We're doomed brother," Mukunzo's words tasted like the coldness of death, as if even speaking of this creature had corrupted them. "We're all dead men. It is only a matter of time." He shuddered and it felt as though a cold hand of death brushed against him.

Together they watched the creature grow smaller on the far horizon until it vanished altogether. It had feasted enough today, but Mukunzo knew it was only a matter of time before it returned.

"We're not doomed brother," responded Bunseki calmly, almost excitedly. "That was Nzambi Mpungu. He is our god. He has come to save us."

"That was not Nzambi."

His younger sibling scoffed. "It has to be. What else could it be?"

"I don't know. Something evil. . . "

• • •

Bunseki grew restless. Since the attack, the ship had drifted aimlessly, partly from the lack of wind, and also because of the revenge Nzambi Mpungu had taken on their captors, the filthy Portuguese Mundele.

In their boredom and fear, their captors quickly found new ways to torture them, for they blamed the Congolese for the monstrous attacking beast. They hung two warriors at a time over the side by their chains. The Bakongo they chose were the weakest among them, those who would not survive the remainder of their journey to Brazil. They had no value. The sailors completely submerged one slave in the water, while the second was allowed to struggle to keep him afloat, but eventually they both became food for the giant fish the sailors called bull sharks.

Bunseki's stomach churned the first time he heard the crunch of a man's leg. The proud Bakongo paddled in his shackles, and struggled to stay afloat, but his leg was ripped off, leaving a slick of blood over the water's surface. It brought more bull sharks to the surface. Unable to ignore the man's scream, Bunseki shuddered.

The water foamed from the frenzied attack. Soon silent, the warrior's insides floated on the surface before being devoured as the second Bakongo's screams ceased.

The Portuguese cheered when the second man's remains vanished beneath the foaming red waters, and then when everything settled down, they did it again. It lasted all through the day, and Bunseki thought the Portuguese all mad. Perhaps they were attempting to appease Nzambi Mpungu with their own sacrifices, but did they not understand that the creature they faced was a protector only of *his own* people, the Bakongo?

With dozens of cruel deaths behind them, the Portuguese looked tired and pale. They filled themselves with strong smelling liquid called rum until they could barely walk. Meanwhile, under orders, Bunseki and his brothers removed body parts and gore from the chains and threw them into the water, but nothing could remove the stench of death from the ship.

Bunseki understood the Portuguese were savages. They deserved the same kind of death. He didn't care what Mukunzo thought, it *had* been Nzambi Mpungu. Their god tried to save them, and he would return and destroy these filthy Portuguese traitors. What did Mukunzo know? He was soft from all his wives, and he had taken Kimpa as his sixth, the girl Bunseki loved, when he could have left her untouched for him to take. It would not have done his brother any harm to show his younger sibling compassion. And now Kimpa was probably dead at the hands of these Portuguese, or worse, she had been turned into a breeding machine for the half-castes who would become the Mundele's prostitutes.

Until the arrival of Nzambi Mpungu, as a giant, shapeless, black bird, Bunseki had believed there was little hope left. But now there was salvation for every Bakongo on the ship. They would be able to return to land soon enough, even if they had to pull the vessel back to shore, walking on the bodies of Portuguese sailors who would soon be dead.

He needed to talk to the Bakongo warriors, rally them, convince them of the true way ahead—they did not need this "New World", and the Vumbi would be ready when they were called. He turned to his brother, noticing the wasted muscles, realising that his power over the other men would have reduced too. And yet he needed his brother one more time for a task that would save them all. He needed to unite the Bakongo so that together, they could lead a revolution against the Portuguese and kill them once and for all. Waiting until they arrived at Brazil was no longer the right choice.

"Mukunzo", he whispered, "we need to trust in Nzambi's winged creature."

"No," demanded Mukunzo, with a light in his eyes that surprised Bunseki.

"Mukunzo, are you soft in the head? This is a sign. We will soon be freed."

"It makes no difference brother. We are already dead. Have you not seen? We will either die at the hands of the Portuguese, as food for the bull sharks, or as food for that monstrous winged creature."

"I disagree," said Bunseki with a fire that burned in his stomach. "Nzambi will come if we ask. He serves us." Ignoring the disbelief in his brother, he closed his eyes and banged out a slow chant on the wooden floor. "*Naaa-zammm-biii. . . Naaa-zammm-biii. . .*" He would have his way. He would lead his people as the new chief, even if his brother would not. Finally, he had found his own moment. He had so long dreamed of commanding.

"You are a fool brother," said Mukunzo.

Bunseki refused to listen and continued chanting. Soon a fever grew amongst the people. The mantra developed a life of its own, and it rippled through the ship. Like a pledge, it was picked up by every Bakongo, passing from one chained warrior to another, to every corner of the ship. The Portuguese yelled at them to stop but they were unable to carry through with their threats, sickened as they were by their rum.

As day became night the chanting continued, and a call to the soul of the founder, Nzambi, he who would rescue them all. Bunseki grew confident in his new found courage because all the Bakongo would see it was he who had first called out to their god. He felt his power grow when the Portuguese retreated to their own area of the ship and left them alone. He realised it was a refreshing change; that the balance of power was shifting. They needed wind to move, he had seen that much in the way the Portuguese commanded their caravel, but Nzambi had taken that gift from them. This was a night where the Bakongo ruled supreme, powered by Nzambi's gift of courage.

The smile on Bunseki's face became one of vexed anticipation, and he ignored Mukunzo's indifference. As brothers they were so close. Yet, even chained they could not have been so far apart.

In the still hour before dawn, Bunseki, his voice hoarse from chanting, felt certain that Nzambi would come and save them, and an ever-growing sense of confidence flowed though him.

The water lapping against the side of their vessel stilled, went quiet. Then it churned and became a torrent in reply. "Mukunzo come," he demanded as he stood and pulled insistently at his brother's chains. "It is time." He was filled with excitement, but he had to all but drag Mukunzo up onto the top deck.

He heard the Portuguese cry out as the shape approached, black like a shadow, yet shimmering like an animal through the invisible heat of a crackling fire. The thick ropey tendrils that thrashed from its underbelly had grown, as if the dead Portuguese had fed its size. Skimming across the water flying silently towards their caravel, it beat at the hot, stifled air. The creature approached, sent by their god, and Bunseki breathed deep with contentment.

There was no breeze to carry the ship forward. Exhausted from lack of sleep after a full night of listening to the Bakongo chanting, Bunseki noticed many Portuguese out on the top deck. They stood at one end, looking on in disbelief, against the backdrop of sunrise. Nzambi Mpungu approached, and Bunseki raised his hand in greeting.

Nzambi flew high above the ship, and Bunseki, opened himself up to his god, waiting for his shackles to vanish, longing to be free once more.

Only Nzambi's wind remained, hot like the parched sun on his face and devoid of any sense of life. It left him bewildered. Surely the god would sense his intentions and do something worthy, something godlike so that Bunseki could fight the Portuguese Mundele.

"Satisfied brother?" asked Mukunzo. "Get down, before you are next to die."

Confused, Bunseki joined his brother on the deck. A musket shot rang out, and then another, and another until the volley was deafening. But there was only one thought on his mind. How was it that Nzambi had ignored him?

• • •

Mukunzo glanced behind and saw the giant monster of a bird turn slowly against a cloudless blood-red sky, as it had done before. It aligned itself with the ship. He pulled at their shackles. "Move towards the edge, Bunseki."

More Portuguese clambered onto the deck, each with a loaded musket. They raised their weapons and fired into the sky.

"Get below, my fellow Bakongo," Mukunzo cried to the warriors, remembering that he had once been a chief of warriors in his homeland and it had always been his destiny to lead, despite their hopeless predicament. "If you can't get below, lay upon the deck."

Yet many of his people ignored him and instead turned to Bunseki, who did nothing but stare, bewildered at his god's false messenger.

The bird-like creature circled, in tighter and tighter arcs, descending a little more each time until it hopped onto the deck. From what might have been one of its many heads, a tangle of grotesque black eyes, like seedpods amidst a mesh of thrashing tongues, glared at them. Then with the swooping motion of its wings, its razor sharp talons like the branches of a dying tree caught up two sailors, ripping the huddled men into clumps of flesh. Blood and chunks of organs and flesh spilled over the deck. A warrior was next to fall.

The Portuguese retaliated by firing repeatedly. Bullets penetrated the creature's black skin; some passing straight through, others tearing flesh, but it had no discernable effect and it kept coming. One giant black eye took in crew and men, stopping at Mukunzo. A cold glare passed him over and he broke into a sweat as it snatched another sailor next to him, ripping open his head to display the pink-grey matter inside. It stood so close to Mukunzo that he could smell its foul oily breath as it gorged on the man's decapitation, sucking on the organ within. It tossed the remains at Mukunzo's feet and he held his breath from the stench.

Bunseki grabbed Mukunzo's arm, but couldn't look away from the creature.

It raised its main head high, threw it back with an upward stare and cried out, a sweet lilting caress. It was compelling. Mukunzo's feet took on life, and he stood. He shuffled towards the blood-soaked bird. Bunseki at his side.

Mukunzo covered his ears, the pain too great, and the compulsion stopped. Seeing the wild expression still in his brother's face, he moved to protect him. "Bunseki, cover your ears." He turned to his warriors. "Cover your ears, men."

Bunseki ignored him. The Portuguese couldn't understand their native Kikongo.

More Portuguese climbed out onto the top deck and walked towards the creature.

"Come, brother." Then Bunseki gestured to a sailor who fell to the ground in front of them, as if they were friends. The sailor did as he was bid, and together they all shuffled over to the man whose brains had been eaten. A Bakongo warrior then fell and joined the dead, and Mukunzo's heart sank. A reminder that the creature did not just favour Bakongo after all.

Mukunzo wrapped cloth torn from the dead sailor's uniform over his ears and held Bunseki back. The creature's calls were muffled, and his voice sounded hollow as he yelled, "Bunseki, wait. You are under a spell." He pulled at his brother's shackles until he stopped. Mukunzo then searched for a key to their shackles, and found one on the fallen sailor's belt. The cloth only offered partial protection, and he felt himself drawn to the creature again, so he called out to Bunseki. "Hold me," he yelled letting go of his ears. He fought the creature's compulsive call as he struggled with Bunseki's shackles, and his brother held him as best as he could with his ears covered.

The creature swept across the deck, grabbing sailors and gutting them with its sharp claws. Others it decapitated, slurping on the marrow of their brain.

When Bunseki was free Mukunzo covered his own ears. "Brother, we must warn our people. Pass the word—cover your ears, find the keys and escape our shackles." Seeing a group of sailors walking to the creature, he said, "Look: destroy the filthy Portuguese Mundele while we have a chance."

"Can't you see brother, Nzambi is already doing that."

Before Mukunzo could respond, Bunseki ran off, and Mukunzo struggled with his shackles. Then he stood and retrieved a musket. He fired on as many Portuguese as he could, stopping only to reload after each shot and unshackle his men.

Slaves grabbed muskets and joined him.

Then the lilting song ceased. Satiated, the creature hopped over to the side of the boat. Spreading its wings, it launched off the bow, climbing into the air with a half-chewed body that fell into the water. The sea below bubbled with rage as the giant toothed bull sharks feasted.

Mukunzo took hope as he examined the bloodied mess of bodies strewn over the deck. Most of the dead were of their captors, but not all. If the creature was truly Nzambi, it would not have slaughtered their own. "Brother," he yelled when he reached Bunseki, "go down and gather the remaining pale-skinned sailors, we will need them to return us home."

Encouraged, Bunseki led the proud warriors, now armed with muskets and knives, below deck. But as it turned out, there was little resistance from the Portuguese, and what few there were had been killed quickly, or thrown overboard. Later when the rage of his people had been satisfied with bloodletting, alone, Mukunzo searched the ship for survivors, but it was futile. Bunseki had ignored his request. Numb, he was unsure what to do.

Returning to the deck where the air was fresh, Mukunzo saw that the slaves rushed out about, and rejoiced. Mukunzo stood back and watched them drink the white men's potions of rum. They gorged on salted pork and hard yellow blocks the Portuguese called cheese. Mukunzo tried some. It might have been made of Bakongo brains, but still tasted delicious after such a prolonged period of near starvation.

Later, when Bunseki stopped dancing in victory, he walked over to Mukunzo who stood away from the celebrations, and smiled. "Not happy with your new freedom, brother?"

Mukunzo shook his head, and glanced around at the still air. "The creature killed Bakongo as often as it killed our enemy."

Bunseki snorted as he puffed his chest proudly, as if it were he who was chief of the people now. Perhaps he was. All eyes seemed to turn to him now when direction was sought. "And yet we are victorious, my brother. Soon the edge of the Congo River will reveal itself, and we can swim to shore, and be free warriors again."

Mukunzo scanned the horizon, and saw nothing. The water was still, not flowing as it should. Mukunzo took a bucket and tied a rope to it, dropped it into the water and pulled it out again quickly.

When he tried to drink its contents he spat out the corrupted taste just as quickly.

"What is wrong Mukunzo?"

"Taste it, the water carries sickness." He couldn't get the taste of salt from his mouth. "I do not think we are on the Congo anymore."

"Then where are we?"

Mukunzo's laughed, but without humour and threw down the bucket, spilling the corrupted water across the wooden deck. "We are lost brother, utterly and totally lost. We cannot get home."

"You are wrong, and I was right to believe in Nzambi. It was my faith that allowed us to do this. We are free men again. There are women on board, perhaps not our tribe, but a wife is a wife, however she be taken. With warriors and women, we can build our village again, and rule free men."

"Perhaps you are right, brother," replied Mukunzo, who carried no strength in his conviction. For the briefest of moments he wanted to believe his brother's impossible dream, "But how do we escape this place? How do we make this caravel move? Do you, or anyone of us, know how to sail as these Portuguese once did?"

"I hear your spite. You think I should have kept them alive?" He paused. "They deserved to die."

"Who is going to turn the ship around now? How do we get home without wind in our sails? We are no less dead unshackled than we were before the creature found us."

"I would rather die proud and free, than rotting in a prison."

Mukunzo nodded. In that, Bunseki was correct, but hope of returning to their homelands seemed lost. They would die out here, when the stored water ran out and the food spent, but Mukunzo didn't think it would come to that. The winged creature, the foe Bunseki so desperately wished to believe was their saviour, would come for them again, before they could hope for an ordinary death.

While the Bakongo danced and celebrated, he watched the empty blue skies. They were devoid of the winged creature, for the moment. He knew it would return when it was hungry again, and take them all.

• • •

In the days that followed, Bunseki watched in disbelief as his control over the newly forged tribe of warriors and childbearing women deteriorated. They ate what food the Portuguese had kept in their hull, but they had been few compared to the chained Bakongo. The men drank the rum until they too fell down with the same illness that inflicted their captors. Many became sick.

No one returned below decks to the stench and memories of imprisonment. Despite Mukunzo's protests, his tribesman ripped down the sails for shelter above deck. Against his wishes, men still able took women, filling them with their seed. He was powerless to stop them, supported as they were by some of the stronger men. And when the barrelled water was nearly empty, they turned against each other, first with fists, and then blades, and finally muskets. Several died. Their corpses thrown overboard to appease the bull sharks, but also to be remove the ever-lingering stench of death. And still the listless sea and sky offered no wind or means to carry them to the banks of the impossibly large river.

Late in the hot, humid day, Bunseki found his brother collapsed towards the rear of the caravel. Gone were the proud muscles, the life in his eyes. He looked a man whose soul was ready to depart this world.

"Mukunzo, no one will listen to me."

His brother grunted.

Bunseki sat, feeling pain inside. His love, Kimpa, had not been among the freed women. "Nzambi will save us!" he said eventually with less conviction.

"Keep saying that brother. Eventually you might believe it."

"But I have saved us. We are free."

Though Mukunzo barely moved, bitter laughter filled the air. It hurt Bunseki. Mukunzo had belittled and disrespected Bunseki as his chief. Bunseki took a step towards his pitiful brother. Willpower alone stopped him from beating obedience into him.

"Is this freedom?" Mukunzo snarled. "I would rather have remained a Portuguese slave than endure this."

"You will not speak to your chief in such a tone."

"So you are chief now?"

"You won't do it."

"You always wanted power, brother, but you never understood the responsibilities of a chief."

"How dare you speak that way to me!"

"I'll speak however I choose. A chief would save us, can you?"

Bunseki went to say more, but noticed Mukunzo's expression change as he looked behind Bunseki. Could Nzambi have returned?

Bunseki turned and faced a gathering of the largest and strongest of the men. Ones he had been unable to control. Their stares were like the coals of fire, and gritted teeth showed between blistered, snarling lips.

"There is no food," said one.

"Nzambi will save us," Bunseki said loudly, standing and taking a step back from their approaches.

"The water is all but gone."

"Nzambi has shown us once that we are chosen. He will do so again."

"Many of us are sick, with witchcraft upon our bellies," said one man.

"And there is no wind to power the belly of this wooden beast," shouted another.

Bunseki shuddered. For the first time since their escape, he was afraid, a fear stemming from the slow, threatening advances of the Bakongo. Many brandished machetes, broken rum flagons and Portuguese knives. "As chief, and speaker to the Winds of Nzambi, you know we will be saved." But, there was less conviction in his words.

"I don't believe you!"

"The god no longer talks to you!"

"You are a liar!"

They shouted and raised their sharpened weapons.

"You have nothing to give!" howled the biggest of the men.

A machete flashed in the heat of the burning sun, ready to cut his head off.

"Wait!" Bunseki cried. He knew they were right. But he had one hope left to appease these men. It would cost him, yet he was willing to pay that price if he must. "Wait, and trust in me one last time."

"Why should we?" asked the warrior with the raised machete.

"Because one amongst us does not believe. Nzambi is not satisfied." He turned to his brother, whose eyes were white with fear. "Until he is dealt with, there can be no rest from the gods."

Mukunzo clambered to his feet, stepping back to distance himself.

Bunseki smiled triumphant. There was nowhere that his weak brother could hide on this caravel.

• • •

Bakongo tied Mukunzo to the mast of the drifting wreck of a vessel, and left him for hours. His skin bled, raw from the cutting rope against his flesh. His mouth was as dry as pebbles. He no longer sweated. And the unbearable pounding in his head was the worst pain of all. He wished now only to die, to find peace, his wives and his children in the next world. He wanted to forget he had ever laid eyes upon the Vumbi, the Portuguese slavers, and the creature, whatever it was.

While he suffered all day and that evening, his brother led the surviving Bakongo on a new fevered chant, much like the previous one. He heard them calling: "*Naaa-zammm-biii. . . Naaa-zammm-biii. . .* "

He watched Bunseki dance, chant, and guzzle the last of the fresh water, all the while holding a knife tight in his hand. The moonlight reflected against its polished metal surface.

"I'll thank you brother," Mukunzo said through a rasping throat, barely forming words, "when you find courage to plunge that blade into my gut. A good death is all I can hope for."

"You will save us all, brother, when the time is right, when Nzambi Mpungu returns to bless us for your sacrifice. But not before."

Mukunzo should have argued, but he no longer cared, nor had strength to find the words. He only hoped the winged creature of nightmares would come soon, so that oblivion would take him. He hoped above everything that it would be his brother that took him, for he could image no worse terror than to be killed by that creature he could not understand. It seemed wrong, fearing that perhaps it would be a death that would never end, if the blacked winged creature took him.

"Stab me now. Call him with my blood."

Bunseki's response was disappointing. "You wish for that, don't you Mukunzo. You wish for a quick end now? But I love you my brother. Nzambi must be appeased when he arrives, not before."

"And where did you get that idea, *little brother*?" he taunted, reminding him who was greater in the true linage of Bakongo chiefdom.

Bunseki raised the blade, and almost took the bait.

Then a screech across the still waters hurt their ears. Bunseki covered his ears. Mukunzo couldn't, and felt drawn to the will of the dark, unforgiving monster. Convinced that the creature was summoned from a spirit realm that was worse than any nightmare, he tried to resist. But still he called out to the creature to take him.

"Brother, gut me now." Finally he found strength to plead, his raspy voice barely a forced whisper.

But Buseki turned to the still waters with the rest of his men and their new wives. As the tangled mass of shadows approached, changing shape more quickly than a thunderous cloud and even more violent in temperament, he grew more concerned.

Mukunzo pleaded. "Now brother! End it for me, please!"

Bunseki turned his gaze from the creature, a monster none of them ever could comprehend, and plunged the knife deep into Mukunzo's belly, twisting and turning until the organs inside began to spill forth amongst the gush of blood.

Pain surged through Mukunzo like nothing he had ever imagined, but he welcomed it. He rode the agony for darkness and oblivion to take him, and yet he remained conscious. He had to see more.

The creature swooped, scooped up several Bakongo warriors and women, stuffing their shredded body parts into its many gorging mouths, and flew on. Blood sprayed like rain, drenching Mukunzo and Bunseki. Men and women screamed, and Mukunzo saw fear in Bunseki's eyes. Finally, the same fear he had seen in the Portuguese.

"I don't understand?" said his brother, dropping the knife. "Where are my gifts? Where is Nzambi's gift to his newest king?"

Then Mukunzo saw the realisation appear in his brother's eyes.

"Mukunzo, what have I done brother?"

Mukunzo managed to smile. "I forgive you brother. Take yourself." Mukunzo felt darkness approach. The pain lessened as a sense of nothing replaced it. "Use the knife, before the creature claims you."

But his brother didn't seem to hear him. "How?" He spoke instead to the night, watched the winged monster return, and gorge again.

The creature turned to face them, and Mukunzo could smell the foul, rotting breath. It stepped closer to Bunseki, hungry mouths snapping and then leaned in.

"I thought I did the right thing. Nzambi Mpungu was supposed to save us . . . "

Mukunzo might have told his brother that it never was their god, that it was only a creature in search of food, but there was no time. For him or Bunseki. As chunks of his brother's organs fell around him, light faded. Sounds vanished. The rasping taste of stone disappeared from his mouth. The pain went away altogether.

And then . . . nothing.

• • • • • • • • • • •

# WOLF NIGHT

## MARGARET MAHY

I

"Babe!" shouted Ivan

"Hey, Babe!" I called back.

And we stood there on the corner, laughing as if the air around us was suddenly electric with jokes, surprised to be meeting again after so much time had flowed by . . . well, maybe, after all, not so very much, for as we stood there, the time between then and now was collapsing in on itself. Nearly three years? It seemed like a moment; it seemed like a lifetime. For I had been away, and, though I had come home again it hadn't seemed like home. I had been twisted into a different shape, and the twisting had hurt me. Well, it was still hurting. Me and my lot—my mum and dad, that is—had set off to travel the world, and then, over in the UK, my father had died. That was the beginning of the twist. I still felt, every morning, as if part of me was dying with him.

"We'll get over this," my mother had said bravely, trying to comfort me, and when it came to getting over things, she certainly set me a good example, because, a year later, she fell in love and married again. Travelling the world can change lives, but not many lives are as changed in the same way as mine. I felt that change back then—I still felt it going on every minute of the day. I missed my father dreadfully, and I did not like my mother's new husband . . . Brook Ardrey. His mere name was like a bad spell to me.

Anyhow my mother and I were home now, and she'd brought her new guy with her (like some sort of souvenir). And here I was, rediscovering this lost place which I had once known by heart. It was both old and new to me. After all, I'd set out as one person and come home as another, which was fine. We all have to change. But over the last few days I'd felt the town all around me, nudging me, always nudging me, reminding me of the girl I'd been back then. These days I mostly existed in a sort of dream, but today I was out on my own, rediscovering places where Dad and I had once been, staring up at suddenly familiar street names (same corner, same cafe on the corner), gazing out towards the sea (same celebrated view), and, suddenly, there he was, materialising as if he were a necessary part of the landscape. Ivan! Babe!

As we laughed we were probably both exploring our memories . . . well, I know I was exploring mine. (How long ago?) Then the clock on the war memorial, set in its circle of grass and garden where two main roads crossed at the centre of town, celebrated our reunion by chiming six times. We both heard it, but we were too busy staring at each other as if, in our different ways, we had discovered lost treasure, and laughing because the discovery was amazing, though of course our very amazement was ridiculous too.

"Where have you been?" I asked as if he had been travelling. "It's ages since . . . "

"I'm in a share house out by the university," said Ivan, nodding over his right shoulder. "Still here. I've just shifted about ten streets to the north carrying a lot of books with me, bogging myself down with study and a part-time job, which keeps me flat out busy." (I wasn't surprised. Kids these days often work long hours and his family weren't all that well-to-do.) "Economics, history, philosophy—weighty stuff! Pins you in one place. So, what about you?"

"I've been flitting about the globe. Lots of different places," I told him. "This way and that,"—(zigzagging my hand)—"Me and my Mum. We've done a lot of creative drifting over the last year or so. Done a lot of changing . . . too much . . . but never mind all that just now."

"Your dad died didn't he," Ivan said. "Word got around. I— well, I was sorry to hear it. Sorry . . . he was a really good guy, your dad was." I could tell he meant it. I think he could see, looking at me, just what a blow it had been to me . . . what a blow it still was, whenever I thought about it.

"Yes, and then my mother married again," I said. "Brook, his name is. Brook Ardrey."

I tried to sound casual about it, but I couldn't keep that twist I mentioned—that inside twist that always made me feel like such a different person, that twist that always hurt me—out of my voice. My words came out all stiff. "We've had to come back for a bit. My gran's been ill. She was needle-sharp when we left but now she's, well, she's sort of slumped. Thinks she's living about fifty years ago."

Ivan looked solemn.

"Sorry to hear it, Babe" he said. "Bad news, even if it did bring you home." Then he added, "I suppose standing still will be a bit of a shock . . . I mean, after all that creative drifting?"

"I've been drifting all right, but it sounds as if you've been burrowing," I said, changing the subject a little. "Philosophy and all that powerful stuff. Deep burrowing! Do you get paid much for philosophy? Does your place cost you much?"

"A bit too much," he said. "Would you like to come in with us? We've definitely got room for one more."

Actually it seemed like a good idea to me because—but a sharp wind blew in on us. I was distracted. "Hey!" I said. "Is that café still down the hill a bit? Have you got time for a cup of coffee?"

"Great," said Ivan. "Let's go, Babe!"

Ten minutes later there we were in that same old café (not the scruffy one down at the bottom of our hill, but the stylish one half-way up, just where the really big houses took over), and we were studying each other, smiling through the faint steam rising from the coffee cups . . . a steam that made us both seem just a little ghostly.

But I was so pleased to see him. My homecoming, even as part of a broken family, was suddenly made real. I somehow imagined my ears pricking up like a dog's ears, anxious to hear every single word Ivan might have to say. Town gossip would tie me into home once more.

"So! Here we are again," Ivan was exclaiming. "I can hardly believe it."

"It's true though," I told him. "It ain't no dream, Babe!"

We both laughed, not so much because anything was funny, but taking pleasure in rediscovered friendship.

Back a few years we'd wound up in the same class. I was a bit ahead of myself and Ivan was lagging behind, which seems funny now, because he was a great reader even then. But we began telling one another about stories we were reading, and swapping the books that imprisoned those stories in cages of words. When we talked about stories we had both read, it was almost like people at a party, clinking glasses and wishing one another adventures and good fortune.

"You lot still rich?" Ivan was asking. "Or have you spent it all travelling?"

"Well, I suppose we're rich enough," I admitted. "But everything's changed. I've never got used to Brook Ardrey."

"So what's wrong with him?" asked Ivan. "I mean, I know he couldn't—could never be like your dad, but is he nasty to you or what?"

Now that was a big question. I didn't mind him asking, but I didn't quite know the answer myself.

"He's good looking," I said, hearing my voice sounding slow and cautious. "And he's sort of masterful, like a hero in a Mills and Boon book. I think my mother loves him being masterful. Anyhow, I get on well enough with him, but sometimes I still find him kind of creepy. I don't know. It might be just that he's so different from my dad. I mean, Brook *tries* hard—tries to move into the space Dad left, and take it all over, which is fair enough, I suppose, because Mum's invited him in—flung the door wide, wide, *wide*!" (I threw out my arms to illustrate.) "But he just *doesn't fit*. Never will! While he's saying something—something playful—to me, his face, his expression I mean, is—" (I heard myself hesitating) "I don't know what it is, but it's *not* playful, that's for sure. And since we've been home I see him looking at Grandma, frowning to himself as if . . . as if she were some kind of computer, and he had to work out a program on her. And sometimes he looks at me as if . . . "

But I had to stop telling him about my mother's new husband, mainly because I couldn't quite explain that look which always seemed so sinister to me. And I couldn't have said even that much to most people—well, I hadn't really said any of it to myself until then. But, even though Ivan didn't know my stepfather or my grandmother, he seemed to catch on to what I was trying to explain. He'd always been good at catching on to vague things and making sense of them . . . as if meanings were dancing around him like moths fluttering around a light, and he was sort of snatching them up as they went by, and then pinning them down in a way that made them real. He hadn't said much about my father dying, but there was something about his voice when he was saying how sorry he was that seemed truly sorry. I knew he meant it. But of course we'd both had a bit of practice at netting words and meanings. It had been our special, private game, I suppose. Apparently still was.

I think we began calling each other "Babe" back when I was about twelve and he was fourteen. It was because of some song at the time—one that we both liked—and as we walked home from school together, we had worked out a plan for capturing the words because once you have the words you have power over the song . . . you can sing it whenever you want to. I was supposed to memorise lines one, two and three. His job was to catch lines four, five and six. If we got a moment to ourselves next day we would sing the song to one another, fitting it together as best we could. "Hey there, Babe!" the second verse began, and soon we started calling one another "Babe'. It seemed a cool thing to be doing. "Hey there, Babe!" we would mutter to each other every morning in class, feeling sophisticated, but careful not to let other kids hear, just in case they started slinging off at us.

Well, in due course we left school the way everyone does, and life began swishing us round and sending us in different directions. I took a gap year, not quite sure just what I wanted to do. Once through my back door, family life took me over in a big way, what with Mum and Dad travelling and quarrelling, which they did back then. And anyhow they had never been impressed with Ivan. Our town was nearly a city, and there were levels in it, not just age levels either, and not just hills and plains. I mean, my lot had all that money lurking in our background, thanks to Gran, and Ivan's family were just getting by, struggling on the edge of everything. Right now, staring at him over the rim of the coffee cup, it was strange to think that someone from a family on the edge could be interested in something like philosophy. It sounded pretty profound. But I had no right to be surprised. Ivan had always been a reader and he had always liked playing tricky games with words, and the thoughts those words expressed.

2

It must be hard for most kids to lose a parent, to have a father or mother somehow tumble away, over and over, out of their lives. As for me, I felt a true piece of myself had died along with my father. Part of me had gone, and would never be part of me again. And even if you get a replacement it doesn't help much. Actually, it can seem as if some sort of treachery is at work. You can even feel a bit treacherous yourself for going along with it.

Brook, my mother's new husband (I can't really think of him as any sort of father), was kind enough to me—kind enough to everyone—and there were times when I even liked him, though always in that puzzled, careful way. Back then I couldn't work out why I felt so cautious about him, but I think I knew from the beginning that he wasn't driven by love. He was driven by a sort of calculation, and I felt that I was being assessed all the time. He was working me out in terms of profit or loss. Mum too! His assessment of Mum somehow ran beneath all the kindness he showed her, and it reduced her to a piece in some game he was playing. I felt she had become a bit less of a person than she had been . . . had become a voice babbling away in the background, loving me or loathing me according to Brook's instructions. I knew Brook felt I wasn't necessary, that I was some sort of leftover intruding into his well-regulated life with my mother. He was certainly mathematical about people, no doubt about it. I often caught him watching Mum and me as if we were numbers that he was trying to add up, and sometimes, when he was being particularly nice to me, or to my old gran (who lived, these days, in a special granny flat connected to our house), I got the strange feeling that he was playing a game of chess with us all, shifting us around on some secret board that only he could see . . . frowning over our places and trying to move us in ways that meant he would win whatever game was being played. Of course I couldn't help believing it must be something to do with money. Gran had all that money tucked away . . . invested, Gran would say in rather an impressive voice, which always made me imagine that her money (which could have been spinning out wild and free, and getting itself spent) was caught in a cage guarded by armed accountants.

"You should spend some of that money on yourself," I heard Brook say to Gran. "Live it up a bit—have a good time." (Just what I had been thinking funnily enough.)

"It's for my granddaughter," she told him. "Some day soon, when she wants to settle down and *marry*," she added, and it sounded as if she were locking an invisible gate on all her wild cash, and in a way on me too. A few years ago she had wanted me to get out into the world and have adventures, but after her stroke, the world alarmed her. These days she wanted me to marry someone reliable . . . wanted me to be looked after . . . to settle down . . . to hold still in the one place forever. Me!

Well, I thought Gran's accountants would need to guard her investments for a long time, because I still went along with her old ideas. I wanted to wander around, to visit a lot of places and have surprises and adventures before I even thought of settling down. Of course if I hadn't existed, then that money would have gone to some other relatives, probably my cousins in Canada. Of course she might have left a bit to my mother, which meant, these days, that it would go to Brook. I was sure Brook thought about that money a great deal, though I had no proof . . . I just felt I could read it as a sort of concentrated interest—a secret obsession—printed out in tiny letters somewhere behind his eyes, flashing on and off at times when he looked at me.

Anyhow, there we were, Ivan and I, bending towards each other across our coffees, gossiping on . . . gossiping on. It was astonishing how easy I felt with him, though we hadn't seen one another for such a long time.

"Another coffee?" he asked, which we both knew was just a way of stretching out our time together. Then he frowned. "Blast! No cash!"

"Me neither," I said. "Never mind. Come up to my place."

It felt so natural to invite him, and I think it felt natural for him to accept. Back a bit we'd sometimes gone to one another's places, even though we lived a long way apart. I knew his parents a little bit, and he knew my mother, though I wondered if he'd recognise her now bossy Brook had taken over. She'd become a bit of a shadow.

The outside air had been transformed by deepening twilight, and though we were walking up streets in a town we had once shared, and were sharing again, it seemed as if the world was mysteriously remaking itself around us. Gardens and front lawns seemed to be disguising something dark tucked in behind them. Familiar gateways suddenly looked as if they might lead to totally strange countries, none of which would have names. I saw a cat skimming across a lawn, and believed it might be a tiger in some Lilliput land. Suddenly, walking there with Ivan, I felt the world around us panting with fantasy. I don't know about him, but right then, up high on the town hills, I felt fantastic, as if I were the one changing the light in the sky, and ordering evening around. But evening can do that to you . . . change an ordinary world into something shifting and remarkable. I half enjoyed that twilit strangeness, even though it also made me a little cautious, rather as if the world might suddenly spring at me.

But at last we turned in at my gate, and ordinary life came bounding to meet us, jaws stretched wide to swallow me up again. We climbed the four steps to the verandah, then stepped across it to the back door, which opened just as I was about to open it myself. There was Brook—that new man of the house— waiting to welcome us, holding the door handle with one hand, extending the other as if he were guiding us in from a storm. My mother was doing what she did so often these days, hovering a little behind him, smiling a smile as much like Brook's own smile as she could make it, unconsciously copying his gestures of welcome.

"I'm glad you're home at last," she said to me. "Brook and I were worried about you." Her expression changed. "Goodness! Is that you Ivan?"

"Sure is," said Ivan.

"I asked him up for a cup of coffee," I explained. "We've both run out of money."

In the end there were five of us. Mum and Ivan and I sat at the table, and my grandmother, lured out of hiding, cuddled herself into a corner of the couch. Once she would have marched around telling everyone what to do, but those days were gone. Brook carried in coffee and biscuits on a tray—he's a wonderful man about the house. It could have been an easy-going, just-before-dinner sort of coffee . . . that's what I had had in mind . . . but for some reason I felt self-conscious, uneasy. Brook left most of the talking to Mum and Gran, who both asked Ivan what he was doing these days, both looking impressed when he mentioned university. But though he wasn't saying much, Brook watched us all intently, his eyes moving from me, to Ivan, then back to me and on to Gran. Once again, it was as if he were trying to nut out a problem, even though there was nothing to work out. After all, what was going on? A friend was visiting me, that was all. Big deal! A visiting friend was pretty normal, even though I hadn't had a chance to catch up with many friends since we'd been home.

"I'd better be getting along," said Ivan at last. "The crowd back at my place will think the Headloppers have got me."

The Headloppers were a gang—a dangerous gang—famous for howling like a pack of wolves as they skulked around the dark places of town. And they were suspected of murdering an old layabout, as well as a girl who had been walking home after her car broke down, but nothing had ever been proved against them. Ivan, frowning to himself, said, "Hey, is there a bank machine anywhere around here? I've run out of cash."

"There's one down the hill in the Woodlands Mall," said Brook. "I'll give you a lift down if you like."

"That's OK," Ivan said. "I can find my way. At least it's downhill from here."

"What about the Headloppers?" said Brook. "The bottom of this hill is real Headlopper territory. Let's be careful."

I was surprised Brook had offered Ivan a lift quite so quickly. It wasn't the sort of thing I'd have expected him to do. He turned towards me. "Come along with us," he suggested. "Have a Friday night walk on the wild side of town."

I was really taken aback. It wasn't like Brook to make such a kindly offer. And people making kindly offers don't usually wear such sharp expressions. Then our eyes met and a warm smile wiped almost all of the sharpness away. Even so, though his face smiled, his eyes remained cool and calculating, as if there were some secret riddle which he just had to answer—as if some plan were forming somewhere in behind them.

3

Wherever you go in cities like ours you find that rich people colonise the hills. After all , rich people like a view and they don't have to *walk* up those hills carrying their shopping, do they? Not if they don't want to. They just point their sleek, well-behaved cars upwards, and vrooom! There they are, high above the rest of the world, able to look out and over and down. Because, of course, once they get onto those hilltops they have wonderful views . . . the city itself, to begin with, then other hills, and sand and sea, if the city is on the coast. I was living in a hilltop home in a street that was never totally taken over by darkness. On fine nights at my house there were stars and sometimes a moon overhead (all very decorative and cheap to run), while down below lay a glittering network of streets pushing light upwards. Of course there were streetlights at our gates, and light shone from certain big windows of the houses around us across hedges and around garden trees, so what with our lights, the stars above and those other lights far below, being able to see at night was something we naturally took for granted. And in the daytime we could look out over a whole patchwork of roofs stitched together with roads, and then further on to the rolling farmland that embraced our particular city, and miles beyond that again to the mountains. I'd grown up with that view, and I suppose there were a lot of times when I didn't particularly notice it. It was there—just there—day after day after day. All the same, though the mountains were unchanging, their peaks, like a distant scribble of darker blue against the blue of the sky, seemed to hold secret significance; sometimes they seemed to be sending me a message I couldn't read. Afterwards I would think that perhaps the mountains had been saying, "Beware Babe! Keep out of the wild woods!"

Once upon a time our hill had been covered in trees. Once upon a time there had been acres of bush—ferns and trees tangled together—along the creek in the gully at the bottom of our hill. But when our town was becoming ambitious, stretching itself out and turning itself into a city, the trees had been felled to make way for yet more houses and shops, and those shops had certainly taken over. Nowadays, once you drove down from the gardens and lawns stretching themselves out over the hills, there wasn't a tree in sight, until you reached the town parks away to the south. For all that, the straggling suburb down below us, old and battered these days, was still called 'Woodlands'.

Woodlands was a hard part of town to enjoy, houses crowded together, crippled buildings holding each other up. And "Woodlands", well, it sounded all open and sunny, a place with groves of beautiful trees, and maybe it had been like that once upon a time. But no longer. Now there was nothing but those tumbling houses, tacky shops and tangled dangerous streets. Walls all mumbling with graffiti, corners alive with violent possibilities. Haunted, of course, by that gang the Headloppers . . . the wild wolves of Woodlands, suspected of two casual murders, though nothing had ever been proved. Anyhow Woodlands was the part of the city I was supposed to keep away from, though there were times we used to zoom down there to the supermarket . . . well, there are always times when you run out of something, and the Woodlands Mall supermarket was easily the closest to us. Besides, the Headloppers chose to be creatures of darkness. They were supposed to hang out in derelict buildings, or shadowy pub doorways, or side streets where the lighting had failed, ignoring the bright invitation of the mall, so we felt safe enough.

Anyhow Ivan and I followed Brook out to the car that had once been my father's, and he drove us down into Woodlands. He seemed to enjoy owning that sleek silver car, and turned it with a flourish into the car park at the back of the Woodlands Mall.

"The shops will be closing," he said, pointing to the back doors of the mall, "but you should be able to get to the money machines without any trouble. I'll meet you round at the front."

Ivan and I scrambled out of the car, and slid in through the back entrance.

Transformation. It was like leaving one world behind us and immediately finding ourselves in another . . . still a real world I suppose, yet somehow insubstantial. I felt, instantly, that I had stepped into a dream that was only partly mine. Something else— something vast and formless—was dreaming along with me, and the dream was springing to life, becoming something more than a dream, becoming something powerful that was able to take charge of everything it touched upon.

It wasn't a late night for shopping, so most of the mall shops were shutting—even that commanding supermarket was on the point of closing down. For all that the mall itself was lit up and there were still a few people walking about, the people seemed to me to be like phantoms. However, there, sure enough, in the heart of the mall, like islands of fantastic promise, were two money machines.

When I had previously come to that supermarket it had always been during the day when there were crowds of people around, which is no doubt why I found it so altered . . . so suddenly strange being there under the spell of night. It was a different place. The mall had become an echoing cave—a tunnel— a strange connection between the real world, left behind us in the car park, and an entirely different world—Woodlands, which had somehow suddenly became mythological. Usually there was some sort of music playing in the mall, but at this time of night it was silent. My shoes squeaked as if they were complaining about what I was putting them through.

"It's like a different world," said Ivan, which is more or less what I had been thinking. "We've walked into another dimension."

I nodded. "At any moment it's going to dissolve, and maybe we'll dissolve too. We'll become a pattern of atoms spinning in space."

"That's almost what we are anyway," said Ivan, looking around rather cautiously. "It's just that a time like this makes us think of what mysteries we are."

It was as if he were speaking the thoughts that ran through my mind, and yet I was a mystery, even to myself . . . such a different person from the one I had been . . . both self and a stranger to self.

The few people walking past us seemed to be moving dreamily as if they were going nowhere in particular, as if they were lost people vaguely searching for some unseen door that would open and allow them to escape. Unfamiliar and haunting echoes rang out in the air around us. A man marched by, striding boldly towards the car park, and for a moment his footsteps sounded to me like cloven hooves striking a floor of stone. Usually there were so many people weaving backwards and forwards that individual steps were lost in the general noise of the crowd, but at this time of night every small sound took on singular significance.

Ivan went up to one of the money machines and fed it his card. It hummed and clicked a little and then money slid out. I'd seen this happen often enough, but at this time of night, at this particular place and in the mood that was overtaking me, I felt that some sort of magic was involved in such obedience and generosity. Those machines seemed more than mere machines, they had become fantastic creatures, mythological beasts under a spell, forced to give up riches when a particular magic password was given, or a secret name uttered. This mood that had been haunting me ever since I came back home to a city alive with memories of my father. There was no actual ghost drifting at my elbow, changing the world as I looked out at it, but for all that I did feel a continual ghostly disturbance deep within myself. Ivan folded the money and put it into a thin brown wallet with his card, then slid the wallet into his jeans pocket.

"Right, let's get going," he said. "Your old man—I mean Brook—will be waiting for us."

"He's *not* my father," I said. "But we'd better hurry. He hates hanging around." Even so, I couldn't help pausing by a bookshop and checking the best sellers arranged in the windows.

"Come on!" said Ivan. "There's a second-hand bookshop a street or two down, and it's a lot more interesting than that one. Not that we've got time to look now. We'd better not keep him waiting."

It seemed to me that Ivan had picked up something odd about Brook, something that was making him anxious.

"Don't you reckon he had a funny expression on his face when he offered to bring us down here?" I said suddenly.

Ivan looked at me but just shrugged.

We came out of the mall, and at once Woodlands seemed to rush towards us . . . a hungry suburb, eager to swallow us up, eager to digest us. The Woodlands lights and sounds belonged to a different dimension again from those we had just left behind in the mall. I reminded myself sternly that they were simply the usual lights and noises that an impatient city makes, as it works its way into the night. Cars and a couple of buses were on the move, murmuring past. Traffic lights blinked monotonously. Just what one would expect. So why couldn't I shake the feeling that the ordinary city had been transformed into a mythical place, run according to different rules from the rules of daylight. Everyday reality had dissolved into some wild and unreliable state. It was crazy I know, but I suddenly believed that the street I stood on was haunted—haunted, perhaps, by the forest that had once possessed the land, dormant these days, sealed under concrete and tar but somehow still there. The shadows that bridged the street seemed tangled—the shadows of great trees rather than of buildings. I half-imagined we were setting out into the ominous forest of fairytale.

For some reason this was a sinister impression. Suddenly I longed to be safely home again—home where lights and shapes were dependable, where a car was a car shut up firmly in a garage and not one of a herd of swollen, hump-backed creatures undulating through the night. And none of the cars I could see looked silver, sleek or shining. There was no sign of Brook at all.

## 4

"He must have lost himself. He'll be here in a minute," said Ivan. I didn't know if he was comforting me or reassuring himself.

Anyhow we stood there waiting, while Woodlands shadows flowed and danced, sometimes curtseying to the lights that brought them into being, sometimes standing rigidly to attention. Brook did not appear.

I thought about him. It was easy to imagine—to suddenly imagine—that he was gambling on me . . . thrusting me into a dangerous world, hoping it would swallow me up. Perhaps seeing me with Ivan had reminded him that some day I might marry . . . that Granny's investments might move completely beyond his reach. Perhaps he was casting me down on a board where the wild forces of the world might sweep me away. I seemed to hear his voice saying, "I told them not to go there. I told them it would be dangerous." Who would contradict him, except Granny and my mother? And somehow I imagined that, though they might weep for me, they would both paper over any secret suspicions and remain silent, Mum because she was so much under the spell of Brook, and Granny because she was no longer the sharp granny she once had been.

The night was emptying out. A darker mood began to settle on us. Somewhere someone howled like a wolf, and then, from down the road, more or less outside a pub, a whole pack howled back. Woodlands was becoming a black fairytale.

"Where *is* he?" Ivan hissed beside me.

"He can't have lost himself," I said uneasily. "This street, Forest Road, is just two corners from the car park at the back of the mall, and it's not as if there are any one-way streets or anything to confuse him. Besides, he knows this part of Woodlands pretty well."

"I don't get into this part of town very often," said Ivan, looking around cautiously. "I feel a bit lost myself right now. Perhaps he's parked further down the road."

"I don't know it very well either," I said. "We sometimes use that supermarket back there because it's the nearest. But we do try to keep clear of it at night, because this part of town can get pretty rough." I paused. "I wish I'd brought my phone but it's in my other coat. I didn't think we'd be gone for long."

"Mine needs recharging," said Ivan gloomily.

By now, the twilight above the Woodlands roofs had deepened . . . had become true darkness. Forest Road, the road we were now standing on, was a luminous, writhing worm, familiar in some ways but not at all reassuring. Doorways and side streets had become black caves, but Forest Road itself held darkness at bay, armed as it was with street lights, along with the glow of passing cars. And, after all, some shops still had bright windows. The people walking past us looked rather more like ordinary shoppers than the drifters in the mall had done. Some of them were even talking to one another in a perfectly normal fashion. It wasn't as if Forest Road was deserted or that people were frightened and anxious. Far from it! The sound of voices—many voices—flowed across the street. "Harry's Drop" said a glowing sign curving over the pub door. There was quite a gang of men standing around that door staring up and down Forest Road. Bottles and glasses clinked, and the pulsing, red tips of cigarettes winked and glowed. In a way all this was ordinary enough . . . just what you might expect. There are lots of pub doorways in a city, and lots of people gathering to smoke and talk and drink. Yet once again that mad feeling pushed in on me—the feeling that we had space or time twisted and we were in a strange dimension. We had strolled through the tunnel of the mall and out into a place trying to disguise itself as part of the city so that it could trick wandering, uncertain people like us, only to consume them when its appetite grew keen.

And now I began imagining that the old trees and ferns which had once flourished here, but which were clamped down these days under the sealed surfaces of footpaths and streets, were breaking free, disguised perhaps, but still making their presence felt to vulnerable people. *You are lost on the woods, in the bush, in the secret, primordial forest of the world. Only now can those ancient woods begin to reveal themselves, as they grow out of the savage darkness that lurks in the crevices of all towns and cities. Cities, those frail frontiers people build to hold the true wild of the world at bay ... the wild and the wolves. The wolves and the wild.* I believed (just for a moment) that the busy men and women walking past us were really savage animals, able to conceal their true nature by taking on human shapes. Woodlands had become something far older and far fiercer than it had ever seemed before—a forest, seeded in prehistoric times, obliged to hide during the day, but able, as the night advanced, to reveal its true self.

"It's really odd," Ivan said. "Hey, night!" he breathed, looking into the air above him as if night were really listening to him. "Where's our transport? Have you swallowed it up?" So I was not the only one feeling that Woodlands was a thin veneer over something ancient and implacable, and that the traffic lights were something different from what they seemed to be . . . night witches, clicking their fingers, maybe. Once again Ivan and I were of one mind. "Let's see if he's parked further on," said Ivan.

So we set off strolling down Forest Road, peering at parked cars, squinting at those other cars that lined up impatiently, waiting for wood witches to click their fingers and turn the traffic lights green.

"Something's happened," said Ivan at last. "Perhaps he got a flat tyre, or broke down. There's room to park along here, and I reckon it should only take about three minutes to drive from the parking lot at the back of the mall around to the front. We must have been waiting for close on fifteen minutes by now. And, come to think of it, why didn't he wait in the parking lot? Why bother to drive round to the front? OK, shall we go back and look in the parking lot just in case he decided to stay there?"

"Or we could phone him, if I knew his number, which I don't, and we could find a public phone which we can't seem to do. I could even ring home and get Mum to come and collect us."

"Or will we live a bit extravagantly and get a taxi? I can probably afford one now, though it would use up most of my money," Ivan suggested.

"I suppose there's a taxi stop somewhere near here. Let's keep an eye open," I said, and off we went again, walking slowly though we had no real place to go. I couldn't be sure how Ivan felt, but I know I felt lost, even though Forest Road was a road I recognised. Well, I knew it in the daylight. Night was transforming it. Once I looked back over my shoulder, up out of Forest Road, high up above Woodlands, and saw little spots of light on the hills behind us. One of those stars was quite possibly the front window of my own home, staring down at the city below.

Ahead of us, a particularly bright street light beamed down at a corner, marking a crossroads. But, bright though it was, it seemed somehow fragile, set in a fierce forest of shadows. From above, the night flowed obstinately down the corrugations of old roofs, poured over into their spoutings and then overflowed, filtering down onto balconies, all of which seemed to be trying to cage darkness—but this was a darkness that would not be contained. Those shadows overflowed yet again, drifting around us, while the windows directly behind the balconies stared blankly out like strange, lashless eyes monitoring the thinning flow of life in the streets of Woodlands.

We reached a stretch of stone wall with no doors or windows that shouted commands at us.

"DIE!" it commanded, in savage sprawling blue paint. "THE WOLVES ARE RUNNING!" it added in urgent scarlet. "BLOOD!" said a small, almost shy message that looked as if it were written in mere crayon. A pink arrow pointed up towards the word "DIE!"

"It's funny to think this place was ever trees," I said, "once upon a time that is." I wanted to remind myself that the city was what I knew it must be, and not some mythical forest.

"Funny that it's still called "Woodlands"," Ivan said, "when it's the dead opposite these days. Mind you, in a funny way it almost feels like . . . " He fell silent.

"I was just thinking that." I stopped and looked around. "Right now, it's all got the feeling of a sort of fierce forest . . . a wild wood . . . hasn't it? Not a tamed forest, all noble trees, but a savage one. And in old fairytales people are scared of forests, they're scared of getting lost. I almost feel we could get lost here. I mean, those people walking past us sometimes seem lost themselves, or sometimes they seem a bit like animals on the prowl." I tried a casual laugh. "We'd better watch out, Babe!"

I was half-joking in the way I said this, turning secret, spooky thoughts into a joke, and yet once I had said it I immediately felt it was true. One woman going past me had a hair style that made it seem, for a moment, as if she had horns sprouting out of her forehead. A guy walked along after her, and I thought at first he had four legs, but it was just the swinging sleeves of a jersey round his waist, casting shadows that mixed with the shadows of his legs and gave him the look of a quadruped.

"Books!" exclaimed Ivan suddenly. "Look! It's that bookshop I told you about. Who'd try running bookshops in this neck of the woods?" And he spun off from Forest Road into one of the many side streets to study a lighted window. I looked up at the sign on the corner—"Robbins Lane" it said—then followed Ivan, and began peering into the window of that small shop. Sure enough, a second-hand bookshop, though it did seem strange to find any sort of a bookshop in Woodlands. Though the window was still lit, there was a notice on the door that said, "Closed".

"Look," Ivan was saying. "I love old bookshops. You never know what you're going to come across. They're like lucky dips."

But I was looking at the name on the window.

"Robbins Books," I read aloud. "Same as the name of the street. I wonder if it's any relation to that Mr Robbins who used to teach us in primary school. He loved reading to us, remember? He loved books."

"All teachers love books," Ivan declared. "Or they ought to. Look! There's an ancient copy of *The Coral Island*. Bit tatty. Still I wouldn't mind reading it again."

"All the books in this window look tatty," I said. "Hey, come on Ivan, let's get back to the mall. Brook might be there by now. He'll be mad if we've kept him waiting."

"It's him who's kept us waiting, Babe," Ivan said. "It's his fault we're still wandering around in the wilds of the city." *Exactly,* I thought as we moved back to the brighter lights of Forest Road.

"I hope he's there. It's so dark—as if all the lights are just there to make other places seem darker."

We were passing a corner. Another narrow alley opened off the main street . . . dark, dark, dark . . . though off in the distance there were stepping stones of light, and a sort of rhythmic movement as if the shadows were dancing to music only they could hear.

"Weird!" I agreed. "Weird, Babe!" and, as I spoke, that darkness in front of us writhed and seemed to shrink back a bit. Someone took shape and stepped towards us.

"Hey! Vannie!" the shadow exclaimed—almost shouted. "Where've you been all my life?"

He was tall, this newcomer, with a long, sharp nose and hair straggling around a face I felt increasingly sure I knew. And the name "Vannie" spoken in that particular voice brought something back to me. I began to remember the school playground and a boy called Dexter Loop . . . Dex. Dangerous Dex. Dex the Devil! But that was ages ago.

"Dex," Ivan said, speaking the name just as I was remembering it, and sounding like me, dismayed perhaps, but only slightly. "How's it all going, man?"

I now remembered Dexter Loop as the leader of a gang of boys, all of them fierce, and revelling in their ferocity, ferocity that had become like a sort of freedom for them. Taken singly they were just ordinary kids, probably a lot of them from the Woodlands part of town, but when they got together they became a single thing, a different thing, a wild pack, a fierce, churning complex organism, many voices blending to become one voice, looking eagerly for trouble, wanting to create trouble just for the thrill of it, and inventing some trouble-chorus all its own if it couldn't find any to join.

Dexter was dressed in black, which was why he had been so hard to see at first, there in the shadows of that ill-lit alley, but there was a yellow symbol on his chest. I knew I had never seen it before and yet, for all that, I felt I recognised it. He had a supremely confident air about him, as if Woodlands was entirely his territory and he was in charge of everything that happened there.

"We run this playground," the school gang would have declared back then. "We're the boss! We're the *wolves*." And back then, in the beginning, they had concentrated their force on lonely or isolated children, of whom Ivan (I suddenly remembered this) was one, calling him "Van" and "Vannie" and making tooting sounds as he walked by. Of course the voice of the older Dexter had deepened into a man's voice, but for me it was still filled with that unpleasant power of the past. He stood looking from Ivan to me and back again, smiling, perhaps trying to trick us into thinking he was friendly. Yet at the same time he was snarling his old wolf's snarl. Hard to tell which was which looking up into a face like his. And suddenly I found I was able to make out that shape on his T-shirt. It was a human shape standing, legs spread . . . without a head. And I knew at once that Dexter must have become a Headlopper.

"What are you doing in this part of town?" he was asking. "Not your sort of place, is it, now you're a uni-ver-sity student?" he mocked.

"Last time I checked, anyone could come here," Ivan replied.

"Could be risky," said Dexter. "There's a lot of savage animals in this neck of the woods . . . all looking for *prey* . . . "

As he said this he grabbed my arm and wrenched me back into the darkness of the alley and *howled* . . . howled like a mad wolf, pouring out a sound both violent and vicious and lonely, from somewhere deep within him. He jerked me back again, and from somewhere out in Woodlands, from somewhere close to the pub I thought, other howlings, fainter but just as menacing, sounded in the night air.

"Hey!" I heard Ivan's voice as I struggled furiously. "Let her go!" Turning my head towards those fingers gripping my shoulder, I took a chance, a lucky one as it turned out. I sank my teeth into Dexter's hand and bit hard. At the same time Ivan found me there in the darkness of that alley and grabbed my free arm, giving an enormous tug. He almost pulled me free. The three of us, Ivan and I pushing frantically against Dexter, struggled there in that dark Woodlands side street. Howling came from Forest Road, but for now it was still two against one. We broke free and began a stumbling run, not back into Forest Road but down that side street towards those distant stepping stones of light.

"Brook!" I gasped. "We must find Brook!"

"I wouldn't bank on it," Ivan grunted. "I reckon he knew what he was doing."

He had voiced my own fears. Brook wouldn't have had a definite plan to do away with me, I thought, just a momentary impulse. Just a gamble with the savage possibilities of a Woodlands night. Worth a try.

Tall buildings seemed to lean over us as if they were responding to Dexter's howling. We reached the place where some of the lower windows flooded the footpath with patches of light, but the upper windows remained tightly closed and dark.

I stumbled as I ran, then stumbled again, kicking against a curb that was almost invisible. I felt sure Ivan was right. I found myself living in a fairytale where anything might be possible. Ivan and me— babes in the wood, deserted, lost. And at that moment a chorus of howling voices—the wolf pack no less—bayed behind us.

"Go right! There!" Ivan hissed, panting a little.

Dexter must have waited for his wolf pack—his Headloppers— to join him. We had a bit of a start on them. All the same, when they howled again in a ragged chorus, they sounded confident . . . and not too far behind. We spun off to the right into a very dark side street, blank windows, locked doors, big rubbish tins. Behind us the howling rose again. The pack were not exactly at our heels but were certainly hunting us, sure of themselves, sure of this part of the city, which was so peculiarly their own. We had no right to be in Woodlands by night. Well, we'd been aliens from the beginning, but now we had been given another part to play. Now we were to be prey to a savage pack. Now, as we ran, we were inviting pursuit.

But when it came to running we did rather better than the wolves behind us, possibly because they had been drinking like Dexter, and we were stone cold sober and driven by fear, and fear can give you urgent wings. Still they followed us, shouting and howling. It wasn't that we had done anything challenging, but those wolves wanted fun, and their idea of a good time was fun at our expense. I didn't know if they wanted to beat us up, or rob us, or tear us to bits and leave our bleeding remains scattered around Woodlands, or perhaps all three. I only know that Ivan and I were both immediately sure we must not let the pack catch us. It didn't matter that we were blameless. We were babes in the wood all right, natural prey, and night had fallen in the forest. None of the ordinary city rules applied in Woodlands at night time. Night was a time of ferocity, and surrender to ferocity. Behind us that voice howled once more, and then the whole pack howled too, with slathering excitement.

"Right!" Ivan cried, and we turned right into a street that I knew must lead us back onto Forest Road. There was enough light for me to see the street sign . . . Robbins Lane.

We had only taken a few steps when Ivan caught my arm and pulled me sideways.

"It's open," he gasped. I had no idea what he was talking about, but I turned as he turned, stumbling over my feet . . . I think they were my own feet, but our running was mixed-up . . . they might have been Ivan's.

The lights of Robbins Book Shop shone in my face. (I could even pick out that tattered copy of *The Coral Island*), and, sure enough, the door, which had been tightly shut and marked "Closed', was certainly open now. Ivan pulled me sideways once more, and we burst into the shop.

The man standing behind the counter, which was loaded with books and newspapers, was indeed the same Mr Robbins who had once taught us at school.

"Hide us," Ivan cried, and once again the howling of the wolf pack sounded outside. "They're after us."

Then a wonderful thing happened. Mr Robbins didn't question us in any way, didn't hesitate. He simply pointed at a deep packing case beside him. I tumbled over into it, and Ivan half fell on top of me. Mr Robbins immediately began covering us with the newspapers from the pile on his counter.

"Stay very still," he said, "just to be on the safe side."

Howling again. Then voices, puzzled but urgent.

"Where—?"

"Where have they . . . ?"

"Must have run in here!"

Through the thin wood of the packing case I could hear scuffling in the door way and those pursuing voices, unintelligible, but definitely threatening.

"Now, what can I do for you lads?" asked Mr Robbins in a crisp, confident voice, a voice that reminded me so clearly of the voice he had used in the school room all those years back. He seemed to be totally without fear. "Is there any particular book you're interested in?"

"Books?" cried Dexter. "No way."

"We were after a couple of kids . . . pickpockets," said another voice. "They ran this way."

You could tell from the sounds that the wolves had burst through the door and were already searching the shop for us. I heard books falling, heard footsteps that I could tell were venturing behind the counter. Someone kicked the side of the packing case.

"There's no one here but me," said Mr Robbins. "You can see that, Dexter. For goodness sake get your pack out of here, and let me get on with my work."

It was strange how authoritative his voice was. It was a voice that expected to be obeyed . . . not fierce, not challenging exactly, just commanding—and commanding in an odd, mild way. Mr Robbins had had years of practice.

"They must have come in here," said Dexter, trying to establish his own authority.

"I have told you . . . I am on my own and working hard," said Mr Robbins. "Please leave me alone to pick up those books you've knocked over, unless you'd like to do it for me?"

Lying tangled and screwed-up under the newspapers, somehow locked into Ivan in a knot I hoped would never come untied, I felt the weight of the books Mr Robbins was putting on the newspapers on top of us. And then I heard, from somewhere in the distance, yet another wolf howl, fainter but unmistakeable.

"Hey! Jake's found them!" shouted Dexter.

"Sounds like it!" cried someone else. There was a scrimmage of feet, the sound of several men trying to get through the door at the same time, and then silence.

"They've gone," said Mr Robbins, his voice gentle but still authoritative. "But stay where you are for just for a few more moments."

We heard footsteps, a scrabbling sound, and a key being turned in a lock. The light changed, what we could see of it. One light—perhaps the one at the front of the shop, the one that had been lighting the window—had been turned off.

"You can get out now, but do it carefully," Mr Robbins said. "They could come past again at any moment. You were lucky you had a good lead on them. Lucky in a lot of ways. They would have looked in the packing case if they hadn't been distracted."

He pointed to a door at the back of the shop. "Go through there. I'll be with you in a moment, and we'll have a cup of tea."

At the back of the bookshop was another smaller room with a door that led out to a yard at the back of the shop. Ivan and I sat in that small room, sat in an anxious way, while Mr Robbins pottered around in the bookshop. Then he came in and looked over at us seriously.

"A cup of tea? Or perhaps not," he said. "You look as if you need to be safe at home. If you go out of the back door there, you'll see my car. Go out to it quietly—it's locked of course, but here's the key—slide into the back seat and keep your heads down. Those so-called wolves could still be stalking you. Give me a minute or two to close up the shop and I'll drive you home."

"Don't they . . . don't the wolves ever bother you?" asked Ivan.

Mr Robbins laughed a little. "I've worked here a long time," he said. "I've got a lot of friends, some of them even tougher than the wolves. And most wolves know I have a gun—a licensed gun—under the counter. All the same, you be careful getting into that car."

"Come on Babe!" I said to Ivan.

"I'll go first, Babe," he replied. "You can be my rearguard."

We did what Mr Robbins had told us to do, breathing hard, slid out the back door of his shop, found the car (no trouble at all) and scrambled into it. A short time later he joined us, and drove us down Forest Road, now almost empty, and up the hill, back up out of the woods.

"It's been quite a night," I said to Mr Robbins. "Lucky for us you were still open."

"It's mostly safe during the day . . . well, safe enough," Mr Robbins said. "But night—well, at night it becomes a different place."

"I'll come back again in the daylight," Ivan promised. "I'll get that copy of *The Coral Island* you've got in the window. Don't sell it to anyone else, will you?"

And at last we came back to my place, high on the hill. Woodlands smouldered angrily below, as if it were furious because we had remade the old fairytale. The story should have ended with our deaths, but in the end we had escaped. Someone closer to home would probably be furious, too.

We said goodnight and thank you yet again to Mr Robbins and made for the front door. Brook's silver car was drawn up outside the garage.

"We won't tell them anything that happened to us," I said. "Let's just make out we missed Brook and then walked home up the hill."

"You think he left us there on purpose, don't you?" Ivan said.

"I *know* he did," I replied. "He thought there might be a chance that . . . " But a moment or two later we were inside, surrounded by light that seemed an entirely different element from the lights that had shifted and moved around us in Woodlands. And there was my gran beaming at us encouragingly, thinking perhaps that, since I was still with Ivan, I was a step closer to doing something worthwhile with my life, even if it was only marrying and settling down. And maybe that's what Brook had felt too. Maybe that's what prompted him to leave us in a dangerous part of the city, taking a chance.

My mother was suddenly hugging me with a strange desperation.

"We've been so worried," she cried, "so worried!"

"What happened to you?" Brook asked, standing behind her like a puppeteer behind a puppet. "I drove around and around, but I couldn't find you. I thought you must have decided to walk home."

"He was so worried," said my mother, echoing herself. "Worried sick."

Brook and I looked at each other. It was a strange glance we exchanged, for I knew (and he knew I knew) that he had abandoned us out of a sort of malice. I read frustration in his glance, before, all in a second, his expression remade itself. All in a second he forced himself to look relieved . . . happy that I was home safely. But I *knew!* I knew, and he knew I knew. What he *didn't* know (I had only known it myself for a few minutes) was that I was planning to leave home. Ivan's place had room for me. Until then I would be doubly on my guard . . . on guard against the stepfather of fairytale. And after all, it was a fairytale Ivan and I had lived through.

Later, saying goodnight to Ivan, I told him, "We were babes in the wood, Babe."

"You're right. We actually were, Babe," he said.

"Babes in Woodlands," I joked, "lost in a way, even though we were close to home. But we were lucky, lucky and quick."

"And Robbins covered us with leaves," he added in a wondering voice, amazed to find he had lived out a fairytale. "Robbins covered us with leaves even if they were leaves of newspaper."

That hadn't occurred to me, but suddenly it seemed that my joke wasn't just a joke about an old story. We had relived it in our own time and in our own way. But maybe that is the way with certain old stories. Maybe they are lived out, over and over again, in one way or another . . . Cinderella . . . Jack the Giant Killer . . . Beauty and the Beast. Maybe they are always springing to life in an uncertain world, over and over again . . . .the same but different.

· · · · · · · · · · ·

# THE KITE

## KYLA WARD

She goes home tonight.
By day she mourns like a wet nurse,
giving her tears to those not her own.
She walks in procession through the necropolis,
beating her breast and tearing her hair;
good figure, long hair and she never stints.
The troupe leader favours her. She always
shares the funeral meal and coin.
But tonight, as torches cluster at the gate
like the bright clouds cluster in the west, she goes home.
Not to the city of the living,
but back into the silent clutter of tombs.
This place is old. The watchmen keep
to the paved roads and crypts with names.
But centuries pass as she walks uphill,
treading shards of sculpture, fragments of stone
and bronze. No lights here, no offerings;
such things attract worse than dogs.
That's why she broke the seals after the funeral,
to keep him safe. She remembers that day:
yellow is the colour of funerals,
of sunlight, disease and the flesh of women.
Now the sky is indigo and wind creeps chill
through a door that she opened, inch by inch,
to a crypt whose first owner had been erased,

barely large enough to contain his outer shell.
Not a good likeness: no likeness at all.
The symbol of a man. They placed it here
and left him. It took her weeks to work the lid aside.
Now her hands sink into linen ripped asunder.
A robber, seeing this, will dig no more,
but he still lies just as he did
when the priest anointed the eyes and mouth
of his mask. A likeness there;
the faintest identity in red and black.
Then they drew the shroud across.
No house since then, no name; for there was
no child and his brother didn't want her.
She did not want him. She was a child herself
when they married. But she knew love.
Red is for the flesh of men. Through bandages,
at last she touches; her feet slip through the crack.
Sinking through shrouds and shawls, the scent
of spices replaced by resin.
Her body measures his.
Her hand explores the coldness of his chest.
Cheek to a shoulder hard and slick
as a carved pillow. Deep in the linen of their bed
she rests. Beside him she can sleep.

•••••••••••

# THE PAST IS A BRIDGE BEST LEFT BURNT

## PAUL HAINES

### I

I'm doing the speed limit in the inside lane on the West Gate Bridge. My rear view mirror reflects a bug-splattered chrome grill. The truck's so close I can't see its number plate. He's speeding up to teach me a lesson. I turn up the radio. The blaring music drowns out the roar of the engine behind me.

Melbourne's cityscape lies under a haze. If it was winter, it'd be romantic: a fog, a morning mist smothering the buildings, hugging tight as it edges out over the bay. But it's summer: bushfire season has just begun and smoke chokes the city. The car's thermometer hits 30 degrees before the clock hits 9am. Today is going to burn.

Four lanes of traffic head towards the city, bumper to bumper, going too fast—four lanes heading out. If I touch the brakes, the truck behind will collect me.

What lesson?

I wonder how long it will take me to cross to the far lane, the outside lane, the lane nearest the water; to stop the car, get out, climb over the barriers, and jump.

### 2

My head is filled with numbers. Inputs equal outputs. Balances, statistics, line counts, record counts, the debits and credits of business, worthless business.

I hate numbers. They're doing my head in.

### 3

I tell my wife about the incident on the bridge.

It's late, almost midnight, and we're lying in bed, almost too tired to talk.

"You okay?" Her eyes are wide in the lamp light. "Don't tell me things like that. You're scaring me."

I tell her not to worry, that it was just an impulse, one of those strange things firing around my head. A crazy thought, that's all.

"Good." She rolls over and flicks off the lamp. "Because you have to look after the baby on the weekends—that's my time off."

Soon, she starts to snore. I lie awake in the dark, trying not to think.

• • •

This is not a cry for help. I'm fine.

I just need to tell someone.

Anyone.

You.

### 4

I used to work with a guy called Matt Halloran. He lived near me and crossed the West Gate Bridge twice a day for two years. Matt, being an engineer, had an interest in the construction of the bridge and he filled me in on a few things I should know.

And you should know, too.

Completed in 1978, after ten years of construction, and at a cost of 202 million dollars, the West Gate Bridge is the second largest bridge in Australia, and is twice as long as the Sydney Harbour Bridge. It boasts eight lanes with a total length of 2,582.6 metres. The river span at its longest being 336 metres, having a maximum width of 37.3 metres, and most importantly, has a height of 58 metres above the water that spills from the mouth of the muddy Yarra River into the Port Phillip Bay below. You can work out for yourself how long it would take to fall 58 metres.

Popular opinion claims that any construction worth its salt needs its share of blood spilled, and the West Gate is no exception. In 1970, two years into the project, the 112 metre span between piers 10 and 11 collapsed, killing thirty-five construction workers. Though it may only be the second longest bridge in Australia, it has the highest body count.

All of this can be found in the public domain.

What you won't find, Matt told me, is that the bridge was originally designed for six lanes, not eight, and that he *never* drives in the outside lanes, the lanes nearest the water.

5

The last vestiges of winter blanket the jutting hills, softening the hidden nooks and crannies.

I'm driving, and I hate it.

The road winds treacherously along the Taieri Gorge . . .

6

I'm Paul Haines. Born thirty-six years ago in New Zealand. Now living in Melbourne, Australia, married to Jules, and have a five-month old daughter we named Isla. I own a house in Yarraville that requires a $2,600 monthly mortgage payment. I work as an I.T. consultant netting $4,000 a month; insurance eats up at least $400 per month, and I don't even know what bills are coming in. Are you doing the sums yet? Dropping to a single income is a killer.

On the side, I pretend to be an SF writer. I've won several awards for my short fiction, and my first short story collection, *Doorways for the Dispossessed,* came out in 2006. It received some good reviews . . . some bad reviews. I'm achieving success, right?

On paper, I guess it can look that way.

Did I mention there is blood in my stool? No? Maybe I'm just not thinking clearly anymore. Are you?

Let's test that. You think this is part of the story? That this *is* a story? Wrong. Not this time.

According to the Australian Bureau of Statistics, thirty percent of all suicides in the last recorded year were males aged between 30 and 34 years old.

I love my daughter more than anything else in this world.

7

Traffic on the Monash freeway heading south out of the Burnley tunnel eases, and I hit 100kmh after weaving through to the fast lane. I'm late for work, and the music is so loud the doors are vibrating. Loud enough to drown out the noise, to bring me back to nothing. The car is the only haven I have to bury myself in sound, to lose myself in music, to make me feel like me, a younger me.

The median barriers are smudged in black tyre skids, and remnants of torn rubber litter the side of the freeway for kilometres. Trucks thunder in the opposite direction, dozens of them, bullying along the road, spouting greasy black bursts of diesel into the air. They blur past, again and again, and in the cab approaching, I see Patrick Lyons behind the wheel. We stare at each other as we pass, him heading north, me south. It can only be a matter of a second, but his face is clear, framed and focused. It's him. He no longer has a short blond crew cut, the hair now longer, down around his ears, like mine used to be. A light fuzz of stubble carpets his cheeks. His blue eyes catch mine.

I haven't seen Patrick Lyons for almost twenty years, and except for the hair, he looks exactly the same as when I last saw him.

It's not possible.

He looks like he's still twenty-one years old.

8

The West Gate Bridge should be haunted.

Sometimes, in the afternoon glare, I see them, migrant workers with crushed limbs and jutting bones, standing on the edge, waiting.

Other times, as the traffic crawls across hot tarseal towards the sunset, I think about what the government calls Soft Targets. I imagine the truck ahead stalling, stalled, waiting for the detonator to ignite the fertilizer bomb in the back.

Brake lights flare red on a truck several cars in front of me. Traffic grinds to a halt.

We wait.

The petrochemical compounds and decrepit factories that make up the western shoreline cast long shadows out over the water. You could buy everything you'd need down there, then take a five minute drive out onto the bridge.

I wonder how long it would take to get out of the car, walk between bonnets and bumpers, past the *No Pedestrian* signs and the number for drivers to call should they see someone on the bridge, and climb over the barrier.

Over one hundred people have jumped since 1990. Seven have survived. Seventy-four per cent of those who jumped from the bridge were male, with an average age of thirty-three. More than seventy per cent were suffering from mental illness.

But not in rush hour.

I'm thirty-six. I've always considered myself, if anything, to be above average.

I don't know why I am thinking this way.

### 9

I've fallen in love with four women in my lifetime. The first two broke my heart, so I broke the hearts of the last two. I still love the last three and hate the first.

I married the third after both our hearts healed because I love her differently and maybe for the way she loves me. Love can be a confusing thing.

I love my daughter more than I love all those women put together. It's not even comparable. When I'm with her, I don't want to be anywhere else. I want to stay in that moment, locked in stasis forever, like a work of art.

I will never get to see what she looks like as an old woman.

### 10

The last vestiges of winter blanket the jutting hills, softening the hidden nooks and crannies.

I'm driving, and I hate it.

The road winds treacherously along the Taieri Gorge, and I constantly brake and shift between gears. I'm a shit driver; I know it and so does everyone in this car . . .

### 11

I installed an automatic sprinkler system for the front yard before the heat of summer kicked in, while we still had a double income. Now that summer's kicking, I can't use the sprinkler due to water restrictions. We use the water from Isla's daily bath for either the front decorative garden or the back herb garden. The bathtub is too small to contain enough water for both gardens.

I thought of buying inflatable water bladders or perhaps a water tank, but even with the rebates offered by the government, I can no longer afford to do it. The government is now talking about taxing people for recycling water as it is impacting on the industrial recycling plants.

I regret spending the money on the automatic sprinkler.

At least, I'm not a farmer. The shotgun is getting a lot more use these days.

12

Matt, my engineer friend, married a couple of years ago and had a son. With these new found responsibilities, he moved his family to Brisbane, where he no longer has to cross a bridge on his way to work.

13

I lie awake in the dark and wonder how I lost myself. When did it happen? Can I pinpoint the year? The week? The event?

After an hour of sleeplessness, I stand in the doorway of Isla's bedroom listening to her soft breathing.

14

My in-laws cannot believe I haven't yet made a will. They also believe that the government gets everything you own when you die if you don't have one. They believe in a lot of things that aren't necessarily true.

I have a life insurance policy, though.

15

To tell you about Lyons, I need to tell you about Lester first, and that means I need to tell you about Otago University.

I chose to attend that university based on three things:

1. It was the furthest university from home;
2. My friend Gavin had gone the year before me, and I regaled in his wild tales;
3. A girl I thought I was in love with was going there, and I thought I could still win her heart.

The third choice made up 70% of my mind—and made it up on the spot. A weighty decision based primarily on impulse.

The day I stepped off the plane, that cold remote Scottish-built town wrapped me up and swept me away. I forgot about the girl I thought I loved, and she dropped out a year later. I'd see her around occasionally, and we'd laugh about old times, but there was never anything there between us. She's unhappily married now to a nice man who drains her personality, moulding her into who they think she should be.

Gavin's wild tales were true. He was struggling to make the grades to enter law school at the time, but he always held sage wisdom for me.

"You learn three things here," Gavin told me one afternoon as I flipped through his record collection. "You learn to drink, to take drugs, and to fuck women."

And in these three things, Lester was my preferred partner in crime.

Gavin's a recluse now, living with a much younger woman with two kids from a previous partner, and has ostracised himself from his parents and siblings. He works the late night shift in a bottle shop. I heard he put on weight and shaved his head. When I try to picture his face, I confuse him with Marlon Brando lost in the Vietnamese jungle, sitting in a dark, wet hut, waiting for someone to come and finish him.

16

I stare at a computer screen watching processes push and massage data from one database table to another. I check transaction volumes and amounts, making sure things tally, that everything adds up; so that when the executive reports are run, everything will be in its place.

I find it easy, and it bores me.

The project is going badly; behind schedule, computer servers falling over—people stressed, very stressed, putting in long hours, working weekends.

Jobs are on the line, media gags, court cases; everything is breaking down including the people around me. The project manager has already been offered as the sacrificial goat, and my manager is resigning in a month's time before his throat is cut, too. He's taking a year off to travel around Australia with his wife and two young sons in their 4WD. I admire him; in a time of crisis when other people are losing themselves, he knows who he is and where he wants to be.

Me? I arrive half an hour late to work each morning and go home early.

### 17

Craig Harris was my best friend between the ages of ten and fourteen. We shared a love of *Mad Magazine*, music, rugby, and his father's *Playboys* and *Penthouses*. We used to read the stick mags in the treehut outside the house they rented—if Merv knew we had them, he didn't seem to care. Eventually, we worked up the courage to actually leave our favourites inside the hut.

That winter wasn't kind. The treehut leaked, and Merv's magazines got soaked and grew mould. By the time summer came around, we were too big to be playing in treehuts anymore.

When Craig was in his early twenties and had returned home to save some money, he noticed his father would slip out after tea but never took the car. By this stage, the Harrises had finally bought their home and Merv—jack of all trades and a poor jack at that—had himself a steady job waterblasting Venetian blinds. Merv had made a decision he intended to live by and stepped up to take on those responsibilities.

After a few weeks, Craig's curiosity got the better of him, and he decided he'd follow his old man. That night, the family had dinner together, and once the plates had been cleared, Merv excused himself and slipped out the back door. Craig watched him disappear around the side of the shed. Half an hour later, Craig stood outside the shed door, his hand hovering over the handle. He pushed open the door to find his father sitting on a chair in the dark, drinking beer from a long bottle, and listening to crackly talkback radio. Merv glared at him but said nothing. Craig shut the door and went back inside. He, too, said nothing.

Merv had stepped up alright.

Craig told me this a few years later, halfway through our second bottle of cheap tequila as the night marked midnight. We were in his shed listening to Mike Oldfield bouncing out of the speakers and off the walls. He was trying out a chair for size. At the time, we laughed. Craig was my best friend between the ages of ten and fourteen. I haven't heard from him in over eight years.

18

A rust-stained grill swallows my rear view mirror. A tuft of red hair matted with dried blood is caught between holes in the grill. The engine roars as the truck changes gear.

I need to make a decision. Speed up or slow down? Or get out of the way? Get to the outside lane.

Something hits the back of my car, shunting me sideways into the barriers.

Lester.

I wake. It's 3am, and Isla's crying.

"Can you get her please, hon?" my wife says sleepily into her pillow.

"Sure." My hands are shaking.

19

I clearly remember the night Lester and I became friends.

We were drunk and walking home from the pub, winding our way along the Leith River in the moonlight. Our breath white frost in the autumn evening air, we talked shit about whether The Cult had sold out and if Pop Will Eat Itself was for real. We stopped at a bridge that crossed the Leith—a metre-wide water pipe ran parallel at ground level.

"It's a rite of passage." Lester turned towards me, his hands buried in the pockets of his denim jacket. Long red locks hung upon his collar, his mullet spiked in front. He climbed up onto the pipe and tapped it with the toes of his Doc Martens. "You have to walk it."

A metre of pipe wasn't much when most of it was curved. I leant over the bridge and looked down. The water in the Leith gurgled several metres below, black and cold. "I'm too pissed."

"That's the rite of passage."

I shook my head and grinned. "You're mad."

He shook his head and scowled. "You're soft, Stevie."

Lester walked out to the middle of the pipe, the sound of his boots loud and intrusive against the night. He made it look easy, matching my pace on the bridge. He even kept his hands in his pockets, though his eyes remained on the pipe in front of his feet.

"Not bad, Lester. I'll buy you a beer." I was impressed. He looked up from the pipe to glare at me. "That's the problem with you soft bastards. You think you—"

And then he wasn't there.

I pulled him shivering from the Leith, and we lay on the river bank laughing, steam rising from our wet and muddied bodies, chests heaving, adrenalin burning through the booze, forever etching that moment in my memory.

That feeling of being alive.

### 20

What? You were expecting a straight narrative. Something linear? Like life, with a start and an end? Life is not like that. It does have a start and an end, but the middle is confusing, disjointed. Life blunders its way forward, staggering through an assault of intrusions that pull you backwards and shunt you sideways.

Life is, has, and always will be haunted by the past.

### 21

Data flows. Fluorescent lights bathe my face. My aching eyes retreat into their sockets. They feel like they're being poached. I need to apply drops daily to ease the irritation.

Someone makes a joke about "going postal" on this project. We all laugh. Though it's not said, we all know this means coming into work with a loaded gun and letting loose.

On the way back from the bathroom, I pass two women talking in the hallway. I see them from the corner of my eye. Something about one of them makes my step falter, and I glance back. Dark hair obscures her face. She is more solid than I remember, but solidity comes with years.

I can't tell for sure, but she could be my first love, an older version of the woman who first broke my heart. Katy Burnett. The only woman I loved that I now hate. I keep walking.

By the time I get back to my desk, the lights are too bright and my eyes are streaming. I feel sick, excuse myself, leave the building, get in the car, and hit the freeway.

I count a dozen late-70s model Ford Falcons, dull red-orange and heavy, on the trip home. Lester drives every one of them. Katy sits in the back of some of them, laughing, her bare legs raised and resting on the headrest of the seat in front of her.

### 22

It's now officially recognised. *Back To Work Blues.* They're talking about it on breakfast television, between reports of bushfires, interest rate rises, water restrictions, and analysis of the best weight loss programs.

I'm pretending not to listen as I focus on Isla batting the toys dangling from the arch of her playmat. Her hands flail; the finger and thumb coordination's not developed yet. She gums me a smile and resumes her batting. My heart melts.

"Maybe that's what you've got," says Jules. My wife has been watching both the show and me pretending not to watch. "Everyone gets it."

"Yeah, maybe, I don't think so." I crouch and kiss Isla's cheek. She wriggles and grunts her appreciation. I grab my car keys and walk towards the front door. "Gotta go, I'm late. Love you."

"Paul?" Jules face hangs low with concern. "Talk to me."

"Hon." I force a smile. "I'm fine, just tired. That's all."

I get in the car and bury myself in the congestion leading towards the bridge. I turn off the music and flick on the radio, searching for a traffic report. There'll be one on talkback for sure.

• • •

Am I having a mid-life crisis?

A mid-life crisis is an emotional condition that can appear in both men and women, usually around the age of 35 to 50 years. The anxiety felt usually focuses on the realisation that the person's life is halfway over, but unhappy marriages, dissatisfaction at work, loss of sex drive can all contribute. I'm not ticking all the boxes here, but I'm certainly giving the pen a good work out.

There are supposedly different neurological reasons why men can't articulate their experiences compared to women.

*What? You want me to articulate those reasons? No can do.*

We want out of the rat race, but we're still The Provider. It's wired into our DNA. We think we're stuck. I spend a *lot* of idle time at work checking this all out. A lot of time.

So am I having a mid-life crisis? You tell me.

I want out, I know that much. But to where?

• • •

Smoke from the bushfires still hangs over the city. I can smell it seeping through the aircon. Across the road, at the petrol station, fuel has hit a new high per litre.

Patrick Lyons fills a rusting, dented Ford Falcon with petrol. He removes the cigarette from his mouth and taps ash onto the forecourt. He grins at me, a good-to-see-you-mate grin: let's catch up over a few beers, smoke some weed, a few lines of speed perhaps, *ha, ha, ha* . . . *Lyons of speed*, sit us down and chew the fat over the past.

He's at least twenty metres away, and his sharp blue eyes drill into mine. He's wired, completely a-grade wired.

He knows where I work. Where I live.

### 23

. . . softening the hidden nooks and crannies.

I'm driving, and I hate it.

The road winds treacherously along the Taieri Gorge, and I constantly brake and shift between gears. I'm a shit driver; I know it and so does everyone in this car, but I'm acting like I don't care, like this is nothing. Logging trucks, enormous and snaking, career full speed head on . . .

### 24

I hardly take drugs anymore. I tell people I still do, to maintain the image I believe I need to maintain—you know, still bucking the system, bohemian lifestyle, that sort of thing—but I usually have an excuse ready if the opportunity for public consumption rears its head.

I used to love it and the twisting corridors it used to lead my mind down. An altered consciousness exploring angles I'd never considered in the straight light of day. But over the years, all the corridors inevitably began to lead in the same direction. Down into darkness.

I found myself thinking about being chopped into pieces with a blunt axe, of being bound naked spread-eagled on a bed while the blade partially severed the inside of my thigh only to stick in fractured bone. This thought kept coming back again and again until I managed to stop myself thinking while under the influence—but then what was the point?

I'd end up sitting alone in a darkened room, with the music down low, listening to the big hush of the nocturnal city, waiting, inevitably, for the sound of wailing sirens to approach—or for Jules to tap on the window.

### 25

"Lyons was my best mate at high school," Lester had told me in my other lifetime. "You'll like him, Stevie."

We'd been on our way to the Cook Hotel for happy hour, three-dollar jugs of beer, pulling our coats tight against the freezing sleet that pricked exposed skin like needles.

"He's not like a lot of them down my way; he's smart." Lester glanced at me, an eyebrow cocked. "He'll beat you at chess."

"We'll see. Haven't met any of your school friends before."

Lester laughed, a harsh sound caught by the wind and swept away. "That's because most of them are dead."

"Eh?"

"Not much to do in Invercargill. So we drove cars. Fast. I've written off two, been pulled out of three others. Lucky to be alive, really. There used to be six of us. Now there's only me and Lyons." Lester pulled open the doors to the pub. Heat and noise poured out into the street. "Black ice is a killer. I wonder if Lyons has earned red laces yet?"

### 26

I scan through the work email registry and phone directories for the surname Burnett. Nothing, and with it, a fleeting instance of relief. Then I scan for the name Katy. She could be married now, and somewhere, deep inside, I feel nauseous thinking that.

There's a Katy on the third floor and one on the fifth. I've only ever met one Katy in my life, and now there's two of them in the same building. I take the lift to the third floor. My eyes are stinging.

### 27

In our first year at university, Lester bought himself a second-hand 1978 redorange Ford Falcon for $5,000. This was two years before I met Patrick Lyons; and therefore, two years before I knew Lester had been involved in at least five serious traffic accidents. I suspect this was why he never had insurance for the car.

I went in that car once with Lester down to the bottle shop to buy a keg of beer and a couple of packs of cigarettes, *B&H Gold, thanks, mate,* for a party. The Sisters of Mercy blasted from the speakers in the doors. The engine growled, the gears ground, and the muscles tensed on Lester's arms whenever he turned the wheel.

He never got to drive that car out of Dunedin. Within two weeks, just before midnight, a lecturer on a $10,000 motorbike crashed into the side of the car as Lester pulled out from the curb after buying a $1.20 steak and cheese pie from the 24-hour dairy.

Without insurance, that pie became the most expensive meal Lester ever had. He had to sell the car and lost almost half of his university savings in the payout.

If only it had been the most expensive lesson he had learned.

### 28

Country roads. Long and meandering. If you want, you can do more than the speed limit. No median barriers. Huge road trains roared along these narrow tree-lined chutes, ploughing through kangaroo and possum.

I tell myself it's a good thing that I'm no longer working in the northern rural areas anymore, that I'm bound to my desk in an industrial suburb and enslaved to the computer chained to it.

No more open roads and open spaces.

### 29

Lester was right. I did like Lyons.

I was expecting a Southern Bogan, and in outward appearances, Lyons didn't disappoint. He kept his blonde hair at a number two buzz, wore black Levis and a black woollen jersey, and sported black Doc Marten boots—with black laces not red.

The man himself, though, was quietly spoken, his conversation intelligent, and his smile comforting. And he bought the first jug of beer. And the second. And the third.

Lyons had run into a spot of trouble with one of the skinhead gangs in Invercargill. He had grown bored with making up $25 foils from the garbage bag of sticky heads he was going to on-sell for the gang and whipped up to the shops for a packet of cigarettes, *B&H Gold, thanks, mate,* and a chocolate milk. It was during this opportune moment that the drug squad busted his house. They found his fingerprints all over the cannabis foils and bags, but they didn't find Patrick Lyons. He kept on walking. At that point, Lyons thought of his good ole buddy Lester and decided that maybe he should check out some honest work opportunities in the not-so-far-away-but-far-enough city of Dunedin.

Lyons moved into our flat. He took the couch in the stairwell/entry area; Lester already had the lounge as his room. We'd sit up smoking pot and drinking beer with the music blasting; our thumbs and forefingers hammering on keys as we battled through computer games.

One night, in the dead of winter as the frost pressed its palms against my bedroom window, something weird happened. For the life of me, I still don't know how. One minute, we'd been killing each other on screen, the next my dick managed to find its way into Lyons's mouth. We sat on the end of my bed where my girlfriend Katy lay wrapped beneath the sheets comatose. I normally had trouble relaxing with oral sex but not that night. I remember Lyons wiping his mouth, and laughing, and his eyes sparkling in the mute light cast from the computer monitor. Later, I realised he looked deranged. Lyons rubbed the shape of Katy's legs beneath the blankets and said we'd better not mention anything.

We went back to the screen. Lyons dispatched a host of Ur-Quan Kzer-Za Dreadnought Fighters to hunt down my already-cloaking Ilwrath Avenger.

He won the game.

I never said a word.

### 30

I'm home late from 'work'. Only the porch light remains lit. I let myself in quietly, trying not to disturb the sleeping family, unsure what excuse I'll use when Jules's interrogation begins. It's the project. Deadlines. Pressure. Won't be for long. The truth is I don't know where I've been for the last few hours.

Before I can get my story right, the hallway light flicks on.

But it's not Jules, and the unprepared lies fall from my lips unspoken.

Lester, naked, pulling on a pair of disintegrating Levi jeans he'd cut down into shorts, emerges from my bedroom, nods at me, and wanders down the hallway. I peer into the open bedroom door. Jules is asleep, huddled under a bundle of quilts.

I follow Lester to the kitchen.

"What are you doing here?"

He ignites one of the burners on the stove, leans in, and lights his cigarette. He drags deep, the embers burn bright, and exhales slowly; his eyes never leave my face.

"I could ask you the same question, Stevie," he says.

He props himself against the stove and taps ash to the floor.

"You can't smoke in here." I grab him by the arm and lead him towards the back door and the courtyard. His skin is cool and damp and stinks of sex.

"What the hell were you doing in my room?"

He laughs, a strangled hiccup, and drops himself into a chair. "Good job, nice house, pretty wife, cute baby. Looks like you made it, eh?"

I shake my head. Something is wrong, badly wrong.

He blows smoke at my face, something I've always hated. "Been fucking yer wife lately?"

At first, I mistake the question for a statement. I should be seething, raging, freaking out. The skin on Lester's arm is melting, the flesh soft and runny. The hair on his head frizzles. I should be feeling something, anything, but I'm not here, no, not at all.

My voice echoes from a long way away. "You try anything on her and I'll kill you."

Lester laughs and flicks his cigarette at me.

"Paul?" Jules stands in the doorway, bleary-eyed, dressing gown pulled tight over pyjamas. "What are you doing out here?" Then more incredulously, "Are you smoking?"

Lester's cigarette burns in my hand, a red sizzle of flesh. His chair is empty. I stamp out the cigarette, go inside, and run my hand under the cold tap in the kitchen.

Jules sniffs the air and stares at the oven; her eyes are suddenly angry. "For Christ's sake, hon, you've left the gas on." She rushes over to the oven and turns the lever to close off the gas. "You've got to be more careful than that; you could have killed us."

I mumble an apology and tell her I'll come to bed soon.

Lester.

It was Lester.

### 31

Numbers. They're fucking with my head.

### 32

I'm driving, and I hate it.

The road winds treacherously along the Taieri Gorge, and I constantly brake and shift between gears. I'm a shit driver; I know it and so does everyone in this car, but I'm acting like I don't care, like this is nothing. Logging trucks, enormous and snaking, career full speed head on, and to let them pass, I keep edging into the loose gravel on the side of the road overlooking the drop into the gorge. The sudden loss of traction sickens me . . .

### 33

I'm sitting in the car waiting.

The lights in her apartment are off. I made sure I left before she did. Maybe she's out, running chores, on a date, or giving some stranger a blowjob in the toilets.

The CD changes. Straitjacket Fits's *Melt* growls slowly from the speakers.

"That's more like it." Lester is in the back seat, his Doc-Martened-feet draped over the shoulders of the front seat.

"I hate this kiwi shit, just elitist varsity noise." Lyons digs his knees into the back of my seat. "Eh, Stevie?" He digs his knees harder. "Eh?"

"I like it," I say. "Just shut up and listen."

They light up joints and talk about the women they've fucked, the booze they've drunk, the drugs they've taken . . .

Here she comes.

I can see her walking towards the door of her apartment in the last remnants of dusk. It looks like her. It has to be her.

Lyons whispers into my ear, his breath fetid, "Go on."

Lester drops his switchblade into the lap of the front passenger seat. "Been fucking her lately?"

I watch her go in. Lights turn on. I get out of the car. Suddenly, I'm at the door and pressing the buzzer to the number of her apartment. The sound is sharp and squat like a constipatory shit ripping a hemorrhoid. I shield my face from the camera.

"Who is it?" The voice is warbled and tinny through the crackling speaker. It could be her; the voice could be hers. I need her to speak more, so I can be sure.

"It's me."

"Who?"

"It's me, Paul."

"Have you got the right address?"

The accent is wrong, but it could be her. "Katy, it's Paul. From uni."

"You've got the wrong address."

The speaker ceases crackling.

Shit. What am I going to do? I need to speak to her. I don't know why. Do we ever know why? My hands start to shake, and I feel faint.

Lester and Lyons are leering from the car windows.

I run back to the car. A section of Lyons's skull, about the size of a saucer, is missing above his right temple. His brain pulses wetly. I jump into the car, slam the door, and grip the steering wheel. I breathe deeply and count the breaths, feeling the air flow in and out, in and out. The car is empty. I put the knife into the glovebox, start the car, and join the congestion leading west and home.

### 34

In my final year of varsity, I buy my first car. A 1978 Ford Falcon, red-orange. Lester's old car. It costs me $1,000, and I buy it mainly to fuck him off. He doesn't speak to me for two weeks.

### 35

I stand by the elevators on the third floor, unable to move, a paralysis seizing my mind. I hold a piece of paper in my hand, the prop for purpose, and I study it furiously, willing my legs to take the steps to circle the floor looking for Katy.

Eventually, I manage to connect with my legs and stumble into a slow walk, seeking out the name plates on the partitions, taking in the faces in stolen glances, recognising only a handful glimpsed in passing or in the canteen. I don't know these people I work with. I have no idea who they are or what they do. I spend my life with strangers, never getting closer than a nod or a polite, stifled hello in a corridor or an awkward silence crammed into an elevator.

The name reads Katy Salisto. The desk is empty. I scan the partition walls for photos, for clues to this woman's life, for confirmation of a link to my past, our past: a chubby-faced toddler grins blurrily; a greyhound wearing a Santa hat; a first aid certificate. There's nothing here I can relate to.

Her keyboard is covered in blood.

A young man with black gel for hair looks up and smiles. "Katy's in the kitchen, mate. Spilt her tomato soup. She'll be back in a minute. Anything I can help you with?"

I shake my head and stare at the carpet as I make my way back to the elevator. I press the buttons and wait. In the distance, a fat elderly Italian woman rushes past with a handful of paper towels.

The bell dings. The doors open.

"Try the fifth floor, Stevie."

Inside, Lyons leans against the wall, half of his face crushed, the skull open revealing the brain. Blood has sprayed over the walls, more pools around his feet.

I step in.

With an arm held together by pulped flesh and bone, he reaches out and presses the number five.

## 36

I stroke Isla's brow, soothing her sobs. It's 3am. Her hair is sweaty and tangled, and I run my fingers gently through it. The pillow is damp with sweat and tears.

"It's okay, baby girl, it's okay. Daddy's here."

Her sobs diminish, and she shudders with an intake of breath. Her skin is hot from crying, and soft, so soft. My heart fills to breaking; I lean into the cot and kiss her gently on the forehead. She sighs.

"Daddy's here, baby girl, don't worry. Daddy will always be here."

When Isla's breathing settles, I creep from the room, slip back into bed, and nestle in against Jules's warm body. I kiss the back of her neck. She sighs.

I fall asleep within seconds, my wife held tight within my arms, our bodies pressed together.

## 37

The night is moonlit and restless. The house lies still. Gentle breathing rises and falls next to me. I slip out of bed and check Isla's room. I hear her snoring: a sound as gentle as a leaf thrummed on the palm of your hand. I listen to her sleeping for several minutes. I'm content, happy, my feet grounded.

I make my way along the darkened hallway to the kitchen to drink some water, hydrate myself, be good, be kind to myself. The room smells of gas, and beneath it, something more pungent.

I turn off the gas handle at the stove. Cigarette butts—B&H Gold—litter the bench.

I realise the other smell is that of burning hair.

## 38

We sit in a café together as tight as a newborn family can be on display in the inner suburbs, chic and trendy, still drinking our coffee. Oh yes, no change in lifestyle here.

Asleep in her pram, Isla's a mess of dark hair sprouting from blankets pulled tight against a soft pouch of cheeks. Sitting opposite me, Jules sips her latte.

She looks tired and beautiful. She smiles at me, happy and alive. I reach across the table and squeeze her hand.

A woman at the next table leans into the pram and coos. "Oh, she's so beautiful."

"Thank you," we say, both proud and embarrassed.

Isla is the most beautiful thing in my world. I could stare at her for hours.

We sip our coffee. Jules yawns. We are too tired to talk to each other. We have nothing to say.

## 39

We're sitting in the Garden Bar on a Tuesday morning, Lester, Lyons, and me. Lyons has had a win on the pokies and has shouted a few jugs of Speight's Draught and that means no lectures for us varsity boys. He's been down Balclutha way for a couple of weeks, doing a couple of odd jobs. I assume he's been drug-running weed. It's what he does.

The pub's empty except for the three of us, and we're sitting outside in the crisp autumn weather because we're smoking a joint.

The barman doesn't say too much as long as we keep it discreet. Lyons also supplies him.

I'm feeling stoned, and the beer is bitingly cold as we ritually scull our first glass. Lyons is rambling on about some young chick fresh out of school he'd spent a couple of days fucking just outside of Balclutha, some dirty bitch who couldn't get enough. Lester and I grin, casting a glance at each other. I've never seen Lyons spading a girl in any of the pubs we've been wasted in this year. Not once. Lester says Lyons has never had a girlfriend. I haven't told Lester about the night I had with Lyons blowing me while we played computer games. I'm not even sure it happened; at least, that's what I tell myself.

At some stage during the drinking, Lyons heads towards the bar to buy another round. Lester yells out, pointing towards Lyons's red shoelaces. "Just what the fuck were you doing down Balclutha, Lyons?"

Lyons grins, obviously proud it's been noticed, but then pulls on his hard face. "Shut it, eh?" he says through clenched teeth and draws his finger across his throat. Then he's at the bar, talking shit, and pushing the empty jugs towards the taps.

I turn to Lester. "So, what's with the red laces? You gonna tell me or what?"

Lester's no longer laughing. He stares at the dregs in his glass, shaking his head. "Nah, he's full of shit. I bet he just put them in himself."

"What does it mean? Come on, man, tell me."

Lester looks up at me, his eyes cool blue in a pool of bloodshot veins. He laughs as if to convince himself things are cool. He glances towards the bar, placing Lyons. "It means you've drawn blood."

I snort. This is just more of their macho bullshit. The Invercargill talk, the tough man attitude they like to throw around when they feel the need for unity, some bond, some better-than-you-fucklander type shit that they try on me often. A fucklander being an aucklander, no capital letters thank you, sir.

"What, like a blood nose or something?"

"Bit harder than that, Stevie."

Lyons plonks three more jugs down on the table. "Bit harder than what?"

"Black laces." Lester and Lyons share a stare, then Lester changes the subject back to the girl Lyons was fucking, but Lyons doesn't want to talk about that.

When Lester goes for a piss, Lyons leans across the table and says quietly, "Be careful of your missus around him, eh? He's going to cut your lunch."

"He's my mate. Why you saying shit like this?"

His eyes are grey steel, boring into mine. I'm withering and cast my eyes away, too stoned, too paranoid . . . the loser. The soft cunt.

"It's what he does." Lyons sits back victorious.

Lester comes back, and we sit in silence, gulping our beer.

40

Katy and I lie in her bed, legs entwined, me inside her, as we watch the TV, relaxed and satisfied. Our sweat mingles on our thighs, and I shift subtly to stay inside her. She presses her arse against my groin. I kiss her shoulder and tell her I love her. She squeezes her vaginal wall around me and says she loves me, too.

On the news is a bulletin for a schoolgirl, age 15, missing from Balclutha for over a week. Her schoolbag and purse have been found and police are currently treating her disappearance as suspicious.

"What's wrong, bubby?" Katy says.

I stare at the TV, my mind back in the Garden Bar. Red laces. Lyons.

"Nothing."

She reaches between her legs and takes my suddenly flaccid cock in her hand.

"It certainly feels like nothing."

I roll out of the bed and pull on my jeans, dressing quickly. My gut churns.

"What are you doing?"

"Nothing, gotta go, sorry, Katy." I kiss her on the cheek.

I'm out the door, and she's yelling at me, not after me, but I don't hear the exact abuse.

I need to talk to Lester.

## 41

Dozens of trucks block the roads, thick steel carcasses grinding the network to a standstill. The morning heat is climbing. As each minute ticks, a degree rises. The hot stench of the city creeps in through the air conditioning.

I sit in my car and increase the volume on the stereo until the bass vibrates through the doors. Lyons sits in every truck cabin, the side of his skull crushed and partially missing. The truck horns blare, and somewhere in my past, I can hear him screaming.

## 42

Numbers fall away, meaningless. What are they to me? An interest rate I cannot control? A mortgage repayment I cannot meet? A deadline I don't care about?

A speedometer reading. A speeding fine. A statistic.

A line of code. An input. An output.

A long way down and gravity is a constant. A statistic.

I'm looking for the wrong things. I'm concentrating on what I have no effect on. I need to look inside. To let go of everything I'm holding onto that was and will now never be. To be content with where I am now.

Of who I am now. A statistic.

I'm so confused, I'm so fucking confused . . .

## 43

My family know nothing about me or my past.

## 44

State highway 85 writhes like an eel in its death throes as it follows the once arduous Pigroot wagon trail past abandoned goldmines and desolate goldfields. The last vestiges of winter blanket the jutting hills, softening the hidden nooks and crannies.

I'm driving, and I hate it.

The road winds treacherously along the Taieri Gorge, and I constantly brake and shift between gears. I'm a shit driver; I know it and so does everyone in this car, but I'm acting like I don't care, that this is nothing. Logging trucks, enormous and snaking, career full speed head on, and to let them pass, I keep edging into the loose gravel on the side of the road overlooking the drop into the gorge. The sudden loss of traction sickens me, and I pull the car—Lester's old red-orange Ford fucking Falcon—back onto the road, trying to look cool in front of the others, while my palms sweat buckets onto the steering wheel.

The car is freezing, the winter air rushing around our ears, fluttering our hair. Lester has the back window down, an escape for his cigarette smoke, even though the cunt knows I hate smoking, and this is his small condolence for my lack of sensitivity to his addiction. Except the fucking window won't go back up.

Lyons is skinning up another joint in the seat next to me. A bottle of harddone-by Jack Daniels rests between his black-jeaned thighs. Lester and Katy are giggling in the back seat, huddling under a blanket together to keep warm. That should be me in the backseat with her, and one of these other pricks driving, but I'm too paranoid, especially with Lester and Lyons's track record with car accidents. No fucking way am I letting them behind the wheel. And like a soft cunt, I'm wearing a seatbelt, all nice and safe and strapped in.

Katy squeals and Lester laughs. I can't see what they're doing from the rear view mirror, and I'm too scared to take my eyes off the road. Lyons leans back over the seat and swats at them with his hand.

"Stop it, ya dirty cunts," he slurs.

I afford another glance in the rear view mirror, but all I can see is their faces, red and laughing.

Lyons leans towards me, his eyes fucked, spit on his lips. "You don't mind, do ya, Stevie?"

I don't need to see the suggestive shapes Lyons makes with his fingers. I know what's going on. I'm the chump in the car. My mates are fucking my girlfriend—the only woman I've ever loved—and right now Lester has his stinking cock out and on her or in her, or she's touching it or . . .

I check the rear view mirror again. Katy's mouth opens slightly, a small loss of control. I know that look. I know when she does that.

Lyons's laughing and blowing smoke in my face. "Eh, Stevie?"

The blanket. I have to get that blanket off them.

They've gone quiet in the back, and under the roar of the V8, I can hear them panting. I fucking know it. If I killed the engine right now, we'd all hear everything, every dirty thrusting furtive wet secret.

I reach back over the seat, fumbling for the blanket, desperate to unmask them, reveal their betrayal. My fingers claw, and I realise the seatbelt is constricting me, so I turn, taking my hands off the wheel for a second, just a second, so I can grab that fucking blanket and despise them openly, denounce them, let the world know what despicable creatures they are.

The tyres slide in the gravel. Lyons screams, and my head bounces off the ceiling as the car turns and tumbles over the bank . . .

I don't know how long I've been sitting here. My hair is wet with blood. The car stinks of petrol. Lyons's door is missing, and so is he. In the back, Lester is wedged between the seat and a half open door. He has no pants on, and his leg is crushed, soaking the blanket red. He's crying. I can't see Katy.

I unclick my seatbelt and force open my door.

"Stevie?" Lester whimpers. "Help me, man, you gotta help me."

Lyons is sprawled nearby in loose rocks, his scalp is bleeding. He stirs and tries to rise, his eyes groggy, looking at me like Christ come to save him.

About twenty metres above us on the bank, Katy lies like a broken doll. Her knickers are around her ankles and I can see the black hair on her cunt as clearly as I can see the blood on my hands.

Lester is pleading now, his voice verging on a whine.

I walk round and kneel down next to him. He reaches for me, but I push his hand out of the way. His eyes widen, then resume their neediness. I take a cigarette—a B&*fucking*H because that's what hard cunts smoke—from the pile spread over his chest where his pack has spilled.

"Stevie? I'm hurting bad."

I nod then walk away while lighting his cigarette. Lyons is staggering to his knees, blood spurting from his scalp in raspberry fountains.

I was hoping Lester would say one of those tough guy lines, something like, "Light me a cigarette, Stevie." But he doesn't, he just whimpers some more. I throw the cigarette into the petrol pooling around the rocks. The car ignites, and Lester screams in earnest. I'm spiralling out of control here, I can feel it consuming every atom in my body, but I can't stop. Lyons tries to run up the bank towards the road, so very far away, but he keeps tripping and sliding back through the loose stones, gibbering. Part of his brain is exposed. What's he going to say? He's a murderer; he's not going to say anything.

I reach the road before he does and flag down a passing log truck. Eventually helicopters arrive, and we are flown to the hospital in Dunedin. The three of them are admitted to intensive care. I'm treated for shock, bruises, and minor cut to the scalp.

Before it goes to court, I change my name and leave for Australia.

### 45

It's four in the morning and someone is standing next to my side of the bed.

I'm awake, nerves frozen, gut aching, and nauseous. My chest tightens, and my breath halts. An indistinct head leans in towards my face, bringing with it the stale smell of cigarette smoke. Outside in the street, the slow rumble of a V8 engine waits patiently.

"Get the fuck up," whispers a voice carried on a wave of spent beer fumes and burnt marijuana.

"Lyons?"

Something cold and sharp presses into my temple. "We've got some unfinished business. All of us."

I slide out of bed and quickly pull on the clothes I'd left on the floor. Jules doesn't move, dead to the world. She inhales a shuddering snort as I leave the room and enter the hallway. Lyons already has the front door open, letting in the balmy night, his partially uncovered brain glistening in the near dark. Under the street light, sits a 1978 red-orange Ford Falcon, its engine growling. Lester peers from the driver's window, his face a mess of burning, weeping skin, his hair singed. He lights a cigarette and winks at me. Lyons ushers me into the back of the car, and Lester floors the pedal. The engine roars as the tyres squeal in anguish, and we're off.

The streets are empty, and Lester accelerates hard, running the red lights all the way, until we're racing up the onramp onto the West Gate Bridge. I can't wind up my window, and the temperature in the car is dropping fast though the air outside feels warm. I pull the blanket on the back seat over my legs and shoulders and huddle into myself, shivering. Lester and Lyons are laughing to each other, their words lost beneath the roar of the engine.

At this hour of the morning, the city is awash with light, the neon of banks and accountants and lawyers announcing the skyline. Beneath the bridge, oily swirls of the Yarra River leak out into the bay, the barbed wire lights of petrol refineries guiding the way.

The Ford is rocketing now, we're doing the tonne, and I'm screaming and screaming and screaming. Lester laughs and Lyons laughs, and there is nothing I can do as the world stretches by in one elongated blur but scream louder and longer than they ever can.

The car stops, engine idling.

Rust has eaten away at the doors. The leather seats are worn and ripped, faded to weakness by a thousand dull hot days. The windows are a web of shattered glass.

"We're here," says Lyons.

Lester throws the gearshift into neutral and kills the motor. His skin smells like frying pork. They get out of the car, cross the road, and go into her house.

I wait in the car, in a frozen South Island winter, and rest my head on the seat in front of me.

I start to cry.

Later, as the sun rises into the morning sky, I'm aware of her sitting next to me in the back seat. My eyes are closed, I'm afraid to look, break the spell. Her fingers stroke my hair back, folding it over my ear, and then she caresses my face.

"I loved you." She kisses my cheek, her lips warm and soft, melting the ice inside me. "I always loved you."

I turn my head slowly, seeking to touch her lips with mine, wanting to hold this moment forever, to not lose her this time. "Katy . . . I'm sorry . . . "

But I'm gone, so far gone. I'm sitting in an abandoned car outside a stranger's apartment while the ones I love sleep in my home on the other side of town.

I get out of the car—it's an old Toyota, burnt out and on blocks—and hail a cab.

46

It's a beautiful summer morning, the blue sky finally showing its hand, the smoke from the bushfires a smudge hovering near the horizon. The cab cruises through the traffic heading west out onto the bridge, while in the opposite direction, rush hour snarls and stalls its way across the West Gate into the city. The sun's stark in the commuters' eyes and warm on my back.

Below, on the Yarra, boats glide out into the bay, and fishermen can be glimpsed on the river banks casting their lines.

It's a good day. It's the best day I've had in a while. I'm weighing it in my hand, and it has an equivalence of my wedding day, a measurement comparable to the weight of my daughter in my arms only a few minutes old. Yes, the clouds are lifting, the ghosts are passing.

I smile and look out on the city, my city, my home.

The cab slows as it reaches the apex of the bridge, indicates as it pulls over into the left outer lane, and eventually, stops. I get out of the car. Over to the right of the bridge, somewhere in Yarraville, plumes of fresh black smoke rise into the air. Sirens blare in the distance. I take a crumpled pack of B&H Gold from my pocket, remove a cigarette, and light it. I throw the pack into the open window of the cab, and it roars off in a rush of V8 fumes, a red-orange blur weaving amongst the traffic and disappears from view.

I climb the barrier. The hot wind whistles through my head as I take a drag on the cigarette and prepare to jump. This is it. Letting go, it's all about letting go.

A leap of faith.

## 48

Numbers.

"Paul! Come here, listen to this!"

Jules yelling from Isla's bedroom. Our baby is nine months old.

"Everything okay?"

"Yes!" Jules's voice bubbles with excitement. "She's saying her first words."

My heart pitter patters, and I'm trying not to run to the bedroom, the coffee I was making left unattended on the bench. I'm hoping, as fathers do, that Isla's first words will be "Dada", as it often is. It seems to be easier for babies to mouth than "Mama", but it will be "Mama", it has to be. Jules is here every day with her, for better or worse. Not that we're competing.

In the bedroom, Jules holds Isla in her arms, near the Mother

Goose calendar that is set to her date of birth. More numbers. Isla knows she's done good, and her gummy grin dribbles enthusiasm. Her pudgy fingers point at the duck on the calendar, amongst the snowman, apple, and skipping girl.

"Duck, duck, duck."

We grin, we hug, we kiss.

We are one.

50

Did you hear me? No? It takes less than a minute.

••••••••••••

# ABOUT THE CONTRIBUTORS

PETER M. BALL's work includes the faerie-noir novellas *Horn* and *Bleed*, and his short fiction has appeared in publications such as *Daily SF*, *Apex Magazine*, and *Eclipse 4*. By day he works for the Queensland Writers Centre. Find him online at **petermball.com** and on twitter @petermball.

LEE BATTERSBY is the author of the novels *The Corpse-Rat King* (Angry Robot, 2012) and *Marching Dead* (Angry Robot, 2013) as well as more than 70 stories, some of which can be found in the collection *Through Soft Air* (Prime, 2006). His work has resulted in a number of awards including the Aurealis, Australian Shadows and Ditmar gongs. He lives in Mandurah, Western Australia, with his wife, writer Lyn Battersby, and an increasingly weird mob of kids. He is sadly obsessed with Lego, Nottingham Forest football club, the Goon Show, dinosaurs and Daleks. He blogs at the Battersblog (**battersblog.blogspot.com**).

DEBORAH BIANCOTTI writes and reads in Sydney. Her first collection, *A Book Of Endings* (Twelfth Planet, 2010), was shortlisted for the William L. Crawford Award for Best First Fantasy Book. Her first novella, "And the Dead Shall Outnumber the Living", has been nominated for a Shirley Jackson Award. Her newest collection, *Bad Power*, is available from Twelfth Planet Press. You can find Deborah online mostly just by Googling her.

JENNY BLACKFORD's eight published stories for adults have received one Honourable Mention from Ellen Datlow and three from Gardner Dozois. Gardner also praised her historical novella *The Priestess and the Slave*; Pamela Sargent called it "elegant". Her first poem for decades was the only poem included in the inaugural Ticonderoga *Year's Best Australian Fantasy and Horror*.

SIMON BROWN has been writing for forty years. He has published novels and short stories in Australia and overseas, and currently lives in Thailand with his wife and two children.

DAVID CONYERS is a science fiction and occasional horror author from Adelaide, South Australia. His books include *The Spiraling*

*Worm* (Chaosium, 2007) co-authored with John Sunseri and *The Eye of Infinity* (Perilous Press, 2011). He is the editor of the anthologies *Cthulhu's Dark Cults* which made the preliminary ballot for the Bram Stoker Award, co-edited with Brian M Sammons the anthologies *Cthulhu Unbound 3* and *Undead & Unbound,* and was co-editor of *Midnight Echo 6: The Science Fiction Issue* with David Kernot and Jason Fischer. He is a contributing editor to *Albedo One,* Ireland's leading speculative fiction magazine. **david-conyers.com**

SARA DOUGLASS grew up in South Australia. After working as a nurse, she completed three degrees at the University of Adelaide, including a PhD in early modern English history. After becoming a full-time writer, Sara moved to Tasmania, where she discovered a passion for gardening. The author of 20 novels, *The Hall of Lost Footsteps* was her only story collection. Sara died on 27 September 2011, aged 54, following a three-year struggle with cancer.

Melbourne based FELICITY DOWKER is a Ditmar and Chronos Award winner and an Aurealis and Australian Shadows Award finalist. Felicity is a founder and contributing editor at dark fiction news and reviews site Thirteen O'Clock (thirteenoclock.com.au). Felicity's debut collection is *Bread and Circuses* (Ticonderoga Publications, 2012). Felicity's short stories have been published in Australian and international anthologies and magazines, including *The Year's Best Australian Fantasy and Horror 2010.* Felicity's most recent work can be found in Ekaterina Sedia's anthology *Circus: Fantasy Under the Big Top* (Prime, 2012), and podcast at Tales to Terrify.

TERRY DOWLING has been called "Australia's finest writer of horror" by *Locus* magazine, its "premier writer of dark fantasy" by *All Hallows* and its "most acclaimed writer of the dark fantastic" by *Cemetery Dance* magazine. His collection *Basic Black* won the 2007 International Horror Guild Award for Best Collection and is regarded as "one of the best recent collections of contemporary horror" by the American Library Association. The *Year's Best Fantasy and Horror* series featured more horror stories by Terry in its 21 year run than any other writer, while London's *Guardian* called his debut novel *Clowns at Midnight* "an exceptional work that bears comparison to John Fowles's *The Magus.*" **terrydowling.com**

JASON FISCHER attended the Clarion South writers workshop in 2007. He has been shortlisted in the Aurealis, Ditmar and Australian

Shadows Awards, and is a winner of the Writers of the Future contest. Jason is the author of over thirty stories, with his first collection appearing soon from Ticonderoga. His "After The World" series of zombie-apocalypse novellas are available from Black House Comics. Jason can be found online at **jasonfischer.com.au**

CHRISTOPHER GREEN was born in the United States. He moved to Australia at the age of 20, attended Clarion South in 2007 and has been published in such places as *Dreaming Again, Beneath Ceaseless Skies*, and *Abyss & Apex*. His work has won an Aurealis Award and been shortlisted for the Australian Shadows Award. At the moment he is attempting to convince himself, with varying degrees of success, that he can write both short stories and novels at the same time. He maintains a blog at **christophergreen.wordpress.com** (also with varying degrees of success).

PAUL HAINES was born in New Zealand in 1970. He moved to Melbourne, and was a graduate of the inaugural Clarion South workshop. The author of three superb dark collections, *Doorways for the Dispossessed, Slice of Life*, and *The Last Days of Kali Yuga*. Author of almost 50 stories and winner of 7 Ditmar Awards, 4 Aurealis Awards, and 4 Sir Julius Vogel Awards, Paul Haines died on 5 March 2012, aged 41, from cancer.

LISA L. HANNETT hails from Ottawa, Canada but now lives in Adelaide, South Australia—city of churches, bizarre murders and pie floaters. Her short stories have been published in *Clarkesworld Magazine, Fantasy Magazine, Weird Tales, ChiZine, Shimmer, Steampunk II: Steampunk Reloaded, The Year's Best Australian Fantasy and Horror*, and *Imaginarium 2012: Best Canadian Speculative Fiction*, among other places. She has won three Aurealis Awards, including Best Collection for her first book, *Bluegrass Symphony* (Ticonderoga). *Midnight and Moonshine*, co-authored with Angela Slatter, will be published in 2012. Lisa has a PhD in medieval Icelandic literature, and is a graduate of Clarion South. You can find her online at lisahannett.com and on Twitter @LisaLHannett.

RICHARD HARLAND's novels and short stories have spanned fantasy, horror and SF, for adult, YA and children's level readers. His recent steampunk fantasies, *Worldshaker* and *Liberator,* have been published in the US, UK, France and Germany, as well as Australia. He has collected six Aurealis Awards in Australia, and the Tam-Tam

Je Bouquine award in France. He lives near Wollongong, south of Sydney, between golden beaches, green escarpment and the biggest steelworks in the southern hemisphere. Richard's website is at **richardharland.net**. His 145-page guide to writing speculative fiction is free at **writingtips.com.au**.

JOHN HARWOOD was born in Hobart, Tasmania, where he grew up in a house full of books, including numerous collections of ghost stories, an interest which would resurface many years later in his first novel, *The Ghost Writer* (Jonathan Cape, 2004). It won the International Horror Guild's First Novel Award for Outstanding Achievement in Horror and Dark Fantasy, and the Children of the Night Award for Best Gothic Novel. *The Séance* (2008), a dark mystery set in late Victorian England, won the Aurealis Award for Best Horror Novel. His latest novel, *The Asylum*, will be published in 2013.

PETE KEMPSHALL is a writer and editor living in Perth, Western Australia. His stories have been published in Australia by Ticonderoga Publications, Twelfth Planet Press and ASIM, and internationally by the likes of Big Finish, Morrigan Books, Dark Quest Books and Apex Publications. He has been nominated for the Ditmar Award for Best New Talent, plus Australian Shadows and Aurealis awards, and blogs about his various writing projects at **tyrannyoftheblankpage. blogspot.com**.

DAVID KERNOT lives in Adelaide and dabbles at science fiction, fantasy, and horror writing. A member of Australia's leading speculative fiction magazine team, *Andromeda Spaceways Inflight Magazine*, his publications include *AlienSkin Magazine*, *AntipodeanSF*, *Aoife's Kiss*, Black House Comics, *Cover of Darkness*, *Midnight Echo*, and Timid Pirate Publishing. Visit **davidkernot.com**.

JO LANGDON was born in 1986 and lives in Geelong. She is a poet and fiction writer, and also a PhD candidate at Deakin University. Her poetry chapbook, *Snowline*, was recently published by Whitmore Press.

MAXINE MCARTHUR is the author of three science fiction novels (*Time Future*, *Time Past* and *Less Than Human*) and numerous short stories. She is a founding member of the Canberra Speculative Fiction Guild, and works as an editor. Her current novel-in-progress also involves early flying machines.

KIRSTYN MCDERMOTT's short fiction has been published in various journals, magazines and anthologies in Australia and overseas. Her debut novel, *Madigan Mine*, received an Aurealis Award for Best Horror Novel, and her second, *Perfections*, is due out later this year. She lives in Melbourne with her husband and fellow scribbler, Jason Nahrung, and can be found online at **kirstynmcdermott.com**

IAN MCHUGH's first success as a writer was winning the short story contest at the 2004 Australian national SF convention. Since then, he has graduated from the Clarion West writer's workshop and sold stories to professional and semi-pro magazines, webzines and anthologies in Australia and internationally. His stories have also won grand prize in the Writers of the Future contest and been shortlisted four times at the Aurealis Awards (for one win). Links to read or hear his stories free online can be found at ianmchugh.wordpress.com.

ANDREW J. MCKIERNAN is a writer and illustrator living and working on the Central Coast of NSW. First published in 2007, his stories have since been nominated for multiple Aurealis, Australian Shadows and Ditmar Awards. His illustrations have appeared in, and on the covers of, various books and magazines and he was Art Director of *Aurealis* Magazine for eight years. He is a founding and contributing editor for Thirteen O'Clock: Australian Dark Fiction News & Reviews (thirteenoclock.com.au). His latest short story, "The Final Degustation of Doctor Ernest Blenheim" appeared in *Midnight Echo 7*.

MARGARET MAHY was an internationally famous children's author, best known these days for having been a Hans Christian Andersen winner in recent years. Prior to that she won many other prizes and awards, not least the Carnegie twice, for *The Changeover* and *The Haunting*. Margaret passed away on 23 July 2012, after a short illness.

ANNE MOK lives in Sydney, where she juggles legal editing by day with fiction writing by night. She is a graduate of Clarion South. Like everyone else, she is working on a novel. Her website can be found at annemok.com.

JASON NAHRUNG grew up in country Queensland and now lives in Melbourne where he works as an editor to support his travel addiction. His most recent long fiction is *Salvage* (Twelfth Planet Press), with an outback vampire novel due out in spring 2012 with Xoum. He lurks online at **jasonnahrung.com**.

ANTHONY PANEGYRES is a Perth author whose writing has recently appeared in *Dotdotdash, ASIM* and *Overland*. "Reading Coffee" was an Aurealis Award finalist for the Best Fantasy Short Story. Anthony is currently working on a novel.

ANGELA (ANGIE) REGA lives in Sydney with her planet hunting partner and two feline familiars. A graduate of Clarion South 2009, Angie's short stories have appeared or are forthcoming in Ticonderoga Publications, Fablecroft, Cabinet Des Fees, Postscripts and Little Fox Press. She is an avid lover of folklore, fairy tales and furry creatures. In more adventurous days, she lived in Chile teaching English and belly-dancing.

TANSY RAYNER ROBERTS is the award-winning author of the Creature Court trilogy: *Power and Majesty, The Shattered City* and *Reign of Beasts.* Her short story collection *Love and Romanpunk* was published by Twelfth Planet Press in 2011. You can find her at her blog (tansyrr.com), on Twitter (@tansyrr) and on the Hugo-nominated podcast Galactic Suburbia. Tansy lives in Tasmania, Australia with a Silent Producer and two superhero daughters.

ANGELA SLATTER is a Brisbane writer of dark fantasy and horror. In 2011 *The Girl with No Hands and Other Tales* won the Aurealis Award for Best Collection and *Sourdough and Other Stories* was shortlisted for the World Fantasy Award for Best Collection. "The February Dragon" (co-authored with Lisa L. Hannett) won the Aurealis for Best Fantasy Short Story. Her work has featured in both US and Australian *Best Of* collections and "The Coffin-maker's Daughter" (from the Stephen Jones edited *A Book of Horrors*) is shortlisted for a British Fantasy Award. *Midnight and Moonshine*, co-authored with Lisa Hannett, will be out in November 2012.

LUCY SUSSEX's award-winning writing includes five collections of short stories, most recently *Thief of Lives* (Twelfth Planet 2011). She has also written *Saltwater in the Ink*, an anthology of C19th emigration writing, and *Women Writers and Detectives in C19th Crimewriting: the Mothers of the Mystery Genre* (both 2010). In addition she has a weekly review column in *The Age* newspaper.

KYLA WARD is a Sydney-based creative who works in many modes. Her latest release is *The Land of Bad Dreams*, a collection of dark and fantastic poetry. Her novel *Prismatic* (co-authored as Edwina Grey) won an Aurealis Award for Best Horror. Her work has appeared in *TiconderogaOnline*, *Shadowed Realms*, *Borderlands*, Gothic.net and in *The New Hero* anthology. RPGs, short films, stage plays and feature articles: if you can scare someone with it she probably has, including programming the horror stream for the 2010 Worldcon. A practicing occultist, she likes raptors, swordplay and the Hellfire Club. To see some very strange things, try **tabula-rasa.info**.

KAARON WARREN's collection *The Grinding House* (CSFG, 2005) won the ACT Writers' and Publishers' Award and two Ditmars. Her second collection, *Dead Sea Fruit* (Ticonderoga, 2010) won the ACT Writers' and Publishers' Award. Her novel *Slights* (Angry Robot) won the Australian Shadows, Ditmar and Canberra Critics' Awards. Her novels *Walking the Tree* and *Mistification* (Angry Robot), both shortlisted for Ditmars. Her stories have appeared in Ellen Datlow's annual anthologies as well as Australian Year's Best Horror, Science Fiction and Fantasy anthologies. Special Guest for the Australian National SF Convention in 2013, Kaaron's latest book is *Through Splintered Walls* (Twelfth Planet, 2012). Kaaron lives in Canberra, with her husband and children. Her website is **kaaronwarren. wordpress.com** and she tweets @KaaronWarren.

# RECOMMENDED READING LIST

Joanna Anderton, "Out Hunting For Teeth" *Midnight Echo #6*
——— "From The Dry Heart To The Sea" *After The Rain*
——— "Flowers In The Shadow Of The Garden" *Hope*
Annette Backshall, "Hunting Rabbits" *More Scary Kisses*
Peter M Ball, "Visitors" *After The Rain*
Alan Baxter, "Dream Shadow" *Winds of Change*
——— "The Seven Garages of Kevin Simpson"
——— "Duty And Sacrifice" *Hope*
——— "Mirrorwalk" *Murky Depths #16*
———"Punishment of the Sun" *Dead Red Heart*
Leigh Blackmore and Richard L. Tierney" Twilight of the Mage
    (poem) *Midnight Echo #5*
Deborah Biancotti, "Shades of Grey" *Bad Power*
——— "Palming the Lady" *Bad Power*
——— "And the Dead Shall Outnumber the Living" *Ishtar*
Isobelle Carmody, "Moth's Tale" *The Wilful Eye: Tales From
    The Tower Volume 1*
Damon Cavalchini, "Renfield's Wife" *Dead Red Heart*
David Conyers and John Goodrich, "The Masked Messenger"
    *ASIM #52*
Shane Jiraiya Cummings, "Graveyard Orbit" *Midnight Echo #6*
——— "The Song of Prague"
——— "The Black Door Apocrypha Sequence: Insanity"
Rowena Cory Daniells, "The Choosing" *Hope*
Sara Douglass, "Black Heart" *The Hall Of Lost Footsteps*
Felicity Dowker, "Red Delicious" *Dead Red Heart*
Terry Dowling, "The Shaddowesbox" *Ghosts By Gaslight*
Thoraiya Dyer, "Fruit of the Pipal Tree" *After The Rain*
——— "The Bird, the Bees and Thylacine" *ASIM #51*
Brendan Duffy and David McDonald, "Just Like Cuckoo" *The
    Epocalypse: Emails At The End*

Mark Farrugia, "Seeds" *Midnight Echo #6*
Jason Fischer, "Goggy" *Midnight Echo #5*
———— "A Clockwork Arthur" *After The World #3: Pack Rules*
Pamela Freeman, "A Moment, A Day, A Year..." *Hope*
Laura E. Goodin, "The Bicycle Rebellion" *Daily Science Fiction*
Clinton Green, "The Hobart Town Whisperer" *After The World #3: Pack Rules*
John Grey, "The Quiet in the Flat Above (poem)" *Midnight Echo #5*
Lisa L. Hannett, "Carousel" *Bluegrass Symphony*
———— "Them Little Shiny Things" *Bluegrass Symphony*
———— "The Short Go: a Future in Eight Seconds" *Bluegrass Symphony*
———— "The Wager And The Hourglass" *Bluegrass Symphony*
———— "Fur And Feathers" *Bluegrass Symphony*
———— "Gutted" *Shimmer #13*
Richard Harland, "An Exhibition of the Plague" *Anywhere But Earth*
———— "Bad Thoughts and the Mechanism" *Ghosts By Gaslight*
———— "Heart Of The Beast" *The Wilful Eye: Tales From The Tower Volume 1*
Robert Hood, "Desert Madonna" *Anywhere But Earth*
Dylan Horrocks, "Steam Girl" *Steampunk!*
Gerry Huntman, "The Bond Penny" *Dread Tales Volume 1: Gears, Coils, Aether & Steam*
Shona Husk, "The Skull Jeweller's Apprentice" *ASIM #50*
Sue Isle, "The Painted Girl" *Nightsiders*
———— "Nation of the Night" *Nightsiders*
Kathleen Jennings, "Finishing School" *Steampunk!*
Pete Kempshall, "All That Glisters" *Dead Red Heart*
———— "Temptation" *Scenes From The Second Storey: International Edition*
Cate Kennedy, "Seventy-Two Derwents" *The Wicked Wood: Tales From The Tower Volume 2*
Rick Kennett, "Rick On the Other Side" *Midnight Echo #5*
Margo Lanagan, "Mulberry Boys" *Blood and Other Cravings*
———— "Into the Clouds on High" *Yellowcake*
———— "The Proving of Smollett Standforth" *Ghosts by Gaslight*
Chris Lawson, "Apologetoi" *Dead Red Heart*
Martin Livings, "The Rider" *Dead Red Heart*
———— and Talie Helene, "The Last Gig Of Jimmy Rucker" *More Scary Kisses*

———— with Alan Baxter, Felicity Dowker, Patty Jansen, Devin
Jeyathuri, Chuck McKenzie, Andrew J. McKiernan, Lezli
Robyn, Daniel I. Russell, Carol Ryles, and Kaaron Warren,
"The Tide" *Dead Red Heart*

Penelope Love, "Lady Yang's Lament" *Dead Red Heart*

———— "SIBO" *Anywhere But Earth*

Robert Mammone, "Shivers" *Big Book of New Short Horror*

———— "The Well" *British Fantasy Society Journal*

Mark McAuliffe, "For Glory" *Eclecticism #15*

Tracie McBride, "H is for Hagiophobia—Symbols of Damnation"
*Phobophobia*

Maureen McCarthy, "The Ugly Sisters" *The Wicked Wood: Tales
From The Tower Volume 2*

Greg Mellor, "Children of the Ashes" *Winds of Change*

Chris Miles, "The Household Debt" *ASIM #51*

Nicole Murphy, "The Fairy King's Child" *ASIM #50*

Jason Nahrung, "Resurrection in Red" *More Scary Kisses*

———— "Messiah on the Rocks" *Anywhere But Earth*

Garth Nix, "The Curious Case Of The Moondawn Daffodils
Murder" *Ghosts By Gaslight*

Tansy Rayner Roberts, "Last Of The Romanpunks" *Love And
Romanpunk*

Jane Routley, "Bats" *Dead Red Heart*

Daniel I. Russell, "Broken Bough" *The Zombie Feed Volume 1*

Carol Ryles, "Snake Charmer" *More Scary Kisses*

Guy Salvidge, "The Kennedys" *Eclecticism #17*

Christopher Sequeira, "Too Many Number 16's" *Midnight Echo #5*

Leife Shallcross, "The Tether Of Time" *Winds Of Change*

Angela Slatter, "Sunfalls" *Dead Red Heart*

Cat Sparks, "Beautiful" *Anywhere But Earth*

———— "The Alabaster Child" *Gutshot: Weird West Stories*

———— "Dead Low" *Midnight Echo #6*

Amanda Spedding, "Shovel Man Joe" *Shades of Sentience*

Nicholas Stella, "Duncan Checks Out" *Midnight Echo #6*

Lucy Sussex, "Sagittaire" *Matilda Told Such Dreadful Lies: The
Essential Lucy Sussex*

Kaaron Warren, "The Rude Little Girl" *Black Static #17*

———— "The List of Definite Endings" *Teeth: Vampire Tales*

———— "A Pot To Piss In" *Voices From The Past*

———— "Lucky Fingers, Five Historical Feasts" *The Conflux
Cookbook*

———— "The 5 Loves Of Ishtar" *Ishtar*
Sean Williams, "The Jade Woman And The Luminous Star"
  *Ghosts By Gaslight*
Suzanne J Willis, "Offerings" *After The Rain*
Kyla Ward, "The Sleep Of Reason (Interrupted)" (poem) *The
  Land of Bad Dreams*
Marty Young, "Desert Blood" *Dead Red Heart*

# AUSTRALIAN & NEW ZEALAND FANTASY & HORROR AWARDS

## THE AUSTRALIAN SF "DITMAR" AWARDS

### BEST NOVEL

*The Courier's New Bicycle*, **Kim Westwood** (HarperCollins)
NOMINEES
*Debris*, Jo Anderton (Angry Robot)
*Burn Bright*, Marianne de Pierres (Random House)
*The Shattered City*, Tansy Rayner Roberts (HarperCollins)
*Mistification*, Kaaron Warren (Angry Robot)

### BEST NOVELLA OR NOVELETTE:

**"The Past is a Bridge Best Left Burnt", Paul Haines (*The Last Days of Kali Yuga*, Brimstone)**
NOMINEES
"And the Dead Shall Outnumber the Living", Deborah Biancotti (*Ishtar*, Gilgamesh)
"Above", Stephanie Campisi (*Above/Below*, Twelfth Planet)
"Below", Ben Peek (*Above/Below*, Twelfth Planet)
"Julia Agrippina's Secret Family Bestiary", Tansy Rayner Roberts (*Love and Romanpunk*, Twelfth Planet)

### BEST SHORT STORY

**"The Patrician", Tansy Rayner Roberts (Love and Romanpunk, Twelfth Planet)**
NOMINEES
"Bad Power", Deborah Biancotti (*Bad Power*, Twelfth Planet)
"Breaking the Ice", Thoraiya Dyer (*Cosmos* 37)
"The Last Gig of Jimmy Rucker", Martin Livings & Talie Helene (*More Scary Kisses*, Ticonderoga)

"Alchemy", Lucy Sussex (*Thief of Lives*, Twelfth Planet)
"All You Can Do Is Breathe", Kaaron Warren (*Blood and Other Cravings*, Tor)

## BEST COLLECTED WORK

**The Last Days of Kali Yuga, Paul Haines (Brimstone)**
NOMINEES
*Bad Power*, Deborah Biancotti (Twelfth Planet)
*Nightsiders*, Sue Isle (Twelfth Planet)
*Ishtar*, Amanda Pillar & K.V. Taylor, eds. (Gilgamesh)
*Love and Romanpunk*, Tansy Rayner Roberts (Twelfth Planet)

## BEST ARTWORK

**"Finishing School", Kathleen Jennings in *Steampunk!* (Candlewick)**
NOMINEES
Cover art, Kathleen Jennings, *The Freedom Maze* (Small Beer)

## BEST NEW TALENT

**Joanne Anderton**
NOMINEES
Alan Baxter
Steve Cameron

# AUREALIS AWARDS

## FANTASY NOVEL

**Ember and Ash, Pamela Freeman (Hachette)**
NOMINEES
*The Undivided*, Jennifer Fallon (HarperCollins)
*Stormlord's Exile*, Glenda Larke (HarperCollins)
*Debris*, Jo Anderton (Angry Robot)
*The Shattered City*, Tansy Rayner Roberts (HarperCollins)

## FANTASY SHORT STORY

**"Fruit of the Pipal Tree", Thoraiya Dyer (*After the Rain*, Fablecroft)**
NOMINEES
"The Proving of Smollett Standforth", Margo Lanagan (*Ghosts by Gaslight*, HarperCollins)
"Into the Clouds on High", Margo Lanagan (*Yellowcake*, Allen & Unwin)
"Reading Coffee", Anthony Panegyris (*Overland*)
"The Dark Night of Anton Weiss", D.C. White (*More Scary Kisses*, Ticonderoga)

## BEST HORROR NOVEL

**No shortlist or winner**
HONOURABLE MENTIONS
*The Broken Ones*, Stephen M. Irwin (Hachette)
*The Business of Death*, Trent Jamieson (Hachette)

## BEST HORROR SHORT STORY

**"The Past is a Bridge Best Left Burnt", Paul Haines (*The Last Days of Kali Yuga*, Brimstone)**
**"The Short Go: a Future in Eight Seconds", Lisa L. Hannett (*Bluegrass Symphony*, Ticonderoga)**
NOMINEES
"And the Dead Shall Outnumber the Living", Deborah Biancotti (*Ishtar*, Morrigan)
"Mulberry Boys", Margo Lanagan (*Blood and Other Cravings*, Tor)
"The Coffin Maker's Daughter", Angela Slatter (*A Book of Horrors*, Jo Fletcher)

## BEST COLLECTION

*Bluegrass Symphony*, **Lisa Hannett (Ticonderoga)**
NOMINEES
*Bad Power*, Deborah Biancotti (Twelfth Planet)
*The Last Days of Kali Yuga*, Paul Haines (Brimstone)
*Nightsiders*, Sue Isle (Twelfth Planet)
*Love and Romanpunk*, Tansy Rayner Roberts (Twelfth Planet)

## BEST ANTHOLOGY

*Ghosts by Gaslight*, **Jack Dann & Nick Gevers, eds. (HarperVoyager)**
NOMINEES
*The Year's Best Australian Fantasy and Horror* 2010, Liz Grzyb & Talie Helene, eds. (Ticonderoga)
*Ishtar*, Amanda Pillar & K.V. Taylor, eds. (Gilgamesh)
*The Best Science Fiction and Fantasy of the Year: Volume 5*, Jonathan Strahan, ed. (Night Shade)
*Life on Mars*, Jonathan Strahan, ed. (Viking)

## BEST CHILDREN'S FICTION (TOLD PRIMARILY THROUGH WORDS)

*City of Lies*, **Lian Tanner (Allen & Unwin)**
NOMINEES
*The Outcasts*, John Flanagan (Random House Australia)
*The Paradise Trap*, Catherine Jinks (Allen & Unwin)
"It Began with a Tingle", Thalia Kalkapsakis (*Headspinners*, A&U)
*The Coming of the Whirlpool*, Andrew McGahan (Allen & Unwin)

## BEST CHILDREN'S FICTION (TOLD PRIMARILY THROUGH PICTURES)

*Sounds Spooky*, **Christopher Cheng (author) & Sarah Davis (illustrator) (Random House)**

NOMINEES

*The Ghost of Annabel Spoon*, Aaron Blabey (author and illustrator) (Viking)

*The Last Viking*, Norman Jorgensen (author) & James Foley (illustrator) (Fremantle)

*The Deep: Here be Dragons*, Tom Taylor (author) & James Brouwer (illustrator) (Gestalt)

*Vampyre*, Margaret Wild (author) & Andrew Yeo (illustrator) (Walker)

## YOUNG ADULT SHORT STORY

**"Nation of the Night", Sue Isle (*Nightsiders*, Twelfth Planet)**
NOMINEES

"Finishing School", Kathleen Jennings (*Steampunk!*, Candlewick)

"Seventy-Two Derwents", Cate Kennedy (*The Wicked Wood: Tales from the Tower Volume 2*, Allen & Unwin)

"One Window", Martine Murray (*The Wilful Eye: Tales from the Tower Volume 1*, Allen & Unwin)

"The Patrician", Tansy Rayner Roberts (*Love and Romanpunk*, Twelfth Planet)

## BEST YOUNG ADULT NOVEL

*Only Ever Always*, Penni Russon (Allen & Unwin)
NOMINEES

*Shift*, Em Bailey (Hardie Grant Egmont)

*Secrets of Carrick: Tantony*, Ananda Braxton-Smith (black dog)

*The Shattering*, Karen Healey (Allen & Unwin)

*Black Glass*, Meg Mundell (Scribe)

## BEST ILLUSTRATED BOOK/GRAPHIC NOVEL

**Hidden, Mirranda Burton (author and illustrator) (Black Pepper)**
**The Deep: Here be Dragons, Tom Taylor (author) & James Brouwer (illustrator) (Gestalt)**
NOMINEES

*Torn*, Andrew Constant (author) & Joh James (illustrator) additional illustrators Nicola Scott, Emily Smith (Gestalt)

*Salsa Invertebraxa*, Mozchops (author and illustrator) (Pecksniff)

*The Eldritch Kid: Whiskey and Hate*, Christian Read (author) & Michael Maier (illustrator) (Gestalt)

## BEST SCIENCE FICTION SHORT STORY

**"Rains of la Strange", Robert N. Stephenson (*Anywhere but Earth*, Coeur de Lion)**
NOMINEES

"Flowers in the Shadow of the Garden", Joanne Anderton (*Hope*, Kayelle)

"Desert Madonna", Robert Hood (*Anywhere but Earth*, Coeur de Lion)

"SIBO", Penelope Love (*Anywhere but Earth*, Coeur de Lion)

"Dead Low", Cat Sparks (*Midnight Echo*)

## BEST SCIENCE FICTION NOVEL

**The Courier's New Bicycle, Kim Westwood (Harper Voyager)**
NOMINEES
*Machine Man*, Max Barry (Scribe)
*Children of Scarabaeus*, Sara Creasy (Harper Voyager)
*The Waterboys*, Peter Docker (Fremantle)
*Black Glass*, Meg Mundell (Scribe)

## PETER MCNAMARA CONVENORS' AWARD

**Galactic Suburbia Podcast**

# AUSTRALIAN SHADOWS AWARDS

## NOVEL

**No award**
HONOURABLE MENTION
*The Broken Ones*, Stephen M. Irwin (Hachette)

## LONG FICTION

**"The Past is a Bridge Best Left Burnt", Paul Haines (*The Last Days of Kali Yuga*, Brimstone)**
NOMINEES
"And the Dead Shall Outnumber the Living", Deborah Biancotti (*Ishtar*, Gilgamesh)
"From the Teeth of Strange Children", Lisa L. Hannett (*Bluegrass Symphony*, Ticonderoga)
"Sleeping and the Dead", Cat Sparks (*Ishtar*, Gilgamesh)

## COLLECTION

**Tales of Sin and Madness, Brett McBean (Legume Man)**
NOMINEES
*Apocrypha Sequence*, Shane Jiraiya Cummings
*The Last Days of Kali Yuga*, Paul Haines (Brimstone)
*Bluegrass Symphony*, Lisa Hannett (Ticonderoga)
*Matilda Told Such Dreadful Lies*, Lucy Sussex (Ticonderoga)

## EDITED PUBLICATION

**Dead Red Heart, Russell B. Farr, ed. (Ticonderoga)**
NOMINEES
*More Scary Kisses*, Liz Grzyb ed. (Ticonderoga)
*The Year's Best Australian Fantasy & Horror* 2010, Liz Grzyb and Talie Helene eds. (Ticonderoga)
*Midnight Echo* #6, David Kernot, David Conyers, and Jason Fischer, eds. (AHWA)

## SHORT FICTION

**"Shovel Man Joe", Amanda J. Spedding (*Scenes from the Second Storey*, Morrigan Books)**
NOMINEES
"Out Hunting for Teeth", Joanne Anderton (*Midnight Echo #6*, AHWA)
"The Sea at Night", Joanne Anderton (*Dead Red Heart*, Ticonderoga)
"Taking it for the Team", Tracie McBride (*Dead Red Heart*, Ticonderoga)
"The Wanderer in the Darkness", Andrew McKiernan (*Midnight Echo #6*, AHWA)

# SIR JULIUS VOGEL AWARDS

## BEST NOVEL

*Samiha's Song,* Mary Victoria (HarperCollins)
NOMINEES
*Dragons Away!* K.D. Berry (Bluewood)
*In The Heart Of Stars*, Warwick Gibson (Patshm)
*Oracle's Fire*, Mary Victoria (HarperCollins)
*Nmemesis*, Pat Whitaker (Cooper's)

## BEST YOUTH NOVEL

*Battle Of The Birds* by Lee Murray (Taramea)
NOMINEES
*Wings*, Raymond Huber (Walker)
*Space Race*, Glynne MacLean (Pearson)
*Fosterling*, Emma Neale (Vintage)
*Rapture*, Phillip W. Simpson (Pear Jam)

## BEST NOVELLA / NOVELETTE

**"Steam Girl", Dylan Horrocks (*Steampunk!*, Candlewick)**
NOMINEES
"The Past Is A Bridge Best Left Burnt", Paul Haines (*The Last Days Of Kali Yuga*, Brimstone)
"Gethsemane", Elizabeth Knox (*Steampunk!*, Candlewick)

## BEST SHORT STORY

**"Frankie And The Netball Clone", Alicia Ponder (*Challenge Issue* 2)**
NOMINEES
"Upon A Star", Debbie Cowens (*Wilywriters*)
"Azif", Lynne Jamneck (*Fantastique Unfettered Issue* 4, M-brane Press)
"Crucible", Dan Rabarts (*Wilywriters*)

## BEST COLLECTED WORK

*Tales For Canterbury*, Cassie Hart and Anna Caro, eds. (Random Static)

NOMINEES

*Aquasynthesis*, Grace Bridges (Splashdown)
*The Last Days Of Kali Yuga*, Paul Haines (Brimstone)
*Matilda Told Such Dreadful Lies*, Lucy Sussex (Ticonderoga)
*Thief Of Lives*, Lucy Sussex (Twelfth Planet)

## BEST PROFESSIONAL ARTWORK

Cover art, Frank Victoria, *Oracle's Fire* (HarperCollins)

NOMINEE

Artwork, Donovan Bixley, *Northwood* (Walker)

## BEST DRAMATIC PRESENTATION

*The Almighty Johnsons*, Simon Bennett, prod., Rachal Lang and James Griffin, writers (South Pacific Pictures)

NOMINEES

*The Devil's Rock*, Leanne Saunders, prod., Paul Campion, dir.

# OTHER AWARDS AND ACHIEVEMENTS

2011: The year of Shaun Tan. After his film based on his picture book *The Lost Thing* won an Oscar for Best Animated Short Film, he won another Hugo award for Best Professional Artist, the Astrid Lindgren Memorial Award, and various national awards like the Ditmar and the Swedish Peter Pan Award, and state awards like the Chronos award for Best Artwork. Hachette Australia and Allen & Unwin were both shortlisted for the Australian Book Industry Awards International Success of the Year for Shaun's picture books *The Lost Thing* and *Tales from Outer Suburbia* respectively.

Jonathan Strahan was again recognised for prominence in the speculative fiction world with a Hugo nomination for Best Editor—Short Form. Sean McMullen was nominated for a Hugo Award for Best Novelette for his story "Eight Miles". James Moloney was awarded a Gold Inky Award (the State Library of Victoria Awards) for his young adult fantasy novel Silvermay.

Mary Victoria saw great success in the David Gemmell awards for her Chronicles of the Tree series, being nominated for the Morningstar (best debut) and the Ravenheart (cover design) awards. The cover for Tansy Rayner Roberts' Creature Court novel *Power and Majesty* took out the Ravenheart award for the gorgeous design by OlofErlaEinarssdottir. Roberts also won the William Atheling Award for Criticism and Review for her "Modern Women's Guide to Classic Who".

Alisa Krasnostein won a Non-Professional Special World Fantasy Award at the World Fantasy Convention in San Diego, California. The

Washington Science Fiction Association this year again recognised Australian small press, as the shortlist for their Small Press Award included the delightful short story "Enid and the Prince" by New Zealand author R.J. Astruc, published in *Worlds Next Door* from Fablecroft Publishing.

• • • • • • • • • • •

# ACKNOWLEDGEMENTS

"Briar Day" © Peter M. Ball. First published in *Moonlight Tuber*.

"Europe After The Rain" © Lee Battersby. First published in *After the Rain*, Fablecroft Press.

"Bad Power" © Deborah Biancotti. First published in *Bad Power*, Twelfth Planet Press.

"The Head in the Goatskin Bag" © Jenny Blackford. First published in *Kaleidotrope*.

"Thin Air" © Simon Brown. First published in *Dead Red Heart*, Ticonderoga Publications.

"Winds Of Nzambi" © David Conyers and David Kernot. First published in *Midnight Echo* #6, AHWA.

"More Matter, Less Art" © Stephen Dedman. First published in *Midnight Echo* #6, AHWA.

"The Hall of Lost Footsteps" © Sara Douglass Enterprises. First published in *The Hall of Lost Footsteps*, Ticonderoga Publications.

"Berries & Incense" © Felicity Dowker. First published in *More Scary Kisses*, Ticonderoga Publications.

"Dark Me, Night You" © Terry Dowling. First published in *Midnight Echo* #5, AHWA.

"Hunting Rufus" © Jason Fischer. First published in *Midnight Echo* #5, AHWA.

"Letters Of Love From The Once And Newly Dead" © Christopher Green. First published in *Midnight Echo* #5, AHWA.

"The Past Is A Bridge Best Left Burnt" © Paul Haines. First published in *The Last Days of Kali Yuga*, Brimstone Press.

"Forever, Miss Tapekwa County" © Lisa L. Hannett. First published in *Bluegrass Symphony*, Ticonderoga Publications.

"At The Top Of The Stairs" © Richard Harland. First published in *Shadows and Tall Trees* #2, Undertow Publications.

"Face To Face" © John Harwood. First published in *Ghosts by Gaslight*, HarperCollins.

"Someone Else To Play With" © Pete Kempshall. First published in *Beauty Has Her Way*, Dark Quest Books.

"Heaven" © Jo Langdon. First published in *After the Rain*, Fablecroft Press.

"The Soul of the Machine" © Maxine McArthur. First published in *Winds of Change*, CSFG.

"The Wishwriter's Wife" © Ian McHugh. First published in *Daily Science Fiction*.

"Love Death" © Andrew J. McKiernan. First published in *Aurealis* #45, Chimaera Publications.

## AVAILABLE FROM TICONDEROGA PUBLICATIONS

## THE YEAR'S BEST AUSTRALIAN FANTASY & HORROR SERIES

THANK YOU

The publisher would sincerely like to thank:

Elizabeth Grzyb, Talie Helene, Peter M. Ball, Lee Battersby,
Deborah Biancotti, Jenny Blackford, Simon Brown, David
Conyers, Stephen Dedman, Sara Douglass, Felicity Dowker, Terry
Dowling, Jason Fischer, Christopher Green, Paul Haines, Lisa L.
Hannett, Richard Harland, John Harwood, Pete Kempshall,
David Kernot, Jo Langdon, Maxine McArthur, Ian McHugh,
Andrew J. McKiernan, Kirstyn McDermott, Margaret Mahy,
Anne Mok, Jason Nahrung, Anthony Panegyres, Tansy Rayner
Roberts, Angela Rega, Angela Slatter, Lucy Sussex, Kyla
Ward, Kaaron Warren, Jonathan Strahan, Peter McNamara,
Ellen Datlow, Grant Stone, Jeremy G. Byrne, Sean Williams,
Garth Nix, David Cake, Simon Oxwell, Grant Watson,
Sue Manning, Steven Utley, Bill Congreve, Jack Dann,
the Mt Lawley Mafia, the Nedlands Yakuza, Amanda Pillar,
Shane Jiraiya Cummings, Angela Challis, Donna Maree Hanson,
Kate Williams, Kathryn Linge, Andrew Williams, Al Chan,
Alisa and Tehani, Mel & Phil, Hayley Lane, Georgina Walpole,
everyone we've missed . . .

. . . and you.


In memory of Eve Johnson (1945–2011)

www.ingramcontent.com/pod-product-compliance
Lightning Source LLC
Chambersburg PA
CBHW020823030726
47496CB00001B/68